SYCAMORE HILL

I was hardly aware that he had pushed himself into a sitting position until I felt his fingers taking the pins from my hair. My eyes widened, and before I could protest, he lowered his head and touched my lips with his in a soft kiss. I moved back away from him, my heart pounding like something wild.

"Don't..." I strained away, wanting to stand up, yet not wanting to.

"We're playing by my rules now. Remember?" he questioned softly, pressing his mouth against the curve of my neck....

Sycamore Hill

FRANCINE RIVERS

A JOVE BOOK

SYCAMORE HILL

A Jove Book/published by arrangement with
the author

PRINTING HISTORY
Pinnacle Books edition published April 1981
Jove edition/August 1985

ISBN: 0-515-08181-7

Jove books are published by The Berkley Publishing Group,
200 Madison Avenue, New York, N.Y. 10016.
The words "A JOVE BOOK" and the "J" with sunburst
are trademarks belonging to Jove Publications, Inc.

PRINTED IN THE UNITED STATES OF AMERICA

To my husband, Rick,
for his encouragement
and support

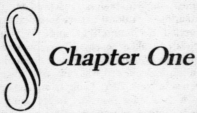# Chapter One

The silver teapot was heavy in my unaccustomed hand. I poured the sweet-smelling brew carefully into a delicate Wedgwood cup. Glancing up nervously, I watched the ascetic gentleman sitting on the silk-brocade settee opposite me. His shrewd gray eyes were narrowed as they roved about the large, elegantly furnished parlor, touching on the most exquisite and expensive of my guardians' many possessions.

"Your tea, Mr. Dobson," I offered quietly. He accepted it with the faintest smile touching his thin lips. Taking one polite sip, he then set it aside indifferently.

"Would you care for a sandwich, sir?" I asked deferentially, lifting a silver platter with open-faced sandwiches delectably displayed by Roberta's expert hand. He declined.

The tension grew inside me. I had never played hostess before, and found sitting in Marcella Haversall's wing chair a great embarrassment. Death had not altered my position in this household. I was still the ward thrust unwelcome upon the Haversalls by my parents' untimely death. And now my guardians were dead, both killed in a carriage accident.

I spread my hands in a futile gesture. "I hope you don't think me presumptuous."

1

"I beg your pardon, Miss McFarland," Dobson said, his attention sharpening on me as he came out of his private reverie. "Why should you think such a thing?"

Explaining would only embarrass both of us more; so I decided to get to the point of his visit. "You're here to discuss my guardians' will, aren't you?"

"Yes," he nodded and then frowned. "This is very difficult." He leaned forward, clasping his hands together between his lean legs. He was having trouble looking at me, and I smiled slightly.

"Please don't distress yourself about my reaction, Mr. Dobson," I told him reassuringly. "I don't expect an inheritance."

"No?" Dobson queried, his mouth tightening. "Why not?"

"Why not?" I repeated, taken aback. "Why, because the Haversalls owe me absolutely nothing. They were remarkably kind to take me in in the first place. I was only five when my parents died of influenza in New York. I simply arrived on the Haversalls' doorstep with a letter from my father and a few possessions. They fed, clothed and educated me as though I were a . . . relation." I could not say that the Haversalls had loved me. They had always been aloof in any emotional sense.

"Charles Haversall was your godfather," Dobson said a trifle sharply.

"Not a blood relation," I repeated.

"Am I not correct in my deduction that you have worked for them since you completed your education? Worked gratis, I might add?"

The Haversalls had asked me to stay with them when I finished school. I had dreamed of making my own life, but felt dreadfully ungrateful when they had talked of their need. After all, they had taken me in when I was a child. They had treated me as their daughter, almost. I was obligated to repay them in some way, and what they asked seemed paltry in comparison to what they had done for me.

So I remained. That had been five years ago. There had never been any discussion of salary, of course. I asked nothing but the room I had occupied since coming to Boston, the meals I took with them and an occasional, cherished hour to read. Life had been satisfactory, if not pleasant.

"I owed my guardians a great deal for their kindness to me," I said, feeling the explanation should not be necessary. Dobson made a sound in his throat.

"Most young women of your age are married with families of their own," he said.

"I've never met any eligible young men, Mr. Dobson." I smiled. "Those I have met were not in my social sphere. They would hardly have looked twice at me."

"I should think they would have looked more than twice, Miss McFarland. You are a very attractive young lady." His compliment was uttered in a most serious way, and I flushed with embarrassment.

Bradford Dobson sighed. "Did you expect nothing at all?" he asked.

"It wouldn't be truthful if I said that. I suppose I expect a small stipend. Not much," I said hastily. "But enough to allow me modest living expenses until I can find a position elsewhere."

Dobson drew a deep breath and then let it out. He stood up and restlessly paced the room for several moments as though something weighty were dragging on his mind. I began to feel frightened.

"This is going to be very difficult," he said more to himself than to me. His face was paler than when he had first arrived, and his eyes burned beneath the thick, dark brows. He finally stopped and faced me, shoving his hands deeply into his pockets.

"The Haversalls made no mention of you in their will, Miss McFarland. Absolutely no mention at all," he told me bluntly.

"They left no provision whatsoever?" I managed after a moment.

"None," he said tersely. His lips were tight. "But . . . but there is a small sum of money that belongs to you in the Haversall estate."

My eyes widened in confusion. "But you just said . . . I'm afraid I don't understand."

Bradford Dobson let out his breath and muttered something I failed to hear clearly. He was obviously very upset and was having difficulty speaking at all.

"Mr. Dobson? Please explain."

"It's what's left of your inheritance."

I stared at him blankly. "My inheritance?" I repeated, completely bewildered now. "But, Mr. Dobson, you just said I had no inheritance."

"Yes, Miss McFarland, you did," he answered.

"Charles Haversall said that my mother and father left a small sum to provide for my education. You mean that some of that money is still left for me?" I asked, hoping for an explanation from him.

"No. I mean that from a very large inheritance from your parents there remains only a little over one thousand dollars." He sank down onto the settee and leaned forward, bringing his face closer. "The letter you spoke of . . . the letter you carried when you arrived here, that was a last will and testament written out by your father before he died. He gave you into Charles Haversall's keeping, permitting him trusteeship over your inheritance, which was to be used on your behalf."

"But there can't have been much."

"There was a fortune," Dobson said flatly.

"You must be mistaken, Mr. Dobson. You're suggesting that the Haversalls stole my inheritance. Why would they do such a thing? They have . . . a fortune of their own. Why, they own the factory, this house, a summer house. You can't seriously believe they would do such a thing!"

"I'm not suggesting. I'm telling you. They did not have as much money as people thought. Charles Haversall never was the most enlightened businessman, I'm afraid. He made some rather disastrous investments early in his career. His family fortune was depleted years ago." Dobson stood again, moving away from me and allowing me time to absorb what he was saying. I felt numb with shock.

"I can't believe it," I murmured.

"I suppose Charles Haversall even managed to delude himself that your money should have been his from the beginning anyway," Dobson grumbled.

"What . . . what did you say?" I stammered, looking up at the solicitor. He turned and looked back at me. He did not say anything for a long time.

"I'm not sure it will help you, Miss McFarland. But I think

you've a right to know everything . . . from the beginning of the story," he said finally. He came back and sat down, facing me with an intent look.

"Charles Haversall ran through most of his family inheritance by the time he was twenty-five. It was about that time that he made the acquaintance of your mother, Lavinnia, through business dealings with her father, George Lambert. Lavinnia was an only child, her mother having died in childbirth. George Lambert was far from being a well man, and Charles Haversall expected to court Lavinnia, marry her and therefore solve all his financial difficulties. But George Lambert was a very astute man, and he recognized Charles for what he was. Lambert made a deal with him when he saw his daughter easily swayed by the handsome young charmer. He agreed to pay off all Charles's debts in exchange for an agreement that Charles would leave Lavinnia alone.

"For a few years Haversall went along with the plan and kept his part of the bargain," Dobson continued. "Then George Lambert died."

The lawyer paused for a moment, trying to arrange his thoughts before continuing. "Lavinnia inherited her father's money, and naturally, Charles Haversall immediately reappeared. With George Lambert out of the way, he expected everything to go his way. He courted Lavinnia, and everyone expected them to marry. They were from the same social sphere and both had been reared in moneyed backgrounds.

"But Charles made a fatal mistake. He introduced Lavinnia to a promising young engineer who had come to work for him after immigrating from Scotland—Terence McFarland, your father.

"I only met him once and very briefly, but I remember him. He had a quick intelligence and a laugh that was contagious. I can understand why your mother was drawn to him. Anyway, after meeting Terence McFarland, Lavinnia lost all interest in Charles Haversall. She married Terence barely two months after meeting him." Dobson shook his head as though amazed at the antics of people.

"It created quite a scandal at the time. I remember it well. To say that people were astounded by what Lavinnia Lambert had done would be to put it mildly. Charles Haversall was from a prestigious family and thought to have unlimited funds behind him. Yet, Lavinnia chose to run off with an unknown and virtually penniless immigrant. Everyone judged him to be the worst kind of opportunist."

Dobson stood up and moved toward the windows. "When they found themselves unwelcome in Boston society, Terence and Lavinnia McFarland moved to New York. Your father started his own company there. He was very successful. Very. Unlike Charles Haversall, Terence McFarland had the Midas touch." He turned at the windows and faced me. His expression was shadowed.

"Your parents felt misplaced guilt over running off and leaving Charles to face the scandal and rumors; so they contacted him when you were expected and asked him to be godfather. Charles accepted to salvage his pride. Then he set about courting another heiress a few years older than him—Marcella Avery. He went through her money in a matter of a few years. He was again in financial difficulties when the influenza epidemic hit New York. Your parents died, and you were sent here.

"Your parents were very young and unduly trusting. The letter you handed over to Charles Haversall was a handwritten will hastily drawn up just before your father died. It gave trusteeship of your inheritance over to Charles. Your father listed certain obligatory terms, of course, but they were kept only minimally. As for the bulk of your inheritance, that went straight into Charles Haversall's private bank account."

I felt curiously numb by all this information. My mouth was dry, but I sat staring into my teacup, not attempting to drink from it. My mind was a turmoil of whirling memories reviewing the 18 years I had lived in this brownstone mansion.

I had seldom been in contact with my guardian as a child. Charles Haversall spent most of his time away from the brownstone and the mercurial moods of his wife, Marcella. When he was home, he ensconced himself in the library with a bottle of expensive French brandy.

From the first, Charles had preferred me out of sight and mind and employed in what he called "worthwhile pursuits." Marcella enrolled me in a day school. When I was at the brownstone, I was relegated to Roberta Gillicuddy's stern care and trained to carry out menial tasks to assist her.

As I grew older, Charles Haversall's interest only changed slightly. I began taking my meals with him and Marcella. Once in a while he would glance over his reports and notice me. The conversation never included me.

When I turned 12, Marcella's interest altered. She was alarmed at my size. I had reached my alarming adult height of 5-8, unheard of for a child my age and most grown women. Marcella looked on me as a freak of nature, and I remembered her barbs only too well. When my beanpole body began to alter, rounding out and filling in, Marcella Haversall became even more alarmed. When I was 16, she decided I was much too endowed for a proper lady, and she took me straight to her dressmaker, who designed bodices to conceal my defects.

My thick fall of auburn hair seemed to annoy Marcella Haversall even more. She had a pale blond beauty that washed out against the colors of the current fashion. She thought my hair wild and untamed and insisted that I coil its sheening mass tightly and hide it beneath a fine pale netting. For the most part, my wardrobe consisted of earth tones. The severely cut styles and carefully coiled mane gave me a prim, austere appearance.

My relationship with Charles Haversall had been almost nonexistent. The one with his wife, Marcella, had been one of reverent servitude. She had been peevishly demanding at times, while at others she had shown surprising kindness. Several times she had given me small gifts at the most unexpected moments. Usually they were things she had received from friends and did not want herself, but they still brightened my drab existence.

It had only been when I talked of leaving that Marcella Haversall used pressures I could not fight. Several times I had approached the subject hopefully, only to have her make me feel guilty and ungrateful for even suggesting I carry out my dreams.

The last time I had brought up the dreaded subject had been four years ago. Marcella had been applying a coat of pale powder to her already-colorless skin while she sat before her vanity. When I made my request, she looked at me through the mirror, her expression wounded.

"Doesn't your lovely room suit you?" she had asked. My room was far from lovely when compared to the other bedrooms in the house, but I had never allowed it to distress me.

"My room is fine."

"Haven't we been good to you, Abigail?" she went on, scarcely hearing my mumbled reply. I knew what was coming and prepared myself. She turned on me, the hurt expression altering to scorn and indignation. "We have been very good to you. And this is how you repay us. You speak of deserting us? You know very well the hardship it's been for us to have you here," she continued, exaggerating their sacrifice, though at the time I was not fully aware. "We've bought your clothes, given you an excellent education, given you a home with affection. And now you talk of walking out on us. Charles has been most generous to you, and he would be terribly hurt for you to do this to him. Why, there is the dinner party next week, and after that the charity ball, and shortly after that there's the Christmas season and its round of parties. You know how Gilly is without your help. She's in her dotage, and the house and kitchen would be in an absolutely dreadful state if you deserted her. But go ahead! Be selfish! Be ungrateful! Don't remember all we've done for you!"

And so I had stayed. And my dependence upon the Haversalls had grown as my prospects had diminished. My life had become centered around their needs, their demands, their expectations of my future. After a while, I stopped thinking of going away at all. When I had precious spare time, I lost myself in books and gleaned my adventures and joy from them.

Now the news Bradford Dobson was giving me shattered the frail network of my life. All that I thought was, was not. All that had been, had never really been. And I could feel nothing.

"Miss McFarland. Miss McFarland," Bradford Dobson beckoned me back to the present. I blinked and then smiled apologetically.

"I am sorry for daydreaming." My statement brought a rather

incredulous expression into Dobson's stiff features.

"Do you understand what I've been telling you, Miss McFarland?"

"Yes. I believe I do." I sounded flat of emotion, and Dobson made an impatient, disbelieving sound in his throat.

"You can't possibly understand, not if you can sit there so calmly! My dear young woman, the Haversalls have systematically stripped you of your inheritance. I don't have the exact sum here with me, but I know it was no small fortune, and well beyond what the Haversall estate contains now. They used your inheritance to buy these expensive things." He waved his hand about the exquisite room. "The Dresden figurines, the rich carpets, the original oil paintings. They went to Europe every year, while they left you here to manage the household. They had dinner parties. They went to concerts, plays, and charity banquets, where they gave away your money. Marcella Haversall spent a fortune on her gowns. And you...." He stopped, looking disparagingly down at my mauve gown. He flushed slightly and shook his head.

"And what did they do for you, Miss McFarland? They did take you in. They did feed you and clothe you and give you an education." His tone was derisive, and then it rose again in indignation. "But you were entitled to the most expensive gowns, the finest Paris could offer. You were entitled to the most exclusive schools, the Grand Tour. Anything. Everything. Instead, Charles Haversall robbed you of everything but a paltry sum. He and his wife treated you as a penniless waif they took in through the goodness of their cold-blooded hearts. They trained you to serve them like some brainless lackey. And now they leave you without even a stipend in their will, without a mere mention, almost destitute. When I think of their deception, it utterly appalls me. And yet you sit there." He looked at me, his face lined and white. "Don't you understand? All this should, by rights, belong to you. But Charles Haversall left his entire estate to an indifferent and insensitive nephew in Maine."

I remembered once Marcella had suggested that if I wanted to leave, Charles could arrange for me to work at the factory. Even now, the thought made me shudder. The people there were heavily overworked and grossly underpaid. I had once overheard Roberta talking to one of the maids about a child who had gotten caught in the machines. Nothing had stopped, and the child's broken body had been pulled free. He had died several days later. The fault had been the lack of safety precautions, but even the child's death had not altered anything. Everything remained as it was. From Roberta's tone, I knew that it had not been the first time something of that sort had happened. Yet, Charles Haversall always maintained that there was not enough money to improve conditions, and if the workers did not like it, they could go elsewhere for work. The workers in Haversall's factory were as bound there as the slaves had been before the war.

I had always sympathized with the workers. I had much in common with them. My life depended on Charles Haversall, and though I longed to be free and independent, each year seemed to make me less so. I had no money and nowhere to go. And I knew the sordid truth. If I had known it years ago, would it have changed anything? Bradford Dobson said that Charles Haversall had carried out the letter of the will. How could I have fought him?

And what about now?

The numbness was wearing off. I began to feel angry, not so much at the Haversalls as at myself. All the years I had allowed myself to be used, when I might have broken away and established my own life. I had hung back from gratitude and loyalty to the Haversalls. Or was that really the truth? Wasn't it more the truth that I had been afraid to leave my dull but secure existence here in this old brownstone? I had seen little of Boston and nothing of the world, and it was frightening to think of setting off on my own.

"I've been such a fool," I breathed, and Dobson's face softened.

"There was no way you could have known what they were doing, Miss McFarland. And even if you had, I doubt if you could have stopped them."

"I should have left years ago before I allowed my life to pass me by!"

The solicitor smiled then. "At the age of twenty-three your life has hardly passed you by," he remarked with some humor.

"You said yourself that most women my age are married with families of their own," I countered with wryness.

"You are a very attractive young woman—"

"Please don't be kind, Mr. Dobson," I said quickly, embarrassed that he should feel he needed to say such a thing. Marcella Haversall had been most clear about my limitations in that area.

"Kindness has nothing to do with it, Miss McFarland," Dobson insisted. "With the right clothes and hair style...." He stopped and spread his hands in an apologetic gesture. "I overstep myself. I do apologize."

"You spoke of my guardian's nephew," I primed.

"Yes. I'm afraid Wendall Haversall wants this house and all his uncle's holdings sold." Dobson lowered the final blow.

"In other words, the new Mr. Haversall wants me out of this house almost immediately," I said, somehow managing to not allow the fear that was beginning to prey wantonly on my nerves to show. Where could I go? What could I do?

"Yes. He already has a prospective buyer."

"He didn't waste any time. My guardian has only been dead ten days."

"What will you do, Miss McFarland?" Dobson asked as delicately as he could.

"I don't know. I...I don't know," my voice shook in spite of my efforts. "Find a position, I suppose," I said with more control. "That would be the most sensible thing to do."

The first thing that popped unwelcome into my mind was the Haversall factory, that looming gray edifice that blighted the landscape of Boston. In my imagination I could hear the men and women moaning as they dragged themselves exhausted to labor in the bowels of the rat-infested building. I could hear the children screaming as they were caught and ground in the merciless machines. I shivered, and my mouth twitched.

"What kind of position, if I might ask?" Dobson pressed.

"I...I don't know," I admitted, licking my dry lips and determinedly pressing away the picture of the factory. "House service...I don't know." The despair of my situation was beginning at last to sink in, and I started to shake.

"You completed your secondary education, did you not?" Bradford Dobson asked, reaching across to pat my hand with his own. Mine were ice-cold and clutched tightly in my lap.

"Yes," I nodded, staring into Dobson's clear, intelligent gaze.

"Would you consider teaching?"

"I'm sure I lack the necessary qualifications, Mr. Dobson," I said with near-certainty. "Boston requires—"

"I wasn't thinking of Boston." He smiled.

"No?"

"No."

"Then where?" I asked, curious now.

"Perhaps out West someplace. Their requirements are not nearly so rigid. You could make a life out there for yourself, Miss McFarland," he suggested.

A quick rush of excitement pushed my gray thoughts away. "I've always had a great interest in California," I admitted.

Dobson's eyes moved assessingly over my face. "You look quite different when you smile like that, Miss McFarland." I was not sure what he meant, and I chose not to answer. "Do you like children?" he asked.

I laughed slightly. "I don't know, Mr. Dobson. I've never been around many young children." I thought of maid Ann's three boys and frowned. "Those I have met hardly qualify as children."

"What do you mean?"

"Annie Callaghan's three boys have been working since they were six. They seem very old. I don't think I've ever seen one of them laugh."

"Factory work."

"The Haversall factory," I clarified. Dobson muttered a sound of disgust.

"The world is well rid of that man."

"That's hardly a Christian thing to say," I commented, but smiled. "If what we are taught in church is true, Mr. Dobson, Charles Haversall should be pitied now that he is dead."

"Perhaps," the solicitor said without conviction. "But it's been my experience to see the takers reaping the rewards of this world while the good Christian men and women suffer.

They say the devil takes care of his own. My vision of hell is not one of fire and brimstone, but rather a place that reeks of greed, lust, and every kind of evil. Charles Haversall will probably relish his eternity."

I stared at him round-eyed with surprise. Then I laughed. "Well, to be completely honest, Mr. Dobson, I hope Charles and Marcella Haversall are not too happy wherever they are."

"In that we heartily agree," he answered. "Now, let's see what we can do about your future."

 *Chapter Two*

The carpetbag grew heavier with each step. I shifted hands, but that afforded me little relief in the heat of the afternoon sun. My mouth tasted of dust. Pausing alongside the dirt road, I dropped the bag and pulled a handkerchief from my drawstring purse. Taking a deep breath, I dabbed at the perspiration that beaded my forehead. I discarded the prim bonnet, pushing it back to rest between my shoulder blades. Then I loosened the top three buttons of my high-neck blouse. It plunged daringly, exposing more than just a little swelling and cleavage above the camisole. I debated rebuttoning it and then gave a shrug. There was no one about to notice my décolleté, and I was too hot to worry about propriety at the moment.

I wondered if the stage had been repaired yet. At the rate I was going, it might come along and pick me up before I was able to reach my destination. Ten miles had not seemed like such a long walk this morning. But it had been cooler then, and the excitement of reaching the end of my journey had been great.

A faint smile twitched as I thought of the picture I made now. Good heavens! If anyone got a look at me at this moment, I would look like a dust-covered recalcitrant of the worst kind. Perhaps I would come by a stream where I could freshen up a bit before arriving in Sycamore Hill. Otherwise I would arrive just as I was: hot, dusty, and exhausted.

Looking up, I was greeted by a cloudless, crystal-blue sky that under other circumstances would have been wonderful. Now I would have welcomed a few clouds. Around me the hills were golden, the only green relief being the waxy spined leaves of huge scattered oaks and other native trees. Not far away was a line of imported eucalyptus trees standing like straight-backed sentinels. There were no flowers about, but the stagecoach driver had assured me that these same dry-grassed hills were covered in spring with golden poppies, blue lupines, sunburst-yellow mustard flowers and red paint brushes.

I might have had more sense, I told myself for not the first time in the past hour. I must have already covered six or seven miles, but I had no way of really knowing. Distances in this hot, dry world of great spaces and few people did not seem the same as in Boston.

Perhaps if I had not run into so many delays before the stage had broken down, I would not have been so precipitate in hiking the last ten miles. The worst delay had come in Sacramento, where my trunk with all the books and teaching materials had been found missing. Central Pacific personnel had not been unduly alarmed, for it seemed such an event was not uncommon. However, the three days it had taken to locate the trunk in Placerville had caused me sleepless nights and an agony of nervous tension. That did not begin to mention my feelings when I was forced to spend three days boarding in a local hotel and paying money I could little afford to spend.

As soon as my wayward trunk arrived in Sacramento, I had boarded the next train to Oakland. Once there, I intended to take the train on to Sycamore Hill. However, as the Fates had it, that train had already departed, and the next would not go for another three days. The station manager had mentioned an old stage line that was still in business. He also warned me that the line had a reputation for frequent breakdowns.

Forty miles lay between Oakland and Sycamore Hill. After traveling a continent, that small distance seemed negligible. I decided to take a chance and ride the disreputable stage. I might have known it would break down not once, but several times.

The last time, the coach had lost a wheel ten miles from town. The driver said it would be several hours before he could effect the repairs. So I had taken to the road with the assurance that my trunk would be dropped off at the general store in Sycamore Hill. Perhaps I would have been wiser to stay with the stage and take my chances on arriving in town. At least then I would have arrived looking like a lady and not something even a cat would hesitate about dragging in.

In spite of all the mishaps, I was filled with trembling excitement. Only at odd moments had I felt real resentment at the Haversalls. Bradford Dobson had been surprised that my attitude had remained so mild. I realized after his disclosures that I had never really known the Haversalls at all, in spite of living under their roof for 18 years. They were strangers to me. Having never become accustomed to luxuries, I did not miss them. Yet, I could not say I did not have moments of bitter resentment about my stolen inheritance. The worst moments were when I realized what a fool I had been to remain out of mistaken gratitude. How they must have laughed at me!

But now I was free. I wondered sometimes if I would have felt so free had I possessed that fortune Bradford Dobson had spoken about. Money carried heavy responsibility. Had I inherited Haversall's factory, I could never have overlooked the despicable conditions of the loathsome place. As it was now, I had nothing but a few dollars remaining from my father's fortune, and ahead of me a position as a schoolteacher for a rural community.

I wondered if I would have that position after the school-board representative had a good look at me. I stopped long enough to brush down my doe-brown skirt. The dust made a soft cloud around me. Sooner or later the sun had to begin its descent, and the noon-high heat would have to dissipate.

Glancing up into the sky again, I thought it must be well after two. Another hill stretched out before me. I prayed that this one would be the last, and beyond it would lie a nice shady community. Sycamores were trees; so surely that meant the town had an abundance of them. Nice, tall trees to cast cooling shadows over my sunburned brow and cheeks and nose by the feel of it.

I was so deep in my thoughts that I failed to notice the gopher hole right in front of me. Stumbling, I fell headlong into the road. Only momentarily stunned, I stood up quickly, straightening my blouse and brushing down my skirt.

"Of all the ridiculous things to do," I mumbled to myself, checking that I had not torn something or scraped anything. "You don't need the Haversalls to make a fool of you. You do such a great job of that yourself."

Then I started to laugh thinking of the picture I must have made a second earlier. It started with a mere jerk of my mouth and then opened into peals of sound. A voice behind me cut it off as effectively as a noose around my neck.

"This is hardly a day to be out pleasure-walking."

Jumping with frightened surprise, I whirled around to face a man sitting above me on a buckboard. His face and expression were shadowed beneath the rim of his hat. In quick perusal I took in the rest of his appearance, noting the clean white shirt that covered a set of decidedly broad shoulders, the leather-and-brass-work belt that circled a lean, hard waist, the brown pants that indicated long, well-muscled legs. He sat comfortably with those legs apart, one booted foot raised on the brake. His hands were relaxed with the reins. I noticed those hands, work-callused but clean even unto the trimmed nails. I felt even more disheveled beside the man's crispness, and a surge of unreasonable resentment stiffened my spine.

With a careless movement, the stranger took off his hat and wiped his forehead with his arm. I was sure it was the heat that made me feel suddenly flushed and light-headed.

He was young, not more than 35, and very attractive in a rugged, tanned sort of way. He had thick, tawny hair, sun-streaked blond in the front. But it was his eyes that caught my immediate, if dismayed, attention. They were the bluest I had ever seen, and they were filled with laughter.

With sudden understanding I realized he had witnessed my ungraceful collapse into the dirt. My face turned an unbecoming beet-red, and the resentment altered to growing irritation.

"You could give a person some warning," I flared, "without sneaking up behind her and scaring her half to death!"

There was the slightest narrowing of those blue eyes, but

the smile changed to a wide grin that disclosed even, white teeth.

"Now, little lady," he drawled, lazily mocking. "You aren't going to pretend it was my presence that brought on that little dance routine you just did."

I deserved that unkind reminder, I thought, immediately regretting my rude outburst. Then I became acutely aware that the man's gaze had dropped to the part of my anatomy that Marcella Haversall had tried to bound. Instinctively I raised my hand only to come in contact with bare skin. Humiliated to be caught in my misdemeanor of propriety, my fingers flew to repair the oversight.

"I liked it better the way it was," the man commented, not intending to spare me anything. I glared up at him. Insensitive, he continued his embarrassing scrutiny of my form.

Snatching up the carpetbag I had dropped, I began to march down the dusty road again. I did not hear the buckboard moving and chanced a quick look back over my shoulder. The man was sitting there watching me with an enigmatic expression. I jerked my head back around, afraid that if I did not watch where I was going, I would stumble into another gopher hole and make a worse fool of myself.

I heard the buckboard move behind me.

"Why don't you sit down and take a load off your feet. You look as though you've walked for miles," the stranger observed unkindly when he drew up next to me. I did have some feminine pride, and I bristled at his blunt assessment of me. I knew I looked a mess, but I did not appreciate his telling me so.

"Thank you very much for your kind observations," I said dryly without looking at him or slowing my pace. Maybe he would take the hint and keep going. I could feel his eyes on me and hoped he blamed the heat for the rush of color. He flicked the reins again, guiding his two sorrels toward the side of the road. They came very close, and I side-stepped. He kept on his path, herding me like an unruly cow until I was pressed off the road.

"What are you doing?" I gasped, just managing to back step yet again before my foot was squashed beneath a large hoof.

"How long have you been walking?" he countered.

"Since eight this morning," I stammered, taking several more backward steps to avoid colliding with the horses. "Will you stop those animals before they walk all over me!"

"Happy to." The man grinned, setting the brake and tying the reins securely before jumping down to tower over me. My eyes widened, and I backed a few more paces while staring warily up at him. Then I began to ease around the buckboard.

"I've no intention of molesting you," he commented derisively. "But I thought you might need a drink of water."

Escape, for the moment, was forgotten. He reached under the seat and pulled out a canteen. I didn't move and he extended his arm offering me the canteen. I smiled.

"Is that all you have? I was praying for a river."

He laughed. "Take it slow," he said when I gulped thirstily from the canteen.

"Oh, that tastes so good," I breathed. "I think I've swallowed half the dust between Oakland and Sycamore Hill." I started to hand back the canteen and then realized I should wipe off the top. With what? I wondered, looking down at my dusty skirt and the soiled handkerchief stuffed into my pocket.

Lean, hard fingers closed over mine. I released the canteen as though his touch burned. A smile bent his mouth as he raised the canteen and drank from it. There was something very intimate about that action, and I felt my embarrassment revived. When he finished, he held out the canteen to me again.

"Would you like another drink?" he asked, a faintly taunting glitter in his eyes.

"No . . . no, thank you," I declined, unable to keep from looking at the finely shaped mouth that had just drunk from the container I had so recently used. He seemed to know what I was thinking and grinned again. Nervous, I fingered the loose tendrils of hair about my face, pushing them back into the serviceable coil. The man watched, and I stopped my tense actions, trying to appear relaxed.

"You're from Boston?"

"How did you know that?" I asked, raising my brows in surprise.

"Your accent. And other things. . . ."

"Other things?"

"No one that I know of would walk dressed like that, carrying a carpetbag, without a canteen in the middle of August. Not if they were from around here. And not if they had any brains."

My mouth tightened, though I saw the teasing light in his eyes. "I was eager to reach Sycamore Hill," I said coolly. "The stagecoach had already broken down twice before, and when it lost a wheel, I thought I'd have a better chance of reaching my destination if I walked. Besides, it was mild enough this morning."

"It starts out cool," he agreed. "But it can end up hotter than hell in the afternoon." I flushed at his easy swearing, and he chuckled.

"What's the matter?" he asked, though I suspected he knew very well.

"Not a thing."

"Boston through and through, aren't you?" he needled.

"What do you mean by that?" I demanded, piqued by his laughter.

"All prim and proper. A little earth language brings sundown into your cheeks."

"I'm not as prim as I look," I flared, his tone indicating some slight at which I took immediate offense.

"Aren't you now?" he asked, raising his brows speculatively. His gaze moved down again, and I tried unsuccessfully to ignore it. My experience with men was almost non-existent, and I was finding this conversation increasingly baffling and disturbing.

"Thank you for the water," I muttered, clutching my bag and turning away.

"Just a minute," he said quickly. "All right," he relented. "I'll try not to tease you anymore. But I think you ought to sit down for a few minutes before you faint dead away. Your face is a little too red."

"I do wish you would keep your observations to yourself, Mr. . . . Mr. . . . ." I searched frantically for a name, then remembered he had not offered one.

"Jordan Bennett," he supplied with a slight smile.

"Mr. Bennett," I finished rather lamely, pulling my eyes determinedly away from his.

"Visiting or staying?"

"Pardon me?" I asked blankly.

"Sycamore Hill. That is your destination, isn't it?"

"Yes, it is."

"And?" He obviously expected an answer whether it was his business or not.

"I'm not sure," I hedged. Jordan Bennett didn't say anything for a minute, but his blue eyes narrowed fractionally on my flushed face.

"You wouldn't be one of Ross Persall's new girls, would you?" he asked almost hopefully.

"No. I've never heard of him," I answered truthfully. There was an oak several yards away, and I walked over to sit in the shade. I dreaded the thought of walking another step and looked up at Jordan Bennett leaning against the tree trunk. Surely he would offer me a ride. No one would be so unkind as to leave a woman walking out here in the heat of the day, I hoped. I did not possess the nerve to ask.

"I'm ... glad to hear that," he said, not really sounding it. I wondered who Ross Persall was.

"Who's Ross Persall?" I admitted my curiosity.

"A local resident," Jordan Bennett answered as evasively as I previously had. I sighed and decided not to press further. Besides, I was too tired to be curious about much of anything. Except for him.

"Are you a local resident?" I asked.

"No."

I waited, hoping for more information. None was forthcoming, but those blue eyes were dancing and obviously seeing right inside my head. My mouth tightened, and I gave a faint shrug to indicate it didn't matter one way or another whether he was or was not from Sycamore Hill. The silence was growing uncomfortable for me.

"Is it always this hot in the summer?" I asked inanely, desperate for anything to say.

"No."

The man was determined to make me angry!

"How far is it to Sycamore Hill?"

"Two miles. Uphill all the way." He was grinning now, and I closed my eyes, saying a silent prayer. It remained unanswered, and I sighed heavily.

"Well?" he drawled.

"Well what?" I asked.

"Aren't you going to ask?" He was laughing at me again, the dreadful man!

"Ask you what?" I pretended obtuseness. There was a long silence, and I looked away, unable to sustain his look. My eyes encountered the road, parched, dusty and pockmarked, but worse, stretching out ahead of me for another two long, painful miles. It wasn't getting any cooler either. I looked back at Jordan Bennett, but couldn't bring myself to voice the question.

"Are you always this stubborn?" he asked with slight impatience. I couldn't explain that it was a matter of reticence, not stubbornness, about asking favors of strangers.

"I give in." He gave a dramatic sigh. "I must be the more curious of the two of us. What's your name first off?" He sounded as though he had made up a list of questions, and I stiffened again.

"Abigail McFarland," I offered hesitantly, and then felt foolish. After all, he had already introduced himself, hadn't he?

"Abigail." He tested the name on his tongue. "A nice, old-fashioned name, if a bit stiff," he commented dryly, and then his eyes widened as some thought, obviously far from pleasant, entered his head. "Good God!" he exclaimed. "I think I know who you are!"

"You do?" I asked blankly. "Why are you looking so thunderous?" I added, alarmed at the sudden change in his expression.

"You're the new schoolmarm, aren't you?" he accused, a wealth of disgust in his tone.

"Well . . . yes," I admitted, bewildered by his reaction to my occupation. I might have been some bug under a rock!

He swore beneath his breath, renewing the color that had recently managed to recede to normal. "I should have known," he muttered and then glared at me as though I had done something criminal. His eyes, when they coursed down over me this time, were derisive and not the least bit friendly. Without another word, Jordan Bennett walked purposely toward his buckboard.

He was going to leave me here! I thought with sudden astonishment. Without thinking, I jumped up and ran after him.

"Mr. Bennett, wait, please," I pleaded. "May I . . . may I . . ." The words wouldn't come. The only other time I had ever asked for anything, I had requested freedom from my guardians. That had been denied to me. I had never asked for anything again.

"No!" he snapped. "If you're about to ask for a ride to town, forget it!" he continued curtly. "A schoolmarm ought to have enough good sense not to be walking on a day like this in the first place," he added tauntingly. "The walk will teach you a lesson."

I tried for levity. "Well, I've learned my lesson." I smiled shakily, hoping he would relent, and still not understanding his contempt for my occupation.

"You'll learn a damn sight more when you reach town," he grumbled, releasing the brake with one fluid motion. His gaze was blistering.

"What do you mean?" I floundered.

"I wouldn't want to ruin the surprise, Miss McFarland," he stated with heavy sarcasm. "And another thing. I'll take odds that you'll be running out of town by the end of the month."

"I'm not as soft as you seem to think I am," I said coolly. Jordan Bennett was unreasonable, unpleasant and definitely not a gentleman.

"No?" His eyes dropped provocatively, further solidifying my impression of him. "You're soft all right. Everywhere . . ." he looked directly into my eyes, "including the head."

I looked at him with hostility matching his own. "Don't let me detain you any longer, Mr. Bennett," I smiled stiffly. A muscle jerked in his jaw.

"Have a nice walk," he retorted in the same testy tone. Then he snapped the reins, not even wasting a backward glance at me. I stood staring after him, unable to believe he really was leaving me out here. Dust billowed out from beneath the wheels and floated back to cover me from head to toe. Frustrated and furious, I pounded the dirt off my blouse and dress, wishing I could scream at him. I wouldn't give him that satisfaction.

Picking up my carpetbag, I forced myself to start walking again. Only two miles, I told myself. Not far. My self-assurance lacked conviction.

"What a horrid man!" I said out loud, glaring down the road where the buckboard went. It disappeared over the rise.

So Jordan Bennett thought I would be running out of town by the end of the month, did he? Well, he would see he was wrong! And what had he meant by that remark? Surely the children of Sycamore Hill were not quite that bad. And what was wrong with being a schoolteacher? It surely did not deserve such unveiled contempt as he had displayed.

My entire body quivered with anger, but after ten minutes' walking, it dissipated. I was exhausted and felt almost as thirsty as I had before the drink from Jordan Bennett's canteen. Only two more miles. Don't think about what he said. It can't be all uphill!

During the rest of my odyssey I could not stop thinking about Jordan Bennett's reaction to my occupation, and his prophecy of my imminent departure. It made my determination to succeed all the more firm, but it also afforded me no comforting thoughts as to what might lie ahead in Sycamore Hill.

 *Chapter Three*

Standing on the rough plank bridge, I gazed tiredly down at the creek below. Young cottonwoods grew along the banks, showing the level of winter and spring flooding by the dead, hugging grasses twisted around their trunks. Now the creek moved slowly, revealing its rocky bottom. I longed to climb down the steep incline and get a refreshing drink. I wished I could take off my shoes and sink my aching, blistered feet into the cold, clear water. Even better would be to submerge my entire body and rid myself of some road dust!

However, all that was impossible, for just beyond the bridge lay a town nestled in the small valley surrounded by oak-covered hills. I knew I was in Sycamore Hill, for at the end of the community's main street arose another hill, this one with a grove of giant sycamores.

Below the sycamores, white crosses and marble markers studded the brown shadows like buttons on dark velvet. At the base of the hill stood a New England-style church with high steeple and brick front steps. Off to the right I saw another church built contrastingly of adobe brick, much in the tradition of a Jesuit mission.

Closer by me and only several hundred yards beyond the bridge lay a two-story building made interesting by gingerbread eaves and red decorative shutters at each of the ten front windows. The raised wooden sidewalk was shaded by an overhang supported by six solid-looking pillars. Just below the walkway were three horse troughs and tying rails. Several saddle horses stood in the sun, chewing distractedly at their bits while their owners lingered somewhere within the establishment.

As I passed the building, I heard noise. Bursts of laughter blended with the sound of a woman singing while someone with a heavy touch accompanied her on an ill-tuned piano.

As I walked into Sycamore Hill, I admired the modest homes that snuggled tightly against businesses along the main street. Each boasted a neat rose garden and white picket fence. Several had vegetable gardens to one side, with squash, pumpkins, tomatoes, bush beans, berries, carrots, peppers, and corn interspersed with brilliant-gold, pungent, bug-repellent marigolds. At one house, there stood an absurd scarecrow on which sat an arrogant magpie almost smirking with disdain.

Black- and English-walnut, maple and pine trees gave shade to the streets that were unpaved and shot out to the left and right. Each bore a name that seemed Catholic or hinted of some founding immigrant—St. Joseph, St. Mary, McPherson, Janssen, St. Paul, Silverton.

On the corner of Silverton stood a fine, sturdy two-story boardinghouse with a small, neatly printed vacancy sign in the front lacy-curtained window. I hesitated and noted with interest the brilliantly overflowing window boxes in front, the porch swing and front wooden steps, the neat garden with sweet peas ranging from deep purple to bright red and pale pink lining the front gate. Two climbing rose bushes alive with honeybees grew lavishly over a latticed arch at the front gate. A large English-walnut tree and two smaller fig trees shaded the yard. To the back I saw another characteristic vegetable garden, and I heard the clucking of hens followed closely by one cocky rooster.

A weary sigh escaped me. Perhaps this pleasant house would be my new home. There was a vast difference between it and the spacious brownstone mansion in Boston. This one bespoke of warmth and hospitality. Here, perhaps, I could develop friendships and make a place for myself. The opportunity had never before been available under the jealous, self-centered guardianship of the Haversalls.

However, there was no time to linger and dream. I noted the sun was well into its descent toward dusk, and I had yet to find the Olmsteads' general store. Arrangements would have been made for my arrival, I was sure. Excitement overrode the pain of my ten-mile walk, and I moved more quickly down the quiet street.

Sycamore Hill had other conveniences. I spotted a tidy tack room with several saddles and bridles displayed in the window, a butcher's shop, another white house indicating a doctor in residence, a tall dark-green building with white trim named Apperson's Feed and Hardware. I wondered briefly if this Apperson was any relation to one after which a street I had seen had been named. Probably. This was the kind of town one would not wish to leave.

I passed a millinery with a window full of charming hats and two stylish dresses on mannequins. Stopping to admire the items on sale, I noted the prices with dismay: I walked on briskly. There was a shoe-repair shop smelling pleasantly of leather and polish on the right, and on the left, a big white-stone bank building. Just beyond that was another less inviting boardinghouse, two saloons and a quaint Italian restaurant with red-and-white-checkered curtains.

I finally spotted a sign announcing Olmstead's General Store. It was only two blocks from the church and the end of town. Parked neatly in front of the store was a loaded buckboard, and I hesitated. Surely that odious man was not there waiting to laugh at me again, I thought furiously. Glancing around, I saw other buckboards. One sat in front of the feed store; another was heavily loaded and standing in front of one of the saloons. That one, I thought with a twist of my lips, was probably Jordan Bennett's.

Feeling more sure of myself, I started forward again. Mounting the steps, I looked curiously at an awesome wooden Indian that stood in front of Olmstead's. Standing beside it, I looked up and down at the headdress, buckskins and hawknose. Then I passed it and stepped into the store.

The first person I saw was Jordan Bennett! He was lounging against the counter, laughing with a woman with pleasant features and long braided hair pinned in a crown on her head. To my humiliation, I felt the color mounting into my face as

Bennett flicked a glance in my direction and then ignored me. Never in my life had I despised anyone quite so much as I did him at that moment. Even the Haversalls had not aroused such resentment.

The woman Jordan Bennett was with gave him a playful slap on the hand and then raised her head to see me standing just inside the door. Her eyes took in my bedraggled appearance as she came around the counter. She smiled, if a bit curiously, and I forced a smile in return. I wondered only briefly if the laughter between Jordan Bennett and this woman had been at my expense.

"May I help you?" the woman asked, stopping only two paces in front of me and eyeing me curiously.

"Yes, I think so," I answered huskily, my throat parched and sore from thirst and swallowed dust. Some of the dust had come from the wheels of Jordan Bennett's buckboard, I thought resentfully, refusing to even look at him. If he intended to ignore me, then that was fine.

"May I speak with James Olmstead? I'm Abigail McFarland from Boston. He's expecting me, I believe," I informed the woman.

Her eyes lighted with excitement and pleasure. "You're our new schoolteacher," she exclaimed brightly. "Oh, I'm so glad you've arrived safe and sound. Did you have a nice trip?" Her exuberance caught me a little off guard. She almost implied that I might have arrived other than well. And then I thought of the picture I must make, and smiled in spite of my discomfort.

"Yes. Everything went well until the last few miles," I told her, casting a brief glance in Bennett's direction and meeting decidedly warning eyes. He straightened from the counter.

"Why don't you get Miss McFarland a cup of your good coffee, Emmy," he suggested. Then he added yet another of his characteristically unkind observations. "Our new schoolteacher looks badly in need of a drink of something."

I glared at him and then smiled at Emmy again. "A glass of water would be very welcome," I admitted, expecting Bennett to laugh. He didn't.

"Oh, yes, of course. Just listen to me rattling on like some magpie. I'm Emily Olmstead, Jim's wife," she said, extending her hand and shaking mine firmly. "This is Jordan Bennett, one of our most illustrious ranchers," she teased him. "You'll have his daughter, Linda, in your class. She's a dear, and as pretty as her mother."

With that announcement I felt a hard lump drop into the pit of my stomach. I avoided looking at Jordan Bennett again, feeling with dismay that it was no wonder he had so decidedly disapproved of me when meeting me on the road. I would be instructing his daughter. And there I had been, looking like some scruffy derelict. I tried to remember every word I had said to the man and hoped I had not been too unforgivably rude.

"The coffee, Emmy," Jordan Bennett prodded with an amused smile.

"Oh, yes, the coffee. I'm sorry. I'll get it now and collect my husband on the way back." She laughed. As she passed Jordan, she tapped him. "Have a pleasant day," she said.

"You too, Em." He smiled slightly, apparently understanding some message she had passed to him. "Give my regards to Jim." Mrs. Olmstead nodded and disappeared behind the curtain to the back storeroom.

I felt a sudden trepidation being alone with Jordan Bennett. Deliberately turning away, I pretended interest in the rows of canned goods, the flour and rice bins and the bolts of cloth stacked neatly on a long table. I heard him move behind me and stiffened with nervous tension.

"Did you enjoy your walk, Miss McFarland?"

I controlled the irritation his amused tone aroused, and forced myself to answer evenly. "Even the last two miles, Mr. Bennett."

"I'm glad to hear it," he murmured, and I could tell he was laughing at me again. I could feel him watching me. "You were about to tell Emmy of our meeting on the road. Take my advice. Don't."

I did turn around then. "Why not, Mr. Bennett? Might it be embarrassing for you?" My tone implied challenge, and his eyes narrowed slightly.

"I don't embarrass easily."

"No, I don't suppose you would at that. One does need a conscience first," I went on incautiously.

"Something you obviously think I lack," he commented dryly, his eyes dancing again. I decided not to answer and hoped my silence would be enough.

The corner of Bennett's mouth curved up. "Listen to me, my dear little Boston grande dame. The first thing you had better learn about being a schoolmarm is not to lounge under shade trees, sharing drinks and conversation with strange men."

His description of our brief encounter sounded scandalous. In embarrassment and rising indignation, I flushed red to the roots of my auburn hair.

"I was not lounging under a shade tree, and you know it, Mr. Bennett," I hissed furiously.

"From my vantage point you were. And the conversation begged a flirtation," he taunted, unmoved by my frustration.

I stared at him in disbelief. "I don't flirt!" I denied hotly. He chuckled, obviously finding my discomfiture greatly amusing.

"I find that encouraging," he drawled, leaning closer so that I had to arch back away from him. He smiled, his eyes glimmering some message that my mind did not fully understand, but my senses did. They quickened until my heart was thudding rapidly. Bennett straightened again as though well aware of his effect on me. His voice became brisk.

"After all, Miss McFarland, there are certain things a town expects of its teacher, one being an untarnished reputation." The unfriendliness was back in his voice and expression.

I blanched at his implication. "There's nothing wrong with my reputation," I was stung to reply in my own defense.

"Not yet, maybe. But a few indiscreet admissions on your part might change that, and you'd find yourself out of a job before you even got started." He made himself perfectly clear.

"Nothing happened that I'm embarrassed about," I said, and then remembered the loosened buttons on my blouse as his eyes trailed down to remind me.

"People always prefer to see the worst. It makes their vicarious living more exciting," he said cynically. "They hear the facts . . . a lone girl on the road, lingering with a man," he went on, insinuating much. He raised his brows provocatively, his eyes moving to my mouth.

"You're vile!" I gasped. "And I don't believe you are the least concerned about *my* reputation," I went on, thinking of his pretty, young wife and daughter. His mouth tightened in impatience.

"There's nothing that can damage my reputation at this point," he said coldly. "I've lived in these parts most of my life, minus a few years. People have already drawn their own conclusions about my questionable character."

In other words, they would believe anything he said above whatever defense I might present, I thought with sudden anxiety.

"Meaning you intend to put a different connotation on our meeting if I should choose to say anything about it," I managed defiantly. "You're even worse than I first thought," I murmured, turning away. Bennett's hand forcibly swung me back. There was a ruthless determination in his hardened expression that warned me against pressing him at all. Seeing my startled and frightened expression, he released me.

"Your intelligence isn't as high as I thought," he commented dauntingly.

"You needn't be so insulting, Mr. Bennett," I snapped back, my fright momentarily forgotten in the face of his remark.

"Everything's been running just fine. I don't need a damn little schoolmarm around to complicate matters," he said, his eyes glittering in odd accusation. "Why the damn hell did you come to Sycamore Hill?"

"I don't know what you're talking about. What do I have to do with anything you're involved in? But as for my reason for being here, this town evidently needs a teacher. And you, yourself, could do with some English lessons, Mr. Bennett. Or can you only promote your own idiocy by using foul language?"

Jordan Bennett stilled to a pulsating silence at my rushed and breathless speech. Then he grinned, his good humor apparently restored. "At least you're true to form. That, perhaps, will be small comfort."

"What are you talking about?" I asked, becoming more and more exasperated.

"Never mind." He dismissed it. "Why don't you take a little friendly advice, Miss McFarland?" he went on in the same friendly manner. "Go on back to Boston and your comfortable parlors and fine-feathered friends."

My chin jerked up as I was reminded of the Haversalls. "You don't know anything about me. So don't presume to tell me where I belong!"

"Oh, I could tell you exactly where you belong, Miss McFarland," he offered, his blue eyes gazing at me in such a way as to bring confused color rushing again into my cheeks. "A man doesn't need a lot of time to know all there is to know about a woman."

"What a prime example of conceit you are," I managed, but I did not sound very convincing.

"I know more about your nature than you think," he continued, gloating over my unease.

"I doubt if you know anything at all, Mr. Bennett."

"I know you'll make a lousy schoolteacher," he prophesied harshly, giving a low blow to my already shaking ego. All the doubts I had voiced to Bradford Dobson when he had learned of this position came flooding back to haunt me. Perhaps Jordan Bennett was right.

"Are you losing your nerve already, Miss McFarland?" Bennett asked. I tilted my chin at a determined angle.

"I will do my very best," I said, hoping he had not seen the sad state my confidence was in. He watched my face as though searching for some indication of weakness.

"I've no doubt you will," he admitted, dismally making it clear that my best would not be good enough. "You'll dig your own premature grave in that godforsaken schoolhouse. I don't doubt it for one minute." He started to say more, but shook his head as Emily Olmstead's voice was heard from the back room. He gave me an unpleasant little smile.

"I should stay and make things really difficult for you," he threatened.

"I don't see how your staying or going will make one bit of difference to me," I retorted truthfully.

"Don't challenge me to show you," he warned, the glitter back in his eyes. "Things are going to be harrowing enough for you without my adding my two-bits' worth."

With that disquieting comment he turned and strode out of the store. I watched him as he jumped onto his loaded buckboard with ease. He untied the reins and released the brake with an impatience born of anger.

"Jim, this is Miss Abigail McFarland," Emily Olmstead said from behind me, drawing my attention away from Jordan Bennett, who was already moving off down the street. I turned with a tense smile, extending my hand to the bullish-looking man with balding head and sharp brown eyes.

"Pleased to meet you, ma'am," he greeted respectfully while looking me over with questioning intensity.

"I'm afraid I had to walk the last ten miles." I tried to explain my state. "The stagecoach lost a wheel, you see—"

"We expected you to come by train," Olmstead interrupted.

"The train wasn't due to leave again for another three days. I was too excited to wait that long." My words were met with a stony look.

"It might have been wiser if you had, Miss McFarland."

"Oh, Jim," Emily cut in. He darted her an impatient look.

"Is her room cleaned yet?" he asked abruptly, and Emily flushed.

"I . . . I hadn't gotten around to going over there yet," she said, and I felt there was more than acute embarrassment in her admission of the oversight.

"I'm sure my room is just fine." I tried to reassure Emily Olmstead. She gave me a very odd little look and then darted another at her husband.

"The school has been closed for over a year," he informed me. "Nobody has been in the place during that time."

That statement aroused a whole series of questions in my mind, but Olmstead's forbidding expression prevented me from asking any.

"You see, we weren't able to find another teacher after—" his wife started to explain.

"You're lucky you didn't collapse on the road in this August heat, Miss McFarland. It's over a hundred degrees, by my guess," her husband interrupted her smoothly, casting her a warning glance that she obviously understood.

"Yes," she agreed at once to his change of subject. "It's too bad someone didn't happen along and give you a ride into town."

What was going on here? First Jordan Bennett with his dire predictions and unreasonable animosity, and now this silent conversation going on over my head. I thought of Jordan Bennett's warning not to speak of our brief roadside encounter. Looking at James Olmstead's slightly disapproving perusal of me, I decided that perhaps silence was indeed the best policy. Especially when I did not know what was going on at all!

"Yes, I would have welcomed a ride," I agreed with a wry smile.

"I think the coffee should be ready now." Emily excused herself. She was back almost immediately with a tray on which sat a cup and saucer, a sugar bowl, a small cream pitcher, a plate of cookies and the welcome glass of water.

"Oh, that's very refreshing," I thanked her, having finished the water first. The tingling of a bell drew my attention as well as that of the Olmsteads.

A heavyset woman walked into the store. As she progressed down the aisle, I noted the small flannel hat perched on her head, with its ridiculous feather protruding and bobbing as she walked. Dark, ferretlike eyes moved over me with avid curiosity.

"Berthamae," Emily greeted. Berthamae only treated Emily to a cursory glance, and then continued to stare pointedly at me.

"You're new in town," she stated the obvious and waited for an introduction.

"Miss McFarland, this is Berthamae Poole," Olmstead supplied. "Miss McFarland is our new schoolteacher, Berthamae." The woman's thick eyebrows shot up.

"Well, it's high time," she emitted sharply before I could even extend my hand in polite greeting. "The town has done without a teacher long enough. That last one was a poor excuse for one," she went on critically.

"I'm sure Miss McFarland isn't interested in the previous teacher's shortcomings," Olmstead cut in, and again there was a quick exchange of glances, this time between Berthamae Poole and James Olmstead.

"Of course, she is," the woman insisted. "She's got to live in that place. She should know about it."

"Did you want something, or not, Bertie?" Emily cut in.

Berthamae Poole relented. "I came for dried lentils, onions, basil, yeast and ten pounds of wheat flour," she answered, quelling her previous course of conversation.

"Then come right this way, if you please," James Olmstead instructed, indicating another section of the store. The woman followed, chin up. James Olmstead was talking fast, his voice very low.

"Don't pay any attention to her," Emily Olmstead whispered close to my ear. "She prattles on just to hear herself talk. Here." She thrust the plate of cookies toward me. "Have a macaroon."

I accepted in silence, casting Berthamae Poole and James Olmstead a curious glance. What had she been going to say about the schoolhouse and the previous teacher? Olmstead had practically taken her by the ear and dragged her away. Another look at Emily was enough to tell me that I would gain no further information from her. She was watching with relief her husband's low-growling conversation with Mistress Poole.

"You will of course stay with us for dinner," Emily informed me. "Then we'll take you up to the schoolhouse." That prospect did not seem one to which Emily Olmstead looked forward.

"School opens the first week of September. That should give you time enough to get the schoolhouse in order again," Olmstead was saying later, between mouthfuls of delicious beef stew and sips of freshly brewed coffee.

"I'm afraid it's a mess," Emily said apologetically.

"After the last teacher resigned, some of the children got it in their heads to vandalize the place," Olmstead said with obvious annoyance.

"You might as well tell her who it was, Jim," Emily told her husband. Then she supplied the answer before he had a chance to swallow another bite of stew. "It was those Poole boys. You met their mother this afternoon. Well, Sherman and Grant, her two sons, are little hellions. I don't suppose I have to tell you who they're named after."

"They'll be in your class," Olmstead said.

"How old are they?" I asked.

"Sherman is fourteen, and Grant is almost thirteen," Emily

supplied immediately. "They're two years senior to our Andrew. He'll be eleven in April." I was informed that Andrew was at a friend's for dinner.

"She'll have plenty of time to meet the children, Em. Bridle that tongue of yours so I can get on with our talk," Olmstead said.

"Yes, dear," she demurred.

"As I was saying, Miss McFarland, the schoolhouse and yard could use some cleaning up. The heavy repairs will be taken care of for you by some of the townsmen when they can spare the time."

"Are there many heavy repairs?" I asked dubiously.

"Two broken windows in front, a couple of smashed desks, a few leaks in the roof, and the back steps from your room need some work. Your quarters are in good condition."

The place sounded like a wreck to me.

"More coffee, Miss McFarland," Emily offered as she began clearing away the dishes.

"No, thank you. May I help you with the dishes?"

"No, but thanks," Emily deferred, stacking the dishes with a clatter and almost scurrying from the room.

"There are other things we should go over," James Olmstead began again, and I reluctantly turned back.

"There are certain rules of conduct that must be maintained."

"For the children?" I asked. I had expected to be able to decide on rules for the children without much interference from the townspeople.

"No, ma'am. For you."

"For me?" I could not keep the surprise out of my voice.

"Of course," he said, giving me a look that indicated he thought I should have known as much. "Your position in this community is a very important one. You are an example for our children, and as such, there are certain strict standards that you must keep."

I braced myself as he continued.

"You will be expected to attend church each Sunday and teach a class there under the authority of our excellent reverend, Jonah Hayes. From your letter and from the reference we received from Bradford Dobson, you have attended church regularly. Isn't that correct?"

"Yes, it is," So far I had no qualms.

"Classes for the children will be from Monday through Friday, beginning at nine in the morning and ending at three in the afternoon. We would have you start school earlier, but there are some children who must ride in from outlying ranches."

"Yes, of course," I murmured in assent.

"The children have not had a teacher for over a year, so you will have to see that they make up the lost time." That was a handicap I had not foreseen.

"How many children are there?" I asked, silently praying there would be few enough that such expectations would not be utterly impossible.

"Sixty-four. Not many for a town this size. Some of the children do not attend because they are needed at home. Others are too young. There will be ten new pupils next year."

The task ahead of me seemed to grow with each word James Olmstead spoke. Sixty-four children! Lessons for all levels! Cleaning the schoolhouse and yard!

"If children have academic difficulties, you will, of course, be expected to tutor them after school hours. If any become sick, you will make up lessons for them to do at home.

"As for your own social conduct, you are not allowed to entertain men in your quarters, nor are you to be alone with a man for any reason other than school business, and then never after five in the afternoon."

"Are you serious, Mr. Olmstead?" I asked, unable to believe he was.

"Absolutely," he said, surprised that I should ask. "They are fairly universal rules, Miss McFarland."

"They seem archaic. I can assure you I have no intention of entertaining men in my quarters, but I am not even allowed to carry on a sociable conversation with a man except on school business?"

"That's correct. You will have as much social contact as you need with the Mothers' League, the Women's Church Guild and the local sewing circles." With what Olmstead had already outlined as my duties, I doubted if I should have the time for any socializing.

"You're expected to attend all town meetings; however, you are not permitted to speak on any issue. You must remain neutral in all political conversations. As for the subject matter in the classroom, limit your teaching to reading, writing and arithmetic. Those are the basics, and anything else is unnecessary frill."

I wanted to interrupt and object, but James Olmstead continued unabated. "Now, about your dress." I stiffened noticeably as he looked me over blandly and nodded approval. "Your present outfit is appropriate to your position, if a bit untidy." After ten miles of walking, what did the man expect! "Ankles, wrists and neck are to be covered at all times. You are permitted to wear browns, grays, black, white or deep green. Anything else you are not. No furbelows. No jewelry except perhaps a plain watch pin. No ribbons, no fancy hairpins. Your hair is to be confined at all times."

"May I take it down when I go to bed?" I asked dryly, unable to resist. Olmstead looked shocked.

"I hope you will not make a habit of speaking in such a manner," he criticized, and I wished I had held my tongue.

"I'm sorry," I apologized meekly. I suddenly felt very tired and depressed. I had thought I had escaped oppressive bondage, but apparently I had cast myself beneath the control of an even harsher master. The new life I had hoped for stretched dismally ahead of me.

Emily Olmstead returned to the dining room, having finished the dishes. She sat down and glanced from her husband to me.

"What have you been saying to Miss McFarland, Jim? She looks positively miserable."

"I've simply been informing her of what is expected of her," he muttered defensively. Emily Olmstead looked sympathetic.

"I suppose you neglected to tell her the good points," she said on a sigh. What good points? I wanted to ask. She answered without a question.

"The children are wonderful. Except the Poole boys, of course. You'll have your hands full with them."

"Em, will you please...." James Olmstead was not going to succeed in silencing his wife this time.

"Reverend Hayes's four sons are perfect little angels, and all very quick-witted. So is Toby Carmichael, the poor waif.

And Hudson Thomas's little girl, Margaret, is a spunky, sweet child. Linda Bennett, Jordan's daughter, is the prettiest and also the quietest, and it's no wonder—"

"Em."

"Katrina Lane is another story altogether. She'll probably turn out to be just like her mother."

"Em!" This time her husband was heard. "Miss McFarland can't be bothered with your senseless gossip," he chastened. "Right now I think she would rather have a good night's sleep. She's got a full day ahead of her tomorrow, cleaning out the schoolhouse."

I wanted to laugh hysterically, but swallowed the urge with a determined effort of will.

"Is she going to stay over there tonight?" Emily gasped, and her husband gave her a baleful look.

"Why shouldn't she? Now, don't start in again, Em. Berthamae took fresh linen over this afternoon and made up the bed for her. She won't notice the dust tonight. The place is perfectly habitable." Emily looked from him to me and then down at her hands clasped in her lap. There were worse bondages, I thought suddenly.

"I shall be fine, really, Mrs. Olmstead. You've been very kind. I'm so tired, I'll sleep like the dead."

Emily Olmstead's rosy cheeks faded white with my reassurance, but she made no further comments. She stared at her husband, but he ignored her.

"Get your shawl, Em," he ordered. She hesitated and seemed about to say something, but her husband's look commanded her obedience.

With the Olmsteads, I retraced my afternoon walk up Main Street. Emily's earlier exuberance was curbed. She hardly uttered a word all the way down the street. When we turned up a side street where Olmstead said the schoolhouse was located, she slowed noticeably, holding back, and then made some excuse to go back to the store. Her husband put his hand beneath her elbow, making her keep pace with him.

The sky was darkening, and a few stars were out. Crickets were chirping. At the end of the street, separated from the last house by several hundred yards, I saw a modest building. It was surrounded by a poorly repaired picket fence that had not been painted in some time. Weeds grew high around the building, which seemed to stare at me with its two broken-window eyes. It looked sad and uncared for in the receding light of day. Off to the left of the schoolhouse were three majestic oaks. Another two grew behind and to the right. There was a broken-down outhouse, and a well in the vee of the hills beyond. On the building itself were bold black letters above the entrance, proclaiming its community function. The place looked as tired, disheveled and lonely as I felt.

Emily Olmstead stopped at the gate. "I'll wait here," she said, ignoring her husband's scowl.

"Em, for goodness sakes."

"I'll wait here," she said, adamant. James Olmstead sighed.

"All right. I'll be out in a minute," he muttered and held the gate open for me. He lit a lantern just inside the schoolhouse door and handed it to me. He pointed across the schoolroom at a closed door.

"Your quarters are right through there," he instructed without moving. Then he went on briskly. "Kindling and wood are out back. We'll keep you supplied with what you need for the schoolroom. It gets cold in the winter. The roof in your room doesn't leak, as far as I know, but if it does, the school board will make arrangements to have someone come by and fix it. You'll be paid at the end of each month. Twenty-five dollars, as we agreed in our letter. Since you've got a place to live, you'll be saving on rent. Food comes cheap hereabouts. It's cattle and farming country, and people will be glad to share what they have with you." Implying that I was to beg for handouts? I wondered. Dear God, my situation is becoming worse by the minute.

"Well, that's about it," he finished and gave me a grim smile. "Speaking on behalf of the community, we're glad to have you here. We hope you stay."

"Thank you," I managed a semblance of a smile. He turned away, eager to be gone.

"Oh, I almost forgot," he said, turning back again. "The well is about two hundred yards back from the schoolhouse. They dug it outside the school grounds so there would be no chance of an accident with one of the smaller children. You'll have to tote your water. There are buckets just outside the back door, but don't forget about the steps. The bottom two are broken."

"I won't forget." My voice sounded flat.

"Good night, then," he said and walked out the door. I heard him speaking in low tones to his wife as they moved away from the gate. I stood in the classroom, which was dimly lit by my lantern, and looked around. The floor was dust-coated. Desks were shoved around. Three of them were smashed and broken in a heap as though someone had intended to build a fire. The walls were gray. Spider webs with their lurking inhabitants suspended from room corners, and jumbled books reclined in a rickety cabinet. The teacher's desk at the front of the classroom was bare except for the dirt that had accumulated with time. A message was scrawled in childish writing across the blackboard. "All who enter here be warned."

As I crossed the room to the door of my quarters, I left footprints in the dust. My heart sank to even deeper depths as I peered into the room that was to be my home. It was sparsely furnished with an old commode containing three small drawers. A washbowl and pitcher stood on top next to a towel and washcloth that had been carefully laid out by Berthamae Poole. The bed against the back wall was narrow but freshly made up. It had one blanket. Another blanket was folded and set on top a small table near a wood-burning stove. Above the stove was a shelf on which stood a tin can with long-stick matches. Hanging on a hook was another kerosene lantern. Drab, faded curtains hung in the one window, effectively blotting out any natural light that might have entered the dreary room. The floor was bare except for the film of dust and grit that had accumulated over a year since the previous teacher had left. Everything about the room was oppressive and pathetic.

There was plenty of work ahead of me tomorrow, I thought with a wry smile. I would not have time for self-pity and thoughts of what might have been had the Haversalls been honest, loving guardians. But the loneliness. Would I be able to bear that?

There was a stillness around me like a shroud. After a few

minutes I became aware of a cricket rubbing its courtship song somewhere in my room. Outside an owl hooted from one of the oaks.

My companions, I thought. Then, putting my hands to my face, I cried uncontrollably.

 *Chapter Four*

After moving the desks from the schoolroom, I spent my first day sweeping out dust and cobwebs. Then I lugged bucket after bucket of water into the place and, setting up a ladder, began scrubbing the grimy walls. By the end of the day I had barely completed half of the room. My hands were raw and chapped by the harsh soap Olmstead had contributed for my cleaning efforts. I looked around at my work and sighed heavily. It was clean, but it did not look it. Depressed, I dumped out the last bucket of dirty water and quit for the day.

With my last few dollars in hand, I dragged myself to the general store and bought some much needed supplies. Olmstead gave me the use of his wheelbarrow to carry my purchases back. By the time I had stashed things away and returned the wheelbarrow, I was so hungry and tired I felt sick. I could not face another minute of work, even to cook, and collapsed without dinner onto my narrow bed. I slept until dawn.

After several unsuccessful attempts to light my wood stove the next morning, I poured kerosene onto the kindling. It worked but almost singed my hair. I cooked a pot of coffee, several brown eggs and warmed a half-loaf of leftover bread Emily Olmstead had given me as a gift. Replete, I felt ready to tackle the schoolroom.

I lugged more water, mixed in more detergent and set to work on the walls on the other half of the room. By that evening my quarters were also scrubbed down. Forcing myself to cook, I made a cheese-rice-and-vegetable concoction that was more nutritious than delicious. Then I took a sponge bath. Falling into bed, I expected to find sleep immediately, but it was impossible. All I could think of was the work yet ahead of me, the lessons I needed to prepare for 64 children; the yard work; the floor scouring; the minor repairs, such as fixing the picket fence, the squeaking doors; the torn bookbindings; the loose chalk tray; the wobbly desks. So many things to do and only a few more days in which to do them. I had never worked so hard in my life.

The third day saw me on my hands and knees scrubbing floors. By the end of that day my back ached from toting water from the well, my legs were sore from walking and getting up and down from the floor, and my arms felt like limbs of wood hanging from drooping shoulders. Yet when I went to bed, I still tossed and turned. The more I needed rest, the more impossible it became. I could not stop thinking of the work that still stretched out before me.

Finally, in frustration, I got up and stood at my window. The first thing I sensed was the disgusting malodorous outhouse, which the children and I were expected to use. Anger made my blood boil.

I would be double-damned if I was going to dig a hole for an outhouse, I decided. If anything was "heavy work," as Olmstead had phrased it, that was! Surely, the kind citizens of this town did not expect that of me as well as everything else they had given Olmstead to outline. More resentful thoughts began to whirl in my exhausted brain, and then an idea struck me. I started to laugh, a jubilant sound in the depressing darkness and glum atmosphere of my austere quarters.

Everything was going to be just fine, I thought with another chuckle. If Olmstead and the rest of his demanding school board did not like my methods of maintaining the schoolhouse, they could always register their complaints with me. I would be more than pleased to listen. I laughed again. However, by that time I hoped my plans would be well started if not completed.

The following morning I was in much better spirits, though still tired and stiff from my strenuous labors. I took care of minor repairs and was satisfied with my accomplishments by the end of the day. The picket fence had all its sticks in place, the door did not squeak anymore, the bookbindings were glued back, and the chalk tray no longer wobbled. I had checked all the desks and found them in good repair. The three smashed ones I used for firewood. Everything was moved back into place again. It was Saturday, and school was scheduled to start on Monday. That gave me the following day to make my lesson plans.

I spent Sunday making lists of projects needed to be done. Then I worked late into the night on lesson plans for the first few days of school. Nervous excitement kept me awake the whole night, and the rising sun found me very apprehensive, but smiling.

Just after eight o'clock I spotted a man riding down the hill behind the schoolhouse. Trailing reluctantly after him were two children on matching pintos. The three stopped for a moment, and the man spoke to the children—one, a girl in a pretty lilac dress, and the other, a boy in somber brown pants and shirt. Then the three rode forward. As they came out of the shadows of the oaks, I recognized Jordan Bennett. Emily Olmstead had not mentioned a son as well.

I hurried from my window to the back door. Just as I started down the steps, I heard the crack and remembered Olmstead's warning about the stairs. I jumped over the last three and heard Jordan Bennett laughing. My heart pounded, and I managed three slow breaths to smother my rush of temper. Then I smiled brightly and strode through the tall grass to meet the approaching trio.

"Are you really that eager?" Bennett grinned.

"Does it surprise you?" I countered with a smile that did not show my nervous tension. "But as for that jump, I forgot about the broken steps."

"You always seem to be doing some dance or other when I see you," he teased, reminding me unkindly of my collapse in the road. I chose to ignore that comment and turned instead to look at the children. Neither resembled Jordan Bennett, but both were beautiful in contrasting ways. The little girl, whom

I assumed to be Linda, was looking surreptitiously through a veil of fair lashes. Her eyes were an unusual violet. The smile on her face was faint with shyness.

The boy, not much older than the girl, was dark-skinned, black-haired and brown-eyed. He looked at me with openly curious appraisal. However there was a tension about him. His thin shoulders and his full mouth looked too hard and firmly set for a boy so young.

"Miss McFarland." Bennett doffed his hat mockingly. "Meet my daughter, Linda, and Diego Gutierrez, the son of my house-keeper. Say good morning to your new schoolteacher, children." His tone irritated me, but I was careful not to show it. Both children mumbled some polite, mechanical response, and I smiled, ignoring the sparkle of mischief that lighted Bennett's eyes.

"Now go into the schoolhouse and get the best seats you can. Today should prove very interesting," he further told them, making it sound like some grand entertainment was in store for them rather than classroom instruction. They obeyed.

Bennett laughed again, and I practiced my willpower with a polite, if somewhat stiff, smile.

"You're looking rather tired this morning, Miss McFarland," he grinned, obviously pleased about it. What a typical Jordan Bennett observation, I thought, stifling the urge to tell him to go home.

"I should be," I commented.

"Oh? Did you do a little work around here?" he asked, glancing around the overgrown school yard I had not yet gotten to. "It doesn't look like it."

My smile stayed plastered to my face, but I knew my eyes were speaking volumes. "Give it a few days, Mr. Bennett, and you might be very surprised."

"I do hope so," he said dryly, the corner of his mouth jerking up in suppressed amusement. "I'll even go so far as to loan you a scythe."

"I'd prefer a horse and plow," I commented coolly. Bennett threw back his head and laughed. Then he looked at me, and something flickered in his eyes.

"That I'd like to see. A fair maid from Boston proper behind a horse and plow. People would come from miles around just to see such a spectacle." There was an odd bite to his words, making it a deliberate insult. I decided to pick up the thrown gauntlet.

"I may be from 'Boston proper,' as you put it, Mr. Bennett," I said calmly, my smile now more a baring of teeth, "but in Boston we have some semblance of manners. As to your 'fair-maid' label, it's misplaced entirely. And I don't appreciate being made fun of."

"I still maintain my first impression," he commented blandly.

I felt momentarily bemused. Then I remembered. "Oh," I sniffed, "that I won't last out the term, you mean. Well, I shall try not to let your opinions prey too heavily on my mind." I waved my hand in airy dismissal. "Will you be returning for the children, or are they permitted to find their way home without your escort?"

"They can make the ride by themselves," he admitted, and I sighed in obvious relief. "But I think I'll come back for them anyway. I want to hear all the gory details of your first day teaching," he added. I did not even attempt a smile that time. I turned around and started to march back toward the school-house.

"Oh, Miss McFarland," Bennett called in overly polite tones. I ignored him and kept walking.

"Miss McFarland," he said, the politeness gone. I let out my breath in irritation and turned around.

"What is it, Mr. Bennett?" I asked, barely managing to keep my voice polite.

He grinned. "You be sure to have a very pleasant day." He succeeded in presenting a cultured Bostonian accent exaggerated just enough to show his derision. I froze for a full second. Then I curtsied prettily.

"Why, how nice of you, Mr. Bennett. And I will do just that as soon as you turn your old cow pony around and ride over yonder hill." I managed a fair attempt at a Western drawl.

He was laughing at me again, satisfied that he had aroused my anger. "See you at three, Abby," he said, further infuriating me by his casual use of such a nickname. He rode off in the direction from which he had come. I stood fuming.

* * *

By ten to nine, 61 children had arrived and were seated in the schoolhouse. The din of noise almost deafened me as I sat at the front desk, looking over my charges and silently gathering my courage. The only quiet children were Linda Bennett and Diego Gutierrez, who had both chosen back-corner seats together. Linda sat watching the ruckus with her hands folded on her desk. Diego watched with wary interest.

Just ahead of them, separated by one desk, was pretty little Margaret Hudson with her sandy-brown pigtails and laughing hazel eyes. She was leaning across the aisle to talk to Patricia Studebaker. Her brother, Chester, was deep in conversation with Toby Carmichael, a red-headed, freckled boy with sad expressive eyes. On the other side of the room Matthew, Mark, Luke and John Hayes, the reverend's sons, chortled gleefully together and looked anything but the angels Emily Olmstead said they were. Other children of outlying ranchers and farmers chattered with friends they had not seen for some time.

Just as I was about to call the class to order, two older boys made a noisy entrance. They laughed boisterously as they slouched down into two front desks. I assumed these were the notorious Poole boys—Sherman and Grant. Their reckless air of defiance and mischief set them apart from the other children and raised my hackles.

"Silence, please!" I tried above the noise. But the children continued to talk. A nervous tingle ran over my skin as the tension built. What if they refused to listen at all? A vision of Jordan Bennett laughing flashed in my mind and gave my voice the added strength it needed.

"Silence, please!" Here and there, children ceased their chatter and looked at me. I waited, looking from one child to another, meeting their silent challenges. All but the Poole boys gave in.

"Whenever you're ready, gentlemen," I said coolly, staring at each boy in turn, anger overriding my nervousness. Something in my expression must have reached them, for they flushed slightly and dropped into silence.

"Thank you," I said quietly and then looked up as a sound at the back of the room attracted my attention. Standing in the doorway was a little girl of about eight. She was dressed in a white pinafore trimmed with pink satin ribbons. On her small feet were high-buttoned white shoes that probably cost as much as my doe-brown dress and jacket. Her dark hair was braided into two long, shiny plaits with pink bows at each end. Her delicate hands were folded in front of her. She looked as though she had come to a party. Her pretty gray eyes looked directly at me, and a little smile flickered nervously across her face.

The woman behind the little girl was dressed in even more finery. She wore a forest-green dress trimmed in brown, much like the one I had seen in the milliner's window on my way up the main street. On her head was a flashy hat with dyed-green and brown feathers. The gray eyes were worldly and cool as they appraised me from head to foot. Then she smiled, a tight, defensive smile, before she moved forward with her daughter in tow.

"My name is Marba Lane, Miss McFarland."

The Poole boys twittered, and I gave them a silencing look. Emily Olmstead had mentioned Marba Lane, but she had not explained her disapproval of the woman. I looked at the woman standing before me, taking in the beauty of her finely boned face. Her makeup was almost theatrical, but done with an expert hand.

"This is my daughter, Katrina."

"We're pleased to have you, Katrina." I smiled at the little girl. "There's a seat over there." I indicated the one in front of Linda Bennett. Katrina looked up at her mother, and the woman nodded. The little girl crossed the room, very aware of the children watching her. I smiled at Marba Lane, and the woman smiled back, all her previous aloofness dissolving from her hard eyes.

"Thank you, Miss McFarland," she whispered, and I stared with surprise at the woman's expression. She turned and walked back up the aisle. A man dressed in an expensive dark suit and white shirt was leaning against the doorjamb, his arms crossed, waiting for her. He was the most handsome man I'd ever seen. Dark-brown hair fell forward on his tanned brow and grew in neatly trimmed thickness over an aristocratic head. He had warm brown eyes that seemed to laugh at the world rather than at me, like Jordan Bennett had a habit of doing.

The man was assessing me. Rather than feeling angry at his perusal, I felt flattered. There was an air of sexual vitality about him that stopped just short of blatancy. His smile was full of charm and a silent compliment.

Marba Lane looped her arm through the man's, and he escorted her out. I noted that he moved with a grace that did nothing to insult his masculinity and only seemed to further emphasize the controlled power of his well-toned body.

I wondered briefly who the man was and then returned my attention to the growing chatter in the room. Once I had regained the children's attention, I wrote several assignments on the blackboard.

As the children worked, I studied them. I noted how they held their pencils, how they concentrated, if they were restless or bored, and I made voluminous notes. As their papers began coming in, I quickly looked them over to form some idea of how much each child knew. Then I began grouping the children by their abilities.

By noon most of the children were well-started in their assignments. I rang the bell and dismissed them for lunch recess and outdoor play. I observed them in their play, noticing which children grouped together and which were excluded. Katrina Lane remained by herself beneath one of the oak trees. Her solemn little face was inscrutable as she watched the other children playing. Linda Bennett and Diego Gutierrez stayed together, talking in whispers and darting glances at the other children.

The Poole boys and the four Hayes boys started up a rowdy game of tag. Their laughter and antics were balm to my tense nerves. When they found a ball under the front steps, they started a keep-away game. When the ball accidentally came flying in my direction, I surprised myself by catching it with ease. My toss back was accurate, and they encouraged me to join in the game. Laughing, I agreed and encouraged more children to join with me.

At 2:30 I had the children clear their desks and pass all materials forward for storing away by Sherman, Luke and Margaret. Then I sat on the front edge of my desk.

"I am very pleased with the way things have gone today for all of us," I began, smiling as I looked from face to face. "From the work you've done today, I will get some idea of where you are and what you need work on."

I paused, folding my hands. "Now, for your homework assignments. . . ." Loud groans issued from the class. I gave a faint, amused smile and imitated their groans with one of my own.

"Yes, homework," I repeated and silently laughed at their woebegone looks. "Tonight I want each one of you to go home and think about what you particularly want to learn here at school. Not just reading, writing and arithmetic, but anything else that is of special interest to you." James Olmstead would have a stroke! "Write it on a slip of paper and drop it in this little box tomorrow morning. You may leave your name off if you wish," I added. Faces were beginning to brighten again. "Also I would like you to write down things you think we should do to the schoolhouse." A chuckle escaped Sherman Poole, and I looked down at him with a wry smile.

"Short of burning it down, of course, Sherman." The children laughed. I waved my hand indicating the drab surroundings. "I'm sure you agree it needs improvement. And if you can forage paint, material scraps, plants, anything you think we could use, we might just be able to make this pathetic old building into a pleasant place to behold."

"What color paint, Miss McFarland?" Andrew Olmstead piped up.

"Anything you can scrounge and that your parents are willing to give," I answered. "We'll leave the outside of the building as it is, but we'll decorate the inside any way you want . . . within reason." I smiled at Sherman's devilish look. "As for the play yard, we'll clean that up little by little and set up a baseball diamond." There were cheers at that announcement. I grinned. "And for those little darlings who get into trouble with the teacher . . ." I eyed Sherman and Grant pointedly, "they can help dig a new latrine for that disgusting outhouse of ours." The children roared with laughter, and Sherman and Grant sank down into their seats with mock fright.

"Well, do you think you have enough to keep you busy and out of mischief tonight?" I asked with a laugh. There was a loud joyous affirmative.

"Then there's just one more thing. From now on, wear

clothes you won't mind getting dirty. We're going to try to make school fun as well as instructive." I raised my brows questioningly as I glanced over the children. "Agreed?"

"Agreed!" they cried.

I smiled. "Class dismissed. I'll see you all tomorrow morning at nine sharp."

There was a mass scrambling for the door and rollicking laughter as the children surged out of the building and ran off in all directions for home. Chores awaited them before they could begin their foraging for the schoolhouse.

Katrina Lane walked out of the schoolroom with the same air of fragile dignity with which she had entered. I watched her with a slight frown. No little girl should be so solemn and withdrawn. She should laugh and enjoy life. I decided to try to make that happen somehow.

Linda Bennett and Diego Gutierrez remained sitting in the back of the classroom. Both looked relieved that school was over. Linda was tracing carved initials on the desk top with her finger while Diego watched me.

"Diego," I said, meeting the boy's intent scrutiny, "your printing is excellent. I'd like you to help John Hayes and Toby Carmichael improve theirs."

The boy's expression closed over. His mouth became tighter. "They won't let me," he told me flatly.

"Why do you think that?" I asked.

"They won't," he repeated harshly, not elaborating. "Just take my word for it."

"Can we try anyway?"

He did not answer, but I could see that he was thinking about it. The idea did not seem to please him. "How about if I just put you in a group with those two boys? Then they can learn from you without having their noses pushed into it," I suggested, feeling that there must be some animosity between the boys. They had not played together in the schoolyard, but then Diego had not once attempted to join in the group games.

"Maybe," he relented only slightly, but did not seem any the more eager. Linda looked up, those marvelous violet eyes clear for a moment of their shyness.

"The other boys won't play with Diego because he's Mexican," she explained candidly. For a moment I did not know what to say, and I knew my face showed my startled state.

"How can you be sure that the other boys feel that way?" I directed my question to Diego. "You didn't try to join in with them in any of their activities. Have you tried before?"

"He came to school two years ago," Linda started to say, but Diego gave her a quelling glance, and she stopped, her finger beginning its tracing again.

"And?" I looked at Diego. He averted his gaze and stared toward the blackboard. There was no defiance in his attitude. Linda looked at him.

"Tell her, Diego," she pleaded softly.

"No," he snapped, glaring at her. "And you'd better not either." There was more pride than threat in those words, and Linda sighed.

"Well, how did it go?" came a deep voice. I looked up sharply to see Jordan Bennett lounging in the doorway, his hat pushed back from his forehead. He directed his question to the children and then glanced briefly in my direction. Linda ran to him, and he lifted her up with an affectionate laugh that did something strange to my stomach. Linda chattered with more animation than she had had all day, while Diego approached with more dignity. Bennett asked a question in fluent Spanish, and the boy answered with one word.

"*Bueno.*" He nodded, smiling up at Jordan Bennett. Bennett looked across the room at me as I busied myself with the children's papers.

"You don't look any the worse for wear," he commented dryly.

"How did you expect me to look?" I managed an amused laugh.

"A little more haggard than you do," he admitted. "But as you said this morning . . . give it a day or two."

Was he really so hopeful of my failure? It was obvious that he had not the least respect for my capabilities. But why was he so antagonistic?

"Are you hoping I'll only last a few days?" I dared ask. That he considered the question seriously with just the faintest twist of his mouth was a slap in my face. I controlled my expression, only the slight upward tilt of my chin indicating that his silence hurt.

"The children need a teacher," he commented. "You'll do as well as anyone else they could find around here."

"Thank you for your vote of confidence," I muttered. I looked away from his penetrating eyes to the two children watching us curiously. "I'll see you both tomorrow." I smiled, hoping Bennett would take the hint and leave. He read my thoughts and gave a low laugh.

"Good afternoon, Miss McFarland." He doffed his hat.

"Good afternoon, Mr. Bennett," I answered politely.

For the next few days school progressed well. I kept the children busy with class assignments. During recesses I gave them a choice of outdoor play or painting in the classroom. Many preferred to plaster the walls with colorful drawings of trees, people, animals and anything else they fancied. After two days the room was a bright art display of varying talents. Several plants sat on my desk and the corner bookshelf. Scraps of material were sewed together by the girls to make colorful curtains for the front windows, which were unrepaired by James Olmstead and his school-board members.

Few difficulties arose between the children. After Diego's initial reluctance, he agreed to move into the group of boys including Toby and Luke. He was welcomed without comment, and the boys began to copy his writing techniques when they heard my praise of his work. Later, Diego began to join in the outdoor games, leaving Linda free to become acquainted with several of the girls her own age. Still overly shy, she became friends with the more extroverted Margaret Hudson, who hardly gave her a chance to speak.

Katrina Lane still remained to herself, even though the other girls made some overtures to her. The only fight that broke out all week was between Sherman and Grant Poole over who was to pitch in a baseball game that had not even begun yet. With pick and shovel, the two boys made remarkable progress on the latrine.

When Saturday came, I was grateful for the day's respite. Though I thoroughly enjoyed the classroom hours with the children, my schedule had proved grueling. Papers and lesson plans kept me up late into the night, and I had to rise early each morning to get everything in readiness for the children. At least, I thought with some satisfaction, the schoolroom had become more cheerful with the children's artistic contributions.

Intending to do my wash, I was in the process of toting water when I heard laughter coming from the front play yard. Coming around from the back, I spied Jordan Bennett coming up the street on his buckboard. Behind him a sturdy horse was tied and following. In the back of the wagon was a hand plow. At a safe distance behind the horse I spotted Sherman and Grant following, laughing between themselves.

From the gleam in Jordan Bennett's eyes I knew that his malicious intention was to make me look a complete fool. Squaring my shoulders, I started forward to meet him at the front gate.

"Good morning, Mr. Bennett," I greeted him pleasantly enough. "How kind of you to come by to plow our play yard for us."

Jordan Bennett laughed. "Nice try," he said in a low voice only I heard. "Just unload it over there, boys," he instructed Sherman and Grant. Matthew Hayes had arrived with two of his brothers. They all were more than eager to oblige Bennett's order.

"The horse and plow are my contribution to your cleanup efforts." He grinned.

"I'm sure I should be very grateful," I said glumly.

"I'll even be kind enough to give you a quick lesson," Bennett went on. I knew he expected me to decline and tell him what he could do with his horse and plow.

"All right," I agreed. "I'm more than willing to learn if it's necessary."

His blue eyes narrowed as he considered me in silence. He jumped down off the buckboard. "We'll see if you have the back muscles for it," he commented. "A woman of your intelligence should be quick enough to learn something as simple as plowing a field. Wouldn't you say?"

"I don't imagine I'll be the first."

With a few succinct instructions he showed me how to harness the horse, which was looking dubious about the whole

thing. I eyed the animal warily, half expecting it to kick me.
Jordan looped the reins about my shoulders, positioned the
plow and stood back. I had watched the play of his hard muscles
through his cotton shirt. He made everything look easy, and
my confidence grew. After taking the plow for a step or two,
he turned the job over to me.

It was not as easy as it looked. I mimicked his movements,
and the knowledge that he and five of my students were watching me gave me added strength. After about ten feet I knew it
would be impossible for me to plow the play yard myself. My
back and arms were already aching.

Pausing to wipe my forehead, I glanced back to see Jordan
Bennett standing there with his arms crossed over his broad
chest. He was enjoying this. He was just hoping I would quit
so he could make another one of his cutting remarks about my
ineptitude. I turned back around, determined to go on.

Something scurried through the grass and startled the horse.
It bolted to the side, jerking the plow out of my hands and
making me fall heavily to the ground. My thigh hit something
hard, and I gasped in pain. I barely had enough time to get
my breath when Jordan Bennett was leaning down, intending
to haul me up like a sack of potatoes.

"I can get up by myself, thank you, Mr. Bennett." I pulled
my arm away from his far-from-gentle touch. I kept my face
averted so he could not see how much my leg hurt. I knew I
had bruised it badly. He disregarded my assertion and grasped
me around the waist to lift me to my feet.

"Are you always so damned stubborn?" he demanded harshly,
his face so close to mine that his breath fanned my cheeks.
"You didn't seriously think I meant for you to plow this damn
yard, did you? Now, what did you do to your leg?"

"It's nothing," I stammered, unable to pull my eyes away
from his. My heart was thudding frantically, and my breathing
was shallow. His eyes narrowed and dropped to my mouth.

"Are you all right, Miss McFarland?" Sherman Poole asked,
running over, his brother in his wake.

"Yes, I'm fine," I said, my voice overly bright. I pressed
Jordan Bennett's hand away from my arm.

"If you want to help, take over the plow," Bennett told the

boys. "That's if you know how!" Sherman, who was gazing moon-eyed at me, did so, while Grant argued that he wanted a turn.

"Look, Miss McFarland, it's easy. I'll have this done in an hour!" Sherman boasted.

"Come on, Sherman. Give me a chance," Grant grumbled.

"Two conquests already. And the Poole boys, no less," Bennett observed sardonically.

"I think I've had about enough of you, Mr. Bennett," I said in a low voice.

"Do you now, Abby?"

"I don't remember giving you permission to call me by my Christian name, let alone cutting it short," I said, growing more irritated by the minute.

"You're more an Abby than an Abigail," he said, his eyes moving with a strange intimacy over my face. "Wide eyes the color of turquoise with gold nuggets, and red hair."

"My hair is not red," I denied, all the while squirming uneasily under his gaze. If he could look at me like that, how did he look at his wife.

"Auburn then, if it makes a difference," he conceded. "I'll bet it would be wild and soft if you ever let it out of that God-awful bun you wear." He reached out to touch it almost as though he meant to remove the pins, and I jolted back, flushing with embarrassment and fright. Flustered, I did not know what to say; so I stepped quickly by him. He was smiling, silently laughing at my reaction to him.

Looking away from his taunting face, I saw James Olmstead striding up the street. He looked anything but approving. Berthamae Poole was coming up the opposite side of McPherson, and her expression reminded me of Marcella Haversall in one of her moods.

"Oh, no," I breathed.

"What's the matter, Miss McFarland? Are your teaching methods about to bring the town citizens upon your head?" Bennett chuckled.

"I don't know what you mean," I evaded, refusing to look at him.

"You know exactly what I mean, Abby," he said softly.

"I've been getting rather interesting reports from Linda and Diego."

"What sort of reports?" I asked, darting him a questioning look.

"Pilfered paints, picture-painting on the schoolroom walls, children digging latrines. Working the children like little slaves when they're not vandalizing community property."

"That's not the truth—" I started defensively, but he cut me off.

"Fine moral example you're presenting, huh?" He raised his brows expressively. "You should be ashamed." He tut-tutted his tongue. "And you have a right to look like a scared rabbit." He glanced at James Olmstead and Berthamae Poole coming to the gate. "If I'm right, you're about to be nailed to the cross."

"I'm sure you'll enjoy staying around to watch," I retorted, walking away from him and forcing a greeting smile at Olmstead.

"Grant Poole!" Berthamae Poole hollered, her face an unbecoming mottled red. "What on earth are you doing behind that plow?" The boy started guiltily and blushed to the roots of his hair as he glanced at me. Sherman was red-faced as well.

"You two boys get over here this minute. If you two are so eager to work, you can just get on home and do the chores!" she shouted at them. Then she glared at me accusingly. "And I'll thank you not to have my sons digging outhouse holes, Miss McFarland!" she huffed furiously.

"Ma—" Grant tried to interrupt.

"Shut your mouth and move!" his mother ordered, and the two boys hot-stepped on down the street, their mother following along with more verbal encouragements. The Hayes boys scattered.

"I thought you understood the rules, Miss McFarland." Olmstead was beginning on me next. "You're not off to a very good start on a number of counts."

I heard Jordan Bennett's approach and silently groaned. What wonderful contribution would he make to this scene? James Olmstead looked from Bennett to me, and his expression was insinuating. "What are you doing here, Jordan?" he finally asked.

Jordan Bennett laughed easily. "Now, hold on just a minute, Jim! You're not implying there's anything between Miss McFarland and myself, are you?" His tone made such an idea ludicrous in the extreme. I came near to hating him.

"No, I'm not," Olmstead said. "But rules are made with good reason. We've got to think of the children. Which brings me to another point, Miss McFarland." He swung back to me. "I've been hearing some things from Andrew that I hope aren't true."

"Since I don't know what you are referring to, perhaps you should enlighten me, Mr. Olmstead," I said with cool dignity.

"I'll just look for myself and save the questions," he said, marching through the gate and up the path to the schoolhouse. I followed slowly, raising fingertips to the throbbing veins in my temple. The painful bump on my thigh hurt as I walked, but I forced myself not to limp, well aware that Jordan Bennett was watching me.

James Olmstead appeared at the top of the steps. "Come in here and explain this appalling mess to me!"

"Yes, Mr. Olmstead," I replied, resigned. When I entered the schoolroom, Olmstead was staring around him as though he could not believe his eyes.

"I couldn't believe what Andy told me this morning until I saw with my own two eyes," he said, still staring at the walls. Then he turned a furious glare on me. "How could you do this?" he demanded. "How could you allow the children to desecrate this schoolhouse in such an unthinkable way?"

I stiffened. "I think it's an improvement over what I found ten days ago," I said in a clear, controlled voice. I heard Jordan Bennett enter the classroom and laugh slightly under his breath. He was really helping matters, wasn't he?

"An improvement?" Olmstead ejaculated, aghast.

"I will admit there isn't a Rembrandt in Sycamore Hill, but they worked hard and did their best to make this schoolhouse a little more pleasant than it was," I told him. I met Olmstead's cold eyes. "Four days of scrubbing and scouring cannot remove dirt allowed to accumulate over a year, Mr. Olmstead. If this schoolhouse was such hallowed ground, why was it allowed to fall into such sad disrepair?"

"She's got you there, Jim." Jordan chuckled. Olmstead's face turned an angry red.

"And what about children digging the latrine out back?" he demanded, ignoring my defenses.

"I had hoped that was one of those heavy chores you referred to when we talked."

"Don't be impertinent, Miss McFarland."

I sighed. "I did not have time to dig a four-foot hole, so the choice goes to those children who refuse to listen or who cause mischief in class."

"Oh." Some of the steam seeped out of his arguments but he was struggling to work up more. He enjoyed asserting his authority.

"Might I ask when you can replace the windows?" I asked, hoping to change the subject. I resented Jordan Bennett's presence intensely.

"There's no hurry to do that," Olmstead said. "It's still summer." He was glowering again. "It seems to me that you're putting off onto the children what you should be doing yourself."

That hurt, for I had tried very hard to be fair. There were few enough hours in a day for me to manage the cleaning, lesson plans and paper-correcting required without being expected to dig latrines and plow play yards.

"It's a matter of choices, Mr. Olmstead," I said with conviction, though inside I was beginning to tremble under the strain of this scene. What would I do if he dismissed me? Where would I go?

"What choices?" he demanded imperiously. "It seems to me you were well aware of your duties the night we discussed them. You agreed to carry them out. You're being paid to uphold them."

"I've only been in town ten days—"

"And you're already off to a bad start," Olmstead interrupted critically.

"Teaching the children has to come first," I said in my own defense, about to reason that my time had not permitted making all the repairs as yet.

"Well, then teach them, Miss McFarland! Painting walls and digging holes isn't in any of the textbooks that I remember!" He glanced around again. "I'll get some whitewash so you can cover these . . . paintings." With that, he marched out of the schoolhouse with a look of satisfaction. My shoulders drooped, and I unconsciously rubbed my bruised thigh.

"You hurt yourself when you fell, didn't you?" Bennett asked from close behind me.

"Nothing that won't mend, Mr. Bennett," I said harshly, looking away from him. My mouth was trembling, and I knew there was little color in my face. Bennett moved closer and put his hands on my shoulders. I jerked away.

"I think you had better leave, Mr. Bennett, before Mr. Olmstead decides to add other misdemeanors to the list he's making against me."

"Such as what, Abby? Indiscreet behavior for being alone with me . . . or are you bent on murder?" He released me, and I spun around.

"You think this is all very funny, don't you?" I flared, blinking rapidly to stop the tears. "Well, laugh your fill and then leave me alone! I haven't got a ranch or a family. If I lose this position. . . ." I stopped. What did this man care whether I lost my position or not? He had made it very clear he did not want me in Sycamore Hill. I managed to regain some measure of control.

"I don't feel like laughing, Abby," Bennett said quietly.

"I'll thank you not to call me that. You have no right!"

Jordan Bennett's expression hardened. "I'll call you any damn thing I please," he retaliated. "And if you think what you've just been through is anything, you're sadly mistaken. Things aren't even warmed up a bit."

I stared at him questioningly, but he was not going to enlighten me.

"I'll say it again. You'll make a very poor schoolmarm."

I did not feel like arguing with him anymore, and I gave a slight shrug of indifference. "Well, we aren't all born with choices, Mr. Bennett."

He turned without another word and strode out of the schoolhouse. I closed my eyes and let out my breath, wondering why I felt like crying.

That night I thought I heard someone moving about in the schoolroom. When I got up and entered the darkened place to investigate, there was no one there. My only company were the shadows from the oaks, and the wind that fluttered through the patchwork curtains.

 *Chapter Five*

The Reverend Jonah Hayes had missed his calling, I thought regretfully as I left the church among the other chastened members of the congregation. The hellfire-and-damnation sermon was still ringing in my ears. I heartily wished that Hayes had offered his rather remarkable dramatic talents to some traveling-show company. The last thing these hard-working people needed was the harangue they received each Sunday like a dose of castor oil. The terrifying pictures of what awaited them if they dared "let the devil in" were enough to keep even the most stout-hearted awake at night. And the weak—woe be to them—were hell bound.

Weakness was defined as sin, and sin, according to the most assured and inspired Reverend Hayes, was anything and everything enjoyable. Even private, unconscious thoughts were subject to the monitoring of Reverend Hayes's God.

I sighed. Surely if a sincere penitent came forward, God would forgive a few indiscretions. However, if Hayes were indeed correct in his interpretation of church doctrine, I could not imagine heaven being populated by anyone but God himself and a sprinkling of three or four saints. What a place to spend an eternity.

No, I thought with conviction. Reverend Hayes's God was

not the same as mine. I preferred the loving, understanding, all-forgiving Father of mankind to the frightening, jealous, possessive avenger who lurked in Hayes's life.

I almost groaned aloud at my own thoughts, for my conception of God was going to add yet another problem in my life. I was to teach Sunday school, and it would be impossible for me to present the tyrannical, unfeeling deity that reigned supreme in Hayes's world. And the good Reverend Hayes was another powerful school-board member!

"Miss McFarland." Emily Olmstead broke into my dreary reverie. "I would like to introduce you to Miss Ellen Greer," she said in formal, almost childish tones of respect. I looked at the small, ancient woman standing next to Emily, leaning heavily on a cane. One arthritically deformed hand lay over another, and her feet were planted slightly apart to hold herself as erect as possible.

Short, frizzled white hair grew over the woman's small head, the only relief from its profusion being an ugly little black hat perched at a precarious angle. Her chin was overlong and pointed with a jutting stubbornness. Soft but wrinkled skin was drawn into emphatic lines pointing to a tight-lipped mouth. She had large ears and a long neck adding to the overall homely picture she made standing there in her somber black dress.

Yet the pair of gray-blue eyes dominated that old, rather awesome face. They were bright and astute, and they looked at me with unembarrassed interest. I smiled, feeling a bit intimidated by the old woman's assessing gaze. I had noticed her once before in church, and I'd wondered who Miss Ellen Greer was.

James Olmstead beckoned his wife, and Emily made a quick apology before darting off to her husband's side. The old woman gave a faint movement of her mouth, which could have been either a smile or a grimace of pain.

"How old are you, Miss McFarland?" she asked in a clear, contralto voice that was very attractive. I thought the question impertinent even for an old lady, and pretended not to hear it.

Miss Greer gave a low laugh. "Apparently lack of respect for your elders is yet another fault of yours."

I stiffened under that assault and barely prevented an angry retort to the woman's rudeness.

"Don't look so testy, my dear," Ellen Greer chided. "I heartily approve," she added conspiratorially. Then she tapped the oak cane. "Come and walk me home. You and I have many things to talk over."

What an imperious old lady, I thought with surprise. However, curiosity made me obey her command. Her pace was slow, and I waited for the old woman to reveal what "things" she had referred to.

"Curse these old legs of mine," Ellen Greer muttered angrily. "They're just about as useless as the licorice sticks Sherman Poole lives on."

I laughed and then quickly apologized, about to explain that it was her statement about Sherman that had amused me so.

"Don't ever apologize, Miss McFarland," Ellen Greer told me. "If you do, that will be the biggest fault on your record."

Before I could comment, she stopped and thrust her cane at a white picket fence. "Open the gate, Miss McFarland," she snapped irritably, and I obeyed. I felt a twinge of resentment at her tone. She had to be the rudest person I had ever met—with the exception of Jordan Bennett!

"You live here?" I asked inanely, looking up almost longingly at the hospitable exterior, for this was the home I had dreamed of as my own on first entering Sycamore Hill.

"Don't ask such stupid questions," Ellen Greer snorted. "Well, come on, Miss McFarland," she went on, impatiently pausing several paces inside the gate. "I haven't got all day."

"I have better things to do with my day than spend it with a discourteous old woman," I said coldly. Ellen Greer's eyes sparkled mischievously, and she laughed delightedly, drawing an astonished look from me.

"I wondered how much you would take from me."

I stared at her, completely baffled. Was the woman in her dotage?

"You've got more spirit than I had at your age, my dear," Ellen chortled. "That may be an advantage, but then again, it may not be. But whatever, I heartily approve of you. Now, please come in and make an old woman's afternoon less of a bore."

Ellen Greer lived in a small room at the back of the board-inghouse. It was furnished with less than my own quarters, but boasted a few plaques on the wall. When I started to read them, Ellen Greer dismissed them.

"Those were in place of a salary increase and a pension," Ellen explained with a sniff for their importance. I read them and turned to look back at her.

"You were the schoolteacher here?" I asked with surprise. No one had ever said anything about who the previous teacher was. This must be the teacher who had quit over a year ago.

"I spent most of my life living in that broken-down shack they call a schoolhouse," Ellen Greer said as she sat in a window chair and tucked a knitted afghan around her thin legs. "Oh, that's better," she sighed. "I just can't walk on these sticks anymore."

"I'm sorry," I started to say and then stopped as I noted the expression of disdain in Ellen Greer's eyes. "I didn't know you were a teacher."

"How were you expected to know?" Ellen asserted. "Emily forgot to mention it. She never was one of my brighter pupils. She would have forgotten her head every morning if the good Lord hadn't sewed it on."

I suppressed a laugh with effort.

"Sit down, girl." Ellen Greer thrust her cane at a chair across the room. "Drag the thing over here so I can have a better look at you."

"It seems to me you looked your fill, Miss Greer." I smiled.

"Don't provoke me," she snapped, her mouth drawing into a tighter pucker, while her eyes sparkled with laughter. "And you have my permission to call me Ellen, since we are fellow teachers."

"Ellen then. And please call me Abigail instead of girl," I commented, liking the old lady in spite of her abrupt manner.

"Abby does you better," she decided, and I was reminded of Jordan Bennett. "I'll call you that, as it pleases me. It's a right of age."

I looked around the room, admiring the crocheted bedspread and the lacy doilies on the small bookshelf that boasted Dickens, Shakespeare, Longfellow, and Dumas.

"My niece allows me to live here on sufferance," Ellen explained without self-pity or bitterness. "She's a nice enough girl, but she would prefer having the extra ten dollars a month this room would bring. And I can't blame her. She's got four hungry, growing children to feed and clothe, and her worthless husband up and died on her ten years ago. Some stomach disorder or another. He wasn't much when he was alive, but at least Amelia didn't have to work at cooking and cleaning for seven boarders."

I thought of the four quiet Bartlett girls: Becky with her lisp, Kathy and Lottie with their bright smiles and inane chatter and Martha, the hardest worker but possessor of the least intelligence.

"How old are you, Abby?" Ellen repeated her first question to me. I did not hesitate this time.

"Twenty-four." My birthday had come soon after I arrived in town.

"You don't look it. But give it time, and you will," she muttered. "Even good children have a way of wearing body and soul down. I bear my wrinkles like battle medals."

"Don't sound so encouraging," I said wryly.

"You may as well know what you're in for, girl. And I don't for the life of me know what's wrong with you that you haven't got a man of your own. It's not the usual thing to have a schoolteacher with your looks. Usually they're old battle-axes like me. What's the matter with you, anyway?"

"Ask James Olmstead. I'm sure he could supply you with several answers to that question," I answered abysmally.

Ellen chuckled. "The children used to call him Tattle-Tom, because he always liked to see and tell the worst about everyone."

"Apparently, age hasn't improved him," I mumbled and then flushed bright red with embarrassment at my wayward tongue. He has been . . . kind." I tried to amend the damage.

"Oh, hogwash and folderol!" Ellen ejaculated in disgust. "James Olmstead isn't what I would call kind. Emily perhaps . . . when she can get away with it. But James? Ha!" She leaned forward from her chair, jabbing her finger toward me. "Now, let's get one thing agreed between us. We'll be honest with each other. I can't abide any more amenities. And being retired now, I don't have to!"

I laughed again.

"Besides," Ellen said more levelly, settling back in her chair and readjusting the afghan, "I've a feeling we're birds of a feather. You're going to need to talk to someone if you intend keeping your wits about you. I had family I could go to when things worried me down. But you have no one, if my gossiping sources are correct." She raised thin gray brows questioningly.

"Your sources are correct," I answered with a faint smile, wondering to whom she had been talking to learn that tidbit of information. "My parents died when I was five, and I was reared by guardians."

"And what happened to them?" she asked, not the least bit hesitant about learning someone else's business.

"They were killed in a carriage accident about six months ago."

"Did bill collectors get the lot?"

I laughed slightly at the old woman's brash nosiness. "A nephew inherited," I answered, without adding the other details of the Haversalls' deception. But it all came back in a second.

"I suspect there's more to that story than you're telling," Ellen said acutely, watching my face. "All right, I won't ask," she relented with a wave of her gnarled hand. "Not today, anyway," she corrected and flashed a smile. "What do you think of Sycamore Hill?"

"It's a nice Western community."

Ellen sniffed. "A very nice, safe answer. Forget the buildings, and let's get down to the people."

"You hardly give a person a chance to breathe, do you?" I commented.

"I learned that during my schoolteaching days. It helped me keep one step ahead of those wild little Indians. If you take my advice, you'll do the same thing. Keep them so busy their little heads spin. Then they won't have time to make your life a misery. And believe me, they can do it! Children have cunning, devious little minds." She waved her hand again, cutting off my comment. "And don't try to tell me they're little angels, all sweetness and light. They'd be abnormal if they were! Even the quiet, dumb ones have some mischief on their minds. As long as they're alive and kicking, that's the way they should be."

"Well, so far they're behaving remarkably well," I insisted, wanting very much to laugh again.

"Give them time," Ellen Greer prophesied. "Right now they're on their Sunday-best behavior. Monday will arrive anytime, and then we'll see what stuff you're made of."

"I do believe you're trying to frighten me off," I replied.

"You'll do just fine. You look soft, but I think there's a determined streak in you." She nodded. "Yes, Abby, my dear, you'll do just fine. Now, who have you met or who do you want to know about?"

I considered a moment before I spoke. "I haven't really met very many people as yet. The Olmsteads, of course."

"Of course," Ellen muttered. "And Bertie Poole, from what I hear."

"Yes."

"She didn't like her boys digging a latrine or plowing the play yard," the old woman chuckled. "When I heard about that, I knew we were going to get on together. The last teacher was in over her head."

"The last teacher? I thought—"

"That I was? No, my dear. I retired five years ago. I worked until I was seventy-five and then couldn't handle it anymore."

"Then who?..."

"A weak little drudge named Prudence Townsend."

"That's not very kind," I admonished.

"No, I don't suppose it is. But she was pathetic as a teacher. She had no business even trying it in the first place. But I don't suppose there was anything she could do. She wasn't the least bit pretty like you, which was at least one point in her favor."

"What an awful thing to say," I emitted, shocked.

"Maybe so," Ellen relented only momentarily, for she went on bluntly again. "She was nice, and that was her problem. The children ran all over her. She wanted to do well, but couldn't keep the horde of barbarians under control. They didn't learn much from her, which was a shame, because the girl had some brains and a lot more education than I did. But it takes

more than formal knowledge to make a schoolteacher. A strong
hand can be more beneficial than ten textbooks."

"I don't think I could use corporal punishment," I admitted.

"You won't have to as long as you have latrines to dig and
play yards to plow," Ellen Greer chortled gleefully. "I would
have loved to have seen the Poole boys at that. Your looks are
going to come in handy where they're concerned. From what
I've heard, both boys have perched you high on a pedestal and
labeled you their first love."

"I wouldn't go so far as that," I disagreed, while remembering the calf-eyed look Sherman had cast me recently.

"Don't be modest! And besides, they show surprising taste,
I'd say. I'd little hope of those two ever showing the least bit
of intelligence, though I know they do have it hidden away
somewhere upstairs beneath all that curly hair."

"They are bright," I agreed.

"They didn't get it from Bertie or Branford. They must be
throwbacks to some other relative long forgotten."

I laughed.

"I had both in my class—the parents first, then the two
boys; so I'm not talking through my hat," Ellen told me defensively.

"How on earth did you ever last fifty-five years?" I asked,
still laughing and thinking her the most outspoken and least
tactful person I'd ever met.

"Following a few basic rules, which I will now kindly pass
on to you," she said seriously. "I kept my thoughts to myself,
believe it or not. I obeyed the rules as closely as possible, and
when I had to break them, I didn't apologize or take any guff
from the likes of James Olmstead."

She tapped her cane on the floor. "And there's another thing
it'll help you to know. Schoolteachers are hard to come by. It's
a thankless job for the most part. Of course, there are bright
spots ahead of you."

"For example?" I asked wryly.

"You may have some gifted student who will make every
dumb one worthwhile."

"You did?"

"Indeed, I did. He only went here until he was fourteen.

Then his mother took my advice and shipped him off back East to finish his schooling. He'd long since learned everything I could teach him, and he was hungry for more. He went on through Harvard and got his law degree. He was even offered a position in the best firm in Boston." Ellen's voice softened, and she looked out the window. "I was real proud of him." She did not speak for a minute and then looked at me.

"Of course, he made some stupid mistakes along the way, like marrying himself a brainless, selfish little society girl." She shook her head in disgust, then waved her hand in her characteristic gesture of dismissal. "Oh, but enough on that. It's ancient history. Anyway, you'll have your bright spots. One Jordan Bennett makes all the Berties worth it."

"Jordan Bennett?" I choked.

"You've met him, have you?"

"Yes." I couldn't help the way I said it, or the way I looked after I said it.

Ellen Greer leaned forward, her sharp eyes curious. "Do I take it you don't like him?"

"You take it correctly," I muttered under my breath. "And believe me, the feeling is mutual."

The gray eyebrows went up. "How do you know that?"

"He makes it as plain as day," I told her.

"He doesn't usually show his feelings. You say he doesn't like you? Does he have some reason to feel that way?" Her gray-blue eyes were studying me again.

"I don't think so, but then perhaps he does," I admitted. "Our first meeting wasn't very cordial."

"Tell me about it," Ellen ordered, sitting forward and leaning on her cane. She was very curious and not attempting to hide it.

"I'd rather not. That's one episode I would prefer to forget."

"You just make me all the more interested."

"The story would disappoint you, believe me."

"Then we'll shelve Jordan for the moment . . . along with those guardians of yours," Ellen Greer decided, but pointed a warning finger at me. "We'll get around to all of them sooner or later, my dear. Mark my word. I may be eighty, but I'm not ready for the boneyard yet, nor is my brain. When curiosity dies, the rest of you might as well follow right along."

"Well, I think you have more than your share of curiosity," I observed with an amused laugh.

"If you were really truthful, you'd call me nosy." Ellen chuckled. "But you're more polite than honest, it seems. We'll have to work on overcoming that handicap if you're planning to make Sycamore Hill your permanent home."

"That is going to be up to Mr. Olmstead, I'm afraid," I told her ruefully.

"No. That's going to be up to you. Forget Tattle-Tommy and just do what you think is best for the children. The rest will fall in line. Now, when are you going to come and visit with me again?" she demanded.

I was pleased she wanted me to come back, and answered, "As soon as I have a spare moment."

"Well, I can't wait that long, Abby," she muttered impatiently. "I'm an old woman and could die at any moment."

"Oh, no! Don't say such a thing," I gasped.

Ellen chuckled again. "I'd better warn you, my dear. I'm not beyond the use of coercion. And I know exactly how to make your conscience smart the most if you stay away too long."

"You're an old harridan," I told her with humor.

"And you, young woman, are very astute. Now be off with you!" She dismissed me like some six-year-old child. "My niece will be in here any minute now reminding me it's time for my afternoon nap." She shook her head in disgust. "You'd think I would have a little peace at my age, but still I have to follow rules!"

I started for the door, but Ellen Greer called my attention back again. "Come for coffee and cake Wednesday at five."

"I will if I can," I promised.

"I'll expect you," Ellen said, a flicker of loneliness appearing before it was squelched. "And, Abby," she went on more gently, "it's been a pleasure talking to you. I may decide to live a couple of extra years just to see what happens to you."

 *Chapter Six*

My second week of teaching began well. I kept my Wednesday appointment with Ellen Greer, and on the old woman's suggestion, decided to teach Bible stories in Sunday School. I would thus avoid a confrontation with the Reverend Jonah Hayes. He could hardly object to verbatim reading from the Bible, and I would have only to pick and choose those stories that best illustrated God's love and forgiving kindness. I did not want to subject my beliefs to ridicule or debate with the fire-breathing reverend, nor did I want to encourage the children to believe that wrath and vengeance reigned supreme.

As the weeks progressed, I began to tackle problems other than the physical appearance of the schoolhouse, testing and lessons for the children. When Katrina Lane continued coming to school dressed in expensive frocks, which she was afraid to get dirty, I decided to talk with her mother. I learned from Katrina that her mother worked in the hotel at the end of Main Street, and that she finished working in the bar at nine o'clock each evening. I wrote a note requesting an appointment and sent it home with Katrina. The following morning Katrina returned, saying that her mother had agreed to talk with me. I was invited to the hotel Friday evening after nine, if that was acceptable. I agreed without giving it a second thought.

The hotel was filled to capacity that evening. The front rails were packed with saddle horses, and several buckboards and carriages were standing at the back. As I came up the street, I could hear the noisy laughter and honky-tonk music. Now and then a man would shout something and more laughter would burst forth.

Entering the open doorway, I went to the desk to ask where I might find Marba Lane. The short, balding man with wire-rimmed spectacles looked at me curiously, then pointed a finger toward swinging doors that hid the crowd in the bar.

"In there, ma'am," he said, pushing his glasses up while he looked at me oddly. "Why don't you sit down over there." He indicated a chair shadowed behind a large potted plant. "Miss Lane will be finished in a few minutes. I'll go and tell the boss you're waiting for her."

The clerk reappeared a moment later, casting me a cursory glance. He did not say anything, but I assumed he had notified Marba Lane's employer that I had arrived. A moment later the swinging doors opened, and the man I had seen accompanying Marba Lane on the first day of school came through. He spotted me in the corner and walked toward me, a charming smile curving his sensuous mouth.

"Miss McFarland," he greeted in a deep, husky voice, and I stood. "Marba is going to be detained a little longer than usual, I'm afraid. We were late getting her show started this evening. The crowd is bigger than usual," he explained. I felt a curious glance sent in my direction by the desk clerk. Then he focused his interest on the register.

"Why don't you sit down? Can I get you something to drink?" the proprietor asked, and I was flattered by his solicitude.

"No, thank you." I shook my head, feeling rather overwhelmed by the man's good looks and charm. The brown eyes were warm and moved over my face quickly, lingering just a second longer on my mouth.

"I should introduce myself," he laughed apologetically and extended his hand. "I'm Ross Persall. I own this place." He held my hand firmly and just a little longer than necessary.

I muttered some amenity. A woman started to sing in the

barroom behind the swinging doors. The voice was pleasant and strong, though lacking in formal training. But it was the lyrics that brought a flush of red up under my skin. Ross Persall was watching me closely, and his mouth tilted up at the corner. The song continued, and raucous laughter blended with the singing and ruthlessly pounded piano. I touched my cheek with my fingertips and wondered if I should leave and come back later.

"Not exactly what you would hear in Boston, is it?" Ross Persall commented not unkindly. I could see no hint of ridicule for my embarrassment in the warm brown eyes, and I smiled.

"This isn't exactly Boston, is it?" I gave a faint laugh. "And quite frankly, I prefer Sycamore Hill."

"I'm glad to hear it. That means you'll be staying on."

"Well, I hope so," I demurred, sitting down again. I glimpsed James Olmstead as he passed the swinging door. He was laughing with all the rest of the men in the bar.

"How are things going at the schoolhouse?" Persall asked me. He put his foot up on a bench and leaned his arms across his raised knee. He seemed in no hurry to get back about his own business.

"I think they are going very well," I said without fake modesty. "The children are eager to learn. That, of course, makes things easier."

"Katrina likes you," Persall informed me.

"That's nice to know." I smiled.

"I can understand why," he said, grinning. "You're not only smart, you're nice to look at." I blushed profusely and wished that Ross Persall would keep his compliments to himself.

"I didn't mean to embarrass you," he apologized. "I take it you're not used to being told how pretty you are?"

I did not think of myself as pretty at all, and I looked up at him with a dubious stare. "I don't want to keep you from your work, Mr. Persall," I said formally, hoping he would take the less-than-subtle hint.

"It can wait." He smiled, understanding me very well. "Besides, I don't think I should leave you on your own out here in the hotel lobby. I saw you noticing James a minute ago. If he finds you out here, you're liable to get into trouble. This isn't exactly Sunday School, you know."

"I'll get into more trouble if he finds you standing over me, Mr. Persall," I told him frankly. He shrugged, unimpressed.

"All he needs is a word in his ear, and he'll leave well enough alone," he said, showing a hint of indifference at what anyone thought. "And call me Ross. Everyone else in town does. Even our good reverend . . ." he said in a lower voice as he winked at me.

"You mean he comes in here?" I asked irrepressibly, and Ross laughed.

"Not for every service. He says he comes to reform a few of my best customers, but I think it's curiosity. A pagan's den, you might say."

"I didn't think I saw you in church." I grinned.

"Could I hope you were looking for me?"

"Not especially," I said truthfully, though I had been curious about him since the first day of school.

"What possessed you to become a teacher?" he asked. "They're usually withered old maids like Miss Greer." Before I had the opportunity to protest his description of Ellen, Marba Lane came floating through the swinging doors in a red dress with plunging bodice. White feathers drifted back from her curling, elaborate hairdo. I stared as I saw the slit up the front of her dress, which exposed long, shapely legs to mid-thigh. With determination I veiled my look of shock and smiled at Marba Lane, who was looking at Ross Persall.

"What little games are you playing now, Ross?" she demanded. "Why didn't you tell me Miss McFarland was here? You knew very well I was waiting for her," she accused.

"Cool down, Marba," Ross said, straightening up. "You had a show to put on, so I kept our little schoolteacher entertained for you."

Marba seemed to dislike that answer even more than the fact that Ross Persall had not told her of my arrival. Her eyes swung to me. I stood, still smiling but feeling decidedly uncomfortable. I could feel the tension emanating from the two people on either side of me, and I wished I understood what was going on.

"I'm sorry you had to hear that," Marba said, jerking her head to indicate the show in the barroom.

"Please don't be," I protested. "You have a very pleasant voice. I enjoyed hearing you." A look passed between Marba Lane and Ross Persall. Marba relaxed slightly.

"I'd almost forgotten that you're not a snob." She smiled.

"Pardon me?" I mumbled.

"We can talk upstairs in my room." And instead of explaining her comment, Marba started up the steps. Ross Persall detained me with a gentle touch on my arm.

"It's been a pleasure, Miss McFarland," he said in a low voice for my ears only. "I hope I'll have the opportunity to speak with you again." Marba had paused on the stairs and was looking down at us with a strange expression.

"I hope Katrina isn't giving you any trouble," Marba said as I caught up with her. She opened her door. The room was lighted by a cut-glass lamp set on a round mahogany table near a window overlooking Main Street. The room was expensively furnished and showed a good decorative sense.

"Oh, no. By the way, where is Katrina?" I asked as I entered the apartment behind Marba. I noticed the open door to the bedroom off to the right. A large double bed with a rich green-satin spread, a polished-brass headboard and a scattering of yellow and white pillows dominated the room. A man's jacket was tossed carelessly over the end of the bed, and I immediately thought of Ross Persall. It was the same kind of dark coat he had worn the first day I'd seen him.

"Asleep in the next room. She usually goes to bed about eight. I don't like her hearing the rabble downstairs," Marba said, stepping behind a screen in the corner to remove her costume. She reappeared a moment later wrapped in a pink-satin robe with a sash tied tightly around her slim waist. The robe fell slightly open at the top, showing off the cleavage of her ample breasts.

"It isn't exactly a place to raise a kid," she continued, sitting down on a loveseat and putting her bare feet up. She indicated that I should make myself comfortable in the chair opposite. "But I haven't got much choice in the matter. I make my living the best way I can," she went on rather defensively.

"You appear to be doing quite well," I said, looking around the room. "This is all very nice."

Marba Lane was watching my face with an inscrutable expression. Her eyes were hard and perspicacious. "Was that what you came to talk about, Miss McFarland?" she asked in a cold voice. "About the way I make my living and how I'm raising my kid?"

I looked at her with surprise. "Good heavens, no. That's your business," I assured her quickly. "Oh, I hope that's not the impression I gave you from my note. Katrina is a very bright little girl and extremely well-behaved. That's not my reason for wanting to see you."

Some of the tension went out of Marba, though her expression was still wary.

"Actually, I wanted to talk about the way Katrina dresses for school," I said.

"The way she dresses?" Marba repeated. She pulled the ostrich plumes out of her hair and tossed them heedlessly onto a table set with a decanter and glasses. "What's wrong with the way she dresses?"

"Nothing, except that she can't really play in those pretty frocks. They're far too nice to get dirty, and so she sits over by the oak and doesn't join with the other children in their games." I leaned forward, my hands clasped. "Doesn't she have something she could wear that she could feel free to play in? Something she wouldn't be afraid to get dirty?"

Marba did not answer for a moment. "And what makes you so sure the other children would let her play with them, even if she did wear something she could get dirty?" she asked almost belligerently. I knew exactly what she was saying, and I hesitated before answering.

"I can't, of course," I admitted honestly. "But by dressing her the way you do, you set her away from the other children. I think Katrina would like to join in their play."

"I don't want my little girl getting hurt!" Marba said harshly.

"She's already hurting, Miss Lane," I said gently. The woman flinched visibly.

"Listen, Miss McFarland," she said sharply, sitting up and leaning forward, her eyes penetrating. "I've been in a lot of towns. And this isn't the first school Kat has attended. Children can be cruel. They hear things from their parents, and then they repeat them to Katrina. I don't want that happening again. Maybe it's better if she does just sit under the oak by herself." Tears glistened in her eyes, and I felt a stab of pity. Reaching out, I touched her hand.

"I can't promise you the same thing won't happen here. But I can promise that I will do my best to see that it doesn't."

"I believe you would." Marba smiled, and then shook her head dishearteningly. "But you see, that's just not enough."

"You said a little while ago that you didn't like Katrina growing up in a hotel," I opened a second try.

"There are worse places."

"Of course. But if you don't want Katrina spending her life here, allow her the chance to adapt to other people. She'll have to get along in the world, Miss Lane. You can't always keep her set apart, and the longer you do, the harder it's going to be on her. The more it's going to hurt when she's faced with leaving you."

"You don't understand." Marba Lane shook her head.

"Maybe not," I relented and sighed. "But I know what it is to be set apart from people. It's lonely, dreadfully lonely."

Marba blinked and considered me more closely. "At least you're accepted in society," she said.

I smiled slightly. "Under very special conditions. We all have our place. Some are more restricted than others. Katrina is bright, attractive and young enough to adapt. Maybe she'll enter social circles larger than the ones you and I are forced to inhabit." She considered in silence, still looking at me thoughtfully. "It is worth a try, don't you think?" I pressed my advantage.

Still not agreeing, Marba leaned forward and picked up the crystal decanter. "Would you care for some apricot brandy, Miss McFarland?" she asked with a sparkle of challenge in her eyes.

"I've always wanted to try it," I admitted with a smile that raised a surprise glance from my hostess. "But I'd better forgo the experience this evening."

"Why?" Marba asked, and I had the feeling she had taken my refusal as an insult.

"Because I saw the chairman of the school board downstairs," I said in a whisper. "And if I mischanced to meet him with brandy on my breath, I would surely be run out of town on a rail."

Marba Lane laughed delightedly. "You know, Miss Mc-Farland, I like you. I like you very much. You're a big improvement over that Prudence What's-her-name dame. I didn't care one little bit when she. . . ." She stopped in mid-sentence and looked down at her glass. . . .

"When she what?" I asked curiously, wondering why she had cut herself off so abruptly and gone so pale.

"Oh, nothing. She just quit teaching rather suddenly, that's all," she finished, dismissing the subject as she sipped her brandy. She had aroused my curiosity.

"Why was the schoolhouse closed so long after she left?" I asked, wondering why Marba Lane had become so restless and white.

"They couldn't find another teacher," she answered hastily, refilling her glass. "No one in town was really qualified to take over other than Miss Greer, of course, and she's too old. Everyone else has their own job and family to take care of."

Perhaps the explanation was as simple as that, I thought. Maybe I was making too much of the schoolhouse remaining unused for so long. But there were more important things to consider than what had happened to the previous teacher, I reminded myself.

"Will you think about what we discussed?" I asked, standing up to take my leave. Marba set her glass down and rose as well.

"Yes, I will," she said, seeming relieved.

"It might help if you talked things over with your daughter. You might even leave the decision to her," I suggested.

"I might just do that." Marba smiled, the color now back to normal in her cheeks. "And, Miss McFarland, thank you for speaking with me about it."

As I walked down the stairs and across the hotel lobby, I heard a familiar voice among the throng in the next room. Startled, I scurried out the front door just as the barroom doors swung back to reveal Jordan Bennett.

My heart was pounding as I skipped down the steps and

hurried along the darkened street toward McPherson Street. I had not seen Bennett since the Saturday he had brought the horse and plow to the schoolhouse. Linda and Diego had ridden to school on their ponies without his escort, and I had been relieved not to see him again. I knew he was avoiding me, and I hoped he would continue the practice. It made my life considerably more peaceful, though I had not succeeded in completely obliterating him from my mind. In fact, I thought of him much too often. Reminding myself that he was married did not seem to make a difference.

After hurrying for about a hundred yards, I slowed my pace to normal, not hearing anyone following me. I let out my breath, realizing that I had been restricting it since hearing Jordan Bennett.

As I turned up McPherson, I gasped in frightened surprise as a hand closed on my arm, yanking me into the shadows of the trees and effectively hiding me from passers-by.

"I thought I recognized that provocative walk of yours," Jordan Bennett chuckled, removing his hand from across my mouth. He had barely managed to cut off my scream.

"What do you think you're doing?" I quavered, wishing I could make out his face more clearly. His other hand trailed away from my arm as he lounged against the tree trunk, looking at me.

"I thought I might ask you the same question."

"What are you talking about? Oh, why am I standing here at all," I muttered furiously to myself and started to move back toward the walkway. Bennett's fingers dug into my arm again.

"What in hell were you doing at the hotel?" he demanded.

"That's none of your business, Mr. Bennett. And just what do you think you're doing!" I gasped again as he gripped my shoulders and pushed me back against the trunk on which he had been leaning. His face came within inches of mine. And my heart was thudding so wildly, I thought he would surely hear it. His eyes were shining through narrow slits.

"I went to the hotel to talk with Marba Lane about her daughter, Katrina," I prattled frantically, afraid of what he intended to do. His fingers eased their painful hold. He studied my face in the faint moonlight.

"Why didn't Marba come to you?"

"Because she works, and I thought it would be easier if I went to her," I said, growing angry that he had frightened me into explaining. Jordan Bennett started to laugh a low laugh that could not be heard beyond a few feet.

"What are you laughing at?" I hissed, trying to shake free of him.

"At you," he answered, continuing the low chuckling as he looked at my indignant expression. "Oh, Abby McFarland, you do amaze me. You really do."

"I think you're drunk," I accused as scathingly as I could.

"Not quite," he disagreed pleasantly, and then leaned close to me again. I stepped back hastily, but the trunk of the tree stopped me again. "But as soon as I see you walk into that schoolhouse, I intend to go back and get pie-eyed."

"You're disgusting," I insulted him, becoming even more angry, as my fury only seemed to amuse him more.

"Run along now." He stepped to one side and bowed low. I moved quickly past him and bent over to emerge from the leafy branches. I jumped forward with a gasp as his hand delivered a hardy slap to my rear. My dagger glance did not even faze him.

"My apologies," he mocked, laughing. "I just couldn't resist an opportunity like that one."

I ran up the street as fast as my long dress would allow me. Entering the dim schoolhouse, I tried to slow the rapid pumping of my heart. I felt like throwing something, anything. And then my eyes caught something written on the blackboard. The words jumped out at me and froze my churning emotions to a jolting standstill: "Leave before it is too late."

The writing was scrawled, the letters uneven and jerky, as though written by an unsure hand. Or a child. It was not the first such message I had received, and I decided to ignore it as I had the others. Some student was probably playing a practical joke on the teacher, I thought with a wry smile.

Yet, that night I did not sleep well. Once I awakened and thought I heard crying, but when I listened intently, there was nothing but nerve-pulsing silence.

 *Chapter Seven*

After I returned from my visit with Marba Lane to find the scrawled warning on the blackboard, several weeks passed without a repeat of the occurrence. I forgot all about it, not even remembering to mention the incident to Ellen Greer during our weekly visit.

Other things also served to distract me. Katrina had begun coming to school in casual gingham dresses and white pantaloons. With encouragement, several girls had invited her to join in group games. While Katrina was coming out of her shy shell and showing a spontaneous gaiety, Diego Gutierrez was running into further difficulties.

Matthew Hayes, in an effort to gain his father's esteem, threw himself in direct competition with Diego, who was showing himself to be easily the most gifted student in the class. Both boys were intelligent and ambitious, but Diego was slightly superior. Matthew Hayes possessed a fierce, quick temper and was showing a tendency to be vindictive.

The competition between Diego and Matthew came to a head one day in the schoolyard. Each had been made captain of a ball team. Diego's team was winning. The two boys, in an effort to get the ball, knocked together accidentally. In a fury Matthew fell on Diego, pummeling him with his fists. Diego was quick and strong. His own temper, never before seen, burst, and he gave the preacher's son several wallops that knocked him to the ground. Not willing to let it go at that, Matthew jumped up as Diego was walking away, and attacked him from behind.

It took all my physical strength to break the two boys apart, while receiving several blows myself. For an instant I was afraid they might succeed in killing one another. Both boys, as well as myself, were breathing heavily as we stood staring at one another. Diego had a black eye, which was rapidly swelling shut. Matthew's nose was bleeding profusely. He howled curses at Diego, who stood looking at the preacher's son with the same contemptuous disgust that I had seen mirrored in Jordan Bennett's face. Afraid to leave the two boys working out their anger without supervision, I decided to put them at opposite ends of the classroom, writing essays on what had happened. As I read them later that afternoon when the children had all gone home, I was appalled at the hatred that had spewed out of Matthew Hayes. Diego's comments were restricted to the facts.

The following day was Saturday, and I set to work scrubbing the schoolroom floor again. A hard rapping at the door announced James Olmstead. He was looking very upset. I dried my hands and waited for him to tell me what was on his mind.

"I've been with some of the school-board members in a special meeting," he began uncomfortably. I steadied my breathing and braced myself, almost sure of what was coming. The two boys were going to be expelled for the fight, and I was about to receive a severe reprimand for allowing the incident to happen in the first place.

"It has come to our attention that Diego Gutierrez beat up Matthew Hayes."

"That isn't at all what happened," I said in surprise. I had suspected that Matthew would go to his father with some tale. I had hoped he would just remain silent on the event.

"What did happen?"

"Matthew Hayes started a fight with Diego Gutierrez over

a ball game. Diego was as badly hurt in the fight as Matthew."

"You shouldn't have allowed it to happen," Olmstead condemned me critically.

"No. I should have seen it coming. The boys have been competing in almost everything."

"Then that makes our decision all the more proper under the circumstances," Olmstead decided.

"What decision? And what circumstances?" I demanded.

"That Diego Gutierrez be removed from this school. His presence alone is enough to cause trouble. We don't want our children exposed to his kind."

"Diego didn't start the trouble. Matthew Hayes did," I insisted angrily.

"Were you there to witness the whole thing?"

"Well, no, but the other children corroborated Diego's story." From Olmstead's expression, the children's decision to side with Diego was another count against him.

"Nevertheless," he disregarded my defense, "he never belonged in this school. He's a Mexican. And he's a bastard. He should not be allowed to socialize with our children."

A bastard! Jordan's? A sick feeling dropped into the pit of my stomach.

"You're slandering the boy, Mr. Olmstead."

"Everybody in town knows what he is," Olmstead told me, though he flushed slightly. "Reva Gutierrez has been living with Jordan Bennett for years."

Oh, God, this got worse by the minute. "Diego Gutierrez has a right to an education whatever the relationship between his mother and Mr. Bennett," I defended.

"Let Bennett send him somewhere else then. That boy doesn't belong with decent people."

I was appalled at the unfairness of Olmstead and the rest of the board members. "And what happens to Matthew Hayes? You won't be helping that boy by solving his problems this way."

"Matthew Hayes will return to school as always."

"Without any disciplinary measures for what he did?" I asked in anger. "He was devious and cowardly in his actions of running to his father with that untruthful story."

"He defended himself," Olmstead asserted firmly, as though refusing to believe anything else.

"Nothing will change your mind, will it?"

"You are to go to Eden Rock and tell Jordan Bennett and Reva Gutierrez of the board's decision."

"You expect me to carry that odious slander against Diego?" I gasped incautiously.

"It's more than obvious you favor the boy. Perhaps your favoritism brought on this whole unfortunate incident."

"I suspect it started long before I ever even heard of Sycamore Hill, Mr. Olmstead. It's a thing called bigotry."

"Don't be impertinent!" Olmstead snapped. "If you want to keep your job, you'll carry out your responsibilities. And one of your responsibilities is to inform Diego and his parents that he is no longer welcome at this school. Is that clearly understood, Miss McFarland?"

I remembered what Ellen Greer had said about teachers being hard to find because the job was a thankless one. I knew that I could refuse to take this message to Diego, but what was the alternative. James Olmstead would go. Or the Reverend Hayes himself. I could well imagine what would be said to Diego in that case. The boy would be terribly hurt with perhaps a memory that would last him his lifetime. I could not allow that to happen.

"I understand you very well indeed, Mr. Olmstead," I said coldly. He flushed slightly under my derisive look, and then left.

I sat down and put my head in my hands. How was I going to tell Diego that he was no longer welcome at school because he had defended himself? What would it do to him? On top of the hurt it would cause him, how was I going to face Jordan Bennett with the board's decision? That I did not approve of it or agree with their reasoning would only make him all the more scornful because I was carrying out their dictates without the courage to fight them. Or could I? What was to stop me from tutoring the boy myself?

Jordan Bennett's illegitimate son. What kind of wife did he have that would allow her husband's mistress and son to remain on the ranch? And Reva Gutierrez? What would she be like?

With my Sunday schedule I had little choice but to leave the schoolhouse cleaning for later that night. I would have to ride out to Eden Rock and speak with Diego, Jordan Bennett and Reva Gutierrez. I gave a harsh, almost hysterical laugh as I remembered that James Olmstead had neglected to tell me how to reach Jordan Bennett's ranch. But the man at the livery stable would know, and I needed a horse and buggy.

When I got to the stable, Charles Studebaker informed me that there were no buggies available, but that Jordan Bennett had donated the gelding for my use. He assured me that the animal was gentle, and having little choice in the matter, I mounted it with some trepidation.

An hour later I was still walking the horse northeast. Studebaker had given me succinct directions. Six miles, stay on the road, turn on the left fork when I came to the bridge.

While riding, I had plenty of time to think. The more I thought, the angrier I became at James Olmstead and his bombastic school board. They thought nothing of hurting Diego by their unreasoning prejudice against his parents. How could I lessen the blow to the boy? Were all people as cruel and deceitful as the Haversalls? I had hoped things would be different out here.

For the first couple of miles I had to slap the horse's rump over and over to keep it going at a steady snail's pace. It had obviously evaluated my mettle as a rider at the onset and knew that it could do as he wished. However, when I neared the fork, the horse grew more interested. It began to walk at a quicker pace, and I felt only vague relief that I would reach the ranch before the following year!

My relief was short-lived. Just past a dried creek bed, the horse's ears perked up and pointed forward. Then it broke into a trot. My head bobbed up and down, and I learned quickly to clench my jaws so my teeth would not crack together every time my rear made bruising contact with the saddle. I could barely focus on the jouncing world passing me by. I kept all my concentration on holding tight to the saddle horn and reins to prevent an ungainly fall in the dirt.

"Whoa, horse," I managed. "Slow down. Easy, boy. Whoa!" I tried every command I could think of to persuade the beast to return to its comfortable snail's pace. It ignored me. My efforts to pull back on the reins were ignored. It clamped its teeth on the bit and was not bothered by my tugging. After a half-mile I started making ignominious offing sounds each time I bounced up and came plopping down.

I saw an immense house set back against an oak-covered range of hills. The details of the tranquil scene were lost on me as I continued beating the horse's rhythm on its back. Its trotting picked up speed, though the horse did not break into a gallop.

My situation struck me as ludicrous. I started to laugh. The sound was forced out of me with each jolt I made, and I laughed even harder. I prayed no one was watching.

The horse trotted on beneath the arch, announcing that I had reached my destination. I saw the hitching rail before the house with relief, but apparently the horse had yet another destination in mind. He yanked hard on the reins, burning my fingers as I tried to steer him to the left. Then he turned right and headed straight for the barn. My laughter ceased.

To my horror and humiliation, I saw Jordan Bennett standing in the yard, arms akimbo, watching me. The horse trotted right past him and into the barn. I wanted to die when I heard Bennett laughing uproariously behind me as the horse finally stopped to thrust his nose deep into a trough of oats.

Then the hilarity of the incident hit me, and I started to laugh again. I laughed until tears were running down my cheeks.

"You nasty old beast." I reprimanded the totally disinterested horse on which I still sat. "How could you do this to me?" I wiped my face and looked back over my shoulder at Jordan Bennett approaching. "You can't know how glad I am that animal has finally stopped," I admitted, rubbing the small of my back and wishing I were in private so that I could rub yet another part of my anatomy. Jordan was still grinning when he reached the large stall.

"You're the first woman I've ever met who could laugh at herself," he said, his eyes sparkling with friendliness.

"What else could I do?" I laughed again. "I'm certainly not the picture of dignity and grace at the moment. Oh, my word, what a ride! I think next time I shall walk." I shook my head ruefully. "I never realized how many muscles the human body possessed, but I'm sure every one is bruised!" I looked around and then down at Jordan Bennett again.

"Now, Mr. Bennett, would you please tell me how to get down off this animal with some semblance of propriety. I won't tell you how I got aboard."

Jordan laughed again. "It's simple," he assured me and reached up to take me by the waist. "Like this." He lifted me down effortlessly.

I had difficulty slowing my breathing when he set me down. His hands were still at my waist, and he had stopped laughing. I felt he was entirely too close, but I couldn't step away from him. When his head started to descend, I did step back instinctively. I came into contact with the horse and felt the heat of the animal against my back. It snorted and continued to gorge itself.

Trying desperately to think of something to say, I flushed. Jordan Bennett's eyes had an unnerving intensity. Though he did not move and his hands dropped from me, I felt we were still too close to one another. All the laughter had gone out of both of us, and there was a pulsating awareness that frightened me.

Say something, I told myself feeling a bubble of panic growing inside me. But it was Jordan who broke the spell. "What brings you all this way to Eden Rock, Miss McFarland?"

His sudden formality and seriousness was enough to bring me back to my senses. The reason for my bruising ride descended on me like a leaden weight. I stared up at him with such distress and embarrassment that he frowned.

"I have to speak with you and Mrs. Gutierrez about Diego." His expression blackened with comprehension.

"About the fight in the schoolyard," he added and made a sound deep in his throat.

"Yes."

The look he gave me was filled with hostility, and I drew into myself, suddenly feeling very vulnerable where he was concerned. "I'll explain the situation to Diego, Miss McFarland," he told me coldly. "It'll hurt less coming from me."

"I would like to speak with him, if you don't mind."

"Oh, I mind all right! What is it? You want to give him the glad tidings?" His mouth was hard and uncompromising.

"You don't understand."

"The hell I don't. I understand only too well, Miss Mc-Farland, high-and-mighty schoolmarm," he sneered. "Does it give you a feeling of power, bringing this kind of news around?"

I stared in disbelief and then pushed past him in anger. He stopped me at the barn door. "Okay, damn it. You can have the pleasure of breaking the good news. But so help me, God," he said through his teeth, "if you make it more hurtful than necessary, I'll personally beat you black and blue. Have you got that in your head, Miss McFarland?"

"Indeed, I do," I said stiffly, turning away quickly so he would not see how much his accusation against me hurt. Someone called my name in an excited voice.

"Miss McFarland! Miss McFarland! What're you doing here?" Linda called and came running down the steps of the ranch house. Diego followed slowly. There was a look on his face that twisted my heart. Linda jumped around me excitedly, chattering on about something that did not even register on my mind. I tried to smile at her but could not take my eyes from the boy's. Did he know already?

"Hello, Diego."

"Buenos dias, Señorita McFarland," he said, using Spanish with a challenging tilt of his head. That hurt even more, because I realized suddenly that this unreasoning prejudice was no new thing to him. What had Linda started to say that first day of school? Something about Diego and school two years ago? Why hadn't I insisted on hearing what had happened? Perhaps I could have prevented this whole miserable situation.

"May I speak with you and your mother, please?"

Diego's eyes showed a telltale moisture, but his full mouth tightened. He breathed in deeply before he spoke and I heard Jordan Bennett mumble something under his breath as he strode away.

"Follow me, please, Miss McFarland."

I followed Diego, noticing how rigidly he held his shoulders. I hardly glanced around the huge living room dominated by a stone fireplace as we passed through. Diego ushered me to the kitchen at the back of the house. Something was cooking, and the smell was tantalizing. I remembered that I had not eaten since daybreak. But I felt slightly sick with a case of nerves.

A small, slim woman stood near the stove. Her black hair was braided and pinned at the back of her neck. She moved with a lithe grace.

"Mama," Diego announced our presence. Reva Gutierrez turned with a smile for her son and then stopped as she saw me next to him. The smile dimmed.

"Miss McFarland has come to tell you that I am not to return to school. Isn't that so, Miss McFarland?" Diego asked. I looked down at him.

"Diego . . ."

"It isn't the first time this has happened," his mother said before I could say more.

I looked between the two of them—the hurt boy standing with quiet dignity, the angry mother. "Well, I do wish both of you would allow me to say what I have to say before you so easily accept the situation."

Reva Gutierrez frowned. "Then say what you wish, and leave us." Diego was silent, eyes averted, chin trembling.

"I'm afraid it is true that Diego's being expelled. The decision was unjust and prejudicial, and I apologize for it."

"Did you make it, Miss McFarland?" Reva Gutierrez demanded sharply.

"No, I had no part in it."

"Then your apology is meaningless," she snapped dismissively. She turned back to her cooking. I knew there was great hurt beneath the anger. Her shoulders were stiff, and her hands were clenching into fists.

"Mrs. Gutierrez—"

"Not 'Mrs.' . . . Señorita Gutierrez. I am not married," the young woman corrected, turning around again. "You see, my son has two things against him. He is Mexicano, and he is a bastard."

Diego's face twisted as he lost control. He turned and fled the kitchen, the door swinging shut behind him.

"How could you do that to him?" I asked faintly, feeling close to tears myself.

"It isn't I who do the hurt to him," Reva said, her accent thickening as the tears started. "It is you! It is the people in the town!"

"I'm sorry, but—"

"Being sorry does not help, Miss McFarland." She dismissed my words with a sharp jerk of her chin.

"I know. That's why I would like to have you bring Diego to me very early each morning so that I can teach him what he would have learned in class," I said in a rush before she could interrupt me yet again. Reva stared at me.

"Bring him to school? . . ."

"If you do not wish to do that, I will come here to the ranch once a week and bring him work and books," I offered.

"You will teach him?" she breathed, her eyes wide and hopeful.

"Diego has a right to his education just as any of the other children, Miss Gutierrez. If you will allow me, I will be honored to teach him all I know. He is a brilliant boy."

Reva Gutierrez stared at me for another moment and then grabbed her apron, putting it up to her face in an effort to hide her emotions. At the same moment someone burst into the kitchen behind me.

"You've got five minutes to get off my ranch!" Jordan Bennett ordered, his expression so fierce, it was terrifying.

"Didn't you hear what I said," he growled when I just stood there, mouth gaping open in fright. He reached out, taking my arm and roughly pointing me toward the door. I gasped in pain and fear.

"Get out!"

"Jordan! *Por Dios!*" Reva cried, the apron dropping from her tear-streaked face. She grabbed at his arm and spoke to him in rapid Spanish. He was not listening to her, his eye fixed on me in barely controlled violence.

"Your horse is out front waiting for you," he raged at me, heedless of Reva pulling frantically at his arm. "If you aren't on it and off my ranch in five minutes, I won't be held responsible for what I do to you. Now get out!"

Shaking almost uncontrollably, I ran through the house and down the front steps. I climbed on the gelding and urged it down the road toward the arch under which I had passed so short a time ago. Watered and fed, the horse responded to my urgency.

About a mile down the road I heard the thundering of a horse behind me. Turning to look back over my shoulder, I saw a black stallion with Jordan Bennett astride. Panic obliterated all reason, and I kicked hard at my mount. I bolted forward, more in surprise by my sudden decisive action than in agreement to follow my dictates. But the stallion stretched out and easily caught up.

Jordan's hand came into my peripheral vision, and instinctively I flinched away, not realizing he was reaching for the reins and not me. The stallion's presence, my twisting motion and Jordan's alarmed shout unnerved the gelding, and it bucked to the side, sending me flying headlong through the air. I felt the sleeves of my dress rip as dirt and rock tore into my hands and forearms. The air was knocked out of me, and I lay motionless.

"Abby!"

Jordan Bennett swung down from his saddle in a fluid motion and came at me. With an agility born of fear, I came to my feet, gasping for breath. Upon seeing my face, he stopped, and something flickered in his expression. I was too frightened to analyze it, and I took a step back.

"Abby," Jordan said more calmly. I still backed away from him, not trusting his anger and remembering the violence of his look only moments before. My arms burned, and I pressed them against me in an effort to stop the pain.

Jordan moved slowly toward me, looking down at his hands. "We'll have to wash—"

"Leave me alone!" I flinched back as he extended his hand toward me.

He dropped his arm and looked at me, his expression strained. "Reva told me about your offer."

Tears of fright and temper burned behind my eyes. "You're insane, attacking me like that."

"Look, damn it!" he exploded in frustration. "If you'd shut up long enough to listen, you'd hear me apologize!"

"It's all your fault!"

"What?" He looked blank.

"Everything! Everything!" I cried, thinking of James Olmstead and what he had told me about Diego.

"What in hell are you talking about?"

"Diego!"

Some of the anger went out of him. "I thought you'd said something to hurt him. I warned you. And I found him crying in the barn," he said in explanation for his earlier violent outburst.

"I wouldn't do anything to hurt him. But you . . . you knew what would happen, didn't you? You knew James Olmstead and his bigoted school board would find some flimsy excuse to expel him, didn't you? And you talk about me trying to hurt him. You're despicable! You're the most miserable human being I've ever met, including the—"

"Be quiet!" Jordan ordered tersely. A muscle jerked in his jaw.

"No! Not before I tell you what I think of you!"

"You've said enough. And you don't know what you're talking about."

"I thought James Olmstead and Reverend Hayes were bad enough. But you're worse," I went on, too angry to think of caution anymore. "You knew what they would do to Diego, and you let it happen."

"Where Diego decides to go to school has nothing to do with me. He made the decision to try Sycamore Hill again. Where else could he go, for God's sake?"

"You ask me that?" I gasped. "You could have sent him anywhere. You have the money to see to his education."

"He's not my responsibility. And even if I did take it on, Reva is too proud a woman to accept any charity."

"Charity!" I stared at him, horrified. "You're even worse than I thought. I can't imagine why Reva Gutierrez even remains in your employ. If it were me, I'd hate you."

"My God! I can't make head nor tail out of what you're saying!" Jordan ejaculated in furious frustration. "Just tell me this. Are you going to do what you said? Will you teach Diego here at the ranch?"

"I'm not going to deny Diego his rights because his father

is an insensitive, irresponsible brute!" I exclaimed. Jordan Bennett became very still. His face hardened into a granite mask.

"Someone told you Diego is my son, is that it?"

"Apparently it's common knowledge. You might as well do him the justice of acknowledging him!" I retorted, suddenly hurting inside and wanting to cry.

Jordan looked away from me and stared toward Sycamore Hill with an inscrutable expression. Then he turned and strode toward his stallion. Mounting, he looked down at me coldly. Something unfathomable passed across his eyes. He gave a harsh, sardonic laugh.

"Wait until they get around to telling you how I murdered my wife."

I stared aghast as he whirled the stallion around and rode at a hard gallop back to the ranch.

 *Chapter Eight*

"Everyone believes that Jordan killed his wife," Ellen Greer answered my question with a disgusted snort. "People always want to believe the worst of others. Don't believe all that hogwash about the 'milk of human kindness.' Most people don't have a kind bone in their bodies, and if they did, they would be ashamed to admit it."

"Ellen," I sighed.

"You got me on a sore subject, Abby. I love that boy."

"He's hardly a boy," I said dryly. "Maybe he's changed since you had him as a student."

"I haven't lost touch with him. He wrote to me regularly when he was studying in the East, and he still drops by on occasion, though not as often as I'd like it."

That was a side of Jordan Bennett I had never seen.

"I'm not blind to his faults, mind you. I know he has a foul, violent temper when he's aroused. It got him into trouble more than once in my school. But that was when he was a boy. He's got more control now."

I remembered the expression on his face when he had burst into the kitchen. How much in control had he been then?

"Even for a patient, placid man, Gwendolyn would have been a trial."

"That was her name . . . Gwendolyn?" I murmured.

"Gwendolyn Bracklin-Reed, to be precise," Ellen said in a stilted, mocking voice that clearly indicated her dislike for the dead woman. "One of the true-blue bloods of Boston, and she didn't want anyone to forget it." That, at least, explained Jordan Bennett's prejudice against Bostonians, I thought.

"What did she look like?" I asked, wondering what kind of woman would attract Jordan Bennett. Ellen gave me a sharp look.

"So you're curious about Jordan's wife, are you? Any special reason?" Those shrewd eyes were alight with mischievous amusement and speculation. I straightened indignantly at the implication and refused to admit to the faint flush that stained my cheeks.

"We can change the subject any time you wish," I managed.

Ellen waved her gnarled hand in reprimand. "Don't be so sensitive, girl, or I might just think you're protesting too much. Besides, it wouldn't do you any good if you were interested in Jordan. He's sworn off women, except for the Friday- and Saturday-night five-dollar type at the hotel. After Gwendolyn, who would blame him? She was enough to make any man wish he had been gelded. And don't give me that wide-eyed, shocked look of yours either, Abby. My frank speaking doesn't embarrass you in the least, and I know it. In fact, I think you thrive on it."

"I think you deliberately try to shock me sometimes," I teased her. "But how do you know so much about his private life?"

"I don't. It's pure speculation. But I know he goes to the hotel on occasion, and I can put two and two together without getting zero."

"Why does Reva Gutierrez stay with him under such circumstances?"

"Reva?" Ellen's eyes opened wide in genuine surprise. "My heavens! Our little town magpies have been busy filling your ears, haven't they?" She leaned forward on her cane, one hand on top of the other. "Does Diego look like Jordan Bennett's son to you, Abby?"

I colored hotly. "I didn't mean to say he was!"

Ellen clucked impatiently. "But that's what you were thinking. You listen to me, Abby. The next time you see Diego, you take a good hard, long look at him," she instructed, her neck stretched out like a defensive old banty hen. "Then decide whether what the gossip mongers in this town say is true."

"He didn't deny it," I muttered unhappily, hoping Ellen was right in her deductions. I did not know why, but it hurt me to believe that Jordan Bennett had fathered Diego. My feelings over him did not bear mulling over. I told myself that no matter how much I disliked the man, I did not like to think him capable of such cruel indifference toward his own son.

Ellen looked astounded and leaned back in her chair. "You mean you actually confronted him with that story? What in the world possessed you to do such a stupid thing?"

I felt like a child caught in some malicious mischief. "I was upset about Diego, and my temper got out of control."

Ellen sniffed derisively. "People with tempers should fetter their tongues. Maybe you and Jordan have more in common than I thought. But I'll tell you this about him. He wouldn't admit or deny anything if his life depended on it. I think he takes amusement in watching people make complete jackasses out of themselves."

"He's done it often enough with me," I admitted miserably. "From the first moment we met."

"You never have told me about that," Ellen reminded me, obviously hoping I would amend the oversight.

"And I don't intend to," I said emphatically, while softening my words with a smile.

"Well, at least I got the story of the Haversalls out of you," she chuckled. "Maybe Jordan will tell me about the other."

Ellen rocked her chair back and forth a few times watching the emotions play across my face. "We were getting around to talking of Gwendolyn, weren't we?"

"We don't have to," I said a little too casually.

"Why don't you be honest and admit you're dying of curiosity about her?" Ellen needled.

"I don't think I want to hear anything about her," I said sincerely. The mere mention of her name caused an uncomfortable feeling in my stomach.

"Well, I'm going to tell you all about her, whether you like it or not . . . and in spite of your supposed lack of interest," Ellen scoffed.

"Gwendolyn Bennett was the most beautiful woman I've ever seen. The kind that makes a man fall head over heels in love and has the ability to make him feel he's the great protector," she said demeaningly. "Men can be such fools. And Jordan is no exception. He took one look at a pair of violet eyes, and the sense he was born with seeped right out his ears." She shook her head in disappointment and disgust.

"I never thought he could be so bamboozled by a woman— or a man, for that matter. But he was. If anything good comes out of that marriage, it will be Linda. She inherited her mother's looks, but pray to God she didn't inherit anything else of hers!"

"How did Mr. Bennett meet his wife?"

"At some big society dinner. He wanted her the first time he saw her, and when Jordan wants something, he goes after it. He didn't have to run very hard to get Gwendolyn though. She heard that he had been offered a position with one of Boston's finest law firms, and she saw money. Their marriage might have lasted if Jordan had stayed in Boston. But he didn't like the people or their rigid social codes. First chance he got, he packed her up and came back to California, where he belongs. I don't think she ever got over the shock of that, and she set out to make his life miserable."

Ellen looked out the back window, where she could see her niece plucking bush beans. I waited, not wanting to admit even to myself that I wanted to know all about Jordan Bennett. He was a frightful man, and I was much too aware of him already. But it didn't seem to matter.

"Gwendolyn had great plans for her life, and a ranch in California had no part in it," Ellen continued. "She didn't want to live here, and she made no bones about it. Jordan wasn't about to let her tantrums drive him back East again. So it was an ongoing war between them. She hated California. She hated the ranch. She hated the people here, and after a while I think she even grew to hate Jordan. She didn't care who knew it."

"But what about Linda?" I asked. Surely there had been something between Jordan and Gwendolyn Bennett for them to have a baby. They must have loved each other for a while after they arrived in California. What went so wrong?

"Linda, I should think, was an unforeseen and unwelcome accident shortly after they arrived in California. Apparently, Gwendolyn got pregnant almost immediately after she and Jordan were married in Boston. She couldn't get rid of the baby fast enough once she was born. Reva took Linda to wet nurse."

"How did Mr. Bennett feel about that?"

Ellen made a grunt. "What do you think? He figured a surrogate mother was preferable to Gwendolyn's open hostility."

"No wonder the little girl is so withdrawn," I said almost to myself. How could a mother reject such a sweet child?

"She may not come to school now that Diego has been expelled," Ellen warned grimly.

"But surely? . . . "

"She loves Diego. She'll more than likely refuse to come to school without him."

"And what about her father's opinion on that?" I asked.

"Jordan Bennett could teach Linda more than you and I put together. And since you've already so magnanimously offered to take care of Diego's education. . . ."

"But it isn't just a question of learning from books, Ellen. Linda needs to be with other children."

"So does Diego. And Diego is like her flesh-and-blood brother. She'll be loyal to him. Do you see the position you've put yourself into, Abby? If the school board ever finds out you're giving Diego private instruction, you are very liable to lose your position."

"Are you trying to suggest I not tutor Diego?" I questioned.

"I'm just saying you should weigh your actions very carefully. You can't change the world, my dear, and trying to do so might get you right out on your ear. Then what good would you be to anyone?"

"There are other positions," I said, defensive of my decision.

"Spoken like a true idiot." Ellen did not spare my feelings. "And if you leave here, what good would you be to Diego Gutierrez, who's the cause of all this? Would you tell me that?" She emitted a disgusted snort. "What a little fool you can be, my dear. Who would give you a reference? James Olmstead? Reverend Jonah Hayes? And what about the other sixty-three children who need you? Diego is one boy. Will you let the others become illiterates so that you can play crusader?"

"There's no sense in arguing, Ellen," I said flatly. "I told Reva Gutierrez I would teach Diego, and I will. If I don't teach him, I will be condoning the school board's position."

Ellen leaned forward again. "It was misplaced loyalty that kept you with the Haversalls while they stole you blind. Look at what they did to you."

"This isn't the same thing," I asserted, angry that she had brought up that subject again.

Ellen sighed deeply and sat back. "No, it isn't. But just don't let your emotions rule you. Do what you have to do to keep your own self-respect, but be as quiet about it as a lamb in a lion's den."

I stood up to leave, asking as I did so if there was anything I could get for her. I got the customary sharp reply that anything she needed she could get up and get for herself. It had almost become a ritual.

"Ellen?" I paused at the door with one final question. "What happened to Gwendolyn Bennett?"

"No one's sure. She died of a broken neck. Jordan said she fell, but the story was never really very clear. Old Tom Hallender, our sheriff, just let the incident drop without too many questions. He was busy trying to solve a robbery at the same time, and people weren't pushing to hang anyone suspected of killing 'the princess,' as they called her. Nobody except Jordan mourned her."

"Then he did love her," I said quietly, feeling a pain knife through me.

"Maybe he still did. Or maybe he just loved what he thought she was the first time he laid eyes on her. Or maybe he just mourned the fact that he ever met her in the first place. Who knows?"

"I suppose Jordan Bennett is a hard man because he's had a hard life," I commented.

"No harder than anyone else around these parts, and a lot easier than some. He has been the cynosure of malicious gossip since Gwendolyn's death. You've heard most of it. Diego was another event for which he gained blame. They also credited him with what happened to Prudence. . . ." Ellen cut her sentence off and looked out the window with a tight, irritated expression.

"Prudence," I repeated. "You mean Prudence Townsend?"

"It's all hogwash and not worth repeating."

"What happened to Prudence Townsend?" I asked, sitting back down opposite Ellen Greer, determined to get an answer this time. Ellen looked at me and shook her head.

"Nothing you'd want to know about, and nothing that would help you in the knowing," she said firmly. I sat waiting, but she just looked at me with her jaw jutted out. I sighed and rose again.

"Besides you, does Jordan Bennett have any real friends in this town?" I asked dryly.

"A few. Emily Olmstead for one, believe it or not. Maybe that's why James is so outspoken about the rumors surrounding Jordan. He always was a jealous little runt."

"Jordan and Emily Olmstead were talking the day I arrived at the general store," I remembered.

"I'll lay you odds that James was nowhere in sight," Ellen snorted.

"As a matter of fact, he wasn't!"

Ellen started to chuckle.

"What's the matter?" I asked, curious.

"You called him Jordan. I thought you disliked the man."

I flushed. "I suppose your calling him by his Christian name rubbed off, that's all." Ellen was watching me with that pensive, sharp-eyed expression that sometimes unnerved me.

"What happened to your hands, by the way?" Ellen asked.

"I fell," I answered tersely.

"How and why?"

"My horse bolted, and I fell off," I said, keeping to the truth without elaborating embarrassing details.

"I don't believe you're telling me everything. Now out with it!" Ellen snapped like the old schoolmarm she was. "How did it happen, and what's it got to do with Jordan? I know it has something to do with him because of the course of our conversation this afternoon."

"I don't intend to go into it," I told her. "It was a needless accident."

"Did Jordan do that?" Ellen asked, distressed now and looking at me oddly.

"It happened exactly the way I told you."

"Well, then, you'd better learn how to sit your horse a little better."

I smiled reassuringly. "I'll be getting more practice," I told her, thinking of my weekly rides to Eden Rock to tutor Diego. I opened the door to leave.

"Abby."

I turned back. Ellen looked disturbed and pensive as she watched me.

"Don't leave yourself open to hurt," she told me. "I think you're more vulnerable than you like to let on."

"I know what I'm doing." I smiled, thinking of the warning she had given me about the school board's finding out about my tutoring.

"I wonder if you do. You might find more at Eden Rock than you can cope with."

It was only after I was walking home that I realized Ellen Greer was thinking of my feelings for Jordan Bennett.

 *Chapter Nine*

A soft, mewling cry awakened me from an exhausted slumber. Lying motionless on my pallet, I strained to hear any sound that might reveal what had roused me from the first sound sleep I had had since finding the warning messages on the blackboard. Again the cry came, softly penetrating the darkness.

Pushing the cover back, I swung my legs off the narrow bed and touched bare feet to a cold, wooden floor. Shadows filled my small room, and I stared at each one until I was able to explain their presence. Rising, I listened. I heard nothing except the same owl who haunted the oak tree, and the symphony of crickets that harmonized in the quiet corners of the building.

Slowly, I tiptoed across my room. The October night was unusually chilly, and I hugged my high-necked nightgown close to my body.

Again the cry came, this time a desperate sound in the darkness, a plea for help. Opening the schoolroom door, I peered in. By straining my ears, I tried to pinpoint where the sound was coming from and what was making it. Then I saw a small, forlorn shadow against the front window. Recognizing the shape, I hurried across the deserted classroom and opened the front door of the schoolhouse.

Sitting precariously on the front windowsill was a small stray black cat. It yowled again, looking at me.

"What are you doing there?" I asked with a laugh. There was a goodly distance between the railing and the sill, and I could not understand how the cat had leaped so far. The cat meowed again and stepped gingerly to the edge, then peered toward me.

"Come on, cat, jump back, and I'll catch you," I held out my hands. The cat sat back distrustfully and yowled again.

I judged the distance between the railing and the cat and realized it would be quite a stretch to reach the animal. I jiggled the railing slightly, and it seemed sturdy enough. The cat was eyeing me wearily as I leaned toward it. When my fingers brushed the fur slightly, it backed away. I had to stretch away even farther, finally managing to get the scruff of its neck. Just as I was lifting the light weight, the railing gave a loud crack. Yanking backward, I just managed to catch my balance as the railing gave way and toppled into the blackness below the steps. My heart was thudding as I looked over the steps and down. It was a good six feet to the hard ground. If I had fallen, I would surely have broken something. I let out a sigh of relief.

"That was close." I laughed shakily, stroking the cat's head with trembling fingers. "The whole schoolhouse seems to be falling down around me. I'll have to have that railing repaired early tomorrow before the children come."

The cat snuggled tightly against my chest as I caressed it. "What were you doing up in the window? And how did you get there, you silly cat?"

The small, scrawny black cat mewed again as I reentered the schoolhouse and shut the door behind me. "I think I have some milk and a little bread. Does that sound good to you?"

Setting the animal down, I rummaged through my small cupboard. The cat meowed plaintively and pressed itself against my legs. Pouring some milk into a saucer, I pinched off pieces of bread to soak. Then I put the meal on the rough-hewn table. Lifting the cat up, I sat down and watched it set to hungry work, lapping up the milk and gulping down the sodden bread.

"Pretty hungry, aren't you?" I smiled and stroked the soft fur. "You're welcome to stay. I've plenty of room. There's no one else but the owl, the crickets and me until the children come for school in the morning, and they'll be delighted to see you here."

The cat arched its back against my hand, and I scratched it. It made an ecstatic sound deep in its throat.

"What shall I call you? How about Orphan? You look neglected enough to be one," I said, continuing the petting. The cat purred on. When I stopped, the cat mewed, then sat down and began its tedious grooming.

I looked around the room and tried to decide where best to put my new friend. Opening a bottom drawer in the commode, I took out several pairs of pantaloons and some soft camisoles before putting in a rough towel. Lifting the cat from the table, I set it in the drawer. Orphan sat down and continued licking her fur.

"There. That drawer is your new home, if you want it," I told her. Then settling back onto my own bed, I sighed. Somehow, even the presence of the small, stray cat seemed to ease the loneliness a bit. Only Ellen Greer had accepted me without conditions, but Ellen only lightened my existence for an hour once a week. Strange how an animal who could not talk to me offered such companionship.

The following morning before seven, I went to the general store, intending to ask James Olmstead to fix the front railing. As I walked up the street, I saw Sheriff Hallender leaning against the wall just outside his office. I gave him a wave and a cheerful greeting. He waved back. Then he shoved his hat back on his head and strode up Main Street to do his early-morning rounds.

Through the window of the store I saw James Olmstead stacking canned goods, and I tapped at the door. Surprised to see me so early, he opened it quickly. I explained about the railing, and he frowned in agitation.

"It'll have to wait," he told me flatly. "I've got too much to do around here to be bothered with the schoolhouse. I'll get to it some other time."

"I'm afraid it can't wait that long, Mr. Olmstead. It's a hazard. One of the children could fall and break a leg. You still haven't fixed the back steps, and I've been there for almost two months."

Olmstead did not appreciate that reminder. "In case you

hadn't noticed, Miss McFarland, I've got a business to run. I haven't got time to go traipsing around, making repairs on the schoolhouse," he growled.

"I know you're busy." I tried for levity. "And I understand how much you have to do. But couldn't you find time to repair the front railing at least? Or perhaps you could find someone else to repair it?"

"And if I find someone else, who's going to pay for the work? I'll tell you this. I won't pay for it!"

"You said that the school board was responsible for any repairs of this sort. Surely they have some fund that would cover the expenses," I said, irritated by his disinterest.

"Kids fall off things every day, Miss McFarland," he said, turning back to the canned goods again. "You're making too much out of it. Just let it go for a while, and when I get the time, I'll fix it."

"I'm sorry, but that's not good enough. It's a matter of safety for the children," I said, determined. "If one of the children falls from the front porch, it will be the school board's responsibility for allowing the railing to go unrepaired."

Olmstead's face turned beet-red with temper. "It won't be my responsibility!" he protested in a loud, booming voice. "The upkeep of that place is your responsibility, and no one else's."

"Mr. Olmstead—" I tried to calm the man. I wished I had our first conversation written down and signed by him so that I would have some proof of my stand. It was too easy for Olmstead and the school board to make vague promises and then flatly deny them when faced with the inconvenience of upholding the agreement. This was only one incident in several. The back steps were still left unrepaired. The roof had leaked during the first rainstorm, and the children had to move their desks. The broken windows in the front were still unreplaced. The front railing was something I could not allow to go unrepaired. It was too dangerous for the children, who used those stairs every day they attended school.

"Don't bother me about this. I've got things to do!" Olmstead interrupted me, impatient and annoyed.

"I cannot be a carpenter and a teacher in one, Mr. Olmstead," I said coldly, my own temper rising. "You agreed to take care of major repairs on the building, and I'm afraid you will just have to find the time to keep that promise."

Olmstead turned around and stared at me in consternation. "How dare you speak to me in that impudent tone," he barked.

"It is not my intention to sound impudent. But, Mr. Olmstead, your own child attends our school. What if Andy were to fall off the porch and hurt himself? How would you feel then?"

He ignored my supposition and hefted a sack of flour onto his back. He marched toward a bin where he intended to empty it. I stood astonished at his rude dismissal of my concerns for the children.

"Mr. Olmstead," I said, schooling my voice to respectful inquiry. Olmstead heaved the sack off his shoulder and dropped it with a thud next to the bin. Then he turned to glare hostilely at me.

"You've got my answer. Do it yourself! I haven't got the time. And if I had, I wouldn't be spending it working on that old schoolhouse. I'll go so far as to loan you a hammer, and the nails are cheap enough."

"Is there something wrong here?"

I turned to look at Ross Persall. He stood in the doorway looking with interest at James Olmstead and me. The drawling voice was casual enough, but I suspected he had heard the last bit of conversation and knew exactly what was going on.

"What can I do for you, Mr. Persall?" Olmstead asked effusively polite. Obviously, Persall was a valued customer and was therefore more important than the safety of 63 children, I thought with exasperation.

"Did you have a problem, Miss McFarland?" Persall asked me with a smile, patently ignoring Olmstead, who was greedily awaiting Persall's hotel order. The storekeeper's face burned, and he looked at me with a warning expression. That bullying look might work on his wife, I thought, but it was not going to work on me!

"Yes, Mr. Persall, I do have a problem. Mr. Olmstead is very busy, and the front railing on the schoolhouse is in desperate need of repair."

"Is that all?" Persall cast a contemptuous look in Olmstead's direction. "I'll get a couple of men on it right away. Olmstead could tell them what's needed, and I'll purchase the materials from Thompson's."

Thompson had recently opened a small store and lumber-yard in competition with Olmstead's business. Olmstead's face whitened, and his eyes flickered with alarm. Persall's hotel order was large and brought in a good deal of income.

"Miss McFarland will have to reject your kind offer, Mr. Persall," he said in a bombastic tone, giving me a cursory glance that was meant to silence my tongue.

"I have no intention of rejecting Mr. Persall's offer, Mr. Olmstead," I said pointedly. His face flushed, and his eyes blazed.

"I think, Miss McFarland, that you have forgotten the rules," he said, looking meaningfully at Ross Persall, who was watching this exchange with a slight smile.

"I will remember your rules when you remember your obligations," I retorted, just managing to keep my voice cool. Olmstead thrust his head forward pugnaciously, but he seemed lost for words. He was not about to offer his time to work on the front railing of the schoolhouse. I knew that I would hear more about my challenge later.

"I'll see you back to the schoolhouse," Persall offered, standing aside so that I could pass through the door.

"What about your order, Mr. Persall?" Olmstead called in obvious dismay. Persall looked at him and walked out behind me without a word.

"I think you have gained yourself an enemy, ma'am," Persall observed as he walked beside me. He put his hand lightly under my elbow as I crossed the street.

"Mr. Olmstead is not counted among my best friends." I smiled ruefully. We turned up McPherson. I felt Ross Persall looking at me, and I glanced at him questioningly. He smiled.

"If Olmstead dismisses you, you can always come to work for me," he suggested lightly.

I laughed. "Doing what? I haven't Miss Lane's talents," I said, thinking of her pretty voice. Ross Persall grinned.

"How can you be so sure about that?"

"My songs are limited to nursery rhymes." I smiled back.

"But I'll bet you have a beautiful body."

I blushed bright-red and turned my face away. He laughed a low, attractive laugh.

"I'm sorry I embarrassed you like that. I forgot you were a lady."

"Marba Lane is a lady," I chastened coldly. Persall gave me a wry look, which I did not like.

"What a prim expression you're wearing," he commented. "Don't you like me?"

"I don't know you," I evaded. Persall laughed again.

"Marba Lane is a lady of sorts, but she's not in your class," he relented.

I decided it was best to not answer. Hopefully, he would not discuss Marba Lane with me. I remembered his jacket on her bed when I visited and was not foolish enough to believe that his relationship with Katrina's mother was entirely innocent. I found it unforgivable that he should speak disrespectfully of the woman. And besides, I liked Marba.

Looking straight ahead, I saw two horses tied at the picket fence surrounding the play yard of the school. One was a small pinto, and the other a large, restless stallion snorting impatiently.

"Isn't that Bennett's horse?" Persall asked, voicing my own nervous thoughts. Linda had not been in school for the past four days. I had not expected to see her until I rode to Eden Rock tomorrow morning. I had intended to speak with Jordan Bennett then about the importance of Linda's being with other children.

Persall followed me up the schoolhouse steps. I paused and indicated the broken railing lying on the ground. "This is what I was speaking of earlier, Mr. Persall. You can see what a hazard it is."

"Anyone who fell off these steps would be sure to break something," he agreed. "Look at the rocks down there. I guess they were left after the foundation was finished. They should be carted away." He bent down and looked at the braces. "Did the railing just topple over?"

"Not exactly. I was leaning against it," I said. "I guess I'm no lightweight."

Ross Persall looked me up and down and grinned. "You're not exactly overweight either. If this thing had been nailed properly, it should have held up fine. It looks like a couple of nails were pulled here." I leaned forward to look for myself, frowning. I glanced at the sill again, remembering my questioning feeling of the night before. How had the cat jumped so far? Or had someone placed her there after pulling the nails that held the railing? But why?

"I'll get one of my men to work on it right away," Ross Persall was saying. I looked at him blankly and then forced a smile. He did not seem disturbed by what he had found, so why should I be? There was probably some logical explanation. The schoolhouse was old. Maybe the nails had jiggled loose over the years, and no one had noticed. Perhaps I was allowing my imagination to carry me away again.

"I appreciate your help, Mr. Persall," I said as he went back down the steps.

"At your service anytime, Miss McFarland." He winked, and there was a roguish glint in his eyes.

When I entered the classroom, I found Jordan Bennett standing in the middle of the room, looking at the whitewashed walls that now covered the children's murals. He turned his head and looked straight at me, something in his eyes telling me clearly that he had heard Ross Persall outside. His first words confirmed it.

"What was Persall doing here?"

"The front railing broke loose. He's going to have one of his men repair it before the children arrive this morning," I answered. I glanced at the far corner where Linda had ensconced herself. The girl was staring at her hands, her bleak expression stating clearly that she did not want to be here without Diego.

"Good morning, Linda," I greeted. "Everyone has missed you."

"Good morning, Miss McFarland," Linda responded politely, casting me a faintly embarrassed smile.

"Linda has been feeling under the weather for the past few days," Jordan said, giving his daughter a smile that drew a blush into her pale cheeks. Then he turned back to me.

"I thought the school board was supposed to take care of

all the repairs on this place," he emitted in a low voice.

"They were, but I'm afraid Mr. Olmstead and the other school board members don't have the time to do the repairs," I explained, wondering just where Jordan Bennett got his nerve to question me so imperiously.

"So you drafted Persall into service?" He raised his brows.

"Mr. Persall offered to help," I answered coolly.

"I'll just bet he did," Bennett grunted. "Persall doesn't know the first thing about repairing anything, but he knows a lot about women." I decided not to ask what he meant by that sneering comment.

"At least he's willing to see that someone does the work. And that's all that's necessary," I said, simmering.

"And beggars can't be choosers," he quoted demeaningly. I glared up at him.

"I don't see you beating down any doors to offer your help, Mr. Bennett," I retaliated. "Now, was there anything else you had to say to me. Because if there isn't, I have work to do before the children arrive."

Jordan's mouth cocked up at one side, and his blue eyes lightened with sardonic amusement. "I wanted to know if you'd changed your mind yet."

"Changed my mind about what?"

"About teaching Diego," he said in a controlled tone. "I figured you would have consulted someone by now about that impetuous offer of yours and learned what a predicament you've put yourself in." He smiled purposefully. "You make a habit of saying things before you think them through." I was reminded of my accusation about him being Diego's father, and I flushed slightly.

"I assure you, I had more than ample time to think things through on the six-mile ride to your ranch," I smiled tightly. "Put your mind at ease, Mr. Bennett. I shall ride out to the ranch tomorrow, and Diego and I will begin his lessons then."

He muttered a colorful expletive under his breath. "Have you no sense at all?" Linda's head came up at her father's angry tone, and he lowered his voice, forcing a smile that did not reach his eyes. "Will you at least give thinking a try, Miss McFarland?"

"Oh, I've been thinking quite a lot lately, Mr. Bennett," I

said, keeping my indignation from showing in my face. I cast a glance at Linda, but she was now reading one of her books. "And would you please leave here before this digresses into another scene?"

"The scene between you and me hasn't even begun yet, Abigail McFarland," Jordan warned. He leaned down so close that I could smell the leather of his jacket. "What if I tell you that you are not welcome at Eden Rock?"

"Reva Gutierrez and Diego don't welcome me?" I raised my brows derisively. "Or are you saying *you* don't welcome me?"

"Would it make any difference?"

"Of course!"

"How so? I own Eden Rock, or have you forgotten that fact?"

"You don't own Diego or his mother, do you?" I snapped. "Or would you prefer that Diego be ignorant as well as an outcast."

A muscle jerked in Jordan Bennett's cheek. I let out my breath.

"I'm sorry. That was unforgivable. But the boy deserves an education, Mr. Bennett. Why should you object so strenuously to my offer?" I tried for reason.

"I'm not thinking about Diego at the moment."

"There isn't anyone else to think about," I said, exasperated. "You ask me if I intend to keep my promise to Reva Gutierrez and Diego. Well, I do. Then you imply you will not welcome me on the ranch. After what I said to you a few days ago, I can understand why you dislike me so much. I spoke in anger. And I'm sorry. But can't we try to put our grievances aside for the benefit of the boy?"

"You bullheaded little bitch!" Jordan breathed in frustration. "You're going to find yourself in a real mess if you persist."

"Are you still hoping I'll leave town?" I asked, gauging his expression. My question caught him momentarily off guard. Then he raked his fingers back through his hair in agitation.

"Do what you want. I don't give a tinker's damn about you." He strode out of the schoolhouse.

"What was that all about?" Ross Persall asked, entering the schoolroom.

"Nothing." I shrugged, feeling confused and oddly depressed. Surely it had not been Jordan Bennett who had written that cryptic note on the blackboard?

"Nothing?" Ross laughed. "I could hear his voice from the gate. What's between you two anyway?"

"Nothing," I repeated, walking to my desk.

"Second enemy you made today," he commented wryly. "You must be the first teacher to arouse so much powerful emotion." He was standing close to the desk, his head bent, as I ruffled through papers. I looked up at him and forced a smile.

"I may be the shortest employed too."

"They won't fire you. It took them too long to find a replacement after what happened to Prudence Townsend," he said softly.

"What did happen to her?" I asked curiously.

"So they didn't tell you. I didn't think they would," he said grimly.

"Well, why don't you tell me?"

"No. It's best forgotten," he decided after a second. "Besides, there are little ears back there in the corner." He indicated Linda, who was watching us. "The kids never knew anything about it. Let's forget it, shall we? You've got other things to think about. I just came back to tell you that one of my men is out there fixing the railing. He'll be done shortly."

"You didn't need to come all the way back to tell me that, Mr. Persall. I would have deduced as much." I smiled warmly.

He grinned. "It was a handy excuse."

When Ross Persall left, I stood, wondering what had happened to Prudence Townsend. Why wouldn't anyone tell me what had happened to her? What was the mystery that surrounded her? There was undoubtedly a scandal, for the mere mention of her name closed mouths like a trapdoor. Had she run off? Had she been fired? Everyone kept telling me to forget about Prudence Townsend, but I knew that it was becoming more impossible to do so each day.

 *Chapter Ten*

On my next visit to the general store I was lucky enough to find Emily handling the business. James was somewhere in the storeroom making an inventory and writing up orders. Emily looked at me apologetically. "Jim told me about the other day," she admitted softly, her eyes darting wearily over her shoulder. "I'm glad Ross Persall had the railing fixed. Jim said it was new only three years ago and that someone must have jimmied with it to break it like that. I'm afraid he blames it on you, Miss McFarland. He says after you allowed the children to paint pictures on the inside walls, they figured they could do anything they wanted to the building."

"I'm sorry he feels that way," I sighed, thinking that although he had been inexcusably rude to me, perhaps he had his own reasons for behaving in such a way. "Maybe he is right about someone pulling the nails out. They couldn't have hopped out by themselves. I just can't think of why anyone would want to do such a thing."

"Someone could have been badly hurt." She leaned forward. "The Poole boys have been building a tree house. Maybe they needed nails."

"Oh, I don't think so, Mrs. Olmstead. And whoever it was, I'm sure they did not intend to hurt anyone."

"I should hope not, but I still think it was the Poole boys." I handed her a list of things I needed, and she began stacking them on the counter in a box. I fingered some soft cotton material with pretty pink and blue flowers on a pale-ivory background. How I would love to have a dress made of this material instead of the drab browns, grays and greens. I wondered how I would look in a flounced skirt with soft, flowing sleeves and sheer lace around a low neckline. A faint, dreamy smile touched my lips.

I moved away from the cloth table, telling myself that clothing wasn't important. But I could not help remembering how Marcella Haversall had indulged herself each season with a dozen new gowns.

Emily was tallying the items as she put them in the box. The last item set in the carrier, she handed me the total. I sighed as I passed across the last of my first month's income. It was another week before I would receive more money, and I would have to be careful in my meals to make these meager stores last. I hoped no unforeseen expenses would crop up, and I wondered if I had been wise to send money to Bradford Dobson for more books. Only a week before, I had received several copies of *Tom Sawyer*, by a new writer named Mark Twain. I had read the book and thoroughly enjoyed it. I knew it would be just right for the Poole boys. I even considered having the better readers present it aloud to the rest of the class as incentive for the younger children to learn more quickly. The gift from the solicitor had been a surprise and a generous thought.

"Miss McFarland," Emily whispered. "I hope you won't take offense, but I think it would be wise if you discouraged Ross Persall."

My eyebrows shot up in surprise. "I haven't been encouraging him. Whatever made you think such a thing?"

"Oh, you wouldn't really have to," she sighed. "He's . . . well, he's got a terrible reputation where women are concerned. He's had several living with him in that hotel of his. That Lane woman is just another one. And she with a daughter!" She tutted disapprovingly. "But it isn't good for you to even speak to him whatever the reason."

"He offered to fix the railing, and under the circumstances I had to accept or let it go undone," I explained. "Your husband didn't have the time to do it, and it was a matter of safety for the children."

"Oh, I understand all that. I didn't mean for you to take offense. James can be so . . . so stubborn when he gets a bee in his bonnet. I'm sorry about that. Really, I am. Please don't be angry with me. I'm only telling you this about Mr. Persall for your own good. He obviously likes you, or he wouldn't have bothered about the railing. Jim said he's never known him to do anything like that for anyone else. Jim was furious!" She glanced over her shoulder again. "Mr. Persall canceled his hotel orders and is dealing with Thompson."

Was that what all this was about, I wondered cynically? Had James Olmstead put Emily up to this little speech about Ross Persall?

I could well understand Olmstead's animosity toward me if what Emily said was true. But what could I do about it? Approach Ross Persall with a plea that he continue doing business with Olmstead? Darrel Thompson was in my class as well as Andy Olmstead. I was in no position to take sides. In all honesty, I preferred Thompson to Olmstead anyway. At least Thompson was courteous and always greeted me with a smile. His wife, Sally, was also pleasant. If I did not like Emily so much, I would take my business to Thompson's along with Ross Persall.

"I'm sorry to hear that," I offered lamely, looking with sympathy at Emily's ingenuous face.

"Oh it wasn't your fault," Emily replied quickly.

"Does your husband agree with that deduction?" I smiled.

Emily flushed and looked down. "He'll get over it."

I picked up my box of supplies. "Miss McFarland?" Emily detained me. "Would you come for tea sometime?"

"I would like that."

"Some of the ladies are coming over this afternoon. Would you like to join us?"

"I'm afraid I can't today. It's Saturday, and I have to . . ."

I stopped, realizing that I was about to blurt out that I was going to ride to Eden Rock to tutor Diego. ". . . To work at the schoolhouse," I finished, feeling guilty for the lie. "Perhaps you'd like to come for tea at the schoolhouse sometime?"

Emily seemed disturbed by that idea. "I'd rather you came to my house," she said frankly, and I frowned. Her aversion was as evident as it had been on the night I had arrived, though I had not thought about it much then.

"Is there something about the place that bothers you?" I asked.

"No! Oh, no. Whatever gave you that idea?" she said with a nervous laugh, looking slightly self-conscious. "I just feel . . . that I spent enough time there as a child. That's all." Olmstead appeared from behind the curtain. Emily jumped at the sound of his voice.

"You've got work to do, Em." He issued his edict. "You haven't got time for idle gossip." She flushed and murmured an agreeable response. I smiled coolly at him and bid her good day.

My ride to Eden Rock was easier the second time. I was surprised that Charles Studebaker was still under instructions to hold Jordan Bennett's gelding for me. I'd been sure that Bennett would take away the horse as a means of preventing my visits to the ranch. I had no carriage and could not afford the rental of one every Saturday with my limited income. I was relieved that the horse was still there for my use. I insisted upon paying the feed expenses and decided to take the horse back to the schoolyard so that it could munch away at the tall grass around the building. Therefore, he served several functions.

When I neared the ranch, I kept tight control on the reins, in spite of the horse's desire to head for the barn again. I wore gloves this time, and my determination won over the horse's. It walked into the yard and with a disgruntled snort stopped at the railing before the house.

Diego came running out on the front steps, a bright smile on his brown face. "Miss McFarland!" He came hopping down the steps. "I was afraid you weren't coming. It's near eleven!"

I had been up since four o'clock. I had completed my housework on the schoolroom before riding to Eden Rock to see to

Diego's lessons, and I was already tired as well as stiff from the long ride. But I smiled brightly back at the boy.

"Surely you didn't think I was going to play hooky." I teased, and he laughed.

"Mama is waiting for us in the kitchen. She has a surprise for you."

"A surprise . . . for me?"

"Si . . . si," he said excitedly. "Something *muy* special. Linda helped her make it this morning while I watched," he announced. I followed him into the house.

This time I was more relaxed and able to admire the rich interior with its expensive provincial furniture, which had obviously been chosen by a woman with immaculate and highbred taste in design. Several heavier pieces of furniture covered in leather kept the room from looking too formal. Except for these pieces and the massive stone fireplace, the living room might have been taken from the Haversall's Boston mansion. I frowned, remembering again my conversation with Dobson. Would I ever forget?

Passing a dining room, I noted a silver tea service on a trolley, and a china cabinet displaying an exquisite set of porcelain, delicately hand painted with china-blue flowers. I tried to envision Jordan Bennett sitting there, legs crossed, sipping politely from one of those delicate cups. I could not. I knew he must have all the amenities to have been so readily accepted in Boston society. A woman of Gwendolyn Bracklin-Reed's breeding would not have been interested, let alone considered marrying, a man without all the necessary social graces and background. Yet, my experience of Jordan Bennett had revealed only the rugged, ruthless side of his nature. I saw him as a man standing legs astride, shoulders squared, head thrown back in defiant challenge and sardonic amusement at the expense of others.

Jordan Bennett was capable of love, for I had seen the way he looked at his young daughter. His eyes mellowed blue and softened with affection. He had a different tone when he spoke to her. I wondered how he would be with a woman he loved. The thought was disturbing, and I pressed it quickly away.

Taking in my surroundings again, I wondered if I was seeing

Gwendolyn's influence in decorating this marvelous house. Had she really hated this place so much? How could she have hated it and yet succeeded in bringing it such a warmth and elegance mingled naturally with the rugged Western hewn-beam ceilings and stone fireplaces? For surely the sheer, lacy curtains that allowed the sun to filter in from the garden were not something Jordan Bennett would have chosen to grace his home. Nor were the decorative figurines and the brocade-covered chairs, nor the love seat and crystal chandelier. Ellen Greer must have been mistaken in her evaluation of Gwendolyn Bracklin-Reed Bennett. No woman would have so carefully filled a home with such treasures if she hated it and the man who inhabited it with her.

When I entered the kitchen, Reva Gutierrez came forward and took my hand. "I am so happy you came back. I am sorry about our last meeting. I was very unjust. You are not like the others at all. Jordan was very sorry about losing his temper with you."

I shook my head, smiling. "There's no need for you to apologize. It was all a misunderstanding."

Reva Gutierrez seemed determined to explain. "Diego went to school once before. He was expelled then also. The other teacher was not like you. She did not have the courage to go against the others."

"There was a fight then also?" I asked, wanting to defer her overly generous attitude about me.

"No," she answered, not elaborating. She frowned thoughtfully and turned away for a moment. "My son is smarter than the others. They are jealous of him. With an education he will have much. They want him to have nothing."

"He must have more than education," I answered. "He will need opportunity also."

"Jordan will make opportunity for Diego," Reva said with assurance. Her tone implied a relationship that Jordan had denied by insinuation. Who was I to believe?

"I have made this in honor of you," Reva said, changing the subject and drawing me forward as she pointed to the table. I stared at the magnificent cake with its bright, decorative icing.

"It must have taken you hours." I admired it. There were

red rosebuds, green leaves and vines, a multicolored butterfly. It was a work of art. "It's the most beautiful cake I've ever seen."

"We will have cake with coffee after my son's lessons," Reva said. "Diego, go and bring your books, *por favor.*"

"*Sí,* mama." He went quickly. When he returned, we set to work. I had brought several books with me, as well as work sheets and writing materials. I assigned enough to keep him busy for the week, keeping him up with the same assignments I had given the others at his level. But Diego was hungry for more, and after watching him work, I knew that I would have to go at a quicker pace with him. His desire to learn was great.

Promising to send for more materials and books, I warned him it might be some time before I was able to get them from the East. My own funds were low until I received my next month's salary, and I did not want to ask Reva Gutierrez for money. I thought of going to Jordan Bennett and asking if Diego could use the books I had seen on several shelves in the living room. But I was already overly aware of Bennett's animosity toward me, and I was afraid that I might make things even more difficult if I were to dare ask him a favor. Perhaps he would offer the boy the materials.

After sharing a piece of Reva's delicious confection and accepting a cup of strong black coffee, I had to leave. It was a long ride back to town, and it was already well past two o'clock. I wished I could linger and get to know Reva, who was a charming, though reticent hostess. Linda had said little, but seemed well pleased to have me on the ranch. Only Diego was talkative and full of questions.

The boy walked out with me to the front of the house. The gelding was there with an empty bucket next to a mounting block. I wondered who had put both there. Tying my skirt, I mounted the horse and gave Diego a wave and I drew around.

I was well across the yard when a familiar voice hailed me. I reluctantly drew in and waited, forcing my face to a calmness I was far from feeling.

"I noticed the horse was tied to the front railing this time," Jordan taunted as he came up to stand next to me. I flushed at his unkind reminder of my last arrival at the ranch. As if I were likely to forget, I thought in exasperation. But I gave a self-conscious laugh.

"Yes, well, I made sure he had plenty to eat before we left town this morning." Somehow, I managed to sound calm, though my heart was doing calisthenics as it always did whenever I looked at Jordan Bennett. He was tall, and the horse with its slightly swayed back had me just above his head. I felt the position put me on a slight advantage, though not nearly enough of one.

"He still managed to down a tidy amount of oats," Jordan commented, and I noted the twitching muscle in his cheek. I always felt a fool when I was around this man. It was easier to laugh at him than allow myself to be the brunt of his joke.

"Who do you suppose is responsible for keeping the school-yard trimmed to the ground?" I asked, smiling slightly. Jordan Bennett laughed. My senses stumbled to a stop and then lurched forward again. He looked so young and reckless when he laughed like that. His eyes were bright, all their usual mockery and hostility gone. I wished my pulse would slow down.

"Studebaker told me the plug was a hay-burner," Bennett commented.

I blinked, hardly aware of what he was saying, but watching the change of his expression with a mesmerized gaze. He stopped and looked at me. Neither of us said anything for a moment, and then he frowned.

"How long did it take you to ride out here this morning?" he asked.

"A . . . about two hours," I answered warily. His mouth had tightened fractionally, and there was an odd glimmer in his blue eyes.

"Did anyone see you leaving town?"

"I didn't pay any attention," I answered truthfully. And then I added lightly, "Should I have been looking over my shoulder the whole way?" My attempt at joviality irritated him.

"That might not have been such a bad idea," he commented dryly.

"If anyone had asked me, I would have said I was taking a ride," I told him, realizing that he was worried that someone would stop me from teaching Diego.

"For seven hours?" he snorted derisively. "What are you going to say when you're asked about that, Miss McFarland? Or why the schoolhouse isn't spotless and disinfected for the coming school week?"

"What makes you think the schoolhouse isn't spotless, Mr. Bennett?" I queried with a daring smile. "You may inspect it anytime you like."

"Anytime? . . . " He provoked me with an insinuating smile. His expression made the color flood my cheeks, and I longed for some quick-witted answer that would wipe the smirk from his handsome face.

"When did you find time to clean that old haunt?" he asked, after a disturbing study of my red face.

"I'm an early riser," I answered tautly. "I'm sure I'm keeping you from your work, Mr. Bennett. So if you will excuse me," I said, loosening the reins in my stiff fingers. His hand came up and covered mine, pushing them down onto the saddle horn. His other hand rested on the cantle. He was much too close for my liking.

"How's Ross Persall these days?" he asked with deceptive softness.

"Oh, for heaven's sake! Not you too!" I sighed in exasperation, unwarranted except that I wanted him to move away. I pulled my hands from beneath his. Then I didn't know where to put them and curled them tightly into fists as I crossed my arms over my abdomen.

Jordan watched my agitated movements and smiled slightly. He eased forward, resting his arm across the horse's back. My knee was against his chest, and I shifted restlessly in the saddle. My color was rising again in embarrassment at his proximity.

"Why are you looking so nervous?" he taunted.

"I've nothing to be nervous about," I snapped.

"What did you mean by your comment? Have you been receiving warnings from other people?"

"Emily Olmstead said something about Mr. Persall having a questionable reputation."

"There's no question about Ross Persall's reputation." Jordan grinned. He need not have added that it was as bad as Emily ascribed.

"I've only met the man a few times. Why all the fuss?"

"I suppose any warning you receive about him will only make you seek him out," Jordan commented unpleasantly.

"And what is that supposed to mean?"

"Just that whatever you're told to do, you do the opposite," he said grimly.

"Maybe it's how and why I'm asked, Mr. Bennett," I managed to say coolly. "And I think it's time I said good day and allowed you to get back to your work," I rattled, my hands going again to the reins when he had moved away from the horse. But quickly Jordan captured my hands in one easy movement, and when I tried to pull away, his fingers tightened painfully.

"Not so fast," he said under his breath. "You don't dismiss me like one of your students." He moved his other hand from the cantle.

"What are you doing?" I gasped in alarm, my eyes widening in my pale face as I felt his hand slide beneath my skirt and curve tightly around my ankle. Through the leather of my high-buttoned shoes I could feel the strength of his fingers.

"You have slender ankles," he commented with a smile. "What's the matter, Miss McFarland? Haven't you ever been touched by a man before?"

"Let me go," I managed through the constriction in my chest. My voice wavered and sounded raspy with tension.

Jordan Bennett's hand moved upward in answer. When it contacted the smooth skin of my calf, I jerked, intending to kick out at him, heedless of any consequences. His fingers caught my ankle, stopping my defense.

"I'll bet you're soft all over." He grinned.

"I'm not very good at parlor games, Mr. Bennett," I answered, shaking.

"If that's true, you'd be wise to stay away from Ross Persall. Parlor games are his favorite pastime." His face was hard, and his eyes blazed. He released me abruptly, and, free of his disturbing touch, my courage returned.

"I'd be even wiser, Mr. Bennett, if I stayed away from you," I said coldly. His mouth twisted derisively as he hooked his thumbs into his belt and stood with his legs splayed.

"I couldn't agree with you more, Miss McFarland," he returned smoothly. "However, since you promised to see to Diego's lessons every Saturday, you've made that virtually impossible. We're going to see quite a lot of one another over the next few months. And believe it or not, I look forward to it!"

"Oh, I'll just bet you do!" I cried, thinking what fun it was for him to ridicule me. "Perhaps Diego should ride to the schoolhouse. I could carry on his lessons there."

"Oh, no, my dear." He shook his head. "I like this arrangement very well. It puts you in the exact position that I want you."

"And where's that?"

"On the crumbling edge of a yawning precipice." He grinned. "And you aren't the least bit sure-footed, are you?" I remembered our first meeting and fumed.

"I'm watching where I'm going now."

"Are you? Are you indeed?" He laughed low and unpleasantly. "It's only a matter of time until you're found out. And you'll get dismissed two minutes after that happens."

"I'm not doing anything wrong," I defended my actions.

"Ah, but that's where you're wrong. You're going about everything wrong. And you're creating a maelstrom of trouble as you go."

"I don't know what you're talking about."

Bennett shook his head, making another low, throaty laugh. "You do know," he disagreed scornfully.

I was beginning to feel very confused. My senses were telling me one thing, while my mind was telling me another. Why didn't I just ride away from this man? Why was I sitting here, allowing him to plant so many seeds of doubt in my mind? I knew the school board would be furious if they ever found out about my weekly trips to Eden Rock on Diego Gutierrez's behalf, but I had resolved that in my own mind. My efforts to help Diego were not interfering with my duties. So there should be no objection to what I did with my own time.

"I can't see how things could have worked out any different from the way they have," I defended myself. "What I do with my Saturdays should be my own concern . . . not the school board's or yours, Mr. Bennett."

"The schoolmistress is to mirror the opinions and dictates of the school board," Jordan said flatly.

"Even if I don't happen to agree with them?" I snapped, my voice higher than normal.

"You should keep your disagreements to yourself. It'd be good practice in self-control."

I ignored the glint in his eyes. "And what about Diego?"

"What about Diego?" he demanded.

"You know very well what I mean about Diego," I retorted.

"A protest could have been leveled against the board's decision."

"By whom?" I asked wryly. "You?"

"You can be very insulting, did you know that?" he uttered in a baleful tone, his eyes narrowing unpleasantly. "Don't you think I'd fight for my own son, Miss McFarland?" he went on sarcastically. His face grew hard as his temper rose. I remembered his previous outburst and realized the incautiousness of my question.

"I'm sorry," I said lamely. I thought of what Ellen Greer had asserted. There was no physical resemblance between Diego and Jordan Bennett, yet the boy shared mannerisms of the older man. I did not want to think about that, for it aroused other questions. If Diego was Jordan Bennett's son, what was Jordan's relationship with Reva Gutierrez now? Surely the woman would not stay if she had been scorned. So that implied that the relationship was an ongoing one. That thought hurt me, and I did not want to analyze my reasons for caring what Jordan Bennett did.

"You *have* confirmed in your own mind that Diego is my son," Jordan said, his mouth curling cynically.

"Do you want me to doubt it?" I had intended to sound flippant, but the words came out almost pleadingly. He muttered a harsh sound.

"No. You go ahead and believe what you want."

"I'm not trying to interfere—"

"It's a little late for that," he interrupted. "You made a promise to the boy, and I'm going to see that you keep it."

"That's entirely unnecessary," I said, stung. "I don't make a habit of breaking promises."

"Then you'll be the first woman I've known who doesn't," he sneered.

"That doesn't say much for the women you've known, Mr. Bennett," I retorted.

He laughed haughtily. "I've known quite a few."

I liked that statement even less than all the others put together. "Well, you don't know me!"

Jordan Bennett looked at me, allowing his eyes to move slowly over my face, lingering for an instant on my mouth and then trailing down to dwell purposefully on my breasts rising and falling with my indignation.

"Not yet, perhaps, Miss McFarland." He smiled slowly.

"Not ever," I asserted definitively and encouraged the gelding to move out.

"Don't count on that!" Jordan's assured voice came from behind me, turning quickly to a taunting laugh.

 *Chapter Eleven*

Another week flew by. As dawn was peering her brilliant golden head over the hills, I set my breakfast dishes into a low pan and poured scalding-hot water over them. Adding a dash of soap, I scrubbed away the residue of my customary scrambled-egg and bread breakfast. I set the old chipped crockery on the table to drain and stepped to the back door and tossed the tepid water out.

Coming back into my warm room, I saw Orphan stretching from her tightly curled sleeping position. She cast me a disgruntled look.

"Good morning, you little beggar," I said cheerfully. I was in the habit now of carrying on one-sided conversations with the cat. "Sorry if I disturbed your majesty, but I've got to get an early start to Eden Rock if I want to be back here by two o'clock to clean the schoolhouse."

Orphan, now well nourished and overindulged with affection, stepped sedately from her commode drawer and glided across the room to rub against my skirt. The cat's long, black tail stood at attention as she arched her sleek back and let out a low rumbling of satisfaction. I leaned down and scooped her up, nuzzling the cat against my neck and stroking the satin back.

"Your milk dish is next to the stove, lazybones," I told the purring animal, which stretched up its neck for my fingers to scratch. "Now, why don't you do your share of the work around here and catch those mice that are walking around at night? Hmmm?"

I set Orphan down next to the milk dish and watched for a moment as she began to lap. It was silly, perhaps, but I had become very attached to the stray cat. I smiled slightly as I thought what people would think if they could hear me talking to the animal in the lonely hours after the children had gone home.

Orphan paused in her meal and sat down. Licking a paw slowly, she wiped her face, clearing away the beads of milk that had collected on her long whiskers. Then she went back to work on the milk.

I stacked several books together, including a new novel that Bradford Dobson had sent as a gift, then bent down to give Orphan a last scratch behind the ears before heading to the livery stable to get the horse.

Charles Studebaker had taught me how to saddle and bridle the gelding when I had explained that I liked to take early-morning jaunts each Saturday. When he had looked at me curiously, I had quickly explained that I needed the exercise and the solitude after a week of working in close quarters with 62 children. He had seemed to understand then, grinning and nodding his gray balding head, his eyes twinkling.

"Frankly, ma'am," he'd said with a chuckle, "I'd understand if you rode that horse straight out of California."

Several homes showed wood smoke coming out of kitchen chimneys. Some hens were cackling in a small coop at the back of a white house. Main Street was quiet, however, and I proceeded quickly to the livery stable before I could be detained by some chance passerby.

Feeling ridiculously happy, I walked with a swing to my skirts, smiling to myself. Sycamore Hill was becoming home to me. I was still having my tussles with stiff James Olmstead. I still carefully plotted my Bible study so that the fire-breathing Reverend Hayes could find no cause for complaint. But I was also making friends. Emily Olmstead, in spite of her husband's discouragement, always greeted me cheerfully and chattered inanely but entertainingly. Charles Studebaker, Marba Lane, and even dubious Ross Persall were friendly acquaintances who might possibly later develop into more. Reva Gutierrez and Diego were still slightly in awe of me, but would gradually lose that stiff formality.

Passing by the boarding house, I looked up and thought with special fondness of Ellen Greer, my closest friend in town— my closest friend in all my life. The old lady was often difficult, but she offered me stimulating companionship for at least one short visit each week.

My thoughts turned to Jordan Bennett. I did not want to admit to myself that I was looking forward to seeing him today. There was no guarantee that I would. After last Saturday's argument he had sent in a ranch hand to escort Linda to and from school.

The horse was saddled and waiting for me in front of the stables. Surprised, I looked past the horse to see Charles Studebaker covered by his work apron and pulling a redhot horse shoe from his forge. He looked up and saw me. He gave me the high sign and then shoved the shoe back into the forge.

"Morning, ma'am," he called, coming out of the shed toward me.

"Good morning." I smiled back, taking my saddle bag and securing it to the cantle.

"What you got in the saddle bag?" he asked, showing the curiosity of a friendly neighbor.

"Books," I answered as I managed to get astride without too much difficulty. Since I was rather adept with a needle, I had altered one skirt into a culotte for riding. It was not the most ladylike way to travel, but I did not have the time nor inclination to learn to use a sidesaddle.

"Looks like you got quite a few in there," he observed. "You going anywhere in particular?"

"Just riding," I said, remembering Ellen Greer and Jordan Bennett's warning, and knowing only too well my precarious position with the school board. "I thought I'd do some school lessons this morning."

"Someplace where it's quiet, you mean," Studebaker said,

"and there's no chance of interruption." He gave me a brief wave as he turned back to the shed and his work.

I enjoyed the morning ride as I turned west and rode through the flat meadow that preceded the rolling hills. Meadowlarks sang, while sparrows dipped and soared. Once I even spotted a tall-eared jack rabbit bounding for cover in the high, pale grasses.

The jarring walk of the horse no longer bothered me and I let my body relax with the rhythmic walk. Remembering my first ride to Eden Rock, I smiled. At least I would arrive with more dignity now. I had learned the horse's weakness and had developed a firmer hand.

Quickening my pace, I narrowed the distance between town and Eden Rock. Ahead of me I saw the ranchhouse and outbuildings stretched out against the hills. Several men were driving a small herd of horses in from the hills. Turning toward the house, I drew my gaze from the riders to the peaceful, wisteria-covered veranda. Reva Gutierrez had seen me and was already appearing at the front steps with a welcoming wave.

"Buenas días," I called and Reva laughed delightedly.

"I did not know you spoke Spanish, Miss McFarland," she said teasingly, and I grinned.

"You've just heard the extent of it!"

Reva was wearing a crisp white blouse with colored embroidery work around the square neckline. The long dark skirt was smooth over her slender curving figure. She looked very pretty and I felt suddenly drab and unattractive. I was several years younger than Reva Gutierrez and yet I felt older and less alive.

"If you would like to learn, I will teach you," Reva offered. I smiled.

"That sounds a marvelous idea. And there are other things you can teach me, Señorita Gutierrez. I would like to know all about *El Día de los Muertos.*"

Reva looked pleased. "We will talk much . . . later. First, we must drag Diego from the corrals. Jordan is breaking horses today and Diego loves to watch. *Ven conmigo,"* she signaled me to follow.

Walking with Reva, I looked about the neat ranch complex. The barn doors were open and I could see a man working inside, pitching hay into the horse stalls. Riding gear was hanging on the wall. Going past the barn and around to the right, I could hear excited voices shouting encouragement and the sound of a horse battling furiously, whining and snorting in outrage at the man on his back.

Reva stepped up onto the fence railing to watch the scene. I moved closer and gasped as I saw a huge sorrel stallion rear on its hind legs and paw furiously at the air while twisting its head fiercely against the bit. Jordan Bennett was astride and grinning like the very devil.

Coming down onto all fours again, the stallion bucked back and forth, twisting frantically to remove the man from the saddle. Jordan moved with the horse easily, shifting his weight to maintain his expert balance. He seemed part of the animal, even his expression mirroring the wild, untamed will as his arm rose and fell with the movement of the stallion.

Moving closer yet, I stared through the rails of the fence fascinated. Horse and rider bolted closer and I jumped back, sure the two were going to pitch right over the railing on top of me. For just an instant, Bennett's narrowed eyes caught my rounded ones. The stallion, sensing his rider's momentary lapse of attention, whirled suddenly to the side and sent Jordan heaving through the air into the dust.

"Jordan!" I cried out, pulling myself up on the fence next to Reva. My heart lodged in my throat as I stared down, sure that I would see him broken and dead in the dust, or being trampled by that rogue of a horse. But he was up almost at once. Dusting himself off with his hat, he glared at the prancing, snorting horse as ranch hands needled him.

"Hey, boss. That ain't like you to get tossed like a babe," one shouted in friendly banter.

"The sorrel isn't as easy as you thought, eh, Mr. Bennett?" another called.

Several men had already jumped down from the fence to help Jordan trap the furious stallion. One man made a leap and grabbed the animal's rearing head, reaching hastily up to hold tightly to the ear. The stallion made a lunge tossing the man up but unable to break him loose. The bared teeth snapped shut just missing the man. The other cowboys held tightly to the saddle while Jordan vaulted up again. The three ranch hands let go at once and made a run for the fence before the infuriated animal could trample them.

More cheers broke the quiet morning air. Jordan's face was fierce with determination. He never once glanced my way again and I felt curiously hurt. I prayed that he would not be killed and suddenly without the least doubt I knew that I loved him.

The contest between man and animal continued, with neither gaining from the other. The magnificent stallion snorted, pawed, bucked and kicked to be free of the man now once again grinning with obvious enjoyment of the animal's spirited challenge. Minutes passed and I watched in awed silence, hardly able to breathe. Once I thought the stallion intended to ram Jordan against the fence but turned back as Jordan set the reins whipping into his hind quarters, making him veer away at the last instant.

Tiring, the stallion reared again and again, lower each time. Then it began to gallop in wider circles around the corral. Jordan let the horse have its head and then after a while drew in the reins slowly, but firmly. The animal slowed and finally came to a prancing stop.

Still maintaining his masterful hold, Jordan pulled back slowly. The stallion snorted fiercely and yanked hard, but was unable to break Jordan's grip. Then, the horse stepped back trying to ease the pull on its mouth. One step and then another. It was what Jordan wanted, and satisfied, he loosened the reins slightly, pressing his knees against the stallion's sweating sides.

The stallion moved forward again, controlled and heeding the rider's command. Jordan rode the horse around the corral again several times and then finally drew the animal in and dismounted. I expected him to look exhausted, but he looked invigorated, blue eyes shining as he swept the perspiration from his brow with the back of his hand.

The animal was breathing hard and shook its head, showing that its spirit was still intact, though curbed by this one man. Moving to the stallion's head, Jordan dug into his pocket and pulled out some treat for the animal. I held my breath again, expecting the stallion to take a large bite and a couple of fingers off Jordan's hand. But the animal's nostrils quivered, and it accepted the lump of sugar, allowing Jordan to stroke its soft nose. I breathed again. Smiling, I felt proud of Jordan Bennett, even knowing I had no right to feel that way.

Sitting at the table in the kitchen, I insisted on helping Reva shell peas for the ranch hands' dinner. Diego was working on a test in another room.

"Your hands are as quick as mine," Reva commented in some surprise, watching me split a pod and shoot the young peas into a bowl with my thumb, then flick the shell into a nearby waste dish.

"I've had my share of practice." I laughed, flicking another empty pod away and picking up a full one.

"You have?"

"Why should that surprise you?"

"Oh, something Jordan said to me last night about Boston ladies," she admitted casually, her own hands moving quickly. I stiffened slightly, but managed to maintain my light smile as I worked on. The thought of Jordan Bennett making disdainful remarks about me during a quiet evening with his mistress hurt unbearably.

"Is Mr. Bennett that well versed in Boston ladies?" I asked disparagingly. Gwendolyn Bracklin-Reed Bennett hardly qualified him as an authority on the breed, I thought agitatedly.

"Jordan went to school in Boston. He said the women there were haughty and lifeless."

Then why did he marry one? I asked myself silently, feeling furious. Reva was watching my face.

"I hope you are not taking this personally, Miss McFarland," she said smoothly. "You are not at all like that."

"Perhaps Mr. Bennett just moved in the wrong circles," I said indifferently, shelling peas with a vengeance.

"Oh, he moved in the best circles," Reva said. "He even married one of the primest stock Boston could offer." Her cold tone drew my attention. "You've been in Sycamore Hill for two months or more, Miss McFarland," she said. "Don't pretend you have not heard about Jordan's wife, Gwendolyn."

"Yes, I've heard a few things."

"Never have I met a more arrogant woman, nor hated one so much."

Reva's veracity embarrassed me, but my averted look did not prevent her from continuing.

"She treated me like so much dirt under her feet. She wanted

Jordan to send me and Diego away, but he wouldn't agree." Her hands halted in their mutilation of the peapods, and she spread them on the table, staring toward the window.

"Diego was just a little boy then . . . a beautiful little boy. Gwendolyn Bennett wanted to possess Jordan, but she could not. She hated Diego because Jordan loved him." Reva looked at me, eyes flashing. "Why should he not have loved Diego?" she demanded fiercely.

"*Señorita.* . . ."

The dark eyes lost their anger and glittered with anguish and confusion. "She called us an embarrassment. My beautiful little boy . . . an embarrassment." Her eyes filled, and her voice softened. "She called him 'Jordan's little bastard,'" she went on, her voice barely audible, and I felt a pain cut into me.

"How could she have been so cruel, Miss McFarland? I was young and foolish once. I fell in love with the wrong man. But she had no right to hurt my boy like that. To say those things about him. . . ." I reached across to touch her hand, not knowing what to say to her.

"Before she came, people thought I was married," Reva told me. "Now they know about Diego, and it is just one more thing they use to hurt him. I would rather they threw stones at me than hurt my son."

I felt my own eyes filling with tears, and I sought uselessly for something to say. Reva looked at me then. Her hand uncurled, and she clasped mine.

"I'm sorry I have upset you. I did not mean to speak to you about this. It is only since Diego left school that I have thought much about it. Perhaps I should take him to Mexico, where he would be among his own people. There no one would doubt me if I said I was a widow. It would be my secret and my son's."

"Surely Mr. Bennett would not allow you to do that. You belong here," I told her.

"Jordan would let me do whatever I wish," she said tiredly, and I wondered if what she really meant was that he did not care enough to stop her from taking his son away.

"I have lived here on this ranch since my father and mother came from Mexico to work for Jordan's parents," Reva explained. "I was eight, a skinny, little, big-eyed girl. Jordan was fourteen then. . . ." She sighed. "Twenty years ago . . . such a long time." She looked at me and smiled. "My son was born in this house. But perhaps all that is not enough to make me belong here. You must be part of the people in order to belong, and the people of Sycamore Hill want no part of me or my bastard."

"Please don't call Diego that."

"It's the truth." Her face contorted in pain.

"But don't you love his father?"

Reva took a long time in answering. There was a distant, sad look on her face. "Even after all this time, and all I've been through because of him, I still love Diego's father."

"Then you must not do anything rash. Whatever anyone says, Diego belongs here. Mexico is a long way from here, and Diego is not a Mexican. He is an American. He was born here and raised here. You can't take him away."

"Tell the people of Sycamore Hill that," Reva said bitterly. "He has brown skin. And everyone around here thinks that all brown people are Joaquin Murietta, riding to steal and kill."

"Fear makes fools of people."

"And fear makes them cruel as well."

"It wasn't the children who wanted your son expelled, *señorita*. A few adults used one child's jealousy to their own purpose. It won't always be that way."

Reva shook her head dubiously. "Jordan was right about you, *señorita*. You know very little about people."

I sat back, stung by her remark and reminded again of her closeness to Jordan Bennett. Reva spread her hands in an apologetic gesture.

"It is true. Some people will change . . . those that wish to do so. But James Olmstead? Reverend Hayes? Branford Poole? Never."

"You blame all for the actions of a few," I said.

"The many allowed the few to do as they wished, did they not?"

I could scarcely deny that, but I wondered if everyone even knew what had happened to Diego, or if they had only heard a twisted view of the incident in the schoolyard. "Perhaps things would be different if everyone was aware of the true circumstances," I said thoughtfully. Reva stared.

"What are you thinking, *señorita?*" Her usual smooth, cream-brown forehead was puckered. I smiled, unable to suppress an impish twinkle of mischief.

"The idea hasn't yet formed itself completely. . . ."

"Please do not get yourself into more trouble because of Diego," she protested, suspicious.

"I'm in trouble most of the time anyway," I shrugged.

"Well, Jordan will be furious with me if you find yourself in further trouble because of us."

"I don't believe that for a moment, *señorita*. Mr. Bennett's sense of humor thrives on my predicaments."

Reva frowned at my taut expression. "You are wrong."

"Well, don't let's worry about what Mr. Bennett thinks. What I do is my own concern and none of his." I launched our conversation into questions about *El Día de los Muertos,* and relieved, Reva gave me a colorful and enthusiastic narration of the holiday rooted in pre-Columbian Indian and Spanish tradition. She explained for how several days she had been preparing for the festive holiday. She showed me several dozen calaveras she had made for other Mexican families employed on Eden Rock, as well as loaves of sweet bread twisted into elaborate shapes. One loaf was a serpent, complete with forked tongue and tail and decorated artistically with red and green icing. Most of the others were shaped into human bones.

I accepted Reva's invitation to her room, and was surprised at the modest quarters she and Diego inhabited at the back of the ranch house, just beyond the kitchen. I had expected Bennett to provide her with more comfortable rooms.

Her room was pleasant enough, and far more spacious than my own. It was painted ivory and draped with lacy curtains and panels of thicker brocade. It was well-equipped with functional furnishings. There were two beds, one on either side of the room. One wing chair covered in brocade stood near the window overlooking the back garden.

Late roses on the lattice just outside the window filled the room with sweet fragrance. A smaller, straight-backed chair stood by a desk in one corner, where Diego's books were stacked beneath a brass lamp.

Pictures on the wall were embroidered and framed in plain,

polished wood. A large, square, cloth-remnant braided rug lay over the wooden floor. There was a pedestal table with a healthy fern near the windows. And just in front of the windows, where the afternoon sun streamed in, was a long, low table covered with a white cloth embroidered with brilliant colors. On the table stood a large, exquisitely carved white-stone crucifix. To the right of it stood a picture of a half-dozen people in somber attire and in a blank-stare pose. The men were hatless and standing behind two women who were seated, one higher than the other. Two children sat at the women's feet. I recognized Jordan Bennett immediately, with his mane of tawny, sun-bleached hair and those magnificent light eyes. He looked no more than 14, tall and lanky and, with his devilish grin, much like Sherman Poole.

Reva picked up the picture. She pointed a long, slender finger to the taller of the two men. He had thick, dark hair that was brushed forward on a high brow. Piercing, hard eyes stared at me out of a ruggedly handsome face with a square, determined jaw. The thin lips were unsmiling and firm.

"This is Jordan's father." Her finger moved to the woman beneath the man's hand. "And his mother." The woman had the same light-colored eyes as did her son, and her hair was blond and braided in a large bun at the nape of her slender neck. She was a delicate-looking woman and seemed mismatched with the giant behind her. Jordan sat at her skirts, legs crossed Indian fashion and hands folded in his lap.

"This is my father and mother." Reva indicated the people to the left of the Bennetts. The man was broad-shouldered and lean, with very black hair and eyes. He had a mustache, well-trimmed and complimentary to his long face. Reva's mother was attractive, with her same darkness, but slightly heavy. The young girl at her feet was thin and big-eyed, as Reva had described herself.

"It's the only picture I have of my parents. It was taken by a man passing through on his way to the goldfields. He was a journalist from the East, and he had a camera that stood on three tall, wooden legs. We'd never seen a camera before. He would set the contraption up and then get underneath all this black draping." She laughed in remembrance. "Then there would be this great flash of light. It was wonderful!"

Reva looked at the picture again. "I heard that he wrote a book about the West, but I've never seen it. I wonder if this picture is in it."

"Were you and Mr. Bennett both the only children in your families?"

"I had two sisters and a brother. My two sisters died in infancy. My brother, Raoul, died when he was ten. I was only three then, and I remember almost nothing about him."

"How very sad."

"It was not uncommon for families to lose so many children. Measles took many. Fevers, dysentery, even hunger." Reva carefully set the picture back on the altar. "It was different for *Señor* and *Señora* Bennett. The *señora* confided a great deal to my mama. They were *amigas*. My mother was strong and used to hard work. The *señora* was frail. She was kind to the people who helped her. She was a great lady. Nothing like that woman Jordan brought home with him from Boston," Reva said, her tone a wealth of comment on her feelings about Gwendolyn Bennett.

"My mama did the cooking, canning, cleaning for Jordan's mama. The *señora* did her sewing. She loved to sew. She taught me to do this work." Reva fingered the exquisite embroidery.

"It's beautiful."

"I will never have the art of the *señora*," Reva said reverently. "But I try. She did such beautiful things. Once, she made me a white ruffled dress for my confirmation. She embroidered pink rosebuds all around the hem. I loved that dress." She smiled. "I still have it packed away in case I ever have a daughter."

Her dream sank painfully into my mind as I thought of Jordan with her, close and loving. An unpleasant feeling curled inside me. I had no right to be jealous, and yet I was. I looked at Reva and envied her so intensely, I thought I would cry. I swallowed hard, looking away.

"The *señora* was greatly admired," Reva told me. "She would have liked to have more children."

"Why didn't she?" I asked, still not looking at Reva.

"The *señor* and *señora* lived apart."

I looked back. "You mean they didn't love each other?"

"Oh, no. They loved one another very much. But Jordan was a large baby, and the *señora* was a delicate woman. She had great pain in childbirth and almost died. She was afraid of having another baby, and the doctor said she would probably die if she did. So she did not sleep with her husband."

My face burned with embarrassment at Reva Gutierrez's intimate disclosure about Jordan's parents.

Reva smiled. "I had forgotten how innocent you are. Of course, that is necessary to your position . . . that you be ignorant of the intimate activities between men and women."

"I'm not totally lacking in knowledge about the facts of life," I said, thinking of the books I had read. My flush receded only slightly.

"You mustn't admit that to the school board," Reva teased. "They might think your great knowledge will corrupt the innocent children." Her mocking tone was in no way unkind, and I smiled.

"It seems so absurd. What is correct and acceptable for other people to feel and know is denied to me because I am a teacher."

"If you had other interests besides your teaching, you would not give your all to the children," Reva disagreed. "That's as it should be. If you had a family, you would not have time to ride to Eden Rock to teach my son. That is why it is best to have a spinster teach; no one else demands her loyalties or efforts. All is for the children's education and betterment."

Reva's explanation was reasonable, but it only emphasized the lonely barrenness of my life stretching before me. It was fine to dedicate one's life to children, but what about when I grew too old to teach? Would I then be like Ellen Greer? Nothing to show for my life but a couple of plaques on a wall, some fond memories and a lonely room at the back of some charitable person's boardinghouse?

I was no different from any other woman. I dreamed of a family of my own, a man I could love, and children I would bear for him out of our love. Perhaps it was even more important to me, because I had no family at all, and the vague memories of security and love were so distant, they only tantalized me.

Loneliness, I told myself often, is a state of mind that can be controlled. But at night, alone in my darkened room with no company but a cat, it was not so easy to rationalize.

The children were becoming more and more my life. Through them I had a purpose. Through them I was able to touch another life, if only for a brief time. My existence would not be completely wasted. Had the Haversalls lived, I knew without doubt that I would have gone on as I had, working for nothing and receiving less than that in return. Yet, now, that time seemed a lifetime away. I did not want to remember them, and pushed my memories away.

"Of course, that does not mean that a virtuous woman like you cannot burn with desire if the right man touches you," Reva continued, giving me a sidelong glance. "Do you burn for anyone, *señorita?*" She was smiling as though she knew something I did not.

"I should say not," I retorted, unable to prevent a picture of Jordan from forming in my mind.

Reva laughed. "How very red you can get, *señorita*. You embarrass too easily. I was only teasing you." She considered me for a long moment then, and a speculative gleam changed her dark eyes. "Jordan said you have met Ross Persall. He is very handsome, no?"

"Yes, he is," I admitted, wondering if she was about to give me another warning about that man.

"Ross knows how to treat a woman. He makes her feel desirable. Women like him very much. Do you like him?"

"I suppose I do," I said, wondering why she should wish to know.

"Ross is very knowledgeable about women—especially those who are lonely and frustrated." Her words were meant to be significant, and I could hardly pretend that I did not understand.

"I've already been warned against the man by half the township," I told her dryly.

"Jordan as well?"

"Especially by him, though I can't think why he felt it necessary to say anything. Mr. Persall merely made some repairs to the front steps of the schoolhouse after Mr. Olmstead informed me he had no time for such duties."

Reva stared at me and then laughed as though at some great joke. Before I could ask her to explain her mirth, Diego entered the room, having finished his test. And for the next few hours we worked together over his lessons. I forgot about the last part of my conversation with Reva Gutierrez. Later, I would understand only too well what she meant about Ross Persall and lonely, frustrated women.

 *Chapter Twelve*

Following Sunday School, cleaning chores in the school-room and lesson planning for the next day, I finally was able to relax and enjoy my stew and warm-bread dinner with Orphan as my companion. I shared my stores with her, and she expounded her gratitude with throaty purrs. She was getting fat, I thought with a smile, remembering the skinny stray kitten she had been when I found her perched on the windowsill. I reached down and scratched her ears affectionately before leaving my room to make my customary evening trips to the well for water.

I was too exhausted to make the ten trips necessary to fill the old metal tub, nor did I feel I could stay awake long enough to heat the water on the wood stove. So I contented myself with one bucket of warm water, just enough for a sponge bath and rinse. One of the luxuries I longed for was a pleasant soak to completely relax my tired muscles. I lathered my hair and then poured the bucket of water over me slowly to rinse away all the soap.

Wrapping myself in one towel, I used another to rub my hair dry. Then I sat brushing it until the thick auburn tresses glistened. My hair was naturally curly, and it floated about my shoulders and back in wild disarray. But it felt good to have it free of its usual confining bun.

Checking my timepiece, I saw that it was later than I had thought. I wanted to go to the cemetery and see the *El Día de los Muertos* procession. Reva had told me that tonight would be the finale of the celebration. Families would walk to the churchyard carrying candles and gifts of food and flowers for deceased loved ones. There would be traditional songs and games for the children.

Though I was not part of the group, I wanted to watch the festivities from the hillside beyond the graveyard. I could sit beneath the sycamores and keep myself warm with my shawl.

So I donned my clothes hurriedly, leaving my hair free for lack of time, as well as a certain defiance I did not want to admit to feeling. I could go around the back way, over the hills, so that no one would see me. I felt reckless and happy.

Skipping down the back steps and hopping over the last two that were still in bad repair, I started out. It was growing dark quickly, and already the air was chilly. I lifted the edge of my skirt and ran along, feeling free and deliciously wicked. My work was done for the moment, but it would start again at dawn tomorrow. For now, just for a few hours, I was not going to think of anything but the beautiful evening, the clear darkening sky and brilliant scattering of stars, the full moon and the festivities that I would at least be able to view from a distance.

As I ran on, I could see the light-filled windows of homes on the hem of town. Smoke curled up from chimneys as dinners were being prepared, and houses warmed against the cool autumn evening. There was the faintest whispering of wind about me, and now and then I could hear the throaty croak of a bullfrog among the cacophony of crickets.

Ahead of me was the hillside cemetery, with the sycamore grove beyond. The procession had already started and was moving into the churchyard. I ran faster, hitching my skirts up until they were about my calves. I had neglected to put on my shoes, and my slippers were thin, just barely enough to protect my soles. I cared nothing about the picture I made with my bare legs showing and my hair winging wildly behind me. There was no one around to care that the dignified, spinster teacher was racing like a hoyden across a field to peek secretly at a celebration.

When I reached the grove, I was winded and had to hold my ribs against the painful stitch in my side. Laughing faintly at my ridiculous behavior, I sank to the ground, which was littered with fallen leaves. More floated down about me as the twigs shuddered against the evening breeze. I drew a deep breath, smelling the damp earth and grass.

Drawing up my knees, I wrapped my shawl-covered arms around them. I craned my neck to see the participants of the procession, but I could not pick out Reva or Diego among the gaily dressed celebrants. The flickering candles added a mystic air to the scene below in the graveyard. People wove their way among the headstones toward the Catholic section. They were singing, but I did not understand the Spanish lyrics, though I thought the melody was beautiful. I closed my eyes and listened with pleasure to the harmonic blending of old and young voices.

"I couldn't believe it when I saw you," came a deep voice beside me, and I jumped with fright. Wide-eyed, I stared up the long length of Ross Persall standing above me. He was grinning broadly as I came hastily to my feet, brushing down my skirts as I did so. I felt foolish, caught in some childish display of mischief, and guilty of the worst sort of indiscretion.

"Don't look so aghast. I won't tell anyone," he assured me, laughing slightly. I stopped my frantic tidying and looked up at him again. His hair was not as neat as usual; it lay forward boyishly. His dark eyes were sparkling with amusement, but there was none of the mockery I always expected from Jordan Bennett.

I relaxed slightly and smiled back at him. "Where were you, Mr. Persall? I didn't see you when I came up here."

"You were in too much of a hurry to be looking around." He grinned. "I had some business at this end of town. I saw the procession and decided to watch for a few minutes. Then I saw a wood nymph racing up the hillside, disappearing in the darkness beneath the trees. I thought I recognized the rather shapely form of our usually dignified teacher, but I had to come investigate to be sure." He was laughing at me, but not in a way as to be offensive.

"And now you know it was." I pretended remorse.

"A not unpleasant surprise."

"I wanted to see the celebration," I explained, indicating the people below. "And when I saw they had already started, I hurried."

"Don't explain yourself. Why don't we just sit down and enjoy the festivities together," he suggested. I remembered James Olmstead's iron rule of avoiding meetings just such as this. Ross Persall seemed to know my thoughts, and his fine shapely mouth curved into a knowing, mocking smile. "There was no one else around to see you or me. So you won't get into trouble for sharing a couple of minutes with me," he said, and his brows rose, giving me a slight challenge.

"I think I will," I decided and sat down again, curling my legs beneath me in a more ladylike position. He stretched out beside me.

"Don't you ever get tired of all the one-sided rules you're expected to follow?" he asked, his eyes sliding down over me and then up again to meet mine.

"Sometimes," I admitted, his perusal not unnerving me the way Jordan's always did. "For example, I see no reason why I can't sit here with you. I enjoy conversing with people."

"The concern isn't about conversing, Miss McFarland, but about what comes after it." He grinned, and I could see what Reva had meant about his effect on women.

"What you're implying need not follow," I told him primly.

"But a man will always try when the woman is as attractive as you," he said, undaunted.

"Shall I take that as a fair warning, Mr. Persall?"

"You can trust me completely, Miss McFarland. I'm not the rogue everyone says. I can be a gentleman if the woman warrants it and the stakes are high enough."

"What do you mean by that?"

"Just that you don't seem the type of woman who would enjoy being trifled with."

"I think that's true of most women."

He gave me a considering look and then smiled. "Not in my experience. Most of the women I've known enjoy trifling."

"I think you're deliberately trying to shock me. And just after you told me that you were trustworthy and not the rogue you're reputed to be," I scolded teasingly.

"You shouldn't believe everything you hear." He grinned again.

"Then I'll take your first warning and run," I suggested, pretending to rise. He reached out and closed his hand over mine. His fingers were strong and warm.

"No . . . at least not yet. I've given you no reason."

"*Yet.*" I laughed. I looked down at him lying on his side in the grass, his hand moving to hold mine. There was a certain sensual quality about him that made me feel quite out of my depth.

"I do believe you are trifling with me, Mr. Persall," I chastened him, drawing my hand away. "Perhaps I should believe all I've heard."

"And what have you heard?"

"Nothing, I'm sure, that would surprise you."

"Tell me," he kindly ordered.

"That you're charming. That you like women, and they like you."

"Do you like me?"

"I'm a woman, aren't I?" I laughed.

"Who's trifling with whom, Miss McFarland," he said with an upward tilt of his mouth.

"We're missing the procession," I reminded him.

"Forget the procession. I'd rather talk."

"I came up here to watch the procession."

"You wound my pride," he sighed. "My company should be more interesting than watching a bunch of Mexicans putting leftovers on graves."

I stared at him, disliking his tone and use of words. "What a dreadful way to put it! They prepare special gifts of food that were favored by their deceased relatives and friends. Their offerings are meant as an assertion of faith!"

"Where did you learn so much about it?" he asked, not the least bit put off by my annoyance, and effectively turning it away.

"Reva Gutierrez told me—"

"Reva? Reva never leaves Eden Rock, at least not since Gwendolyn Bennett told the town about Diego's relationship to Jordan. Reva used to come in quite a lot before that."

"Yes, I heard about that. Did you know Gwendolyn Bennett?"

Ross did not answer for a moment. "Slightly," he said finally, and there was a look in his eyes I could not fathom. "You've learned a lot in your short time in town, haven't you?"

"I don't know what you mean," I hedged, realizing my error too late.

"You couldn't have met Reva unless you've been to Eden Rock. And I wonder what you were doing out there." I was glad of the darkness that concealed my guilty flush. When I did not answer, he gave a slight laugh. "Jordan works fast."

"Mr. Bennett has nothing to do with my visits to Eden Rock."

Ross chuckled. "Well, you needn't worry. I'm not going to tell the school board anything. I'm hardly on speaking terms with the preacher, and James Olmstead is a pompous ass I would just as soon avoid."

"I've been tutoring Diego," I volunteered, not wanting him to think my reason for going to Eden Rock had anything to do with Jordan Bennett.

"Defiance." He smiled.

"Well, I don't agree with Diego's expulsion, and until I can find a way of having him reinstated, I intend to see that he keeps up with his lessons."

"I don't see why you should concern yourself. The kid is Bennett's bastard. Let him worry about it."

I found Ross Persall's statement offensive. "Ellen Greer says it's all a vicious rumor."

"Ellen Greer is just a bit biased," Ross said. "She doesn't believe he murdered Gwendolyn either."

"But you do, I suppose."

He sighed. "Let's forget the sins of Jordan Bennett, shall we? I'm much more interested in learning about yours."

I had not liked the subject, but his abrupt disregard of it bothered me. Did he really believe Jordan had killed his wife? Somehow I could not believe it. Perhaps because I did not want to believe it.

I relented. "I've no real sins with which to regale you. Dreadful, isn't it?"

"Not even one little one?" Ross teased.

"Scores in my mind," I admitted, "but none committed."

Ross took a blade of grass and began nibbling thoughtfully at the end of it. "Those are the best sins of all. Tell me about yours."

"I do believe you're serious," I emitted with a laugh.

"Of course. What's more interesting than discussing one's sins . . . committed or merely considered."

"Well, then, let's discuss yours. I'm sure they're far more interesting than mine."

He grinned devilishly. "Perhaps, but I'm afraid we haven't near enough time to even start on mine."

"What a shame."

"Let's just leave it at the fact that I enjoy bending rules now and then."

"Social or legal?"

Ross Persall laughed. "On occasion, both."

We went on to talk of other things, and I found him a fascinating companion. He knew much of the valley history and a great deal about the local people. Some of his stories were shockingly funny and usually at the expense of someone's overly stiff propriety. Some of his stories were not so funny. It was from Ross that I learned about Tom Hallender, the aging local sheriff.

Two decades before, three gunmen had come into town intent on evil-doing. Tom Hallender had been only a deputy then. The local sheriff had left town, afraid for his own life. Hallender had been forced to face the three gunmen himself when they had broken into a local establishment and raped a woman. He had called a challenge to the three men, who had laughingly accepted. The gunfight had taken place on Main Street.

Tom Hallender was not a quick draw, but he was deadly accurate and had a strong will to survive. The three gunmen had outdrawn him and had succeeded in hitting him, but Tom Hallender had emerged the victor. He suffered three gunshot wounds, one bullet grazing his side and chipping a rib. He had dropped and rolled, but not soon enough to avoid the second bullet, which hit him in the knee. Firing off two shots, he killed two gunmen. But the last gunman managed to get off two more shots before he was felled by Hallender. One of the outlaw's bullets missed its mark, but the other passed through the deputy's shoulder.

The lawman had recovered quickly from the two flesh wounds, but he never fully recovered from the shattered knee cap. The doctor had used a metal disc made by the blacksmith to replace Hallender's patella. Fortunately, the daring medical experiment had prevented him from being crippled, but it brought frequent pain and made him limp.

"He doesn't look like a man with such courage," I said, thinking of the lean man of middling height. His thinning gray hair was always carefully brushed from a center part, and placid gray eyes looked out above a thick nose. His solemn mouth was hardened slightly by the thin, well-trimmed mustache.

"No, he doesn't," Ross agreed, tossing away another blade of grass. "I was surprised when Bradford Poole told me the story. He was a kid then, and remembers it firsthand. He said he'd watched from an upstairs window." Ross shook his head. "I was making critical remarks about the sheriff, and that's how the story came up at all. I guess everyone around here figures everyone's heard about it."

"What kind of critical remarks?"

"There was a bank robbery two years ago. Three men killed a teller and got off with a hundred thousand dollars."

"That's quite a fortune."

"By anyone's standards," he agreed.

"And what about the criminals?"

"One of them was wounded. Hallender went after them, but he said he only found the one man. His buddies had murdered him when he slowed them down."

I gasped. "How awful."

"But as for the other two, they got clean away. Not a clue as to where they went or what happened to the money. Two of them were recognized by one of the tellers."

"Who were they?"

"A trio called the Woodland brothers. They had pulled a couple of other robberies in the Oakland area and points north of there. It was the younger brother Hallender found."

I stared at Ross. "You mean they killed their own brother?"

"I doubt if they were really related," he commented with a shrug. "But with that kind of animal, you never know what they'll do."

"And this was two years ago," I said quietly, in awe. "Have they robbed anyone else since then?"

"There have been rumors, but nothing substantiated. One hundred thousand dollars will carry them a long way."

I sighed and looked down the hill. "Everyone's gone!" I remarked with surprise. I had been so engrossed by my conversation with Ross Persall that I had failed to see the last celebrants leaving for home. I had missed most of the celebration as well.

"So they are." Ross chuckled, not surprised at all. "We're all alone now."

"Stop teasing me." I gave a push at the arm he started to put around my shoulders.

"Aren't you afraid I might seduce you?" His eyes gleamed with laughter.

"Not in the slightest," I answered and stood up, brushing the autumn leaves from my skirt.

"So you do trust me."

"Don't sound so disappointed. That's a good foundation for a friendly relationship."

Ross gave a deep-throated laugh. "A friendly relationship, huh?"

"Purely platonic," I emphasized, drawing my shawl more tightly around me as I felt the cold. I laughed at his rueful expression.

He came to his feet. "You're more of a brat than those sixty-odd children you beat sums into," he drawled.

I laughed again. "I've enjoyed our little chat, Mr. Persall."

"Ross," he coaxed.

"Ross," I agreed, unable to think of him any other way now.

"I hope we can do it again."

"So do I," I said candidly, then frowned as I realized that it would be virtually impossible.

"Why don't we make arrangements for that to happen right now?" he suggested with a raised brow.

"Another clandestine meeting?" I teased.

"Put a little excitement into our lives." He grinned.

"I don't dare put any more in mine," I sighed, thinking of the chance I ran riding to Eden Rock every Saturday. If the board were to hear. . . .

"We can meet by the old water tower east of town. I can be there at eight each evening," Ross whispered encouragement. "It's not far from the schoolhouse, and no one goes there much."

I looked up at him through the concealing veil of my lashes. There was a warm blaze in his eyes, a sensuous curve to his mouth. Perhaps Ross was not as trustworthy as I thought.

"I don't think so," I declined.

"You don't trust me after all," he said ruefully.

"Let's just say I think it's wise to leave things like this. We've had an enjoyable evening."

"Those who are always wise have life pass them by, my dear Miss McFarland." His faintly mocking tone lacked the bite of Jordan Bennett's usual barbed comments.

"Woefully true, perhaps. But I'm not in any kind of position to test your theory. I'm sorry."

"Then at least let me see you back to the schoolhouse."

My luck with the school board was thin enough. "I don't think so."

"Oh, wise and ever-cautious maiden," he needled.

"Good night, Ross." I smiled and turned away to walk down the hill. I was almost to the bottom of the incline when I turned to look back up where I had sat with him. Ross had walked down the other way along the fence of the cemetery. He was standing beside a marker just beyond the boundaries. He leaned down slightly and dropped something onto the ground. Then he straightened and walked on without another look at the lonely grave.

I stood for a long moment in the shadow of the hill, then curiosity got the better of sense. I walked briskly back along the line of the hill and moved toward the grave. It was unkept, with weeds growing over the low mound of dirt, which had started to sink in on its resting inhabitant. One wild flower lay at the base of a cross that bore no identification. The flower rustled against the night air and then rolled off the mound, flipping away with the wind.

For a long time I stared at that grave, wondering what poor soul was buried there just beyond the enclosed cemetery. What had the person done to be so excluded from the peaceful, resting places of the others? Was there no one who cared about the person who lay here beneath the cold earth, only a wooden marker to say he had once lived?

But Ross Persall had cared. Not much perhaps, but enough to place one wild flower on the grave.

Suddenly, for no explicable reason, I felt very cold. Drawing my shawl more tightly around me, I turned away and walked back toward the darkened schoolhouse.

 *Chapter Thirteen*

When I came down over the hill and saw the schoolhouse, I was struck by the silence. It was so quiet, my ears rang. Even the crickets and the owl that inhabited the oak seemed hesitant to perform their customary night concert. I stood motionless in the dark shadows of the oak, feeling vaguely uneasy but unable to explain the sensation. I stared at the lonely, dark building that was now my home.

How ironic, I thought, that during the daylight hours from Monday through Friday the place resounded with the chatter and laughter of children at work and play. But at nights and on the weekends it sat in lonely desolation, inhabited by only me, Orphan and some active, noisy mice.

The chill I had felt at the grave returned when I saw a faint illumination move across a side window of the schoolhouse. For a moment I had thought I had seen a woman. Then I admonished myself for being so foolish and letting my fanciful imagination control my good sense. What would another women be doing in the schoolhouse this late at night?

I walked across the open area between the oak and the back steps. As I started up, I heard something in my room. There was a scurrying and a desperate mewling sound. Orphan, I

161

thought in alarm, and opened the door quickly, wondering what was the matter with her.

The cat gave a panicky yowl as she saw her escape made possible, and she darted past me. Turning, I saw her bound down the steps and race madly across the grass, clawing her way up the oak.

"Orphan, what is the matter with you?" I asked, reaching inside the doorway to grab a match. I struck it, lit the lantern and glanced quickly around the room. After finding everything in good order, I looked back out toward the oak.

"Come on down, you silly cat," I beckoned. She refused to budge from her high perch, and I wondered if she could get down. She made a plaintive meow.

"You got yourself up there, so I'm afraid you'll have to find your own way down," I called to her.

Orphan had no intention of coming down from the tree. I gave a faint shrug and quietly closed the door behind me. Sometimes that cat acted very strange indeed. I despaired of ever getting her to catch the schoolroom's resident mice; she never wanted to enter the classroom at all.

My room seemed colder than the night air outside. Rubbing my arms, I moved to the stove. There were still red-hot coals burning, and it seemed strange that their heat had not kept the room from growing so chilly. I picked up several more pieces of wood and stoked the coals, then dropped them in to burn. Holding my hands over the fire, I warmed myself. I thought of my conversation with Ross Persall and smiled slightly. Tonight had been a pleasantly quiet interlude with a very handsome and charming man. Tomorrow would be another demanding, yet exhilarating day with my children. I was growing very satisfied with my life.

A sound from the schoolroom drew my attention. Those mice, I thought with annoyance. Perhaps I would have to find myself another more adventurous and courageous cat to team with my stray. Orphan was a fine companion, but sadly lacking in natural hunting talents. I could always invest in traps. Olmstead stocked a variety. I did not like that thought, but something would have to be done if the little creatures began working on the children's texts and the modest paper supply. When another sound came, I thought I had better investigate.

Opening the schoolroom door slowly, I peered in, not eager to find some larger relative of the mouse family in residence. The cold air hit me almost physically, raising an army of goose bumps upon my skin. Even the thick shawl was no protection. I pushed the door even wider and stood staring into the darkness. I could make out the shapes of the children's desks and that of my own. The texts were stacked neatly on the shelves, and the can of pencils on top was undisturbed.

I heard nothing now. Surely mice would scurry for cover, wouldn't they? An odd prickling sensation was growing at the nape of my neck. Stepping farther into the room, I peered around again.

No movement. No sound. Intense, ear-ringing silence greeted me. And that chill. What had made the noise? I wondered. And why was it so cold in this room? The broken windows, I answered myself silently. Yet, it had not seemed so cold outside.

As I started to turn back to my room, something caught the corner of my eye. There was another message on the blackboard. Almost afraid, I moved into the room to read what the practical joker had chalked there this time. Two words were written in a neat hand—not in the scrawled writing as had the other, more menacing messages been written.

"Go away." Simple and direct, I thought wryly. I muttered an impatient sound and picked up the eraser. As I rubbed out the irritating message, I thought I heard something.

"Abigail..."

My heart began to pound as I strained to hear every sound. I did not move, but stood like a statue, my hand still raised and clutching the eraser. Again, that chill hit me like an unseen force.

And there was something else! The smell of lavender. It permeated the room, strong and cloying. I was panting in alarm, but I forced myself to ease my arm down and place the eraser gently back in the chalk tray. Turning slowly and staring around the darkened room for the intruder, I found there was no one there. No one at all.

I sensed a faint, moaning sound, as though someone were

crying with his face muffled in a pillow. Then, again, that intense, almost tangible silence. A sudden gust of wind blew the patchwork curtains into the room, whipping them about wildly for an instant. Then they lay still. Even the scent of lavender was gone.

It was a full minute before I became aware that the crickets had started to chirp again. The old owl hooted from the oak, and I heard Orphan meow and scratch at the back door. I drew in my breath and let it out again, still nervously staring around the schoolroom.

Had I imagined the entire episode? Everything was in place. There was the usual night sounds—the creaking of the building, the insects and birds outside. What had frightened me so much a moment ago, filling me with unreasonable dread?

Perhaps that lonely grave outside the cemetery had distressed me more than I realized. Perhaps it had begun a chain reaction of imaginings. I knew my imagination had fuel enough to feed it. Perhaps that lonely marker had pushed my fantasies into nightmarish proportions. With a last, slow look around the schoolroom, I turned away.

When I reentered my room, it was comfortably warm. The lantern I had lighted cast a welcoming glow over everything. Orphan scratched again at the door, letting out a summoning cry. When I opened the door, she came in unhesitantly and rubbed herself against my skirt as she always did.

Shaking my head, I gave a faint laugh at the wild thoughts of only a moment before. I had even wondered if there was a ghost inhabiting the schoolhouse. Now, in the warmth and glow of my room, I realized how utterly ridiculous that thought was. I had let the desolation of that lonely grave affect my good, solid common sense. Ghosts, goblins, witches. The stuff Halloween was made of, and Halloween just passed. How people would laugh if they were to know what an impressionable schoolteacher they had hired, I thought. Well, I would not give them the entertainment of admitting such nonsense. I gave Orphan a bowl of warm milk. Then I removed my clothing and put on my nightgown. In spite of my reasoning, however, sleep was a long time in coming.

* * *

During the week that followed I tried not to ponder the strange occurrence in the schoolhouse. In the daylight hours I didn't have much time to think about that evening, because I was so involved with the children. Even during the late afternoon, when I cleaned the schoolroom, and early in the evening, when I cooked for myself and planned lessons for the following day, I was able to keep my thoughts from distressing me. However, it was later, when I blew out the lantern and snuggled deeply into the blankets of my lumpy cot, that all reason fled. Well after midnight, even rationalizing was far from comforting when strange noises filled the schoolhouse, when my room was at its darkest and coldest.

Orphan's strange behavior further increased my uneasiness. She flatly refused to enter the schoolroom, and sometimes a frightened yowl would erupt from her, startling me awake in the blackest of night. Somewhere in my reading I had remembered that cats were believed by some to be the familiars of witches and therefore had uncanny knowledge about the supernatural. Perhaps Orphan sensed a presence I was afraid to acknowledge. Such thoughts proved even more frightening to me, and I wondered if the concentration of my experience was not unlike reading horror stories to oneself after dark.

Yet, sometimes late at night I would awaken for no reason and lie in a state of cold sweat and tension, listening for something I could not explain. For the most part I would recognize the nighttime sounds—the owl in the oak, the mice in the rafters, a cricket in the corner, a toad beneath the back steps. As soon as I made the identification, my fear dissipated, and I wanted to laugh at my foolishness. Yet, there were other sounds that I could not rationalize. Twice since the night I had returned from my sojourn with Ross, I again heard a woman crying. Neither time had I dared leave my bed to investigate.

When I first experienced "the occurrence," as I came to call it, I had immediately dismissed the possibility of a ghost. Then I rethought the matter. While I clung desperately to the mental haven of disbelief, my instincts told me I was wrong. This woman of the schoolhouse did, in fact, exist.

Being a Christian, I therefore believed in an afterlife. So how could I reasonably not believe in ghosts who were supposedly the disembodied spirits of the dead. Souls, as the church would define them. I knew what frightened me, of course. This spirit had, for some reason, not departed this world for the next. She was living here in the schoolhouse . . . with me.

It seemed strange that I should be so sure that the ghost was a woman. I had never seen her. And the crying was so faint, it was hard to discern as male or female. After all, men cried as well as women. Why shouldn't the ghost be a man? Yet, I knew, without any doubt, that the ghost was female. But who was she? And why was she here? And why was she so dreadfully unhappy?

Gradually, as several more weeks passed, the fear I felt at the visitations lessened and evolved into other emotions. The ghost had never tried to harm me. The only unpleasantness I experienced at her presence was the alarming cold. Everything else I felt was brought on by my own emotions. I began to wonder about her. Whatever was grieving my nocturnal companion must be the reason her soul had not departed this world. If I learned her secret, perhaps that would release her. And give me a night's peace!

Once, I dared enter the schoolroom when I heard her crying in the night. There was nothing. Not even the flickering of the curtains. And the crying stopped almost immediately when I opened the door.

"You're looking tired, Abby," Ellen Greer observed during our Wednesday-afternoon visit three weeks after I had become aware of something strange going on in the schoolhouse. I continued to sip my coffee, then glanced up at her through the veiling of my lashes.

Considering how I had felt the first time I experienced the visitation, I hesitated in confiding the story to anyone else. They might think me completely mad, even Ellen Greer, who I considered my closest and only real friend. I could imagine what she would think if I were to tell her that there was a ghost inhabiting the schoolhouse. She might laugh at such nonsense, or she might be alarmed and worried that my position had proven entirely too much for me.

"I haven't been sleeping well," I said simply. Ellen looked concerned.

"What's on your mind?"

"Lots of things, I suppose."

"Don't brush me off, girl! Something is bothering you, and I want to know what it is this minute."

I laughed at her characteristically demanding nosiness. "Ghosts and goblins, actually," I said, lowering the cup and saucer to my lap. "They're making too much noise in the schoolhouse to allow me a good night's sleep." I made it all sound like a joke, but something flickered in Ellen's eyes.

"Now, is that a fact?"

"Were you ever bothered by noises in the schoolroom, Ellen?" I asked, trying to keep the tremor out of my voice.

"I can't say I was, but then I was so tired by the end of the evening that nothing could have awakened me."

"Maybe I'm overtired." I shrugged, staring down into my cup and thinking that perhaps my first thoughts on the matter were correct and that my imagination was merely overworking itself.

"Maybe you're drinking too much coffee at night," Ellen suggested.

"Maybe it's that simple."

"Maybe, maybe, maybe!" she snapped. "Have you been hearing a lot of silly stories around town?" she demanded, and I looked up curiously.

"What kind of stories?"

"You tell me."

"You're being very vague, Ellen."

"So are you," Ellen snorted. "We don't usually play these kinds of games, my girl. Now, out with it."

"All right," I sighed, giving her a self-deprecating smile. "I believe there's a ghost living in the schoolhouse."

Ellen Greer did not seem the least bit surprised. But she was 80 and perhaps past the age of being surprised by anything.

"You don't think I'm crazy?" I asked with a laugh.

"No. I think someone is playing an elaborate Halloween trick on you."

"Halloween passed us weeks ago."

"That doesn't mean that active little minds aren't working on some mischief. Schoolteachers are always prime targets, or haven't you learned that yet?"

"I've had the garter-snake-in-the-desk routine, Ellen. It's

not something like that, I'm sure. There really is something there. I can feel it. There's a cold feeling in the schoolroom sometimes. But never during the day."

"Of course not," Ellen said wryly.

"I'm serious," I said in growing frustration.

"I know you are, and that's precisely why I choose not to be."

"Oh, Ellen. . . ."

"Don't you 'Oh, Ellen' me, my dear. You're letting your imagination run away with you on the evidence of a few unexplained sounds and shadows. I didn't think it of you." She shook her head. "I was sure you were a sensible young lady, not some flighty nitwit who sees ghosts and goblins in every shadowed corner."

Her sharp tone and criticism made my throat ache with restrained tears, and with difficulty I flattened all expression from my face. I had had long practice doing that with the Haversalls, but Ellen could cut deeper than they ever had. She looked at me for a long moment and sighed. "I've lived in that schoolhouse," she added quietly. "I know how eerie it can be sometimes, with the owls hooting and the crickets making their infernal racket out in the tall grass and even inside your very room. Your imagination draws demons out of little nothings, especially when you're exhausted. When you're all by yourself, sounds become magnified and distorted."

I shook my head, meeting her eyes. "No, Ellen. I can hear a woman crying. I know the difference between frogs croaking, mice gnawing and all the rest of the noises my little companions contribute. I can hear a woman crying! And you won't convince me otherwise with all your—"

"Don't get yourself so worked up," Ellen soothed. She leaned forward and rested her gnarled, arthritic hands on the crook of her cane. "There's an explanation, my dear, but it isn't a ghost. There's no such thing. They're something made up centuries ago by some mother or father wanting to keep their pesky children in bed at night."

"You go to church, Ellen. You believe in heaven and hell. So why won't you believe me about this? We have to have some form when we die, don't we?"

Ellen snorted and leaned back in her chair again. She shook her head, looking at me like a worn but still patient parent. "'From ashes to ashes, dust to dust,' as the Good Book says. That's what I believe in, Abby. What makes man worth any hereafter, if there was such a place, which I heartily doubt. People remember us as we were during our life on this god-forsaken earth. That memory, be it good, bad, or indifferent, is about as much as any of us can hope for after we're dead and buried. God created us perhaps, but I'm inclined to believe he regretted that mistake and wants nothing further to do with us." She sighed deeply.

"My dear, heaven and hell are right here," she further explained her views, tapping her cane hard on the floor as emphasis. "Your loneliness is part of your hell. Seeing your students learning is part of your heaven. And as for my attending church like some faithful follower, it's my only social activity of the week."

Ellen chuckled. "Hayes is a pompous, ignorant baboon, but he's entertaining to watch. I relish the way he shouts himself red in the face, making his veins stand out at the temples. He scares the very mischief out of the weakhearted. Did you see Berthamae's face last Sunday when Hayes howled down at her of the sins of idle gossip? And Howard Donlevy turned white when the good reverend told the congregation that God is listening to our every word. I've never heard anyone cuss with the finesse that Howard exhibits. He's an artist with the way he punctuates his sentences with hells and damns."

I knew that Ellen was trying to distract me from my thoughts, but her methods were not working and only succeeded in increasing my curiosity about the spirit in the schoolhouse. Her very determination to sidetrack me made me wonder just what she really did believe.

"There is something there in the schoolhouse, Ellen," I said quietly, dogmatic. Ellen stopped her flow of talk and looked at me. Her mouth tightened.

"There isn't anything in that schoolhouse now that hasn't been there since it was built fifty-odd years ago," she told me firmly. "There's only a lonely woman who gives up her own dreams to help others have the means of achieving theirs."

"Did Prudence Townsend leave because of the ghost?" I asked, displaying my own determination to have some answers.

Ellen issued an impatient snort and tapped the fingers of her right hand on the arm of her rocker. "No. Prudence Townsend did not leave because of any ghost," she retorted indignantly. She did not meet my eyes, however, but looked away from me and out into the garden now turned under and fertilized for spring planting.

"Then why did she leave?" I asked, still pressing the matter.

"Leave be on the subject of Prudence Townsend!" Ellen snapped, her eyes swinging back to me. I saw with surprise that she was really angry, more angry than I had ever seen her.

"That girl was a damn fool, plain and simple! Now, just forget about her!"

I knew I would not do as Ellen so belligerently instructed. However, I would respect her wishes and not bring up the subject of Prudence Townsend with her again. There was no sense in doing so, for I would get no answers to my questions from Ellen Greer. And as for the ghost that inhabited the schoolhouse, I would have to find other sources of information concerning that as well.

# Chapter Fourteen

Trouble seemed to roost on my shoulders. As long as my ideas remained in opposition with James Olmstead's and the Reverend Jonah Hayes's, there was little I could do to alleviate the growing tension of my life.

Since arriving in town, I had become the hub of controversy. First, I had allowed the children to paint murals on the schoolroom walls, an act in itself that had raised eyebrows, made tongues wag and heads shake. Then I had used physical labor to work out the mischievous energies of my resident miscreants. My teaching methods were next to come into the critical arena. Games and dramatic play had no place in a classroom, according to Olmstead and the goodly Reverend Hayes. I knew that my methods were unorthodox and highly unconventional, but both men had demanded results, and the techniques were working. The children were learning, and they were enjoying themselves in the process. The way they learned seemed of little import.

Most of the parents graciously reserved comment about me. There were some exceptions, of course. Berthamae Poole had been very indignant when she found her two boys digging the latrine. However, since then, she had forgiven and even praised me when her sons showed marked improvement in their basic skills. They surprised her even more by reading during the evening rather than playing poker.

I had earned Reverend Hayes's eternal ire by refusing to teach the stories he selected for Sunday School. He had suggested Adam and Eve being cast from Eden, the destruction of Sodom and Gomorrah, Job, and the great flood to start with during the first month. However, I had put those aside and taught the stories of Ruth, the raising of Lazarus, the blind man who was given sight, and the meeting of Jesus and the woman beside Jacob's well.

Angry and frustrated, Reverend Hayes had said that the children were not getting the proper attitude about God's power. They should fear His wrath, he'd said. I had argued that everyone should live with the knowledge of His love and forgiveness. He cited passages from the Bible, and I did likewise, which only increased his distrust and dislike of me.

With the antagonism between me and Olmstead and Hayes, I knew it would be difficult to have Diego Gutierrez reinstated in school. However, I intended to try as much for his sake as for Matthew Hayes's, since the latter was still in disgrace with his classmates.

My first attempts to discuss the matter with James Olmstead and the goodly reverend met with dismal failure. Once, Olmstead simply turned on his heel and stormed from the storefront into the back room, where he had remained so long, I had little choice but to leave in frustration. Reverend Hayes proved even more illusive. He was always on his way out to visit some member of the congregation who was in dire need of his spiritual guidance. The reverend seemed oblivious of his eldest son's dilemma. It was when Matthew came to me in tears that I decided I would have to press until the matter was resolved.

My opportunity came sooner than I expected. I needed a few sundries and went to the store following school on Friday afternoon. When I entered, I spotted James Olmstead perched precariously on a tall ladder, rearranging some canned goods. Below him, arms crossed and talking leisurely, stood Reverend Hayes. I smiled slightly, wove my way among the tables and positioned myself at the base of the roost and in front of Rev-

erend Hayes. The latter eyed me with the same imperious gaze
that terrified most of his parishioners. Then he looked up at
James Olmstead, who had not yet noticed my daunting presence.

"Good afternoon, gentlemen," I said pleasantly enough.
Hayes's quelling look was not going to veer me off my purpose.
Olmstead looked down and mumbled some disgruntled greeting. He continued to work, obviously hoping I would take the
hint and go away.

"I wish to speak with both of you about the reinstatement
of Diego Gutierrez in school," I opened bluntly. They knew
very well what was on my mind, and I might as well jump
right into the fire with both feet as to roast on the edges.

Reverend Hayes's thick brows rose with a shot, and those
frightening eyes chilled. His facial muscles became set. Olmstead merely issued an impatient snort.

"When are you going to leave that alone, Miss McFarland?"
the reverend asked tiredly. I saw Emily standing silently behind
the counter. She looked up once and then quickly lowered her
head to pretend concentration on a grocery list handed to her
by Berthamae Poole. I could expect no assistance from them.
Emily was cowed by her bullying husband, and Berthamae
Poole shook with fear of the reverend.

"I'm afraid I cannot do that. Diego was expelled more than
a month ago for a minor incident—"

"Minor incident!" Reverend Hayes boomed. "You call my
son's bloody nose a minor incident?"

"Diego Gutierrez suffered a blackened eye that swelled shut,
Reverend Hayes," I said quietly, managing to keep my voice
steady and reasonably calm in the face of Hayes's quite alarming anger.

"He deserved it," he stated, still in a loud voice, not caring
who heard him. The two women at the counter were frozen,
but if ears could grow to indicate interest, there would be two
sets as tall as a jack rabbit's.

"That little Mexican devil was beating up my son for no
reason. He deserved to get a black eye. He deserved a good
hiding as well, and if you were doing your job properly, Miss
McFarland, you would have used the switch on him in front

of the children so that they would all know what happens to bullies."

"Diego did not beat up your son," I said coolly.

"That's not what I was told!" he stormed.

"I know that," I said in an attempt to be soothing, but knowing it was like throwing sand in the face of an angry bear.

"You said you were not even there when the fight started," Olmstead reminded me, a glint of satisfaction in his eyes.

"I was in the schoolroom tutoring one of the children," I agreed. "However, I was informed by several of the children who witnessed the entire affair that it was Matthew who hit Diego first and not the other way around."

"My son said Diego Gutierrez started the fight," Hayes insisted stiffly.

"And if you discussed the episode with him now, I believe you would find his story different."

"Why should his story be any different now than it was then?" Olmstead asked, coming down from his perch agressively. I stepped back out of his way. "Have you threatened the boy to make him change his mind?" he continued. "Your favoritism for the Mexican is well-known, Miss McFarland."

I wondered if he was deliberately trying to incite my anger. If that was his intention, he was succeeding remarkably well. I drew a deep breath, striving for some control over my anger.

"I do not threaten children, Mr. Olmstead," I said indignantly. "And I find such a question highly insulting."

Olmstead flushed as I stared at him. I knew that my expression said more than was politic, but I could not help but feel he was contemptible.

"Matthew's grades have dropped since the boy was expelled," Hayes told Olmstead, obviously implying there was a connection.

"Matthew's grades have fallen," I agreed frankly. "His work has suffered greatly since the incident with Diego. He is under a great deal of strain."

"Strain you have put on him, no doubt," the reverend was quick to say.

"The strain of a guilty conscience and social pressure," I said calmly. "Since Matthew used you and Mr. Olmstead to finish a fight he started and could not finish successfully, the children have ostracized him. They liked Diego Gutierrez, and they refuse to forgive Matthew his deceit and method of revenge."

"And you encourage their behavior?" he demanded, outraged that the children should so despise his son.

"Indeed, I do not. But it changes nothing in the way they feel. Children understand justice, and they know that Diego did not receive it."

"You are impertinent!" Hayes said with a whitening around his mouth.

I did not speak for a minute. "I understand that you did not have all the facts," I said slowly, wanting only to accomplish my goal and not further antagonize these two men.

"I have the facts. My son gave them to me."

"I suggest you speak with him about the incident again," I said and then looked at Olmstead. "You should speak with your son as well, Mr. Olmstead. He witnessed the incident as did Margaret Hudson, Sherman Poole and Toby Carmichael."

James Olmstead looked uncertain for the first time. Reverend Hayes's expression remained unchanged. I began to suspect that there was more than his son's bloodied nose behind his dislike of Diego Gutierrez. I was afraid I knew what it was, and it would be very difficult to fight.

"Whatever happened that day, the boy doesn't belong in our town's school. He shouldn't be allowed to mix with good children," Reverend Hayes began.

James Olmstead looked at Hayes with an admiration I found impossible to understand.

"Would you please explain?"

"I shouldn't think that would be necessary," Hayes sniffed.

"I'm afraid it is!"

"The boy is Mexican, and he is born out of wedlock. He does not belong with decent people."

I was shaking and hoped it did not show. "You deny the boy his rights because of two things over which he has no control?"

"That boy has no rights as I see it, Miss McFarland. And I won't allow him to be reinstated into the school so that he can further blight our good children with the sin of his birth."

I stared speechlessly at Hayes, the anger blooming inside me until I trembled with it. "Your Christian understanding shows no bounds, does it?" I managed, but my sarcasm eluded him.

"I'm glad you finally understand our position, and agree," he said, obviously satisfied with the conversation's outcome. My mouth dropped open and then clamped shut.

"You completely misunderstand me, Reverend Hayes," I said through my teeth. "I meant that you and Mr. Olmstead here are—"

"I told you once before that Diego was no concern of yours, Miss McFarland," interrupted a harsh and all-too-familiar voice. I swung around and saw Jordan Bennett standing well inside the general store, legs astride and arms akimbo. I wondered how long he had been there and how much he had heard. I cast an accusing glare at Hayes and Olmstead, who were staring fixedly at the tall, broad-shouldered man dominating the room. I hoped Jordan had heard everything and would now do something about Diego's plight.

Jordan's blue eyes glittered dangerously, and I could feel the anger coiled inside him, ready to spring out. But he was not looking at James Olmstead nor at the Reverend Jonah Hayes. He was looking directly at me as if I were some despised rodent he'd just caught in a trap. I looked back at him, feeling confused and not just a little frightened by the intensity of his silent accusation. What was he accusing me of now? I wondered. I felt a tinge of irritation mingled into my emotional upheaval that the sight of him always caused.

"Why don't you carry on with your own business and leave Diego to me?" he asked in a voice that was not in the least polite. My eyes widened, and then I felt myself bristling like a hedgehog.

"I could do that, Mr. Bennett, if I knew that you planned to do something about this whole, unforgivable situation," I said in a scarcely controlled voice.

Something flickered in Jordan's eyes, but I was in no condition to analyze it, nor care if it meant repercussions later.

"Who do you think should take responsibility for Diego?" he asked in a quiet, hard voice.

"We all have a responsibility to Diego," I said adamantly, then felt the astonished stares of Olmstead and Hayes. I looked back at them, ignoring Jordan Bennett.

"What are you talking about now, Miss McFarland?" Hayes ejaculated with impatience, his loud, deep voice carrying throughout the store, and I was sure he would be heard outside in the street as well. My chin jerked up.

"You deny Diego Gutierrez his right to an education because of . . . because of personal prejudice. Every other child in this community is at the mercy of your arbitrary decision-making. What you deny Diego today, you could deny tomorrow to Toby Carmichael because he's a waif without parents, or Margaret Hudson because she's outspoken about her opinions, or Katrina Lane because her mother has to work in a hotel casino."

"There's no reason to suggest expulsion of Toby or Margaret. Both attend church regularly," Hayes assured me. "But you may have a point about Katrina Lane. I've been thinking about that girl and her mother lately."

Olmstead's gaze turned to Hayes, and he looked surprised. The lines in his forehead deepened as he was undoubtedly thinking about Ross Persall's hotel order going to Thompson permanently if Katrina were to be expelled.

I could not believe I had heard Hayes correctly. Jordan Bennett's strong fingers closed around my upper arm, and he turned me forcibly toward him. "However important you may think you are, your responsibility concerning the children starts when they walk into your classroom in the morning and ends when they walk out of it at the end of the day," he said in a low, harsh voice. His fingers bit into me when I started to protest. "Now will you get out and let me handle this, especially since you're so damned sure you know what's best for Diego!"

"But, I can't go . . ." I stammered, my mouth trembling under his vehemence. I thought of what the minister had just said concerning Katrina.

"You should have stayed in Boston. Damn it, woman! When are you going to learn to shut up and listen? Now get out of here! Unless you want to stay and make things worse!" He almost flung me toward the aisle leading to the front door. I had not the courage to defy him again.

Standing on the wooden sidewalk above the dirt street, I

controlled my inclination to burst into tears of anger, frustration and hurt. Jordan Bennett was at the center of my mangled feelings, though I knew the other two men were the ones at whom I should be angry. Hayes more than Olmstead, for I had not been mistaken in seeing Olmstead's recognition of the minister's bad judgment. Perhaps that was good, and he would begin to lean more my way if only for monetary reasons.

I rubbed my temples, feeling the onslaught of a torturous headache. I had wanted to help Diego, and had only succeeded in making matters worse by mentioning Katrina Lane. Surely that vile man who dared call himself a servant of God would not really expel Katrina. If he did, he would have to find Sycamore Hill another teacher, I resolved. Fear entered my consciousness as I thought of that possibility. What would I do if it came to that? I had no savings. Everything extra I had managed to extract from my teaching income had gone into buying books from an Eastern mail-order house. Where would I go to live? I knew I would have to vacate the schoolhouse.

That thought was not entirely unpleasant, for I had not enjoyed living in that place with its strange sounds and oddly chilling breezes that made me certain of a presence I did not want to acknowledge. For all my reasoning, for all my insistence that I was curious, I was afraid of whatever else lived in the schoolhouse. And whatever Ellen Greer said, there was something there. I could feel it.

It was well into late afternoon, and I knew I should return to my quarters. But I could not face them. I needed to walk, to get away from Sycamore Hill, to get away from the responsibility that lay so heavily on my shoulders.

Jordan Bennett was wrong. I had to feel responsibility for the children beyond the time they spent in the classroom. My job was not from nine in the morning to three in the afternoon. It was from the time I got up until I went to bed, and even beyond that when I dreamed of incidents that happened during the day.

My life was immersed in my occupation. Sometimes I felt smothered by it, as I did at this moment when things were going so badly. But I owed the children everything I could give them. What they learned from me would shape their lives.

Other things came into it, of course. I did not think myself omniscient, but they had a right to learn basic skills, and I had the right to teach them more if I thought it necessary.

One of the things I longed to expand was tolerance. There seemed to be so little of it, even within myself, as I could not bring myself to tolerate the Reverend Jonah Hayes.

An afternoon wind whipped my skirts back against my legs. I could feel the chill biting into me, but I did not stop my walk. The sycamore grove was up ahead of me, and I headed for it as though a haven. I remembered the conversation I had had with Ross Persall, and wished for his company again. He had made me forget what I was for a while. He had made me feel attractive and desirable. He was not like Jordan Bennett, who made me feel ridiculous, stupid and like a child.

On the way up the hill I passed the lonely grave where Ross had dropped the wild flower. I hesitated. The wooden cross was tilted sideways as the body beneath began to decompose and the soil caved in on it. Leaning down, I straightened the simple marker.

"Who are you?" I whispered. "And why are you here and not inside the cemetery?"

Only the cold wind responded. I stood up and continued up the hill, feeling very depressed. I sat for a long time beneath the sycamores, which were now almost denuded of their big, bright-yellow leaves. I thought of little but the beautiful land around me. I looked beyond the town at the rolling hills with their sentinel oaks and tried to think of nothing. When I finally got up to leave, it was well after dark, and the stars were out in multitudes above me. Below, lights shone in home windows where families were gathered to discuss the events of the day.

Never had I felt so lonely.

For just an instant I wondered where Jordan Bennett was, and I felt such painful longing that I wanted to cry. How could I be so attracted to a man who so frequently clashed with me? Then I thrust him from my mind. It was a futile gesture, as his image remained like an engraving.

Walking back by way of the hills along the edge of town, I listened to the night sounds. I wondered if I would hear the ghost tonight, and I prayed for one uninterrupted eight-hour rest. I rubbed my arms against the cold, but did not increase my pace. There was no hurry to reach the schoolhouse. I had set food out for Orphan before going to the store. My stomach growled, and I remembered that I had started out to buy some supplies. There was little in my larder, and none of it appealed to me at the moment.

As I came down the hill, I hesitated. I looked at the schoolhouse and tried to make myself feel that I was coming home. I could not. I lived there in that place, but it was not my home. It was somewhere to lay my head. I counted myself lucky that I had an occupation that filled me. I could satisfy my needs by living for the children. Wasn't that what Ellen had said? I smiled slightly. I would have to work so hard that I did not have energy to indulge in useless self-pity.

When I entered the back door of the building and walked into my room, I was surprised to see that the fire was still going in the stove. It was burning very low, but the embers shone red. I flicked open the grate and pushed in another log to last the night. It was a luxury I could ill afford, but I needed to feel warm, and a crackling fire always made me feel better no matter how depressed I was. There was something that answered a primeval need in the flickering flames. My mind became soothed as my body was warmed.

I walked to the door of the schoolroom. I stopped, reached out and then retracted my hand. I was unhappy enough without searching out something that would aid in giving me a sleepless night. But it drew me. Reaching out again, I turned the doorknob and pushed inward.

The schoolroom was empty. I felt nothing, and oddly, I was disappointed. The front window had been grudgingly repaired by Olmstead last week, and there was no breeze to raise the patchwork curtains the children had made. I hugged myself against the chill and stared down at the scrubbed floorboards, feeling even more dejected. Had *she* even gone away to leave me alone?

A faint noise drew my attention. I trembled slightly as I stared into the darkened corners searching for her. I saw nothing, but I knew I had heard something. I felt someone watching me.

"Are you there?" I whispered, surprised that my voice did not sound strained. "Please, come and talk to me."

A hand touched my shoulder.

A sharp gasp erupted from my throat, making a high sound of fright. I swung around so fast, I lost my balance and started to tumble over backward, when strong, masculine hands grabbed me.

For an instant I felt blackness closing around me. I was engulfed in waves of dizziness. I shut my eyes tightly. My breath was coming in fast, jerky gasps. My heart was thundering out of control.

"Who were you expecting?" demanded a hard voice. "Ross Persall?"

I opened my eyes and stared up at the intruder. "Jordan!" my voice rasped. The room was too dark to read the expression on his face, but he was standing rigidly in front of me, his hands still biting painfully into my shoulders.

"What are you doing here, Mr. Bennett?" I strived for some control. I fairly squeaked when I spoke. Though the fright had dissipated, other more unnerving emotions began to keep my breath and heart in rapid motion.

Jordan did not answer for a moment. I could feel his eyes boring into me, and his anger was growing to a hard tension that was almost tangible.

"Who were you expecting?" he repeated.

"No one."

I could hardly admit to him that I was looking for a ghost and asking it to speak to me. He would either laugh or think I had lost my mind. I could not bear another scene with this man. I just wanted him to go away and leave me in peace. So I took refuge in as much dignity as I could muster. Placing my hands firmly against his chest, I pushed back so that he freed me. Then I stepped back several paces more, though still facing him.

"I was not expecting anyone," I said with measured calm, "and certainly not you creeping around in the dead of night. What are you doing here, Mr. Bennett?" I asked again.

"I've been waiting for you," he answered tautly.

"Here?" I looked around the darkened schoolroom.

"No. In there." He jerked his head, indicating my quarters.

"You've been in my room?" I stammered, the thread of control unraveling. "For how long . . . and how did you get in there?"

"Since early this evening. And you left the back door open," he said dryly. "Almost as though you were expecting a visitor." His voice was insinuating and very unpleasant.

"There's never been any need to lock my door. But I will from now on, you can be sure of that!"

"Indeed?" he retorted mockingly. "Every night and against all comers?"

I frowned at him, wondering what was making him so upset. I could feel his anger crackling in the air.

"It's been a very long day," I said tremulously. "I'm tired."

"Where have you been, damn you?"

If I thought of telling him to mind his own business, it passed so quickly from my mind, I did not realize it. His tone made anything but the truth a direct challenge. I did not know what he would do, and I did not want to find out.

"I walked up to the sycamore grove."

"You've been up on that hill for six hours?" he asked. He quite obviously did not believe me. "Who have you been with?"

"I have not been with anyone. And what business is it of yours anyway?" I cried, the bravado rising. I felt as cornered and desperate as any animal in the woods stalked by a hunter.

Some of the tension seemed to drain from Jordan. "It's damn cold in here," he observed in a quieter, more controlled voice. "Let's go back to your room and have our talk."

"I would like to go back to my room. But not with you. And I'm not in the mood to talk with you either!"

He took a couple of steps toward me and grasped my wrist. Pulling me after him, he entered my room and shut the door behind us. Releasing me, he leaned back against it, his arms crossed. The candlelight showed the hard, uncompromising set of his face and the glitter of his blue eyes.

"Sit down, Miss McFarland!" he ordered in a cold voice. I sat. A humorless smile tilted his mouth. "Now, was that so damned difficult?"

I was shaking, and efforts to stop it were to no avail.

"If you're trying to frighten me, you're doing an excellent job of it," I said, only afterward wondering at the wisdom of such an admission.

"You're frightened? Miss McFarland, you don't frighten easily enough!" he told me. "Someone should take you in hand, Abby," he said more calmly now that he had gotten his way.

I did not try to argue with him. I sat in the chair by the table staring at him fixedly. My expression seemed to bother him. Jordan frowned and let out his breath. "Stop looking at me like that! I'm not going to hurt you, for God's sake!"

Too much had happened that day, and I was perilously close to losing control and crying. I looked away from him and blinked rapidly. My fingers twisted together in a knot on my lap, and I swallowed convulsively. I am not going to cry in front of this dreadful man, I told myself fiercely.

"Diego is reinstated. He'll be back in school Monday morning," Jordan said tiredly. He was rubbing the back of his neck as though it ached. He did not look at me as my eyes swung back to him with that announcement.

"Oh!" My fingers loosened their death grip on each other. "But how did you ever manage?"

"After you almost made a complete mess of the whole thing?" he finished wryly. "Hayes is at the mercy of pressures himself. And you needn't worry about Katrina Lane. I don't think he'll be doing anything to her."

"Oh, thank God," I sighed in relief. "I was so afraid he was serious about removing her as well as not allowing Diego to come back."

"He was."

"I just don't understand that man!"

"Obviously not, or you would have handled the situation a damned sight better than you did." The irritation was back in his voice. He moved away from the door. There was no place for him to sit except on my bed. Jordan Bennett stepped away from that restlessly and began to finger my possessions. He touched my brush and comb set lying on top of the old dresser. He picked up a chipped cup and set it back on the shelf, glancing over the cabinet with its meager boasting of supplies. Then he picked up a book and read the title.

"You go in for heavy reading," he commented, opening the new volume of Greek plays Bradford Dobson had sent.

"How did you get Reverend Hayes to reinstate Diego?" I asked curiously.

"I have my methods of dealing with people like him," Jordan said in a cool voice. He was reading the inscription Bradford Dobson had written on the inside cover: "'With much admiration and wishes that this will supply you with hours of cathartic enjoyment. Your servant always, Bradford Dobson.'" Jordan was frowning. "Who's Bradford Dobson?"

"He was solicitor to my late guardians."

"Young or old?"

"What possible difference could that make to you?" I asked in confusion.

"None." He snapped the book shut and dropped it on the bed.

"I liked Mr. Dobson very much. He was very kind. In fact, he was the one who helped me find this position."

"You call that kind?" Jordan gave a harsh laugh.

"I had to find some way to make a living."

Jordan looked at me. "Why didn't you just marry some poor fool? That's what most women do, isn't it?"

"I can't speak for most women, Mr. Bennett, but for myself, I could not marry just to have a roof over my head or food on the table."

"There are men who could supply you with more than just room and board," he commented idly. "You could have beautiful clothes, jewelry, whatever you wanted . . . under certain circumstances."

"And for what price?" I asked dryly, thinking about the loss of self-respect. Then I wondered what I would say if Jordan Bennett were to propose such a marriage arrangement to me. But, of course, he was speaking generally, not specifically. It's always easy to be objective when your own emotions aren't involved.

"You know very well at what price, Abby. You aren't that naïve." He looked at me with such an intimate scrutiny that I could scarcely misunderstand his meaning. I wondered if he was deliberately trying to embarrass me. If he was, I was not going to give him the satisfaction of knowing he had indeed succeeded. I was stonily silent and kept my expression blank.

"Well?" he drawled. "What would you say to such a proposal, if any man were tempted to offer you one, that is?" He made the possibility seem very remote and made me feel like the least attractive woman in the world.

"A woman who accepted such a proposal would be little more than a prostitute," I answered in a flat tone of indifference.

He raised his brows derisively. "Harsh judgment for the majority of womankind."

"You're very cynical. Could it have anything to do with your own personal experience?" My question was rhetorical, but I could hardly believe I had mouthed it at all. I prepared myself for a storm.

Jordan Bennett's eyes narrowed to slits. "How very incautious you can be," he said in a low voice, a tilt to his mouth. "But you are right. My wife was little more than a whore, but what she lacked in genuine emotion, she well made up for in skill."

A pain started in the pit of my stomach and spread through my system at the thought of Jordan with his wife. I kept my face bland. He watched me closely, almost as though he was assessing the effect of his words.

I stood up. "You've told me about Diego. Thank you."

He smiled sardonically. "You're welcome."

"It's very late," I said with a lift of my brows. I looked pointedly toward the back door.

Jordan grinned. "Trying to get rid of me?"

"Quite frankly, yes!" I answered bluntly. "Now please leave. You know the rules."

"The rules be damned. You don't care about them, and neither do I," he dismissed my reason.

"I do care! I don't want to lose my position here."

"You enjoy being alone so much?" His smile was taunting.

"Have you said all you intended to say, Mr. Bennett?" I fumed. "If you have, please leave my room!"

Jordan rubbed the back of his neck again and cast me a disgruntled look. "Believe it or not, I came to thank you for the time you've spent with Diego. If you hadn't stayed out half the night, I wouldn't be here now. I'd be back at the ranch and in bed instead of standing here arguing with you!"

"You could have let the news wait until tomorrow," I snapped back. "You knew that I would be riding out for Diego's regular lessons."

"I thought I'd save you the ride," he retaliated with some sarcasm. "I never wanted you on my ranch in the first place, if you'll remember."

A lump of pain caught in my throat, and I swallowed hard. "Yes, I remember." I paused and ran my fingers nervously over the table, keeping my eyes averted from his. "And I'm sorry."

"There are a couple of other things I wanted to say before I leave." If anything, his voice sounded harder than before. I wanted to tell him to please say them quickly and make his departure, but thought it best to say nothing at all. He had paused for an instant as though expecting some comment, and when none came, he shifted his weight.

"Can we sit down and talk like civilized people?" he asked in a tone hardly conducive to peace making.

"We can try." I smiled faintly. I sat down at the table again. Then I looked up at him. He was watching me with an enigmatic expression. Then he glanced around for another chair. Seeing none, he sat on my bed. He leaned forward, clasping his hands between his knees.

"First off, I wanted to tell you to deal very carefully with Hayes. He's an . . . intense person and not very predictable."

"I could say that about other people in the community," I said with wry humor.

He glanced up and gave me a rueful smile. "You fit that description yourself, Miss McFarland," he said dryly.

"I didn't have myself in mind."

"And another thing," he said briskly, looking directly into my eyes with unnerving intensity. "I'm not sure Diego will show up on Monday."

"You plan to keep him home at the ranch?" I asked in surprise, my fingers splaying out on the tabletop.

"No, I am not planning to keep him at the ranch," he said. "You're jumping to all the wrong conclusions again."

"Then why?"

"Because he was hurt by all this mess . . . damned hurt. He may not agree to come back to school. I'd think you would understand why he wouldn't be particularly crazy about the idea of returning for more of the same medicine."

"It won't happen again."

"You don't know that for sure."

"The mess was brought on by adult interference," I told him. "And since you've taken care of that part of it, Diego will only have to contend with the children. One, actually— Matthew Hayes. And believe me, Mr. Bennett, that boy is more than willing to come halfway. He's learned his lesson."

Jordan shook his head slightly. "We'll see, won't we?"

"Diego has more courage than you give him credit," I said rather primly.

Jordan smiled. "You think I'm maligning my own son, is that it?"

"No. I think you're being overprotective."

Jordan laughed. "Not too long ago you were saying I did not protect him enough."

"Yes." I nodded, watching the change in his appearance. He was magnetic when he laughed. He heightened all my senses.

"The boy needed time to lick his wounds," Jordan explained. "And Matthew Hayes needed time to learn a few things as well. Maybe the two of them can sort things out between them. That would be the ideal solution."

"I agree."

Then came a momentary silence before Jordan muttered under his breath. "My God."

"What's the matter?"

"You agreed with me." He grinned.

I smiled, genuinely amused. "A precedent!"

Jordan's grin softened. I wanted to look away from him, afraid he would see more in my eyes than I was willing to have him see. He suddenly seemed too close to me, the room too small and intimate for his dominating presence. His eyes were charting courses over my face, lingering too long on my mouth. My lips parted slightly as my breath seemed to lodge in my chest, unable to pass the thundering of my heart.

Jordan stood up as though he could not stand to be still any longer. He looked away from me toward the door. A muscle worked in his jaw. "I'd better be going," he said unnecessarily. That he wanted to leave quickly was obvious, and strangely enough, it hurt.

I stood up as well, smiling with an effort. "I'm glad you came to talk with me," I said sincerely. Jordan looked at me then.

"I'm not sure I am," he said. Embarrassed color flooded into my face.

"I'm sorry you feel that way, and I won't detain you any longer. Please tell Diego I will look forward to seeing him on Monday."

Jordan stepped by me and put his hand on the door, but did not open it. He seemed to be debating with himself. I couldn't stand it.

"So, what are you waiting for?" I demanded, stepping forward, my hands balling into fists. "Why don't you leave?"

He looked down at me, and the expression in his eyes drove me further into my anger. I reached out, shoving his hand aside and grasping at the doorknob to pull it open. "Here, let me help you, Mr. Bennett!" I twisted the handle and pulled, but Jordan's hand came up to hold the door shut.

"Don't push me too far, Abby!"

"Just leave! You were so eager to go a minute ago. Well, go on and leave!"

"Oh, hell!" he muttered fiercely below his breath.

Then Jordan's hands descended on my shoulders, turning me full against him. I looked up in alarm as he pressed me back against the door. His body held me still as his mouth came down to cover mine. I struggled to be free, but he took advantage of my movements to mold us even closer together. I tried to cry out, but he only used that advantage to deepen his kiss, to invade my mouth with his tongue. Then I did not want to be free.

Sensual madness invaded my mind and body so that I wanted to be closer to Jordan's warmth. I wanted to open his wool shirt and feel the texture of his skin beneath my fingers. I wanted to press myself against the hardening muscles and be encompassed by his strength. I pushed his jacket back to be nearer, and he impatiently shrugged out of it, letting it slide to the floor. His fingers came up and raked the pins from my hair. He was heedless of the shamble he was causing. Then he was kissing me again, his mouth moving from mine to plunder my ear and then trail down my neck. When he raised his head, a groan escaped. He started to step back away from me.

"Jordan . . ." I sighed. My hands came up almost of their own volition to encircle his neck and draw his head down again.

"My God!" he rasped, his hands pulling me forward again. My hips were grinding against his. Then he swore beneath his breath. He reached up and grabbed at my wrists.

"Let go, Abby!" he moaned. "For God's sake, let go of me before I finish what we've started."

He dragged my hands free and shoved me back. I stood shaking before him, but the emotion that raked me was not fear. He looked at my face, his own strained and hard, his eyes dilated to blackness.

"I made the mistake of entering your territory," he ground out with an effort. "I swore to myself I wouldn't, and by God, I won't again!" he told me intensely.

I stared at him dumbly for a moment before his rejection sank into my brain. Then the first cold tendrils of understanding crept in to make me feel shamed and dirty. How could I have allowed him to kiss me like that? And worse, why had I responded to the point that I did not care anything about my self-respect? I should have known he would look at me like some creature he did not want to recognize. What did he think of me now? That I responded to any man as I did to him?

Jordan reached out and tilted my chin up, forcing me to look at him squarely. I felt confused by the emotions that still raged inside me, frightened by his anger and hurt by his in-difference. Oh, dear God in heaven, what was happening to me? How could I have fallen in love with this man?

"You're ashamed already," he said, half-compassionately, half-derisively, his eyes glittering. "Be thankful I didn't take what you offered so magnanimously."

I shut my eyes against the look in his. He released me.

"Stay away from Eden Rock, Miss McFarland. That's my

territory. And if you ever come near it, we'll play by my rules then. The consequences and your sensitive Boston feelings be damned."

He snatched up his jacket and then walked out the door, slamming it behind him. I stood for a long time staring at nothing and feeling utterly miserable and humiliated. Then I undressed and went to bed.

Once during the night I awakened. I thought I heard something moving about in the schoolroom and bumping into a desk, making a scraping sound over the floor. But when I listened intently for more movement, I heard nothing. Exhausted, I fell back to sleep.

In the morning I found the note scrawled across the blackboard. "Go back to Boston." The words brought Jordan Bennett into my mind.

 *Chapter Fifteen*

Just as Jordan Bennett had warned, Diego Gutierrez did not return to school the following Monday morning. When he did not come Tuesday or Wednesday, I began to consider riding to Eden Rock to talk with him in spite of Jordan's dire warning to me. What could the man do to me? He had already done his worst from my viewpoint. He had made me recognize irrefutably that I was in love with him, while he held me in his contempt.

Thursday morning Diego returned to school. Linda walked in with a wide smile on her face, and I looked up to see Jordan in the doorway, his hand on Diego's stiff shoulder. There were other children already in class, and they jumped up to welcome Diego back. The wary expression on the boy's face began to dissolve, and after a moment he smiled.

My heart was doing acrobatics at the sight of Jordan, but after the first glimpse of his grim expression, I avoided his eyes. A faint flush crept into my cheeks, and my body felt cold with shame as I remembered our last meeting and his words before departing. What must he be thinking of me as he stood there watching Diego take his usual seat next to Linda at the back of the classroom? I was afraid to even contemplate it.

I was thankful that the children were so involved in chattering with Diego that they failed to see my embarrassed expression. I felt Jordan watching me, but refused to look at him again. After a moment he turned back and strode out of the room without a backward glance. My stomach muscles slowly relaxed.

For the rest of the week things settled back to normal. Jordan rode in with the children now that the rainy season was well underway and the journey was sometimes hazardous. He never lingered after seeing the two children inside the door. I sank everything into my teaching, classroom preparation and cleaning of the schoolhouse. I worked until I was too tired to dream or even be frightened by whatever else lived in the schoolhouse with me.

I worried a great deal about Matthew Hayes. He regretted his actions against Diego, primarily because the children despised him for it. Even after Diego returned, Matt was treated to jibes and taunts. He was ostracized from the yard play. His schoolmates even shunned him in class. Whenever there were teams to draw up, Matt was last to be included. His grades fell, and he never raised his hand to answer class questions. When I called on him, he just stared at his hands and said nothing. I caught the looks cast in his direction and saw the tortured look in his eyes.

A few days after Diego's return to class I found Matt sitting hunched over on the front steps of the schoolhouse. All the children were around back, playing beneath the cloud-strewn late-fall sky. I came down the steps and sat down next to the miserable boy.

"Matt," I said softly and saw how he drew inside his shell. He looked away as I leaned forward, but not before I saw his chin trembling and his eyes filling with tears. This wouldn't do at all, I thought unhappily. I moved closer and put my arm around the boy's rigid shoulders. As I began to talk with him, he gradually relaxed until finally the hurt poured out in shuddering sobs.

"But . . . but they hate me, Miss McFarland," he cried. "They won't have anything to do with me." He leaned forward so that his face was hidden against his knees. I hugged him closer.

I whispered that things would work out if given time. Everyone does something that they regret, but they can't allow it to ruin their lives. He had learned from what had happened, and he would be a better, stronger person for it. I wasn't just speaking to Matt Hayes; I was remembering my own transgressions with Jordan Bennett.

Matt mumbled that none of the children would ever talk to him because of Diego. He knew it was his fault, but he wanted to change things so that he would have some friends again. I suggested he talk with Diego.

"He'll never speak to me," Matt said assuredly, looking up at me. He was frightened by the very idea.

"You owe him an apology, Matthew. If you started with that, perhaps the two of you could sort things out. You both have a lot in common."

"My father says . . ." he started, but I patted his hand, knowing by his expression what his father had said.

"Never mind what your father said," I dared. "You have to make your own decisions about people, Matt. You talk with Diego."

"He won't listen, Miss McFarland." He shook his head, his shoulders sagging.

"You have to have the courage to try, Matt. If that doesn't work, we'll figure something else out to get you back in good stead with the children."

Matthew looked up at me uncertainly. "I didn't think you liked me."

I frowned and wondered how much my personal feelings had influenced the boy's depression. He was right when he said I had not liked him after what he had done. I had found his behavior despicable. Since then, however, he had changed, and I had watched with respect and sympathy as he had tried to make amends. The boy deserved a second chance. Didn't everyone?

"I didn't like what you did, Matt. There's a difference between that and not liking you," I told him gently.

Over the next few days I watched painfully as Matthew Hayes tried to muster courage to speak to Diego. Each time he started out to approach the other boy, Diego's friends got

in the way. Not wanting there to be witnesses to his attempt
at peace making, Matthew always turned away. The week came
to an end, and nothing had been resolved.

With Monday I watched in great hope that Matthew would
be able to carry out his intentions. But his courage seemed to
have failed completely, and he stayed away from everyone,
sitting between the old oak while the other children played.
He watched with pale intentness. I was afraid if the two boys
did not work things out soon, Matthew's rightful regret would
change into renewed and bitter resentment.

Things had gone far enough, I decided. It was time I stepped
into the situation.

During the noontime break on Wednesday I decided that it
was time to get the two boys together. I called Matthew and
Diego into the classroom. The children all stopped playing and
watched the two boys enter the schoolroom. I saw some of
them approaching and told them to go back to their play. Reluctantly, they did so.

Inside the classroom Diego looked at Matthew with wary
dislike. Matthew was chewing nervously at his lower lip and
staring fixedly at his feet.

I took a deep breath. "I think it's time you two boys sat
down together and talked things over."

"We've got nothing to talk about," Diego said in a hard,
defensive voice. Matthew looked at me as though to say, "I
told you so." I frowned, hoping I looked sufficiently stern.

"I beg to differ, Diego. You two have a great deal to talk
about. And talk you shall. You are both to go back into that
corner," I indicated a corner reserved for quiet study, "where
you will not be disturbed, and you are to discuss what happened
here over six weeks ago. Is that clearly understood?"

The boys went, Diego grudgingly mumbling something under his breath in Spanish, and Matthew as though he were on
his way to the gallows. They sat for several moments in complete silence, looking everywhere but at one another. I sat at
my desk working on some papers and saying a silent prayer.
Then I heard the low mumble of Matt's voice. He was talking,
head down, looking at his hands. Diego was staring at the top
of the boy's head.

And then Diego was talking. I decided I should leave the

boys alone now that they had started speaking to one another. Checking on the children in the yard, I waited ten minutes before reentering the classroom. When I did, I found Diego sitting by himself in the back of the room.

"Where's Matthew?"

"Probably home crying to his papa." Diego sneered unpleasantly.

I sighed, wondering if I had made another grievous error in placing the two boys together. "All right. What happened, Diego?"

"We did what you told us to. We talked."

"Did Matthew apologize to you?"

"*Sí*. But you don't expect me to believe that gringo, do you?" His expression was hard.

"Matthew Hayes is very sorry, Diego."

"He's sorry because the other *niños* want nothing to do with *cabrón* who runs to papa whenever things don't go his way!"

"I don't think Matthew will do that again. He learned a lot from what happened, Diego. Did you?"

"Where is he now, then, Miss McFarland?" Diego demanded, standing up. He looked angry, but there was something else beneath it. He was afraid everything was starting again. "He's probably home crying to his father about what I said to him."

"And what did you say to him?" I asked, beginning to really doubt my methods. I started to wonder what the repercussions were going to be to both Diego and Matthew. Perhaps Jordan Bennett was right in his assessment of my abilities and my place.

"I told him his apology didn't mean anything to me. I didn't like him before, and I don't like him now. He's getting just what he deserves!"

I sighed heavily, feeling very disappointed with the outcome of my plan, and not knowing where to go from here. "I'm sorry you didn't believe Matthew, Diego. He has wanted to apologize since you came back, but was afraid you wouldn't believe him."

"Well, why should I?" Diego demanded, unconvinced and decidedly antagonistic.

"Please sit down." He obeyed, his mouth tight, his eyes

narrowed and shoulders rigid.

"When you go home tonight, I want you to think about something. Think long and hard." I paused. "I want you to think about anger, jealousy, prejudice and intolerance, in fact, all the things that you can think of that make this world of ours a difficult and sometimes impossible place in which to live. I want you to think hard about your feelings concerning Matthew and why you feel that way."

"I know what I feel about Hayes. And I know why," Diego said caustically. I gave him a stern look.

"May I finish?"

Diego looked shamefaced.

"Now, when you finish thinking about those things, I want you to pretend you are Matthew Hayes." Diego's expression was sullen. I continued doggedly. "I want you to think about every aspect of his life. When you're finished with that, write it all down on paper and give it to me."

Diego let out an angry breath. "I don't see why I'm the one being punished. He started the fight, and I got expelled."

"He started it, yes. But he wants to finish it in the manner it should have been finished long ago, and you don't want to let him, do you? You want to hurt him more than he hurt you." I reached out and took Diego's hand. "You're not feeling anything any different than anyone else would feel under the same circumstances. But I happen to believe you're bigger than that."

"What do you mean?" Diego looked at me cautiously.

"It takes a very big man to forgive. It's easy to hold a grudge, Diego. But what does it accomplish, and who does it hurt most? You think about that too."

"It seems to me you're giving me a lot to think about," he said with a rueful smile. I smiled back at him.

"A very lot," I agreed. "But no less than I will ask of Matt."

"Matthew's father probably won't let him come back to school," Diego announced glumly, still sure of his assessment of Matthew's intentions.

I shook my head. "Let's give Matt a chance to prove himself, shall we?"

"I'm not sure I want to come back to school tomorrow just so I can get kicked out again."

"Oh, Diego. I think you've a little more courage than that,

haven't you?" I told him solemnly. I squeezed his hand. "You give me the written part of your assignment when you feel you've thought everything over enough. All right?"

"*Sí.*" He nodded.

I found Matthew sitting outside on the front steps. His knees were drawn up, his head hidden in his arms. I talked with him about much the same thing as I had with Diego, and I repeated my assignment. He agreed more readily than Diego, wanting desperately to do anything in order to rejoin his peers.

When Diego saw Matthew sitting in his usual place minutes later, he looked surprised and then relieved. The rest of the children cast curious looks between the two boys, and several times I had to reprimand a couple of them for trying to speak to the two boys about what had happened during the lunch hour. Margaret was finally assigned extra work for continuing to draw Diego into conversation, and Luke and Mark were given spelling words to write to keep them occupied. Otherwise, the rest of the afternoon passed without incident.

However, the following morning Matthew's father stormed into the schoolroom before any of the children had arrived. His face was livid, and his voice boomed out in its usual bullying fashion. "Just what are you trying to do now, Miss McFarland?" he demanded in a raging voice. "Luke told me this morning that you had Matt in here talking with that other boy yesterday."

"The boys needed time to talk things over," I started to explain, but Reverend Hayes was in no mood to listen.

"I don't want my boy having anything to do with that . . . illegitimate son of a Mexican charwoman! It's bad enough that I had to reinstate him, but I'll not have that son of Cain mixing with my own son!" He stormed on and on until my head began to throb. Then he strode out of the schoolhouse without allowing me the opportunity to state my own opinions.

Shortly after the scene with Jonah Hayes, Diego and Linda arrived. Diego handed me a note from Reva, and I read it with a feeling of dismal resignation. I was slightly relieved to find that she understood what I was trying to do and condoned it only if I could see that Diego was not put in any kind of position to be hurt.

Several days after I had spoken with both boys, I saw Mat-

thew approach Diego in the schoolyard. The children stopped
to watch, some curious, some hoping for a renewed battle.
Diego looked around him at the faces of the children and then
at Matthew. He said something to the boy in a low voice.
Matthew held out his hand. I held my breath, waiting. Slowly,
Diego held his out in acceptance. I felt an overwhelming pride
in the two boys then, and my eyes filled with thankful tears.
They would never be close friends perhaps, but at least they
had learned something about one another, and about life.

Just before Thanksgiving I intended to make a personal visit
to each family to discuss the progress of their children. I made
voluminous notes and planned out what I must say to each
parent.

The first conferences went exceedingly well. I had dreaded
the visit to Reverend Hayes, but was surprised when he treated
me with restraint. Not once did he raise his voice to me, though
I could see how much he wanted to.

I did not know what to do about my conference with Reva
concerning Diego, and especially my most dreaded conference
with Jordan about Linda. I remembered only too well how he
told me to stay clear of Eden Rock, but surely he would not
quarrel with my intentions of discussing his daughter's progress
in school? Then I struck upon a possible solution to my dilemma.

In the prim note to Jordan I asked him to come to the
schoolhouse for our parent-teacher conference. I suggested he
bring Reva Gutierrez with him so that I could talk with her
about Diego. That way, I said also, they would save one trip
to town. However, the following morning Linda brought a
sealed envelope from her father. As I tore it open with shaking
fingers, my heart was racing. I don't know what I had expected,
but it was not what I read. Jordan's handwriting was a strong,
dark scrawl. One word was written in the center of the sheet
of white Eden Rock stationery: "Coward!"

"Daddy said that he would be glad to see you at Eden Rock
Saturday morning, Miss McFarland," Linda informed me, the
tone of the words an indication that she was parroting her father.
Then she looked closely at me. "Are you feeling all right,

ma'am? Your face is a funny red color."

"I'm fine. Just fine," I said and gave her a quick reassuring smile. I sometimes wished I had never met Jordan Bennett.

When I awoke on the Saturday before Thanksgiving, I found a clear sky. It was the first in days, and I thought it ironic that it should fall on the one day I would have to waste sparring with Jordan Bennett.

By seven o'clock I was astride a horse and on my way to the ranch. When I reached Eden Rock, just past nine, Reva was waiting. She informed me immediately that Jordan had ridden off early on some ranch business. He had not said how long he would be gone, but she expected him back because he had mentioned my visit the previous evening. I fumed silently, sure that he had disappeared deliberately to irritate me and delay my departure.

Reva and I talked over coffee. There was not a great deal to cover, since I had been tutoring Diego only weeks before, and Reva knew his progress. Gradually, I relaxed and forgot that I was in the one place that Jordan had warned me to avoid at all costs. I reasoned that I had no worries since he had relayed his welcome via Linda.

Diego and Linda traipsed into the kitchen near noon, looking for something to eat. When they said they had not seen Jordan, Reva decided not to hold lunch until his return. She ladled out four bowls of beef-and-vegetable soup, and cut slices of freshly baked bread. There was churned butter and the special treat of quince jelly. Nothing had tasted as good to me in a long time.

"I'm pleased to see how much you enjoy your food," Reva chuckled as she watched me down my last bite of bread. I flushed slightly.

"How could I do anything else when you're such a fine cook," I said sincerely.

"I imagine you are a very fine cook yourself, *señorita*." She smiled and I shook my head.

"What skills I did possess I've forgotten since I started teaching. I'm afraid there isn't time."

"Then what do you eat?"

"Don't look so concerned." I laughed. "I'm far from starving."

"What will you do for Thanksgiving?" she asked.

"Why don't you come here for Thanksgiving?" Linda enthused, but I shook my head.

"No, thank you, Linda. That's very nice of you to ask, but I . . . I have other plans," I lied. The thought of spending Thanksgiving on Eden Rock under Jordan's baleful eye was unthinkable. I looked at Reva and, remembering her relationship with him, felt suddenly desolate.

"I think I'd better be going," I said, standing up. "Thank you very much for the splendid meal, Reva."

"You mustn't leave," she said in alarm. "Jordan will return at any moment. You haven't had your conference with him."

"I'm afraid I can't wait any longer," I apologized. "I've stayed much too long already. I've very much enjoyed our visit. Perhaps Mr. Bennett could ride into town early next week, and I could talk with him then."

"Yes, I suppose that would be fine," Reva said with a nod. "He's been riding into town much more often then he used to. He used to go in only when he had to do so. Now he seems to go one or two times a week. Sometimes more often." She was looking at me intently.

Probably to spend time drinking at the casino, as I had seen him that one night more than a month ago, I thought.

The minute I rode past the front gate of the ranch, I felt immeasurably relieved. I did not look back, afraid I might see Jordan riding in, and I would have no choice but to go back and talk with him. I had told Reva that I enjoyed the visit. It was partially true. When I was able to force out of my mind her possible relationship with Jordan, I could like her very much. Then a picture of her in his arms would surge unbidden into my mind, and I would feel sick with envy.

The less I thought about Jordan Bennett, the better my piece of mind. I did not need to fuel the fire that burned in my mind and body. I wanted to extinguish it forever, to feel nothing for that man but the same indifference he felt for me. People said he had murdered his wife. People believed that Diego was his illegitimate son. But everything was forgotten the moment he had taken me in his arms. I had thought of nothing when he had kissed me. I had reveled in him when his hands had moved on my body. Only sense and realization had come later when he had been the one to stop what he himself had started. I would not have had the strength of mind to have done so. I wondered if that was what hurt the most.

The sun was high, and this was a precious Indian-summer day. It was not a day to depress myself with thoughts about Jordan Bennett. My afternoon was virtually free. I did have schoolwork to do, but nothing that I could not do this evening or tomorrow afternoon following church. I could ride for as long as I wished, or as long as this horse was willing.

So I turned west and rode along the foothills. I began to feel warm and pushed my bonnet back to bounce against my shoulder blades. The river was nearby, and I turned northeast toward it. When I reached the riverbank, I let the horse walk along at a clopping slow pace as I looked at the water shimmering with the sunlight. It meandered along below the hills heading north. I had followed it for some time when I saw an idyllic place for a private swim.

Just below me was a stretch of sand and a deep pool beneath an overhang of willow and alder trees. They were almost nude of their leaves, exposing the river that would be completely hidden in the spring. I gazed at the spot, thinking that I would come back here in May and take advantage of this place for a cool bath.

I needed to stretch my legs; so I rode down the incline to the highest alder. There I tied the horse up. I walked the last several yards to the riverbank. I hunkered down, sifting my fingers through the golden leaves, then grasping some. I tossed them like a pagan offering on the water and watched as they caught in the sluggish current.

A mischievous smile tugged at my lips as I wondered what James Olmstead and the goodly Reverend Hayes would think if they knew what I was planning for springtime relaxation. Then a surge of defiance hit me.

It had been several months since I had had a real bath. I had used my three-bucket washing method, which was far from pleasant, although functional. I looked at the pool and thought how wonderful it would be to really submerge myself in fresh, clean water.

Why shouldn't I do something wild just once? Debating with myself, I looked down longingly at that deep pool of clean water. Then I made up my mind.

Casting several wary glances around, I began to disrobe hurriedly. In only a moment I was undressed completely. And without further hesitation I stepped into the chilly water. Initially, I only went into the water up to my thighs, then I submerged my body up to my neck. I thought about wetting my hair and wavered. Then, with a laugh, I pulled the pins from my severe bun and let my hair cascade down into the water. I leaned back until it was wet to the scalp, then began a leisurely backstroke around the pool.

My body became used to the cool water. I relaxed and sat back on my heels so that the water near the bank was up to my chin. I closed my eyes and listened to the birds. I had been in the pool almost ten minutes when I heard a horse whinny from somewhere up the hill. A shock of alarm and panic went through me as I jerked around and looked up.

There was no one up there but my horse. I thought briefly of some passerby seeing me in the pool. I laughed at the thought. What would the people in town say if they heard of their prim schoolmarm bathing naked in the river? I envisioned Reverend Hayes's outraged, horrified expression, and I laughed again. Yet, I decided that it was time to get out, dry off and get back into my clothes before just such a possibility arose. The reality would not be amusing at all.

Once back in my brown skirt and high-necked starched white blouse, I wondered what to do about my hair. I sat down and used my fingers to spread it out over my shoulders. Its weight soaked my blouse, but as I kept pushing my fingers through it, the heat from the sun dried it until it glistened like copper.

Looking up, I judged it to be near three o'clock from the position of the sun. I reached up and felt my hair again. It was not quite dry, but it would have to do. Raking my fingers through it, I gathered it tightly at the nape of my neck and twisted it back into its customary style. I set the long pins in to hold it securely. I brushed my skirt free of sand and leaves as I stood, and then I started back up the hill, where my horse was still munching contentedly at some grass.

I felt like walking for a while; so I took the reins and led the horse up the hill. When I reached the top, I started to mount. Then I heard someone give a cough, as though wanting to make his presence known while not alarming me. I looked behind me, but saw no one. I pressed my hand against the horse, and it stepped aside as I glanced under its neck.

Jordan Bennett was leaning against an oak, a blade of grass between his teeth. He was grinning.

A flash of surprise coursed through me, and at the same time I thanked God he had not been there an hour before. I turned to look down the hill. From where he stood, he had a perfect vantage point of the pool, while remaining concealed from below. I looked at him again, and something in his laughing eyes made me feel suddenly very shaky and unsure of myself.

"How . . . how long have you been there?" I asked faintly. He pushed away from the tree and walked toward me. When he was standing just in front of me, he removed the straw from his mouth and flicked it to the ground.

"You have a small birthmark about five inches above your right knee. Rather nicely positioned on the inside of your thigh," he answered, the grin widening wickedly. I felt the blood leave my face and then surge back until my cheeks were on fire. The whinny had not come from my horse, I thought too late. I looked away from Jordan and saw his stallion tied a short distance away, also well out of sight of the pool.

Damn him! I thought furiously. Damn him all to hell! "You're even more a rogue than I thought!" I cried.

"Is that possible?" He laughed, enjoying my discomfort.

"If you had any decency in you at all, you would have gone away. And what are you doing here anyway? I'm not anywhere near your precious ranch!" I spoke wildly.

"You are on my ranch, Miss McFarland," he told me. There was a certain glint in his eyes that warned me of consequences to come. It brought back all the feelings he had aroused that night in my room.

"I am not," I insisted shakily.

"You have the typical female sense of direction." He laughed again. "You're a full mile inside Eden Rock boundaries." I stared up at him, dubious. He raised his hand and pointed south.

"You see that line of low hills where the eucalyptus are? That's the start of my land."

"Well, I didn't know," I said, quietly defensive while wondering that mess I had gotten myself into now.

"Too bad," he said softly. "For you, that is."

"That still doesn't alter things," I replied, blinking fast as my mind started to whirl madly. Just what form would his threat take, I wondered frantically. What was he possibly thinking to have that look back in his eyes? "You should have made yourself known earlier or, better still, ridden away!"

"I don't know a man alive who would ride away from the scene I just enjoyed," he answered. His eyes moved down, lingering on the rapid rise and fall of my breasts. He smiled.

"Any gentleman would have," I said fiercely. His eyes came back up to mine, and he laughed out loud.

"You think so? How very little you know about men, my dear Miss McFarland."

"Well, I'm not going to stand here arguing with you about it," I managed, turning quickly away to escape, but he moved quickly as well. He slapped my horse hard on the rump, sending him cantering off with a start.

"Why did you do that?" I gasped in dismay, staring at Jordan. Then I turned to look at my horse a distance away. I started to run after it, but Jordan's arm looped around my waist and lifted me off the ground. His mouth was next to my ear.

"Don't you remember what I told you about coming onto my territory?"

I tried desperately to pry his fingers loose. "Let . . . go of me . . . Mr. Bennett," I gasped, kicking and twisting.

"Not this time!"

My heart thudded. "The message you sent by way of Linda implied safe passage," I said quickly. "Now put me down!"

"Nothing doing." He laughed. "And I did offer you 'safe passage,' as you call it, to the ranch house for the purpose of discussing Linda's progress in school, not safe passage to wander around on my land and then bathe naked as a jaybird in my river."

"Then put me down, and we will talk about Linda," I pleaded, squirming. He set me on my feet again, and I hastily rearranged my clothing, stuffing my blouse back into my skirt. My face could not have been redder, nor my heart racing faster.

"Talk away," he said, crossing his arms. And I did. I talked out of desperation. I was relieved that he was listening!

"Why don't we sit down?" he suggested. "I don't know about you, but I'm getting hot standing out here in the sun."

Jordan indicated the shade beneath the big oak. He started toward it, and I had little choice but to follow. When he sat down, I hesitated. I could hardly stand above him like this and finish telling him about Linda's progress and educational needs. So I slowly sat down, eyeing him warily. He smiled slightly, his eyes mocking. Then he plucked another straw to chew on.

"You were saying that Linda has some difficulties in expressing herself," he prodded.

"She's very shy, except with Diego," I managed. Then I continued slowly, finally launching into some suggestions on how he could help her. He nodded. When I finished, I cast around for something more to say.

"Seems I've misjudged your teaching abilities," Jordan said casually. He had reclined on the grass, his head supported by his hand. "But I still think you're better suited for other things." His expression was unreadable. I was not sure what he meant by that cryptic statement; so I was not going to take either offense or pleasure in it.

"I enjoy teaching very much," I said frankly. He was studying me, and I shifted restlessly. "Well, that's all I have to say," I told him nervously. "Do you have any questions?"

"I've a lot of questions, Miss McFarland," he said wryly, a smile pulling up the corners of his mouth. My heart lurched.

"What did you want to know?" I asked.

"How is it you've never gotten married?"

My mouth tightened, and I started to get up. His hand caught my wrist, preventing me from rising.

"Well?"

"That's not the kind of question I meant!"

"You didn't qualify yourself." His thumb caressed the inside of my wrist. I pulled back, disturbed by the intimate touch. But his hold was unyielding though painless.

"I never met anyone I wanted to marry," I stammered. He

looked at me closely, his expression changing slightly.

"Did you have many suitors?" He was taunting me again.

"If you must know the truth, I didn't have any!" I was stung to admit. I pulled back again, but he retained an even firmer hold on my wrist. His eyes narrowed fractionally.

"You expect me to believe that?"

I tried to tell myself it did not matter what he thought about me. Then I knew it did matter. What Jordan thought of me mattered very much.

"It's true. I was hardly in a position to meet any men, and if I had, it wouldn't have mattered anyway."

He frowned, uncomprehending. "What do you mean?"

"My guardians, the Haversalls, were not my relations," I explained. "I was not in their social sphere. I did not mingle with their friends, and I never had the opportunity to make friends of my own."

"Why not?" He was still frowning.

I remembered the hours of work I had done for the Haversalls. The way I had answered their needs as charwoman, scullery maid and lady's hand servant. I thought also of the fact that the Haversalls had stolen my inheritance while making me more and more dependent on them. I remembered the gratitude Marcella Haversall had reminded me I owed them, and how guilty I had felt each time I had contemplated leaving them and making a life of my own elsewhere. I remembered the day in the parlor, talking with Bradford Dobson and learning the real state of affairs. My throat closed, and I averted my face from Jordan's.

"What are you thinking about, Abby?"

I shook my head. "It doesn't matter. It was a long time ago and best forgotten."

I was hardly aware that he had pushed himself into a sitting position until I felt his fingers taking the pins from my hair. My eyes widened, and before I could protest, he lowered his head and touched my lips with his in a soft kiss. I moved back away from him, my heart pounding like something wild fighting for freedom. He looked at me with that faintly mocking smile, his eyes very blue. Then he began to lower his head again.

"Don't . . ." I strained away, wanting to stand up, yet not wanting to.

"We're playing by my rules now. Remember?" he questioned softly, now pressing his mouth against the curve of my neck. I shuddered ecstatically. My eyes drooped closed, then opened wide again as his hand moved from my face to my breasts. I pushed it away.

"I'm not very good at parlor games, Mr. Bennett!" I reminded him tremulously. I pressed my hands against his chest. I wanted to escape. He set his weight against me so that I fell backward onto the grass.

"Nor am I, Miss McFarland," he agreed mockingly, smiling down from above me.

"Please, let me go." I twisted and started to kick out, but he put one leg over mine to still my struggles.

"Nothing you can say is going to stop me," he said frankly. "I'm going to do what I've wanted to since I first saw you walking along the road in the middle of August, carrying that ridiculous threadbare carpetbag of yours." He leaned down and kissed me then, and there was no gentleness in it, only a sensual demand he intended me to meet. When he raised his head, my mouth was trembling.

"Tears won't work with me, Abby," he murmured. "Especially when I know there's no reason for them."

I turned my head away as his lowered again. "You don't understand. . . ." He had rejected my love once before, leaving me feeling bereft and ashamed. And yet, I wanted him again even more than I had that first time in my room. I was afraid, so afraid of why he was doing this.

Jordan nuzzled my neck, nipping me slightly. "I understand that some things defy all the rules and reason in the world, like what we feel for each other," he was saying. "You won't admit it yet, but you want me as much as I want you. If I didn't know that, I wouldn't be here with you now." He pulled me full against him as he rolled sideways to relieve me of his weight.

"Now, kiss me back, damn you," he challenged softly, and because I really wanted to, I did.

What fears and reservations I had dissolved with Jordan's expert love-making. I cared about nothing except that he hold me, kiss me, possess me. My response was instinctive and irreversible, and I knew that he reveled in it, taking all that I was willing to give and demanding that which I was afraid at the last second to relinquish. I felt as though I belonged in Jordan's arms, and that whatever was in his past did not matter at all. What mattered was now and the ecstasy of giving myself to him completely, because I loved him.

It was only afterward that I realized how self-defeating one's mind can be, how we convince ourselves of fairy-tale endings and knights who are not dressed in tarnished armor.

Jordan said nothing after his possession. His hands continued to stroke my body as though exploring newly claimed territory. I lay silently beside him, my eyes closed, wanting desperately to hear him say he loved me. When he still said nothing, fear began to gnaw at me. Surely he must now know how much I loved him after what I had just given to him. But still he said nothing, and his hands stopped their caressing as he stared up at the sky above us. The warmth he had created with his ardent love-making cooled, and I felt a hard lump in my throat.

Pushing himself up, Jordan looked down at me, his eyes moving over my body in a sensual perusal that gave me an uneasy feeling deep in the pit of my stomach. He bent down and nibbled at my ear. Then he gave a throaty laugh, a sound of male triumph.

"You don't look like a Boston lady now, my dear Miss McFarland," he said sardonically. His hand moved from my face in a long caress down the length of my body to rest on my bare thigh. "In fact, you look anything but a lady."

A chill grew inside me until I thought I would die of it. He gave me a quick kiss before straightening again. He was saying something about the ranch, but my mind was still focused on his indictment of my behavior of moments before. Shakily, I sat up and reached out for my clothes.

I could feel Jordan watching me, looking over the body he had recently claimed like something he had bought for a bargain at a bawdyhouse.

"Don't dress yet, Abby. There's the whole afternoon."

I avoided his hand when he reached out to touch me. I wondered if I could even stand, I was shaking so hard. But I had to get away from him. He had only wanted to use me like some whore, and I had been fool enough to let him. There had been no love inside him when he had possessed my body, only a carnal need.

I stood up, frantically pulling on my clothes and fastening them with trembling fingers. I stuffed my blouse heedlessly into my skirt. Jordan was dressing leisurely, watching me with an expression of amusement. He pulled on his pants, clasping his belt buckle. I was so ashamed of what I had done that I wanted to die on the spot. Had I really allowed Jordan to make love to me here on the grass, right out in the open like some field animal? Tears blinded me. Jordan was pulling on one of his boots when I bolted toward the horse standing about a hundred yards away. Jordan caught me and swung me around to face him.

"What in hell is the matter with you now?" he demanded insensitively, staring at my tear-streaked face. I did not even stop to think what I was doing.

"I hate you!" I spat at him, pulling my arm back and lashing out at him, striking him hard across the face. His expression mirrored astonishment, and then a black rage. I saw his hand coming at me and did nothing to avoid it. I stumbled back from the blow, and my cheek burned like fire.

Yet, somehow his action was what I wanted. It relieved some of the emotional ravagement I felt, leaving me with a numbing shock and a physical pain I could hide behind.

Trembling violently, I put my hand up and touched my face. Jordan was staring at me, white-faced. He raked his fingers back through his hair, and I saw that his hand was shaking.

"If you hate me, you've a damned strange way of showing it." He was looking at me as though he detested me. "What you hate, my dear Miss McFarland, is your own precious self. Because you gave me everything without making conditions first," he hurled at me, his mouth twisting bitterly. I turned away and ran, unable to bear any further rejection and humiliation.

"Abby!"

I kept running. Reaching my horse, I swung myself up, my skirts hitching about my knees. I did not care.

"Abby!" Jordan shouted again, not moving from where he was. "So help me, God. If you run from me now, to hell with you!"

I kicked my heels hard into the horse's side, and, unaccustomed to such rude treatment, he lurched forward with a start. I wished he would gallop faster. Not once did I look back at Jordan Bennett standing in the open field above the river pool.

 *Chapter Sixteen*

"Abby, my dear, what's wrong with you today?" Ellen asked. "You haven't been listening to a word I've said for the past half-hour. Am I that dull in my dotage?"

"No, Ellen. I'm sorry," I apologized quickly. "I've just got a lot on my mind."

"Well, out with it, girl. It's obviously bothering you. You look as though you haven't slept a wink in weeks. Now, what's the matter?"

"There isn't anything the matter," I insisted. "Just . . . just a lot of school things I've got to do. You know, Christmas is coming up in less than three weeks. I'm supposed to have a program for the parents."

"Poppycock," Ellen grumbled. "That's not what's eating you, and don't try telling me it is. Now, I've asked you a question, and I want an answer."

"Well, you've had the only answer you're going to get!" I snapped with rudeness. Ellen's eyes widened.

"My, my, we're touchy today, aren't we?" She clucked her tongue. "Whatever this 'nothing' is, it's serious. I'd bet a dollar on it." She squinted her pale eyes at me. "It isn't that darned ghost business again, is it?"

I could lie and say it was. I had heard the woman crying on occasion, but I was too unhappy to care if there were a dozen ghosts inhabiting the old schoolhouse.

"I've had some problems with James Olmstead and Mr. Hayes," I said, hoping she would be satisfied with that. Actually, I had not had an argument with either of them in over a week, which was surprising.

"Yes. That wouldn't surprise me." She chuckled. "I heard about the scene at the general store a while back. My niece told me all about it, and she heard it all from Berthamae, naturally. That woman has a mouth as big as the Grand Canyon." She chuckled again. "I also heard that Jordan arrived at an opportune moment. The report had it that you were about to be hung by your thumbs."

The last person in the world I wanted to think or talk about was Jordan Bennett. I felt as though what had happened between us the week before was written clearly across my forehead. "This woman gave her body to Jordan Bennett without benefit of clergy!"

"Mr. Bennett didn't appreciate my 'interference,' as he so kindly called it," I told Ellen.

She was watching my face with her usual shrewdness. "Jordan's a sensitive man, and don't give me that look of yours, my girl. He is! He's probably still annoyed with you for thinking he fathered Diego."

"I don't imagine it matters what I think about Mr. Bennett," I told her stiffly and stood up. "I really must be going, Ellen. I've got . . . I've got a lot of school things to plan out for the next week or two. The holidays are coming, and we should give a program for the parents. And. . . ." I was rambling, searching for excuses, and I knew it. Worse, Ellen knew it. I gave a faint smile of apology and turned to leave.

"Abby . . ." Ellen called softly, and I looked back questioningly at her over my shoulder. "Abby, dear, whatever is bothering you . . . if you ever want to talk about it, I'm always here. And I hope you know that whatever you say to me will be kept in strictest confidence." Her tone was gentle and sympathetic. How much did this intelligent woman see?

"Yes, I know." I nodded, unable to say more. I turned away,

hoping she had not seen the tears. I shut the door quietly behind me and then leaned back against it. I loved Ellen Greer like a mother. I longed to put my head on her lap and cry out the whole dreadful story. But I was afraid that her affection for me would change to shocked disapproval.

Rubbing the tears away quickly, I told myself I had to get control. What was done was done, and I couldn't change anything. I had made a fool of myself, giving myself to a man who cared absolutely nothing for me. It had happened, and I couldn't alter that fact. It was best not to dwell on what had happened, not to relive the shame and hurt of his blunt assessment of me only minutes after making love.

Jordan had said I was no lady, and I had not been when I had given myself to him with such abandoned wantonness. I remembered his triumphant laugh and the way he had looked at my body, like something he owned. I should hate him. I should tear him from my mind. Yet, I only felt a longing for him that grew worse as the days passed. I couldn't stop thinking about him. Jordan had been right when he said I hated myself, not him. I wondered if other women felt this aching need for a man's possession.

Drawing a deep breath, I left the boardinghouse. I smiled at Margaret Hudson's mother as she called a greeting to me from the opposite side of the street. I paused to gaze in pretended interest at the new display in the milliner's window.

The bell on the door tinkled as someone started out.

"Good afternoon, Miss McFarland," Marba Lane said in her husky voice. I looked up from the lacy confection in the window and smiled warmly, very pleased to see her.

"Hello, Miss Lane." She was wearing a beautiful lilac dress, trimmed with ivory lace and pink ribbons. A glorious flowered hat crowned her elaborately dressed raven hair.

"What a lovely ensemble," I breathed candidly. "Are they Mrs. Apperson's creations?"

"Thank you." She smiled, well pleased with my reaction to her finery. "But, no, they're not Georgia's creations. I saw the designs in a French magazine and asked her to copy them for me."

"Well, you look very beautiful. Lilac suits you."

"Don't pay her such compliments, Miss McFarland. She'll get bigger-headed than she already is," came a teasing voice. Ross Persall walked out of the shop, just behind Marba.

"Good afternoon, Mr. Persall," I greeted.

"And to you, ma'am." He grinned, and there was a teasing light in his eyes at my formality.

"Katrina tells me that she has a part in the school play," Marba said, ignoring Ross's taunt. She seemed pleased and proud of the prospect.

"An angel, no less," Ross added dryly. Marba shot him an annoyed glance. She appeared to be very defensive of her daughter.

"Yes," I answered. "She's going to sing one of the carols. She has a charming voice."

"It's very kind of you to let her be in the play, Miss McFarland," Marba said gratefully, and I looked at her with some surprise.

"No, Miss Lane. It has nothing to do with kindness. Katrina is an intelligent child with a definite talent. I'm proud to have her in my class and very glad that she wants to be in the play."

Marba's face was very still and controlled. She smiled tightly. "Even if her mother happens to be a dance-hall entertainer?"

"I don't see how that should make any difference," I said, but understanding what she meant. "Besides," and I smiled, "I happen to like Katrina's mother very much. She's a very charming lady."

Marba's eyes grew bright. "It's no wonder Katrina thinks so highly of you," she said softly. "Come on, Ross." She looped her arm through his. "We'd better go before other less-open-minded people use this chance meeting against Miss McFarland."

A natural impulse made me reach out and touch Marba's gloved hand. "Miss Lane?" I redrew her attention. She hesitated. "It's more important what we think of ourselves."

"Not always," she answered, her dark eyes clouding.

Again, I reacted on impulse. "As soon as school is out and the confusion dies down, I'd be very pleased if you'd come for tea." Marba Lane looked astonished.

"I don't think . . . I don't think that's a wise idea," she said.

Ross Persall had an odd look on his face. He seemed totally unaware of Marba's fingers clutching at his arm. He was looking at me.

"I have a few people in this town I would call real friends, Miss Lane," I said, thinking of Ellen and Charles Studebaker, Elvira Hudson and Ross Persall. "I would like to include you among them."

Marba's mouth trembled slightly, then she smiled. "I'll remember that, Miss McFarland. Thank you. But because I like you, I won't accept your offer. Good day."

It was well past ten p.m., and my table was still strewn with the children's homework assignments. I had corrected most of them, but had got caught up in writing suggestions on a few. That lead me on to an idea for a class project, which I jotted down on a separate sheet and added to yet another pile of papers. Stopping, I got up, stretched my aching muscles and went to the stove to replenish my cup of coffee. I stood with a chipped mug in one hand, while the other rubbed mechanically at the small of my back. How I would appreciate a nice, soft chair for these long hours of paper-correcting, rather than the straight-backed wooden one someone had probably discarded years ago.

A tap at the back door startled me. I glanced questioningly at the closed portal, wondering if I had really heard something. Who would be coming by at this time of night? The three discreet taps sounded again.

Leaning against the door, I pressed my ear to the wood. "Who is it, please?" I asked, cautious not to unlock the door until I knew who was there. I had begun locking my door since finding Jordan Bennett in the schoolroom.

"Ross."

"Ross?" I repeated, then unlatched the door and swung it back in alarm. "Is something wrong with Katrina . . . or Marba?" I asked, immediately thinking that must be the reason for this unprecedented visit. I checked my pin watch. It was well after ten o'clock.

Ross stood, leaning his hand against the doorjamb, smiling down at me apologetically. "No." He shook his head. "I was out and saw your lamp was still burning. I thought if you weren't busy, we might talk for a while." He looked past me at the paper-strewn table. "I hope I didn't interrupt something important."

"I was correcting homework papers," I answered automatically, but frowning slightly. "What are you doing walking around at this late hour?"

"It isn't late by my standards. In fact, this is just about the busiest time of my day. But I felt restless tonight, and I didn't want to face the crowd at the casino. Look, Abigail, if this will get you into trouble, I'd better be on my way. I only figured I could stop at all because of the lights being out all the way up McPherson."

Ross Persall knew very well that if anyone were to pass by and see him on my doorstep, my teaching career would be finished. He seemed very sure that no one was about. I smiled and gave a faint laugh. "It will probably land me right in the fire pit, but I don't really care anymore. Come on in. It's cold out there."

Ross stepped into the light and looked around my small room with unveiled interest. He was wearing a heavy jacket, rather than his usual dark suit coat.

"Not much, is it?" he commented wryly.

"What a thing to say about my home," I teased in mock indignation. "It's quite adequate really. I don't need a lot of space for my work."

"They might have at least got you some new curtains and something besides that same old moth-eaten rag rug."

"Let me take your coat, unless this visit is going to be so short you needn't take it off."

He looked contrite. "I'm sorry." He removed his coat, but simply tossed it over onto my bed. "I'll get the other chair from the schoolroom," he said. When he returned, he set it up against the opposite side of the table. He crossed his arms and straddled the chair.

"Can you finish your work while we talk?" he asked, watching me make a quick check mark next to a wrong arithmetic sum.

I nodded. "I've only got a few more papers, Ross. And then I can give you my undivided attention," I teased.

"That's all I came for." He grinned and then watched me work over the sheets. "What you said to Marba today . . ." he said and then stopped.

"What about it?" I asked, not raising my head. I shoved the completed paper aside and picked up another.

"That was nice of you."

I glanced up with a frown. "I didn't say it to be nice. I said it because I meant it."

His mouth tilted up at one corner. "I've no doubt you did, Abigail."

"She doesn't have much of an opinion of herself, does she?" I said quietly.

"Marba has been through the mill more than once in her twenty-eight years," he said in a bland tone. "She's hardly going to think she's a grand lady."

"I've found her very warm-hearted," I said. He seemed amused.

"Yes. She's that," he said wryly, reaching into his pocket to pull out a long, slender cheroot. "Do you mind if I smoke?"

I shook my head, still watching his face with curiosity. Just what was this man's relationship with Marba Lane? And why did he speak of her so disparagingly. As he lit the cigar, he watched my face. His own expression was veiled by the curling smoke.

"What are you wondering about?" he asked after inhaling deeply and letting it out slowly. I shook my head, reverting my attention to the last papers needing correction.

"You know, there isn't anything you can't ask me, Abigail," Ross assured me softly. "If you're curious about my relationship with Marba, don't be. There was something between us for a while, but it's long since over."

I looked up and directly into his dark, compelling gaze. "I don't like the way you talk about her."

His brows moved up slightly. "How do you mean?"

"Critically."

"I like Marba. She's a fine woman." He drew another deep breath from the cheroot and let the smoke out with a slight tilt back of his head. The smell was not unpleasant. "I just don't happen to have any interest in her anymore."

I didn't say anything, and he smiled at me.

"On the other hand, I find you very interesting. You're educated, very attractive . . . and innocent."

I laughed. "I've been warned about you, Mr. Persall. So don't think you can woo me with words," I teased him. His gaze narrowed, but he still smiled.

"Who's been warning you? And what have they been saying?" he asked in a taunting voice.

"I won't give you my source, but I was told you were an expert when it came to lonely, frustrated women," I blurted out with my usual unthinking candor. Something flickered across his face. It was there and gone so fast that I couldn't define it. Then he grinned devilishly.

"Are you frustrated, Abigail?"

"The good Reverend Hayes and James Olmstead are enough to frustrate anyone," I said with a smile. Ross laughed deep in his throat, a pleasant, wholly amused sound. I wondered what I had said to give him such enjoyment.

"What a priceless piece of innocence you are." He chuckled. Then he noticed that the ash on his cigar was getting dangerously long. He glanced around. "Where's the little enamel ashtray?"

"What enamel ashtray?" I raised my brows, looking around. "I've never seen one."

He looked momentarily disconcerted, and then gave a laugh. "Doesn't everyone have an ashtray around?"

"Here, use this," I said, shoving a saucer across the table to him. He frowned, and then tapped the ash loose to fall into the dish. He didn't say anything as I finished correcting the last three papers. Ross Persall seemed very deep in his own thoughts.

When I finished my work, we talked about Sycamore Hill. He asked me questions about myself, and strangely, I didn't hesitate in answering. I told him a great deal about my life with the Haversalls, more than I had admitted to Ellen Greer, my closest friend. I only wondered briefly why it was so easy to talk to Ross Persall. Perhaps it was his eager interest or his quietly receptive manner. Perhaps it was simply the right time for me to talk. Whatever it was, I confided many of my feelings.

We did not spend the entire time talking about me however.

I asked many questions, and Ross told me much of his own poverty-stricken childhood in Louisiana. His family had once held a great deal of land and a beautiful plantation house. Much of the property had been confiscated after the Civil War and divided into small 40-acre plots for the slaves. Only a few years after that the land had fallen into the hands of Northern carpetbaggers. Ross's father had drunk and gambled away whatever money the family had left following the war.

"He had a taste for expensive French brandy," Ross said in a dry, bitter tone. Cleveland Persall had died drunk, leaving an ailing wife and one young son. Ross's mother died when he was 14. He hustled small jobs for nickels and dimes, doing anything he could find. He learned that he had his father's interest in gaming, but possessed a talent the deceased man had lacked. He developed his skill, made some connections in New Orleans and started as a dealer in a casino near the docks. From there, he became a manager with a small percentage of the profits. By the time he was 23, he had amassed enough to strike out on his own. A fight with a jealous husband had made it wise for him to head west.

"It's not difficult to make money gambling if you use your head. It's a matter of strategy, knowing the cards and the odds," he told me, his face animated. I smiled at his enthusiasm. "I'll bring a deck and teach you to play poker," he promised.

It was well after one a.m. when Ross Persall got up to leave. My eyelids had begun to feel very heavy, and I had unsuccessfully tried to stifle several yawns.

"I'd like to come back," he said, standing near the door, pulling on his heavy jacket.

"I don't know if that's such a good idea, Ross," I told him, knowing that I had broken the rules tonight, and I did not want to make a habit of it.

He did not respond for a second. Then he smiled. "We've been very naughty tonight, haven't we?" he mocked my guilty conscience. "Breaking all Hayes and Olmstead's rigid rules. Tell me you didn't enjoy yourself," he dared.

"I did. Very much," I admitted.

"How scandalous," he teased. "If the good Reverend Hayes knew you had spent five minutes with me, he would be sure that something very wicked had taken place." He chuckled.

"No doubt he would," I said thoughtfully.

"His poor little wife is pregnant again," Ross told me, unabashedly grinning. Then leaned down and looked into my startled face. "That's why Hayes is so suspicious of everyone . . . because he's so deliciously wicked himself."

"Ross, you're terrible," I said, embarrassed. Then I laughed.

Ross straightened, still grinning like a mischievous boy. "Now what do you say? Can I sneak back in the night to visit with you every now and then?" He raised his right hand and looked suddenly solemn, though his eyes sparkled. "Just to talk, I swear."

"Stop it." I was still laughing.

"You've a right to some relaxation, you know," he drawled. "It's not as though we're doing what Hayes is. We've just been talking." He grinned devilishly again. "What's wrong with that?"

"Nothing."

"Besides," he dropped his voice conspiratorially, "I can be very, very discreet when the situation warrants it. Trust me."

"Go home," I ordered in mock sternness, refusing to answer one way or the other. He studied my face for an instant, and then his eyes glinted. He left without another word.

Arguing with a man like Ross Persall would have been like arguing with Daniel Webster himself. I was not even going to attempt it. I suspected that anything I might say, any arguments I might raise against his return, would be gainsaid.

I knew Ross Persall would return. And because I was lonely and enjoyed his company, I would welcome him, despite the rules. I had totally forgotten what Reva Gutierrez had said about Ross. He was an expert when it came to lonely, frustrated women.

Chapter Seventeen

My stomach was knotted into a queasy mass of nerves, and a nauseating headache was beginning to develop. I had not been feeling well for the past week, but I knew it was due to this evening. The children were presenting their Christmas play to the parents. I had no worries about them; they knew their parts well, their costumes were finished and waiting, and the refreshments were prepared and ready to be set out by the children and myself following the show. The schoolhouse had never looked so festive, with pine cuttings, painted cones, a small decorated tree, and bright crayon drawings of Christmas scenes and even soap snow in the windowpanes.

What had my stomach churning was the fear of seeing Jordan Bennett again, and having to speak to him. It had been six weeks since he had made love to me on the grass above the river pool. It had been two weeks since I had even glimpsed him in town. He had been coming out of Olmstead's store as I had rounded McPherson. I had halted, conquering the urge to dart behind a tree and hide. Jordan had mounted his big stallion and started down Main Street. I forced myself to walk on, keeping my head high and face blank of emotion, though every sense I possessed seemed overly aware of him. He rode right by me, casting me one glance that made me remember with renewed and intensified shame every detail of what had taken place between us on that grassy slope.

If such a brief glimpse of him could do that to me, what would happen this evening when I had to face him and talk with him? I prayed he would not come. I prayed something would take him far, far away. Perhaps ranch business. Perhaps he would simply not wish to come.

The children were arriving. Margaret Hudson walked in with her parents and then went into my room to change into her costume. The Hayes boys came with their father and mother. The Reverend Hayes seemed very subdued, but watchful. I suspected he was hoping for some great blunder on my part so that he could dismiss me. Elizabeth Hayes looked wan and tired. Beside her domineering husband, she seemed almost a nonentity. I pitied her being married to such a man.

Toby Carmichael, Chester and Harold Studebaker and Sherman and Grant Poole arrived next. Their parents wandered in soon afterward. Charles Studebaker greeted me warmly and returned several books he had borrowed. Berthamae seemed impressed with the children's decorations and moved from arrangement to arrangement, admiring the handiworks. Katrina Lane arrived with her mother and Ross in tow. Marba looked very uncomfortable, but Ross grinned at me with a conspiratorial wink. I couldn't help but flush slightly, thinking of our conversations after most of the townspeople were long asleep. He had come by twice since the first visit, and each had been as entertaining as the one before.

Every time the door opened, my heart lurched. I felt sick and dizzy with tension. Ellen Greer arrived, dressed somberly, with a simple brooch at her thin neck. She was leaning heavily on her niece's arm, but raised a gnarled hand in hello and then took a seat toward the back of the classroom. When I saw Reva, I tried to still the trembling of my knees, knowing that right behind her must be Jordan. I focused my gaze purposely on Diego and Linda, who came rushing in together. With a few words to me, they went quickly into the back room to throw on their costumes for the play. I forced myself to look up and meet Jordan's blue, enigmatic gaze. My hand knotted convulsively at my side.

"Good evening." My greeting encompassed both Reva and Jordan. Reva chattered gaily, very excited about the evening ahead. Her son had a major part in the presentation, and she was proud. She looked around at the other parents, and there was a definite tilt to her head that dared them all.

Jordan had not said a word, but he was watching me. I wished he would look elsewhere, for his studious gaze was unnerving me more and more by the second. I could feel my cheek fluctuating between tingling heat and cold whiteness. Apparently satisfied by what he saw, he turned away. My relief was short-lived. A gnawing pain ate at my stomach as I saw him smiling and talking with Marba Lane across the room.

I moved about, showing people where to sit. Ellen stayed me with a hand to mine. "Are you feeling all right, Abby?" she asked in a low voice. "You look very pale tonight."

"Just a case of nerves," I said with a smile. "I'll be fine just as soon as everything begins and goes smoothly."

"Everything will go very well, my dear." She patted my hand. I wished she had resorted to her usual biting humor, then perhaps I could have snapped out of this dreadful state of nerves. My eyes drifted toward Jordan again. He was still talking with Marba, throwing back his head and laughing now at some witty remark she had made. Ross was laughing with them. He turned as though sensing my attention, and he smiled at me. I forced myself to smile back.

Looking at my pinwatch, I saw that it was time to begin. I entered my room and shut the door behind me. Then I shushed the children. "Is everyone ready?" I asked in a cheerful tone, smiling at each one of them in encouragement. I was as nervous as they were—perhaps more so. My hands felt clammy. My head was floating with a strange kind of dizziness, and I felt nauseated. I took a deep, slow breath.

"I'm so excited, I feel faint," I admitted to them laughingly. Several giggled and seemed to relax by my disclosure. "Matthew, do you have your lines ready?"

"Yes, ma'am."

"Everyone is into their costumes?"

"Yes, ma'am," they all replied in hushed tones, wide-eyed with excitement.

"Well, then, as they say in the theater, 'break a leg.'" I

leaned forward. "But not really, please." They giggled again.

I went out, leaving the door slightly ajar so that they could hear me. Taking another deep, calming breath, I stepped onto the low platform and leaned back against the edge of my desk, with my hands clasped in front of me. People saw me come from my room, and they grew quiet. I carefully avoided looking in Jordan Bennett's direction, though I was aware his eyes were on me from the moment I came from my quarters. Marba Lane seemed more relaxed and was even smiling, her first tension dissipated. How I wished mine was! Ross was smiling at me with encouragement. Then I let my eyes trail over the other faces, picking out the friendly ones—Elvira Hudson, Ellen Greer, Charles Studebaker, Emily Olmstead.

My heart was doing a nervous polka in my chest as I said my first few words of greeting and introduction. Once those were out with a voice that was thankfully unbroken, though slightly more breathy than usual, I felt my control returning. I went on to talk a little more about our play, an adaptation of Dickens's *A Christmas Carol*. I gave a brief synopsis of the story, explaining that due to a lack of time, we would act only the key sections. And then I introduced Matthew Hayes as our narrator. He marched forward with great dignity, his nervousness apparent in the slight shaking of the papers in his hand as he began reading in a slow, careful voice. I sat near the door where I could signal the children for their entrances. Sherman Poole came on first as Scrooge. There was some laughter from the parents as they saw the tall, lanky boy dressed and made up as an old man. Sherman grinned sheepishly and then launched into his threatrical debut with gusto.

The play went very well. Toby Carmichael made a darling Tiny Tim, but it was Grant Poole as Father Christmas who brought down the house with laughter when he tripped over his costume and almost fell flat on his face. By the time the end came, everyone was thoroughly enjoying themselves, even Reverend Hayes. The children lined up on the small platform and made their giggling, now-confident bows to the applause of their proud parents. Then they scurried back to change into their costumes for the nativity scene and caroling.

Some of my nervousness returned as I again stood in front

of the filled schoolroom and spoke to the parents about the carols and the history of the nativity scene. I allowed the children five minutes for their quick change. We had rehearsed this many times, and I knew by a light tap on the door when they were all ready. I paused for a moment, looking at the door.

The youngest girls came out first, dressed in their party best with paper wings and little halos. The parents twittered proudly among themselves. Then the boys came, scrubbed and combed and looking a little too innocent to be credible. I suppressed my smile as I looked at Sherman's solemn look.

A space had been cleared at the front of the classroom, and here Margaret and Diego knelt together as Joseph and Mary. A small doll was wrapped and lay in a basket. Luke, Harold and Chester were the Wise Men following the star held aloft by Matthew Hayes.

With me conducting, the children sang "Silent Night, Holy Night." Their harmony was not always perfect, but never had I heard them sound more wonderful. Katrina Lane sang the second-verse solo as the other children hummed harmony. Her voice was pure and delightful, and she looked every bit the angel she was dressed.

When the song was over, the children grinned delightedly. I smiled back, gave them a broad wink and said they were dismissed. The parents were clapping and standing up to greet their children, who were pouring down off the platform to receive their well-earned compliments.

As I turned around, I felt another wave of dizziness, and a clammy chill came over me. It passed quickly, but left the same annoying nausea with which I had been too often plagued lately. I felt all the color draining from my cheeks. Turning quickly away from the attention of the parents, I headed toward my room where there was a chance of privacy and the excuse of a half-dozen trays of cookies waiting to be set out. Once there, I closed my eyes and took several deep breaths. The nausea abated slightly, and my head stopped swimming.

"Can I help you, Miss McFarland?" Elvira Hudson asked from behind me. I turned around and smiled with forced brightness. I gladly accepted her offer and indicated two trays she could carry out to the table while I took the grounds from the coffeepot. The smell of the rich brew revived my ill feeling. Usually I loved the smell of coffee, but not lately.

Breathing through my teeth, I lugged the heavy commercial pot Ross had loaned me across the room to the refreshment table. Then Elvira and I began distributing the treats. As people came by for cookies, they paused to congratulate me on the Christmas program. I glimpsed Jordan at the far side of the room, talking again with Marba Lane. She looked toward me several times as she spoke, and I wondered if they were discussing me. Jordan's arms were crossed over his chest, and he was smiling slightly. It was a friendly smile he had rarely turned on me, except the one time I wanted so desperately to forget.

Everyone in town had come for the program. Even Sheriff Tom Hallender was there. He stopped at the table when the others had moved on. I noticed that his hair was growing very white at the temples, and he looked tired and drawn.

"You're doing a fine job of teaching, ma'am," he commented. "I haven't had any need to chase down truants lately."

Ross walked up to stand next to Tom Hallender. "With a teacher as pretty as Miss McFarland, who would want to play hooky?" He grinned. I was now used to Ross's flirtatious manner, and for once I didn't flush.

"Do you plan to stay in Sycamore Hill?" Hallender asked.

"Yes," I answered, and then added with a smile that I hoped I would be allowed to stay. It was up to the school board as to whether my contract would be renewed at the end of the year. If it was, I could stay on permanently unless some unforeseen conflict arose.

"Oh, they'll renew it all right," the sheriff said, seeming very sure. "There isn't anyone around these parts that would want to work day and night in this place." His words seemed to mean something other than the usual duties that went along with teaching, and I had started to question him when the good Reverend Hayes approached with his wife on his arm.

"Tom, how are things with you?" The minister nodded greetings to the sheriff. Ross was standing next to Hallender, but Reverend Hayes looked right past him, and fixed his cold eyes on me. The only evidence of Ross's reaction to the deliberate snub was a faint twitch in his cheek. He sipped at his coffee and then moved away from the table.

"The Christmas program was done fairly well," Reverend Hayes said, and I was pleased by that compliment, the first of any degree at all that I had received from him.

"Thank you very much." I smiled. "I thought Matthew did remarkably well with his narration. Didn't you? He does very well in any oral presentation."

"You showed sound judgment selecting him to do it," the minister agreed proudly. "Your judgment was a little lacking in some others however," he added after a pause. Hallender looked at the reverend with obvious interest. Elizabeth Hayes peered up at her husband pleadingly. When she squeezed his arm, he patently ignored her.

"I don't understand," I said.

"You never cease to amaze me, Miss McFarland," Reverend Hayes said with a stern shake of his head. "How could you possibly have a Mexican boy play Joseph? It's unthinkable! And that barmaid's daughter as an angel? What a lack of taste and discretion!"

Angry color came into my face. I hoped that Diego and Katrina were nowhere close by to hear such vile prejudice.

"I'm sorry you feel that way," I said levelly. "The children elected Diego to play Joseph, and as for Katrina, she has a beautiful voice and is a charming child."

"Luke would have been an excellent Joseph," the minister insisted, flatly ignoring my explanation about how the parts were chosen.

"Luke would have done well, yes," I agreed, trying desperately for calmness. My stomach was churning again, and I wished that the conversation would end so I could escape outside for a breath of cool night air.

"If you agree with me, you should have chosen him," Reverend Hayes told me briskly. "Joseph should have been played by a white child."

I started to tremble. I straightened up. The impatience from my own physical discomfort made me speak candidly. "I know a little about geography, Reverend Hayes. Jesus was born in Bethlehem, not in London. It's highly unlikely that Christ would have been white . . . or blond . . . or blue-eyed. It's more reasonable to assume he would have been dark-skinned, probably very dark, since he was a carpenter and therefore must have spent a good deal of time outside in the sun. And he traveled, walking over the land to preach the gospel to the people. He would have been brown, Reverend Hayes, very, very brown!"

There were curious eyes on us, but I had kept my voice low enough so that others did not hear me. Hayes's mouth was a hard line of anger and indignation. He gave me a long, eloquent look and then spoke in a hiss to his pale wife.

"Get the boys! We're leaving!" She scurried away to collect her four sons. Hayes did not move, and I noticed the color in his neck. I knew my own color was very high. There was a great deal more I wanted to say to this man, but I knew that I had already said quite enough. More than enough, as it was.

"June can't come soon enough, Miss McFarland. I suggest you begin looking for other prospects more suited to your temperament," he hissed, hitting me at my most vulnerable point—my survival. The color washed out of my cheeks as he watched with immense satisfaction the effect of his words. I felt the nausea welling inside me as I watched him walk across the room and leave with his family. I closed my eyes and lowered my head.

"The life of a public servant is about as thankless as they come, isn't it?" Tom Hallender said. I looked up, and he smiled sympathetically. "God knows, you have enough work to do without having to take that kind of abuse. Beats me why you do take it, Miss McFarland. A young woman like you, well-bred, pretty. You should be able to find some position in a more exciting place—San Francisco, for example. There must be lots of things there that would be more rewarding and interesting than teaching farmers' kids the alphabet and numbers while taking a lot of rough talk from a preacher who thinks you're kin to the devil himself."

He shook his head, a bitter twist to his mouth. "I've worked for this town for thirty-six years. You want to know what I'll get when I have to quit because I'm too old to handle the job? I'll get a gold watch, if I'm lucky."

I thought of Ellen Greer and her two plaques. Ellen had been fortunate enough to have a niece who was willing to give her room. What would the school board have done to reward her for 50 years of service to the community if Ellen had had no one?

"I was surprised you even stayed on. You must have heard about this place." He glanced around the schoolroom.

"May I have more coffee, Miss McFarland?" Elvira Hudson cut in, casting Tom Hallender a warning look. He stared back at her blandly. "Brady Apperson wants to discuss last year's robbery with you, Tom," she told him. Hallender's eyes narrowed.

"What about it?" he asked defensively. I remembered what Ross had said about the sheriff's being unable to solve the crime.

"He has a theory about how the robbers got away and where they went."

Hallender gave a derisive snort. "Maybe he'd like to take over my job," he muttered bitterly as he set down his cup. "He can have it!" He cast me an apologetic shrug. "We've a lot in common, you and I, Miss McFarland. Neither one of us has any life we can call our own." He walked away.

"Don't let Tom upset you, Miss McFarland," Elvira said, leaning forward to pat my hand. She looked at my face with concern. "Are you feeling all right? You look quite pale."

"I just need some air." I smiled weakly. "Excuse me."

I turned away and moved as quickly yet inconspicuously as possible across the room to my door. Perhaps the solitude would make the nausea and dizziness subside. With my door closed behind me, I took several deep breaths, but they did not help this time. I knew I was going to be sick. My fingers fumbled frantically at the back door. I could not face the stench of the outhouse, and I thought of fleeing to the privacy of the old oak beyond the well. But I would never make it. I stumbled down the back steps and made it to the wall of the schoolhouse. My stomach heaved, and I retched several times. Nothing came up for I had not been able to eat all day. When the spasms were over, I leaned weakly against the wall.

"You're in a fine state of nerves, aren't you?" Jordan whispered right behind me, his hands grasping my shoulders at the same instant he spoke. I jerked. My muscles went rigid. My heart began pounding at an alarming pace. To my further humiliation, I was sure I was going to be sick again. I started to shake, fighting desperately for control.

"Go away," I groaned, another wave of nausea rising. I tried to pull away, but he drew me back against him, bracing me.

"Calm down, Abby. You've got yourself all wrought up. Take a couple of deep breaths," he instructed. I obeyed, praying I would not be sick in front of him again.

"Please, please just go away," I begged, tears of frustration blurring my vision. Jordan's fingers kneaded my shoulders.

"You needn't be embarrassed. I've seen people sick before."

I shook my head, closing my eyes and clamping my mouth shut. The wave swelled up and then graciously receded.

"I'd chance a bet that this is all due to your fear of facing me after what happened between us at the river," he murmured with a taunting laugh. I yanked my shoulders, trying to be free of him. His fingers bit into my flesh, holding me still. He lowered his head and whispered harshly against my ear. "What did you expect me to do tonight? Announce to the damned township that we made love?"

My muscles loosened as the dizziness returned. I felt too miserable to fight him or speak. I wanted to turn toward him and seek the comfort of his arms around me. But there was no comfort there. Only exquisite torment and later, shame.

Jordan caressed my shoulders again. His fingertips moved over and down to trail along my collarbone. I closed my eyes as a sigh escaped me. He continued the massaging, slowly drawing me back against his chest. His face moved against my hair. He lowered his head, and his lips roved down as he kissed the curve of my neck. I shuddered, feeling a fire kindled in my body.

"Abby," he breathed against my skin. "Abby, it was good between us. Why did you run away from me like that?"

Memory returned. In the space of a second I remembered every detail of what had happened by the river, and what he had said to me afterward. All the shame I had felt then flooded back, and I gasped with the agony of it.

Twisting, I tried to free myself. Jordan's fingers tightened painfully as he swung me around. The sudden movement set my head reeling sickeningly.

"Leave me alone," I stammered.

"I should, by God. I don't know why I bother with you. I've never chased after a woman in my life. But I want you . . . and I know you want me." The admission seemed torn from him against his will.

"No." I shook my head. My hands reached up to press futilely against the strong muscles of his chest. "You're wrong."

I saw his mouth turn up in a sardonic smile. "No? Do you want me to prove it to you?" he demanded in a low, challenging voice. "It'd be damned easy, Abby. Damned easy. I'm not a novice where women are concerned," he went on relentlessly, reminding me that he had already had one wife and still might have a mistress living with him. A picture of his arms around Reva Gutierrez, his mouth taking her, tormented me.

"But you're the most passionately responsive one in my experience," he said harshly, his head moving down as though he intended to prove his point and his power over me. I began to struggle in earnest then, and the suddenness of my fight bought my momentary freedom. He reached for me, and, desperate, I raised my hand to slap out at him as I had done once before. His fingers closed so tightly around my wrist, I thought the bones would be crushed.

"You'll come out the loser in any slapping contest you wage against me," he ground out through his teeth. "Don't you remember what happened the last time?" His temper seemed barely in check, and I could feel the violence coiled inside him.

I stared up into his blazing eyes and saw the rigid fury in his expression. My eyes opened very wide in fear. He stared down at me, seeing my fixed, still expression. The rage died, and the grimness left his face. His fingers loosened their agonizing grip, allowing the circulation to return. He started to say something when I heard someone saying my name.

"Abigail." Ross was coming around the corner of the building. "Abigail, where are you?" His voice was low.

Jordan's mouth twisted cynically, his eyes never leaving my face.

Shaking, I turned away. "Over here, Ross," I answered. Jordan released my wrist abruptly, his expression accusing.

"So it's 'Ross' and 'Abigail,' is it? What else is there to this sudden intimacy that's sprung up between the two of you?" he demanded, barely moving his lips as he spoke.

"What're you doing out . . . Jordan!" Ross said, coming around the stairs and stopping as he saw the tall man standing in front of me, blocking my escape. Ross stared at Jordan and then looked at me. "What's going on out here?"

"You tell me," Jordan said in a low, growling voice. Ross looked at me again, and I felt a guilty flush heat my entire body. The darkness thankfully hid the embarrassed color. Jordan was looking at me now, and then back at Ross. There was a decidedly cynical twist to his mouth.

"I overheard Missus Hudson saying you looked ill," Ross explained. "I was worried about you. Are you all right?"

"She's fine. It's just a case of nerves," Jordan answered for me. His tone implied dismissal, and Ross's concerned expression changed as he cast a cold look at Jordan. Then he looked at me again.

"Are you?"

I nodded.

"We've got to talk," Jordan said to me.

"Just what's going on?" Ross repeated. There was a hard edge to his voice that I had never heard before. I looked up at Jordan. I loved him so much, I wanted to die of it, but I was sure that what he felt for me was nothing even close to that emotion. And I had already been a fool once over him.

"No. We've . . . we've nothing more to talk about, Mr. Bennett."

Jordan assessed my expression. He let out his breath in exasperation. "Have it your own way," he snapped. I watched him walking away and felt bereft. I felt Ross watching me closely, but I didn't care.

"What was going on out here between the two of you?" Ross demanded in a whisper.

"Nothing." I shook my head, feeling suddenly exhausted. At least the nausea had passed.

"Were you really sick?" he asked, a dubious expression on his face. I looked at him and suddenly realized that Ross Persall was jealous. It surprised me very much.

"Yes, I was. Mr. Bennett must have heard me."

"What did he mean about you and him having something to talk about?"

"School business," I lied. Ross did not take his eyes from my face. But after a second he accepted my answer.

"We'd better go back in, or people are going to get suspicious," he said. "You go first. I'll wait for a couple of minutes."

I started to move away, but his hand at my elbow stopped me. "Abigail..." he whispered, then seemed to change his mind. His hand dropped to his side. "Go on. We'll talk about Jordan Bennett later."

When I reentered the schoolhouse, Elvira Hudson came over to ask if I were all right. I forced a smile, saying I was fine now and that I had only needed to get some air. She seemed satisfied. I looked around the room until my eyes settled on Jordan. He was standing beside Reva, his hand possessively beneath her elbow as he leaned down to whisper something to her. My heart plunged into the pit of my stomach.

Reva looked up at Jordan curiously and then nodded. I focused my attention back on Elvira. I tried listening to her inane, friendly chatter. I did not notice Ellen Greer looking between me and Jordan with discerning eyes, nor did I see the faint raise of her gray brows as Ross Persall came back into the schoolroom and glanced once in my direction.

My face whitened as I saw Reva coming toward me with Diego and Linda. Jordan was moving across the room, behind them.

"Miss McFarland, we have to go home," Diego said with obvious disappointment.

"Jordan says he's got business to take care of at the ranch," Reva explained.

"We want to wish you a very merry Christmas, ma'am," Linda said, beaming.

"Thank you, and I wish you all the same," I murmured, and smiled back tremulously. Reva spoke to me for a moment. Her friendliness made me feel dreadfully guilty and ashamed for loving Jordan. Linda hugged me, and Jordan watched grimly. I looked up at him, praying that everything I felt was well-hidden. His eyes were cold. His mouth tilted up at one side in a mirthless smile.

"Have a pleasant holiday, Miss McFarland," he said in a

dry tone, his gaze flicking toward Ross Persall with an added silent message. Stung by his insinuation, I let my own eyes move to Reva as she steered the two children toward the door.

"I wish you happiness with your family, Mr. Bennett," I said with a jerk of my chin. His eyes narrowed on my face for a moment. Then he strode off toward the door, where Reva waited for him.

I remembered what the reverend had said in his angry parting. "June can't come soon enough. . . ."

For the first time I agreed with him.

 *Chapter Eighteen*

Whatever seemed to be ailing me got worse during the next week. I lost weight, and my clothes seemed to hang on me. The sickness was worse during the morning, sometimes so bad that I was hardly able to get out of bed. I could hold down no food except a slice of bread and some milk late in the afternoon. I debated going to the doctor, but decided against it. I had not the funds to pay him, nor buy the prescription he might give me. And, I reasoned, whatever bug I had would best be fought off with plenty of rest. Ten days of holiday stretched out for that purpose.

However, my sleep was fitful, filled with nightmares. Sometimes I awoke to crying, and I would lie in an exhausted stupor, unable to feel anything but aching awareness of my back muscles. As the days passed, my turquoise-and-gold eyes seemed to dominate the pallor of my face. I felt drained of energy.

With the children out of school, I saw no one. I passed my time making preparations for the coming classes. I visited Ellen once, but hardly listened to what she said to me. I excused my placid state and went home to rest.

A few days after the children's Christmas program I was surprised by a visit from Elizabeth Hayes. She tapped lightly at my back door, identifying herself with her soft, self-deprecating voice.

"I hope I'm not bothering you," she apologized as I invited her in and she saw the papers and books spread out on my table. It was a brisk morning. The sky was clouded over, warning possible rain that night. Elizabeth was huddled inside a thick woolen shawl that all but swallowed her in its mass, pregnant or not.

"Of course not," I was hasty to reply. "Would you care for something to drink?" I offered hospitably. "Coffee?"

Elizabeth Hayes grimaced. "I can not abide the smell when I'm in a family way," she admitted with a faint flush of self-consciousness. I sat down, folded my hands on the table and waited for her to tell me why she had come.

"I came to apologize for Jonah," she said softly. It seemed strange to hear the stalwart Reverend Hayes called with that affectionate inflection. There was a softness in Elizabeth Hayes's expression that clearly indicated that while Jonah Hayes was harsh and a bully to some, he held no fear for this woman.

However, I felt that any apology from Hayes should have come from him personally, if it were to mean anything. I doubted that he had sent his wife; yet I felt sorry for the gentle lady who lived with such a tyrannical man. With Hayes, four active, mischievous sons and another baby well on the way, Elizabeth had much with which to cope.

She smiled at me with soft appeal. "He's not a bad man."

"Oh, please," I said, embarrassed. "I'm afraid I was at fault for what happened after the Christmas program. I have no tact whatsoever when my temper gets aroused."

Elizabeth gave a laugh of genuine amusement. "Neither does Jonah, I'm afraid. He can be terribly gruff and unfair when he's angered. And he's been very angry with you several times."

I smiled. "Yes. So I've noticed."

"He admires you."

My eyes opened wide with incredulity. "He does," she insisted, seeing my disbelief. "Oh, he doesn't agree with you, but he respects your spirit."

"He as much as told me that my contract will not be renewed come June," I informed her.

The reverend's wife shook her head. "Yes, I know. He was upset that he had said that, and I think he will just forget about it. He can't say he's sorry, but he tries in other ways to show he is."

Now that she was warm, Elizabeth let her heavy shawl fall back off her thin shoulders. She was wearing a dark-brown wool dress with plain white collar and cuffs. The only relief to the severe outfit was a pretty enamel bird at her neck.

"He hasn't always been so uncompromising," she said thoughtfully. "He has always been a serious man, a very feeling one. It's only since we lost our little girl that he's seemed angry with the world and his faith in God has been tested."

She shook her head. "I don't suppose I should even be talking about all this with you, but," she looked up at me and smiled slightly, "you've been so good for Matt, and I would hate to see you leave Sycamore Hill. Mark and Luke like you very much, and, well, little Johnnie loves you. His first love." She smiled, her hazel eyes sparkling. "And you know how that is." She spread her hands, and her expression grew serious all of a sudden. "I almost think Jonah is a little jealous of it all. He likes to be in total command, and now he finds that you have a great deal of influence over the way our boys think."

"How old was your little girl?" I asked hesitantly, afraid my question would open old wounds, and yet wanting to know what had made Hayes the way he was.

"Four . . . and so beautiful." Her eyes misted, and she blinked quickly. I saw her hand unconsciously smooth over her growing abdomen in silent prayer. "She contracted chicken pox when we were in Kansas. She wasn't a very strong child. She died in Jonah's arms. I was afraid he would go mad with his grief." Her mouth trembled in remembrance. "And there were the two boys—Matt was three, and Mark only one. By the grace of God, they did not become ill." She sighed, and then smiled at me again. "I pray this baby will be another little girl like our Ruth, only stronger. I shall name her Rebecca."

"I hope you have your little girl." I smiled. I liked Elizabeth Hayes very much. There was a gentle strength about her that made her a most admirable woman.

"Jonah's father was a preacher," Elizabeth began again. "He

was a truly dreadful man." She smiled. "Fierce, unforgiving, the hellfire-and-damnation kind of minister," she said with a sparkle in her eyes. "Jonah didn't want to be like him. I'm afraid he's becoming that way and doesn't even realize it."

"Why does he have such prejudice against Mexicans?"

"When we first came here, some young *bandidos* vandalized the church. Two got away, but one was caught. He said something to Jonah that truly horrified him. Blasphemy, but what exactly, I don't know. He wouldn't tell me."

"But that's no reason to despise all Mexicans," I said.

"No, it's not," she agreed. "But Jonah has not been reasonable about many things since Ruth died. I wish I knew what to do," she sighed. "He seems to get worse as the years pass."

"Have you tried sitting down and talking with him about it?"

"I don't know that it would do any good. If I were to say anything to him, he would look on it as a betrayal of our love. It would hurt him too deeply."

"Would he listen to anyone else?"

"The only person that he truly respects here in Sycamore Hill isn't even a church member any longer—Jordan Bennett."

I felt the color rising into my face and quickly turned away. Standing, I busied myself at the stove, setting on a kettle for tea. I wanted to do anything to hide my shaking hands and the crimson flush that had swept into my cheeks at the mere mention of Jordan Bennett's name. I took down two cups from the shelf and removed the lid from the canister. "It . . . it surprises me that the reverend would think so much of him," I managed.

"You mean because of all the gossip about his wife's sudden death?" she asked with a rueful smile. "Don't look so surprised, Miss McFarland. A minister's wife hears many things from many people."

"I suppose so." I turned away, measuring out the tea and putting it into the kettle. I did not possess a tea ball; so I had to carefully sift out the leaves when the brew was made.

"I don't believe the stories," Elizabeth said. "People disliked Gwendolyn Bennett very much. She was from a wealthy family in the East, and she hated living in California. She never tried to make friends with anyone. Everyone was aware that her marriage with Mr. Bennett was not a happy one. They simply jumped to conclusions when she was brought into town on the buckboard."

"How did she die?"

"Her neck was broken. Because little was said about how it happened, people chose to believe that Mr. Bennett did it himself. So sad really. I think he is a decent man. I don't believe he would murder anyone."

"I've heard he has a violent temper."

"I've never seen him angry," she admitted. "But he's a loving father."

"Your husband believes Mr. Bennett is Diego Gutierrez's father. That was part of his decision to expel the boy."

Elizabeth looked up and sighed. "Yes, I know. It's strange that all that doesn't affect his respect for Mr. Bennett. Men and women usually lay blame for such unfortunate situations on the woman involved. The man is forgiven his momentary lapse, while the woman and child suffer for the indiscretion for the rest of their lives."

"Then you believe it's true?"

"I don't know. It's possible, I suppose. They have lived together for years. And neither one of them has ever denied the story, though I shouldn't think they owed anyone any explanations. But I really don't know if it is true."

"I don't believe it," I said quietly. Even as I said it, I wondered if my belief was colored by my love for Jordan. Perhaps I did not want to believe it anymore.

"I was told that Mr. Bennett's late wife was very beautiful," I said a moment later. I turned toward the kettle again as the water began steaming. I tried to sound casual, hoping my interest in Jordan's life was not too obvious. Why didn't I just leave well enough alone? But I could not. I never stopped thinking about him.

"Oh, yes." Elizabeth nodded. "She was exquisite. But I've never seen a more pathetic creature."

"Pathetic?"

"She came from a wealthy family and undoubtedly had everything her own way until she married Jordan Bennett and came to live in California. Out here she was despised by everyone, and it was her own doing, I'm afraid. She was beautiful, and knew it. There was an arrogance about her that immediately made people dislike her. She was bitter and resentful about having to live here." Elizabeth shook her head, her expression mirroring her pity. "She was so young, and she had so much to be thankful for—a lovely little daughter. . . ."

"Do you care for sugar? I can't offer you cream or milk. I haven't any at the moment."

"No, thank you. This is just fine." Elizabeth Hayes lifted the mug and sipped gingerly at the hot brew. "This is very good." We sat in companionable silence. Elizabeth sighed and then leaned forward to rub the small of her back.

"Are you feeling all right?" I asked, concerned. Her face seemed quite pale with the strain. Then it cleared with a bright, amused smile.

"It all goes along with being in a family way," she said with a faint flush. "Sometimes every muscle in my back seems to be protesting the coming of this baby. But at least I can be thankful that the morning sickness is letting up some."

"Morning sickness?"

"They call it that because it comes mostly in the morning. Some women are unfortunate enough to have it all the time. I suffer from it for the first few months, and then it goes away. Sometimes I feel a little faint, but that passes also." She leaned across the table and patted my hand. "Don't look so worried, Miss McFarland. I've been through this five times before. This is my sixth baby."

"Yes . . . yes . . . well, I hope you will be feeling better," I stammered as my mind whirled with horrifying thoughts.

"I hope I haven't embarrassed you by talking about it," she apologized.

"Oh, no, no." Backaches? Dizziness and nausea? Fainting spells? Oh, dear God in Heaven. . . ."

Elizabeth Hayes finished her tea and stood up, pulling her shawl up around her shoulders again. "I've kept you much too long, and you're so kind. I'm very grateful for what you've done for the boys, Matt especially. He must learn to stand on his own two feet." We shook hands at the door, and she told me not to be so upset about her husband's angry threat. I wished her well and closed the door.

Trembling, I sat down at the table again. My stomach churned sickeningly, and my head began to ache with tension. Now I knew what was wrong with me. It only seemed impossible that I had not realized it sooner. I was carrying Jordan Bennett's child!

That night I lay awake for hours, trying to think. No solution presented itself. Never once did I consider going to Jordan with the news of my condition. To suffer further humiliation or rejection from him was unthinkable.

Was I ever to be a fool? Hadn't I been fool enough over the Haversalls? And then Jordan? How could I have let myself fall in love with a man who cared nothing for me except as a trollop to roll with in the field when he needed satiation? What a mistake I had made giving myself to him in such abandonment, never once thinking of the consequences! And now I would pay, and so would my unborn child.

I thought of what the situation would be when my condition became known. It would not be long before I would not be able to keep it secret. It would be obvious to everyone. Then I would lose my position, my livelihood, small though it was. Then what would I do? Would I be able to keep my pride, or would I have to crawl to Jordan and beg his help? I would rather die!

Could I run away? But where could I go? And how would I leave? I had no money, and who could loan me enough to start somewhere new. And how could I even start somewhere else when I had an infant to care for? The situation seemed to grow worse and worse as I contemplated it.

Perhaps I could save some money over the next few months. But I could see no way to save enough to support myself for even two months. Who could I stay with? Ellen in her tiny room overlooking a garden? What would she think of me if I were to tell her of my condition? I pressed my hands tightly over my face, wishing I could die.

By morning I had no answers, and my head and body ached from lack of rest. The nausea only further reminded me of my dismal, terrifying future. It was Sunday, and I was expected at church for services and Sunday school. Mechanically, I dressed and gathered my things together.

Somehow I managed to get through the morning, though my thoughts were far away and frightening in nature. When people looked at me, I wondered if they guessed my secret, though I knew that was impossible. It was only my own guilt that was torturing me.

Ellen stopped me as I was heading back for the schoolhouse. "You look dreadful, child. What are you doing to yourself?"

"I haven't been sleeping well," I answered.

"Why don't you come over, and we'll talk?" she suggested, her face even more wrinkled with her obvious concern over me. I felt miserable.

I hesitated at her invitation, thinking what she would feel about me if she were to learn the truth. Could I tell her? Could I stand to have her affection change into shock and contempt? I swallowed hard, feeling tearful and wanting desperately to run away.

"I don't think—"

"Don't give me any of your lame excuses, Abby," she said sharply. "You're on vacation, and your time is your own. Now, you can spare me an hour or two. You're coming for lunch. Do you understand?" she said, speaking to me as though I were a truant.

I could not help but smile at her manner. How I loved this domineering old tyrant!

"All right," I agreed.

Her pursed mouth twitched with satisfaction. "Then come along, and we'll have no further arguments about it."

A short time later we sat in her room. The day was as bleak as I felt, and I cast about frantically for something to say to lighten the mood that had come with me. Ellen's niece brought in a pot of coffee and two cups, and my barely settled stomach began to turn. Ellen poured out a cup.

"You'll have to come get it, Abby. My hands are too shaky for passing it across to you," Ellen instructed.

"No . . . no, thank you. I don't feel like having any coffee right now."

Ellen looked at me sharply. "You look drawn."

I tried to relax my facial muscles and smile, but my stomach was tightening alarmingly. Without answering, I shook my head.

"You're ill!" Ellen said.

The wave passed, and I opened my eyes and let out my breath slowly. "I'll be all right in a moment."

"How long has this been going on?" Ellen demanded, annoyed at the idea of my being sick. "Elvira Hudson said you didn't look well the night of the Christmas program. And when you came back in, you looked positively ready to faint. Now you're ill again. Have you seen Doctor Kirk?"

"No. There's no need."

"I disagree. You can't go on like this, Abby. You look a wreck. You've lost weight, and you don't need to lose any. Now, don't be so stubborn and ridiculous. I'll talk to Doctor Kirk myself and arrange an appointment for you."

"No!" I cried. "It's up to me whether I see a doctor or not, and I don't want to see one!"

Ellen was silent but watchful. My face flushed under her speculative glance.

"It's nerves, that's all. Really. There's no need to concern yourself, and I wish you wouldn't!" I said, hoping she would stop staring at me in that peculiarly discerning way of hers, as though she could see right inside my head. I was sure she had guessed what was wrong with me.

"And just what do you have to be nervous about?"

I lowered my head, feeling the guilty color staining my face. "Reverend Hayes suggested I start seeking another position," I managed finally, grasping that excuse and hoping it would satisfy her.

She relaxed slightly and gave an impatient sigh. "Yes. So I heard. You were tactless to say the least. When are you going to learn to avoid that man and keep your mouth closed. You have Diego reinstated, and Matthew Hayes has learned his lesson. Don't expect to work miracles by rearranging the reverend's head."

I laughed, for just an instant forgetting my problems. "How did you manage to be tactful all those years, Ellen?"

"Good question," she muttered, then sniffed. "I think everyone was just a little scared of me. I had most of this township in my schoolroom at one time or another, you know."

"You've been around long enough."

"Don't be impertinent!" she snapped, and then laughed with

me. She waggled her finger at me. "But don't you think you've sidetracked me. I've had experts try that over the years. Now, what's bothering you?"

"It's nothing that you can help me with, Ellen," I said honestly.

"Is it the same thing that's been bothering you for some time?" she pressed, but gently. I rubbed my temples.

"It's all interrelated." I looked up at her, not even trying to conceal the anguish I felt. "But I can't talk about it. Not with you. Not with anyone."

For a long time Ellen did not say anything. She was deep in her own thoughts. I shifted restlessly, my hands feeling very cold. What if I told her?

"Did Jordan find you outside the schoolhouse?" she asked suddenly, her eyes piercing.

My mouth opened and then shut. "Was he looking for me?" I parried, knowing it was useless.

"Abby . . ." she said warningly.

"Yes. We talked," I wearily admitted.

"And what has Ross Persall to do with you?"

"Ross?" I gasped. "Nothing. We're friends."

"Women are never friends with a man like Ross Persall," she snorted derisively.

"Well, I am. We've talked on occasion, and he seems very nice."

"Charming is a better word." She sniffed.

"You don't know him," I said defensively.

"No. But I don't expect it's any great loss." She pointed to the sandwiches. "Come, come. Eat something." I shook my head. "At least try," she said with concern. I picked up a half, handling it for a moment before forcing myself to take a small bite. I chewed the spongy mass and swallowed.

"You left the schoolroom in such a hurry, I was worried about you," Ellen admitted, having munched a bite of her own sandwich. "Then Jordan disappeared for a long time, and he came back in looking like thunder itself. You returned looking like death warmed over, and Ross Persall followed a few minutes later, watching you with a possessive air. And I saw him cast Jordan more than one accusing look. Now, what does all that mean?" She raised her brows slightly.

"I was sick. Mr. Bennett happened by at the most inopportune time. We argued a bit, then Ross Persall came by and simply misunderstood what was going on. There's nothing between Ross and me for him to feel possessive."

"And Jordan?"

My face turned a guilty red.

"Abby?"

"There's nothing. . . ." I started to lie, and then couldn't. I shook my head and felt the tears welling into my eyes, blinding me.

"Abby . . ." Ellen said softly, her voice so gentle and tender, it was my undoing. I started to sob. I put my hands over my face. I heard her get up from her chair by the window and move across the room. Her arm came around my shoulders.

"Abby . . ." she repeated, and the distress was evident in her tone.

"I'm sorry."

"Don't be. I've known there was something wrong for some time now. Won't you trust me, dear?"

"I can't talk about it. I can't." I looked up at her through my blurred vision. Her arms came around me, cradling me against her.

"You could tell me anything. It wouldn't matter. I love you like my own daughter."

I pulled away, feeling the full weight of my guilt. I looked up at her. I could not stand it. I got up and hurried to the door.

"Abby! Please, let me help you!" Ellen pleaded.

My fingers closed around the knob, and for an instant I leaned my forehead against the door. "Oh, Ellen," I moaned. "You wouldn't love me if I told you. You'd never even want to see me again."

By some minor miracle no one saw me hurrying back to the schoolhouse. No one saw me go out the back door and run past the well and out into the rolling hills, where I could find a few hours' solitude and peace. I had to think. I had to find some way to work things out.

It was very late when I returned to my room. As soon as I walked in, I knew someone was there. The teakettle was on and was steaming madly. Upon checking, I found it almost empty. The door to the schoolroom was ajar, and I went in.

For a moment I didn't see anything. Everything seemed to be in its place. Then I saw someone sitting in the chair at my desk. My heart stopped and then started again in a rapid drumbeat. I moved forward slowly, straining my eyes to see who it was. There was no movement.

Then I recognized her. Her pale eyes were wide open and staring, her mouth sagged in a soundless scream. The fingers of her right hand clutched at the front of her dress.

"Ellen?" I rushed forward and touched her. She was freezing cold. She slid sideways into my arms.

"Ellen! Ellen!"

She was dead.

 *Chapter Nineteen*

Clouds darkened overhead, threatening to add another deluge to the storm that had already swelled creeks and puddled the streets. The wind whipped wildly through the sycamore grove, making the branches groan with protest. The last few leaves released their weakened hold and spun off dizzily. Everywhere, the world seemed gray and cold.

A crowd followed six men bearing a small pine box on their shoulders. They moved slowly up the street and through the gate of the cemetery. People drew tightly together to ward off the cold. The men lowered the box, setting it on slats across a yawning hole. Here and there people sobbed or spoke in low, aggrieved voices. Reverend Hayes moved forward, flanked by Jesuit Father Anthony from Sycamore Hill's only other church, St. Joseph's. Ellen Greer had been a shared servant of the town, and her funeral was a joint concern.

Father Anthony spoke first, briefly and poignantly, summarizing Ellen Greer's career and years of unselfish service to the people. Reverend Hayes spoke then, his voice subdued as he talked of Ellen's strength of mind and character and of the debt everyone owed her.

Jordan Bennett, as one of the pallbearers, stood at the front.

His face was pale and controlled. The dark suit he wore looked expensive. It was an Eastern cut, and it made him seem remote and all the more a stranger to me.

The eulogy became a drone of sound against the wind. Words were lost. I watched as the six men, Jordan among them, lifted the small, poor casket and took the slats away. I closed my eyes. I wanted to blot out the picture of Ellen being set into that cold, dark grave at the top of the hill. The words "ashes to ashes, dust to dust" drifted to where I was standing, slightly apart from the crowd. I winced when I heard the thud of soil as it was dropped in upon Ellen.

". . . You can tell me anything. I love you like my own daughter. . . ." Ellen's voice came to me. Tears burned and then coursed down my cold cheeks. "Abby . . . Abby . . . please let me help you. I love you like my own daughter. . . ."

The pain in my chest was excruciating. If only I had been there, perhaps I could have helped her. But Doctor Kirk said she had died almost instantly of a heart seizure. He said she had been ill for a number of years. But if I had been there, I could have comforted her. I could have held her close to me so that she would not have been so afraid. I could have told her how much I loved her. I had never told her. But I had not been there when she needed me. And Ellen had died alone in that cold, haunted schoolhouse.

"Miss McFarland," someone said softly. I opened my eyes and saw Ellen's niece, Sadie, standing before me. She held out something. The little package was loosely tied with parcel string. "I think my aunt would have wanted you to put these up in the schoolhouse somewhere. They're her service plaques," she explained, her voice wobbly. I took them and nodded. I was unable to speak. Fifty years of teaching, two small bronze plaques. I stood silently, tightly gripping the pieces of memorabilia that represented Ellen's entire life.

A picture of Ellen's face flickered in my mind's eye. She was smiling that taunting smile of hers and wagging her gnarled finger at me. Then another picture superimposed itself. I saw her face in death, eyes open in fear, mouth in a silent scream for help. And she had been alone. All her life, Ellen Greer had been alone, even in the end.

People moved past me down the hill. I felt their stares. Everyone knew that Ellen had died in the schoolhouse. Everyone knew I had discovered her body. Some, hearing my screams, had sent Tom Hallender to investigate.

I overheard one townswoman saying to another, "Did you see Miss Greer's face that night? She saw something. That's what killed her. She saw something there in that place. I'm not sending my little girl back there, that's for sure."

Had Ellen seen the ghost? Was that what had frightened her so badly that she had suffered the fatal seizure? I stared back into the faces that passed me. Jordan was approaching. His eyes were seeking mine and rendering some message I was incapable of comprehending in my grief over Ellen. I turned away quickly and made my way down the hill to the gate. I felt like walking; so I started back along the fence and up toward the grove. I had stopped by the lonely grave with its wooden marker when Tom Hallender caught up with me.

"Miss McFarland, could I have a minute of your time, please?"

When I did not answer, he moved closer. He looked at the plaques clutched in my hand. "Not much to show for fifty years, is it?" he said bluntly, repeating my private thoughts of only moments before. I wished he hadn't.

"There are other things more important, Sheriff," I answered quietly, wanting him to leave me alone with my grief.

"Seems to me the town could have given her more than two plaques, a cheap pine casket and some sentimental words over her grave," he went on brutally frank. I flinched.

"Everyone respected and loved her," I said shakily.

"Sure. So much so that if it hadn't been for her niece's husband owning a boardinghouse, Miss Greer would have rotted in some charity home somewhere," he continued ruthlessly. The cold possible truth of his words made me recoil.

"Is this why you wanted to talk with me?" I emitted tremulously. "Because if it is, I would just as soon not hear more!"

"I know you cared for Miss Greer." He disregarded my plea. "You were good friends with the old lady. I don't think she would have wanted the same kind of life for you."

His comment about Ellen being an old lady irritated me,

and my mouth tightened. "I don't know what you're talking about."

"I mean working for fifty years and then getting nothing for it but what you've got in your hands." He indicated the loathsome plaques. Why wouldn't he just go away and leave me alone?

"It doesn't matter," I whispered painfully.

"It should then," he said, irritated. "You'll be just like her, you know. Working here year after year, giving everything you've got to people who don't care a penny about you. Then when you're old and of no more use to them, they'll kick you out and expect you to fend for yourself."

Of course, that would not happen to me. I would not be allowed to stay here in Sycamore Hill. Not once my secret became known. But somehow that did not matter now. I did not see so far ahead. I did not want to see any farther ahead.

"You shouldn't be so concerned, Mr. Hallender. And I don't know why it should matter to you so much what happens to me."

"Because I'm in the same position Miss Greer was, only I haven't got a niece with a boardinghouse," he said bitterly. "I wouldn't want to see the same thing happening to you as well. Someone's got to get out."

"I don't understand." He wasn't making any sense to me at all.

"It's so simple. I've got a little money saved. I'll loan it to you so you can go someplace else and start anew."

My eyes opened wide. "Why should you want to do that for me?" I hardly knew this man, and yet he was offering me his savings. Why?

"Just what I said, Miss McFarland. So you don't end up like Miss Greer, wasting your life for people who just don't give a damn."

"I don't see teaching as a waste of my life, Mr. Hallender," I assured him honestly, smiling ruefully. A flicker of impatience plus something else passed quickly across his face. He looked down at the grave by which I was standing.

"Beats me why you would even want to go back to that place with everything that's happened there."

"You mean because Ellen died there?" I asked, and then shook my head. "It doesn't frighten me." There were other things worse.

"She isn't the only one who died there," he said calmly. I did not say anything for a moment, but my heart was thudding with alarm. He looked down at the grave again.

"Please explain," I managed finally.

"There was a teacher just before you—"

"Prudence Townsend. Yes, I know."

"You're standing by her grave," he said, and I stared down in surprised horror.

"But I understood she was a young woman," I stammered.

"Younger than you, I'd guess."

No one had ever told me that Prudence Townsend was frail or sickly. I looked down at the grave, at the wooden cross where the earth had sunk in slightly. "How did she die? And why is she buried here, outside the cemetery?" I asked in a hushed tone.

"She was buried here because the priest said she couldn't be buried in consecrated soil," he answered my second question. "A couple of men dug this grave in the dead of night so the children would never know about it. It didn't even have a marker. No one knows who put this one up."

"But I don't understand. Why all the secrecy? Why was she buried here?"

"Because Prudence Townsend hanged herself, Miss Mc-Farland," he said quietly, and there was a cold expression on his face.

"Dear God," I gasped. "But why?"

"Who knows?" He shrugged, disinterested. "Probably couldn't stand the loneliness. But that's why they had trouble finding another schoolmistress. Word got around these parts about what happened. No one wanted to live in that place, not after someone hanged herself there. People are superstitious, even if they don't like to admit it. Some were saying Miss Townsend was still there."

I could feel my face turning very white as Hallender continued. "So Hayes said he'd write East to one of the schools." And the head of the school had by chance been a friend of

Bradford Dobson. "They all decided among themselves to keep the story about Miss Townsend a secret. They let the place go until you came." He gave a harsh, mocking laugh. "They were all half expecting you to come running out of there the first night. When you didn't, they figured all the stories about the ghost were just that—stories. You wouldn't have stayed on in there otherwise."

Staring at the grave, I thought of the ghost in the schoolhouse. Now I knew who she was and why she was there. She was not a figment of my imagination.

"She hanged herself from the front beam. The one nearest the desk. I figured she tossed the rope up over the beam, tied it around her neck and then jumped off the desk."

I shuddered.

"She must have figured it would break her neck," he went on. "But it didn't. She must have kicked for quite a while before she finally died."

I pressed my hands over my ears. "Don't . . ." I felt him watching my face. I felt sick.

"I'm sorry," he said when I finally lowered my hands. "My offer still goes. Why don't you think about it?" I did not answer, and he looked grim. "I hope what I've told you hasn't upset you too much." I stared at him. "But you did ask," he said defensively. Then he walked off, leaving me standing beside Prudence Townsend's grave.

Heedless of the darkening sky, I wandered in the hills behind town, finding the solitude my grief craved. I cried for Ellen, whom I had loved. Then I sank into a tortured despair over my own situation. When it became noticeable that I was pregnant, I would lose my livelihood. What would I do then? Could I go to Jordan and ask his help? No. I shook my head at the thought. I had some small bit of pride left, and I would rather die than ask his help. I did not want to live on his charity, while suffering his eternal contempt.

That depressing notion kept repeating itself in my mind. I thought about Prudence Townsend. She had hanged herself because she could no longer bear the loneliness. I knew it was Prudence who haunted the schoolhouse, but now the supernatural was less frightening to me than the natural state of my own life, and the dismal future.

It began to drizzle, and the dampness slowly seeped through my shawl. I hardly noticed, but continued to walk, head down, thoughts whirling in answerless questions and confusion. When the sky opened up, weeping its torrents down upon me, I ran for shelter beneath one of the ancient oaks that were scattered about. By the time I reached one, I was bone-cold and drenched to the skin. I waited for what seemed an eternity before deciding that the storm would not abate for hours. I would have to go on.

The water streamed down from my face. My clothing stuck to me, weighing me down. Trudging down the slopes, I saw the schoolhouse, like some pathetic relic, in the storm darkness of late afternoon. The rain was beating its primitive cadence on the leaky roof. Water cascaded down, pouring onto the grass of the schoolyard. Little rivulets had already formed and were running down McPherson. Puddles grew in the center of the street. By morning the streets would be mud.

Exhausted and freezing, I dragged myself up the back steps. I snatched up the bucket, knowing I would need a hot bath if I were to avoid a chill. After dumping my sodden shawl on the floor, I headed back out into the rain to get water from the well. When I returned, I set the filled bucket on the stove and bent to take kindling from the box. My fingers were numb and clumsy, and I had to strike the long match several times before it ignited.

It seemed forever before the fire was going strong. While I waited for the water to heat, I stripped out of my wet clothes and dried myself with a rough towel. Wrapping myself in a blanket, I sat down near the stove, waiting for the chill to melt from my bones.

I felt like a drowned rat with my hair plastered against my head and my skin bloodless-white and goose-bumped. Finally, the water began to steam, and I gingerly lifted the bucket down from the stove and poured the contents into my bathtub. Testing the water, I waited another few minutes before stepping in and kneeling down. I washed my body with a washcloth and then dried myself again. Some of the chill was gone, but I was still cold. I pulled on my nightgown and wrapped myself in the blanket like a caterpillar in a cocoon. Then I huddled near the stove for warmth.

I must have dozed off, for when I next looked at the fire, it had burned down to orange coals. I stoked it again and wondered if I would ever feel warm. When I awakened later, it was well into night. I stood up, feeling stiff and sore. I sighed deeply and rubbed my back, remembering with a wry smile what Elizabeth Hayes had said about the symptoms of pregnancy. I had every one. I lay down on my bed.

There was a scuffling noise in the schoolroom. It was too early for my lady of the schoolhouse, I thought, and I was too despondent to care anyway. Nothing seemed to matter anymore. Ellen was dead. Jordan did not love me. I was alone. Oh, God, I was so alone.

I dozed again, wrapped in my blanket. When I was awakened later, the rain was still pounding on the roof. A leak had opened in the center of my quarters, and I got up to put something beneath it. The ping of drops against the metal bucket sounded loud in the room. I lay for a long time, listening to it. In time my eyes closed slowly, lulled by the rhythmic beating of rain on the roof and the droplets splashing into the bucket. Then I heard the crying.

Every few minutes it would start, softly and plaintively. It had happened so many times before, it had ceased to alarm me. But now there was added meaning to it. I remembered Tom Hallender's story about Prudence Townsend and how she had died in the schoolroom. I remained still on my narrow, lumpy cot, but gradually I began to feel restless with the continued desolate moaning that came from the other room. I unwrapped the blanket from my legs and got up. The floor was icy beneath my bare feet, but I had no slippers. I drew the blanket up around my shoulders and cuddled inside it.

Again the crying started. Almost unaware of what I was doing, I entered the schoolroom. It was freezing cold, and there were several leaks puddling the wood floor. As soon as I had opened the door, my lady of the schoolroom had stopped crying. I wondered if it were all illusion, as Ellen had once said. Then I remembered her face in death. Terrified, trying to scream. Had she seen the ghost? Or had the expression only shown fear that death had come to claim her? After all, I had never seen the ghost. I had only heard the faint crying and once smelled an essence of lavender. Was I now allowing Tom Hallender's story to strengthen my beliefs that the ghost did in fact exist?

I looked about the room, and there, on the beam closest to my desk, hung a rope. There was a noose at the end. I shuddered. I remembered the details of Prudence Townsend's death, as related by the sheriff. Had the ghost put the rope there? Where had it come from? Once before, it had been there, and I had pulled it down in a moment of fear-filled panic. Now that I understood, it did not seem so frightening somehow. I approached it, staring at it with a cold feeling in the pit of my stomach. No emotion seemed to penetrate. I felt curiously numb. Then I looked at the desk and chair, and once again I remembered Ellen.

I am alone, I thought, suddenly bereft. Totally, forever alone.

As though sharing my pain, the lady of the schoolroom began to cry again. It seemed to come from nowhere . . . and yet everywhere, surrounding me like a shroud. My skin goose-bumped. The faint lavender scent I had experienced once before drifted into the room. I turned slowly, expecting to see some physical evidence of her presence. But there was nothing, and the crying stopped again. The room was filled with the sound of rain beating on the roof. I stood in tortured stillness until my muscles ached. My eyes roamed the room, searching. There was nothing but the shadows dancing on the walls.

I thought of the funeral, and an image of Jordan flashed in my mind. My hand slowly moved down over my abdomen, and a desolation so fierce filled me that I felt pain from it. My baby . . . and Jordan's. It was here inside me, waiting for life.

What then? A child unloved by its father, shunned by the community because of the sins of its mother? To be labeled a bastard all his life? The word ricocheted through my mind, growing louder. A bastard. Jordan's bastard. I thought of Diego and the pain I sometimes saw in his expression. A confusion and longing mingled. Did I want that for my baby? And what was the solution? I thought of Prudence Townsend hanging from the front beam, and suddenly her act seemed my only answer.

"Prudence?" I whispered softly into the darkness. Nothing.

"Prudence. . . ." A faint sobbing sounded. "I know why you're here. I understand. The sheriff told me how you died."

My eyes drifted to the rope suspended from the beam. I reached out and fingered it. For an instant a bubble of hysteria caught in my throat. Then I felt empty and still inside, almost as though I were already dead and the fighting was over.

The crying had begun again, low and plaintive in the darkened room. I knew Prudence was here with me.

"Prudence," I whispered shakily, again reaching out to touch the rope dangling from the beam. "I have no one either. No place to go." The crying softened and then stopped altogether. There was a strange hush in the room.

My eyes opened wide as I saw something across the room. It defied description, but sent an instinctive shivering up my spine. Gasping with terror, I jerked back, colliding hard with my desk and falling sideways.

I was frantic to escape. I rushed toward the front of the schoolroom, bumping into desks and tripping against things in the darkness. My breath rasped. My heart thundered. I reached the door and twisted feverishly at the knob.

"Abigail. . . ."

Something hit me from behind. I cried out in shock and pain. Then blackness engulfed me.

 *Chapter Twenty*

From somewhere outside, birds were singing. My head ached abominably, and I did not want to open my eyes. But I have to get up, I reasoned. I was so cold, and the only way I would get warm was to get close to the fire. As cold as I was, it must have gone out. I reached down, thinking that I could pull the covers up more tightly. But my fingers encountered only my nightgown and then moved to touch bare wood beside me.

Forcing my eyes open, I stared upward and saw the beamed ceiling overhead. What was I doing in the schoolroom? I fought off the wave of dizziness and nausea as I pushed myself up. I pressed my hand against my head. It throbbed, and I fingered a lump encrusted with blood beneath my hair. How had that happened?

Disoriented, I sat up completely and hung my head down to keep from fainting. I tried to remember. Then pieces of the night before began to return. Had I dreamed it all? I had certainly not dreamed up the lump on the back of my head. But what about the rest? I wondered, looking around the room. There was no rope suspended from the front beam, and everything seemed normal except for a few desks shoved from their usual positions.

Had Prudence Townsend tried to kill me? No, that wasn't

right. I had wanted to kill myself, and then she had come at me. Then something had hit me from behind, and I fainted. But I had been at the front door of the schoolhouse. My head was spinning, and I closed my eyes. Nothing made any sense, and it hurt my head to think about it.

First things first, I thought. I'm so cold. I've got to get the fire started and warm myself before I catch pneumonia.

The fire was out, and the woodbin was empty. Sighing, I dragged myself into some clothes, pulled on stockings and shoes and started out the back door. The sunlight hurt my eyes and sent a throbbing pain through my head. I stood wavering at the top of the steps, holding tightly to the railing. Thank God, James Olmstead had finally fixed the back steps, I thought. I started down, carefully, because I was dizzy and unsteady on my feet. I should stop and sit down. But I'm cold, my mind argued back and forth with itself. The sooner I get the firewood, the sooner I can build the fire and get warm.

At the bottom of the steps my head was hurting so badly, I knew I would have to sit down for a minute. But before I could, I fainted.

"Abby . . . Abby . . ." The familiar voice roused me. My eyelids flickered and then opened. I stared up into Jordan's taut face, meeting his concerned gaze in confusion. "What in blazes happened to you?" he demanded harshly. "I found you at the bottom of the steps in a dead faint."

I still could not believe Jordan was here. I forced my eyes away from him, afraid he would see too much in my face. The stove came into view, and the cabinet. Orphan was meowing at the back door, demanding her morning bowl of milk. I winced as I pushed myself up.

"Ohhh, my head," I groaned, reaching up to press my hand against the throbbing spot. Jordan roughly pushed my hand away and drew me forward into a full sitting position. My hands instinctively pressed defensively against his chest.

"I know you can't stand having me touch you anymore," he said in a hard voice. "But take my word for it, I'll be a gentleman." I closed my eyes, wishing my heart would stop its erratic beating. I could feel the hard muscles of Jordan's chest beneath my fists, and I curbed the desire to spread my fingers.

"You've got yourself quite a goose egg," he commented, and I felt warm breath against my hair. "What did you do to yourself, for God's sake. Fall down the stairs?" His voice was still hard and dictatorial. Bristling at his tone, I pushed back and then wished I hadn't. My head spun sickeningly.

"Just take it easy for a minute. I've got to clear the blood away," he said in a surprisingly gentle voice. It was almost my undoing. With a damp cloth he swabbed the spot. I sensed the exact moment when his mood changed. His hand moved from the nape of my neck to my shoulder. His touch was subtly gentler.

"Abby. . . ."

I had to say or do something before Jordan knew the power he had over me. "I . . . I don't feel well."

He gave a throaty laugh. "And it's no wonder." His hands moved in a lingering caress down my back. I took my hands from his chest and clenched them tightly together.

"Please let go of me."

Jordan stiffened slightly, and then his hands dropped away. He remained sitting on the cot, and I could feel his eyes boring into me. Then he got up and turned away. "How did it happen?" he asked in a curiously flat voice.

"What?"

"The bump on your head, what else?" he said harshly, raking his fingers back through his tawny hair and casting me an impatient glance over his shoulder.

"I'm not sure," I managed, thankful that he had moved away. My senses were returning. I swung my feet from the cot.

"You'd better not stand up just yet," he suggested. My head was swimming again, and I gave a faint laugh.

"Don't worry. I won't."

"Did you fall down the steps?"

"No. Something hit me last night."

Jordan's gaze became piercingly intent. "Last night? You've been out there since last night?"

"No. In the schoolroom."

"Then what were you doing on the back steps?"

"I woke up in the schoolroom, and I was so cold. The fire was out, and I didn't have any wood in the box. So I went out to get some. I guess I fainted."

I pressed my fingers against my temple. I heard Jordan move, and I looked up as he stalked out the back door, slamming it behind him. I stared in confusion, thinking he had gone away. What had I expected? For him to care? Hadn't I learned anything?

A moment later the door opened, and I looked up. Jordan scowled at me. "Is your head hurting you again?"

"N-no . . ." I brushed the tears away quickly, averting my eyes from his.

He dumped a load of wood in the bin and set to work on the stove.

"What are you going to do?" I asked, feeling stupid the moment the question was uttered.

"What does it look like I'm doing?"

"You don't have to do that. I can . . ."

The look he gave silenced me. "No. I don't, do I? I wonder why I'm bothering."

"Why are you then?" I asked, stung.

He exhaled sharply, but ignored my question.

When the fire was restarted, Jordan stood up and turned around. I had been watching him, remembering what it had been like being loved by him. There was a warm, curling sensation in the pit of my stomach, and it seemed to be spreading. When he looked at me, I looked away defensively.

"Do you want to sit by the fire? You'll get warm faster than sitting at the other end of the room," he commented dryly, his eyes coolly enigmatic. I did not answer. Nor did I move. "I'll stand by the door if it makes you feel any safer."

The bitterness of his tone made me flinch. But I stood up and moved slowly across the room. The dizziness had lessened, and so had the throbbing. I sat down at the table, remembering the last time he had been here and what had happened then. My face felt warm, and I kept looking at my hands. Jordan stood by the door, his arms crossed over his chest. I could feel him watching me, and I knew there was no gentleness in his expression.

"You said you were hit from behind," he prompted, and I looked up. I thought I saw real concern for me written on his face, but his expression was quickly shuttered.

"I guess that's what happened. I'm not sure. I don't know," I muttered.

"When did all this happen?"

"I don't know. About one or two in the morning, I suppose."

"What were you doing in the schoolroom at one or two in the morning? Were you expecting a visitor?" His tone was faintly accusing, and I looked up at him, bewildered. His expression was unreadable, but he studied my bemused face with slow intensity, as though expecting to find something very unpleasant there.

"You're not making sense," I said. His mouth softened.

"Neither are you. You'd better start at the beginning."

Jordan could stand there so aloof, while I sat here knowing I carried his illegitimate, unborn child. He was asking that I confide in him even though he cared nothing for me other than as someone he had taken for a few ecstatic moments on a hillside above the river. I shook my head. "No. I don't want to talk about it with you," I said hoarsely. "You'd never believe me anyway."

"Why don't you try me?" There was something in his voice that made me want very much to trust him. I swallowed convulsively, wondering why he had come here and wishing that he had not.

"Just go away. You'd never believe me."

"Abby, give me a chance." He moved away from the door to stand in front of the table. His closeness did awesome things to my insides. I had to say something; so I blurted everything out at once in a tense question.

"Would you believe me if I told you that I saw Prudence Townsend in the schoolroom last night?" I asked, attempting a self-deprecating smile that failed dismally.

He looked at me, and his mouth tilted up gently at one side.

"Before or after you hit your head?"

I knew he was only teasing me, but too much had happened recently for me to appreciate his humor or the reason behind it. Tears burned as I glared up at him. "I knew you wouldn't believe me! I should have kept it to myself! You love making fun of me. I should have learned a long time ago how much you enjoy laughing at me. Why don't you just go away and leave me alone?!"

"Abby. . . ." he shook my shoulder.

A sob escaped, and I clamped my jaws shut, speaking through my teeth. "Go away."

"You can't seriously believe there's a ghost here, can you?" he asked rationally. I started to laugh, a high-pitched sound that stopped as an agonizing pain shot through my head.

"We'd better get you to Doc Kirk," Jordan decided, putting a hand beneath my elbow. I thought of the baby I was carrying, and my eyes opened wide. That's all I would need! The doctor learning of my condition, and word spreading like wildfire through town.

"No!" I jerked my arm away. "I won't go to the doctor!"

"Don't be a fool! You've probably got a concussion. It's nothing to fool around with."

I took a deep, steadying breath. "I'm all right. It's just a little bump on the head," I said.

"Oh, for God's sake!" Jordan muttered in frustration.

I put my head in my hands. "Just go away, Jordan. Just please, go away and leave me alone."

There was silence for a moment, and then his fingers pressed comfortingly on my shoulder before dropping away. He came back around in front of me. Leaning down, he put his hands on the table. "You were saying about Prudence Townsend," he prompted again. I shook my head slowly. "Tell me, Abby. I'm not going to laugh at you."

"Not out loud maybe," I muttered bitterly.

"Abby."

I looked up at him. "She's here! She is!" He did not say anything, and I searched his face. "I saw her, Jordan."

He straightened. "Then we'll go from there." He gave me a slow smile. "Would you mind terribly if I sat down?"

I sighed. "There's a chair just inside the schoolroom door."

When he was seated, I felt frozen with tension. I was afraid to look at him again, sure that he would see how much I loved him. I wondered what he would say and how he would look if I blurted out that I was carrying his baby. But I would never suffer that humiliation.

"Start at the beginning," Jordan urged.

"I . . . I heard her crying again."

"Again?"

I glanced up and then away. "I've heard her crying since the first. Ellen said it was just the night sounds—animals, boards creaking, that sort of thing. But it wasn't. It was . . . Prudence Townsend."

"How long have you known about Miss Townsend?"

"I didn't know who she was, not until yesterday after Ellen's funeral." I stopped, refusing to allow myself to think of Ellen now. I would only cry again and make a further fool of myself in front of Jordan. I swallowed hard before continuing in a ragged voice. "I've walked by that pathetic little grave outside the cemetery many times before. I was always curious about it, but never asked anyone. Sheriff Hallender stopped to talk to me, and he told me about her . . . and what she did to herself."

I shuddered at the memory of that conversation, and then I remembered last night. My arms goose-bumped again, and I stared at the schoolroom door fixedly, half expecting her to appear there in front of me. Jordan did not say anything, and I was scarcely aware of his intent regard.

"What does she have to do with the bump on your head?"

I blinked. Then I focused on him. "She was crying again last night, and I went into the schoolroom. I wanted to talk with her. She . . . she appeared. I ran. I could feel her right behind me, and I went toward the front door. I opened it, and she said my name. Then something hit me in the back of the head. The next thing I remember, it was morning, and I was lying in the schoolroom."

Jordan frowned.

"You don't believe me, do you?" I demanded bitterly.

"You've got a bump on your head," he said, offering me a faint smile.

"You think I'm just another lonely schoolmarm letting her imagination carry her away."

"Are you?"

"She exists, I tell you," I said doggedly.

"You said this ghost of yours was the cause of Ellen's death."

"I'm only guessing about that. It was the look on Ellen's face," I said, shutting my eyes against the memory. "I've overheard people talking about it. There are others in this town who believe Prudence Townsend is haunting this place. They just decided not to share the information with me when I came."

"Understandable," Jordan muttered wryly.

"Very!" I agreed. "Though it wouldn't have mattered much."

"What do you mean?"

"I had a total of two dollars in my bag. Where would I have gone?" I spread my hands. "But she didn't threaten me then. It was just the crying at night and knowing she was here."

"You're sure someone isn't playing an elaborate joke on you?"

"A rather macabre joke, wouldn't you say?" I snapped. "And it's been going on for four months."

"Maybe someone wants you out of the schoolhouse."

I looked at him. "There are at least three people who have voiced that wish. Mr. Olmstead and the Reverend Hayes are two."

"And the third?"

"You."

Jordan's eyes darkened. "You know just how to irritate the hell out of me, don't you?"

Orphan meowed again, plaintively. "I've got to feed my cat," I said quickly.

"Forget that damn cat," Jordan growled. "It can wait. If it were worth its salt, it'd be filled up with mice. This place must be crawling with them."

Orphan sensed she was not wanted, and she scuttled out the cracked window.

"What else can you tell me?"

"Isn't that enough?" I asked, sincerely appalled.

"Is there any physical evidence of what happened?"

I thought hard for a moment. "There have been notes scrawled on the blackboard. And twice there's been a rope over the front beam," I told him hesitantly.

"Where's the rope? I'd like to have a look at it."

"Gone. It was there last night. It wasn't there this morning."

"Are you sure it was there in the first place?"

"Yes!"

"All right. Don't get upset," he said soothingly. "What sort of notes?" I related them to him. "Anything unusual about the writing?" Jordan then asked.

"The messages were printed at first, and they weren't very neat."

Jordan stood up and paced restlessly about the room. I watched him, unable to look away. Would I ever be able to forget this man? I remembered the first time I had seen him on the road. I had responded to him even then. My life stretched before me, arid and loveless. Then I thought of his child, and my hand crept down protectively. Somehow I would find a way, even without Jordan Bennett.

"What's the matter?" Jordan asked. I blinked and looked away, realizing that he had been looking at me.

"Nothing."

"Don't give me that, Abby. What is it? Are you sick again? You've been sick an awful lot lately, haven't you?" He eyed me curiously.

"I'm perfectly all right," I replied stoically. Jordan gave me a withering look. Then he moved toward the door.

"Jordan?" I appealed, and he looked back at me, his mouth tightly drawn, eyes narrowed.

"Did you have something else you wanted to tell me?" His expression was hard and unyielding.

"No, I guess not. I think I've told you quite enough as it is," I said tiredly. Jordan's expression grew even colder. "You don't believe she's in there, do you?" I looked toward the schoolroom door and shivered.

"I think something very strange is going on around here," he admitted, relenting only slightly. He pushed his heavy jacket back from his belt and shoved his hand into his pocket in a casual, careless stance. He obviously was not much concerned, I thought, hurt by his indifference. Yet, I still wanted him to stay. I ached to tell him about our baby.

"Someone wants to scare you out of here," Jordan said thoughtfully. "But I doubt if it's a ghost. There's a more rational explanation than that one."

"What do you think I should do?" I asked shakily, wanting him to make the decision for me. His mouth tightened again.

"Since you won't take my advice and see Doc Kirk, I think you should lie down and rest," he said curtly. That had not been what I meant, and he knew it. His answer seemed to confirm my feelings that, while he had listened to my incredible story, he was not much concerned over it. Any thought of confiding in him about the baby dissipated with his look. Unable to bear his indifference, I averted my eyes. He yanked open the door and left.

It was only after he had gone that I wondered why he had come to the schoolhouse in the first place.

After fixing myself a light breakfast of warm toast and tea, I did as Jordan suggested and lay down on my cot to rest. Surprisingly, I slept for hours, and awakened feeling somewhat refreshed. The dizziness was gone, though the lump on the back of my head was still tender to the touch.

Deciding that cleaning was too strenuous, I busied myself making class plans for the new year. I scanned textbooks and jotted down possible assignments that would be fun and informative for the children.

Around four o'clock I prepared a small can of stew for dinner. Then I toted water from the well. My headache returned with the heavy work, but it lessened when I bathed in the warm water. By the time I emptied the tub and set it away, it was after six and already dark. The sky had been overcast that afternoon, and I wondered if there would be another storm tonight. I remembered the leaks in the schoolroom, and I decided to set out some pans to prevent too much water damage. Having done that, I went to bed.

A loud crash and a muffled oath awakened me. I felt dazed with sleep for a moment, and then heard another crash. Someone was in the schoolroom. I remembered what Jordan had said that afternoon about someone wanting to scare me into leaving, and I felt a sudden surge of anger. Was this all a hoax designed to terrify me? I shoved back the covers and tiptoed across to the lantern near the door. Hurriedly, I struck a match and set it to the wick. Then I opened the door, intending to confront the mischief-maker and demand an explanation.

The front door of the schoolhouse was ajar. I hooked the lantern on the bar just inside my door and walked into the classroom. A pan was upside down and moved from where I had set it earlier. A puddle of water was splashed on the floor beside it.

Footsteps were coming up the front landing. I looked up,

startled and saw someone standing in the doorway.

"Abby!"

"You!" I breathed.

"I saw the light in your room. What's going on?" Jordan asked.

"What are *you* doing here?" I demanded in turn. He had stepped into the room, closing the door behind him. His eyes moved slowly about the room and then came to rest on me.

"I came to see your ghost, what else?" he answered mockingly. He looked away and noticed the pan. "Did the cat kick over the pan? Or did Prudence Townsend?"

I didn't like his tone, but answered nevertheless. "Orphan won't come into this room at night," I told him flatly. "But something kicked it over."

"Not some*thing*—some*one*."

"I don't see much difference," I said wearily. He was looking at me, and the lantern light from behind me cast enough illumination for me to see the tautness of his expression. His eyes moved down slowly, taking in my long, loose hair tumbling around my shoulders and down my back, and the white nightgown I was wearing. I was unaware that the light behind me clearly silhouetted my body.

"Abby. . . ."

My heart thudded wildly at his hoarse tone. He came slowly toward me, stopping just in front of me. For a long moment he did not move. Then his hands came up to my shoulders, caressing and gentle. I tilted my chin up as his mouth descended. His lips touched mine in a soft, testing kiss. I knew then I should draw away, but I didn't want to. He lifted his head and looked down into my face. Opening his jacket, he drew me against him, pulling his coat back around me. Then he kissed me again with devastating effect. His kiss went on. One lingering caress led to another. The heat of his body grew like a furnace through the thin-cotton fabric of my gown. I knew Jordan was fully aroused. Knowing that my effect on him was as fast and as profound as his on me was headily intoxicating. The blood sang wildly in my ears, and my heart drummed in a frantic race with his.

Jordan moved restlessly, pushing back far enough so that I saw his eyes were dilated and bright. His hand shook as he raised it to my face. Then he kissed me again.

"You know I want you, Abby. Let me make love to you. Here. Now," he breathed against my mouth before taking it again.

Want . . . not love, my mind cried painfully. He only wants to use me again like he did at the river to relieve his physical need for a woman—any woman.

Jordan sensed my withdrawal. His embrace tightened. "Abby," he groaned in protest. "I need you." His hand moved down my spine to the small of my back, pressing me hard against him so I could have no doubt. My own need of him almost threatened to overcome my pride. I struggled slightly, afraid if I remained any longer in his arms, I would forget everything but this moment and the intense desire for his possession. Jordan kissed me again, roughly passionate. I pulled my mouth away, knowing I had to say something, anything, to stop what was going to happen.

"I haven't forgotten your obligations to Reva even if you have," I managed, grasping at the first thing that came into my head. Jordan's caress stopped abruptly. He didn't move, and his stillness was worse than anything I had ever experienced. Irrationally, I wanted to reach up and kiss him, to apologize for the lost moment and the words that meant nothing.

His fingers bit into my shoulders as he shoved me away. His eyes were still dark and bright but with another emotion equally as primitive as passion.

"That was as effective as a cold shower," he ground out.

"You do owe Reva something," I said, not wanting to allow myself to relent and apologize. Jordan's look was full of hostility.

"You still persist in believing Diego is my son." He sneered at me. When I did not answer, he went on. "I'd be proud to have a son like him. But, no, damn you. He is not my son. I've never been with Reva . . . not in that way. I grew up with her, for God's sake. It would have been like bedding my own sister." His fingers reached out, pinching painfully around my jaw and tilting my face up with a jerk. "Or do you think me capable of that sin as well?!" He released me and stepped away as though afraid of what else he might do if he remained too close to me.

"You wanted me to believe it was true," I whispered, remembering the implications he had made himself.

He looked at me in utter contempt. "You believed exactly what you wanted to believe! You heard just what you wanted to hear! I thought if you had time to think things through, you'd have the sense not to believe all the gossip. Until now, I've never explained myself to anyone. I didn't think it would even be necessary with you. But you're no better than anyone else. In fact, you're worse! You're the lowest kind of hypocrite there is. Have you ever analyzed your actions, Miss Abigail McFarland? You turn up your Boston nose over what you *imagine* is going on with Reva, while you spread yourself like a whore for me in a field above Altadena Creek!"

I recoiled from him as though he had struck me physically in the stomach. My face paled, and my eyes filled with tears. "Get out. I don't ever want to see you again," I managed chokingly.

"Only too happy to oblige," he answered harshly, but his own face was pale and drawn. "Only one other thing before I go. Just for the record, I didn't murder my wife. She was drunk and fell down the stairs while I was working five miles from the ranch house. That's how she broke her neck. I didn't do it! When you invite the ladies in for tea, shovel that into their cups along with the sugar!"

Jordan turned and strode out the schoolhouse without a backward glance. A moment later I heard his horse galloping away into the night. I sank down onto a chair and felt miserable. I wouldn't blame him for hating me. My hand smoothed down over my abdomen. I shut my eyes and bent down, too desolate even for tears anymore.

"Well, well, well," came a satisfied voice from the doorway to my room. I looked up and stared in frightened surprise at the man standing there. "I couldn't have planned things better myself." The man heaved something at me. A length of rope snaked across the floor to my feet. I stared at it in horror, seeing the noose at the end. Then I looked up again.

Tom Hallender unholstered his gun and aimed it at me.

 *Chapter Twenty-one*

"Pick up the rope, Miss McFarland," Hallender instructed me coldly. I did not move. I was unable to tear my eyes from the black barrel of his gun. His hand was steady, and he moved his thumb slowly to cock the hammer. It made a deadly click, sending a shock of terror through me.

"I said pick up the rope," he ordered in a low voice.

I bent forward at the waist, feeling blindly for the rope at my feet. My eyes never once left his gun. I could not comprehend what was happening. Only yesterday Tom Hallender had been friendly, concerned about my welfare and future. Now he stood here in the shadows of the schoolroom, holding a gun on me. It did not make sense. Nothing seemed to make sense anymore, I thought. I could feel a rise of hysteria, which I choked down.

"What are you going to do?" I asked, my voice not seeming to be my own. The sheriff looked intent and determined.

"It's not what I plan to do. It's what you're going to do to yourself," he told me, and his eyes dropped to the rope in my hand. I blinked, confused. Then my heart stopped. It started hammering again in hard, alarmed staccato thuds that sent a surge of adrenaline through my system.

"I don't understand," I murmured, terrified that I did.

"You're going to hang yourself just like Prudence Townsend did."

My eyes widened, and my lips parted in a silent gasp. I watched as he moved slowly into the room, limping from his old wound. He unhooked the lantern as he came. He set it on the desk and leaned back negligently. He put his left arm across his chest, bracing his gun arm. The barrel never wavered from my head, but he carefully returned the hammer, and I breathed again.

"I'll give you a little assistance, of course," he said with a wry smile.

I strove for calmness. "Why should I want to do such a thing?" I asked shakily.

"Loneliness." He shrugged indifferently. "Tonight is Christmas Eve. Ah, I can see you've forgotten what day it is, Miss McFarland. And no wonder, with your friend Miss Greer dying on you, and then your lover walking out on you. But tonight is Christmas Eve, all right, and everyone else in this miserable, ungrateful town is home with their family, eating and drinking Christmas cheer," he said bitterly. He gave a harsh laugh.

"They aren't giving a thought to people like you and me who give our lives for them. They don't think to invite us," he jabbed at his own chest, "into their homes to share their wealth." His eyes were glittering resentfully in the dark. "You and I mean nothing but to save their skins, protect their belongings or educate their brats. That's the truth, Miss McFarland, and you know it!" His mouth moved up into a humorless grimace.

"But I don't feel that way, Mr. Hallender," I said quietly, wondering if the man had gone mad in his bitterness.

"But that doesn't matter," he shot back. He hesitated before he went on in a lower voice. "It takes a strong person to live alone. And, Miss McFarland, you're not a strong person. Or more to the point, people won't think you were once they find you swinging from that rafter up there." He pointed up to the front beam with the barrel of his gun.

"But why?" My voice was shaking uncontrollably. The coil of rope in my hand felt as heavy as lead.

Hallender's eyes had never once left mine. My question

seemed to discomfort him. "It's your own fault it's come to this," he accused. "You should have taken the notes I left seriously. But you didn't. I thought the noises and crying would do the trick. But you weren't buying any of that either. So I pulled the nail from the front railing, hoping you would break your leg or neck reaching for that stray cat I set on the sill. But, hell, no!" he snarled angrily. "You were lucky and rescued the little nuisance without hurting a hair on your damn head."

I remembered Orphan perched on the windowsill that dark night. I had wondered how such a small kitten could have got herself into such a high, precarious place. And Ross Persall had said the railing had been tampered with.

"Then I tried offering you a loan yesterday," Hallender continued dismally. "After Miss Greer's funeral you looked like you were ready to get away from Sycamore Hill. But you turned me down. That left me with no choice. I had to kill you. I thought I had last night, but it seems you have a very hard head, Miss McFarland," he said dryly.

"You hit me?"

He made an affirmative movement of his head.

"And you're the one who has been making all the crying noises and eerie sounds?"

"None other."

"But I don't understand why you're doing all this? What have I ever done to make you want to do these things . . . or to kill me?"

"I don't want to hurt you. I don't want to kill you," he told me harshly. "But I have to. Like I said, it would never have come to hanging you if you'd taken my earlier warnings seriously. Now I've got no choice but to kill you."

I licked my lips tensely. "But I saw Prudence Townsend. How did you manage that?"

His eyes left mine for the first time, but only for an instant. Then he smiled slightly. "Good try, but it won't work. If you saw anything, it was out of your own imagination. There's nothing here, Miss McFarland—nothing that is except you and me. And in a little while it'll be just you hanging up there, dead." He jerked his head upward to indicate the beam, and I swallowed hard.

"It won't be slow like it was for her," he assured me almost kindly, and I felt the hysterical impulse to laugh. Then I recalled his vivid picture of Prudence jerking frantically at the end of the rope as it slowly strangled her. Kicking and kicking.

Hallender straightened away from the desk, impatient to get on with his deed. "Bring the rope over here."

I couldn't have moved even if I had wanted to. I licked my lips again. The back of my neck felt wet with perspiration.

"Come on. You're not making this any easier for me."

"Why should I?" I gasped, affronted and terrified. He wanted me to make things easy for him?!

"Stalling isn't going to do you any good," he muttered.

"You should at least tell me why you're doing this!" I cried, desperate for time.

"Money," he retorted simply. "The 'root of all evil,' as our self-righteous minister would tell you."

"Money? But how are you going to get money for murdering me?" I asked, bewildered.

"The money is stashed here. You've been sleeping over it for months."

"I don't know anything about any money," I said blankly.

"Well, since you're going to die for it, I might as well tell you about it." Hallender settled back against the desk again. I felt a moment's reprieve.

"Three men robbed the bank a year ago. They got off with a little short of a hundred thousand dollars," he explained, and raised his brows expressively. "Now do you get it?"

I stared at him, remembering the stories I had heard about the robbery. "You mean you organized the robbery?"

"I had nothing to do with the robbery," he said, irritated by my suggestion. He shifted restlessly. "I'm the sheriff, remember? It was my job to go after those thieves and get the money back . . . and bring them in any way I could. Well, I caught up with them. They backtracked on me and tried to set up an ambush. But it backfired. I got them instead. One at a time, Indian style. But I risked my neck doing it."

My eyes widened as comprehension sank in. "You mean you murdered those men and kept the money from the robbery?"

Hallender's mouth tightened, and the knuckles of his gun hand stood out, white. "I told you I risked my life for that money. It's mine by rights. The town owes me something for thirty-six years and a bum leg."

"That . . . that may be true, Mr. Hallender. But one hundred and fifty thousand dollars?"

"How much is a man's life worth? I've been lamed once for this town. I got a couple of pats on the back for that. If I'd been killed, they would have given me a pine box. I'm taking that money!"

"But why didn't you just take the money then and keep going? Why did you come back here?"

"If I'd done that, I'd never have had any peace. I've been a lawman near all my life. I know what goes on. My face would have been plastered all over the state . . . and country for that matter. I'd have had someone on my trail for the rest of my life. No, thank you." He shook his head. "It was better this way, hiding the money and waiting until I could retire. That way it'd just be another unsolved robbery where the thieves got away with it. In time I could go someplace far away and enjoy my good fortune."

"Why don't you just take the money now and go?"

"I wouldn't be out of here five minutes and you'd be setting the town on me," he declined.

"But you could have come in here any time I was out, or at night when you were pretending to be Prudence, and moved the money somewhere else. Why didn't you do that? Why do you have to kill me?"

"You think I just stuck it in a desk or something?" He laughed. "All that money? Ten big bags of it, Miss McFarland! No, ma'am." He laughed then as though greatly amused and satisfied with himself.

"Where?" I asked, glancing around as though I might see it.

He laughed again, slapping his leg in obvious enjoyment. "You've been sleeping on it for months."

"What?" I breathed. "My cot?"

"It was the most obvious place I could think of, but which others would discard for the same reason. It's sewn right into your mattress. In fact, there isn't much mattress stuffing left in that bed of yours." He laughed again. "Everything went perfectly. I was careful when I brought the money up here, but someone heard me working in here. They spread the word that it was that schoolmarm's ghost. People just avoided this place all that much more. After Miss Townsend killed herself, people didn't want to come up here anyway. But after they heard about the sounds, they really stayed their distance. I never expected them to find another schoolteacher so soon—not sooner than a year anyway. And by that time it wouldn't have mattered. I'd have retired, come up here and got my money and been out of the state. But then you showed up," he said in resigned dismay.

"I didn't expect you to find the money, even though you were sleeping on it. But it still worried me. What if you were one of those women who stashes her savings inside her mattress instead of in the bank? It really worried me." He gave a harsh sound in his throat.

"People won't believe I killed myself," I said quietly, sounding more assured than I was.

"You think not?" He raised graying brows derisively. "There are plenty of reasons I can think of why people will believe it." He smiled unpleasantly. "You've been acting mighty strange lately, kind of dazed and depressed. I'm not the only one who's noticed it. I overheard Sadie saying her aunt was concerned about you, and that's why she went to the schoolhouse. But if that isn't enough, there are plenty of other reasons."

"Like what?" I stalled for more time to think.

"I overheard a damned good one just before I came in. Bennett! Couldn't be more perfect if I had planned it myself. There were rumors that Miss Townsend killed herself because she fell in love with someone and was scorned by him." He frowned slightly. "I wonder if that was Bennett too. Pretty active fellow." He smiled slightly. I remembered what Margaret Hudson had said, and I wondered if I had just been another of his amorous victims.

"Nobody will believe it. Everyone has seen the antagonism between Jordan and myself," I told him.

Hallender grinned mockingly. "But he was your lover, wasn't he? I heard that much. He was pretty blunt about it. 'Spreading yourself like a whore in a field about the creek,' I think is the way he put it," he said crudely, bringing a humiliated flush to my pale cheeks. "I never figured you for the type. But Bennett ought to know, huh?" Hallender's eyes looked down over me speculatively, and a cold feeling spread through me.

"Nevertheless," I stammered, "people won't believe it."

"Bennett was right when he said people believe gossip." Hallender shrugged. "Everyone believes he killed his wife. I know he didn't, of course."

"How do you know?"

"What faithless things women are," he grunted. "You believed it too." He shook his head slightly. "No wonder he was so mad."

"How do you know?" I repeated, the answer very important to me.

"Being sheriff, I had to know all the facts of what happened so as to decide if a warrant had to be issued. He told you the truth. From what I heard from witnesses at the ranch, his high-and-mighty bitch of a wife was little better than a lush. And I smelled the brandy on her myself when Bennett brought her body in that day. That Gutierrez woman was there in the house when Mrs. Bennett had her accident. Mrs. Bennett had been drinking. Her usual morning relaxation, I suppose," he sneered. "And apparently she was coming down the stairs for another bottle when she tripped on the rug. The doc said she was probably dead before she hit the bottom. Broken neck." Hallender snapped his fingers. "Just like that." He paused, shifting the gun slightly. "An accident. But people prefer to believe the worst."

Ellen Greer's words almost exactly, I remembered. I had been no better than anyone else. I was in love with Jordan Bennett, and yet I had always had some doubt. No wonder he hated me. I closed my eyes, remembering his face as I had last seen him. What would he think when they found my body? Would he blame himself, adding to his already unhappy situation?

"But all that has nothing to do with me," I muttered, looking at Hallender. I had to find some way out of this mess.

"No? A lot of scandal surrounds Bennett. You've heard it. It would just take a small hint here and there to add your suicide to his other list of sins. Pretty, young schoolteacher falls for rich rancher; he scorns her; and she kills herself," he rattled off unemotionally. "Not a new story, but believable enough for my purposes."

Hallender was right. People would believe it. Even my own mood and actions of the last weeks would serve to strengthen the story. When Hallender exposed the sordid rumor of my relationship with Jordan, that would only add to the reasons he had already catalogued of why people would believe I had taken my own life.

Hadn't I contemplated it only last night when I had believed mistakenly that I had seen Prudence Townsend? Some instinctive desire to survive must have probed my subconscious. What other explanation was there for what I had seen?

"It's time to quit the talking," Hallender said ominously. He jerked the gun in a silent order. "Pick up the rope," he repeated. My hands were perspiring. "Pick it up," he said yet again.

I made my decision. If I was going to die, it wasn't going to be by hanging. I let the rope fall from my fingers. He cocked the hammer again, and I waited silently.

"Pick it up, damn you!"

I shook my head, unable to speak.

"You think I won't shoot you, is that it?" he snarled. Something in his eyes told me he was uncertain. And I knew why. If he shot me, he would arouse the town. Everyone would know I had not killed myself, and his story would be useless. Suspicions would be rampant, and people would begin asking questions, wanting to know why I had been murdered. What would be the motive?

What if I jumped up and ran? I wondered suddenly, my heart pounding. If he pulled the trigger instinctively, he wouldn't miss this close. And besides, he was an expert marksman as well. But would he fire? Was I willing to find out? As though sensing my thoughts, Hallender straightened and moved forward.

"If you shoot me, everyone will know this is murder," I told him shakily. His mouth flattened out into a hard line. He moved forward relentlessly. The gun seemed to stretch out closer.

"I could shoot you point-blank in the head. It'd still look like suicide," he whispered chillingly. Sweat ran between my breasts as he put the barrel of the gun up against my temple.

"Where would I get a gun, Mr. Hallender? I couldn't afford to buy one on my income, and if I could, it would have been from Olmstead or Thompson. They both would know I had no gun," I reasoned. No one was going to help me out of this. I thought of Jordan and realized with sudden regret and dismay that he had been watching the schoolhouse, protecting me. Something I had told him must have aroused his suspicions.

But Jordan was gone now. I was alone. I looked up at Hallender's narrowed, cold eyes and knew that he would give me no mercy. The barrel of his gun yawned at me bigger than Ellen's open grave. If I was going to live, I would have to rely on my own intelligence to manage it.

Hallender took a couple of steps back. "Pick up the rope," he repeated harshly, shifting with obvious impatience. My heart drummed loudly in my ears, and my head began to ache so badly, I thought it would burst. His knuckles whitened as he held the gun. I could see that his hand was not quite steady. I waited to hear the explosion of noise and feel the pain shattering my head. A cold numbness and unknown resolve began to possess me. Hallender had spoken the truth. He did not want to kill me, and I was not going to let him. Not if I could prevent it.

"Who will find my body, Mr. Hallender?" I asked in a soft, amazingly calm voice.

He frowned. "I don't know, and I don't much care."

"But you should. You're a decent man, I think. Wouldn't you care if a small, innocent child were to happen in here and see your handiwork? Would you want a child to live with that for the rest of his or her life?"

"I could always come back tomorrow," he offered. The possibility obviously disturbed him.

"On what excuse? You're not a parent. I've done nothing to warrant a visit from the sheriff. They haven't forgotten the robbery, have they?"

"Shut up!" he ordered tersely. His voice was loud in the still room. "I'll think of something," he said more quietly. "No kid will find your body, I assure you, for your peace of mind," he said sarcastically. "Now pick up the rope, damn you!"

"I won't. You can't expect me to make it that easy for you."

"I could bash in your brains," he threatened, taking a step forward so that I thought he was really going to do it. I flinched back. "Bennett would be blamed. A lovers' quarrel. Everyone knows he has a vile temper. They'd believe he killed another woman. They like you. Maybe this time they'd even hang him. It's been a while since the town's seen a good hanging."

It could happen, I thought wildly, and then stilled the fear. I could not think of all the possibilities now. I could only try to find a way to escape. "Jordan's no fool, even if everyone else is. I told him about the sounds I had heard. He was suspicious. He didn't believe Prudence was here. Why do you think he was here tonight, Mr. Hallender? He was watching the schoolhouse. Maybe he's watching now."

"I don't believe you," he said succinctly. "You had a lovers' quarrel. That much I heard. And I watched him ride over the hills before I came in through your room. Bennett's gone."

I decided to try another tactic. "What has he ever done to you? Wasn't he your friend? You'd have his death on your conscience as well as mine if the town did put him on trial and hanged him."

"Shut your damn mouth!" he snarled furiously. His gun hand shook violently, and I thought for an instant he was going to pull the trigger without even realizing what he was doing. He paused and then suddenly holstered his gun, hammer back in place, and grabbed up the rope.

I did not hesitate. I bolted past him for the door. He swore vilely and kicked out his bum leg to trip me. I heard him grunt in pain. Then his fingers became tangled in my free hair, drawing me up short with a cry. I stumbled and fell to my knees. My scalp was stinging, and I was sure he was going to rip my hair right out.

"Let go! You can't hang me!" I cried, grabbing at his hand. I fought as I felt him trying to sling the noose over my head. I twisted around and kicked out hard with my bare feet. I felt my toes and soles crush into him. He gave a high-pitched screech of pain and doubled over. I struggled up and frantically threw off the rope. Hallender's fingers came out, grasping blindly until they fastened on my nightgown. The top buttons ripped away as I strained forward toward the door of my room. I turned to hit his hands loose.

"You bitch . . ." he gasped. His face was a grimace of agony, but his eyes were blazing with feral rage. I grunted and gasped with my violent efforts to beat free. He loosened one hand, doubling it into a fist as he swung at me. He caught me across the side of my jaw. I tasted blood as I dropped to my knees. He grabbed my hair, pulling my face up as he hit me again and again until I was senseless.

"You had to make it hard, didn't you?" he groaned. "You had to fight me! Well, your lover Bennett will get blamed for the mess I've made of your face," he went on. Then he looped the noose around my neck as I lay prostrate on the floor. My fingers clutched at the rope, but he yanked hard. I gasped for air. He dragged me across the floor. Then I heard the rope slap against the rafter above. He was hauling me up. My feet were off the floor. I was kicking. The rope burned my neck. I choked. The circulation was cut off in my fingers as the noose tightened. I fought, the muscles of my arms straining with all their strength.

God, help me. I am dying! My vision blurred as I choked, gagging against the bounds of the rope. I kicked one last time.

Then suddenly I was falling. I hit the floor hard, and the slackened rope loosened about my neck as my fingers continued their pulling. I dragged in air painfully, staring around me for Hallender. I yanked frantically and managed to pull the noose off.

Hallender was falling backward against the desk in an effort to escape the fleeting, white form that was trying to engulf him. The sheriff hit the lantern, knocking it onto the floor. It shattered, and kerosene splashed out onto the floor at Hallender's feet. The lighted wick made the fuel explode into flames that licked up the man's legs. He screamed in pain, the animal sound tearing into my brain. When he ran for the door, I did not stop to think of what he had just tried to do to me. I stumbled up and chased after him, shouting his name.

Hallender's body was engulfed in flames by the time he reached the street. He staggered and fell. Dropping down next to him, I rolled him over in the mud, trying frantically to extinguish the flames. Lights were going on in houses close by. People were coming out, staring up the street in curiosity.

"Help me! Help me!" I cried. Hallender's screams of agony

were making me cry out as though I were burning. I tried to pound out the flames.

A few people started running up the street. Two men reached me and helped me roll the sheriff over until the flames were completely smothered. Hallender's screams changed to moans as he writhed in agony. The exposed flesh was blackened and bloody, the smell of burned skin and muscle sickeningly sweet in the air. He moaned, delirious, twisting against the efforts of the men, who were trying to comfort him.

There was nothing else I could do for Tom Hallender. I averted my face as the two men bent closer to talk to him. I could not bear his agony, and I stood up. Looking back up the street, I saw flames flickering through the window of the schoolhouse. I bolted forward. "The schoolhouse!" I cried in dismay. "Someone help me put the fire out!" I started to run back.

"Let it burn!" shouted one of the men. "Miss McFarland, let it burn!"

In confusion, people were looking at Hallender's charred body and then at the burning building down the street. The sheriff began to scream again as the two men carefully lifted him.

I ran down the street, through the schoolhouse gate and up the path to the front steps. Dashing into the building, I ripped curtains from the front windows and slapped at the flames that were destroying my desk and the front seats of the classroom. My arms rose and fell, rose and fell; yet my efforts seemed to only whip the fire into further fury.

Running to my room, I grabbed the bucket of water from the stove. I hauled it back into the schoolroom. After shoving the curtains into the water, I beat again at the flames with the drenched cloth. I worked feverishly, but the fire was still gaining, licking over the wooden floor and catching books and papers, spreading farther and growing increasingly, hellishly hotter.

Finally I took the bucket and cast the water over my desk in hopes that I might save something. Weakened, my fingers lost hold of the handle, and the bucket thudded heavily onto the floor on the other side of the desk, into the burning inferno and out of reach. Smoke was everywhere, and I could hardly breathe. I reached out and grabbed Ellen Greer's two bronze plaques.

Then I thought of the money, the savings of farmers and ranchers in the valley around Sycamore Hill. If nothing else could be salvaged, that must be. I managed to reach my room again, although the fire was now eating at the wooden framework of the schoolroom and creeping closer to my quarters. My precious books were catching fire, but there was nothing I could do. I reached my bed, coughing in the iron-gray air. I yanked at the mattress and pulled it from the narrow bunk and onto the floor.

Had I grown so weak? I fought to drag the mattress across the floor to the back door. I coughed, my lungs burning with the acrid air. It was hot, and the flames were illuminating the frame of the classroom doorway. In a minute this room would be engulfed.

Where was the rain now? God, please, let it rain again! I prayed fervently, all the while jerking frantically at the mattress. I managed somehow to drag it out onto the steps. Getting it down to the ground was easier, but it was a muscle-aching chore to drag it through the wet grass to a safe distance. Only when I stopped did I notice that the back end of the mattress had caught fire. I beat it out with my hands.

Then, blessedly, it did begin to rain. A deluge fell from the black clouds. Fire and water sizzled and hissed in mortal combat.

I sank down, my body shaking with physical exhaustion. I stared up bleakly at the schoolhouse, which was still burning in the torrent of rain. The roof was almost gone. The flames reached out the windows, blackening the sides of the building. There would be little worth salvaging by the time the storm extinguished the fire. I had dropped Ellen Greer's plaques in my room.

In my mind's eye I saw my burned books; the children's art; the blackened, destroyed desks and walls. My head was beginning to throb, and I groaned, pressing my fingers to my temples. My face felt stiff and swollen. I sank farther down as though the rain were a weight on my shoulders. Finally, keeling over, I lay numb on the grassy slope beneath the oak.

"Abby. . . ." A deep, anxious voice entered my consciousness. "Abby." I felt strong hands on me, turning me onto my back. The rain was cold on my face. The man lifted me in his arms. As he carried me, my head bounced against the hard muscles of his shoulder. My eyes flickered open, and I saw people standing around and then walking alongside as I was carried down the street high in his arms. I heard people talking.

"Is she going to be all right?"

"What happened to her face?"

"Tom Hallender died. Burned to death!"

"The sheriff admitted he had the money! It was in the mattress Miss McFarland dragged out of the schoolhouse!"

The man carried me on down Main Street, with people following. The voices rose and fell around me as I wavered in and out of consciousness. My head hurt, and I groaned. The man's arms tightened protectively, drawing me still closer to the warmth of his body. "You'll be all right," he whispered, his voice hoarse with worry.

"You can't take her there!" someone said in protest. "Get her out of the rain! Maybe Sadie will let her use Miss Greer's old back room."

"I've got a new boarder. Sorry."

I was cold and shivering. The rain kept coming, but it had softened to a drizzle. I could feel my nightgown clinging to my chilled skin. My protector carried me on, effortlessly. I could hear the rapid beat of his heart. I felt it against my breast as he held me cradled next to him like a child.

A door opened and closed behind us. I heard noise and more voices, then silence. Someone touched my brow with gentle fingers. Through a haze of pain and exhaustion I opened my eyes. My vision was blurred.

Marba Lane moved closer, her soft fingers pressing the damp hair away from my cheek. "Put her in my room, Ross. I'll take care of her."

I heard no more.

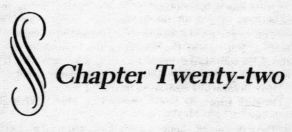

Chapter Twenty-two

Doctor Patrick Kirk's head was slightly bowed, and his eyes were narrowed with concentration as he listened through his stethoscope to my rapidly drumming heart. I knew how fast it was racing, and I also knew that he could tell just how frightened and tense I was at this examination. Would he begin to wonder why?

I watched the doctor's face closely for some indication of what he was thinking. Finally, he straightened up, pulling the medical instrument from his ears and letting it dangle against his white shirt and tweed vest. He looked at my distraught face.

"I want you to understand that anything, absolutely anything I learn from my examinations is strictly confidential."

The flood of color washed in and out of my cheeks like waves on a white-sand beach. Then I swallowed hard. "You know."

"That you're pregnant? Yes. From my first examination. About seven weeks, I'd say."

I closed my eyes tightly. "Will the baby be all right?" I asked, thinking of the events of the last few days and the violence and physical exertion of the previous night.

"Then you want this child?"

I opened my eyes and looked at him. My hand crept down to my abdomen, and I thought of Jordan. I loved him, but I would never share his life except through this baby I carried. "Yes, I want this baby very much," I whispered.

"In that case you were very lucky. You've a strong constitution. The baby is well-set. I don't think you'll have any problems." He smiled kindly. "I should tell you that I suspected you were pregnant the night of the Christmas program."

"Yes?" My eyes widened. "How?"

The doctor's hand came up as his fingers lightly traced beneath my eyes to my cheekbones. "I noticed the faintest mask of pregnancy. I doubt anyone else would have paid any attention. But I guess I'm always on the lookout for new patients." He smiled like an old friend, and my tension left me. I could talk to this man without fear or embarrassment.

"How soon will I be able to travel?" I asked.

Dr. Kirk frowned, then he rubbed his chin. "What about the father?"

"The father doesn't know. I don't think he'd want to, Doctor," I said, anticipating what he would say next. "And . . . and this situation is more my fault than his. He doesn't love me, and I wouldn't want him to feel he had to marry me." The words dragged out painfully.

"How far are you intending to travel?" he asked after a careful study of my face and deciding he would not be able to change my mind. My eyes burned.

"As far as possible." Marba had come into the room this morning to tell me that there had been a $1,500 reward for information leading to the capture of the bank robbers and return of the money. That would take me quite a distance and leave me enough to live on until the baby was born.

"How are you traveling?"

"By coach some of the way, then by train."

"Well, so long as it isn't by horseback and you're not going too long a distance by coach, I don't see any problem. Just some common sense, and let your body be the guide. If you start aching or cramping, rest. Don't push yourself!" He smiled wryly then. "Try to keep the worrying to a minimum, if possible. And as soon as you get settled, contact a physician."

"Thank you." I stared down at my clutched hands, tears welled into my eyes.

He patted my shoulder soothingly. "I wish you luck, Miss McFarland." He left.

I lay back in bed, feeling the heavy weight of my situation on my chest. The door cracked slightly, and someone tapped.

"Mind if I come in for a visit?" Ross asked, entering anyway. He walked to the bed and drew up a chair. "Doc said you'd be as good as new in a couple of days."

I forced a smile. Ross's face softened, and he picked up my hand. "You're beautiful, even with black eyes. How's your head? Doc said you suffered a concussion. You have to take it easy for a while. Just lie back and let me wait on you." He pressed his mouth against the palm of my hand.

"You're quite the heroine in town now." He grinned. "Everyone is buzzing about how you risked your life to go back into that schoolhouse to drag out the bank's money. What are you going to do with the reward? Blow it away on pretty dresses?"

"I don't think so." I smiled. "Probably use it for something more sensible than that." I couldn't tell him yet that I was leaving. I remembered the tone of his voice as he had lifted me. I remembered flashes of his face when he lay me on this bed. How I wished Jordan Bennett had looked at me like that, just once.

"Is the schoolhouse completely destroyed?" I asked, hoping he would believe the tremor in my voice was due to worry about the fire.

"No. The rain had already pretty well soaked the place before Hallender accidentally started the fire. The storm put it out in a short time. There's not much to salvage, I'm afraid. It's a shell, though your quarters are still intact. You aren't planning to go back there, are you?" He seemed surprised and disturbed.

"No." I shook my head. "No, I won't go back there."

"I picked up your things. You can stay here as long as you want."

"I feel awful about putting Marba out of her own bed."

"Why should you? Marba likes you." He gave a slight

chuckle. "I think she enjoys playing the role of benevolent nurse." I did not like his tone.

"I'm very grateful to her, Ross."

Ross relented. "Marba's a good woman."

"I'm glad you're aware of that."

He laughed under his breath. "You sound just like a school-marm when you talk like that."

"I should." I smiled slightly.

Ross clasped my hand between his and stared into my eyes, his own darkening with emotion. "Abigail, I think you know how I feel about you." I was unable to keep the dismay from my expression, and he sighed ruefully. "Don't say anything right now. We'll give it a little more time."

There was nothing time would change in my feelings for Ross Persall, but I couldn't tell him that. I hoped he did not feel about me what I felt for Jordan Bennett. I wouldn't want anyone to hurt that much. And soon I would be gone.

"I haven't thanked you yet," I stammered self-consciously, wishing there were some way to make him feel nothing but friendship toward me.

Ross stood looking down at me. "That's not necessary."

"I wish there were something I could do."

Ross leaned down. "There is one thing," he whispered. "What?"

"Let me kiss you," he breathed. I liked Ross Persall. I was grateful to him, but when he put his mouth on mine, I felt nothing but vague acceptance. His kiss was gentle at first, then he started to probe my lips with his tongue. I drew away immediately, feeling repulsed. Jordan's kisses had been far more intimate, but my reaction had been drastically different.

"I'm sorry," I murmured, unable to look at him.

He sighed again, resigned. "You really are an innocent. I don't believe a man has ever really kissed you before. If you gave me a chance, you might find you'd like it."

I was not about to blurt out my knowledge on sexual response. Better his ego remain intact, than disillusion him about my response to his kiss. No man would ever touch me again, not in the way Jordan Bennett had. All I had, I had given. And there was no more for anyone else.

"I think you should let Miss McFarland rest, Ross," Marba said from the doorway, her eyes cold and sparkling. Her gaze flickered from my flushed face to Ross. He walked indolently across the room and paused beside her, his mouth quirking up at one side in a taunting smile. Then he looked back at me, his expression tender.

"I'll be back to see you later."

Marba shut the door after him with a sharp thud. Then she turned. I could see nothing but warmth and friendly concern in her smile as she approached the bed and took the seat that Ross had recently vacated.

"I hope you didn't misunderstand . . ." I started, attempting an explanation for what she had just seen.

"I didn't. It doesn't concern me except that I'd hate to see you get hurt, Miss McFarland."

"Please, call me Abby."

Marba smiled and touched my hand. "Abby, then. I like you very much, you know. But you're very naïve about men, I think. Ross is a little out of your league."

"I'm not in love with him," I told her frankly, hoping it would allay any of her possible fears or hidden jealousies.

"I'm glad. I'd hate to see you making the same mistakes I did when I was younger," she said, her eyes sad. "We women can mistake passionate embraces for declarations of love." She shook her head. "Don't overlook Ross's character flaws, Abby. It would be a terrible mistake."

"Ross has been very kind to me," I felt impelled to say in his defense.

"Ross? Kind?" Marba raised her brows and gave me a tight smile. "How very little you know about Ross Persall. I hope you never learn any more than you know right now."

After a hearty lunch, which Katrina delivered to my room, I lay back against the pillows, allowing exhaustion to take over. When I awakened, it was dark outside. I heard voices in the other room. The door cracked slightly, and, not wanting to see anyone, I closed my eyes and feigned sleep.

"Leave her alone, Ross," Marba said sharply, and I heard the door creak again as he drew it partially closed, turning to answer her.

"Why don't you butt out, Marba? This isn't any of your business," he said bitingly.

"I like Abby. I don't want to see you hurt her."

"You're jealous!" Ross accused, not without a tinge of satisfaction tainting his voice.

Marba did not speak for a moment. "I'm not jealous," she then said quietly, "I stopped loving you a long time ago. Katrina's father taught me a lot about men like you. I knew what you were before I ever let you touch me."

"Then why did you?"

"Hope, maybe. A foolish dream. I don't know. What does it matter now? But please leave her alone," Marba pleaded. I stared at the door, seeing movement as Ross stepped away. He didn't shut the door, and I could still hear what was going on, though I wished I didn't.

"Did you ever stop to think that I might love Abigail?"

"I'd be happy if you did," she said, sounding sincere. "But you haven't got it in you to really love anyone. It's not your fault. It's just the way you are. You always want the unattainable. You have to try and make every woman fall in love with you. Even that poor, pathetic creature, Prudence Townsend...."

I sat up, unable to stop listening now.

"What do you know about her?" Ross asked, his voice dropping.

"I know you used to go see her late at night. And whenever you were around, she watched you. Oh, Ross! Did you add her to the notches on your bedpost too? Did you feel any guilt when she hanged herself? I don't doubt for a second that she did it because she was in love with you. She was a dreadful little snob with her ridiculous airs of importance, and I hated her for the way she treated Katrina. But she didn't deserve your brand of calculated cruelty."

"I'm sorry she did that," Ross said in a flat tone of defensiveness. "But I don't feel any guilt about it. Why should I? I didn't give her the rope. I never made her any promises."

"But you did make love to her."

"I accepted what she gave, sure. Who wouldn't? But then she started talking about settling down and getting married.

The last time I saw her, she was boring me with gushy talk about my making a fine father, and wouldn't I like to have a son just like me someday. My God! Can you imagine me with a kid strapped around my neck like a millstone for the rest of my life? I thought I was doing her a favor when I quit seeing her."

"You just stopped seeing her? Without any explanation?" Marba asked, quietly expressive.

"Well, what the hell! What was I supposed to do? It would have been worse if I had dragged it out any longer. And she knew anyway how the whole affair was going to end . . . or she damn well should have. She was the worst kind of clinging vine."

"Oh, Ross."

I didn't listen anymore. Sagging back against the pillow, I suddenly knew exactly why Prudence Townsend had killed herself. She had been carrying Ross Persall's child.

Standing at the window the following morning, I saw Jordan riding into town. He passed over the crest of the hill beyond town and rode right beneath my window. My heart jolted at the sight of him, and I watched as he continued up Main Street, stopping finally in front of Olmstead's store. Had he heard anything about what had happened at the schoolhouse? But how could he have? And what possible difference would it make?

Sighing heavily, I leaned my head against the window frame. I kept the curtain drawn back so that I could gaze out with Sycamore Hill stretching before me. My eyes kept straying back to Jordan's sleek stallion as it shifted impatiently at the rail. Jordan came out of the store and stood unmoving on the steps. He rubbed the back of his neck in a weary gesture. Then he descended the steps hurriedly and gracefully swung up into the saddle. He paused once on his ride back up Main Street, casting a long glance up McPherson to the burned-out school-house. Then he came back toward the hotel.

My heart began to pound. Drawing back so that I could not be seen from the street, I continued to watch Jordan. I was unable to tear my gaze away. Could he feel me watching him?

Jordan slowed as he came abreast of the hotel. My heart

was thundering in my chest. He drew his horse in and then dismounted. When he walked into the hotel, I gripped the material of the curtains in an agony of tension and hopeful longing. Was he stopping to see me, or did he have another reason for coming here?

Five minutes later Jordan reappeared. Raking agitated fingers through his hair, he remounted and turned back toward the road out of town. He set his horse at a leisurely trot that quickened almost immediately as he crossed the bridge. I watched him galloping away, thinking I would never see him again. Finally he disappeared over the rise of the hill.

I turned away, heedless of the tears that streamed down my face. Crossing the small room, I sank down onto the bed and gave myself up to sobs of desolation. "Oh, Jordan. . . ."

I never once noticed Katrina watching me silently from the doorway.

Most of the swelling in my face from Hallender's beating had gone down after the first few days. The bruises were still ugly, though they were gradually fading to yellow and purple across my cheekbones and eyes. My head no longer hurt, but I still suffered from dizziness now and then, though not from the blow Hallender had given me. Morning sickness still beset me each day, and I tired easily. Since seeing Jordan ride away, I had little appetite and was listless and depressed most of the time. I felt guilty for Marba's attempts to cheer me. And Ross was constantly coming in to visit me. Doctor Kirk was the only one who understood my mood and the reason for it.

A week after Ross had carried me to the hotel, the Reverend Hayes came to see me. I prayed he had not come to argue or sermonize on my shortcomings. He had not, and he sat down after making a swift study of my face. He looked slightly horrified by it. Then he got right to the point of his visit. "Doctor Kirk says you're doing well. Will you be ready to restart classes in, say, another week?"

"Don't you think I'd frighten the children?" I asked with a slight smile. He flushed a bit. I regretted my comment immediately and smiled apologetically.

"The schoolhouse is unusable, I know," he said. "But there's always the church. There's plenty of room there. We could set things up temporarily, until a new schoolhouse could be built. There are already plans underway."

"That sounds good." I nodded.

"Then you agree to restart classes in a week?" He seemed greatly relieved.

"I'm sorry. No."

"Do you need more time?"

"It's not that." I swallowed heavily. "I'm leaving Sycamore Hill."

Hayes sighed, not surprised by my announcement. "If you do that, you leave us all in an awful lurch," he said almost blandly. I felt guilty, but I knew there was no way I could stay on. Hayes would be the first to tell me to leave if he knew the truth of my condition.

"I'm sorry about that. But I . . . I just can't stay. I hope you understand." There was no way he could understand the real reason for my wanting to leave. I hoped that he would believe my intimation that it was the experiences at the schoolhouse that made me wish to resign.

"You could at least do us the courtesy of remaining until we find a replacement."

"It was my understanding that it took you a year or more to find one after . . . after Miss Townsend . . . died."

Hayes looked down. "I don't expect it will be any easier to find another this time," he muttered, disgruntled by the prospect. When he glanced back up at me, he seemed momentarily discomforted. "I can understand your hesitation, of course," he said. It was the closest he had ever come to an apology.

"I hoped you would," I murmured inanely, feeling guilty for the unuttered lies that hung in the air. My experience with Hallender was enough to make anyone wish to leave. Let Reverend Hayes believe it was reason enough for me.

Hayes shifted uneasily in his chair, his eyes moving about the room in vague curiosity. He cleared his throat. "Elizabeth told me about her talk with you," he began with obvious embarrassment. "I know we've never gotten on. Is that part of the reason you're leaving?"

"No, please," I said, embarrassed as well. "I know you

were always concerned with what was best for the children. It's just that we didn't agree on some things. I wasn't always very tactful."

"The children need you, Miss McFarland," Hayes said, relieved but determined. "You've done a good job with them since you came. Your teaching methods aren't, well, aren't always orthodox." He smiled. "But they were learning," he added quickly, afraid I would take offense.

"Thank you for that." I smiled slightly.

"You can't just leave them high and dry now," he went on. It was just the sort of guilt appeal that the Haversalls had used on me when I had suggested leaving to begin my own life. It had worked then, and under different circumstances it would have worked now as well. The choice had always been there for me to make before if I had had the strength to follow through. Mistaken gratitude and guilt-ridden responsibility had bound me then. Now it was the birth of my child. There were moments when I almost rejoiced with the knowledge of the baby within me. Other times I felt almost overcome with fear of our future.

"I'm sorry," I said quietly. Hayes looked at me for a long moment.

"There's no way I can change your mind, Miss McFarland?"

"No. I am sorry."

He stood up. "I won't say I like your decision," he told me frankly. "You did your job in spite of our differences. If you need a reference, I'll give you a good one." At my surprised look, he seemed almost insulted. "I'm a fair man. In your shoes I don't suppose I'd want to stay here either."

I could not look at him.

"Good day to you, Miss McFarland. And good luck," he said flatly, putting on his hat as he left the room.

"You're really leaving then," Marba said regretfully. "Isn't there any way we can change your mind?" Katrina held a plate of cookies in front of me, but I shook my head having no appetite for them.

"No, thank you, Katrina." I glanced up at Marba sitting across from me. "I really can't stay, Marba," I told her unsteadily.

My plans to depart on the Oakland stage in the morning were already made. I had even purchased my ticket, and my few possessions were packed and ready in my carpetbag and small trunk. The bank president had been by the previous day to give me the reward for returning the bank money. I had not wanted to accept it, but had little choice. I needed it to support myself until the baby was born and I could find employment. The money belonged to the people of Sycamore Hill, and under any other circumstances I could not have accepted the reward at all. It was only right that all of it should have been returned. However, pride had to be set aside due to necessity and circumstances.

"Please," Katrina added to her mother's appeal. The little girl's eyes were filled with soulful pleading. Never had I felt more guilty and dreadful.

I reached up and cupped her sweet face. "I'm sorry, sweetheart. But I just can't."

Her eyes filled. "Even if . . . even if Mr. Bennett asked you to stay? Would you if he asked you?" she pleaded.

The shock of her unexpected question caught me completely off guard. What could Katrina know about my relationship with Jordan Bennett? I wondered in near panic, hoping that my feelings didn't show on my face. My smile wavered. "It wouldn't make any difference," I managed to answer. It would never happen, I added to myself.

"Katie, what makes you ask such a thing?" Marba queried, looking between her daughter and me.

Katrina turned. "I saw Miss McFarland crying. She . . . she said his name."

I felt Marba's eyes turn on me in a curious stare.

"Go wash your face, honey," Marba instructed her daughter gently. "Then would you go downstairs for a while so that I can talk with Miss McFarland alone?" Katrina nodded her small bowed head. She shuffled dejectedly out of the room.

As soon as the door closed behind her, I stood up and walked uneasily to the window, looking down on Main Street. I could feel Marba watching me closely. We had talked many times since I had come to the hotel. After the first night I had moved into the room next-door. Marba had come often to sit with me, and we had covered a myriad of subjects, though never touching on anything too highly personal.

"Abby?"

"The weather has cleared," I said quickly. "I thought it would be raining again this afternoon and even tomorrow when I leave. But it's clear." I winced, thinking of tomorrow morning. I closed my eyes and saw Jordan's face. I opened my eyes again, trying to purge myself of him. What was the use?

"I always suspected there was more to your leaving than what happened with Hallender," Marba said quietly, ignoring my efforts to avoid the subject. I turned and gave her a purposeful, surprised look.

"What else could there be? I should think that experience would be enough."

"Oh, yes, for anyone else. But not for you." She smiled kindly. "You love the children, and you feel a heavy responsibility toward them. I remember how upset you were two days ago, when Hayes came to see you and ask you to stay on. You would, I think, if something else hadn't entered into your decision. How does Jordan Bennett fit in?"

"He . . . he doesn't," I answered. I gave a self-conscious laugh. "I don't know what Katrina was thinking. She must have been mistaken." I turned away, unable to look Marba in the face.

"Oh, Abby," she said sympathetically.

My fingers moved back and forth on the sill as I tried to block out all thoughts of Jordan and my leaving tomorrow morning. "He's not the reason I'm leaving," I said truthfully. I'm leaving because I'm going to have his baby, I added silently to myself.

"Does he know you're leaving?"

"Everyone knows. I'm sure he does too," I said, unaware of how revealing my tone was. "Anyway," I turned around with a forced smile of brightness, "I'm looking forward to my trip, I've . . . I've missed the East Coast."

"Maybe Ross should ride out and tell Jordan."

"No! No! Please!" My face whitened with fright. "Don't ask him to do that. You don't understand, Marba. Please, promise me."

"All right. Please don't get so upset."

I rubbed my hand across my face, taking deep, calming breaths. "I'm sorry. That was silly of me," I muttered and gave a self-deprecating laugh. "I'm not myself lately."

"Diego and his mother would like to know. They owe you a lot for the tutoring you did," she tried again.

I shook my head. "It's better if I just go. I've said enough good-byes in the past few days to last me a lifetime. I couldn't. . . ." I did not finish, nor did I need to do so. Marba seemed to understand. I sat down again, and my fingers plucked idly at my skirt. She watched me. The silence was uncomfortable, and I stood up again. I began to pace.

"Maybe if you stayed on, things would work out. I don't think Jordan Bennett is indifferent to you," Marba suggested.

I gave a bleak laugh. "Oh, he's not indifferent to me. He despises me. I let him. . . ." I stopped, realizing almost too late what I was about to blurt out in my misery. I let out my breath.

"Abby." Marba's voice was full of question and concern.

"I believed all the gossip about him. I was a fool where he was concerned. I did everything wrong; I said everything wrong." I stopped and looked at her. "Believe me, Marba. Jordan Bennett will rejoice when I get on that stage tomorrow."

Marba looked at me long and hard. Then she changed the subject.

 *Chapter Twenty-three*

It seemed fitting that I should leave town by the Oakland stage. My trunk and carpetbag were heaved up and secured to the roof, and Ross helped me into the cab. He held my hand a little longer than necessary.

Looking back out the side window, I forced a bright smile at Marba who was standing with sad-eyed Katrina on the walkway. Others had come to say good-bye—Matthew Hayes and his brothers, the Poole boys, Margaret Hudson, Chester and Harold Studebaker with their father, and little Toby Carmichael. Elvira Hudson stood with Emily Olmstead, and Elizabeth Hayes was with Dr. Kirk. They all seemed hopeful that even at the last moment I would change my mind and stay. I looked at the doctor, and he smiled, giving me a slow nod of understanding. My smile wavered and then stiffened with purposeful determination. The coach started off, and I gave one last wave and a lingering look at the friends I was leaving. I had only been in Sycamore Hill for five months, and they had been trying ones. But the small town had become my home, more so than Boston had ever been.

I averted my eyes and did not look back again. A hard knot

of pain swelled in my throat. My chest ached. I refused to cry. The time of crying was past. I had my baby to think of now, and I would not let it be born into sadness. I had enough money to start new somewhere, perhaps even San Francisco if I could bear being that close to Jordan. I had already decided I would tell everyone I was widowed. My child would never know differently and would grow up believing that he or she had been conceived in love and marriage. I would give my baby enough love for two parents, and I would work hard to make sure that my child would never lack for security.

But San Francisco was too close. Perhaps Sacramento. Or maybe north to Portland, Oregon, or even Seattle, Washington. I did not want to go back to the East again. There was nothing there for me, and I loved the West. What did it matter where I went as long as I was far enough away from Sycamore Hill and Jordan Bennett to protect my baby from the truth?

Would my child look like Jordan? A boy with brown hair, sun-streaked-gold in summer. A boy with sharp blue eyes and a quick intelligence. A boy that would grow tall and broad-shouldered. A sharp pain knifed me in the pit of my stomach as I thought of that possibility. It would be agony to have a son who would grow more like Jordan every day. Yet, it would be wonderful too.

The coach bounced and jolted as it rolled over the storm-puddled road. It climbed slowly, winding through the hills. Then the road dipped, and we quickened our pace. If all went on schedule, I would reach Oakland by late afternoon. I would stay on for a day in a hotel near the train station. Tomorrow I would decide where I was going to settle.

My back ached from the constant jarring motion as we bounced along. We stopped twice to water the horses, and I walked around, shaking the stiffness from my limbs after seeking the privacy of the bushes away from the road. Then on we went. Finally exhaustion overcame discomfort, and I slept.

When I awakened, the stagecoach was stopped. Turning my head, I saw the sun dipping toward the west. We were out of the hills, but there was no sound of a bustling city outside. The stagecoach driver was talking to someone, and I listened with vague interest.

"Just tie your horse up back there. He's lathered pretty bad, isn't he? Looks like you've been riding hard. We've only got about ten miles to go, and I'm on schedule. So I'll take it easy. It won't hurt to be a little late. It's happened plenty of times before." The driver laughed.

Someone answered from the back of the coach, but I could not make out the words. Reins slapped against the back luggage carrier as the stranger tied his mount to the stagecoach. I sighed heavily and leaned my head back again before once more closing my eyes. When I'd left town, I had been thankful that I was alone. I had not wanted, nor felt able, to carry on polite conversation with anyone.

The door opened, and the vehicle dipped against the weight of the man stepping in. The wheels creaked and started to roll forward again. We were on our way. Ten more miles, the driver had said. Could I feign sleep that long? I felt my silent companion watching me. After a few moments I slowly opened my eyes. I encountered an intense blue gaze from the dust-covered, sweat-stained man sitting opposite me.

"Jordan!" I breathed in shock and confusion, my eyes widening as I straightened in the seat. A surge of happiness and hope bloomed inside me and then quickly evaporated into frightened suspicion. Why was he here? He had obviously ridden hard to catch up. He looked drawn with exhaustion. The lines were deep around his eyes and mouth.

He let out his breath as though he had been holding it for a long time. Then he wearily rubbed the back of his neck. "My God!" he muttered. "What a run you've given me."

I stared at him in growing dismay. Had he guessed why I had left? Had someone told him? Dr. Kirk? No. He didn't know Jordan was the father of my baby. Marba? No. She had promised not to tell him anything. Why had he come after me? I wondered in panic-stricken silence.

"I thought you were going to marry Ross."

I gasped. "Ross? What made you think that? Just because I stayed at the hotel?"

"Ross told me he planned to take care of you on a permanent basis."

"Ross said that?"

"Why else do you think I stayed away?" he demanded harshly. "When I found out what had happened, I came to the hotel to talk with you. He greeted me with that piece of news. I just rode out and stayed at the ranch."

"I thought you knew I was leaving," I murmured.

His eyes snapped. "How could I? You didn't let me know! And I didn't have any idea of what your plans were other than what Ross told me. I didn't know until Matthew Hayes rode out this morning with news from his father that school was closed until further notice. Matthew told me that you had left this morning on the Oakland stage." Jordan's face was taut and white.

"Why are you here?"

His eyes moved away from mine. He put his booted foot up on the seat, resting his arm on his knee as he rubbed his beard-shadowed face. He looked at me again, but his expression was unreadable. "I wanted to apologize."

My heart sank.

"I'm sorry about what happened at the schoolhouse. I should have been there." His face was lined, his frown deepening as he assessed my face. "Are you all right now? Jim Olmstead said Hallender beat you up pretty badly." His face became very pale. "I should have been there! I should have stayed to keep an eye out for you. I shouldn't have left you alone at all. I knew something was going on in that place. And I left you."

"You don't owe me any apology." I smiled weakly. "I said some terrible things to you."

"About Reva? When my temper had a chance to cool down a little, I knew you had said that because you were afraid. You knew what I wanted. . . ."

I flushed and looked quickly down at my hands. My knuckles were white.

"Abby," he said softly. "Abby, I'm sorry."

"You . . . you haven't a thing to be sorry about." I shook my head, unable to look up at him again. I wished he had not come. This only made things harder. It only emphasized how much I loved him for the man he was.

"Is that why you're leaving? Because of what happened to you? Or is there something more?"

"Why else?" I asked, glancing up with sudden trepidation.

"I thought maybe . . ." He stopped and looked away. "Never mind."

"What did you think?" I asked. My heart was pounding in tension. Did he know? Did he suspect why I was really leaving?

His mouth curved up in a smile that didn't reach his intense blue eyes. "I thought maybe you wanted to get as far away from me as you could."

"I suppose that's partly true," I admitted with a sigh.

Jordan winced. "I deserved that. I've behaved like the biggest ass alive with you," he said in self-contempt. I started to protest, but he jerked his head in a cutting way. "I'm going to explain a few things to you."

"You don't owe me any explanation about anything."

"You've got to understand about Gwen."

"No!" I averted my eyes so he wouldn't see the look of pain his wife's name caused.

"I met her at a dinner party given by the university dean," he began, ignoring my protest.

"Please. I don't want to hear any of it. It's nothing to do with me."

He gave me a quelling look and continued with his usual ruthless determination. "He was introducing me as 'a young attorney with promise,'" he said dryly. "I met Gwen's father first, and then he introduced me to Gwen. She was beautiful, and I was attracted to her. So I started seeing her on a regular basis. I thought I loved her enough to marry her. She agreed to my proposal. When I made plans to return to the West Coast, we argued. She tried every kind of argument and pressure to keep me in Boston. I knew about that time that I didn't really love her and that we should break off the engagement. That's when she told me she was pregnant."

My face stiffened and went very pale.

"She thought that would change all my plans about returning here, but it didn't. So she miscarried."

I gasped. "You make it sound like she planned to lose your baby," I said, slightly defensive. Jordan just looked at me.

"We stayed in Boston for another six months, and she conceived Linda."

What he was saying hurt. I thought of Jordan with his wife, making love with her, and it gnawed at my insides. I looked at Jordan. His face was implacable and cold.

"I wanted my child born on the ranch; so we came west despite Gwen's tantrums. She hated everything about California. She was still hoping she could make me go back to Boston, but when she finally realized she couldn't, she started to drink. It started as a means of hurting me. Then I don't think she could stop herself. It was like a sickness. Thank God, Reva was there to take care of Linda," he said, looking away and staring out the window as the land rolled by. A muscle worked in his jaw.

"During one of her binges Gwen told me her first pregnancy and the miscarriage had been a neat little invention to keep me in Boston."

My mouth gaped open at him. He still stared grimly out the window.

"She told me I could have been a famous, rich attorney who would rub elbows with the Boston elite, instead of a dime-a-dozen rancher in California." His mouth twisted in bitter memory. "The age-old female trick to get a man to marry her, and I fell for it like a fool. We both suffered for my stupidity."

I felt very cold. I was grateful that Jordan did not know or suspect anything about the baby I carried. He would believe I intended doing the same thing Gwendolyn Bracklin-Reed had done—trapping him into an unwanted marriage.

Jordan looked at me, his mouth drawn down, his eyes glittering with remembered anger. "Can you have any idea how I felt when she told me that? I think I could have killed her, but by that time I pitied her. She couldn't help what she was. She had been reared to put status above everything, to look for a man rich enough and socially accepted enough to give her all her dreams. We didn't want the same things. But she could never accept that. She made my life, and her own, a misery." He leaned back. "I swore when she died that no woman would ever get to me again. I'd been a fool over one once, and I wasn't going to be again for any price."

The hardness of his face eased, and his mouth turned up in a half-smile as he looked at me again. "Then you came along, stumbling along the road like some lost, dust-covered waif. You remember what happened?"

"I fell flat on my face," I muttered with a self-contemptuous smile.

"And you laughed at yourself. I liked you before you ever turned around. And when you did. . . ." He shook his head, and his smile softened. "Then I realized who you were, and knew what would happen if you showed up in town with me by your side. You wouldn't have had a job waiting for you."

"I understood that later. But you might have explained."

"I wasn't in an expansive mood by that time. All I could think of was what a waste of a beautiful woman. Then I realized where my thoughts were leading."

I concentrated on keeping my expression cool. What Jordan was saying made me happy, because I knew he had been attracted to me from the first. But it changed nothing. If he found out I was pregnant, he would remember Gwendolyn Bracklin-Reed's tactics in trapping him. He would feel obligated to marry me, and what attraction he had would be destroyed like the fragile, meaningless thing it was. Hadn't it happened once before?

"I waited around at the store to make sure you got there all right. Then I tried to explain why I left you walking."

"My reputation." I smiled slightly. "I know. I realized later when Mr. Olmstead listed the rules."

"I wanted you to keep your job." Jordan smiled, and there was a certain look in his eyes that made my heart pound.

"Every time you spoke with that Boston accent of yours, I was reminded of the fact that you were Boston-born and bred. Marriage to the right man, love or not. But I was still attracted. I thought myself a fool all over when I found excuses to see you. The more I saw you, the less you were like what I expected. But it seemed every time we met, we argued for some reason or another. Then you accused me of being Diego's father."

I flinched. "I'm sorry."

He gave a harsh laugh. "I was almost glad you believed it," he admitted. "It was the excuse I needed to leave you alone. If you thought all the gossip was true, then I could. . . ." He shook his head in self-derision. "It didn't work. I still wanted you, whatever the town was telling you about me. I enjoyed baiting you." He smiled. "It was better arguing with you than making love to anyone else."

He stopped. His eyes were searching for something in my face. I concentrated on showing nothing. Want, not love, I reminded myself. And Gwen's trick, I must remember that. Jordan must not know how I felt and what I carried inside me.

Jordan sighed. "Then the schoolhouse. When I found you outside. . . ." He stopped. "And then the business about a ghost. I stayed around that night to watch over you. When I saw the lantern was lit, I came in at a run. You were standing there with the light behind you. I never wanted a woman so much as I did then. I didn't stop to think. It's a good thing you did say what you did, or I would have made love to you there, on the floor."

As he had in the field. I remembered what he had said there, and I remembered what he had said at the schoolhouse. It was all true. I was a hypocrite of the worst kind, and I had spread myself like a whore for him. I tried desperately to steady myself.

"Abby," Jordan said softly. "Abby, please don't look like that." He leaned forward, his hand starting to reach for mine. I pressed back jerkily. He stopped.

"I wanted you so much," he said softly, his eyes not leaving me. "I hurt with wanting you. I thought you felt the same, and when you pushed me away, I got mad. I wanted to hurt you because you could just draw back from me so easily when I needed you so damned much." He let out his breath. "I didn't stop to think. When you mentioned Reva, that hurt. That you could think that of me. God, it really hurt! And I wanted to hurt you as badly." He searched my face. "I did, didn't I?" I did not answer, and he looked down at his hands.

"And then I just left you alone . . . and vulnerable. And Hallender damn near killed you. My God," he said shakily, and he looked up at me with tortured eyes. His hand shook slightly as he reached across to lightly touch my face. "It still shows where he hit you."

I drew back from his touch, afraid of what I would show.

He felt guilty about what had happened to me. I could see that. But it still changed nothing. I forced a smile. "I'm all right now, really. You mustn't feel you were to blame for what happened. That's ridiculous. What did you think you should have done? Remained there in the hills, guarding me? Hallender waited until you were gone. He wasn't going to do anything as long as there was a chance someone would see him. So don't take any responsibility." I did not want him to feel guilty or obligated in any way.

"There's something else I have to tell you," Jordan said slowly. When I had drawn away from him, he had leaned back, careful to keep his hands on his legs so that I knew he wasn't going to try and touch me again. He let out his breath, his eyes moving uneasily away from mine. He moved restlessly, seeming suddenly very taut and discomforted. All his self-assurance had gone. "About what happened at the river . . ." he said slowly, and I flinched.

"I'd rather not talk about that, if you don't mind."

"No, I don't suppose you do."

He shifted again, and his fingers coursed through his hair and then rubbed the back of his neck. His eyes flickered to mine and then away. I frowned. This was a side of Jordan I did not know. He was afraid, and more, he was embarrassed.

"I had a plan," he sighed, the words dragging out.

"A plan?"

He did not speak for a moment, and I watched his face in growing confusion.

"Things couldn't have been worse between us after I came to see you in your room after Hayes reinstated Diego. You remember that night?"

How could I ever forget? I thought.

"I knew something was going on between you and Ross. He let it slip to me that he knew you were tutoring Diego, and he couldn't have found out from me. Everyone else on the ranch was careful not to say anything either, knowing what it would mean to you if word got out. So that left you. You were seeing Ross, and you trusted him enough to tell him. You trusted Ross Persall, but you couldn't trust me. I was jealous as hell. So I made a plan."

He paused again, frowning. "I knew you responded to me after that night in your room." My face turned red. "I wanted you," he went on, "and I sure as hell didn't want Ross Persall getting anywhere near you. I thought if I could just get you away from town and alone for a while, things would take their natural course. I thought everything had worked out. And then you said you hated me. I slapped you. You ran away."

"I slapped you first."

"Hell," he breathed. "Anyway, I thought if I'd succeeded in getting you pregnant, you'd have to come to me."

I stared at him, eyes wide, mouth open in a silent "oh."

"I figured it worked well enough for women getting what they wanted, it ought to work as well for a man. Despicable, I know," he said, reddening. "But I. . . ." He stopped. "Oh, God, there's no excuse for that, and I don't blame you for hating me."

"But I don't hate you. Just tell me why you wanted me to come to you," I pleaded, needing to know. I was filled with hope.

For a moment Jordan did not answer. Then he looked into my eyes. "Do you have to go, Abby? Couldn't you change your mind and come back? I wouldn't push you." He stopped and shook his head. "No, I can't promise I wouldn't." His voice was very dry, and he smiled mockingly.

"Jordan, please. Tell me why."

"I guess you deserve your pound of flesh. . . ."

"Jordan. . . ." I leaned forward, putting my hands on his legs. He flinched as though in pain.

"I love you," he said simply.

"Oh, Jordan. Was that so hard?"

His eyes moved over my face, and his expression changed drastically. He leaned forward so that our faces were close. "Abby," he said, warningly, and I laughed joyously.

"I love you!" I cried.

Neither one of us moved for a full second. Then we were kissing hungrily, unable to get close enough, wanting to be skin to skin and even closer. It was Jordan who finally drew back. He was trembling, and he gave me a slightly baleful smile. "We'd better stop," he rasped. "We can't be more than a mile from Oakland, and I'd hate to shock the driver or get arrested."

I laughed again. Joy was bursting inside me like Fourth of July fireworks.

"I thought you looked happy when you first opened your eyes and looked at me a while ago," Jordan said. "Then you went all cold, and I didn't know what to think. But I thought anything was worth trying to get you to come back."

"I thought you'd guessed why I left."

"Guessed what?" He frowned.

My laughter softened and stopped. "That your scheme worked."

His brows drew down. "What do you mean?"

I smiled and moved his hand over my abdomen. His eyes dropped sharply, and then he looked up at me. "You're pregnant?" I nodded, now slightly afraid of how he would take the news.

"That's why you were sick," he said. "I thought it was nerves." Then his eyes narrowed and glittered with arrogant accusation. "And you were leaving! My God, Abby!"

I spread my hands. "I didn't think you'd want to know. I thought you. . . . Oh, Jordan, don't you remember what you said to me that day at the river?"

"Before you ran off?" he asked, thinking back.

"Yes."

"Not really. I never did understand what made you turn on me like that. Especially after—"

"You said I wasn't at all a lady. You said—"

He put his fingers on my lips, and his mouth curved wryly.

I flushed, and he went on. "Abby, the last place in the world a man wants his woman to behave like a lady is in bed . . . or in a field next to a river." His eyes were laughing. He pulled me forward, giving me a hard, punishing kiss. Then he drew back. His eyes grew serious.

"I half expected you to go cold on me that day, to just ward off my efforts to make love to you. But, my God, you came alive! I've never felt so wonderful. Like I owned the whole damned universe as long as I had you. And then you hit me. You looked at me like you hated me, and you ran away. I couldn't understand it. One minute, hot and giving everything to me, the next, cold and hating."

"But I thought. . . ."

"Never mind. I understand now, I should have been able to figure it out then." His smile became teasing. "I assure you, honey, you're a lady everywhere you ought to be." He drew me onto his lap and held me tightly. Then his hand moved down to my abdomen. "You're feeling all right now?" he asked, his voice full of concern.

"I feel wonderful," I said truthfully. What was a little morning sickness compared to this!

"And you were leaving," he said shakily, faintly accusing. "Without even telling me about the baby. Where in hell were you going?"

"I hadn't decided. Oregon. Washington. I didn't know. Just away." I couldn't stop touching him, looking at him, and I knew that the feeling was mutual.

"If Matthew Hayes hadn't ridden out to the ranch this morning, I don't know when I would have come to town and found out you'd gone. I might never have found you again. And I would never have known about our baby." He held me tighter. "By damn," he said harshly, "I ought to beat you!"

I chuckled softly. "I'd rather you sought other ways to punish me, if you think you must."

He cupped my chin, tilting my face up to his. His eyes were brilliant with laughter and comprehension. "You call that punishment?"

I tried to look serious. "Isn't it?"

His mouth trailed down the side of my neck. "Maybe I'm not understanding you. Maybe you should tell me exactly what you mean," he teased.

"I always tell my students to use their imaginations."

"I've got a vivid imagination," he breathed against my mouth. We did not speak for a long time. Then Jordan lifted me and set me back on the seat opposite him. "You'd better stay put," he said hoarsely. "The stage driver be damned."

"What do we do when we get to Oakland?" I asked, thinking of a wedding ceremony.

Jordan laughed. "What do you think?" Jordan was not thinking about a wedding. What he was thinking was very obvious.

I smiled mischievously. "Don't you think you should marry me first?"

"You'll get your church wedding all in due time, Miss McFarland. But not in the next twenty-four hours," he told me. "Now, wipe the dust off your face, button up your blouse and act like a lady . . . for a little while anyway," he commanded.

I made a face at him, but for the moment at least, I obeyed.

FRANCINE RIVERS

writes historical romance with a passion!

**"A dynamic writer...
Francine Rivers is class!"**

—BARBRA WREN
Barbra's Critiques

_____ 07433-0 **KATHLEEN** $3.50

_____ 06823-3 **THIS GOLDEN VALLEY** $3.50

Prices may be slightly higher in Canada.

SECOND EDITION

VISUALIZING

HUMAN GEOGRAPHY

Subir Basak/Flickr/Getty Images

VISUALIZING
HUMAN GEOGRAPHY

SECOND EDITION ————————————————————————————————————

ALYSON L. GREINER
OKLAHOMA STATE UNIVERSITY

WILEY

VICE PRESIDENT AND
  EXECUTIVE PUBLISHER   Petra Recter
EXECUTIVE EDITOR   Ryan Flahive
DIRECTOR OF DEVELOPMENT   Barbara Heaney
MANAGER, PRODUCT
  DEVELOPMENT   Nancy Perry
EDITORIAL PROGRAM ASSISTANT   Julia Nollen
ASSOCIATE DIRECTOR, MARKETING   Jeffrey Rucker
MEDIA SPECIALIST   Anita Castro

SENIOR MARKETING MANAGER   Suzanne Bochet
SENIOR CONTENT MANAGER   Micheline Frederick
SENIOR PRODUCTION EDITOR   Sandra Rigby
PRODUCT DESIGNER   Howard Averback
CREATIVE DIRECTOR   Harry Nolan
COVER DESIGN   Harry Nolan
PHOTO RESEARCHERS   Billy Ray, Teri Stratford,
  and Sheena Goldstein
PRODUCTION SERVICES   Furino Production

Front cover: Subir Basak/Flickr/Getty Images
Back cover: AFP/Getty Images

This book was set in New Baskerville by codeMantra., printed and bound by Quad Graphics. The cover was printed by Quad Graphics.

ISBN: 978-1-118-52656-9
BRV ISBN: 978-1-118-70127-0

Printed in the United States of America
10 9 8 7 6 5 4 3 2 1

Preface

How Is Wiley Visualizing Different?

Wiley Visualizing differs from competing textbooks by uniquely combining three powerful elements: a visual pedagogy, integrated with comprehensive text, the use of authentic situations and issues from the National Geographic Society collections, and the inclusion of interactive multimedia in the *WileyPLUS* learning environment. Together these elements deliver a level of rigor in ways that maximize student learning and involvement. Each key concept and its supporting details have been analyzed and carefully crafted to maximize student learning and engagement.

1. Visual Pedagogy. Wiley Visualizing is based on decades of research on the use of visuals in learning (Mayer, 2005).[1] Using the Cognitive Theory of Multimedia Learning, which is backed up by hundreds of empirical research studies, Wiley's authors select visualizations for their texts that specifically support students' thinking and learning—for example, the selection of relevant materials, the organization of the new information, or the integration of the new knowledge with prior knowledge. Visuals and text are conceived and planned together in ways that clarify and reinforce major concepts while allowing students to understand the details. This commitment to distinctive and consistent visual pedagogy sets Wiley Visualizing apart from other textbooks.

2. Authentic Situations and Problems. Through Wiley's exclusive publishing partnership with National Geographic,

Visualizing Human Geography has benefited from National Geographic's more than century-long recording of the world and offers an array of remarkable photographs, maps, media, and film from the National Geographic Society collections. These authentic materials immerse the student in real-life issues in human geography, thereby enhancing motivation, learning, and retention (Donovan & Bransford, 2005).[2] These authentic situations, using high-quality materials from the National Geographic Society collections, are unique to Wiley Visualizing.

3. Interactive Multimedia. Wiley Visualizing is based on the understanding that learning is an active process of knowledge construction. *Visualizing Human Geography* is therefore tightly integrated with *WileyPLUS*, our online learning environment that provides interactive multimedia activities in which learners can actively engage with the materials. The combination of textbook and *WileyPLUS* provides learners with multiple entry points to the content, giving them greater opportunity to explore concepts, interact with the material, and assess their understanding as they progress through the course. Wiley Visualizing makes this online *WileyPLUS* component a key element of the learning and problem-solving experience, which sets it apart from other textbooks whose online component is a mere drill-and-practice feature.

Wiley Visualizing and the *WileyPLUS* Learning Environment are designed as a natural extension of how we learn

Visuals, comprehensive text, and learning aids are integrated to display facts, concepts, processes, and principles more effectively than words alone can. To understand why the visualizing approach is effective, it is first helpful to understand how we learn.

1. Our brain processes information using two channels: visual and verbal. Our *working memory* holds information that our minds process as we learn. In working memory we begin to make sense of words and pictures and build verbal and visual models of the information.

2. When the verbal and visual models of corresponding information are connected in working memory, we form more comprehensive, or integrated, mental models.

3. After we link these integrated mental models to our prior knowledge, which is stored in our *long-term memory*, we

build even stronger mental models. When an integrated mental model is formed and stored in long-term memory, real learning begins.

The effort our brains put forth to make sense of instructional information is called *cognitive load*. There are two kinds of cognitive load: productive cognitive load, such as when we're engaged in learning or exert positive effort to create mental models; and unproductive cognitive load, which occurs when the brain is trying to make sense of needlessly complex content or when information is not presented well. The learning process can be impaired when the amount of information to be processed exceeds the capacity of working memory. Well-designed visuals and text with effective pedagogical guidance can reduce the unproductive cognitive load in our working memory.

[1] Mayer, R. E. (Ed.) (2005). *The Cambridge Handbook of Multimedia Learning.* New York: Cambridge University Press.
[2] Donovan, M.S., & Bransford, J. (Eds.) (2005). *How Students Learn: Science in the Classroom.* The National Academy Press. Available online at http://www.nap.edu/openbook.php?record_id=11102&page=1.

Wiley Visualizing is designed for engaging and effective learning

The visuals and text in *Visualizing Human Geography 2e* are specially integrated to present complex processes in clear steps and with clear representations, organize related pieces of information, and integrate related information with one another. This approach, along with the use of interactive multimedia, provides the level of rigor needed for the course and helps students engage with the content. When students are engaged, they're reading and learning, which can lead to greater knowledge and academic success.

Research shows that well-designed visuals, integrated with comprehensive text, can improve the efficiency with which a learner processes information. In this regard, SEG Research, an independent research firm, conducted a national, multisite study evaluating the effectiveness of Wiley Visualizing. Its findings indicate that students using Wiley Visualizing products (both print and multimedia) were more engaged in the course, exhibited greater retention throughout the course, and made significantly greater gains in content area knowledge and skills, as compared to students in similar classes that did not use Wiley Visualizing.[3]

The use of *WileyPLUS* can also increase learning. According to a white paper titled "Leveraging Blended Learning for More Effective Course Management and Enhanced Student Outcomes" by Peggy Wyllie of Evince Market Research & Communications[4], studies show that effective use of online resources can increase learning outcomes. Pairing supportive online resources with face-to-face instruction can help students to learn and reflect on material, and deploying multimodal learning methods can help students to engage with the material and retain their acquired knowledge. *WileyPLUS* provides students with an environment that stimulates active learning and enables them to optimize the time they spend on their coursework. Continual assessment/remediation is also key to helping students stay on track. The *WileyPLUS* system facilitates instructors' course planning, organization, and delivery and provides a range of flexible tools for easy design and deployment of activities and tracking of student progress for each learning objective.

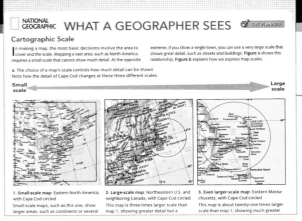

Figure 1: What a Geographer Sees: Cartographic Scale (Ch. 1)
Through a logical progression of visuals and graphic features such as the arrow and circles, this illustration directs learners' attention to the underlying concept.

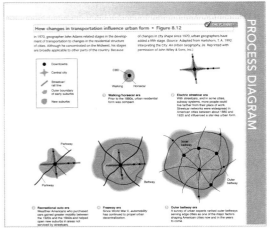

Figure 2: How changes in transportation influence urban form (Figure 8.12)
Textual and visual elements are physically integrated. This eliminates split attention (when we must divide our attention between several sources of different information).

Figure 3: Before and after gentrification (Figure 8.17)
Photos are paired so that students compare and contrast them, thereby grasping the underlying concept.

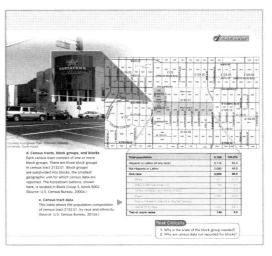

Figure 4: What a Geographer Sees: U.S. Census Geography (Ch. 6)
From reality to abstraction: Linking a photo of a place to its position on census tracts and then showing the data derived from that tract helps students understand how geographic data are produced.

[3] SEG Research (2009). Improving Student-Learning with Graphically Enhanced Textbooks: A Study of the Effectiveness of the Wiley Visualizing Series. Available online at www.segmeasurement.com/

[4] Peggy Wyllie (2009). Leveraging Blended Learning for More Effective Course Management and Enhanced Student Outcomes.

How Are the Wiley Visualizing Chapters Organized?

Student engagement requires more than just providing visuals, text, and interactivity—it entails motivating students to learn. Student engagement can be behavioral, cognitive, social, and/or emotional. It is easy to get bored or lose focus when presented with large amounts of information, and it is easy to lose motivation when the relevance of the information is unclear. Wiley Visualizing and *WileyPLUS* work together to reorganize course content into manageable learning objectives and relate it to everyday life. The design of *WileyPLUS* is based on cognitive science, instructional design, and extensive research into user experience. It transforms learning into an interactive, engaging, and outcomes-oriented experience for students.

The content in Wiley Visualizing and *WileyPLUS* is organized in learning modules. Each module has a clear instructional objective, one or more examples, and an opportunity for assessment. These modules are the building blocks of Wiley Visualizing.

Each Wiley Visualizing chapter engages students from the start

Chapter opening text and visuals introduce the subject and connect the student with the material that follows.

Global Locator Maps, prepared specifically for this book by the National Geographic Society cartographers, help students visualize where the area depicted in the photo is situated on Earth.

Geographies of Development

BHUTAN'S QUEST FOR GROSS NATIONAL HAPPINESS

Imagine your own Shangri-la—that is, an idyllic place. What place on Earth, if any, comes closest to matching that? Did the country of Bhutan come to mind? Most likely it did not, although in recent years this small mountainous state nestled between India and China has occasionally been described as a Shangri-la. This designation has less to do with Bhutan's striving to be a perfect place and more to do with its physical setting and its ideology of development.

Until the early 1970s, Bhutan was among the world's most impoverished countries. Then, King Jigme Singye Wangchuck conceived a development strategy that would balance economic growth with environmental protection, Bhutanese cultural traditions, and democratic governance. He envisioned a path to development that, in his words, would bring "gross national happiness."

Bhutan has since invested heavily in education and health care. In the early 1980s Bhutan had an adult literacy rate of 23%...

... achieve development in a way that is environmentally sustainable and socially conscious.

This chapter covers different facets of development such as ways of measuring and mapping development and income inequality. It also introduces the major approaches that have shaped development efforts.

Global Locator

ASIA
BHUTAN

NATIONAL GEOGRAPHIC

CHAPTER OUTLINE

What Is Development? 264
- Economic Indicators
- Sociodemographic Indicators
- Environmental Indicators
- Development and Gender-Related Indexes
- Environment and Development
- Where Geographers Click: Human Development Reports

Development and Income Inequality 277
- The Gap Between the Rich and the Poor
- Factors Affecting Income Distribution
- Globalization and Income Distribution

Development Theory 282
- The Classical Model of Development
- Dependency Theory
- World-System Theory
- The Neoliberal Model of Development
- Poverty-Reduction Theory and Millennium Development
- What a Geographer Sees: Poverty Mapping
- Video Explorations: Solar Cooking

Chapter Outlines anticipate the content.

CHAPTER PLANNER ✓

☐ Study the picture and read the opening story.
☐ Scan the Learning Objectives in each section:
   p. 264 ☐ p. 277 ☐ p. 282 ☐
☐ Read the text and study all figures and visuals. Answer any questions.

Analyze key features
☐ Geography InSight, p. 276
☐ Process Diagram, p. 283
☐ What a Geographer Sees, p. 288
☐ Video Explorations, p. 290
☐ Stop: Answer the Concept Checks before you go on: p. 277 ☐ p. 282 ☐ p. 290 ☐

End of chapter
☐ Review the Summary and Key Terms.
☐ Answer the Critical and Creative Thinking Questions.
☐ Answer What is happening in this picture?
☐ Complete the Self-Test and check your answers.

Chapter Introductions illustrate key concepts in the chapter with intriguing stories and striking photographs.

263

The **Chapter Planner** gives students a path through the learning aids in the chapter. Throughout the chapter, the Planner icon prompts students to use the learning aids and to set priorities as they study.

WileyPLUS Experience the chapter through a *WileyPLUS* course. The content through *WileyPLUS* transports the student into a rich world of online experience that can be personalized, customized, and extended.

Wiley Visualizing media guides students through the chapter

Wiley Visualizing in *WileyPLUS* gives students a variety of approaches—visuals, words, illustrations, interactions, and assessments—that work together to provide students with a guided path through the content. But this path isn't static: It can be personalized, customized, and extended to suit individual needs, and so it offers students flexibility as to how they want to study and learn.

Learning Objectives at the start of each section indicate in behavioral terms the concepts that students are expected to master while reading the section.

WileyPLUS

Every content resource is related to a specific learning objective so that students will easily discover relevant content organized in a more meaningful way.

Language Diffusion and

LEARNING OBJECTIVES

1. **Explain** how political, economic, and religious forces can affect the diffusion of language.
2. **Identify** factors contributing to linguistic dominance.

What social and geographic factors contribute to the spread, or diffusion, of languages? In our discussion of language families, we learned that the spread of agriculture may have facilitated the historic spread of languages. If we take a broader perspective, we can see that technology and human mobility can contribute significantly to language diffusion. Historically, ships, railroads, and other forms of transportation opened physical

Sanctification • Figure 5.13

Process Diagrams provide in-depth coverage of processes correlated with clear, step-by-step narrative, enabling students to grasp important topics with less effort.

WileyPLUS

Interactive Process Diagrams provide additional visual examples and descriptive narration of a difficult concept, process, or theory, allowing the students to interact and engage with the content. Many of these diagrams are built around a specific feature such as a Process Diagram.

Geography InSights are multipart visual features that focus on a key concept or topic in the chapter, exploring it in detail or in broader context using a combination of photos, diagrams, maps, and data.

Maps from the **National Geographic** collection and maps created for this text by NGS cartographers immerse the student in a variety of real-life issues in human geography.

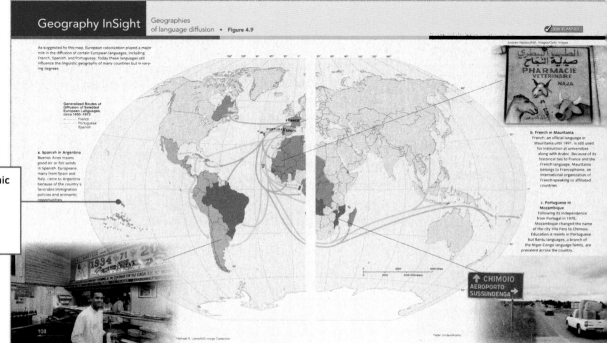

Geography InSight — Geographies of language diffusion • Figure 4.9

What a Geographer Sees highlights a concept or phenomenon that would stand out to geographers. Photos and figures are used to improve students' understanding of the usefulness of a geographic perspective and to enable students to apply their observational skills to answer questions.

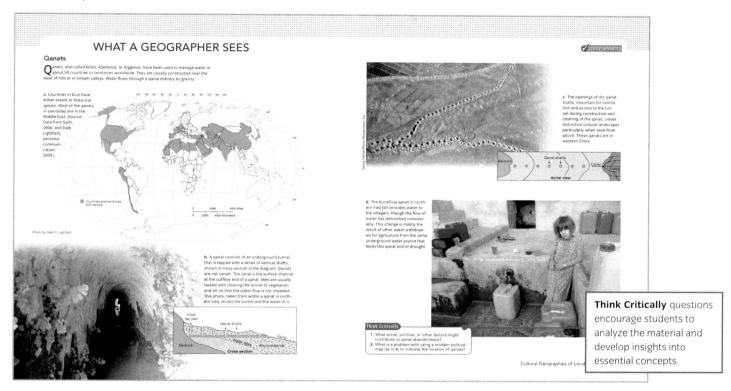

WHAT A GEOGRAPHER SEES

Qanats

Qanats, also called *karez*, *khettaras*, or *foggaras*, have been used to manage water in about 50 countries or territories worldwide. They are usually constructed near the base of hills or in stream valleys. Water flows through a qanat entirely by gravity.

a. Countries in blue have either extant or historical qanats. Most of the qanats in use today are in the Middle East. (*Source:* Data from Salih, 2006; and Dale Lightfoot, personal communication, 2009.)

c. The openings of the qanat shafts, important for ventilation and access to the tunnel during construction and cleaning of the qanat, create distinctive cultural landscapes particularly when seen from above. These qanats are in western China.

b. A qanat consists of an underground tunnel that is tapped with a series of vertical shafts, shown in cross-section in the diagram. Qanats are not canals. The canal is the surface channel at the outflow end of a qanat. Men are usually tasked with clearing the tunnel of vegetation and silt so that the water flow is not impeded. This photo, taken from within a qanat in northern Iraq, shows the tunnel and the water in it.

d. The Kunaflusa qanat in northern Iraq still provides water to the villagers, though the flow of water has diminished considerably. This change is mainly the result of other water withdrawals for agriculture from the same underground water source that feeds this qanat and of drought.

Think Critically
1. What social, political, or other factors might contribute to qanat abandonment?
2. What is a problem with using a modern political map (as in a) to indicate the location of qanats?

Think Critically questions encourage students to analyze the material and develop insights into essential concepts.

In each chapter, the **Video Explorations** feature, researched by Joy Adams of the Association of American Geographers, showcases one of more than 30 **National Geographic videos** from the award-winning NGS collection. The videos are linked to the text and provide visual context for key concepts, ideas, and terms addressed in the chapter.

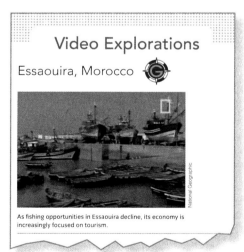

Video Explorations

Essaouira, Morocco

As fishing opportunities in Essaouira decline, its economy is increasingly focused on tourism.

Where Geographers Click showcases a website that professionals use and encourages students to try out its tools.

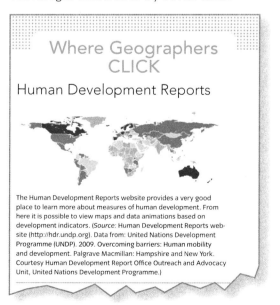

Where Geographers CLICK

Human Development Reports

The Human Development Reports website provides a very good place to learn more about measures of human development. From here it is possible to view maps and data animations based on development indicators. (*Source:* Human Development Reports website (http://hdr.undp.org). Data from: United Nations Development Programme (UNDP). 2009. Overcoming barriers: Human mobility and development. Palgrave Macmillan: Hampshire and New York. Courtesy Human Development Report Office Outreach and Advocacy Unit, United Nations Development Programme.)

WileyPLUS Streaming videos are available to students in the context of *WileyPLUS*, and accompanying assignments can be graded online and added to the instructor gradebook.

In concert with the visual approach of the book, **www.ConceptCaching.com** is an online collection of photographs that explores places, regions, people, and their activities. Photographs, GPS coordinates, and explanations of core geographic concepts are "cached" for viewing by professors and students alike. Professors can access the images or submit their own by visiting the website. Caches on the website are integrated in the *WileyPLUS* course as examples to help students understand the concepts.

Geo Media Library is an interactive media source of animations, simulations, and interactivities allowing instructors to visually demonstrate key concepts in greater depth.

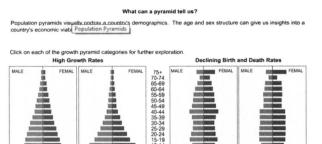

What can a pyramid tell us?

Population pyramids visually portray a country's demographics. The age and sex structure can give us insights into a country's economic viab[ility]. Population Pyramids

Click on each of the growth pyramid categories for further exploration.

WileyPLUS In **Google Earth™ Links, Tours, and Activities**, photos from the *WileyPLUS* eBook are linked from the text to their actual location on the Earth using Google Earth. Tours and activities created by professors engage students with geographic concepts addressed in the text. Contributing professors include Randy Rutberg, Hunter College (New York); Jeff DeGrave, University of Wisconsin-Eau Claire; and James Hayes-Bohanan, Bridgewater State University.

Coordinated with the section-opening **Learning Objectives**, at the end of each section **Concept Check** questions allow students to test their comprehension of the learning objectives.

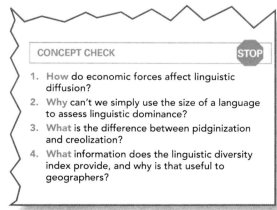

CONCEPT CHECK   STOP

1. **How** do economic forces affect linguistic diffusion?
2. **Why** can't we simply use the size of a language to assess linguistic dominance?
3. **What** is the difference between pidginization and creolization?
4. **What** information does the linguistic diversity index provide, and why is that useful to geographers?

WileyPLUS At the end of each learning objective module, students can assess their progress with independent practice opportunities and quizzes. This feature gives them the ability to gauge their comprehension and grasp of the material. Practice tests and quizzes help students self-monitor and prepare for graded course assessments.

Student understanding is assessed at different levels

Wiley Visualizing with *WileyPLUS* offers students lots of practice material for assessing their understanding of each study objective. Students know exactly what they are getting out of each study session through immediate feedback and coaching.

The **Summary** revisits each major section, with informative images taken from the chapter. These visuals reinforce important concepts.

Ecosystems 358

- An **ecosystem** includes the living organisms, their physical **environment**, and the flows of energy and nutrients cycling through them. Ecosystems exist at a variety of scales, from a local estuary such as the one shown here, to a desert that spans several countries. The Earth's interconnected ecosystems constitute the **biosphere**.

Ecosystems • Figure 12.1

Rich ReisING Image Collection

- The **First Law of Ecology** expresses the principle that the environment is an interconnected web that includes people, and that human actions have environmental consequences.
- The environment is also a form of **natural capital**, which includes its **nonrenewable** and **renewable resources**. When ...

- Most of the proved oil reserves are concentrated in the Middle East. The single greatest consumer of the world's oil is the United States. In the United States, oil and natural gas production from shale formations is changing the energy landscape.
- Coal, the most abundant of fossil fuels, presents a number of environmental challenges when extracted and used. Mountaintop removal, depicted here, remains a controversial technique, and burning coal is linked to mercury pollution and **acid rain**.

Understanding mountaintop removal • Figure 12.11

Troy Fleece/BAP/Wide World Photos

- Though not a fossil fuel, uranium is a nonrenewable resource used to produce nuclear energy. Worldwide, nuclear energy constitutes a minor part of the ener...

What is happening in this picture? presents an uncaptioned photograph that is relevant to a chapter topic and illustrates a situation students are not likely to have encountered previously.

What is happening in this picture?

NATIONAL GEOGRAPHIC

Rickshaw pullers move through the streets of Kolkata, India. Rickshaw pullers provide an affordable means of transportation around the clock as well as year-round. Unlike cars and buses, rickshaw pullers can still navigate inundated streets during the monsoon rains. But city officials consider rickshaw pullers a reason for traffic congestion and have proposed banning them.

AFP/Getty Images

Think Critically
1. What does this photo suggest are some other causes of traffic congestion?
2. Could rickshaws be considered a sustainable form of urban transportation? Why or why not?

Think Critically questions ask students to apply what they have learned in order to interpret and explain what they observe in the image.

Critical and Creative Thinking Questions challenge students to think more broadly about chapter concepts. The level of these questions ranges from simple to advanced; they encourage students to think critically and develop an analytical understanding of the ideas discussed in the chapter.

Critical and Creative Thinking Questions

1. Will Internet voting ever replace the use of traditional polling places? What geographic and political conditions would be most conducive to such change?
2. List some advantages and disadvantages of majority-plurality and proportional representation systems.
3. Do some fieldwork in the area where you live and identify a relic boundary. What processes led to the creation of that boundary?
4. Not all ethnic groups are nations. Why?
5. Under what circumstances might devolution become a centrifugal force?
6. A political geographer might argue that the Berlin Conference was an exercise in gerrymandering. Explain what is meant by this statement and take a position on it.
7. What similarities and differences are there between the division of Germany after World War II and the division of Cyprus?
8. Review the geographic composition of the UN Security Council, shown in the diagram. Does it need reform? Why or why not?

Permanent members (China, France, Russia, United Kingdom, United States)
Nonpermanent members (elected by the General Assembly and serve for two years)
- African
- Asian
- Latin American
- West European and Other
- East European

Self-Test
(Check your answers in Appendix B.)

7. The population pyramid shown here _____.
   a. depicts a low sex ratio
   b. indicates that rapid population growth in the future is likely
   c. depicts a low age-dependency ratio
   d. all of the above

United Arab Emirates

Males   Females
80+
75–79
70–74
65–69
60–64
55–59
50–54
45–49
40–44
35–39
30–34
25–29
20–24
15–19
10–14
5–9
0–4
15 10 5   0   5   10 15
% of population

8. Which statement about the rate of natural increase (RNI) is false?
   a. The RNI can be used to calculate population doubling time.
   b. The RNI expresses the difference between births and deaths in a population.
   c. The RNI can be negative or zero.
   d. The RNI for a country today is usually 5% or higher.

9. A key component of Malthus's thought was that _____.
   a. population growth would stimulate technological innovations
   b. people would voluntarily control and lower fertility
   c. population growth increased geometrically relative to the food supply

11. Fiji, a country located in the South Pacific Ocean to the east of Australia, has a stage 2 profile. Explain what this means according to the demographic transition model.

12. What stage of the epidemiological transition is associated with resurgent infectious diseases?
   a. stage 1   b. stage 2
   c. stage 3   d. stage 4

13. Label the four major components of Lee's conceptual framework for migration theory.

14. Net migration expresses _____.
   a. the difference between in- and out-migrants
   b. the rate of population growth
   c. the ratio of male to female migrants
   d. the value of migrant remittances

15. Which type of migration has historically been most closely linked to the growth of cities?

Visual end-of-chapter **Self-Tests** pose review questions that ask students to demonstrate their understanding of key concepts.

Why *Visualizing Human Geography 2e?*

We live in an ever-changing world in which geographical knowledge is central to the well-being of our communities and society. Perhaps nowhere is the urgency of geographical knowledge made clearer to us than through issues involving the local, national, and global impacts of climate change; the earthquake, tsunami, and nuclear disaster in Japan; or the civil war in Syria. Simultaneously, technological innovations continue to open new horizons in mapping and techniques for visualizing geographic information that enable us to see, explore, and understand local and global processes as never before. What a challenging and invigorating time to be either a student or an instructor of geography.

Geographic literacy

Visualizing Human Geography 2e provides a fresh, new pathway for building geographic literacy and introducing students to the richness of geography, including its many different approaches, perspectives, techniques, and tools. Geographic literacy seeks to endow students with geographic and analytical skills to be creative and capable decision makers and problem solvers. More specifically, geographic literacy includes:

1. fostering the skills of spatial analysis so that students gain an understanding of the importance of scale and can evaluate and interpret the significance of spatial variation;

2. enhancing students' comprehension of the interconnectedness of social and environmental dynamics, and the implications of this for people's livelihoods, their use of the Earth, and environmental change;

3. cultivating global awareness in students and exposing them to divergent views so they are prepared and equipped to participate in an increasingly interconnected world; and

4. educating students about the advantages and limitations of tools such as GIS and GPS in the acquisition and use of geographic information.

A fundamental premise guiding the presentation of material in this book is that such key geographical concepts as place, space, and scale cannot be divorced from a study of process. In other words, questions of why and how are vital to our understanding of where activities, events, or other phenomena are located. Thus, every chapter contains at least one Process Diagram in order to show the diverse factors and complex relations among them that drive social and environmental change.

Human geography is well suited to a visually oriented approach for three reasons. First, maps and images are fundamental tools of geographers that help to reveal patterns or trends that might not otherwise be apparent. Second, within the practice of human geography there is a longstanding tradition of studying cultural landscapes for evidence about such processes as diffusion, urbanization, or globalization in order to more fully understand social difference and to assess human use of the Earth. Third, many human geographers are interested in representation, including the kinds of images that are used by different agencies and entities to characterize places, regions, people, and their activities. Therefore, a visual approach enables a more complete instructional use of photographs, maps, and other visually oriented media to explore and evaluate the significance of different representations.

Other features of this book include:

- content that reflects the latest developments in geographic thought;

- coverage of geographical models and theory as well as their real-world applications;

- top-notch cartography;

- accurate and up-to-date statistics;

- an appendix devoted to understanding map projections.

Organization

Visualizing Human Geography 2e is a college-level textbook intended for use in introductory human or cultural geography courses. Students need not have had any previous coursework in geography to use this book. The structure of the book is based on a 12-chapter framework suitable for institutions using either the semester or quarter system. The chapters are arranged according to conventional practice. Globalization and gender issues are covered throughout the book. The outline below provides a brief overview of the content of each chapter.

- **Chapter 1, What Is Human Geography?** This foundational chapter introduces students to the discipline of geography and the subfield of human geography. It covers the key concepts of nature, culture, place, space, spatial diffusion, spatial interaction and globalization, and scale. One section of the chapter explains and gives examples of the applications of geographic tools including remote sensing, GPS, and GIS. Students are also introduced to possible careers in geography.

- **Chapter 2, Globalization and Cultural Geography.** This chapter expands on the process of globalization introduced in Chapter 1, then moves to the cultural impacts of globalization such as the diffusion of popular culture and local responses to it. The chapter also explores the commodification of culture through case studies of the diamond industry, representations of indigenous culture, and world heritage. The chapter uses the term *local culture* instead of *folk culture* and examines geographies of local knowledge, including traditional medicine.

- **Chapter 3, Population and Migration.** Such fundamental concepts as population density, fertility, mortality, life expectancy, and their regional differences are discussed and explained in this chapter. Population pyramids, the rate of natural increase, and the demographic transition model are used to examine population change. The chapter also introduces theories about population growth, resource use, food insecurity, and migration, and discusses the patterns of global migration.

- **Chapter 4, Geographies of Language.** Linguistic diversity is an important theme throughout this chapter. Present-day and historical factors help anchor the discussion of the distribution of languages and language families. The relationships among linguistic dominance, status, geographic space, and language endangerment are also covered. The chapter closes with a discussion of dialect geography and toponyms.

- **Chapter 5, Geographies of Religion.** The contrasting geographies of six major religious traditions are discussed in this chapter: Judaism, Christianity, Islam, Hinduism, Buddhism, and Sikhism. The concept of civil religion is introduced and is used to explore the emergence of sacred places and spaces. The chapter addresses the tension between modernism and traditionalism in religion, geographical aspects of religious law, and the origins, diffusion, and globalization of Renewalism. The concept of geopiety provides one way of considering the connections among religion, nature, and landscape.

- **Chapter 6, Geographies of Identity.** Chapters 4, 5, 6, and 7 cover different facets of identity, and this chapter expressly examines race, ethnicity, sexuality, and gender. The chapter treats race as a social construction and examines geographies of racism produced in South Africa during apartheid. The chapter also addresses the complexity of ethnicity, the representation of ethnicity and identity on censuses, theories of ethnic interaction, ethnic conflict, and environmental justice. The section on sexuality and gender challenges students to think about the geographic implications of a heterosexual norm, and the persistence of gender roles and gender gaps.

- **Chapter 7, Political Geographies.** Crucial to this chapter are the development of the state, the geographical characteristics of states, and the geographical implications of centripetal and centrifugal forces as well as separatism and devolution. Discussions of the United Nations and European Union provide contrasting studies of supranational organizations. The topic of global geopolitics is explored through a mix of traditional and contemporary theories as well as globalization and terrorism. Students are introduced to the fundamentals of electoral geography and ways in which cultural landscapes can be used to convey political power and ideologies.

- **Chapter 8, Urban Geographies.** This chapter opens with a discussion of the different types of urban settlements, global patterns of urbanization, the development of megacities and primate cities, and urban hierarchies. The next section of the chapter focuses on models of urban structure. This is followed by a study of the impact of public policy on residential change and urban redevelopment. The extent of urban poverty and the causes of slum formation are detailed, and the chapter closes with a discussion of trends in urban planning.

- **Chapter 9, Geographies of Development.** Students learn what development is, what makes it a normative project, and how it can be measured using development indicators or indexes. The chapter discusses the geography of income inequality, one expression of uneven levels of development, then turns to an examination of the evolution of development theory. Students are introduced to dependency theory, world-system theory, neoliberalism, and poverty-reduction theory, among others, and their geographical ramifications. Students also learn about the technique of poverty mapping.

- **Chapter 10, Changing Geographies of Industry and Services.** This chapter explains distinctions among primary, secondary, tertiary, quaternary, and quinary types of industry. It introduces commodity dependency and staple theory. Students learn about the origins and diffusion of the Industrial Revolution as well as the impact of Fordism and flexible production on manufacturing in the core. The chapter distinguishes between outsourcing and offshoring, and addresses the emergence of newly industrialized economies, export-processing zones, and the globalization of commodity chains. The chapter also examines the process of deindustrialization, characteristics of postindustrial societies, changing patterns of employment in manufacturing and services, and gender mainstreaming.

- **Chapter 11, Agricultural Geographies.** This chapter follows the chapter on industry because agriculture has been and is still strongly influenced by technological change and systems of industrial production. The chapter identifies three major agricultural revolutions and distinguishes between the Green Revolution and the Gene Revolution. Students are encouraged to think about types of agriculture as agricultural systems, and the global distribution of several examples of subsistence and commercial agriculture is discussed. The chapter also covers the impacts of agriculture on the environment, sustainable agricultural practices, the impact of globalization on agriculture and dietary practices, and the causes of the recent global food crises.

- **Chapter 12, Environmental Challenges.** The nature and functioning of ecosystems provides a framework for this chapter. A discussion of the concept and process of environmental degradation leads to an examination of Garrett Hardin's work on the tragedy of the commons and common property resources more broadly. The chapter covers the geographical aspects of the distribution, use, and consumption of all major nonrenewable and renewable energy resources. Students learn about the greenhouse effect, global warming, carbon footprints, and land-use and land-cover change. The chapter closes with a discussion of international policies on greenhouse gas reductions.

New to this edition

This Second Edition of *Visualizing Human Geography* incorporates new content and pedagogical features, including:

- **Up-to-date content.** Throughout the text, the information and data have been updated to reflect the most recent data available at the time of the revision. All world maps have been revised to show the newest country, South Sudan.

- **Enhanced visuals.** The photos, maps, charts, and diagrams in every chapter have been scrutinized for their clarity, relevance, and pedagogical effectiveness. Many maps and diagrams have been revised, and a wide variety of new photos have been added throughout. Multipart figures now consistently include overarching captions that clarify the relations among the different parts of the figures. In support of the book's emphasis on active learning, additional critical thinking questions have been incorporated into a number of photo and figure captions.

- **New *Ask Yourself* questions.** These are short answer closed-ended questions that are linked to a visual. Each chapter has one or more of these features. The *Ask Yourself* questions are designed to help students engage with the core content presented in the visual. The use of closed-ended questions with answers provided at the back of the book ensures that students have a way to obtain immediate feedback on their comprehension of concepts at different points in the chapter.

- **New coverage of important topics.** This edition continues the practice of incorporating examples and discussions from relevant current affairs.

- **Chapter 1** includes new visuals that enhance the coverage of the scope of geography, including the relationship among human and physical geography, environment–society dynamics, and the major subfields of geography.

- **Chapter 3** features a completely revised, updated, and expanded section on migration with several new photos and illustrations. Instead of using a regional framework, the migration section is now organized around the following topics: migration principles, internal migration, international migration, and immigration to the United States. This new organization now includes a discussion of amenity migration, counterurbanization, historical and contemporary patterns of immigration to the United States, and the categories of immigrants on which the U.S. immigration system is based.

- **Chapter 4** has been revised to include an expanded discussion of the Kurgan and Anatolian hypotheses about the origins of the Indo-European language family.

- **Chapter 6** expands the coverage of gender issues with a new discussion of women in the military. The chapter also includes new visuals in its coverage of ethnicity and the U.S. Census, and incorporates an expanded discussion of the conflict in Darfur.

- **Chapter 7** introduces new content on the euro-zone crisis, including the topics of sovereign debt and austerity, and features updated coverage of gerrymandering.

- **Chapter 8** revisions include an augmented discussion of redlining and the impact of neighborhood rating systems on the social geography of the city, as well as a discussion of housing patterns and residential segregation. New material has been added on urban poverty and the collapse of the housing market in the United States.

- **Chapter 9** has been revised to incorporate the newest development indexes, specifically the inequality-adjusted human development index and the gender inequality index. This chapter also includes new illustrations to help students understand the changes in levels of development experienced by different countries over time. A new *Geography InSight* feature focuses on environment, tourism and development in Costa Rica. A discussion of the Occupy Wall Street movement has been added to the section on income inequality.

- **Chapter 10** has been reorganized to incorporate expanded coverage of services, including a discussion of growth in the service sector. A new *Geography InSight* feature enhances the discussion of types of services, and a revised *Process Diagram* relates steps in the manufacturing processes to manufacturing value added and profit captured using the example of an iPad.

- **Chapter 12** now includes a new section on the production of oil and natural gas from shale as well as a *Geography InSight* feature that examines the new geography of oil and natural gas production in the United States, landscape transformation associated with it, and the advantages and disadvantages of fracking. The chapter also includes revised sections on global environmental change and nuclear energy.

Also available

Earth Pulse 2e. Utilizing full-color imagery and National Geographic photographs, *EarthPulse* takes you on a journey of discovery covering topics such as *The Human Condition, Our Relationship with Nature, and Our Connected World*. Illustrated by specific examples, each section focuses on trends affecting our world today. Included are extensive full-color world and regional maps for reference. *EarthPulse* is available only in a package with *Visualizing Human Geography*. Contact your Wiley representative for more information or visit www.wiley.com/college/earthpulse.

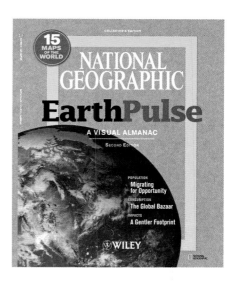

How Does Wiley Visualizing Support Instructors?

The Wiley Visualizing site hosts a wealth of information for instructors using Wiley Visualizing, including ways to maximize the visual approach in the classroom and a white paper titled "How Visuals Can Help Students Learn," by Matt Leavitt, instructional design consultant. You can also find information about other texts published in our program. Visit Wiley Visualizing at www.wiley.com/college/ visualizing.

Wiley Visualizing

Wiley Custom Select

Wiley Custom Select gives you the freedom to build your course materials exactly the way you want them. Offer your students a cost-efficient alternative to traditional texts. In a simple three-step process create a solution containing the content you want, in the sequence you want, delivered how you want. Visit Wiley Custom Select at http://customselect.wiley.com.

National Geographic Videos

Researched by Joy Adams of the Association of American Geographers the **Video Explorations** presented in each chapter of the textbook, are just some of the 30+ NGS videos available to provide visual context for key concepts, ideas, and terms addressed in the textbook. Streaming videos are available to students in the context of *WileyPLUS*, and accompanying assignments can be graded online and added to the instructor gradebook.

Book Companion Site www.wiley.com/college/greiner

All instructor resources (the Test Bank, Instructor's Manual, PowerPoint presentations, and all textbook illustrations and photos in jpeg format) are housed on the book companion site (www.wiley.com/college/greiner). Student resources include self quizzes and flashcards.

PowerPoint Presentations

(available in *WileyPLUS* and on the book companion site)

A complete set of highly visual PowerPoint presentations—one per chapter—is available online and in *WileyPLUS* to enhance classroom presentations. Tailored to the text's topical coverage and learning objectives, these presentations are designed to convey key text concepts, illustrated by embedded text art. Lecture Launcher PowerPoints also offer embedded links to videos to help introduce classroom discussions with short, engaging video clips.

Test Bank (available in *WileyPLUS* and on the book companion site)

The visuals from the textbook are also included in the Test Bank by Carolyn Coulter, Atlantic Cape Community College. The Test Bank has a diverse selection of test items including multiple-choice and essay questions, with at least 20 percent of them incorporating visuals from the book. The Test Bank is available online in MS Word files as a Computerized Test Bank, and within *WileyPLUS*. The easy-to-use test-generation program fully supports graphics, print tests, student answer sheets, and answer keys. The software's advanced features allow you to produce an exam to your exact specifications.

Instructor's Manual (available in *WileyPLUS* and on the book companion site)

The Instructor's Manual includes creative ideas for in-class activities, discussion questions, and lecture transitions.

Guidance is also provided on how to maximize the effectiveness of visuals in the classroom.

1. **Use visuals during class discussions or presentations.** Point out important information as the students look at the visuals, to help them integrate separate visual and verbal mental models.

2. **Use visuals for assignments and to assess learning.** For example, learners could be asked to identify samples of concepts portrayed in visuals.

3. **Use visuals to encourage group activities.** Students can study together, make sense of, discuss, hypothesize, or make decisions about the content. Students can work together to interpret and describe the diagram, or use the diagram to solve problems, conduct related research, or work through a case study activity.

Image Gallery

All photographs, figures, maps, and other visuals from the text are online and in *WileyPLUS* and can be used as you wish in the classroom. These online electronic files allow you to easily incorporate images into your PowerPoint presentations as you choose, or to create your own handouts.

Wiley Faculty Network

The Wiley Faculty Network (WFN) is a global community of faculty, connected by a passion for teaching and a drive to learn, share, and collaborate. Their mission is to promote the effective use of technology and enrich the teaching experience. Connect with the Wiley Faculty Network to collaborate with your colleagues, find a mentor, attend virtual and live events, and view a wealth of resources all designed to help you grow as an educator. Visit the Wiley Faculty Network at www.wherefacultyconnect.com.

How Has Wiley Visualizing Been Shaped by Contributors?

Wiley Visualizing and the *WileyPLUS* learning environment would not have come about without lots of people, each of whom played a part in sharing their research and contributing to this new approach.

Academic Research Consultants

Richard Mayer, Professor of Psychology, UC Santa Barbara. Mayer's *Cognitive Theory of Multimedia Learning* provided the basis on which we designed our program. He continues to provide guidance to our author and editorial teams on how to develop and implement strong, pedagogically effective visuals and use them in the classroom.

Jan L. Plass, Professor of Educational Communication and Technology in the Steinhardt School of Culture, Education, and Human Development at New York University. Plass co-directs the NYU Games for Learning Institute and is the founding director of the CREATE Consortium for Research and Evaluation of Advanced Technology in Education.

Matthew Leavitt, Instructional Design Consultant, advises the Visualizing team on the effective design and use of visuals in instruction and has made virtual and live presentations to university faculty around the country regarding effective design and use of instructional visuals.

Independent Research Studies

SEG Research, an independent research and assessment firm, conducted a national, multisite effectiveness study of students enrolled in entry-level college Psychology and Geology courses. The study was designed to evaluate the effectiveness of Wiley Visualizing. You can view the full research paper at www.wiley.com/college/visualizing/huffman/efficacy.html.

Instructor and Student Contributions

Throughout the process of developing the concept of guided visual pedagogy for Wiley Visualizing, we benefited from the comments and constructive criticism provided by the instructors and colleagues listed below. We offer our sincere appreciation to these individuals for their helpful reviews and general feedback:

Visualizing Reviewers, Focus Group Participants, and Survey Respondents

James Abbott, Temple University
Melissa Acevedo, Westchester Community College
Shiva Achet, Roosevelt University
Denise Addorisio, Westchester Community College
Dave Alan, University of Phoenix
Sue Allen-Long, Indiana University – Purdue
Robert Amey, Bridgewater State College
Nancy Bain, Ohio University
Corinne Balducci, Westchester Community College
Steve Barnhart, Middlesex County Community College
Stefan Becker, University of Washington – Oshkosh
Callan Bentley, NVCC Annandale
Valerie Bergeron, Delaware Technical & Community College
Andrew Berns, Milwaukee Area Technical College
Gregory Bishop, Orange Coast College
Rebecca Boger, Brooklyn College
Scott Brame, Clemson University
Joan Brandt, Central Piedmont Community College
Richard Brinn, Florida International University
Jim Bruno, University of Phoenix
William Chamberlin, Fullerton College
Oiyin Pauline Chow, Harrisburg Area Community College
Laurie Corey, Westchester Community College

Ozeas Costas, Ohio State University at Mansfield
Christopher Di Leonardo, Foothill College
Dani Ducharme, Waubonsee Community College
Mark Eastman, Diablo Valley College
Ben Elman, Baruch College
Staussa Ervin, Tarrant County College
Michael Farabee, Estrella Mountain Community College
Laurie Flaherty, Eastern Washington University
Susan Fuhr, Maryville College
Peter Galvin, Indiana University at Southeast
Andrew Getzfeld, New Jersey City University
Janet Gingold, Prince George's Community College
Donald Glassman, Des Moines Area Community College
Richard Goode, Porterville College
Peggy Green, Broward Community College
Stelian Grigoras, Northwood University
Paul Grogger, University of Colorado
Michael Hackett, Westchester Community College
Duane Hampton, Western Michigan University
Thomas Hancock, Eastern Washington University
Gregory Harris, Polk State College
John Haworth, Chattanooga State Technical Community College
James Hayes-Bohanan, Bridgewater State College

Peter Ingmire, San Francisco State University
Mark Jackson, Central Connecticut State University
Heather Jennings, Mercer County Community College
Eric Jerde, Morehead State University
Jennifer Johnson, Ferris State University
Richard Kandus, Mt. San Jacinto College District
Christopher Kent, Spokane Community College
Gerald Ketterling, North Dakota State University
Lynnel Kiely, Harold Washington College
Eryn Klosko, Westchester Community College
Cary T. Komoto, University of Wisconsin – Barron County
John Kupfer, University of South Carolina
Nicole Lafleur, University of Phoenix
Arthur Lee, Roane State Community College
Mary Lynam, Margrove College
Heidi Marcum, Baylor University
Beth Marshall, Washington State University
Dr. Theresa Martin, Eastern Washington University
Charles Mason, Morehead State University
Susan Massey, Art Institute of Philadelphia
Linda McCollum, Eastern Washington University
Mary L. Meiners, San Diego Miramar College
Shawn Mikulay, Elgin Community College
Cassandra Moe, Century Community College
Lynn Hanson Mooney, Art Institute of Charlotte
Kristy Moreno, University of Phoenix
Jacob Napieralski, University of Michigan - Dearborn
Gisele Nasar, Brevard Community College, Cocoa Campus
Daria Nikitina, West Chester University
Robin O'Quinn, Eastern Washington University
Richard Orndorff, Eastern Washington University
Sharen Orndorff, Eastern Washington University
Clair Ossian, Tarrant County College
Debra Parish, North Harris Montgomery Community College District
Linda Peters, Holyoke Community College
Robin Popp, Chattanooga State Technical Community College
Michael Priano, Westchester Community College

Alan "Paul" Price, University of Wisconsin – Washington County
Max Reams, Olivet Nazarene University
Mary Celeste Reese, Mississippi State University
Bruce Rengers, Metropolitan State College of Denver
Guillermo Rocha, Brooklyn College
Penny Sadler, College of William and Mary
Shamili Sandiford, College of DuPage
Thomas Sasek, University of Louisiana at Monroe
Donna Seagle, Chattanooga State Technical Community College
Diane Shakes, College of William and Mary
Jennie Silva, Louisiana State University
Michael Siola, Chicago State University
Morgan Slusher, Community College of Baltimore County
Julia Smith, Eastern Washington University
Darlene Smucny, University of Maryland University College
Jeff Snyder, Bowling Green State University
Alice Stefaniak, St. Xavier University
Alicia Steinhardt, Hartnell Community College
Kurt Stellwagen, Eastern Washington University
Charlotte Stromfors, University of Phoenix
Shane Strup, University of Phoenix
Donald Thieme, Georgia Perimeter College
Pamela Thinesen, Century Community College
Chad Thompson, SUNY Westchester Community College
Lensyl Urbano, University of Memphis
Gopal Venugopal, Roosevelt University
Daniel Vogt, University of Washington – College of Forest Resources
Dr. Laura J. Vosejpka, Northwood University
Brenda L. Walker, Kirkwood Community College
Stephen Wareham, Cal State Fullerton
Fred William Whitford, Montana State University
Katie Wiedman, University of St. Francis
Harry Williams, University of North Texas
Emily Williamson, Mississippi State University
Bridget Wyatt, San Francisco State University
Van Youngman, Art Institute of Philadelphia
Alexander Zemcov, Westchester Community College

Student Participants

Karl Beall, Eastern Washington University
Jessica Bryant, Eastern Washington University
Pia Chawla, Westchester Community College
Channel DeWitt, Eastern Washington University
Lucy DiAroscia, Westchester Community College
Heather Gregg, Eastern Washington University
Lindsey Harris, Eastern Washington University
Brenden Hayden, Eastern Washington University
Patty Hosner, Eastern Washington University

Tonya Karunartue, Eastern Washington University
Sydney Lindgren, Eastern Washington University
Michael Maczuga, Westchester Community College
Melissa Michael, Eastern Washington University
Estelle Rizzin, Westchester Community College
Andrew Rowley, Eastern Washington University
Eric Torres, Westchester Community College
Joshua Watson, Eastern Washington University

Reviewers of *Visualizing Human Geography*

Joy Adams, Humboldt State University
Frank Ainsley, University Of North Carolina – Wilmington
Jennifer Altenhofel, California State University – Bakersfield
Jessica Amato, Napa Valley College
Christiana Asante, Grambling State University

Greg Atkinson, Tarleton State University
Timothy Bawden, University of Wisconsin – Eau Claire
Brad Bays, Oklahoma State University
Mark Bonta, Delta State University
Patricia Boudinot, George Mason University

Michaele Ann Buell, Northwest Arkansas Community College
Henry Bullamore, Frostburg State University
Kristen Conway-Gomez, California State Polytechnic University – Pomona
Carolyn Coulter, Atlantic Cape Community College
Christina Dando, University of Nebraska – Omaha
Jeff DeGrave, University of Wisconsin – Eau Claire
Ramesh Dhussa, Drake University
Dixie Dickinson, Tidewater Community College – Virginia Beach
Christine Drake, Old Dominion University
James Ebrecht, Georgia Perimeter College
Istvan Egresi, University of Oklahoma
William Flynn, Oklahoma State University
Piper Gaubatz, University of Massachusetts
Jerry Gerlach, Winona State University
Stephen Gibson, Allegany College of Maryland
Charles Gildersleeve, University of Nebraska- Omaha
Jeff Gordon, University of Missouri – Columbia
Margaret Gripshover, University of Tennessee- Knoxville
Joshua Hagen, Marshall University
Helen Hazen, Macalester College
Marc Healy, Elgin Community College
Bryan Higgins, SUNY – Plattsburgh

Juana Ibanez, University of New Orleans
Edwin Joseph, Grand Valley State University
William Laatsch, University of Wisconsin- Green Bay
Heidi Lannon, University of Wisconsin – Oshkosh
Robin Lyons, San Joaquin Delta College
Kenji Oshiro, Wright State University
Siyoung Park, Western Illinois University
Bimal Paul, Kansas State University
Cynthia Pope, Central Connecticut State University
Albert Rydant, Keene State College
James Saku, Frostburg State University
Anne Saxe, Saddleback College
Roger Selya, University of Cincinnati
Dean Sinclair, Northwestern State University
Anne Soper, Indiana University – Bloomington
Christophe Storie, Winthrop University
Tim Strauss, University of Northern Iowa
Ray Sumner, Long Beach City College
Joseph Swain, Arkansas Tech University
Richard Wagner, Louisiana Tech University
William Wheeler, Southwestern Oklahoma State University
Pat Wurth, Roane State Community College
Donald Zeigler, Old Dominion University at Virginia Beach

Survey Respondents

Gillian Acheson, Southern Illinois University
Joy Adams, Humboldt State University
Frank Ainsley, University of North Carolina – Wilmington
Victoria Alapo, Metropolitan Community College
Jennifer Altenhofel, California State University – Bakersfield
Robert Amey, Bridgewater State College
Brian Andrews, Southern Methodist University
Donna Arkowski, Pikes Peak Community College
Christiana Asante, Grambling State University
Michele Barnaby, Pittsburg State University
Steve Bass, Mesa Community College
Sari Bennett, University of Maryland, Baltimore County
Kathryn Besio, University of Hawaii – Hilo
Keith Bettinger, University of Hawaii
Phil Birge-Liberman, Bridgewater State College
Mark Bonta, Delta State University
Fernando Bosco, San Diego State University
Henry Bullamore, Frostburg State University
Rebecca Buller, University of Nebraska – Lincoln
John Burrows, Talladega College
Perry Carter, Texas Tech University – Lubbock
Lisa Chaddock, San Diego City College
Wing-Ho Cheung, Palomar College – San Marcos
Jerry Coleman, University of Southern Mississippi Gulf Coast
Kristen Conway-Gomez, California State Polytechnic University – Pomona
Carolyn Coulter, Atlantic Cape Community College
William Courter, Santa Ana College
G. Nevin Crouse, Chesapeake College
George Daugavietis, Solano Community College
Bruce Davis, Eastern Kentucky University
Jeff DeGrave, University of Wisconsin – Eau Claire

Lorraine Dowler, Pennsylvania State University
Anthony Dutton, Valley City State College
Markus Eberl, Vanderbilt University
Gary Elbow, Texas Tech University
Chuck Fahrer, Georgia College & State University
Johnny Finn, Arizona State University
Roxane Fridirici, California State University – Sacramento
Robert Fuller, North Georgia College & State University
Benjamin Funston-Timms, California Polytechnic State University – San Luis Obispo
Jerry Gerlach, Winona State University
Michael Giammarella, CUNY – Manhattan Community College
Omar Godoy, LACCD – East Los Angeles College
Banu Gokariksel, University of North Carolina
Marvin Gordon, University of Illinois at Chicago
Qian Guo, San Francisco State University
Steve Graves, California State University – Northridge
Angela Gray, University of Wisconsin – Oshkosh
Joshua Hagen, Marshall University
Katherine Hankins, Georgia State University
Timothy Hawthorne, Ohio State University
John Hickey, Inver Hills Community College
Miriam Helen Hill, Jacksonville State University
Larissa Hinz, Eastern Illinois University
Doc Horsley, Southern Illinois University
Ronald Isaac, Ohio University
Ryan James, University of North Carolina – Charlotte
Duncan Jamieson, Ashland University
Wendy Jepson, Texas A & M University – College Station
Chad Kinsella, Kentucky Community & Technical College
Marti Klein, Cypress College
Richard Kujawa, Saint Michael's College

Margareta Lelea, Bucknell University
David Lemberg, Western Michigan University
Anne Lewis, Allegany College of Maryland
Joseph Lewis, Ohio State University
David Liscio, Endicott College
Lee Liu, University of Central Missouri
James Lowry, University of New Orleans
Ronald Luna, University of Maryland
Kerry Lyste, Everett Community College
Taylor Mack, Louisiana Technical University
Michael Madsen, Brigham Young University
Christine Mathenge, Austin Peay State University
Richard McCluskey, Aquinas College
Frank McComb, Georgia Perimeter College – Clarkston
Mark Meo, University of Oklahoma
Diane Meredithn, California State University – East Bay
Silva Meybatyan, University of the District of Columbia
Pam Miller, College of Eastern Utah
Linda Murphy, Blinn Community College
Natalia Murphy, Southern Arkansas University
Hemalatha Navaratne, Borough of Manhattan Community College
Tom Newton, Kirkwood Community College – Iowa City
Kenji Oshiro, Wright State University
Seth Parry, Emmanuel College
Dan Pavese, Wor-Wic Community College
Michael Pesses, Antelope Valley College
Ingrid Pfoertsch, Towson University
Nathan Phillippi, University of North Carolina – Pembroke
Colin Polsky, Clark University
William Price, North Country Community College
Larshale Pugh, Youngstown State University
Melanie Rapino, University of Memphis

Eike Reichardt, Lehigh Carbon Community College
Robert Ritchie, Liberty University
Julio Rivera, Carthage College
Alicia Roe, Inter American University of Puerto Rico – Metropolitan
Karl Ryavec, University of Wisconsin – Stevens Point
James Saku, Frostburg State University
Samuel Sawaya, Sinclair Community College
Andrew Scholl, Wittenberg University
Anita Shoup, CUNY – Hunter College
Steven Silvern, Salem State College
Michael Siola, Chicago State University
Sarah Smiley, Morgan State University
Lisa Stanich, Lakeland Community College
Herschel Stern, Miracosta College
Mary Tacy, James Madison University
Jane Thorngren, San Diego State University
Dan Turbeville, Eastern Washington University
Richard Tyre, Florida State University
David Unterman, University of North Carolina – Greensboro/
   Sierra College
Wendy Welch, University of Virginia's College at Wise
Ben Wolfe, Metropolitan Community College – Blue River
Louis A. Woods, University of North Florida
Dawn Wrobel, Moraine Valley Community College
Patricia Wurth, Roane State Community College
Leon Yacher, Southern Connecticut State University
Keith Yearman, College of DuPage
Lei Xu, California State University – Fullerton
Laura Zeeman, Red Rocks Community College
Robert Ziegenfus, Kutztown University of Pennsylvania
William Zogby, Mohawk Valley Community College
Kathleen Zynda, Erie Community College – North Campus

Students and Class Testers

To make certain that *Visualizing Human Geography 2e* met the needs of current students, we asked several instructors to class-test a chapter. The feedback that we received from students and instructors confirmed our belief that the visualizing approach taken in this book is highly effective in helping students to learn. We wish to thank the following instructors and their students who provided us with helpful feedback and suggestions:

Christiana Asante, Grambling State University
Mark Bonta, Delta State University
Patricia Boudinot, George Mason University
Michaele Ann Buell, Northwest Arkansas Community College
Hank Bullamore, Frostburg State University
Chuck Fahrer, Georgia College and State University
Marti Klein, Cypress College
John Kostelnick, Illinois State University
Kerry Lyste, Everett Community College
John Menary, Long Beach City College
Siyoung Park, Western Illinois University

Cindy Pope, Central Connecticut State University
Larshale Pugh, Youngstown State University
Stacey Roush, Montgomery Community College
James Saku, Frostburg State University
Roger Selya, University of Cincinnati
Tim Strauss, University of Northern Iowa
Amy Sumpter, Georgia College and State University
Nicholas Vaughn, Indiana University Bloomington
Pat Wurth, Roane State Community College
Donald Zeigler, Old Dominion University at Virginia Beach

Dedication

I dedicate this edition to my husband, Luis Montes, and also to all of my in-laws, "out-laws," and family members for their support and understanding over the years.

Special Thanks

Visualizing Human Geography 2e has benefited in countless ways from the many thoughtful and generous contributions of others. I owe a special thanks to Publisher Jay O'Callaghan and Executive Editor Ryan Flahive for their steadfast commitment to this book and their ability to assemble such an amazing project team. It is an honor to work with so many dedicated, creative, and professional people.

I am especially grateful to have had the opportunity to work with Developmental Editor Rebecca Heider, who has been a wonderful source of novel and inspiring ideas. Her crisp exposition has improved the clarity of concepts and artwork throughout the book. The book's style, structure, and cohesiveness has also benefited from the comprehensive vision of master craftswoman, Nancy Perry, Manager of Product Development. My thanks also go to Julia Nollen, Editorial Assistant, for her invaluable assistance with the art manuscript and the cheerful disposition with which she provided day-to-day guidance on this project.

Micheline Frederick, Senior Content Manger, and Sandra Rigby, Senior Production Editor, have provided expert oversight and leadership on this edition. I am deeply indebted to Senior Marketing Manager Margaret Barrett and Jeffrey Rucker, Associate Director, Marketing, for all of their hard work and unflagging dedication to this book. It has been a real pleasure working with Jeanine Furino of Furino Production, a skillful and conscientious manager with a keen eye for detail. This edition would not have been possible without the superb work of codeMantra, the compositor, and Mapping Specialists, for their cartography. All the new photos have been made possible by the indefatigable efforts of Sheena Goldstein, Senior Photo Editor, Billy Ray, Photo Editor, and Teri Stratford, Photo Researcher. In addition, I sincerely appreciate the guidance and assistance on permissions provided by Christine Moore, Associate Development Editor.

I also wish to thank the students and instructors who have provided feedback on this book; I welcome your comments at any time. To all of my colleagues in the Department of Geography at Oklahoma State University, thank you for being so collegial and supportive.

About the Author

Alyson L. Greiner is Associate Professor of Geography at Oklahoma State University. She earned her PhD in Geography from the University of Texas at Austin. She has taught courses on cultural geography, world regional geography, the history of geographic thought, and the regional geography of Europe, Africa, and the Pacific Realm. She regularly teaches undergraduate, graduate, and honors students. She has received a Distinguished Teaching Achievement Award from the National Council for Geographic Education. From 2009-2012 she served as a Regional Councilor for the Association of American Geographers. Her scholarly publications include *Anglo-Celtic Australia: Colonial Immigration and Cultural Regionalism* (with Terry G. Jordan-Bychkov) and several peer-reviewed journal articles. She is presently the editor of the *Journal of Cultural Geography*.

Preface

Matthew Brown/ASSOCIATED PRESS

1

What Is Human Geography? 2

Krzysztof Dydynski/Lonely Planet Images/Getty Images

2

Globalization and Cultural Geography 34

MUSTAFA OZER/AFP/Getty Images

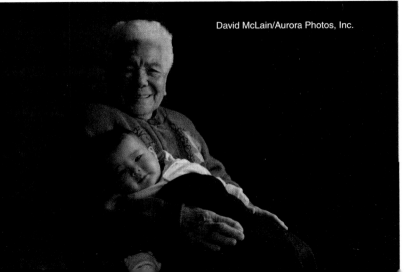

David McLain/Aurora Photos, Inc.

Courtesy Alyson Greiner

© avneesh kumar/Demotix/Demotix/Demotix/Corbis

Pavel Rahman/©AP/Wide World Photos

Alexandre Meneghini/©AP/Wide World Photos

Joe Raedle/Newsmakers/Getty Images, Inc.

Behrouz Mehri/AFP/Getty Images

Getty Images/FlickrSelect/marin.tomic

Oliver Berg/dpa/Landov LLC

Multi-part visual presentations that focus on a key concept or topic in the chapter

A series or combination of figures and photos that describe and depict a complex process

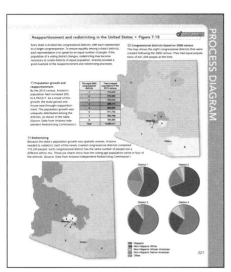

VISUALIZING
HUMAN GEOGRAPHY

1

GEOGRAPHY, INQUIRY, AND SEEING THE LIGHT

Can you find your hometown or city on this image of the Earth at night? Bigger cities and more urbanized or built-up areas shine the brightest. Japan appears very brightly lit because the country is highly urbanized and has a high density of commercial and industrial activity. Try to find the trans-Siberian railroad in Russia or interstates in the United States to see how night lights reveal human activity.

Why do the spaces of illumination vary from one continent to another? What inferences can you make about well-lit places and settlement patterns, wealth, or environmental modification? Geographers ask these and similar kinds of questions. Embedded within such questions are concepts relating to location, place, space, region, scale, distribution, and inter-connectedness. Thus, geographical inquiry has its roots in a fundamental curiosity about the world.

However, there is more to geographical inquiry than simply asking questions. Geographers also step back when studying a topic or phenomenon and examine relationships between data in order to generate new insights about how the world works. In this way, geographical inquiry and analysis contribute to the development of geographical theory—knowledge that advances our understanding of the social, spatial, regional, and ecological facets of our world.

Simply stated, this book is designed to introduce you to geographical inquiry and theory through a perspective that emphasizes people and the spatial variation in their activities around the world. This chapter introduces human geography and illustrates how geographers approach their work, including some of the tools they use.

CHAPTER OUTLINE

CHAPTER PLANNER ✓

- ❑ Study the picture and read the opening story.
- ❑ Scan the Learning Objectives in each section:
  p. 4 ❑   p. 12 ❑   p. 23 ❑
- ❑ Read the text and study all visuals.
  Answer any questions.

Analyze key features

- ❑ Geography InSight, p. 6 ❑   p. 24 ❑   p. 29 ❑
- ❑ Process Diagram, p. 16
- ❑ What a Geographer Sees, p. 21
- ❑ Video Explorations, p. 23
- ❑ Stop: Answer the Concept Checks before you go on:
  p. 11 ❑   p. 23 ❑   p. 29 ❑

End of chapter

- ❑ Review the Summary and Key Terms.
- ❑ Answer the Critical and Creative Thinking Questions.
- ❑ Answer What is happening in this picture?
- ❑ Complete the Self-Test and check your answers.

Data courtesy Marc Imhoff of NASA GSFC and Christopher Elvidge of NOAA NGDC. Image by Craig Mayhew and Robert Simmon, NASA GSFC

Introducing Human Geography

LEARNING OBJECTIVES

1. **Describe** the scope of geography and its main branches of study.
2. **Outline** the four main geographical approaches to the relationship between nature and culture.
3. **Explain** how geographers study landscapes and regions.

W e are going to let you in on a little secret: Geography majors go places—in their careers, that is. They also have a lot of fun in the process. This is quite likely because geography is a discipline that encourages people to find a topic or region they are passionate about and explore its many different dimensions. Are you interested in music? Music geographers are needed to understand the globalization of hip-hop as well as its local variations. If you are a sports fan, sports geographers help identify optimal locations for stadiums, golf courses, and other athletic facilities. If your passion is nutrition or health, medical geographers help track and limit the spread of epidemics and study ways to improve people's access to medical care. See *Where Geographers Click* to learn more about careers in geography.

Some nongeographers rather naively thought that globalization would make geography irrelevant. Globalization, they claimed, made the world smaller, more accessible, and therefore, easier to know and understand. Meanwhile, geographers politely noted that globalization was not a new phenomenon and that geography had, to the contrary, taken on even greater relevance. For example, understanding the consequences of global climate change on different countries, agricultural production, and coastal populations demands geographic awareness. Similarly, we cannot solve the problem of poverty until we know better its geographic dimensions— where it occurs, how spatially extensive it is, who it affects, and how it is related to access to resources, such as land, water, and housing. Globalization has moved geography to center stage. Simultaneously, improvements and innovations in technology have expanded the geographer's toolbox. These new tools include ways of acquiring data about the Earth with improved GPS

Where Geographers CLICK

Careers in Geography

© DNY59/iStockphoto

Visit the Jobs and Careers section of the Association of American Geographers (AAG) website for career preparation tips, job listings, and other resources.

receivers, higher resolution satellite imagery, and new ways of visualizing this information with virtual globes such as Google Earth.

The word *geography* derives from Greek words (*geo* + *graphia*) meaning *to write about or describe the Earth*. As previously noted, however, geography is much more than a description of the Earth or a factual listing of countries, their capitals, and resources.

Geography consists of two main branches: physical geography and human geography (**Figure 1.1** on the next page). Physical geography focuses on *environmental dynamics* (e.g., water quality, soil erosion, forest management) whereas **human geography** focuses on *social dynamics* (e.g., economic development, language diffusion, ethnic identity). Some physical and human geographers focus on *environment–society dynamics* and work on topics that span both branches of the discipline (e.g., vulnerability to environmental hazards, impacts of fossil fuel consumption, social consequences of global climate change). The unity of geography as a discipline stems from a shared philosophy that recognizes the urgency of better understanding the spatial aspects of human and environmental processes and using geographic knowledge to generate solutions to the social and environmental challenges in our world.

> **human geography**
> A branch of geography centered on the study of people, places, spatial variation in human activities, and the relationship between people and the environment.

Human geography, like the discipline of geography more broadly, is both a science and an art. The science of human geography stresses the importance of acquiring adequate knowledge about specific processes, events, or interactions in order to explain why they occur or produce the particular outcomes that they do. For example, a human geographer studying migration seeks to explain the causes and consequences that propelled people to move from one place to another.

In contrast, the art of human geography emphasizes a different way of knowing that focuses less on explanation and more on understanding and meaning. The human geographer studying migration also learns about the experiences of the families that migrated and the ways they dealt with challenges in order to better understand the perceptions, feelings, and meanings of the move to the people who made the journey. Thus, the artistic and scientific aspects of human geography are complementary.

Nature and Culture

What do the words *nature* and *culture* mean to you? At first they seem straightforward, but the longer you think about them the more you realize that they both have a variety of different meanings. For example, nature can refer to the intrinsic qualities of a person, or to the outdoors, and culture can refer to taste in the fine arts or to customary beliefs and practices. Because of this definitional looseness, geographer Noel Castree (2001, p. 5) calls *nature* "a promiscuous concept." The same can be said about *culture*.

Nevertheless, these concepts are so fundamental to the practice of geography that we should examine them briefly here.

Very broadly speaking, **nature** is the physical environment; it is external to people and does not include them. People, because of their capacity for intellectual and moral development, are the bearers of culture, and it is culture that distinguishes people from nature. When understood in this way, these concepts yield a dualistic framework that sets nature and culture in opposition to one another.

This **nature–culture dualism** has had a significant impact on ways of thinking about social difference. During the 18th century, some European scholars used this distinction between nature and culture to argue that it was the human capacity for culture that made people *superior* to nature. This line of reasoning was subsequently extended and used to rank societies. So, for example, non-Westerners were seen as being closer to nature than so-called civilized and cultured Westerners, and therefore inferior. Although the origins of these ideas are difficult to unravel, they matter because the way we see human societies in relation to nature and to one another affects not just how we use the environment but also how we interact with others.

Today, many geographers and other social scientists reject the nature–culture dualism because of the way it separates nature from culture. These scholars stress instead that people—in spite of their capacity for culture—are very much a part of nature. This perspective is central to **cultural ecology**, an important subfield within human geography that studies the relationship between people and the natural environment.

When conceptualizing the relationship between people and nature, cultural ecologists and other geographers recognize several different approaches. We discuss four of these next: environmental determinism, possibilism, humans as modifiers of the Earth, and the Earth as a dynamic, integrated system.

Environmental determinism The position that natural factors control the development of human physiological and mental qualities is called **environmental determinism**. We can trace the intellectual roots of environmental determinism in Western thought to the ancient Greeks, who speculated that human diversity resulted from both climatic and locational factors. For example, plateau environments seemed to produce people who were docile.

The two main branches of the discipline have given rise to three broad areas of emphasis. On the diagram, colored terms identify major subfields.

Stephen J. Stadler

CANTIERI del MEDITERRANEO

a. Mount Vesuvius rises behind Naples
Mountain geography includes the study of alpine soils, landscapes, and environments.

GEOGRAPHY

Physical geography   *Human geography*

Biogeography   Mountain geography

Environmental dynamics   Geography of snow and ice

Meteorology/ climatology   Geomorphology

Coastal/marine geography

Cultural geography   Economic geography

Geography of religion   Population geography

Social dynamics

Medical geography

Political geography   Geography of language

Cultural ecology   Urban geography

Environment-society dynamics

Climate change   Agriculture and land use

Energy geography   Water resources

Development

Hazards/vulnerability/resilience

b. Tourists in the Dominican Republic
Economic geography studies tourism trends, patterns of trade, as well as business location data.

© Holger Mette/iStockphoto

The Asahi Shimbun via Getty Images

c. Devastation in Japan from the Fukushima-Daiichi nuclear accident
This accident—the result of an earthquake, tsunami, and planning oversights—reveals the interconnectedness of people and the environment.

Ask Yourself

1. On the diagram, why are the borders between the different areas of emphasis shown as indistinct?
2. Using the photo in **a**, explain how the study of mountain geography could lead to a study in environment–society dynamics.

Introducing Human Geography **7**

The four elements and environmental determinism • Figure 1.2

Some ancient scholars thought that all natural phenomena, including people, were made up of the four elements in varying degrees. Environmental determinism attributed cultural difference to human traits that reflected these four elements and were strongly shaped by physical factors, including climate.

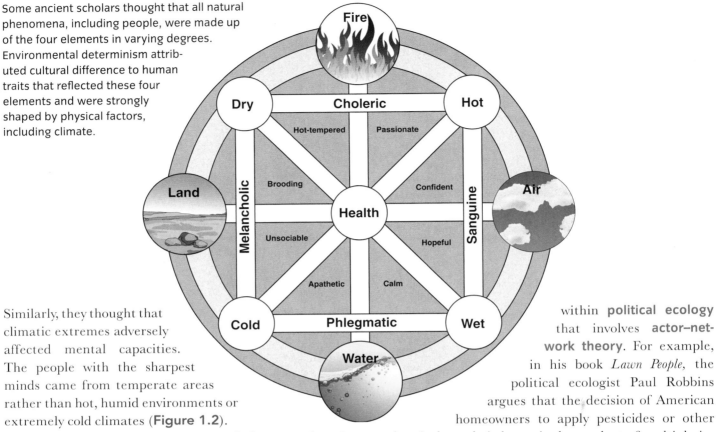

Similarly, they thought that climatic extremes adversely affected mental capacities. The people with the sharpest minds came from temperate areas rather than hot, humid environments or extremely cold climates (**Figure 1.2**).

Environmental determinism prevailed among American geographers during the early 20th century and then fell quickly into disfavor. Three major criticisms of environmental determinism prompted this change in perspective. First, geographers found overly simplistic the linear, cause–effect relationship that forms the basis of environmental determinism. People, they argued, are more than automatons that simply respond to stimuli, such as the prevailing winds or temperatures in a specific place. Nonenvironmental factors, such as systems of government and law, also help explain human diversity. A second criticism of environmental determinism is that similar natural settings do not produce the same cultural practices or human behavior. Third, environmental determinism tends to contribute to ethnocentric interpretations of sociocultural differences. It is therefore not much of a surprise that some ancient Greek scholars attributed the flourishing of the Greek civilization to the temperate climate of the Mediterranean.

In recent years a radical reinterpretation of environmental determinism has emerged

political ecology
An offshoot of cultural ecology that studies how economic forces and competition for power influence human behavior, especially decisions and attitudes involving the environment.

actor–network theory
A body of thought that emphasizes that humans and nonhumans are linked together in a dynamic set of relations that, in turn, influence human behavior.

within **political ecology** that involves **actor–network theory**. For example, in his book *Lawn People*, the political ecologist Paul Robbins argues that the decision of American homeowners to apply pesticides or other chemicals to their lawns is the product of multiple interacting factors. These factors include the supply of and demand for lawn chemicals, the importance of property values, community pressure to maintain a well-kept lawn, lawn aesthetics (e.g., ideas about how a lawn should look), and the lawn itself (**Figure 1.3**).

Actor–network theory challenges the idea that people have free will. Rather, nonhuman entities gain agency (the ability to exert influence) by virtue of the networks of relations in which they are embedded. As Robbins observes, "the nonhuman world does have an active, ongoing, and crucial role in directing the conditions of the economy and the character of human culture" (2007, p. 137). Unlike environmental determinism, actor–network theory gives agency to natural factors as well as anything human-made (e.g., lawns, machines, or laws) but not in a simplistic cause–effect relationship.

Possibilism Reactions against environmental determinism in the early 20th century gave rise to **possibilism**—the view that people use

Actor–network theory • Figure 1.3

Actor–network theory acknowledges that our surroundings influence us. The lawn, the availability of fertilizers, and aesthetics influence human behavior by prompting a homeowner to mow, fertilize, and maintain it. (*Source:* Adapted from Robbins, 2007.)

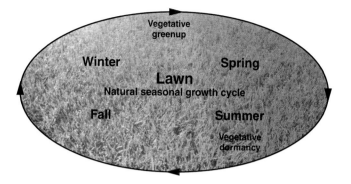

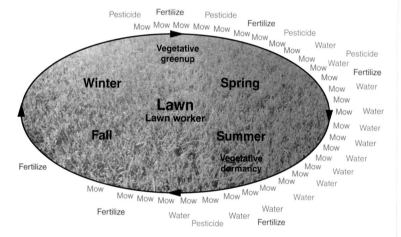

agency, the ability of people to modify their surroundings. He observed that, over time, human activities transform natural landscapes into **cultural landscapes**. Significantly, Sauer's work helped raise awareness of the human role in landscape change. Visually, evidence of humans as modifiers of the Earth is all around us, from our cities to our cultivated agricultural fields (**Figure 1.4**).

An important extension of the humans as modifiers of the Earth approach involves seeing nature as a *social construction*—an invented concept derived from shared perceptions and understandings. This perspective acknowledges that people shape the natural environment through their practices *and* their ideas about what nature is or should be. A good example of this involves the idea of wilderness in the United States. The environmental historian, William Cronon, has shown that in the 18th century wilderness was equated with wasteland, but by the 19th century wilderness was strongly associated with natural beauty.

Earth as a dynamic, integrated system In this approach, geographers see people as intricately connected with the natural world. Two key principles sum up this approach: (1) the Earth functions as a system made up of diverse components that interact in complex ways; and

their creativity to decide how to respond to the conditions or constraints of a particular natural environment. The word *constraints* is important here because it indicates that the environment is seen as limiting the choices or opportunities that people have. Possibilists, then, do not completely reject the idea of environmental influence; however, they are reluctant to view the environment as the sole or even the strongest force shaping a society. Thus, a possibilist sees technological diversification as one mechanism for expanding the range of choices a society has.

Humans as modifiers of the Earth A different approach to the relationship between people and the environment was advanced by geographer Carl Sauer (1889–1975), beginning in the 1920s. Sauer rejected environmental determinism and emphasized instead human

Mattias Klum/NG Image Collection

An extreme cultural landscape? • Figure 1.4

If your country lacks snow-covered mountains, why not manufacture them? This mountain-themed resort facility is in the United Arab Emirates and features year-round skiing even though outside temperatures rarely dip below 70° Fahrenheit.

Formal, functional, and perceptual regions • Figure 1.5

A wide variety of business, government, and planning agencies make decisions based on spatial information related to these three types of regions.

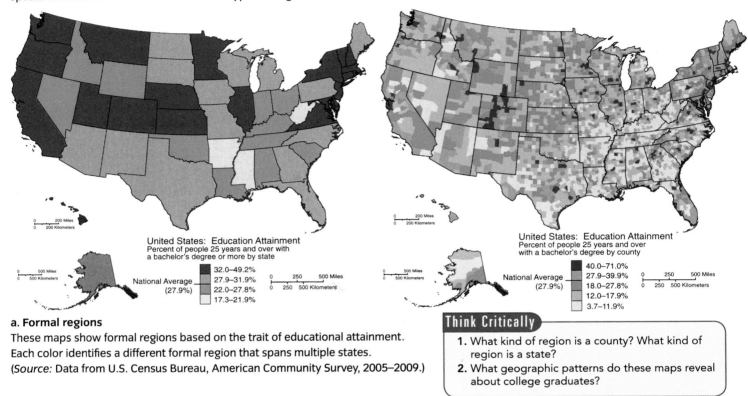

a. Formal regions
These maps show formal regions based on the trait of educational attainment. Each color identifies a different formal region that spans multiple states. (*Source:* Data from U.S. Census Bureau, American Community Survey, 2005–2009.)

United States: Education Attainment
Percent of people 25 years and over with a bachelor's degree or more by state

National Average (27.9%)
- 32.0–49.2%
- 27.9–31.9%
- 22.0–27.8%
- 17.3–21.9%

United States: Education Attainment
Percent of people 25 years and over with a bachelor's degree by county

National Average (27.9%)
- 40.0–71.0%
- 27.9–39.9%
- 18.0–27.8%
- 12.0–17.9%
- 3.7–11.9%

Think Critically
1. What kind of region is a county? What kind of region is a state?
2. What geographic patterns do these maps reveal about college graduates?

(2) the Earth is constantly changing as a result of natural and human-induced events. We explore these ideas further in Chapter 12.

Cultural Landscapes and Regions

As we have discussed, culture is sometimes used to refer to a person's intellectual improvement through education, particularly the development of an aesthetic appreciation for the arts. In other instances, culture refers to beliefs and practices—such as dietary customs, religious beliefs, and so on—held in common by a group of people. Thus, a cultural group shares certain traits or elements of culture. This understanding of culture guided much of the practice of human geography until the late 20th century. More specifically, two long-standing approaches to the study of culture emphasize reading the cultural landscape and performing regional analysis. The emphasis on cultural landscapes reflects Carl Sauer's influence on geography, especially his view that culture is the driving force for landscape change.

Reading the cultural landscape works from the premise that the cultural landscape constitutes a rich repository of information about cultural beliefs and practices. In other words, the cultural landscape resembles a *palimpsest*—a parchment that, though cleaned, still bears the traces of what was previously inscribed on it. To a human geographer, the visible expressions of culture—for example, the settlement patterns, the structures people build, the architectural styles they choose, and the ways people use land—all provide clues about people's values, identity, and more broadly, their cultures.

Regional analysis involves studying the distinctiveness of regions. In the United States, this might include understanding how and why the South differs from New England culturally, economically, and politically. Or, regional analysis might examine the ways in which the War in Iraq (2003–2011) altered the demographic and religious makeup of the country's provinces, and the ramifications of these changes.

Types of regions Geographers identify three types of regions: formal, functional, and perceptual. A **formal region** is an area that possesses one or more unifying physical or cultural traits. Unlike formal regions, a **functional region** is an area unified

David Sucsy/Getty Images

b. Functional region
A university campus is a functional region. On the University of Texas campus, the Tower is part of the Main Building, an administrative node that includes the president's and provost's offices, among others.

Courtesy Alyson Greiner

c. Perceptual region
Chickasaw Country is a perceptual region in Oklahoma that is associated with the territory of the Chickasaw Nation, depicted in dark blue in the photo. History, politics, recreation, tourism, and even aspects of the physical geography of an area can shape the characteristics of perceptual regions.

by a specific economic, political, or social activity. Every functional region has at least one node, usually the business, office, or entity that coordinates the activity. For example, each state in the United States constitutes a functional region with its state capital serving as the node. In contrast to both formal and functional regions, **perceptual regions** derive from people's sense of identity and attachment to different areas. The borders of perceptual regions tend to be highly variable since people often have very personal reasons for perceiving an area a certain way (**Figure 1.5**).

Culture reconceptualized Recently, certain geographers have stressed the point that we should think of culture as an abstract concept, not as a material item or collection of cultural traits. According to Don Mitchell, for example, "There's no such *thing* as culture" (emphasis added) (1995, p. 102). By this he means to caution people against trying to limit culture to specific and fixed habits of life. In his view, the visible and tangible expressions of culture are important, but they need to be understood in their dynamic context—in relation to prevailing economic, social, political, and other factors.

Similarly, other geographers stress that an understanding of culture that defines the term as a way of life fails to recognize other crucial aspects of culture. Consequently, over the past several decades there has been a significant reconceptualization of **culture** that draws on the following three attributes:

1. Culture is a social creation that reflects diverse economic, historical, political, social, and environmental factors.
2. Culture is dynamic, not fixed, and can be contested. This is illustrated by the phrase "culture wars."
3. Culture is a complex system. Through interactions with one another, people create and express culture, and in turn, culture shapes and influences people.

> **culture** A social creation consisting of shared beliefs and practices that are dynamic rather than fixed, and a complex system that is shaped by people and, in turn, influences them.

The significance of this reconceptualization of culture is that it seeks to make the practice of human geography even more vigorous. For those who work within the reading the landscape approach, this reconceptualization

© Rich Legg/iStockphoto

Culture, power, and landscape • Figure 1.6

We can read the cultural landscape to discern that this gated residential community is exclusive. If our approach is informed by a fuller understanding of culture, however, we are better equipped to examine the invisible dimensions of power, identity, or class, for example, that also factored in this community's establishment.

of culture means that sometimes what remains on the landscape provides only a partial understanding of the complex and dynamic forces that created it. Consider, for example, gated residential communities (**Figure 1.6**).

CONCEPT CHECK　　　　　　　STOP

1. **What** is the focus of cultural ecology?
2. **How** does actor–network theory conceptualize the relationship between people and the environment?
3. **How** are formal, functional, and perceptual regions different?

Thinking Like a Human Geographer

LEARNING OBJECTIVES

1. **Contrast** the concepts of place and space.
2. **Distinguish** between spatial variation and spatial association.
3. **Identify** four different types of diffusion.
4. **Explain** the relationship between globalization, spatial interaction, and time–space convergence.
5. **Review** the different scales used in geographical research.

All you need to begin to think like a human geographer is a curiosity about places in the world, whether they are nearby or far away. This curiosity might spur questions similar to those we raised about nighttime illumination in the chapter opener, or it might prompt questions about the connections between different places.

Thus, to think like a human geographer is to cultivate a perspective that includes a consideration of one or more of the following: (1) place, (2) space, (3) spatial diffusion, (4) spatial interaction, or (5) scale.

Place

When geographers use the term **place** they are referring to a locality distinguished by specific physical and social characteristics. Every place can be identified by its *absolute location*, or position, reckoned by latitude and longitude on the globe, as well as its **site** and **situation** (**Figure 1.7**).

Places matter because they contribute to the social, political, and economic functioning of our

> **site** The physical characteristics of a place, such as its topography, vegetation, and water resources.
>
> **situation** The geographic context of a place, including its political, economic, social, or other characteristics.

Site and situation • Figure 1.7

By considering site and situation, we can make sense of the location and context of any place. What aspects of Istanbul's site and situation make it strategic?

© Robert Preston Photography/Alamy Limited

a. Physically, Istanbul occupies a hilly site adjacent to a deep harbor and has grown on both sides of the Bosporus, a narrow and strategic waterway that connects the Mediterranean and Black seas. From left to right across the hilltop are the Hagia Sophia, now a museum, and the Blue Mosque.

b. These maps depict the situation of Istanbul, Turkey's largest city, in relation to the surrounding bodies of water, the rest of the country, and neighboring regions. By virtue of its situation, Istanbul straddles the regions of Europe and Asia.

MUSTAFA OZER/AFP/Getty Images

c. Istanbul's growth as a major port stems from attributes of its site and situation along an important strait. What this photo does not capture, however, is the dynamic nature of a place's situation. Numerous ferries and cargo ships ply the surrounding waters, but a workers' strike or inclement weather can quickly alter Istanbul's situation.

world. Indeed, the tourism industry capitalizes on the fact that no two places are identical and that people enjoy experiencing these differences. Places are also important because they provide anchors for human identity. When you meet someone for the first time and are learning about that person's identity, you typically ask, "What is your name?" and then "Where are you from?" The reverse is also true: Your sense of identity derives in part from your own place-based experiences. Geographers use the term *sense of place* to refer to the complex, emotional attachments that people develop with specific localities. The feeling of belonging is strongly linked to a person's sense of place. Similarly, a part of the collective identity shared by cultural groups often involves their sense of place and the feeling that they belong in a specific place.

Space

If place refers to a specific locality, then **space** refers to either a bounded or unbounded area. Geographers identify two different kinds of space: absolute and relative. *Absolute space* refers to an area whose dimensions, distances, directions, and contents can be precisely measured. Geographers often draw an analogy between absolute space and a container in that it is possible to know a container's boundaries, dimensions, and contents. In fact, a formal culture region is a good example of a container-like space. The concept of absolute space dominated the practice of geography until about the 1960s. Until then, geographers were strongly interested in the study of regions. Since the 1960s, however, the concept of relative space has gained prominence.

Relative space refers to space that is created and defined by human interactions, perceptions, or relations between events. Relative space is defined less by precise boundaries and more by *contingency*—the idea that the outcome of human interactions and perceptions depends on who and what are involved. A good example of relative space and its contingent character is the space of trade. For trade to occur between two countries, each must be able to supply the products the trading partner needs and enter into a mutual agreement to do so. The contingency of trade, then, depends in part on the countries' ability to continue to supply the desired products and to maintain favorable diplomatic relations. When two countries or businesses engage in trade, they create a relative space of trade that exists between them as long as these contingent conditions are satisfied.

Relative space • Figure 1.8

If absolute space resembles a container, then relative space resembles a network of linked nodes, also referred to as a hub-and-spoke network. In the context of social networking, nodes or hubs represent individuals. (*Source:* Adapted with permission from The Monitor Company Group, L.P.)

As the trade example shows, political and economic interactions can shape the creation and production of relative space. So, too, can social interactions. In this way, relative space is socially produced. Social networking sites such as Google+ and Facebook provide great examples of this. When you log on and chat with your friends, you are creating and participating in a relative space. It is indeed fascinating, and even a little overwhelming, to think about the millions of relative spaces created not just on the Internet but globally, as people, businesses, and organizations interact. Can you list the different relative spaces you are a part of on a daily basis? More importantly, do you see how the concept of relative space involves horizontal linkages, as well as networks or webs of connections that defy containment (**Figure 1.8**)?

In the course of this discussion we have set up a dichotomy between absolute and relative space. However, the two concepts can and often do overlap. We realize this connection when we think about the relationship between perceptions and space. For example, how does human behavior change when people move from one space to another? How does your own behavior change as you go from home or your dorm to a classroom or to the library? These buildings and rooms have characteristics of both absolute and relative space in that they are bounded, physical spaces but also zones or fields of perception and interaction. The fact that the range of acceptable behaviors changes from one space to another suggests that our perceptions of space can be significantly shaped by many factors, including power relations.

These relations between space and power, or authority, have been informed by the work of French philosopher and historian Michel Foucault (1926–1984). Foucault has

spatial variation
Changes in the distribution of a phenomenon from one place or area to another.

spatial association
The degree to which two or more phenomena share similar distributions.

distribution
The arrangement of phenomena on or near the Earth's surface.

shown, for example, that the power relations associated with space have a way of regulating and controlling—or as he calls it "disciplining"—human behavior. Look again at Figure 1.8. Where is the power in this network?

Grasping these aspects of space is a key part of understanding how the world works. Consequently, human geographers adopt and emphasize a *spatial perspective* in their work. That is, they pay particular attention to the variations from one place or space to another in society and environment–society dynamics. **Spatial variation** and **spatial association** are other key concepts geographers use; both concepts build on an understanding of **distribution** (**Figure 1.9**).

Spatial variation and spatial association • Figure 1.9

Adopting a spatial perspective helps to identify and explain distributions.

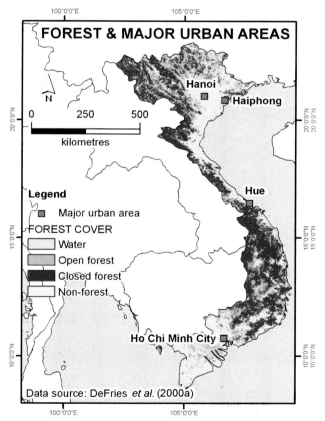

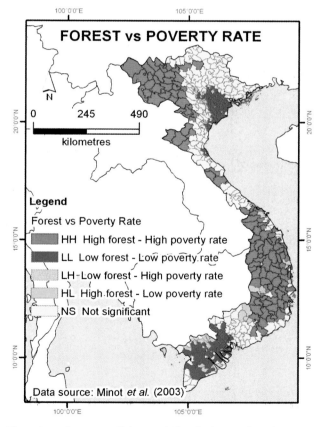

a. The spatial variation of closed forests in Vietnam changes markedly from north to south across the country. ▶ **What are some likely reasons for this?** (Figure 1.9 images from Sunderlin, Dewi, and Puntodewo, 2007, p. 17; used with permission from CIFOR, www.cifor.cgiar.org.)

b. There is a strong spatial association between forest cover and poverty rates in Vietnam, although this does not necessarily mean that one phenomenon has caused the other. Understanding this association demands an investigation of other factors, including economic forces, political policies, historical developments, and social practices.

Understanding hierarchical diffusion • Figure 1.10

Hierarchical diffusion involves cascading or stair-stepping from one level or rank to another. In this example, BigApple Togs, a hypothetical fashion chain headquartered in New York City, launches a fashion innovation that is diffused hierarchically through the company.

President and CEO

| Rank ❶ | VP Purchasing
New York City | VP Marketing
Los Angeles | VP Sales
Los Angeles | VP Finance
New York City | VP Investors
New York City |

| Rank ❷ | Manager
Pacific Region
Los Angeles | Manager
Mountain Region
Denver | Manager
Midwest Region
Chicago | Manager
Northeast Region
New York City | Manager
Southeast Region
Atlanta |

| Rank ❸ | Sales Staff
Seattle
Portland
San Francisco | Sales Staff
Salt Lake City
Santa Fe
Phoenix | Sales Staff
St. Louis
Minneapolis
Omaha
Columbus
Oklahoma City | Sales Staff
Boston
Philadelphia
Pittsburgh | Sales Staff
Norfolk
Nashville
Little Rock
New Orleans
Miami
Dallas |

a. The organization chart for BigApple Togs forms the framework in which the hierarchical diffusion of ideas can occur down through the ranks.

Spatial Diffusion

How does fashion, news, gossip, a flu virus, or the latest high-tech gadget spread through a population and from one place to another? These questions get at the core of **spatial diffusion**. Because spatial diffusion may occur rapidly or slowly, depending on the circumstances, time is always an essential dimension of diffusion.

> **spatial diffusion**
> The movement of a phenomenon, such as an innovation, information, or an epidemic, across space and over time.

Geographers recognize four different types of diffusion: relocation, contagious, hierarchical, and stimulus. Migration is the most common type of *relocation diffusion*. *Contagious diffusion* occurs when a phenomenon, such as the common cold, spreads randomly from one person to another. In contrast, *hierarchical diffusion* occurs in a top-down or rank-order manner. See **Figure 1.10** for an explanation of hierarchical diffusion.

Stimulus diffusion occurs when the spread of an idea, a practice, or other phenomenon prompts a new idea or innovation. A great deal of stimulus diffusion affects the production and marketing of goods. We can see this readily in the automobile and fast-food industries, for example. The idea behind a successful product often triggers applications of that principle in other settings—whether it is a certain body style on a vehicle or the development of a new kind of fast-food restaurant.

Studies suggest that spatial diffusion often involves a mixture of types. The diffusion of H1N1 flu since April 2009 provides a good example. This flu virus was first detected in Mexico. It spread contagiously within Mexico and to persons in neighboring U.S. states. It then spread to New York City via the relocation diffusion of several students who had vacationed in Mexico. Contagious and relocation diffusion subsequently played a role in the worldwide spread of the disease, which was eventually classified by the World Health Organization as a *pandemic*—an epidemic on a global scale. Not only do the different types of diffusion often work simultaneously, but the presence of *absorbing barriers*—

b. In addition to the downward diffusion through the ranks of employees, there is also hierarchical diffusion from smaller to larger cities.

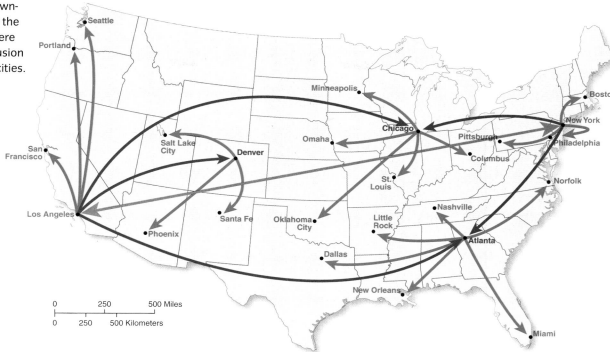

① The President and CEO launches a new design. Knowledge of this innovation diffuses hierarchically to members of the top level (Rank 1) of the organization in the company's main offices in New York and Los Angeles. People at lower levels do not yet hear about it because knowledge of the innovation by-passes or leapfrogs them.

② Individuals from Rank 1 hierarchically diffuse the idea down to people in Rank 2, located in major regional offices. A geographical leapfrogging also occurs because the managers work in different cities.

③ Individuals from Rank 2 spread the innovation to people in Rank 3, located in smaller cities around the country.

physical, legal, or other obstacles that stop diffusion—and *permeable barriers* can also affect both the rate and the direction of spatial diffusion.

Spatial Interaction and Globalization

We live in an increasingly globalized world. **Globalization** refers to the greater interconnectedness and interdependence of people and places around the world. Globalization propels and is propelled by **spatial interaction**—the connections and relations that develop among places and regions as a result of the movement or flow of people, goods, or information.

The term *spatial interaction* was first coined by geographer Edward Ullman in 1954, several decades before the word *globalization* was invented and popularized. For Ullman, a transportation geographer, the study of geography was synonymous with the study of spatial interaction. He identified three factors that influence spatial interaction: complementarity, transferability, and intervening opportunities.

Complementarity exists when one place or region can supply the demand for resources or goods in another place or region. In other words, complementarity provides a basis for trade. Leading coffee producers, such as Brazil, Colombia, and Indonesia, help satisfy the demand for coffee in major consuming regions, such as western Europe and North America, and create a condition of complementarity. Spatial interaction as a result of complementarity can involve short or long distances. Complementarity also exists when people travel from their homes to a movie theater or a gas station.

Complementarity stems from spatial variation. Such spatial variation may relate to the availability of natural resources or to particular economic conditions. For example, countries with scarce coal resources look to coal-rich countries to satisfy their demand for this resource. Economic conditions that are associated with spatial variation and

Justin Guariglia/NG Image Collection

NATIONAL GEOGRAPHIC

Transferability • Figure 1.11

Since the 1950s, the standardization of containers for movement by ship, tractor-trailer, or train has altered the transferability of freight by reducing the friction of distance.
▶ **How has the transferability of mail or photographs changed through time?**

lead to complementarity include low costs of production and economies of scale. Low labor or transportation costs, for example, may make the production of a good less expensive in one place than another, giving that place an economic advantage. Similarly, the ability to create an economy of scale can stimulate complementarity. An *economy of scale* refers to the reduction in the average production cost of an item as a result of increasing the number of items produced. Because certain costs are fixed—for example, the cost of machinery or equipment for an automobile assembly line—lower average costs per vehicle are obtained by producing more of them.

A second factor that influences spatial interaction is **transferability**—the cost of moving a good and the ability of the good to withstand that cost. High-value goods that are not bulky and can be easily transported, such as jewelry, have high transferability. Low-value, bulky goods, such as rocks or hay, have low transferability. In general, goods with low transferability are more likely to be used near their source. Transferability is affected by the *friction of distance*, or the way that distance can impede movement or interaction between places. Historically, distance has deterred spatial interaction, but changes in modes and speeds of transport have reduced the friction of distance (**Figure 1.11**).

Intervening opportunities constitute the third factor that influences spatial interaction. An **intervening opportunity** is a different location that can provide a desired good more economically. Like the friction of distance, intervening opportunities can alter the spatial interaction between places. If you usually stop at the same gas station to fill up your car but decide to frequent another gas station because you have noticed it has lower prices, you have taken advantage of an intervening opportunity. Intervening opportunities are important because they help reconfigure the flows and relations between places. In addition, intervening opportunities point to the importance of accessibility. For geographers, *accessibility* means the ease of reaching a particular place. Different measures of accessibility exist. Accessibility is most commonly expressed in terms of travel time or cost. The greater the accessibility of a place, the lower the travel time to or from it. Public facilities, such as parks and libraries, are considered highly accessible because there are usually no fees to use them.

Distance is an important aspect of the accessibility of a place, but, as the previous example suggests, other aspects can be just as important as or even more important than distance. A business may locate a branch office in a place that is more distant from the market in order to take advantage of lower rents. Alternatively, accessibility can be expressed in terms of a place's *connectivity*— that is, the number and kind of linkages it possesses. Such linkages might include airports, the presence of interstate highways, or the availability of high-speed computer networks. Fiber-optic cables, technology that permits much faster transfer of data compared to copper wires, has helped connect the globe (**Figure 1.12**).

Distance decay In 1970, geographer Waldo Tobler, an expert in spatial interaction modeling, made the following observation: "[E]verything is related to everything else, but near things are more related than distant things." This simple statement, known as *Tobler's first law of geography*, highlights how spatial interaction is affected by **distance decay**. Within cities, population density usually diminishes with increasing distance from the downtown area. Similarly, people are will-

> **distance decay**
> The tapering off of a process, pattern, or event over a distance.

ing to travel a few miles to a grocery store and will do so hundreds of times over the course of a year, but most people are not willing to travel long distances to reach a grocery store. Consequently, distance decay can be an important factor when deciding where to locate

Spatial interaction and connectivity • Figure 1.12

Spatial interaction occurs in myriad ways as, for example, when you text message a friend, journey from home to work, or transfer funds electronically. Technologies, such as cellular networks, submarine cables, and telephone land lines, facilitate long-distance and international spatial interaction, although the map makes clear the global unevenness of these linkages. (*Source: College Atlas of the World*, 2007.)

NATIONAL GEOGRAPHIC

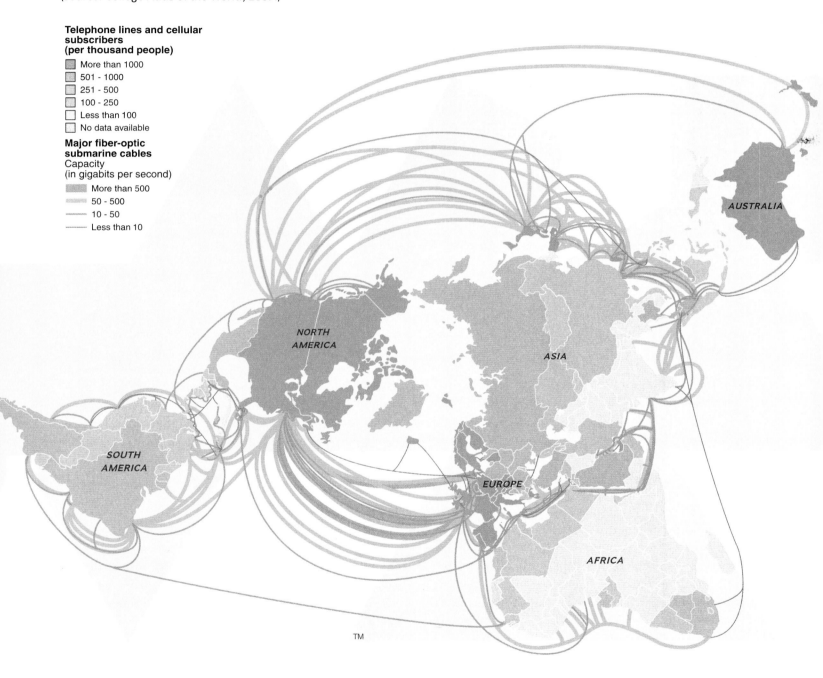

Telephone lines and cellular subscribers (per thousand people)
- More than 1000
- 501 - 1000
- 251 - 500
- 100 - 250
- Less than 100
- No data available

Major fiber-optic submarine cables
Capacity (in gigabits per second)
- More than 500
- 50 - 500
- 10 - 50
- Less than 10

Distance decay • Figure 1.13

Certain offenses, such as burglaries, sometimes demostrate distance decay.

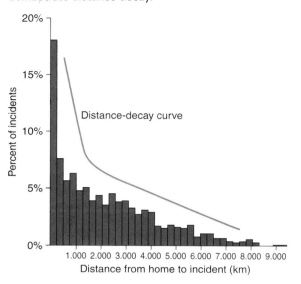

a. Burglars more often commit their crimes closer to home. (*Source:* Adapted from Block and Bernasco, 2008.)

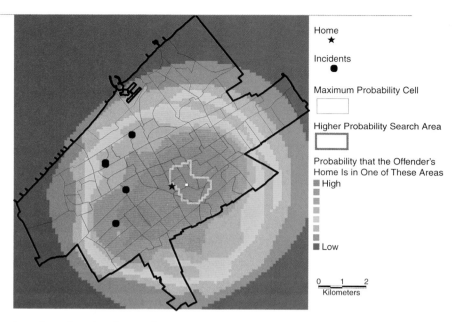

b. Using what they know about distance decay for burglaries, investigators mapped incidents in The Hague, Netherlands, to identify the area where the burglar likely lived, thereby narrowing their search. (*Source:* Block and Bernasco, 2008.)

certain businesses or public services. It turns out that distance decay can factor in the patterns of some criminal offenses (**Figure 1.13**).

Time–space convergence As we saw previously in our discussion of transferability, technological innovations in transportation and communication have made it possible to reduce the friction of distance. When this happens, places seem to become closer together in both time and space. This process is known as **time–space convergence**, and it highlights the importance of relative distance. Whereas absolute distance refers to the physical measure of separation between points or places in meters or feet, for example, *relative distance* expresses the separation between points or places in terms of time, cost, or some other measure. Globalization does not alter the absolute distance between places, but it can change their accessibility as more places become interconnected. Moreover, globalization can reduce the friction of distance, bringing about a change in our sense of relative distance and making it seem as though distant places have become closer together.

Is it possible that even as time and space appear to converge, social relations experience a lengthening or distanciation? The sociologist Anthony Giddens argues that the same technological innovations that lead to time-space convergence also create *time–space distanciation*, the elongation of social systems across time and space. Such social distanciation occurs as remote interaction—for example, e-mail or cell phones—becomes more prevalent than face-to-face interaction. In his view, even writing is a technological innovation that leads to time–space distanciation.

Geographic Scale

The concept of scale is so fundamental to geography that many geographic works give direct or at least indirect attention to it. In its broadest sense, **geographic scale** provides a way of depicting, in reduced form, all or part of the world. For example, every globe is a scale model of the Earth.

Two classes of geographic scales exist: map or cartographic scale and observational or methodological scale. A *map or cartographic scale* expresses the ratio of distances on the map to distances on the Earth. Geographers also distinguish between large-scale maps and small-scale maps (see *What a Geographer Sees*).

WHAT A GEOGRAPHER SEES

 **THE PLANNER**

Cartographic Scale

In making a map, the most basic decisions involve the area to cover and the scale. Mapping a vast area, such as North America, requires a small scale that cannot show much detail. At the opposite extreme, if you show a single town, you can use a very large scale that shows great detail, such as streets and buildings. **Figure a** shows this relationship; **Figure b** explains how we express map scales.

a. The choice of a map's scale controls how much detail can be shown.
Note how the detail of Cape Cod changes at these three different scales.

Small scale ⟵――――――――――――――――――――――――⟶ **Large scale**

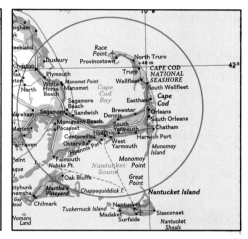

1. Small-scale map: Eastern North America, with Cape Cod circled

Small-scale maps, such as this one, show larger areas, such as continents or several states, but in less detail.

2. Large-scale map: Northeastern U.S. and neighboring Canada, with Cape Cod circled

This map is three times larger scale than map 1, showing greater detail but a smaller area.

3. Even larger-scale map: Eastern Massachusetts, with Cape Cod circled

This map is about twenty-one times larger scale than map 1, showing much greater detail but a much smaller area. (*Source:* Maps 1, 2, and 3 from College Atlas.)

Verbal scale: 1 inch represents 36,000,000 inches or about 568 miles on the ground	**Verbal scale:** 1 inch represents 12,000,000 inches or about 189 miles on the ground	**Verbal scale:** 1 inch represents 1,750,000 inches or about 28 miles on the ground
Ratio scale: 1:36,000,000	**Ratio scale:** 1:12,000,000	**Ratio scale:** 1:1,750,000
Fractional scale: 1/36,000,000	**Fractional scale:** 1/12,000,000	**Fractional scale:** 1/1,750,000
Graphic scale:	**Graphic scale:**	**Graphic scale:**
0 KILOMETERS 600 800 1000 0 MILES 200 400 600 800 1000	0 KILOMETERS 200 300 0 MILES 100 200 300	0 KILOMETERS 30 40 50 0 MILES 10 20 30 40 50

b. Map scales can be expressed verbally, as a ratio or fraction, or graphically.
The advantage of a fraction or ratio scale is that it works for any unit of distance. In the fraction and ratio examples for the Cape Cod map, 1 unit on the map represents 1,750,000 of the same unit on the Earth. Geographers frequently use centimeters or inches as units, but they could use any unit, even something whimsical, such as the width of an iPhone.

Ask Yourself

1. What type of map scale is most desirable if you plan to use a copier to reduce or enlarge a map?
2. How does the perspective in a map differ from the perspective in a satellite image?

Observational or *methodological scale* refers to the level(s) of analysis used in a specific project or study. This might include the body, home, neighborhood, city, region, country, or global scale. When geographers talk about the range of observational scale, they say that it extends from small scale (the level of the body) to large scale (the global level). This is the opposite of how they use the terms *small-scale* and *large-scale maps*. With observational scale, the most detailed level of analysis is the body, whereas large-scale maps have the most detail. As with cartographic scale, the choice of observational scale always involves a sacrifice between the area covered and the level of detail of the data.

The body or self constitutes an important scale because it provides a basis for personal and individual identity (**Figure 1.14**). It also helps us see how scale relates to spatial differentiation and social control. In Western society, for example, the home has historically been characterized as a kind of private space and female domain. This contrasts with the realms of politics and work, which have often been characterized as a kind of public space and male domain. In this way, ideas about the female or male body can contribute to the development of segregated spaces. For another example that illustrates the importance of the scale of the body, see *Video Explorations*.

In addition to the different levels of observational scale, it is important to remember that scales are often interdependent. We see this in globalization as things that were once popular on a local, regional, or national scale expand to the global scale. Similarly, we are reminded of the interdependence of scales in the way that an anti-Muslim film that was made in the U.S. and appeared on YouTube triggered protests in the Middle East and Southeast Asia in 2012.

Contested bodies • Figure 1.14

The body is personal space and a scale that we control. Or is it? This photo shows Hind Ahmas, the first woman in France fined for wearing a full-face veil. France banned the wearing of these veils in public.

Franck Prevel/Getty Images

Video Explorations

✓ THE PLANNER

Teeth Chiseling

National Geographic

In Indonesia, a chieftain's wife undergoes teeth chiseling to enhance her beauty. To this Sumatran group, beauty is more than skin deep; it is a matter of balance between the soul and body. At what point might cultural standards of beauty become a form of oppression?

CONCEPT CHECK STOP

1. **Why** does a formal region resemble absolute space?

2. **What** is meant by a spatial perspective, and how does it relate to the practice of geography?

3. **What** makes hierarchical diffusion more systematic than contagious diffusion?

4. **How** does globalization affect relative distance?

5. **Why** is the body considered a significant scale?

Geographical Tools

LEARNING OBJECTIVES

1. **Explore** how remote sensing works.
2. **Explain** the data structure of a GIS.
3. **Review** some of the applications of remote sensing, GPS, and GIS.

An appealing facet of geography is the ability to use a wide variety of research tools. This includes a mix of exciting and relatively new technologies—such as GPS devices, satellite images, geographic information systems, and interactive maps—as well as more traditional and long-standing research tools, including maps, photographic documentation, archival resources, and interviews.

The tool that has been most closely associated with geography is the map, a simple but powerful means of visualizing the world. Please see Appendix A to learn more about map projections and the challenges of representing the spherical Earth on a flat surface. This section focuses primarily on the more recent technological tools, in part because they have significantly expanded the geographer's toolbox. First, however, we need to distinguish between *skills* and *tools*. Skills are a product of our aptitude and learned abilities, whereas tools are the instruments we use to improve procedures or techniques, such as data gathering or visualization.

Like other scholars, geographers seek to cultivate their observational, analytical, and writing skills. Often, it helps to know another language, as well as statistics. Carrying out fieldwork, including extended or repeated visits to a research site or sites, is another skill many geographers hone. Those geographers whose fieldwork involves a great deal of outdoor exploration in remote places where daily luxuries, such as safe drinking water and air conditioning are not readily available, often describe themselves as "muddy-boots geographers."

Remote Sensing

When you scan the road in front of you as you drive, you are, in effect, engaging in a type of **remote sensing**—acquiring information about something that is located at a distance from you. In this case, the human eye acts as a *sensor* that responds to the stimulus of light and transmits certain signals to the brain. For geographers, remote sensing uses instruments or sensors to detect Earth-related phenomena and to provide information about them. As the term *remote sensing* suggests, the sensors are always located at a distance from the subject being studied. With greater reliance on satellite-mounted sensors, the distances between the sensor and

Innovations in sensor and computer technology have led to improvements in resolution (the detail we can detect), as well as a virtual explosion in the different uses for remotely sensed data. Today, for example, it is possible to obtain remotely sensed images with sub-meter (less than 3 feet) resolution.

Earthquake epicenter

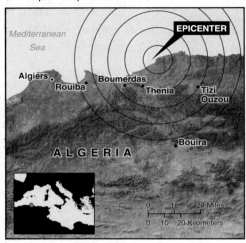

Collapsed apartment

Claude Paris/©AP/Wide World Photos

a. The earthquake that struck Boumerdes, Algeria, on May 21, 2003, registered a magnitude of 6.8 on the Richter scale and caused the deaths of more than 2,200 people. Structural damage in the city was severe and spatially variable.

b. The availability of high-resolution remotely sensed data with submeter resolution makes possible the rapid identification of structural damage across the affected area, because building collapse produces an identifiable textural signature not present in areas where buildings have not collapsed.

c. Using these textural signatures, geographers can then create maps identifying regions with significant percentages of collapsed buildings. Identifying high-damage areas is essential to relief coordination following a natural disaster.

Textural change between before and after images

☐ Modest ☐ Significant ■ Extreme

Increasing textural change due to building collapse →

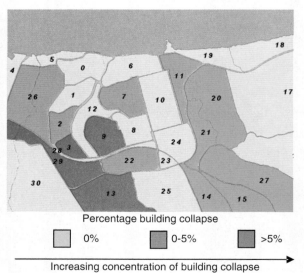

Percentage building collapse

☐ 0% ☐ 0-5% ■ >5%

Increasing concentration of building collapse →

the target of study can be considerable, often spanning thousands of kilometers.

Many of the early applications of remote sensing involved detecting conditions in the natural environment, especially in the area of weather monitoring and forecasting. Human geographers are increasingly making use of remote sensing to study such things as the spatial extent of urban areas or to track oil spills and other

d. The collapse of buildings changes the cultural landscape, in effect creating more edges. Visually, we can see this pattern in the more chaotic and brighter appearance of the images, but the use of software to detect these changes speeds up the analytical process. Identifying high-damage areas is essential to relief coordination following a natural disaster.

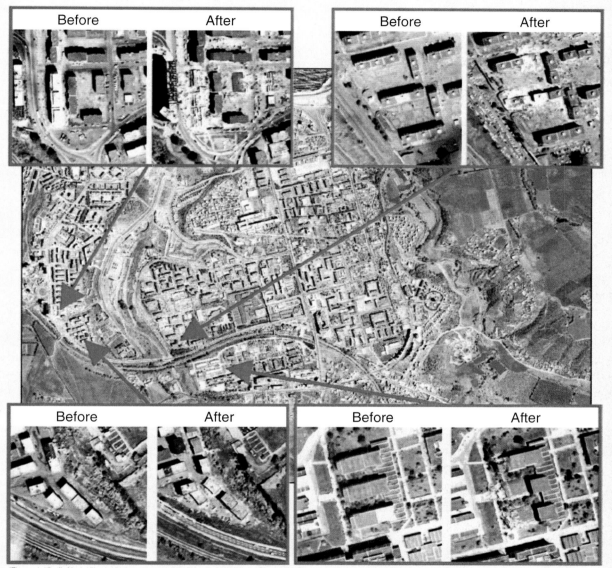

(Figure 1.15a (left), 1.15b, 1.15c images courtesy Beverley J. Adams, Charles K. Huyck, B. Mansouri, R. T. Eguchi, M. Shinozuka. 2004. Application of High-Resolution Optical Satellite Imagery for Post-Earthquake Damage Assessment: The 2003 Boumerdes (Algeria) and Bam (Iran) Earthquakes. In *Research Progress and Accomplishments 2003-2004*, MCEER-04-SP01, MCEER, University at Buffalo, pp. 173–186.)

forms of water pollution. Some recent studies suggest that remotely sensed data on nighttime lights, as shown in the chapter-opening photo, might provide a basis for estimating populations in countries that do not have reliable censuses, or even estimating the wealth of a region. Those who study natural disasters are also able to use remote sensing to document and record the extent and damage caused by fires, hurricanes, or other natural hazards (**Figure 1.15**).

GPS applications • Figure 1.16

GPS technology helps to locate features on Earth and understand how individual and group patterns of mobility vary.

a. Cell phones equipped with GPS receivers make it possible to use location-based services to find friends in your area.
▶ **Is this kind of geographic awareness a benefit or hindrance to personal security?** (*Source:* NG Maps.)

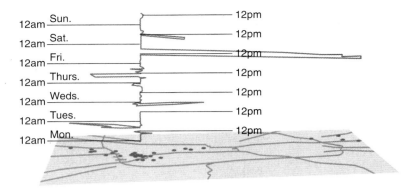

b. This diagram shows the time–space paths of a female teenager in one week in Marion County, Indiana. The dots represent waypoints (intermediate destinations) collected via a GPS-enabled cell phone as the young woman traveled from home and back. The squiggly lines to the left or right of the vertical axis represent the distances traveled away from home at different times. ▶ **How might time–space paths vary by age, gender, or ethnicity?** (*Source:* Wiehe *et al.*, 2008.)

Global Positioning System

A **global positioning system (GPS)** uses a constellation of artificial satellites, radio signals, and receivers to determine the absolute location of people, places, or features on Earth. A GPS receiver uses the time it takes to receive a signal from a satellite to calculate how far away the satellite is. When radio signals are simultaneously transmitted from multiple satellites, it is possible to apply the geometric principles of triangles to determine the latitude, longitude, and altitude of locations on Earth.

When you use a GPS device (which basically functions as a receiver), you are tapping into a system that has been developed and funded by the U.S. Department of Defense. Thus, the term *global positioning system* refers specifically to the system developed by the United States and more generally to the use of multiple satellites as a way of locating things on or navigating between places on Earth. Although the first GPS satellite was put into orbit in the 1970s, GPS did not provide global coverage until 1995. Since then, civilian use of GPS has boomed, and annual global sales of GPS devices regularly amount to several billion dollars.

Like remote sensing, GPS has greatly expedited our ability to acquire data about the Earth. For example, locational information for map features can quickly be acquired

and transferred to computers to make or update maps. GPS is regularly used to confirm the legal boundaries of property, to track and inventory different species of plants and animals, and to monitor conditions in agricultural fields. GPS has contributed to the growth in precision farming. For example, GPS can be used to record information on soil types, moisture, or pest infestations at different locations in a field. When this kind of information is combined with GPS-ready agricultural machinery, it is possible to manage pesticide application so that it is applied only where needed and in the smallest amounts possible, preventing waste.

Within the past decade, locational information has become a valuable commodity, as demonstrated by the rapid growth in location-based services. A *location-based service* (LBS) uses the location of a GPS receiver to provide information about nearby businesses and sometimes even people. For example, you can use a smartphone to search for nearby restaurants or ATMs and to find friends with GPS-equipped smartphones who are in the area (**Figure 1.16**).

GPS technology raises a host of thorny ethical questions. Often there is a fine line between a service and surveillance. Law enforcement officials can use GPS to track the locations of parolees, and parents can use it to know the whereabouts of their kids. Geographers Jerome Dobson and Peter Fisher coined the term *geoslavery* to refer to "a practice in which one entity, the master, coercively or surreptitiously monitors and exerts control over the physical location of another individual, the slave" (2003, pp. 47–48). In what other ways might GPS compromise personal privacy?

Geographic Information Systems

Many people—geographers and nongeographers alike—enjoy poring over paper maps and studying them for the patterns and trends they show. Of course, paper maps do have their limitations. If you need to know the area covered by a lake, for example, doing the calculation manually can be labor intensive and time-consuming. Just imagine trying to manually compute the area covered by lakes in a single country. The emergence of **geographic information systems (GIS)** has its roots in this very issue: how to improve the functionality of maps and the spatial analysis of *georeferenced data*—that is, data tied to locations on Earth.

There are two ways to georeference data: directly and indirectly. The most common system used for direct georeferencing is latitude and longitude. For in-direct georeferencing, locations may be given by street address, zip code, school district, census tract, or other spatially defined entity (for which latitude and longitude could then be obtained). We can obtain georeferenced data from various sources, including paper maps, satellite imagery, aerial photography, and GPS devices, to name a few. A GIS, then, refers to a combination of hardware and software that enables the input, management, analysis, and visualization of georeferenced data. The usefulness of GIS as a tool stems from its ability to relate different kinds of georeferenced data (**Figure 1.17**).

A GIS can link data, reveal new relationships, and visualize them with maps. In a GIS, maps are interactive, enabling a user to click on a map feature and obtain information about it, to turn different data "on" or "off" for viewing, and to query the data. Another facet of GIS is that

GIS data structure • Figure 1.17

Every GIS is built around two types of information: spatial and attribute.

▼ **a.** Spatial data consists of the latitude and longitude of the boundaries, cities and rivers shown on this map. Attribute information describes the geographic features, and is stored in tables like these for Venezuela, Lima, and the Amazon River. (*Source:* NG Maps.)

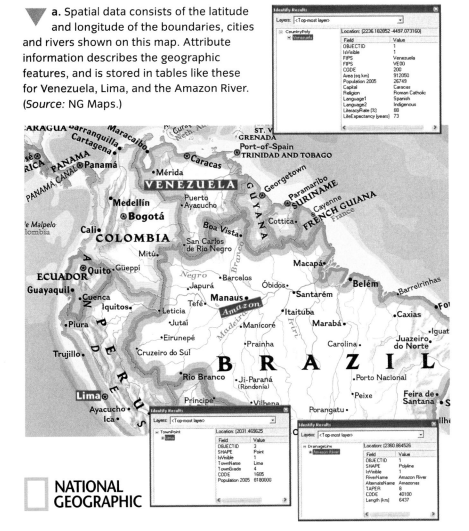

▼ **b.** Georeferenced data are stored in a computer in one of two formats.

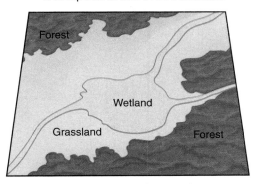

Vector data uses latitude and longitude coordinates to represent geographic features as points, lines, or other complex shapes.

Raster data uses equally-sized cells to represent features. Here, each pixel contains a value that identifies the land cover: 1–forest, 2–grassland, and 3–wetland.

it can accommodate statistical analysis and perform calculations, such as identifying the most optimal route between locations.

One way to conceptualize this is to think of a GIS as a kind of database that stores information in different layers (**Figure 1.18**).

GIS data layers • Figure 1.18

GIS incorporates the ability to combine, through overlays, a wide variety of georeferenced data. In these examples, cities, roads, and rivers are represented by vector data whereas raster data is used to show elevation. (*Source: College Atlas of the World*, 2007.)

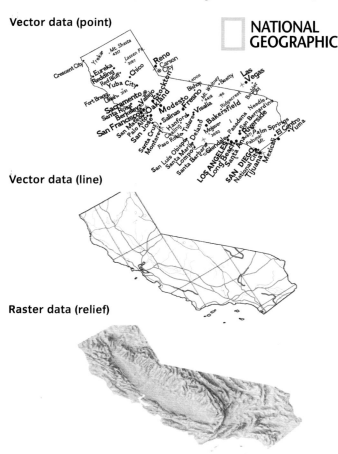

Vector data (point)

NATIONAL GEOGRAPHIC

Vector data (line)

Raster data (relief)

Vector and raster data combined (political)

The possible applications for GIS are mind-boggling. For example, GIS has been used in Jamaica to evaluate proposed sites for new schools by examining the terrain and road network in combination with demographic data on the numbers and ages of school children. GIS has also been used to track deforestation in Bolivia over time and, through modeling, to rank and predict areas vulnerable to future deforestation. With support from the Food and Agriculture Organization of the United Nations, water resources, including inland fisheries in Sub-Saharan Africa, are being studied with a GIS to predict fish yield and to help local communities plan for adequate food supplies. In Iowa, GIS has been used to study the spatial associations between demography, ecology, and the incidence of West Nile virus (**Figure 1.19**).

As a tool, GIS has tremendous potential to help solve problems, model social and environmental conditions, and make planning decisions. For students and others who are thinking about career plans, GIS has dramatically transformed employment prospects for geographers by opening up a wide range of job and career options across the public and private sectors.

There are, however, three major criticisms of GIS. One is that to do GIS requires that users have access to the necessary hardware and software. Most GIS software is proprietary and has the greatest functionality on today's newest and fastest computers. Even though the prices for both computers and GIS software have become more affordable, purchasing just the minimum components can still cost a few thousand dollars. In addition, before you can use your GIS, you need data. Some GIS data are publicly available at no charge, but this is not always the case. Thus, you may have to purchase customized data from a GIS services firm or employ personnel to conduct fieldwork to obtain the data. These hardware, software, and data-related costs have prompted people inside and outside the GIS-user community to point out that GIS is still not very accessible.

A second and related criticism is that, given its constrained accessibility, GIS reinforces one power divide in society such that only those individuals and institutions that have the requisite financial resources can purchase and use GIS. This limitation has ramifications for map-making and for decisions made based on GIS-derived maps and analysis. On the one hand, access to GIS means we can make more maps than ever before. On the other, it is important to ask, Who is making those maps and whose economic, political, or other interests do they serve?

A third criticism of GIS is that it promotes a detached and strongly Western view of the world. It is entirely

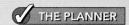
West Nile virus (WNV) is a disease that can be transmitted to humans and animals by certain mosquito species. The first outbreaks of WNV occurred in the United States in 1999. Nationally, Iowa and several other Midwestern states have recorded a high incidence of the disease. These maps illustrate the use of a GIS to study disease incidence. (*Source:* DeGroote et al., 2008.)

a. This map was created by overlaying a dot map of disease incidence on the map of population density. The scale of the study was conducted at the level of census block groups (a subdivision of a census tract). If WNV occurred in a block group, its center point is shown.

b. Census block groups have been overlaid on a land cover map of Iowa. Darker boundaries indicate block groups recording occurrences of WNV between 2002 and 2006. Using this map and the previous one, we can see that WNV is more concentrated in the western part of the state and associated with agriculture and row crops.

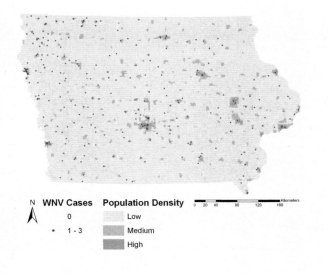

N | WNV Cases | Population Density
| 0 | Low
• | 1 - 3 | Medium
| | High

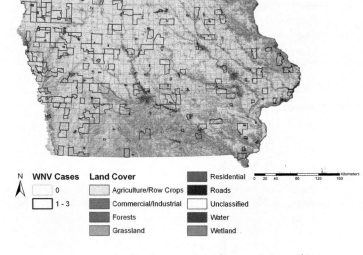

N | WNV Cases | Land Cover | | Residential
| 0 | Agriculture/Row Crops | Roads
| 1 - 3 | Commercial/Industrial | Unclassified
| | Forests | Water
| | Grassland | Wetland

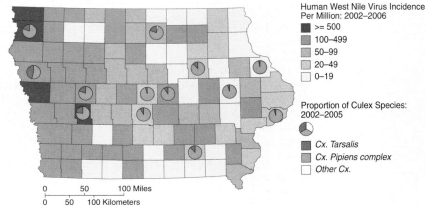

Human West Nile Virus Incidence
Per Million: 2002–2006
- >= 500
- 100–499
- 50–99
- 20–49
- 0–19

Proportion of Culex Species:
2002–2005

- Cx. Tarsalis
- Cx. Pipiens complex
- Other Cx.

c. Several *Culex* species of mosquito are the most significant transmitters or vectors of the disease. This map shows disease incidence and mosquito species by county. ▶ **How might agricultural practices such as irrigation and animal feeding operations be associated with the spread of WNV?**

(Figure 1.19 images courtesy of J. P. DeGroote, R. Sugumaran, S. M. Bend, B. J. Tucker, and L. C. Bartholomay. 2008. Landscape, demographic, entomological, and climatic associations with human disease incidence of West Nile virus in the state of Iowa, USA. *International Journal of Health Geographics* 7(19). Original publisher: BioMed Central.)

possible to do GIS by simply sitting in front of a computer and never visiting the site being studied. What impact might this style of work have on the way decisions about a place are made? Although there have been some strides toward incorporating local knowledge into GIS, how places in the world are represented in a GIS remains anchored to concepts of absolute location, defined boundaries, and contemporary political states.

CONCEPT CHECK STOP

1. **How** does remote sensing incorporate the concept of scale?

2. **How** does a GIS incorporate and make use of georeferenced data?

3. **What** are some limitations of remote sensing, GPS, and GIS?

Summary

1 Introducing Human Geography 4

- The discipline of geography consists of two main, and some-times intersecting, branches: physical and human. The scope of **human geography** is broad and encompasses the study of places, spatial variation, and human–environment relationships.

- The terms **nature** and **culture** rank among the most complex words in the English language. Dualistic thinking that separates nature from culture has shaped Western thought, but many geographers reject the **nature–culture dualism**.

- Very broadly defined, **cultural ecology** focuses on the relationships between people and the environment. Four different ways of understanding that relationship include **environmental determinism**, **possibilism**, humans as modifiers of the Earth, and the Earth as a dynamic, integrated system. Of these, environmental determinism has received the most strident criticism.

- **Political ecology**, a branch of cultural ecology, places greater emphasis on the role of economic forces and power relations in shaping nature–society dynamics. **Actor–network theory**, for example, seeks to reinsert a consideration of environmental influence in such studies.

- Culture can refer to shared beliefs and practices of a group. Reading the **cultural landscape** and performing **regional analysis** have long been associated with this conceptualization of culture. Regional analysis frequently involves the study and mapping of **formal regions**, like the ones shown on the map, as well as **functional** and **perceptual regions**.

Formal, functional, and perceptual regions • Figure 1.5

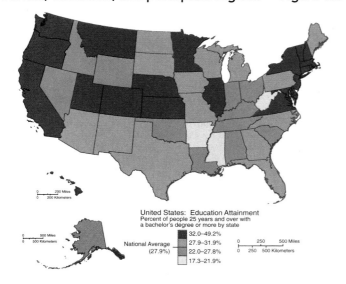

United States: Education Attainment
Percent of people 25 years and over with a bachelor's degree or more by state

National Average (27.9%)
- 32.0–49.2%
- 27.9–31.9%
- 22.0–27.8%
- 17.3–21.9%

- There has been a significant reconceptualization of culture within human geography. This reconceptualization sees culture not only as a collection of cultural traits but also as a social construction that is dynamic and contested.

2 Thinking Like a Human Geographer 12

- Geographical inquiry is informed by five key topics or approaches, including **place**, **space**, **spatial diffusion**, **spatial interaction**, and **geographic scale**.

- Places are essential to the spatial functioning of society. Different attributes of **site** and **situation**, depicted in the photo, convey information about the geographic context of a place.

Site and situation • Figure 1.7

MUSTAFA OZER/AFP/Getty Images

- When geographers talk about space, they are referring to either absolute or relative space. Spatial diffusion occurs when some phenomenon spreads across space, but such diffusion is rarely a uniform process. Thus, the study of diffusion is also intimately associated with questions about **distribution** and **distance decay**.

- The practice of adopting a spatial perspective, whether that includes studying **spatial variation**, **spatial association**, or how people create and perceive relative space, distinguishes geography from other fields of study.

- Spatial interaction increasingly fuels **globalization**, but the particular geographies of globalization are shaped by complex contingencies related to uneven diffusion, complementarities of trade, and the accessibility and connectivity of places.

- We perceive the effects of globalization through **time–space convergence** in the way that distant places seem to become closer together as technologies reduce travel time and cost. Although the geographic scale of the globe remains unchanged, time–space convergence affects relative distance.

- From the paper map to the interactive map, the geographer's toolbox continues to expand through technological advances related to **remote sensing**, **GPS**, and **GIS**. Remote sensing has extended the visual horizons of geography by enabling us to see and detect things not visible to the naked eye. GIS has improved our ability to examine spatial associations and visualize them, especially by creating maps such as the ones shown here, and overlaying them.

- These exciting technologies do raise serious ethical questions about privacy and surveillance. GPS has been criticized for its potential to contribute to geoslavery.

GIS data layers • Figure 1.18

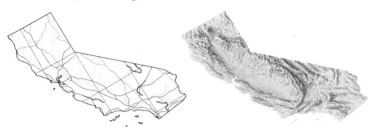

Key Terms

- actor–network theory 8
- complementarity 17
- cultural ecology 5
- cultural landscape 9
- culture 11
- distance decay 18
- distribution 15
- environmental determinism 5
- formal region 10
- functional region 10
- geographic information system (GIS) 27

- geographic scale 20
- global positioning system (GPS) 26
- globalization 17
- human geography 5
- intervening opportunity 18
- nature 5
- nature–culture dualism 5
- perceptual region 11
- place 12
- political ecology 8
- possibilism 8
- raster data 27

- regional analysis 10
- remote sensing 23
- site 12
- situation 12
- space 14
- spatial association 15
- spatial diffusion 16
- spatial interaction 17
- spatial variation 15
- time–space convergence 20
- transferability 18
- vector data 27

Critical and Creative Thinking Questions

1. Applying what you have learned about diffusion, is it feasible to close borders between countries when an epidemic appears to be intensifying and becoming global in scale?

2. Do national parks and protected areas reflect a nature–culture dualism? Explain your reasoning.

3. Do you agree with the actor–network theory? Discuss your answer.

4. Propose a GIS project and identify the spatial and attribute data you would need to conduct it.

5. Plan a research project that would enable you to cartographically depict the boundaries of a perceptual region.

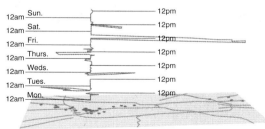

6. Keep a geographical diary in which you record the times and the places you go during a week. (You can also do this by collecting waypoints if you have a GPS-enabled cell phone or other GPS receiver.) Use the Internet to find a suitable base map and plot out your time–space paths, using this figure as an example. If you know how, you could even make a mash-up and include photos of your favorite places.

What is happening in this picture?

A flash mob protest assembles in Terminal 5 at Heathrow Airport in London. Flash mobs are large groups, often coordinated via social networking sites, that gather in a public place for a specific purpose.

Think Critically

1. How does a flash mob challenge taken-for-granted notions of space?
2. What type of diffusion drives flash mob formation?

Steve Parsons/PA Wire/AP Photo

Self-Test

(Check your answers in Appendix B.)

1. Which of the following statements about place is FALSE?
   a. Studies of place may begin with a consideration of site characteristics.
   b. Every place has a unique absolute location.
   c. The situation of places can change.
   d. Sense of place is related to the ability to navigate.

2. Which of the following is most closely associated with relative space?
   a. a GPS receiver
   b. trade between two cities
   c. site
   d. formal regions

3. _____ diffusion, shown here, involves _____, where certain individuals or places are skipped because of their rank or status.
   a. Stimulus; bypassing
   b. Contagious; overlapping
   c. Stimulus; randomization
   d. Hierarchical; leapfrogging

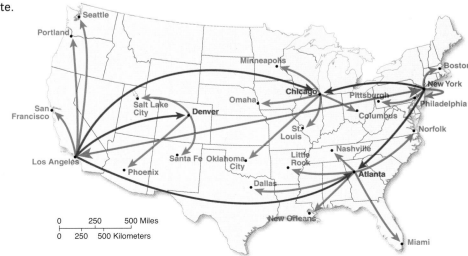

4. As discussed in the chapter, key factors that influence spatial interaction include all of the following except _____.
   a. transferability
   b. intervening opportunities
   c. complementarity
   d. relative distance

5. What spatial process is illustrated in this graph?
   a. distance decay
   b. connectivity
   c. accessibility
   d. hierarchical diffusion

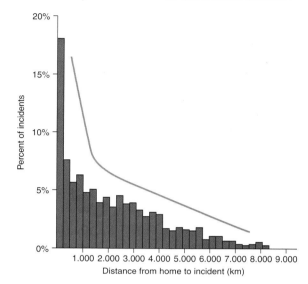

6. Globalization and time–space convergence affect our perception of _____.
   a. culture
   b. relative distance
   c. regions
   d. absolute distance

7. The statement, "there is no such thing as culture" is most closely associated with _____.
   a. the nature-culture dualism
   b. actor–network theory
   c. culture reconceptualized
   d. stimulus diffusion

8. Which of the following situations is not likely to involve remote sensing?
   a. measuring the extent of an oil spill
   b. overlaying different mapped datasets
   c. identifying a pest infestation in an agricultural field
   d. locating new settlements in rural areas

9. GPS is associated with all but one of the following. Which item does not belong?
   a. absolute location
   b. navigation
   c. location-based services
   d. indirect georeferencing

10. Which of the following statements does not describe a characteristic of a GIS?
    a. A GIS can relate settlement density to elevation.
    b. A GIS can use raster or vector data.
    c. A GIS can use directly but not indirectly georeferenced data.
    d. A GIS links attribute data to spatial data.

11. As discussed in the chapter, which of the following is not a major criticism of GIS?
    a. If all the data are on the computer, GIS users may feel no need to know a place firsthand.
    b. Because of its reliance on state or regional data, GIS can reinforce conventional views of society.
    c. GIS data may not be publicly available for a specific place or project.
    d. GIS is a recognized low-cost solution to decision making and planning.

12. Consider this statement: "Houses constructed with steep roofs or heavy thatch roofs are just two examples of responses to wet environmental conditions." Which viewpoint does it best express?
    a. possibilism
    b. Earth as a dynamic system
    c. environmental determinism
    d. cultural ecology

13. A good example of a functional region is _____.
    a. Red Sox Nation
    b. a wealthy residential community
    c. the area served by a TV station
    d. an area with a high percentage of college graduates

14. An approach that uses the cultural landscape as a clue to people's values and priorities is _____.
    a. reading the landscape
    b. political ecology
    c. regional analysis
    d. actor–network theory

15. This photo illustrates _____.
    a. the presence of a permeable barrier
    b. the concept of contagious diffusion
    c. the existence of a perceptual region
    d. the presence of an absorbing barrier

Courtesy Alyson Greiner

THE PLANNER ✓

Review your Chapter Planner on the chapter opener and check off your completed work.

Globalization and Cultural Geography

TATTOOING AND GLOBALIZATION

If you have a tattoo, what does it mean to you? If you don't have one, do you want one? Tattooing has a long history and is geographically widespread. It has been practiced by Samoans for more than 2000 years. To Samoans, the tattoo is a mark of distinction. Boys are often tattooed at puberty with designs extending from their waist down to their knees. Thigh tattoos are common among women, as shown in the photo. Among New Zealand Maori males, full facial tattoos employing spiral designs are not unusual, and some Maori women have tattoos on their chins, although these practices were more widespread in the past.

The late-18th-century Pacific voyages of Captain Cook helped increase the popularity of tattooing among Westerners. Even as tattooing became common among European and American sailors, who favored the armband style of tattoo, Christian missionaries working in the Pacific region sought to curb the practice because they considered it unholy.

Tattooing is a good example of a globalized cultural practice that has become extremely popular in Western countries. Despite the globalization of tattooing, diverse local practices endure though they have changed over time. Tattooing therefore reveals the fascinating interplay between events at local and global scales.

In this chapter we examine the cultural impacts of globalization, beginning with some background on globalization and the important role that large corporations play in shaping popular culture, including cultural practices and patterns of consumption. We also consider the diverse expressions of local culture and local knowledge.

Courtesy Samoa News Archives

CHAPTER OUTLINE

CHAPTER PLANNER ✓

- ❏ Study the picture and read the opening story.
- ❏ Scan the Learning Objectives in each section:
  p. 36 ❏   p. 40 ❏   p. 44 ❏   p. 50 ❏
- ❏ Read the text and study all figures and visuals. Answer any questions.

Analyze key features

- ❏ Geography InSight, p. 46
- ❏ Video Explorations, p. 52
- ❏ Process Diagram, p. 53
- ❏ What a Geographer Sees, p. 56
- ❏ Stop: Answer the Concept Checks before you go on:
  p. 40 ❏   p. 44 ❏   p. 50 ❏   p. 59 ❏

End of chapter

- ❏ Review the Summary and Key Terms.
- ❏ Answer the Critical and Creative Thinking Questions.
- ❏ Answer What is happening in this picture?
- ❏ Complete the Self-Test and check your answers.

Globalization

LEARNING OBJECTIVES

1. **Provide** evidence to illustrate the process of globalization.
2. **Account** for the development of contemporary globalization.
3. **Describe** the flow of capital around the world.

In Chapter 1, we defined the concept of **globalization** as those processes contributing to greater interconnectedness and interdependence among the world's people, places, and institutions. Some of the clearest expressions of globalization can be found in the geography of the foods we eat and the clothes we wear. In the ingredients listed on some brands of trail mix, for example, we learn that the raisins are a product of the United States, Chile, Argentina, South Africa, and Mexico; and the almonds and cashews are products of Africa, India, and Brazil. Garment labels on certain T-shirts and jeans proclaim "Made of 100% U.S.A. materials. Assembled in Costa Rica." You may not be someone who scrutinizes the labels on the things you buy, and that is partly the point. We have grown so accustomed to the global sourcing of the products we use every day that we do not realize how much a part of our lives globalization has become or what makes globalization such a significant development.

Contemporary Globalization

Globalization stems from the expansion of capitalism and international trade. If we approach globalization purely from the standpoint of scale, we see that globalization is not an entirely new process. The trade in spices from Asia and Africa to Europe illustrates a connectedness that developed at the global scale as early as the 15th century. However, *contemporary globalization*—the focus of this chapter—is a more recent development that has been underway since the 1960s and has been especially rapid since the 1980s and 1990s. Even though the concept of globalization has long existed, use of the word *globalization* did not become commonplace until the 1980s.

Contemporary globalization differs significantly from historical examples of globalization because of the greater degree of financial, political, and cultural interdependence that now exists. The spice trade extended horizontal or international connections between places. Since the 1960s, however, globalization has involved both an ongoing **horizontal expansion** via rapid flows of goods, people, and ideas between places, and simultaneously a kind of **vertical expansion** as well, especially through the development of policies, such as trade agreements that formalize linkages and strengthen them like a deep root system. Thus, we can think of globalization as a process that both widens and deepens connectedness. As we saw in Chapter 1, globalization is both a cause and an effect of spatial interaction (**Figure 2.1**).

Five major factors have encouraged globalization:

1. The quest for global markets associated with *capitalism*. This includes searching for locations where goods can be produced and distributed efficiently.
2. Technological advances, especially in the areas of transportation, telecommunication, and digital computers.
3. Reduced business costs, such as lower costs for long-distance transportation.
4. An increase in the flows of financial **capital**, as a result of trade and international investments.
5. Policy, including laws and institutional arrangements, that supports the four previously mentioned factors.

> **capital** Financial, social, intellectual, or other assets that are derived from human creativity and are used to create goods and services.

One policy development in the expansion of globalization was the creation of the World Trade Organization (WTO) in 1995 (from its precursor, the General Agreement on Tariffs and Trade [GATT]). The WTO's primary purpose is to establish and enforce the rules of trade. Today more than 150 countries belong to the WTO.

International tourism and globalization • Figure 2.1

Tourists now travel to the ends of the Earth, including Antarctica, shown here. Growth in international tourism highlights the importance of mobility to globalization. Worldwide, the number of international tourist arrivals reached 990 million in 2011, an 83% increase since 1995.

Global Flows of Capital

Globalization is marked by large flows of capital around the world. Multinational corporations have emerged as major players in the global economy, and foreign direct investment has increased. A **multinational corporation (MNC)** (also called a transnational corporation, or TNC) owns offices or production facilities in one or more other countries. These overseas operations are referred to as *foreign affiliates*. Some business experts more narrowly define an MNC as a corporation that derives at least a quarter of its revenue from its foreign operations. For example, General Electric (GE) is headquartered in the United States and has various business operations in more than 100 countries. In recent years more than half of the company's revenue has come from its overseas business endeavors.

A few statistics help underscore the importance of MNCs in the global economy. Today there are 82,000 MNCs with 810,000 foreign affiliates, up from 37,000 MNCs and 170,000 foreign affiliates in the early 1990s. Some of the largest economic entities in the world are MNCs. In 2011, each of the three largest MNCs—Royal Dutch Shell, ExxonMobil, and Walmart Stores—earned revenues in excess of $400 billion. The revenues for each of these MNCs exceeds the value of all goods and services produced in many countries, including Denmark, Greece, Ireland, Malaysia, Egypt, and Nigeria among others (**Figure 2.2** on the next page).

MNCs go abroad to gain new markets, lower the costs of labor and production, or acquire a needed resource. MNCs transfer money from their home countries to foreign or host countries to finance their overseas business activities. This process is known as **foreign direct investment (FDI).** For instance, purchasing or constructing manufacturing plants or equipment in the host country is a form of FDI. There is considerable disagreement over the impacts of FDI. On the one hand, FDI increases the flow of cash in a country and can help promote economic activity, raise employment, and lead to the transfer of knowledge, technology, and infrastructure. On the other hand, FDI can make it difficult for local companies that lack comparable

Multinational corporations • Figure 2.2

The distribution of MNCs and their operations in other countries, or foreign affiliates, reveal the globalization of business. (*Source:* Data from UNCTAD, 2008.)

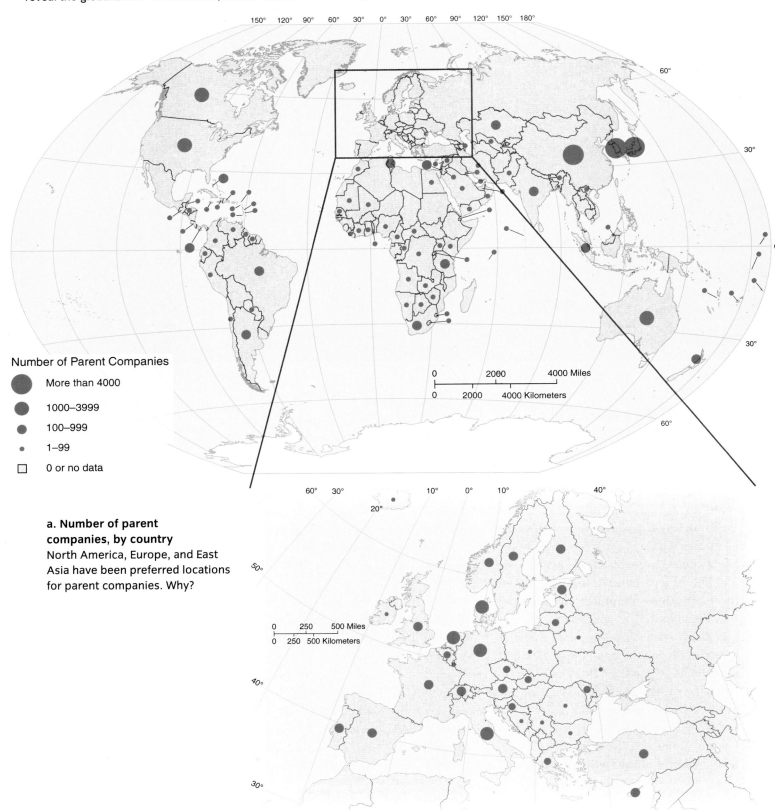

Number of Parent Companies

- More than 4000
- 1000–3999
- 100–999
- 1–99
- 0 or no data

a. Number of parent companies, by country
North America, Europe, and East Asia have been preferred locations for parent companies. Why?

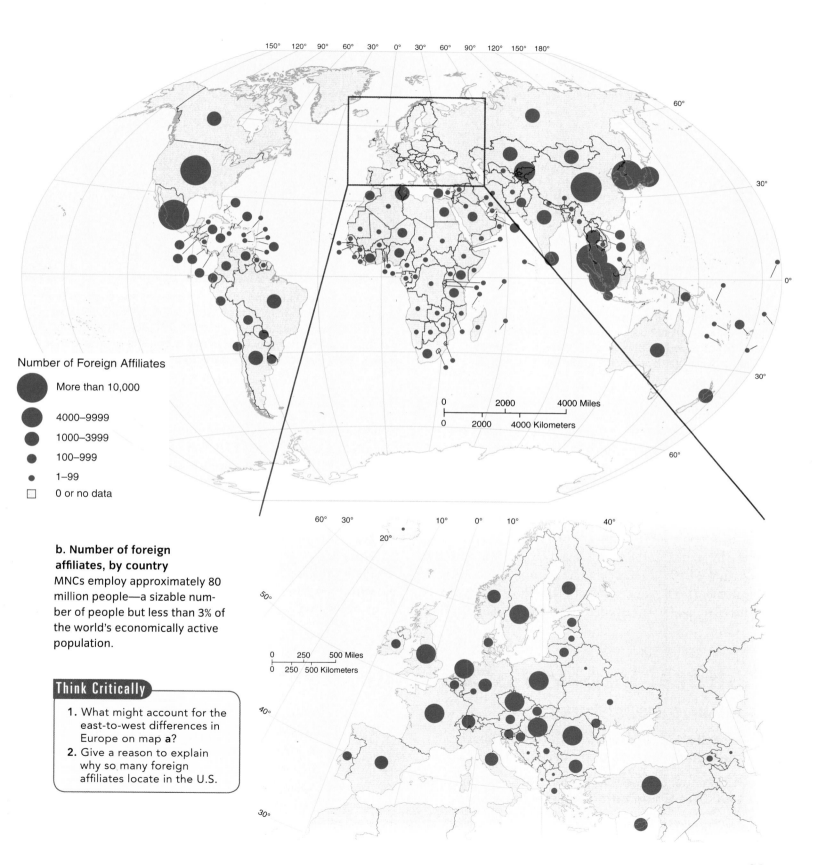

b. Number of foreign affiliates, by country

MNCs employ approximately 80 million people—a sizable number of people but less than 3% of the world's economically active population.

Think Critically

1. What might account for the east-to-west differences in Europe on map **a**?
2. Give a reason to explain why so many foreign affiliates locate in the U.S.

Number of Foreign Affiliates

- More than 10,000
- 4000–9999
- 1000–3999
- 100–999
- 1–99
- 0 or no data

Flows of foreign direct investment (FDI) into different regions • Figure 2.3

Growth in FDI reflects globalization, but FDI inflows are geographically uneven.

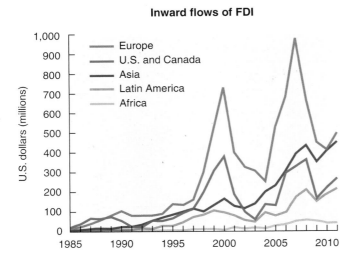

Inward flows of FDI

a. Wealth attracts FDI. Europe usually surpasses all other regions in the value of FDI inflows, sometimes quite substantially. Sharp declines correspond with recessions and other changes in the investment climate. (*Source:* Data from UNCTADstat, 2012.)

REUTERS/Mohamed Nureldin Abdallh/©Corbis

b. New building construction supervised by a Chinese engineer is an example of Chinese FDI in Sudan. Historically, most trade occurred among developed countries. As globalization proceeds, trade and investment among developing countries in Asia and Africa continue to grow. ▶ **Why might Sudan be attractive to Chinese companies?**

financial resources to compete with MNCs. Because FDI helps a company improve its business, the main benefactor is the MNC, not the host country. Similarly, there is no guarantee that a country that receives FDI will also receive transfers of knowledge or technology, in part because of patent protection. Despite the debate over the impact of FDI, flows of FDI have increased dramatically since the 1990s and largely in tandem with the growth of MNCs, though they remain spatially uneven (**Figure 2.3**). The total value of FDI inflows now exceeds $1.5 trillion annually, with almost half of it flowing to developed regions. Regional totals can disguise this geographic unevenness: FDI inflow into Portugal is about one-fifth of the flow into the United Kingdom.

CONCEPT CHECK STOP

1. **How** is capital associated with globalization?
2. **How** is contemporary globalization distinguished from historical globalization?
3. **What** are the advantages and disadvantages of foreign direct investment?

Cultural Impacts of Globalization

LEARNING OBJECTIVES

1. **Identify** and discuss three theses addressing the cultural impacts of globalization.

2. **Explain** how Americanization, McDonaldization, and Coca-Colonization are intertwined.

3. **Distinguish** between neolocalism and glocalization.

Globalization is a complex phenomenon that has many different dimensions. Thus far we have focused on some of the economic aspects of globalization. In subsequent chapters we will explore some of the political, industrial, environmental, and other dimensions of globalization. In this section we investigate the impacts of globalization on cultural difference through an examination of some facets of **popular culture**. Popular culture encompasses products that are mass-produced—for example music, video games, TV shows, cars, clothing—as well as widely held attitudes about preferred forms of leisure, recreation, and entertainment. Popular culture is heavily influenced by mass media, including TV broadcasting, the motion picture industry, the Internet, and

popular culture
The practices, attitudes, and preferences held in common by large numbers of people and considered to be mainstream.

traditional forms of book and newspaper publishing. Rapid change, as seen in the way fads come and go, is a characteristic of popular culture.

Views about the cultural consequences of globalization are related to our understanding of spatial diffusion. In Chapter 1 we discussed spatial diffusion and noted that it often occurs via a combination of methods, for example via *hierarchical diffusion* and *contagious diffusion*. In some instances, *reverse hierarchical diffusion*—in which diffusion occurs in a "bottom-up" manner—also plays an important role (**Figure 2.4**).

Reverse hierarchical diffusion • Figure 2.4

Walmart provides a rare example of a company that expanded through reverse hierarchical diffusion, growing from a single, small-town location to a multinational corporation with more than 10,000 stores in 27 countries.

a. Walmart's beginnings
The first Walmart opened in the small town (population 6000) of Rogers, Arkansas, in 1962. Its forerunner was Sam Walton's 5&10 store.

b. Walmart store openings: 1970–1974
During the first years after the company's founding, new stores opened in other nearby small-town locations in the region. (*Source:* Adapted from Graff and Ashton, 1993.)

◄ **c. Walmart store openings by county size**
It was not until the late 1980s and 1990s that new stores concentrated on the larger markets associated with major metropolitan areas. (*Source:* Data from Graff and Ashton, 1993.)

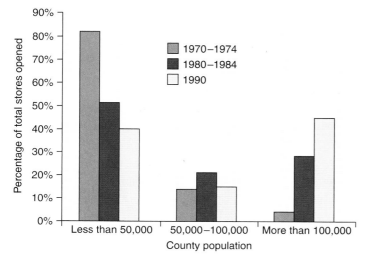

Ask Yourself

Approximately what percentage of stores did Walmart open in counties with more than 100,000 people from 1970 to 1974? In 1990?

Social scientists have proposed a simple but useful framework to help us make sense of the cultural consequences of globalization. This framework consists of three key ideas or theses: the homogenization thesis, the polarization thesis, and the glocalization thesis.

Homogenization

According to the homogenization thesis, globalization makes cultural tastes, beliefs, and practices converge and become more alike. The global diffusion of fast-food franchises, restaurants, hotel chains, and big-box retailers, such as Walmart, is often cited as evidence of the homogenization thesis. In the 1970s, before the word *globalization* was coined, geographer Edward Relph developed the term **placelessness** to draw attention to the loss of the unique character of different places and the increasing standardization of places and cultural landscapes (**Figure 2.5**). In the 1990s, writer and cultural critic James Howard Kunstler lamented what he saw as the emergence of a "geography of nowhere," primarily because of so much standardization in the American landscape. The epitome of "nowhere" is the cookie-cutter residential subdivision where every house looks alike.

It is clear that the products and services of some American companies, such as Nike, Microsoft, Google, and Walmart, have achieved a global presence and visibility. Similar developments have occurred in the fast-food,

soft drink, and entertainment industries—the source of many American cultural icons. The term *McDonaldization* refers to the standardization of eating habits—specifically through the provision of fast food eaten on the go, out of styrene packages or paper wraps. In addition, the global reach of the Cartoon Network—broadcast in over 160 countries—now surpasses both McDonald's and Coca-Cola.

The homogenization thesis is tied to the notion that economic processes shape cultural practices. These economic processes are largely attributed to the expansion of capitalism, and although the United States is not the sole driver of globalization, the country exerts a great deal of economic and cultural influence. Consequently, homogenization is widely understood to bring **Americanization**. The pervasive presence of American products involves the expansion of U.S.-owned MNCs. Some proponents of Americanization point out that it is much more than just a diffusion of goods; Americanization also involves the spread of values and attitudes, such as consumerism, freedom, and individualism. Critics of Americanization note that even though MNCs do employ local workers and managers, the bulk of the profits accrue to the multinational corporation, not the foreign country or the local economy where their franchises or branch plants are located. Thus, they see the diffusion of American corporations and brands as an expression of American economic, political, and cultural hegemony or dominance. The term *Coca-Colonization* implies that the hegemony of MNCs creates a set of power relations similar to those that exist between a country and its colonies, producing a kind of imperialism. For example, a Starbucks located on the grounds of the Imperial Palace in Beijing was widely seen by Chinese as cultural imperialism. Controversy over the presence of this Western chain at such a preeminent Chinese cultural site forced the store's closure.

> **Americanization**
> The diffusion of American brands, values, and attitudes throughout the world.

Polarization

According to the polarization thesis, globalization contributes to a heightened sense of sociocultural identity that serves to fragment people and trigger social disorder and instability instead of creating a standardized global culture. Those who subscribe to the polarization thesis believe that rather than homogenizing the world, globalization has unleashed powerful separatist forces that have heightened concerns about security not just for individu-

Courtesy Alyson Greiner

Placelessness • Figure 2.5

Despite the preponderance of American companies visible here, this photograph was taken in Australia and illustrates the standardization of cultural landscapes beyond the United States.

Cultural flows and neolocalism • Figure 2.6

Globalization encompasses complex movements of economic, political, and cultural ideas and practices, including resistance to them.

Reuters/Robert Sorbo/Landov LLC

a. Beliefs, practices, and products do not only flow from the Western world to other parts of the globe—they also flow out from non-Western places. Japanese anime (from *animation*) and cosplaying (costume role-playing of anime characters) have become very popular in North America, Europe, and Australia.

Courtesy Alyson Greiner

b. Local ordinances established by area communities or collective preferences can resist some of the homogenizing forces of globalization. Building codes in Santa Fe, New Mexico have favored the area's Pueblo revival architectural style shown here.

als but also for countries. They point to the fact that numerous wars and struggles over identity in the Balkans, the Caucasus, and Africa have coincided with the spread of globalization, as has the prevalence of global terrorism. Similarly, globalization has made possible and, with the Internet, has even facilitated the extension of cross-border criminal networks. Although the homogenization and polarization theses are quite popular in the media, many scholars find that they tend to oversimplify how globalization works because they depict globalization as having a single and fixed outcome. However, many scholars doubt that we will witness a complete homogenization of culture or landscape. They argue that human creativity tends to resist uniformity and that there will always be some people who refuse to conform. Furthermore, scholars stress that globalization is not unidirectional from the West to the rest of the world. The diffusion of tattooing discussed at the start of the chapter is an example of cultural practices spreading to the West. The existence of Indian and Ethiopian restaurants in London or Toronto also illustrates the multidirectional nature of globalization.

Similarly, globalization has as much to do with connectivity as it does with polarization. As the previous discussion

of the polarization thesis shows, globalization not only creates homogenizing forces, it can also stimulate local awareness. **Neolocalism** is a term coined by geographer James R. Shortridge to describe a renewed interest in sustaining and promoting the uniqueness of a place (**Figure 2.6**).

Glocalization

The glocalization thesis provides a third framework for understanding the cultural consequences of globalization. **Glocalization** occurs when a multinational corporation alters its business practices to reflect local preferences. From a geographic standpoint, glocalization is the result of the bridging of the local and global scales to create what is sometimes called the *local-global nexus*. Stated differently, there is always a dynamic relationship between local and global forces such that local forces become globalized and global forces become localized. Glocalization is a conceptual framework for understanding the impacts of globalization, as well as a business strategy. Globalization expert Jan Nederveen Pieterse (2009, p. 52) draws attention to

> **glocalization** The idea that global and local forces interact and that both are changed in the process.

Glocalization • Figure 2.7

In India, where cows are sacred to Hindus and Muslims avoid consuming pork, the menu often features the McVeggie, a beefless burger, the Chicken Maharaja Mac, and a variety of other vegetarian and nonvegetarian options but no beef or pork products.

David Pearson/Alamy

the local-global nexus with the maxim that "all business is local" (**Figure 2.7**).

Glocalization is also the subject of considerable debate. Because MNCs pursue glocalization so purposefully and strategically—in order to win consumers and gain profits—some experts see the adaptations MNCs make to local markets as somewhat superficial. They stress that glocalization provides an outward appearance of heterogeneity that disguises the overall standardization of business and cultural practices. Other specialists counter this by pointing out that what matters is how people use glocalized products, and the meanings they associate with them. For example, people can and do create informal gathering places at coffeehouses and diners, which builds community and sense of place.

CONCEPT CHECK

1. **What** are the strengths and weaknesses of the homogenization and polarization theses?
2. **How** are Americanization, McDonaldization, and Coca-Colonization similar to and different from one another?
3. **What** evidence supports the glocalization thesis?

The Commodification of Culture

LEARNING OBJECTIVES

1. **Discuss** how commodification can shape cultural practices and meanings.
2. **Explain** how representation and commodification relate to the notion that culture is contested.
3. **Explain** what is meant by heritage dissonance.

As we discussed in Chapter 1, the term *culture* is a social creation consisting of shared beliefs and practices that are dynamic rather than fixed. Culture is a complex system that is shaped by people and, in turn, influences them. Mani-festations or expressions of culture take both material and nonmaterial forms. **Material culture** includes the tangible and visible artifacts, implements, and structures created by people. Furniture, dwellings, musical instruments, and tools are all examples of material traits. **Nonmaterial culture** is not tangible and is associated with oral traditions and behavioral practices. Examples of nonmaterial traits include recipes, songs, knowledge, or philosophies shared by word of mouth, and the way we behave in certain circumstances as when we greet people. **Cultural geography** is a branch of human geography that emphasizes human beliefs and activities and how they vary spatially, utilize the environment, and change the landscape.

Cultural geographers are extremely interested in the **commodification** of culture. Slavery commodifies human beings, while online dating services commodify the procedures for meeting and getting to know prospective partners. Plasma collection centers and sperm banks reflect the commodification of bodily fluids. Seeing what's available on eBay quickly reveals the extent of commodification.

Commodification is closely associated with **consumption**. Cultural geographers note that consumption both influences and is influenced by culture. Your cultural background influences the things that you use, but these items also shape the interactions you have with other people. Commodities affect social relationships. Prenuptial agreements, in which couples agree before they marry to the division of their property should they divorce, provide a good illustration of how commodities shape social relationships.

Commodities also affect social relationships because they communicate meaning. Think, for example, about the different social messages that your clothing, jewelry, car, house, or apartment send about you. Commodities become symbols of ideas and values. People who share the same cultural background share the same codes for interpreting these symbols and their meanings.

Advertising, Commodification, and Cultural Practice

Advertising is one of the main forces affecting patterns of consumption locally as well as globally. Simply stated, advertising is designed to influence consumer behavior, and it does so by the clever manipulation of images, text, symbols, and slogans. In this section we explore some of the connections between geography, advertising, and consumption through developments involving diamonds. This example highlights some of the ways in which commodification can shape cultural practices.

Do you agree that gems have intrinsic value? Globally there are enough people who do to sustain a lucrative market for them. Among Westerners, diamonds have long been considered the most precious of all gems. The average amount spent by grooms on a diamond engagement ring now exceeds $3000, double what they would have paid if they had made their purchase in 1995. If they shop at

---

> **commodification**
> The conversion of an object, a concept, or a procedure once not available for purchase into a good or service that can be bought or sold.
>
> **consumption**
> Broadly defined, the use of goods to satisfy human needs and desires.

Tiffany's, the renowned luxury diamond retailer, they can expect to pay, on average, $10,000 for a diamond engagement ring. But diamonds are not scarce, so how can they command such high prices? The answer is a complicated mix of economics, geography, history, and marketing.

Think about the diamond commercials and advertisements you have seen. If you believe that "a diamond is forever," you have accepted one of the diamond industry's most familiar and durable advertising slogans, first launched in the United States by De Beers in 1947. The diamond industry cultivates the idea that diamonds are associated with everlasting love, will retain their value over time, and are symbols of beauty, preciousness, happiness, and status. Also, diamond marketers have strongly conventionalized—even ritualized—the act of giving a diamond engagement ring.

The history of De Beers is instructive in understanding the commodification of diamonds. De Beers began as a mining company in the late 19th century in what is now South Africa. The Englishman Cecil Rhodes established De Beers and sought to control the worldwide diamond industry by acquiring the diamond mines in the region. Under the direction of the Oppenheimer family in the 20th century, De Beers established a diamond **cartel** that controlled the supply of diamonds and therefore the demand for them.

De Beers solicited contracts with other diamond producers to bring them into the cartel; as a result, for the better part of the 20th century the company controlled between 66% and 80% of the global supply of rough, unprocessed diamonds. This control gave the company the power to decide when to sell diamonds and also to determine the selling price. Even though diamonds are not scarce and can actually be manufactured, the De Beers cartel succeeded in creating the illusion that diamonds are in short supply by carefully controlling the quantities of diamonds they made available for sale.

In the late 1980s and 1990s, a number of events helped to break the De Beers monopoly. New diamond mines opened in Russia and Canada. Russia only participated in the cartel during some years, while Canada did not participate at all. Diamond mining companies in Australia and Angola also remained outside the cartel. Diamond prices have fluctuated in recent years, but are expected to remain high because of strong demand in Asia.

> **cartel** Entity consisting of individuals or businesses that control the production or sale of a commodity or group of commodities—often worldwide.

Diamonds are a good example of a natural resource that gains value through commodification, marketing, advertising, and globalization.

▼ a. Diamond mining and conflict

Diamonds are extracted from underground mines, surface mines, and river alluvium. "Diamond diggers" sift alluvium in Sierra Leone. Diamonds fuelled civil wars in several African countries.

Candace Feit/The New York Times/Redux Pictures

Schalk van Zuydam/©AP/Wide World Photos

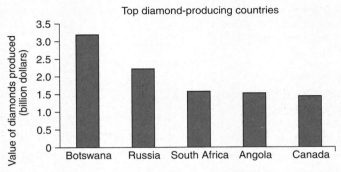

Top diamond-producing countries

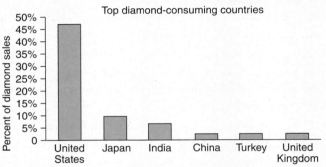

Top diamond-consuming countries

▲ c. Leading diamond producers and consumers

The geography of diamond production differs considerably from the geography of diamond consumption. Diamonds are mostly marketed in nonproducing countries (green). The United States has no commercial diamond production, yet the country has by far the greatest demand for diamond jewelry. (*Source:* Data from KPMG, 2006.)

▲ b. Diamond-related conflict

Sheku Conteh lost his hand during the conflict period in Sierra Leone. Because it is difficult to trace the origins of a diamond, the Kimberley Process Certification Scheme was developed to solve the problem of conflict diamonds. However, difficulties enforcing the certification scheme mean that conflict diamonds still exist.

d. Japanese newlyweds

Rare was the Japanese bride who wore a diamond engagement ring a few decades ago. But Japan's economic recovery after World War II generated increased consumerism, and marketing promoted diamonds as symbols of modernity, status, and purity. Today, Japan is the second-largest diamond jewelry market after the United States. ▶

Itsuo Inouye/©AP/Wide World Photos

Developments in Angola were among the first to draw attention to the problem of **conflict diamonds** or *blood diamonds*, but diamonds also factored in bitter conflicts in Sierra Leone, Liberia, and the Democratic Republic of the Congo. In response to public concerns, many diamond retailers now certify that the diamonds they sell are not conflict diamonds (**Figure 2.8**).

Sports, Representation, and Commodification

The discussion of diamonds shows how successful some enterprises are at shaping cultural practices, both locally and globally. Commodification is not limited to material culture, however. Commodification also influences nonmaterial culture and increasingly involves indigenous and local communities, in part because it presents opportunities for commercial transactions and economic gain. The Maori are the indigenous peoples of New Zealand. One facet of Maori nonmaterial culture that has been heavily commodified within the past decade is the **haka**, a collective, ritual dance (**Figure 2.9**).

The commodification of the haka has been hotly contested for two key reasons. The first reason is that, as Maori scholars have pointed out, the haka is not actually a Maori war dance and the rugby players do not use authentic haka moves. The second reason involves ownership and control of Maori culture. In 2000, some Maoris began to seek a greater share of the profit that both Adidas and the New Zealand Rugby Football Union (NZRFU) were making on contracts for the televising of All Blacks games. Representatives of the NZRFU commented that their use of the haka was not for commercial purposes. When Maoris raised concerns over violations of copyright in response to Adidas featuring the haka in a commercial and on billboards, lawyers for NZRFU argued that it was not possible to prove who created the haka or who had ownership of it.

If you are not Maori, the controversy over the haka may seem insignificant. Nevertheless, there are at least two crucial points to take from this discussion. The first is that culture is contested. Culture is so contested because people derive a good part of their sense of identity from it. The second and related point is that the controversy over the haka involves questions of ownership as well as cultural boundaries. For example, who should have a say in the use of cultural symbols, such as the haka or the representation of peoples and their cultural practices? Also, are there

The haka • Figure 2.9

Peter Morrison/©AP/Wide World Photos

Global Locator

AUSTRALIA NEW ZEALAND

NATIONAL GEOGRAPHIC

Before a match, members of the New Zealand rugby team, the All Blacks, gather in the middle of the field and perform the haka, an ancient ritual dance consisting of a series of loud chants, body slapping, forceful movements of the arms and legs, and jumping. The goal is to psych up the members of the All Blacks team and intimidate their opponent.

The dissonance of heritage • Figure 2.10

The exclusion or oppression of a group can contribute to conflicting views of heritage.

a. Hundreds of Native Americans in Oklahoma protested the centennial celebration of the state in 2007. To them the celebrations recalled a heritage rooted in treaties with their nations that the U.S. government failed to uphold and in the taking of Native American land for the purposes of white settlement.

b. Robben Island was the notorious prison for South Africa's anti-apartheid protestors, including Nelson Mandela, former president of South Africa and Nobel Peace Prize winner. To the indigenous San people, some of whom were also imprisoned there, the place symbolizes oppression by European colonialists. ▶ **What might the heritage of Robben Island mean to former prison staff?**

limits to the aspects of culture that can or should be commodified? If so, who sets those limits? These issues are all the more complicated by the friction between Maoris and New Zealanders of European descent, and the long-term prejudice the Maori have encountered since colonial days.

The Heritage Industry

Questions about commodification and authenticity also surround the **heritage industry**, which has experienced considerable growth since the 1980s. This growth is closely associated with a shift in the meaning of heritage. Geographer David Lowenthal, for example, has tracked the evolution of this term. Until very recently, heritage referred to property transmitted to an heir. It also included cultural practices relating to inheritance and the management of one's estate through wills and trusts. Today, however, **heritage** more commonly refers to any contemporary use of the past. For example, even radio stations that play "classic rock" are using a kind of heritage.

> **heritage industry**
> Enterprises, such as museums, monuments, and historical and archaeological sites that manage or market the past.

The creation of heritage attractions frequently involves the commodification of the past. The heritage industry, in effect, packages the past for sale. In order for it to have broad appeal, the idea of heritage has to be simplified, sanitized, and made entertaining. These views underscore the fact that heritage is characterized by **dissonance**—the quality of being inconsistent. Heritage dissonance expresses the idea that the meaning and value of heritage vary from group to group.

In their book, *Dissonant Heritage: The Management of the Past as a Resource in Conflict*, J. E. Tunbridge and G. J. Ashworth identify two main reasons that heritage is always dissonant. The first reason involves the opposing uses of heritage. For example, many heritage sites are also sacred sites. Allowing tourists at these sacred sites has the potential to lead to conflict. The second reason involves the *particularism* of heritage. That is, the meanings and uses of heritage are group-specific. Simultaneously inclusive and exclusive, heritage creates an inconsistency or dissonance in its meaning. The dissonance of heritage is clearly revealed in multicultural societies where heritage is frequently contested (**Figure 2.10**).

World Heritage

World or **global heritage** refers to sites perceived to have outstanding universal value for all of humanity. Geographer Douglas Pocock has noted that identifying extraordinary sites dates to at least the Classical Greek identification of the Seven Wonders of the World. The movement to protect and preserve world heritage, however, gathered its momentum in the 1960s and 1970s and has been led by UNESCO, the educational, scientific, and cultural organization of the United Nations.

In 1972, UNESCO adopted the Convention Concerning the Protection of the World's Cultural and Natural Heritage. This paved the way for the creation of a World Heritage Committee (WHC). One of the charges of the WHC was to generate a World Heritage List of cultural and natural sites deemed to possess outstanding universal value. In 1992, the list was modified to incorporate cultural landscapes that reflect different facets of the relationship between people and the environment.

Pocock argues that adding cultural landscapes to the World Heritage List marked a significant shift to a broader vision of heritage that is not limited to material evidence. For example, a particular landscape may be associated with significant religious, social, or other meanings regardless of the presence of tangible artifacts. Since this change in 1992, a World Heritage property might be a cultural site, a natural site, a cultural landscape, or a mixture of these (**Figure 2.11**).

World Heritage sites • Figure 2.11

Travel Ink/Getty Images, Inc.

The concept of world heritage has evolved and the number of designated sites has increased.

a. The event that linked UNESCO with world heritage was the impending destruction of the Abu Simbel temples by the formation of Lake Nasser behind the Aswan High Dam in Egypt. UNESCO considered Abu Simbel, built in the 13th century BCE, an irreplaceable cultural resource and in the 1960s arranged to disassemble the two temples and reassemble them on land above the waters of Lake Nasser.

Robert W. Nicholson/NG Image Collection

Lake Nasser

Locations of the Abu Simbel temples today

Original locations of the Abu Simbel temples

b. The first cultural landscape recognized in the World Heritage List was New Zealand's Tongariro National Park. Originally included as a natural site on the World Heritage List, in 1993 its listing was revised to recognize it as a cultural landscape with major religious significance to the Maoris.

Zephyr/Science Source

Latin America and the Caribbean 14%

Africa 9%

Middle East 7%

U.S. and Canada 4%

Asia and the Pacific 21%

Europe 45%

c. Nearly 900 sites are now recognized World Heritage sites, but the greatest geographic concentration of them is in Europe. Thirteen percent are located in the three European countries of Italy, Spain, and France. (*Source:* Data from UNESCO, 2009.)

UNESCO World Heritage List

Guy Vanderelst/Getty Images, Inc.

At the UNESCO website, you can view a map of World Heritage sites and learn more about them.

The World Heritage List has been celebrated for its role in raising awareness about global cultural resources and sometimes for triggering the development of new tourist sites (see *Where Geographers Click*). But the World Heritage List has also been criticized for four main reasons. First, it reflects a Eurocentric bias with an overrepresentation of sites in Europe, including buildings and properties associated with Christianity. Second, when World Heritage sites are identified, tourists often expect that the site will be accessible to them, regardless of any competing uses of the site or their state of repair. Third, these sites can be very expensive to maintain. Fourth, critics question whether there really can be such a thing as global heritage. They base this criticism on the point, made earlier, that heritage is group-specific.

CONCEPT CHECK   **STOP**

1. **How** does the history of the De Beers cartel illustrate the connections between commodification and cultural practice?
2. **Why** is the commodification of the haka a contentious issue?
3. **Why** is the World Heritage List both celebrated and criticized?

Cultural Geographies of Local Knowledge

LEARNING OBJECTIVES

1. **Define** local knowledge.
2. **Distinguish** between traditional and allopathic medicine.
3. **Explain** the relationships among local knowledge, gender, and cultural ecology.

Earlier we introduced the concept of popular culture. Historically, geographers and other social scientists have drawn a distinction between popular culture and folk culture, with *folk culture* referring to groups of people whose members share similar cultural traits, live predominantly in rural areas, and whose livelihood is minimally connected to the global market economy. The basis for this distinction between folk and popular culture stems from social changes related to the rise of capitalism and the spread of industrialization.

When this two-part classification was initially conceived in the 19th century, the labels "folk society" and "urban society" were used. At the time, folk society was synonymous with preindustrial society and urban society was associated with development. Thus, the term *folk* is problematic because of the way it suggests a less advanced group of people and makes those groups classified as folk cultures seem like quaint curiosities representative of a bygone era. A folk culture was understood to include those people who represented the common folk (as opposed to the elites) and whose cultural artifacts were handmade, not mass-produced. But this practice of excluding the customs of local elites introduces a bias and also calls into question the usefulness of the term *folk culture*. Because of these criticisms and in light of ongoing globalization,

> **local culture** The practices, attitudes, and preferences held in common by the members of a community in a particular place.

especially the greater interconnectedness of the global economy, we prefer instead to speak of **local culture**.

How do local cultures make decisions about natural resources? What factors do they take into consideration when planting or harvesting, preparing food, or caring for the sick? The complicated answers to these kinds of questions depend on the people we are talking about and on the knowledge they possess, as well as on the political, economic, environmental, and social circumstances in which they live. For a long time scholars have recognized that people acquire, share, use, and transmit knowledge in many different ways. But it is only recently that researchers have begun to understand and appreciate the importance of local ways of knowing. In this section we explore cultural geography through a discussion of local knowledge.

Local Knowledge

Geographers and other scholars use the term **local knowledge** to refer to the collective knowledge of a community that derives from the everyday activities of its members. Three characteristics help clarify the meaning of local knowledge:

1. Local knowledge is usually transmitted orally and is rarely written down. In many cases, oral transmission is supplemented by activities or stories that help to demonstrate a procedure or reinforce a particular practice.
2. Local knowledge is dynamic and continuously evolving—changing to reflect the acquisition of new observations and information.
3. Local knowledge does not exist as a single, monolithic entity. Rather, numerous reservoirs of local knowledge are retained by different individuals and groups within a community. It may be more suitable to talk about *local knowledges* instead of local knowledge.

In the past, Western thinkers assumed that local knowledge and land-use practices were outmoded, even inferior. Geographer Jim Blaut argues that these kinds of prejudices were part of the European **rationality doctrine**, prevalent during the lengthy period of European colonialism, when non-Europeans were perceived to

> **rationality doctrine** The attitude and belief that Europeans were rational and non-Europeans, especially colonized peoples, were irrational.

be irrational and childlike. By the 1950s and 1960s, Blaut notes, Europeans attributed a scientifically deficient mentality to their colonial subjects. This vision contributed to the emergence of **diffusionism**—the view that the diffusion of Western science, technology, and practices to other peoples would enable them to advance socially and economically. Ironically, diffusionists—many of whom were geographers—overlooked the importance of place as well as the relevance of local knowledge.

Most researchers today share the view that awareness of the local context—including local knowledge—is essential. Because local knowledge provides a framework for individual and community problem solving, not only on a day-to-day basis but also over the long term, it contributes to and informs **sustainable development**—an approach to resource use and management that meets economic and social needs without compromising the resources for future generations. Moreover, an awareness of local knowledge provides insights on the **social capital** of a particular community, which affects how decisions on matters such as resource use are made.

> **social capital** The social ties, networks, institutions, and trust that members of a group use to achieve mutual benefits.

Geographies of Traditional Medicine

Traditional medicine is an important reservoir of local knowledge that varies considerably from one place to another. Those who practice traditional medicine carry different titles, including healer, herbalist, bone setter, and spiritualist. A healer may acquire her or his knowledge from an experienced elder, or may be trained at a university. Despite its name, traditional medicine can actually be conventional, particularly if it is widely practiced by the general populace or forms the basis of a country's health care system. Alternatively, traditional medicine might only be practiced in special circumstances.

> **traditional medicine** Medical practices, derived from a society's long-established health-related knowledge and beliefs, that are used to maintain or restore well-being.

Most approaches to traditional medicine share two attributes: They tend to be holistic and personal. A **holistic approach** to medicine sees health as encompassing all aspects—physical, mental, social, and spiritual—of a person's life. A **personal approach** to medicine means that it is quite possible for two people to have the same

Video Explorations

Leeches for Curing Illness

National Geographic

This video introduces Ayurvedic medicine, a holistic form of medicine common in India.

symptoms but receive different treatments. Traditional medicine is usually contrasted with **allopathic medicine**, sometimes called modern or Western medicine. The oldest form of medicine practiced by humankind is traditional medicine. Allopathic medicine, by contrast, developed in conjunction with advances in biology and chemistry, the rise of the experimental method, and the invention of new technologies, including the microscope.

> **allopathic medicine** Medical practice that seeks to cure or prevent ailments with procedures and medicines that have typically been evaluated in clinical trials.

Traditional medicine in India grew out of *Ayurvedic* beliefs and practices (in Sanskrit *ayurveda* means "the science of life") based on the sacred Hindu text, the Vedas. It emphasizes the maintenance of harmony between a person and her or his environment, through such techniques as the use of herbal and oil treatments (see *Video Explorations*).

A similar ancient theory exists in Chinese traditional medicine and involves the *yin* and *yang*—opposing forces that, if out of balance, can result in illness. An important facet of Chinese traditional medicine is **acupuncture**, which has been practiced for at least 2500 years (**Figure 2.12**).

> **acupuncture** An ancient form of traditional Chinese medicine that promotes healing through the insertion of needles into the body at specific points.

Traditional medicine is geographically widespread; however, since many countries do not keep statistics on the practice or use of traditional medicine, it is difficult to draw comparisons between traditional medicine and allopathic medicine. Also, because there are very few systems of licensing practitioners of traditional medicine, there is no easy method to keep track of them. Studies conducted in Zambia, for example, indicate that there are 44 traditional healers for every allopathic doctor in the country. In addition, the position of traditional medicine within a country's health care system varies considerably.

Traditional medicine is fully and officially part of the national health care system in just four countries of the world: China, North Korea, South Korea, and Vietnam. In China, for example, the country's constitution grants traditional medicine legal authority to be practiced and used. It is official policy in China that allopathic and traditional medicine should coexist. Thus, a patient can visit either kind of doctor, and health insurance will provide full coverage for the visit, diagnosis, and treatment. Similar practices exist in North Korea, South Korea, and Vietnam, where the national health care system recognizes and supports both traditional and allopathic systems of medicine. In Japan, by contrast, most medical schools train physicians to practice allopathic medicine, though it is often possible for students to take classes in *kampo*, Japanese traditional medicine.

In Western countries the term *complementary and alternative medicine* (CAM) is now preferred to *traditional medicine*. CAM is sometimes described as the adoption of traditional medicine within an allopathic system. The United States is much like Japan in its long-standing emphasis on the training of allopathic practitioners. However, in 1998 the United States created the National Center for Complementary and Alternative Medicine within the National Institutes of Health in order to support and advance research on CAM.

Globalization and the cross-cultural exchange of ideas and practices associated with health and well-being have contributed to the rise in CAM. Another important reason for the growing popularity of CAM is its affordability, particularly when compared to allopathic medicine.

The diffusion of acupuncture • Figure 2.12

THE PLANNER

Acupuncture is now one of the most recognized forms of traditional medicine in the West. How did knowledge of acupuncture diffuse?

❷ 6ᵀᴴ century CE
Knowledge of acupuncture diffuses to Korea and Japan with the Buddhist religion. A Chinese medical text was given to Japan in 552 CE and ten years later a Chinese acupuncturist visited the country. Subsequent visits to China by Japanese monks studying medicine also helped diffuse knowledge of acupuncture.

❸ 8ᵀᴴ–10ᵀᴴ centuries
Acupuncture diffuses to the area of present-day Vietnam via trade.

To France

❶ Several centuries BCE
Acupuncture originates in ancient China.

The Silk Road

❺ 19ᵀᴴ century
Acupuncture probably arrived in North America as early as the 1800s via at least two pathways: Chinese immigrants who continued to use acupuncture, and information transfer with the medical community.

From China

❹ 10ᵀᴴ–16ᵀᴴ centuries
The diffusion of acupuncture to the West likely followed the Silk Road, an ancient trade route. Tenth-century Persian medical texts mention acupuncture. French Jesuits working as missionaries in East Asia during the 16th century brought back information on acupuncture and helped its diffusion to Europe.

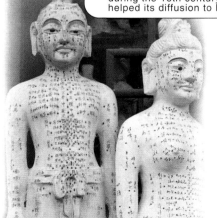

hanhanpeggy/iStockphoto

a. One of the first references to the use of needles for therapeutic purposes appears in a text called *The Yellow Emperor's Classic of Internal Medicine*, which was compiled between about 480 and 220 BCE. These models, labeled in Chinese, show the body's acupuncture points.

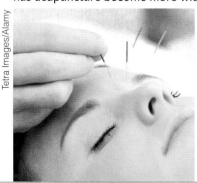

Tetra Images/Alamy

b. Following its arrival in the West, acupuncture was marginalized for a long time by practitioners of mainstream, allopathic medicine. Only since the 1970s has acupuncture become more widely accepted and available within the United States. In the 1980s, acupuncture became eligible for coverage under some insurance plans.

The global resurgence of traditional medicine • Figure 2.13

CAM is increasingly a part of medical practice in countries where allopathic medicine has dominated.

Richard Levine/Alamy

a. CAM may include the use of herbal medicines, now estimated to have a global market value of $60 billion. Yearly spending on CAM exceeds $2 billion each in the United States, Canada, and the United Kingdom.

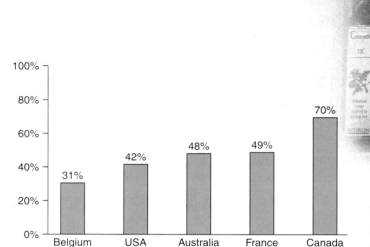

b. The graph shows the percentage of population in selected developed countries that has used CAM at least once. Even in countries where allopathic practices prevail, people indicate a willingness to try CAM. ▶ **What might account for the difference between the United States and Canada?** (*Source:* WHO, 2002.)

One of the concerns about CAM, however, centers on its safety with respect to the variable and inconsistent regulations on practitioners and remedies. Nevertheless, recent studies show that in several countries where allopathic medicine has prevailed, high percentages of people report using CAM (**Figure 2.13**).

Cultural Ecology and Local Knowledge

Local knowledge embodies a great deal of information about the environment. Indeed, approximately 75% of the plant-derived pharmaceuticals available today have been developed from plants used in traditional medicine. As we have seen, the specific knowledge an individual accumulates depends on her or his gender, age, status, wealth, and life experience. Significantly, the local knowledge possessed by one group may not be readily shared with members of another group. Often, an important reason for this is that the knowledge accumulated by certain members

of the community is considered specialized knowledge. Therefore, cultural practices shape the ways in which local knowledge is acquired and shared.

Gender and traditional medicine In the case of traditional medicine, women, men, or both may be the repositories of the specialized knowledge depending on where we are and the community involved. A study of South African villages found that men, especially those 50 years of age or older, tended to have more extensive knowledge of plant resources for medicines than did the women. Within Talaandig communities in the Philippines, however, women accumulate more knowledge about lowland herbs, whereas men accumulate more knowledge about forest herbs. The reason for this gender-based distinction involves daily work and roles: Men spend more time in forest environments engaged in agricultural pursuits. In towns in Amazonia, however, women typically are the primary repositories of knowledge of medicinal plants.

They frequently cultivate such plants in their yards and gardens, and they share knowledge about the plants with other women.

Water resources, local knowledge, and gender

It is not unusual for local knowledge about a given topic, such as medicinal plants or water resources, to reveal an intimacy of awareness about place and ecology. San communities in the Kalahari Desert of southern Africa, for example, once utilized *sip-wells* as part of their strategy for obtaining water. They learned that water, though not visible on the desert surface, collects in and below the sands in certain locations. By using straws from plant parts, they could sip water from the sands and store the water in ostrich eggs for use at a later time.

Both women and men play important roles in managing water resources, although their influence tends to vary by scale and location. Broadly speaking, men exert more influence at the regional, national, and international scales, whereas women have more influence at the household scale and, depending on the place, sometimes also at the village and community scales. Across Sub-Saharan Africa, about one-fourth of women in rural households require 30 minutes or more a day to collect water. However, in some instances women spend the better part of a day collecting water for household use. Where manual or mechanized pumps have been installed at well sites, a number of cultural (and ecological) changes have occurred. Use of the pumps reduces the amount of time spent collecting water. Moreover, maintaining the pumps—a job initially allocated to men—is increasingly performed by women who are more invested in pump maintenance and water sanitation because of their role in managing daily and household water needs. In the eastern regions of Nepal, however, some well pumps have been installed in places that lack adequate privacy for women to bathe—a reflection of the fact that women were not included when information about water usage was obtained.

In parts of the Middle East, North Africa, Central Asia, and Mediterranean Europe, one facet of the local knowledge about water resources involves **qanats**. These ancient systems have long provided villages with water for agriculture and household consumption. Construction and maintenance of the

> **qanat** A system of water supply that uses shaft and tunnel technology to tap underground water resources.

qanats as well as decisions about how much water to allocate to different families and for different purposes have historically been carried out by men, while women have been responsible for water collection. To understand how qanats work, see *What a Geographer Sees* on the next page.

Vernacular architecture The study of **vernacular architecture** has been closely associated with human geography for well over a century. Cultural geographers maintain that vernacular architecture provides valuable insights on human use of space—whether in terms of the layout of a house or building, or of the design of a village or settlement. According to Paul Oliver (1997, p. xxiii), vernacular architecture is an architecture "of the people." More specifically, vernacular structures

> **vernacular architecture** The common structures—dwellings, buildings, barns, churches, and so on—associated with a particular place, time, and community.

are customarily owner—or community—built, utilizing traditional technologies. All forms of vernacular architecture are built to meet specific needs, accommodating the values, economies and ways of living of the cultures that produce them.

Vernacular dwellings and structures often incorporate locally available materials and resources and are adapted to environmental conditions as well as cultural practices and needs. In China, building traditions usually reflect awareness of cosmic forces, which the geographer Ronald Knapp refers to as **mystical ecology**. One example of mystical ecology includes **feng shui**, the art and science of situating settlements or designing cultural landscapes in order to harmonize the cosmic forces of nature with the built environment. The concepts of *yin* and *yang* that

> **mystical ecology** The interrelationship between an awareness of cosmic forces and human use of the environment.

we discussed in relation to acupuncture are also relevant to *feng shui*. The cosmic force or energy known as *chi* or *qi* (pronounced *chee*) not only controls the interaction of *yin* and *yang* but is also believed to be visibly expressed in the physical landscape. Thus, an auspicious site has positive *chi*. Assessing the characteristics of a particular site according to feng shui principles is complex and includes the lay of the land and the location of water sources. Indeed, *feng shui* literally means *wind and water*.

WHAT A GEOGRAPHER SEES

Qanats

Qanats, also called *karez*, *khettaras*, or *foggaras*, have been used to manage water in about 50 countries or territories worldwide. They are usually constructed near the base of hills or in stream valleys. Water flows through a qanat entirely by gravity.

a. Countries in blue have either extant or historical qanats. Most of the qanats in use today are in the Middle East. (*Source:* Data from Salih, 2006; and Dale Lightfoot, personal communication, 2009.)

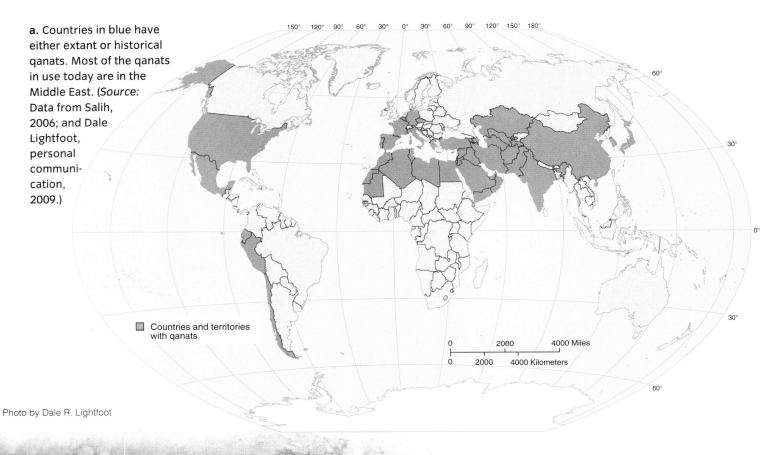

Countries and territories with qanats

Photo by Dale R. Lightfoot

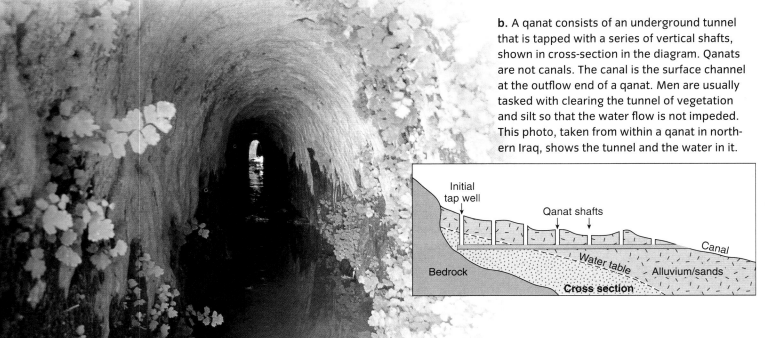

b. A qanat consists of an underground tunnel that is tapped with a series of vertical shafts, shown in cross-section in the diagram. Qanats are not canals. The canal is the surface channel at the outflow end of a qanat. Men are usually tasked with clearing the tunnel of vegetation and silt so that the water flow is not impeded. This photo, taken from within a qanat in northern Iraq, shows the tunnel and the water in it.

Initial tap well

Qanat shafts

Canal

Water table

Bedrock

Alluvium/sands

Cross section

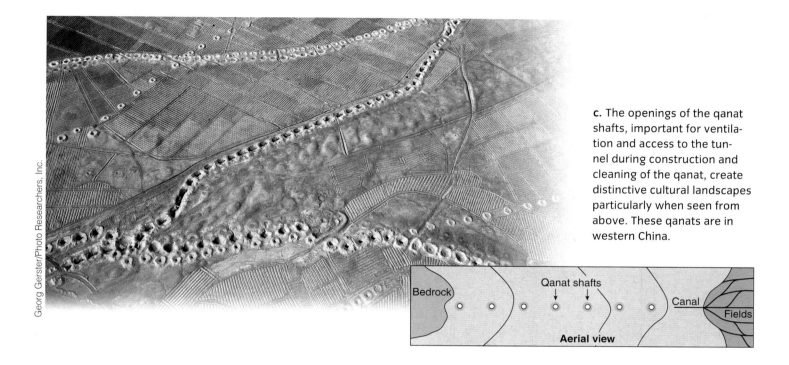

Georg Gerster/Photo Researchers, Inc.

c. The openings of the qanat shafts, important for ventilation and access to the tunnel during construction and cleaning of the qanat, create distinctive cultural landscapes particularly when seen from above. These qanats are in western China.

Bedrock | Qanat shafts | Canal | Fields

Aerial view

d. The Kunaflusa qanat in northern Iraq still provides water to the villagers, though the flow of water has diminished considerably. This change is mainly the result of other water withdrawals for agriculture from the same underground water source that feeds this qanat and of drought.

Photo by Dale R. Lightfoot

Think Critically

1. What social, political, or other factors might contribute to qanat abandonment?
2. What is a problem with using a modern political map (as in **a**) to indicate the location of qanats?

Architecture and the environment • Figure 2.14

Vernacular architecture expresses local knowledge and sheds light on the relationships between people and their environment.

Alison Wright/NG Image Collection

a. Mongolian nomads dwell in buildings known as *ger*, or yurts, with walls consisting of a circular lattice frame and a roof supported by slender poles. The entire structure is covered with felt and can be collapsed for transport to a new location.

b. Vernacular principles sometimes influence popular architecture. This rest stop in Germany was designed according to feng shui. The site's mountain backdrop and nearby creek generate positive chi. The wavy roof, colors, and materials evoke the five elements of feng shui—wood, earth, metal, fire, water—and harmonize with the environment.

Stefan Puchner/picture-alliance/dpa/AP Images

Krzysztof Dydynski/Lonely Planet Images/Getty Images

c. This church in Colombia is built from "Giant Bamboo" or guadua (*Guadua angustifolia*). Guadua, which grows in Colombia and Ecuador, has been used for housing by the indigenous people for centuries. Guadua is increasingly favored as an earthquake-resistant building material.

A tenet of *feng shui* is that wind disperses *chi* but water can help contain it. Thus, some of the most auspicious sites are those that are backed by high, rolling hills or mountains, have lower hills to the front, and are adjacent to flowing water. Worldwide, vernacular architecture displays tremendous variety in building techniques, styles, and materials and often influences current building practices (**Figure 2.14**).

CONCEPT CHECK STOP

1. **How** have Western views of local knowledge changed over time?

2. **How** has the status of traditional medicine changed over time?

3. **Why** are gender differences relevant to resource management?

Summary

✔ THE PLANNER

1 Globalization 36

- **Globalization** extends the interconnectedness and interdependence of people and places in the world. Although globalization existed before the term was coined, geographers recognize that contemporary globalization differs from its historical precedents. This is because the world is experiencing a widening and deepening of economic, cultural, and political interconnectedness not seen before.

- **Capital** refers to those assets that stem from human creativity and are used to create goods and services. One of the hallmarks of globalization is the increased circulation of financial capital.

- Today, **multinational corporations (MNCs)** are a significant component of the global economy. They not only dominate global trade, but they also influence the flow of financial capital especially through **foreign direct investment (FDI)**, as shown here.

Flows of foreign direct investment (FDI) into different regions • Figure 2.3

Reuters/Mohamed Nureldin Abdallh/©Corbis

2 Cultural Impacts of Globalization 40

- Globalization's impacts on society are complex and diverse, and are most readily discernable by trends in **popular culture**.

- When examining the cultural impacts of globalization, geographers and other social scientists have identified three key theses: the homogenization thesis, the polarization thesis, and the glocalization thesis.

- While diffusion can occur in two or more directions, the fact that many American companies and products have achieved a global presence raises concerns about **Americanization**.

- **Glocalization** (shown in the photo) and **neolocalism** challenge the view that the cultural impacts of globalization flow only or primarily from the Western world to the rest of the world.

Glocalization • Figure 2.7

David Pearson/Alamy

3 The Commodification of Culture 44

- Culture can be expressed in tangible or intangible ways, giving rise to the distinction between **material culture** and **nonmaterial culture**. **Cultural geography** is the branch of human geography that studies the impact of human beliefs and activities on other groups and the environment.

- A **cartel** controls the production or sale of a commodity. **Commodification** converts an object, a concept, product, or procedure formerly not available for purchase into a good or service that can be bought or sold. Commodification is related to **consumption,** which is encouraged by advertising. As noted in the discussion of diamonds, advertising can even influence cultural practices. In the case of the **haka**, shown here, advertising helped commodify an aspect of Maori nonmaterial culture and demonstrates the contested nature of culture.

The haka • Figure 2.9

Peter Morrison/©AP/Wide World Photos

- It can also be said that the **heritage industry** involves the commodification of the past. The particularism of **heritage** means that it is always characterized by **dissonance**. The identification of **world (**or **global) heritage** sites has been both celebrated and criticized.

4 Cultural Geographies of Local Knowledge 50

- **Local culture**, often contrasted with popular culture, refers to place- and community-specific ways of life that differ from but are not untouched by globalization and more mainstream beliefs and practices.

- **Local knowledge** encompasses the collective knowledge of a community that derives from the everyday activities of its members. In every community there are multiple repositories of local knowledge. These are the individuals and groups who retain specialized knowledge for different activities. Understanding how decisions about resources are made within a community often reflects the influence of **social capital**, gender, age, and other factors.

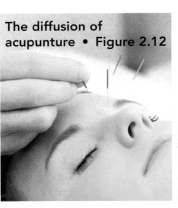

The diffusion of acupuncture • Figure 2.12

Tetra Images/Alamy

- Historically, European views of non-Europeans (especially colonized peoples) were influenced by the **rationality doctrine** and **diffusionism**.

- **Traditional medicine** is a kind of local knowledge that is often contrasted with Western, or **allopathic,** ways of practicing medicine. Traditional medicine is widely practiced around the world, and some facets of it, such as **acupuncture** (see photo), have become more mainstream and globalized.

- Local knowledge often reveals an intimate awareness and understanding of the environment, highlighting the importance of cultural ecology. **Vernacular architecture** encompasses the local building traditions and wisdom of a particular community. A more complete understanding of vernacular architecture, **qanats**, and **mystical ecologies** such as **feng shui** demands an awareness of local knowledge.

Key Terms

- acupuncture 52
- allopathic medicine 52
- Americanization 42
- capital 36
- cartel 45
- commodification 45
- conflict diamonds 47
- consumption 45
- cultural geography 44
- diffusionism 51
- dissonance 48
- feng shui 55
- foreign direct investment (FDI) 37

- globalization 36
- glocalization 43
- haka 47
- heritage 48
- heritage industry 48
- holistic approach 51
- horizontal expansion 36
- local culture 51
- local knowledge 51
- material culture 44
- multinational corporation (MNC) 37
- mystical ecology 55
- neolocalism 43

- nonmaterial culture 44
- personal approach 51
- placelessness 42
- popular culture 41
- qanat 55
- rationality doctrine 51
- social capital 51
- sustainable development 51
- traditional medicine 51
- vernacular architecture 55
- vertical expansion 36
- world (or global) heritage 48

Critical and Creative Thinking Questions

1. Using what you have learned in this chapter, would you say that consumerism is an expression of democracy? Explain your reasoning.

2. In what ways do different genres of music express resistance to or acceptance of forces of globalization?

3. The United States has contributed very little to the globalization of sports. Why?

4. Is distance education a form of commodification? Explain your reasoning.

5. What is meant by the commodification of nature? Give examples to support your interpretation.

6. What are some consequences of commodifying public goods such as water?

7. Study the residential architecture in your hometown. Can you identify any vernacular styles? If so, what patterns do you observe in the distribution of those styles?

8. Use this photo to discuss how vernacular architecture relates to the emphasis within geography on environment-society dynamics.

Alison Wright/NG Image Collection

What is happening in this picture?

People from the country of Myanmar, formerly known as Burma, protest the South Korean multinational Daewoo International Corporation and its recent foreign direct investment in a natural gas project off the country's coast.

Think Critically

1. Why are many people around the world suspicious of foreign direct investment?
2. More broadly, why is there dissent against globalization?

Apichart Weerrawong/©AP/Wide World Photos

Self-Test

(Check your answers in Appendix B.)

1. As discussed in the chapter, list two of the major factors driving contemporary globalization.

   _____

   _____

2. To a country receiving foreign direct investment, benefits may include all but one of the following. Which item does *not* belong?

   a. FDI supports small, local businesses.

   b. FDI improves a country's cash flow.

   c. FDI can increase employment.

   d. FDI can transfer technology.

3. Placelessness is most closely associated with which thesis about the impacts of globalization?

   a. the homogenization thesis

   b. the polarization thesis

   c. the glocalization thesis

   d. the Americanization thesis

4. The spread of Walmart stores shown in this diagram illustrates _____.

   a. glocalization

   b. neolocalism

   c. hierarchical diffusion

   d. reverse hierarchical diffusion

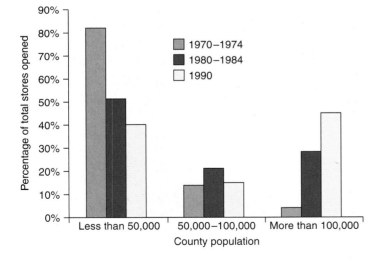

5. _____ is a pejorative term that implies that culture flow is unidirectional; _____ counters the view that homogenization is inevitable.

   a. Neolocalism; globalization

   b. Polarization; dissonance

   c. Coca-Colonization; glocalization

   d. Americanization; reverse hierarchical diffusion

6. This McDonald's menu from India is an example of _____.

   a. globalization and glocalization

   b. glocalization and diffusionism

   c. glocalization and neolocalism

   d. cultural dissonance and Americanization

David Pearson/Alamy

7. List two limitations of the term *folk culture*:

   _____

   _____

8. Based on the discussion of the commodification of diamonds, which of the following statements is FALSE?

   a. The demand for diamonds is generally greatest in countries that do not mine them.

   b. The De Beers cartel helped ritualize and spread the practice of giving diamonds as gifts.

   c. The De Beers cartel used advertising to create an illusion of diamond scarcity.

   d. Blood diamonds have little to do with commodification.

9. Which of the following is *not* a characteristic of vernacular architecture?

a. The design of vernacular architecture seems at odds with its surroundings.

b. Vernacular architecture can tell us about human use of space.

c. Vernacular architecture is an architecture of the people.

d. Vernacular architecture can reveal shared beliefs such as mystical ecologies.

10. Which of the following is *not* a criticism leveled against the World Heritage List?

a. There is no such thing as global heritage.

b. Listed sites are not always made available to the public.

c. Listed sites display a Eurocentric bias.

d. Profit from tourism to listed sites is not returned to the local communities.

11. Which of the following terms cannot be used to describe local knowledge?

a. oral

b. evolving

c. monolithic

d. nonmaterial

12. Using the accompanying map as a guide, briefly explain the diffusion of acupuncture.

13. _____ long affected development policies and contributed to _____.

a. Dissonance; sustainable development

b. The rationality doctrine; diffusionism

c. Traditional knowledge; sustainable development

d. Local knowledge; health care

14. Allopathic medicine is _____ and _____; traditional medicine is _____ and _____.

a. expensive; requires formal training; inexpensive; never requires formal training

b. holistic; impersonal; informal; spiritual

c. widespread; personal; indigenous; targets specific ailments

d. nonholistic; associated with the West; holistic; individual

15. In terms of qanat systems, what is a primary function of the circular features shown in this picture?

a. to capture water for underground storage

b. to provide access for cleaning

c. to provide a place to install a mechanized pump

d. They don't have a particular function.

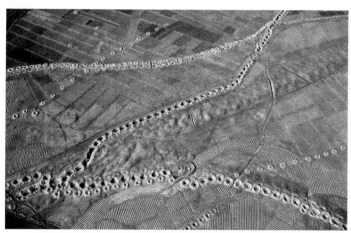

Georg Gerster/Photo Researchers, Inc.

THE PLANNER ✓

Review your Chapter Planner on the chapter opener and check off your completed work.

Population and Migration

POPULATION CHALLENGES AND OPPORTUNITIES

The world achieved a major milestone on Monday October 31, 2011. Do you recall what it involved? On that day the global population reached 7 billion. Just 12 years earlier, the world population had reached 6 billion. In your lifetime, the world has achieved two new population milestones. To put this in perspective, world population reached 1 billion in 1804, but it took most of human history to do so.

A world with so many people presents challenges that involve quality of life issues, employment prospects, and sustainability. When populations grow, demands on the environment and on public services also increase. This photo shows a public swimming pool located in China, where going swimming is sometimes disparagingly referred to as "boiling dumplings" because people can bob up and down but do not have room enough to swim.

As we can see, total numbers of people matter, as do issues of access to goods, resources, and amenities. The characteristics of a population are also important, and approximately 43% of the world's people are under the age of 25. The world has never had as many youth as it does today. Young people represent opportunity. They bring energy and creativity to the workforce and have tremendous potential for driving change.

For population geographers, then, there are several important dimensions to the study of population that deserve attention. These include factors affecting population growth and decline, population composition, and migration. This chapter provides an introduction to these and other facets of population geography.

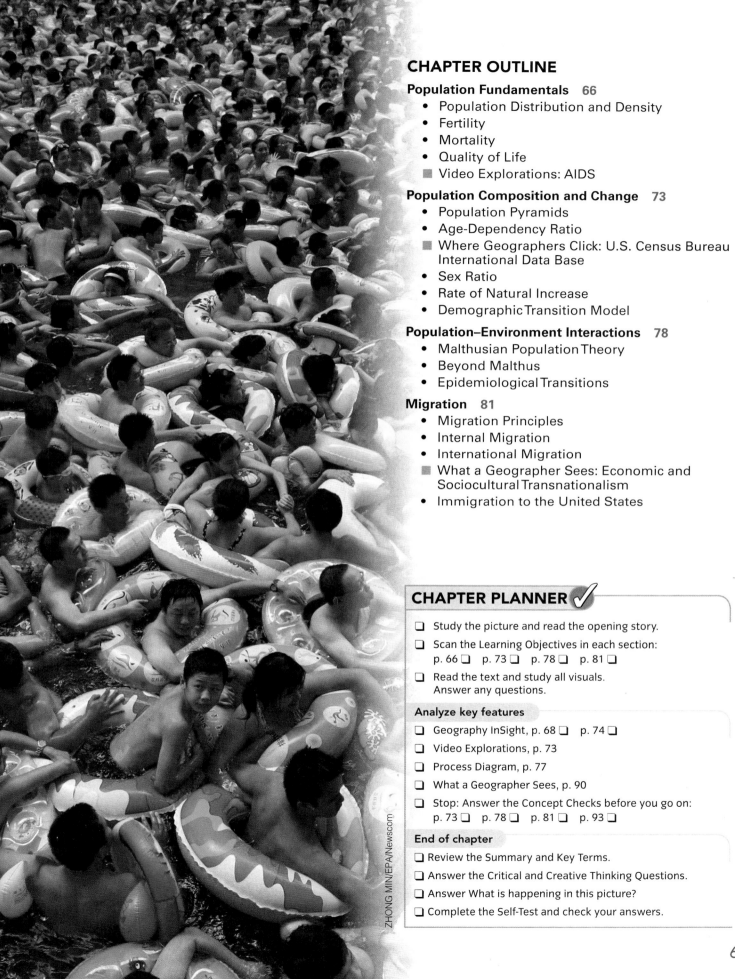

ZHONG MIN/EPA/Newscom

CHAPTER OUTLINE

CHAPTER PLANNER ✓

☐ Study the picture and read the opening story.

☐ Scan the Learning Objectives in each section:
p. 66 ☐   p. 73 ☐   p. 78 ☐   p. 81 ☐

☐ Read the text and study all visuals.
Answer any questions.

Analyze key features

☐ Geography InSight, p. 68 ☐   p. 74 ☐

☐ Video Explorations, p. 73

☐ Process Diagram, p. 77

☐ What a Geographer Sees, p. 90

☐ Stop: Answer the Concept Checks before you go on:
p. 73 ☐   p. 78 ☐   p. 81 ☐   p. 93 ☐

End of chapter

☐ Review the Summary and Key Terms.

☐ Answer the Critical and Creative Thinking Questions.

☐ Answer What is happening in this picture?

☐ Complete the Self-Test and check your answers.

Population Fundamentals

LEARNING OBJECTIVES

1. **Describe** how population is distributed around the globe.
2. **Identify** the factors affecting fertility rates.
3. **Identify** the factors affecting death rates.
4. **Explain** how life expectancy and infant mortality are a measure of quality of life.

The example of the crowded public swimming pool in China provides a useful starting point for thinking about the relations between people, space, place, and more broadly—**population geography**. As we saw in Chapter 1, population geography is one of the major subfields of human geography. Population geography draws on demography, the statistical study of characteristics of human populations, but goes beyond it to address how and why populations differ in their distribution, density, composition, change over time, and interaction with the environment. The study of migration is also a major component of population geography.

> **population geography** The study of spatial variations among populations and population–environment interactions.

Population Distribution and Density

As illustrated in **Figure 3.1**, the world's 7 billion people are unevenly distributed.

Global population distribution • Figure 3.1

The fundamentals of population geography build from a familiarity with the spatial configuration of the world's population.

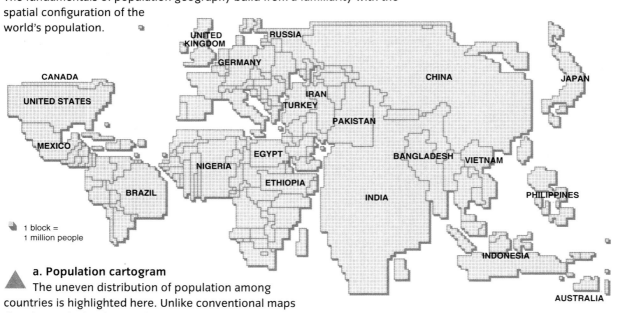

a. Population cartogram
The uneven distribution of population among countries is highlighted here. Unlike conventional maps that depict the land area of countries, on this cartogram the size of a country is shown in proportion to its total population. At a glance, you can visualize how China's population dwarfs that of Russia, for example. (*Source:* NG Maps.)

1 block = 1 million people

b. Population, in millions, and as a percent of world total
The 10 most populous countries are shown compared to the population of all other countries combined. Together, China and India account for 37% of the global population—almost as much as all those other countries. (*Source:* Data from Population Reference Bureau, 2012.)

China, 1,350, 19%
India, 1,260, 18%
Other countries, 2,923, 41%
United States, 314, 5%
Indonesia, 241, 3%
Brazil, 194, 3%
Pakistan, 180, 3%
Nigeria, 170, 2%
Bangladesh, 153, 2%
Russia, 143, 2%
Japan, 128, 2%

Density expresses the number of people, structures, or other phenomena per unit area of land. When population geographers want to know about the pressure a population exerts on the land, they calculate the population density. More specifically, population geographers use two different measures of population density: **arithmetic density** and **physiological density**. To calculate the arithmetic density, you divide the total population by the total land area. One limitation of the arithmetic density is that it does not distinguish between types of land in an area, some of which may be inhospitable. The physiological density takes into account how much of the land is **arable land,** that is, how much of the land can be used for agriculture. To calculate the physiological density, you divide the total population by the total area of arable land. See **Figure 3.2** to understand how and why arithmetic and physiological densities vary from country to country.

> **arithmetic density** The number of people per unit area of land.
>
> **physiological density** The number of people per unit area of arable land.

Fertility

Populations are dynamic, and two of the most important causes of population change include births and deaths. In its broadest sense, *fertility* refers to the ability to produce offspring. More narrowly, however, fertility refers to the births within a given population. Fertility and *mortality*—the incidence of death within a given population—are affected by biological, social, economic, political, and cultural factors.

Population geographers use two important measures of fertility: the **crude birth rate (CBR)** and the **total fertility rate (TFR)**. Of these measures, the CBR is the most familiar, but it is also a more general measure. Thus, it is "crude" in the sense that it reflects childbearing trends within society as a whole rather than by specific age group. Globally, the CBR ranges from 6 in the small European principality of Monaco to 46 in the African countries of Mali, Niger, and Zambia. The CBR for the world is 20, while that for the United States is 13.

The TFR helps population experts to gauge family size and predict future population

> **crude birth rate (CBR)** The annual number of births per 1000 people.
>
> **total fertility rate (TFR)** The average number of children a woman is expected to have during her childbearing years (between the ages of 15 and 49), given current birth rates.

trends. When the TFR is 2.1, a population is said to be at the **replacement level**—the fertility rate necessary for a population to replace itself. For example, it takes two children to replace a couple. It may seem that the replacement level should be 2.0 exactly. It is slightly higher than this because some people will not have children. When the replacement level is achieved, the population will eventually stabilize if deaths stay the same and migration has no impact. TFRs at or near replacement level signal that a population may be stabilizing.

Factors influencing fertility Direct and indirect factors affect fertility at the individual and societal levels by creating conditions that increase or diminish the likelihood of becoming pregnant. Direct factors are both biological and behavioral. Natural sterility is a biological factor. Behavioral factors that directly affect fertility include the percentage of women who are married or in sexual union, as well as the prevalence of contraceptive use.

Indirect factors include those diverse cultural, social, economic, and political circumstances that influence the desire to have children and may prompt changes in behavior and, thus, fertility. For example, fertility in the U.S. has dropped since the onset of the recession in 2007 in part because economic factors such as high unemployment and concerns about economic uncertainty have diminished fertility desires. Some economic factors have the opposite effect, however. Across the developing world, children are considered an economic investment because they will be able to work and contribute to the family's income. Although Americans tend to expect their parents to have retirement savings or pensions, in many developing countries children may be the sole source of financial support for aging parents.

It is difficult to pinpoint a single factor that controls fertility; rather, complex associations among factors are often involved. Poverty tends to be associated with higher fertility, but the relationship between poverty and fertility is complicated because the poor are also more likely to have lower levels of education. Studies now indicate that literacy is linked to delays in marriage and childbirth, as well as lower rates of teen pregnancy. Because of these complex factors, fertility varies depending on the

People tend to cluster, revealing favored environments as well as strategies for supporting high population densities.

a. Dot map of population density

Globally, the pattern of densely and sparsely settled regions suggests that people tend to prefer to live in certain natural settings, such as on level land and away from deserts. Nearly 70% of the world's people live within 400 kilometers (250 miles) of a coast and on just 10% of the Earth's land. (*Source:* NG Maps.)

© KIM KYUNG-HOON/Reuters/Corbis

c. Dense urban population

The global distribution of population is increasingly urban. Indeed, cities are home to half of all people on the planet. In Tokyo, subway workers push people onto trains, ensuring high arithmetic densities in each subway car during the rush-hour commute.

Country	Total population	Land area (square km)	Arithmetic density (people per square km)	Arable land (percent)	Arable land (square km)	Physiological density (people per arable square km)
Japan	128,000,000	364,000	352	12	43,680	2,930
Egypt	82,300,000	995,000	83	3	29,850	2,757
Bangladesh	153,000,000	130,000	1,177	55	71,500	2,140
China	1,350,000,000	9,570,000	141	15	1,435,500	940
United States	314,000,000	9,162,000	34	18	1,649,160	190
Australia	22,000,000	7,682,000	3	6	460,920	48

b. Arithmetic and physiological densities

The higher the physiological density is, the greater the pressure that a population exerts on land that is used for agriculture. Bangladesh records high arithmetic and physiological densities even though the country has a high percentage of arable land. (*Source:* Data from Population Reference Bureau, 2012; CIA, 2009.)

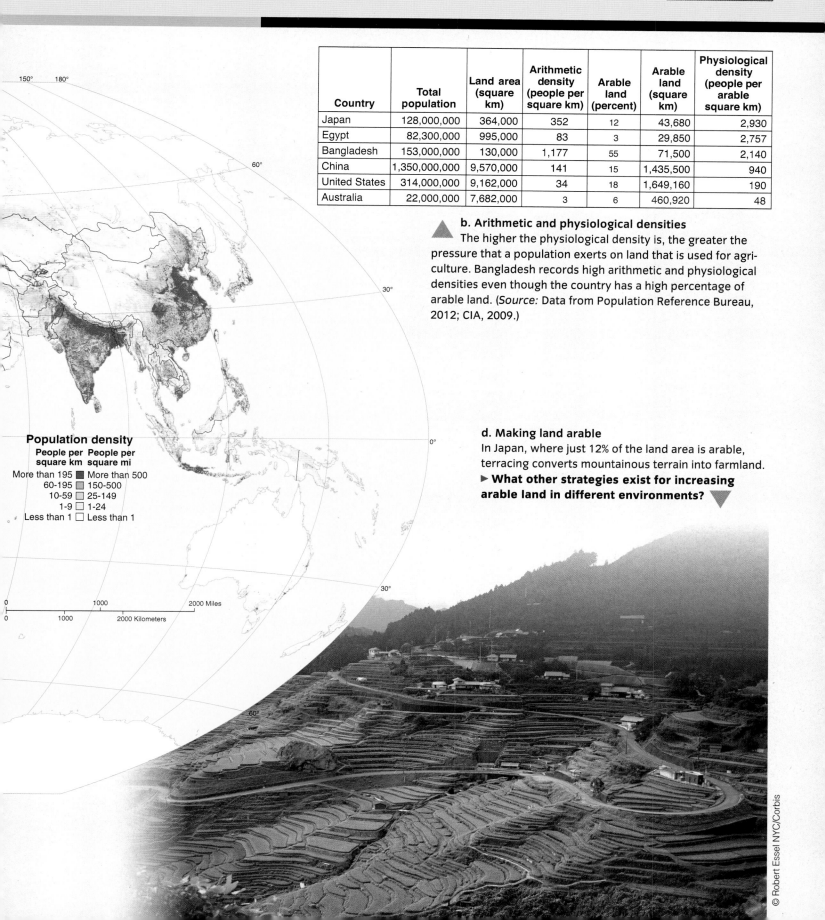

Population density

People per square km	People per square mi
More than 195	More than 500
60-195	150-500
10-59	25-149
1-9	1-24
Less than 1	Less than 1

0   1000   2000 Miles
0   1000   2000 Kilometers

d. Making land arable

In Japan, where just 12% of the land area is arable, terracing converts mountainous terrain into farmland.

▶ **What other strategies exist for increasing arable land in different environments?** ▼

© Robert Essel NYC/Corbis

region, country, or social group being studied. **Figure 3.3** illustrates some of this variation.

Population control policies

Governments can influence fertility by introducing policies to promote or limit population growth. Such population control policies are, respectively, *pro-natalist* or *anti-natalist*, and usually involve incentives to change reproductive behavior and, consequently, fertility.

A country with a declining population may want to raise fertility in order to avoid having to rely on immigration to fill its labor needs. Although France's TFR of 2.0 is not high by global standards, the country has one of the highest fertility rates in Europe. Many experts attribute this to pro-natalist policies that give tax concessions to families with three or more children, subsidize day care, permit parental leave, and prevent women from being fired while on maternity leave.

China likely provides the most familiar example of a country that has implemented an anti-natalist policy. Out of concern that explosive population growth would undermine the country's development, the Chinese government began to promote smaller families several decades ago. By 1979, fertility rates in China had dropped below three children per woman.

Government officials did not consider this dramatic decline in fertility sufficient, however, and in 1979 China implemented the *one-child policy*. This policy was never intended to apply uniformly to all of China's people or its geographic regions. Thus, the implementation of the policy has and continues to vary demographically and spatially. For example, certain ethnic minorities are permitted three children and rural couples are permitted two children if the first child is a girl and the births are separated by at least five years. By the early 1990s, China's fertility had dropped below replacement level. See **Figure 3.4** for additional discussion of the policy and recent developments.

Global dimensions of fertility • Figure 3.3

Globally, fertility rates are falling—quite rapidly in some places.

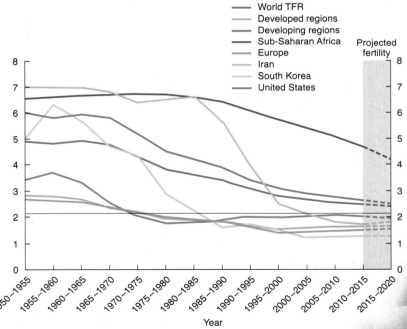

a. Nearly 80 countries have TFRs at or below replacement level. Iran's example is instructive: During the 1950s, Iran's TFR was 7.0 but today it is below replacement level. Europe, with a TFR of 1.6 has even lower fertility. The two most often cited reasons for the global decline in fertility are improved standards of living and the education of more women. (*Source:* Data from UNDESA, 2009.)

Lynn Johnson/NG Image Collection

b. Sub-Saharan Africa records some of the highest fertility rates in the world, often in excess of 5.0. In Ghana, shown here, the TFR dropped from 6.4 to 4.0 between 1998 and 2008. Among Ghanaian women with high school or postsecondary education, the TFR falls to 2.1.

Population control in China • Figure 3.4

China's one-child policy has important geographical dimensions. The policy was conceived at the national scale but has always been implemented at the local scale. For example, local areas were assigned birth quotas, and couples had to request permission to have their first child.

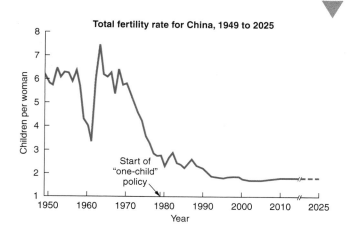

Bruce Dale/NG Image Collection

a. Translated from Chinese, this billboard from the 1970s reflects the government's "later, longer, fewer" message, a voluntary anti-natalist strategy prior to the one-child policy. It promoted marriage at a later age, longer periods of time between pregnancies, and fewer pregnancies.

Randy Olson/NG Image Collection

b. The steep fertility decline underway prior to 1979 leads some experts to question whether the one-child policy was necessary. (*Source:* Adapted from Riley, 2004.)

Total fertility rate for China, 1949 to 2025

(Graph: y-axis "Children per woman" from 1 to 8; x-axis "Year" from 1950 to 2025. Fertility rate starts around 6 in 1950, peaks near 7.5 in mid-1960s after a dip around 1960, then declines steeply through the 1970s. An arrow marks "Start of 'one-child' policy" around 1979, with rates leveling near 1.7 through 2025.)

c. Enforcement of the one-child policy has, until recently, been strictest in urban areas. Faced with an aging population, Shanghai in 2009 began encouraging couples, who themselves were from one-child families, to have two children.

Mortality

Like fertility, patterns of mortality also affect population change. A standard measure of mortality is the **crude death rate (CDR)**. Today, no country has a death rate in excess of 23. Globally, some of the lowest death rates—1 to 2 deaths annually per 1000 people—have been recorded in the Middle Eastern countries of Qatar and Kuwait. In contrast, some of the highest death rates occur in the African countries of Lesotho (23) and Sierra Leone (20), a result of the ongoing AIDS epidemic and poor access to medical care.

Natural and social factors can increase mortality. For example, natural disasters can lead to temporary increases in the death rate. Prior to Hurricane Katrina, the death rate for Orleans Parish, where New Orleans is located, was 11.3. More than a year after the storm, the death rate was 14.3—an increase of more than 26%. Many medical officials believe that the higher death rate was the result of ongoing stress associated with the personal, financial, and psychological hardships Katrina wrought.

The state of the health care system is another factor that affects death rates. Poor countries often cannot afford to provide vaccinations or purchase medicines needed to manage preventable diseases. Countries affected by wars and violent social upheaval are likely to experience increased death rates.

crude death rate (CDR) The annual number of deaths per 1000 people.

Although poorer countries often have high death rates, having a high death rate does not necessarily mean that a country is less developed. A country that has a high proportion of elderly people will, typically, have a high death rate regardless of the country's wealth. For example, Sweden has a much higher proportion of elderly people than Honduras and its death rate is 10, whereas the death rate in Honduras is 5. Thus, we should remember that the death rate cannot tell us about the quality of life or health in a country.

Quality of Life

Two demographic measures that reflect quality of life are life expectancy and infant mortality. **Life expectancy** is the average length of time from birth that a person is expected to live given current death rates. Women have slightly longer life expectancies than men. Globally, the life expectancies for both men and women have risen substantially in the past century, from about 29 years in 1900 to 70 years today. Population geographers have recently identified places called *blue zones* that have exceptionally long-lived populations (**Figure 3.5**).

Life expectancy can decline if the level of poverty increases or if a country experiences a social upheaval. Following the breakup of the Soviet Union, Russia experienced a decline in its life expectancy, especially among men. In 1990 life expectancy for Russian men was 64 years, by 2000 it had fallen to 59 years; today it is 63 years. By contrast, the life expectancy for Russian women is 75 years. The social and economic trauma of Russia's reforms, as well as high rates of alcoholism among men, help account for these differences.

Globally, the impact of HIV/AIDS on life expectancies varies. In wealthier countries, better access to medical care and pharmaceuticals has helped bring life expectancies of persons living with HIV/AIDS close to normal. Elsewhere, however, HIV/AIDS has reduced life expectancies by as much as 20 years. Lesotho and Botswana, southern African countries, have life expectancies of 48 and 51 years, respectively. (See *Video Explorations*.)

The second key measure that indicates the quality of life in a particular population is the **infant mortality rate**—the number of deaths of infants under one year of

NATIONAL GEOGRAPHIC

Life expectancy • Figure 3.5

The expected length of a person's life has much to do with access to medical care, nutrition, and sanitation. Therefore, life expectancy data can reveal disparities in health and well-being.

b. Okinawa, Japan is a well-studied blue zone, with 50 centenarians (persons 100 years or older) per 100,000 people, a rate four to five times higher than that in other countries with high life expectancies. Here, a 102-year-old Okinawan holds her great-great-granddaughter. Lifestyle choices related to diet, exercise, and social involvement with others are thought to help explain these patterns.

Okinawa, Japan

Life Expectancy at Birth (in years)
- 70 or older
- 60–69
- 50–59
- 40–49

a. Life expectancy varies between countries, but Africa has the lowest life expectancies of any continent. (*Source:* NG Maps.)

Video Explorations

AIDS

National Geographic

AIDS is an acronym for Acquired Immune Deficiency Syndrome, a disease caused by the HIV virus. In Sub-Saharan Africa, HIV infection is spread primarily via heterosexual intercourse. Across the region, mortality from AIDS remains high, with significant long-term social and demographic consequences.

age per 1000 live births. High infant mortality rates signal that inadequacies exist in the health care given to pregnant women and to newborn babies. At the start of the 20th century the infant mortality rate for the United States was over 100. Today the infant mortality rate is about 6, just slightly higher than the rate in the European Union. In many Sub-Saharan African countries struggling with malnutrition, unreliable access to safe water, and/or civil strife, infant mortality rates approach and sometimes exceed 100.

CONCEPT CHECK   STOP

1. **What** are two different measures of density, and why do population geographers need them?
2. **What** is the significance of replacement level fertility?
3. **Why** is mortality rate not a good indicator of quality of life or health in a country?
4. **How** does life expectancy vary around the world?

Population Composition and Change

LEARNING OBJECTIVES

1. **Describe** how population pyramids display population data.
2. **Explain** how to calculate the age-dependency ratio.
3. **Summarize** the factors that may contribute to an imbalanced sex ratio.
4. **Identify** the components used to measure population change.
5. **Describe** the differences among the four stages in the demographic transition.

We can describe every population in terms of its composition—that is, in terms of the characteristics of the specific groups within it. Take, for example, the student population of your college or university. We can ask: How many students are between the ages of 18 and 22? How many students work part-time? What percent of the student body commutes? What is the ratio of men to women? For population geographers, this kind of information creates a demographic picture of the variations within a given population.

Significantly, population composition also provides valuable clues about how a population is likely to change in the future. For example, college recruiters target areas with large populations of high school students. Similarly, the types of television shows and advertisements change from afternoon to evening as the composition of the viewing

population changes. One tool that gives us a glimpse of the composition of a population is the population pyramid.

Population Pyramids

The vertical axis of a **population pyramid** depicts age cohorts—groups of people born in the same time span. Most population pyramids use five-year cohorts and begin with the youngest age group, which includes infants and children up to 4 years of age.

> **population pyramid** A bar graph that shows the age and gender composition of a population.

The age cohorts on the left of the vertical axis usually represent males, while the age cohorts on the right side of the vertical axis represent females. The horizontal axis indicates the percentage of the total population. Population pyramids can be grouped into three categories with

Population pyramids help to visualize the age and gender composition of a population. Their shape derives mainly from the birth rate, and they can be grouped into three categories: rapid growth, slow growth, and population decline. They can also help us visualize demographic impacts of significant past events. (For all graphs in Figure 3.6: *Source:* Data from U.S. Census Bureau International Data Base, 2012.)

a. Rapid population growth
A broad base, as seen in the population pyramid for the Philippines, indicates that birth rates have been and continue to remain high, that there is a high percentage of young people, and that the country's population is increasing rapidly.

b. Slow population growth
The base of Australia's population pyramid is starting to resemble a column, with similar numbers of births each year and slow population growth.

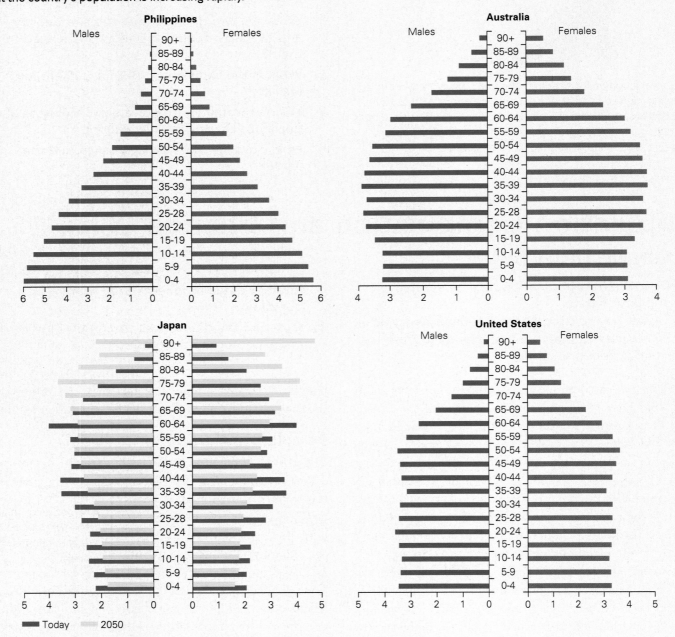

c. Population decline
A shrinking base, as we see on Japan's population pyramid, indicates population decline. If this trend continues, Japan will have an inverted population pyramid in 2050.

d. Baby boom
The shape of a country's population pyramid can be transformed within a lifetime or a generation. Find the bulge that includes persons born between 1946 and 1964; it represents the baby boom generation born in the United States after World War II.

distinct shapes: rapid growth, slow growth, and population decline. See **Figure 3.6** for a discussion of these categories and follow the link in *Where Geographers Click* to view some animations.

Age-Dependency Ratio

You can use the population pyramid in **Figure 3.6a** to estimate that 34% of the people in the Philippines are below the age of 15. What percentage of the country's population is over the age of 65?

Demographers pay close attention to the number of people younger than 15 and over 65. People in these groups are termed *age dependents* because most of them do not work on a full-time basis. The **age-dependency ratio** helps countries to predict and plan for how their society will change. Countries with a youthful population need to ensure that there is sufficient classroom space and that there will be jobs available as these youths age.

> **age-dependency ratio** The number of people under the age of 15 and over the age of 65 as a proportion of the working-age population.

To calculate the age-dependency ratio, you divide the number of age dependents by the working-age population (the number between ages 15 and 64) and multiply the result by 100. Look again at Figure 3.6a. In the Philippines 39% of the population (40 million) are age dependents, and 61% (63 million) are of working age. The Philippines has an age-dependency ratio of 63:100—that is, for every 100 people between the ages of 15 and 64 there are 63 age dependents. In contrast, Japan's age-dependency ratio of 60:100 results mainly from the high percentage of elderly. The closer to 100, the higher the age-dependency ratio. By comparison, Costa Rica's age-dependency ratio is 44:100, but Iraq's is 85:100.

Where Geographers CLICK

U.S. Census Bureau International Data Base

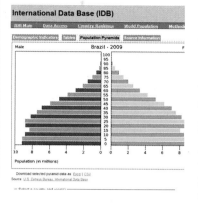

You can look at population pyramids for most of the world's countries at the U.S. Census Bureau International Data Base website. You have to first select a country, click submit, and then select the population pyramids tab. With a little practice, you can compare population pyramids for different years and set the population pyramids in motion. (*Source:* U.S. Census Bureau.)

Sex Ratio

Another way to examine the composition of a population is with the **sex ratio**. In normal conditions, more males are born than females, giving a slight imbalance. The natural sex ratio is 105:100, meaning 105 boys are born for every 100 girls.

> **sex ratio** The proportion of males to females in a population.

Diverse forces can create disparities between the number of men and women in a population. Men have higher mortality rates than women in virtually every age cohort. Women live longer, and you can see this in the population pyramids in Figure 3.6. War usually has a disproportionate impact on the male population; immigration can also affect the sex ratio (**Figure 3.7**).

Sex ratio in the United Arab Emirates • Figure 3.7

The United Arab Emirates recruits laborers from other countries for its industries.

a. Foreigners constitute more than 80% of the country's labor force. South Asians, shown here, are heavily concentrated in construction jobs.

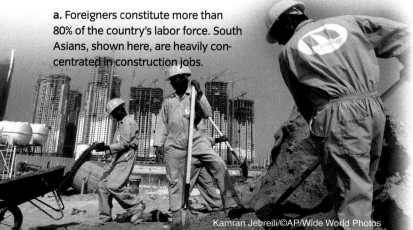

Kamran Jebreili/©AP/Wide World Photos

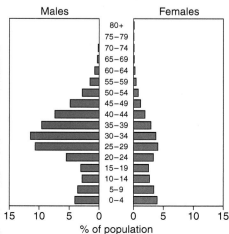

b. The population pyramid reveals how reliance on migrant labor has massively altered the country's sex ratio. For the entire population, the sex ratio is 219:100; for 15- to 64-year-olds, the sex ratio rises to 274:100.

Some Asian countries, including India and China, have high sex ratios. India's sex ratio is 113 but rises to 123 in some northwestern states. In 2011, China's sex ratio was 118. In China's rural provinces, where couples are permitted a second child if their first is a girl, the sex ratio for second births exceeded 160. In both countries, a strong cultural preference for boys is partly responsible for these disproportions, but in China the one-child policy also likely plays a role. The extremely imbalanced sex ratio for second births points to the practice of sex selective abortions to ensure at least one boy. What are some possible long-term effects of such uneven sex ratios?

Population geographers track the spatial variations that result from population growth or decline. To do this, they need to know about changes over a given time within a population. In the next section, we will concentrate on the changes to the population through births and deaths. Later in the chapter, we will look at changes to the population through immigration (in-migration) and emigration (out-migration).

Rate of Natural Increase

A population experiences natural increase when the number of births exceeds the number of deaths. To calculate the **rate of natural increase (RNI)** population geographers subtract the death rate from the birth rate and convert

> **rate of natural increase (RNI)** The percentage of annual growth in a population excluding migration.

that number to a percentage. For example, in 2012 the birth rate for the world was 20 per 1000 and the death rate was 8 per 1000. The difference is 12 per 1000, which, when converted to a percentage, yields a rate of natural increase of 1.2%. This figure may seem low, but we should keep in mind that even a small percentage increase translates into a large number of persons. In 2012, the world population grew through the addition of about 85 million people.

The rate of natural increase can be zero, as in Austria, where both the birth rate and the death rate are 9 per 1000. A negative rate of natural increase indicates that the death rate is higher than the birth rate and there is a natural *decrease* in the population. With a birth rate of 11 and a death rate of 15, Ukraine presently has a negative rate of natural increase. **Figure 3.8** shows how the rate of natural increase varies around the world.

Population geographers use the rate of natural increase to determine the number of years it takes a population to double. The **population doubling time** gives us a sense of the pace at which a population is growing. To calculate the population doubling time, you divide the number 70 by the rate of natural increase. This calculation gives a population doubling time for the world of 58 years (70 ÷ 1.2). The current rate of natural increase for Ethiopia is 2.4%, giving it a population

Rates of natural increase around the world • Figure 3.8

The rate of population growth for the world is declining, and has been for the past several decades. Even so, the population of the world will continue to increase because of its young age structure and rising life expectancies. (*Source:* Data from Population Reference Bureau, 2009.)

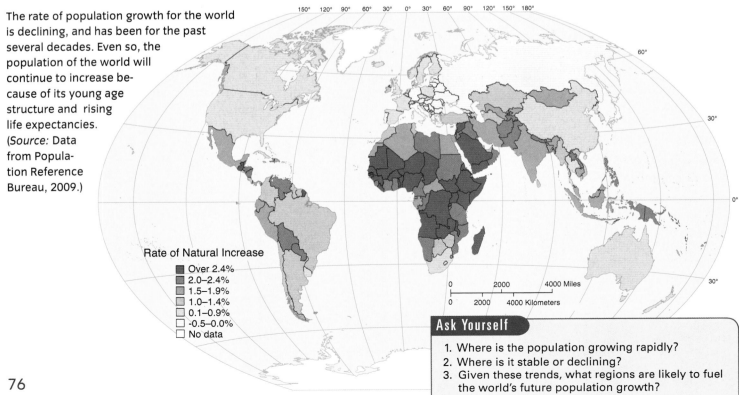

Rate of Natural Increase
- Over 2.4%
- 2.0–2.4%
- 1.5–1.9%
- 1.0–1.4%
- 0.1–0.9%
- -0.5–0.0%
- No data

Ask Yourself
1. Where is the population growing rapidly?
2. Where is it stable or declining?
3. Given these trends, what regions are likely to fuel the world's future population growth?

Demographic transition model • Figure 3.9

The demographic transition model is derived from population trends in western Europe before, during, and after the Industrial Revolution. It consists of four stages.

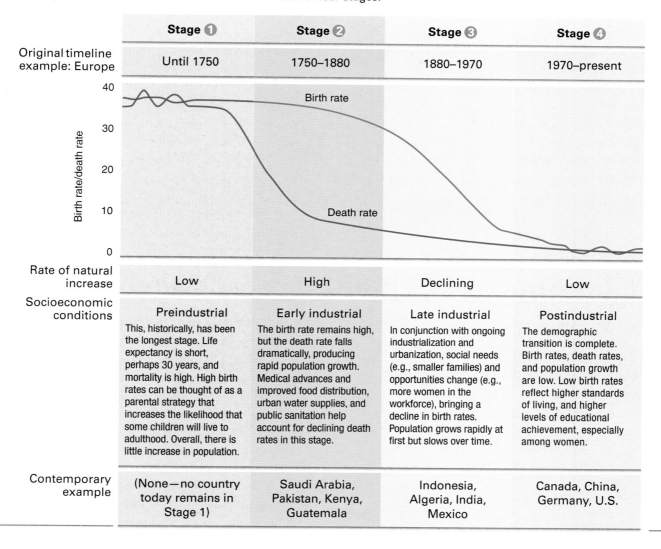

	Stage ❶	Stage ❷	Stage ❸	Stage ❹
Original timeline example: Europe	Until 1750	1750–1880	1880–1970	1970–present
Rate of natural increase	Low	High	Declining	Low
Socioeconomic conditions	**Preindustrial** This, historically, has been the longest stage. Life expectancy is short, perhaps 30 years, and mortality is high. High birth rates can be thought of as a parental strategy that increases the likelihood that some children will live to adulthood. Overall, there is little increase in population.	**Early industrial** The birth rate remains high, but the death rate falls dramatically, producing rapid population growth. Medical advances and improved food distribution, urban water supplies, and public sanitation help account for declining death rates in this stage.	**Late industrial** In conjunction with ongoing industrialization and urbanization, social needs (e.g., smaller families) and opportunities change (e.g., more women in the workforce), bringing a decline in birth rates. Population grows rapidly at first but slows over time.	**Postindustrial** The demographic transition is complete. Birth rates, death rates, and population growth are low. Low birth rates reflect higher standards of living, and higher levels of educational achievement, especially among women.
Contemporary example	(None—no country today remains in Stage 1)	Saudi Arabia, Pakistan, Kenya, Guatemala	Indonesia, Algeria, India, Mexico	Canada, China, Germany, U.S.

doubling time of just 29 years. In contrast, Spain has a rate of natural increase of 0.2% and a population doubling time of 350 years. One important limitation of population doubling time is that it treats population growth as fixed at today's current rate. For this reason, population doubling time is not used to predict future population size.

Demographic Transition Model

The **demographic transition model** grew out of several studies of population trends in Europe. Broadly, this model relates changes in the rate of natural increase to social change as a result of urbanization and industrialization. More specifically, it describes a common demographic shift from high birth and death rates to low birth and death rates over time (**Figure 3.9**).

Using what you know about the relationship between the rate of natural increase and the demographic transition, you can refer again to Figure 3.8 to identify other countries that have stage 2, 3, or 4 profiles.

More important than assigning a country to a specific stage is that we understand why a country has a certain demographic profile. As we have seen, economic, social, and political factors affect demographics. In turn, these factors are bound up with development, a topic we discuss in greater detail in Chapter 9. Moreover, the demographic transition model has serious limitations. Because it does not take migration into account, it presents only a partial picture of population change, and the model cannot be used to make predictions. Finally, because the model is based on western Europe's experience, it is not directly applicable to developing countries where experiences with urbanization and industrialization have been very different. For example, Nigeria's death rates have fallen and more than half of its people live in cities, but major declines in fertility have not occurred.

CONCEPT CHECK STOP

1. **What** are the three basic shapes of population pyramids?
2. **Why** do population geographers pay attention to age-dependency ratios?
3. **Where** do highly imbalanced sex ratios exist, and why?
4. **How** does the rate of natural increase vary around the world?
5. **How** does the rate of natural increase change from stages 1 to 4 of the demographic transition, and why?

Population–Environment Interactions

LEARNING OBJECTIVES

1. **Summarize** Malthusian population theory.
2. **Contrast** the neo-Malthusian and cornucopian theories.
3. **Define** epidemiological transition.

The chapter opener referred to the crowded conditions at a public swimming pool in China. From a more global perspective, is there a limit to the number of people the Earth can support? How are population size, quality of life, and the state of the environment related? These complex questions have long challenged many thinkers. The study of **population ecology** examines the impacts populations have on their environments as well as the ways in which environmental conditions affect people and their livelihoods. In this section, we discuss some past and present theories that address different population–environment interactions.

Malthusian Population Theory

One person whose ideas have received a great deal of attention for more than two centuries is the English economist Thomas Malthus who, in 1798, published *An Essay on the Principle of Population*. Malthus wondered whether society could be perfected so that people everywhere could enjoy prosperity and well-being, but he came to the rather pessimistic conclusion that rapid population growth was a major cause of human poverty and misery.

Malthus was writing at a time when England was in stage 2 of the demographic transition and its population was rapidly increasing. Perhaps these factors influenced his argument that the food supply increased arithmetically—from 1 to 2 to 3 to 4, for example—but that population increased geometrically—from 1 to 2 to 4 to 8 to 16, and so on. The result, he claimed, was that the number of people in a country would quickly exceed their food supply. According to Malthus, *positive checks* such as famine and disease would then spread, raise mortality, and reduce the population. In essence, population size was held in check by a country's food-producing capacity. To avoid such dire events, Malthus, who was also an Anglican clergyman, argued that people would need to implement voluntary *preventive checks* such as postponing marriage and practicing sexual restraint. For Malthus, this was extremely unlikely. As he explained, "towards the extinction of the passion between the sexes, no observable progress whatever has hitherto been made" (Malthus 1997, p. 80).

Beyond Malthus

More than two centuries after the publication of his *Essay*, Malthus's work still prompts debate about overpopulation and population growth. **Neo-Malthusians** are those who share the same general views of Malthus. They argue that, because the world's resources are limited, there is also a natural limit to the number of people the Earth can support at a comfortable standard of living. This limit is known as the world's **carrying capacity**. Some Neo-Malthusians consider the world overpopulated now. In their view, overpopulation not only outstrips the food supply, it ultimately threatens human existence by causing loss of biodiversity, resource scarcity, environmental degradation, and economic decline. Neo-Malthusians see the recent spate of food riots and concerns with climate change as evidence of the dangerous consequences of population pressure.

One of Malthus's critics was the development theorist Ester Boserup, who, beginning in the 1960s, argued that increases in population size and density lead to innovations that make it possible to expand the food supply. Boserup's argument provides a good example of **cornucopian theory**—a theory that human ingenuity generates adaptive strategies that lead to human well-being. Cornucopians reject the idea that there is a carrying capacity and see larger populations as a stimulus for economic growth and prosperity. (The word *cornucopia* means "horn of plenty.") Improvements in life expectancy that have come with population growth and increased consumption support the cornucopian position.

With respect to Malthus's argument, history has shown it to be incorrect in two respects. First, although world population has grown rapidly, it has not grown geometrically. Second, Malthus failed to anticipate that food production could be so dramatically expanded. Since 1970, for example, global production of cereal grains and livestock has increased significantly, in large part because of numerous improvements in agricultural implements and techniques (**Figure 3.10**). These shortcomings aside, Malthus did recognize the important role that indirect factors have on fertility through his concept of preventive checks. Indeed, neo-Malthusian thought shaped the population control and family planning strategies adopted in many parts of the developing world after World War II.

To this point our discussion has presented two sides in the debate over Malthusian population theory. Not everyone fits so neatly into the Malthusian or cornucopian camps, however. Those who occupy a third position—the "social critics"—focus less on the issue of population growth or size and more on problems of access to and distribution of food and other resources. Social critics point out that although there is enough food produced in the world to feed everybody, shortcomings in our economic, political, and institutional systems create **food insecurity**, meaning that people do not have physical or financial access to basic foodstuffs. Food insecurity is not just a concern of other countries;

Agricultural production and population • Figure 3.10

Between 1970 and 2010, the world's population grew from 3.7 to 6.8 billion, global production of cereal grains more than doubled, and global production of livestock nearly trebled. These comparisons show that the rate of growth in output of cereal grains and livestock has exceeded that for population. (*Source:* Data from FAOSTAT, 2012.)

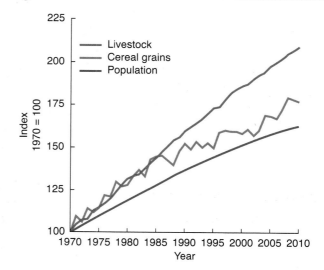

it exists in different magnitudes in all U.S. states. Many factors contribute to food insecurity, such as poverty, war, and civil strife, and natural disasters (**Figure 3.11**).

Epidemiological Transitions

The study of health and disease, like the overpopulation issue discussed previously, also brings together the study of people and the environment. When we take a long-term and global approach to trends in health and disease, we can discern notable shifts in mortality and disease prevalence. Borrowing from the model of the demographic transition introduced earlier in the chapter, we call these shifts **epidemiological transitions**.

To understand these transitions, it helps to distinguish between communicable and noncommunicable diseases. *Communicable diseases* spread from person to person via the transmission of pathogens (disease-causing organisms). *Noncommunicable diseases* such as cancer are influenced by genetic, environmental, and lifestyle factors (smoking, poor diet, inactivity). They cause the body to deteriorate, usually over long periods of time.

Today scholars recognize three epidemiological transitions. The first transition took place up until about 1750 and was characterized by a prevalence of epidemics attributed to communicable diseases such as smallpox and the Black Death. The second transition began about 1750 and continued to about 1980. It is primarily associated with a decline in deaths from communicable diseases as medical science, hygiene, and sanitation improved, and a rise in deaths from noncommunicable diseases. This transition was first observed among the most developed countries. We can see this shift playing out by comparing the leading causes of deaths between high- and low-income countries (**Table 3.1**). Globally, more people die from noncommunicable disease than infectious diseases. Although infectious diseases still rank as leading causes of death in low-income countries, deaths attributed to heart disease and stroke are on the rise. It is important to note, however, that another dimension of the second epidemiological transition involves increasing prevalence of noncommunicable diseases among the poor, mainly because of changes in lifestyle habits.

Food insecurity • Figure 3.11

Food insecurity occurs when a population lacks access to basic food as a result of physical or financial limitations.

a. Stunted growth is a sign of chronic food insecurity and malnutrition. Iodine deficiencies also impair health. Food insecurity in North Korea is most severe in the northeastern provinces, where level and arable land are in short supply. North Korea's food insecurity stems from poverty but is complicated by environmental conditions and the policies of its repressive government. (*Source:* DPRK, 2005.)

b. North Korean workers bag donated wheat. The cost of fertilizer has been beyond the means of this impoverished country. Officially, U.S. policy is not to use food aid for strategic purposes. However, the United States often does stipulate that the distribution of such aid be monitored. ▶ **Does this make food a political tool?**

Leading causes of death Table 3.1	
Low-income countries	**High-income countries**
1. Lower respiratory infections	1. Coronary heart disease
2. Diarrheal diseases	2. Stroke
3. HIV/AIDS	3. Lung cancers
4. Coronary heart disease	4. Alzheimer's/dementia
5. Malaria	5. Lower respiratory infections
6. Stroke	6. Pulmonary disease
7. Tuberculosis	7. Colon/rectum cancers
8. Low birth weight	8. Diabetes mellitus
9. Birth trauma	9. Hypertensive heart disease
10. Neonatal infections	10. Breast cancer

Source: WHO, 2011 [causes of death, 2008]

The third transition, underway since about 1980, is characterized by the emergence or resurgence of infectious diseases, a process that is often associated with environmental change. Lyme disease, which is spread to people by deer ticks, is a resurgent disease in the northeastern United States. Deforestation of New England during and after colonial settlement diminished deer habitat. As suburbanization expanded, forests have regrown and attracted more deer. Malaria is resurgent in the East African highlands, where warmer temperatures have been recorded and malaria cases have increased in higher elevations—places that were once too cool for the mosquitoes that transmit malaria.

CONCEPT CHECK STOP

1. **How** has Malthus's theory been criticized?
2. **What** are the implications of neo-Malthusian and cornucopian perspectives for resource use?
3. **How** do the three epidemiological transitions differ?

Migration

LEARNING OBJECTIVES

1. **Identify** Ravenstein's principles of migration.
2. **Distinguish** among the different types of internal migration.
3. **Describe** global patterns of international migration.
4. **Explain** how the origins of immigrants to the United States have changed over time.

Thus far, we have focused our discussion of population change on the relationship between births and deaths in a given population. There is, however, another important factor that contributes to population change: migration. Migration matters because it can lead to the redistribution of people in a country or region, and may alter its ethnic, linguistic, or religious composition.

> **migration** Movement from one territorial or administrative unit to another associated with long-term or permanent change in residence.

Migration is one kind of spatial or geographic mobility, but not all population movements are migrations. In general, migration is understood to involve population movement across a territorial boundary as, for example, when moving from one county, state, or country to another.

Emigration refers to the out-migration or departure of people from an area, whereas **immigration** refers to the in-migration or arrival of people in a new location. As we learned in Chapter 1, migration is a form of relocation diffusion.

Net migration is the difference between immigration into and emigration from an area in a given period of time, such as a year. When the number of people moving out of an area exceeds the number moving in over the same time period, then net migration is negative. Population growth or decline depends not only on net migration but also on natural increase (births minus deaths). We can use the **demographic equation**, expressed as natural increase plus net migration in a specified period of time, to calculate population change in an area. The demographic equation reminds us that population and migration are closely connected.

Migration Principles

Migrations can involve small or large numbers of people, and can take place over short or long distances or periods of time. Migration is not solely a "one-way" movement of a migrant from an origin to a destination; it encompasses pendulum-like, "two-way" movements as well. For example, *circular migration* occurs when the same individuals make repeated or periodic moves between an origin and one or more destinations. "Snowbirds"—retirees who move from northern locations in the United States to warmer destinations in the South where they spend the winter—are circular migrants.

Ravenstein's principles Most migrations share several characteristics, which were called the *laws of migration* when first proposed in 1885 by the British demographer E. G. Ravenstein. Today, we tend to think of these as principles built around the following six points:

1. Most migrations cover short distances and do not cross international boundaries.
2. Migration involves two opposite processes: dispersion (the departure of migrants from a place of origin) and absorption (the arrival of migrants in a place of destination).
3. Migration flows produce counterflows.
4. Urban areas are common destinations of long-distance migrants.
5. Urban residents tend to be less likely to migrate than rural residents.
6. Women migrate more than men within their country of birth, whereas men more frequently migrate beyond their country of birth.

Ravenstein was one of the first researchers to draw attention to gender differences in migration. Recent trends, however, show that women increasingly participate in international migration and do so as frequently as men. When speaking of counterflows, Ravenstein explained that a flow of migrants into a city will often produce a counterflow of city residents to suburbs. Migrations can also generate counterflows back into the area of origin. Counterflows can include the movement of people, knowl-

edge, or resources. For example, the spread of information about a destination back to family members at the origin is considered a counterflow.

Ravenstein also observed that as the distance traveled during a move increases, the number of migrants decreases. Thus, he highlighted the role of distance decay in migration flows and noted that all migrations, through the processes of absorption and dispersion, involve spatial interaction. Still, an important question remains unanswered: What specific factors influence people's decision to move? We explore these factors more fully in the following section.

Push and pull factors The decision to migrate is a complex one. We call migration a highly selective process because not everyone migrates. People must consider many things, such as the opportunities a new place presents, the challenges of living and working away from one's home community, the cost of the move, as well as how and when the move will occur. Often, social networks—systems of personal ties and communication—play an important role in migration. More specifically, all migrants confront a combination of **push factors** and **pull factors**.

The social scientist Everett Lee revisited Ravenstein's work in order to develop a theory of migration. An important part of Lee's theory centered on migration as a decision-making process that is compelled by the personal perception of many different variables (**Figure 3.12**).

> **push factors**
> Unfavorable conditions or attributes of a place that encourage migration.
>
> **pull factors**
> Favorable conditions or attributes of a place that attract migrants.

Internal Migration

Internal migration occurs when people move within a country, from one county, state, or region to another. Ravenstein's principles remind us that most migrations are internal largely because distance acts as a barrier to migration. There are an estimated 740 million internal migrants worldwide. The study of internal migration has shed light on the causes of migration and shows that internal migration can be classified into two broad categories: migration from rural locations, and migration from urban locations.

Drivers of internal migration In the past, internal migration was largely understood as a response to a

Migration theory • Figure 3.12

Everett Lee identified four categories of factors that affect the decision to migrate. Someone considering migrating from London to Dallas, for example, would weigh positive (+), negative (−), or neutral (0) factors associated with the origin and destination. She or he would also consider intervening obstacles and personal factors. (*Source:* Adapted from Lee, 1966.)

1. Area of origin
+ Close to friends and family
+ Cultural amenities
+ Public transportation
0 Fewer sunny days
− High cost of living

2. Area of destination
+ Lower cost of living
+ Job prospect
0 More sunny days
0 English-speaking
− Hot summers
− Would need a car

© nicholas belton/iStockphoto.

3. Intervening obstacles
• Understanding immigration requirements
• Obtaining a visa
• Moving expenses

4. Personal factors
• Always wanted to live in the U.S.
• Will be far from family
• Will have to make new friends
• Hard to find good fish and chips

Think Critically

1. How can this model accomodate household or community-level factors?
2. What influence might a previous migration experience have on the decision to migrate?

particular problem such as a drought. Today, however, migration experts see internal migration as part of a systematic strategy to sustain or improve one's livelihood. For example, the migration of one or more family members can be part of a household strategy to alleviate poverty or avoid situations of food scarcity.

As we saw in our discussion of Lee's migration theory, diverse push and pull factors propel and inhibit migration. Studies of internal migration reveal that three major factors greatly influence the migration decision. These factors are: age, employment concerns, and natural or environmental amenities.

Migration experts agree that one's age has a strong bearing on both the decision to migrate and the likelihood of doing so. Migration rates among young children who are not yet teenagers are very high, reflecting the fact that their migration is tied to the movement of their parents. In contrast, families with teenagers tend to have low migration rates. Young adults aged 20–34 tend to have the highest migration rates, with these rates falling steadily as they age. Often, a small increase in migration takes place at retirement age.

Job opportunities constitute some of the most important drivers of internal migration and are even more salient when a long-distance move is involved. Job opportunities include wage differentials, and specifically the prospect of earning higher wages or gaining year-round work in a particular destination. Moving to take a job, or to take advantage of the perceived potential for finding a job because of job growth, also propels internal migration.

Natural or environmental amenities are the desirable characteristics of places. Even though the perception of what a natural amenity is varies from person to person, studies of the characteristics of favored environments point to the importance of moderate temperatures year-round, abundant winter sunshine, varied physical landscapes, proximity to water, and low summer humidity. Not all migrants move with amenities in mind, however. As a general rule, amenity migrants are more affluent and seek to live a specific kind of lifestyle.

Rural out-migration
Rural out-migration involves either rural–rural migration or rural–urban migration. In developing regions of the world, rural–rural migration constitutes one of the most persistent forms of internal migration. Unfortunately, however, we know less about the volume and flow of rural–rural migrants than any other kind of internal migration. This dearth of information stems from the fact that movement from one rural area to another is often not recorded or tracked in government censuses.

Rural–rural migration has long had a seasonal dimension to it. Rural communities and individuals move to find employment in seasonal jobs associated with forestry, fishing, or agriculture. High rural population densities, land scarcity, or land degradation may also prompt rural–rural migration.

In India, rural–rural migration remains one of the predominant forms of migration, though it has been declining in recent years. The composition of these migration streams varies significantly by gender, with men moving primarily to seek employment and women moving to join their spouses. For women, these rural–rural flows are described as "marriage migration," and occur because of the longstanding practice of marrying someone from another village. More than 75% of women who migrate between rural locations in India identify marriage as the reason for their move.

Occasionally rural–rural migration rivals rural–urban migration. Data from Nepal show that nearly 70% of the country's internal migrants move between rural locations whereas just over 25% move from rural to urban locations. More specifically, the predominant rural–rural migration flows in Nepal carry people from hill areas to the more agriculturally productive valleys.

Historically, rural–urban migration has contributed greatly to the growth of cities. Within some countries, rural–urban migration has strongly transformed the livelihoods and residential patterns of certain native peoples. In New Zealand, most Maori now live in cities rather than on their native lands (**Figure 3.13**).

On a global scale, the movement of people from the countryside into cities was a defining aspect of the 20th century, occurring most rapidly between 1950 and 1975. When we look more closely, however, we see that in spite of this broad trend, rural–urban migration has varied from one country and region to another. These variations can partly be explained by remembering the regional differences in the experience of the demographic transition. In the United States, for example, rural–urban migration became more prevalent as the Western frontier closed in the late 19th century and remained a major force for urban growth in the United States until the 1970s.

China's experience with rural–urban migration has been even more recent. In what has been called "the largest [migration] in human history" (Chan, forthcoming), 440 million Chinese are estimated to have moved from rural to urban destinations in the period from 1979 to 2010. For many years, rigid government policies restricted internal migration in China. These policies created the *hukou system*, a means for registering all Chinese citizens based on whether their household was located in a rural or urban area. This system affected migration because it prohibited people from changing their classification. Although a rural resident could move to another rural location, she or he could not move to an urban location. Since the 1980s, a series of reforms have altered the hukou system, and enabled a massive reshuffling of China's population.

China's effort to control rural–urban migration is not unusual. At the government level, rural–urban migration has long been perceived as a process that exacerbates other urban problems. Most countries have policies that prevent or seek to curb rural–urban migration. Such policies have not been very successful. Even in China, for example, the registrations of approximately 150 million people do not reflect where they actually live. The term "floating

Rural out-migration • Figure 3.13

The departure of rural residents for other rural or urban destinations has long been associated with employment prospects.

a. An important agricultural area known for its flat land, Nepal's Terai region has been a major destination of migrants moving from other rural areas, especially from the mountains were farming is less lucrative.

© Bruno Morandi/Hemis/Corbis

b. Sporting their iconic Bowler hats, these indigenous Aymara women sell goods on the streets of La Paz. The Aymara, once predominantly rural, now increasingly live in Bolivia's cities.

© James Brunker/Alamy

population" refers to these people. Experts now recognize that rural–urban migration is unavoidable, but not solely negative since many people do raise their income and gain access to better services such as health care.

Urban out-migration There are two types of urban out-migration: urban–urban migration and urban–rural migration. Urban–urban migration takes one of three general forms: movement from one city to another city, movement from a city into a nearby suburb, or movement from one suburb to another. As a region gains more cities and urban residents, urban–urban migration tends to become more frequent. Thus, urban–urban migration is more common among developed countries and in developing countries with high levels of urbanization.

Migration between cities has been a more important component of internal migration in the United States and Western Europe since the 1950s and 1960s, and in Latin America since the 1980s. Today, urban–urban migration is the most prevalent form of internal migration in Latin America. For example, nearly 75% of the internal migrants in Brazil have moved between urban locations. Historically, the largest cities in the region such as Mexico City or São Paulo have been favored destinations, however, migration to mid-sized cities is increasingly common.

In developed countries, some of the most frequently cited reasons for moving from city to suburb or suburb to suburb have more to do with the desire to have a better house, neighborhood, or school system than with the search for a job. In developing countries, however, there are often two streams of urban–urban migrants. One stream consists of lower class laborers who do move in search of work, and the other stream consists of members of the middle and upper classes who move for lifestyle reasons.

Urban–rural migration involves moving from metropolitan to nonmetropolitan destinations such as small towns or rural locations. When people migrate from urban to rural destinations they contribute to **counterurbanization**, the deconcentration of population in an area. The United States has experienced two episodes of counterurbanization: in the late 1970s and early 1990s. In each of these periods nonmetropolitan areas experienced net migration, reversing the historically dominant pattern of rural–urban migration. Amenity migrants, especially retirees and affluent urban professionals, fuel much of this migration. Popular destinations include the Rocky Mountain West, the Sierra Nevada mountains in California and Nevada, northern New England, and the upper Great Lakes.

Contrary to popular opinion, counterurbanization in conjunction with urban–rural migration has also been underway in West and Southern Africa since the 1970s. In Africa and other parts of the developing world, however, urban–rural migration resembles circular migration. In many instances, the people who become urban–rural migrants are those who previously were rural–urban migrants and are returning home. Such migrants may leave the city because they cannot obtain a job or afford to live there, as happened during the financial crisis that affected Southeast Asia in the late 1990s. It is important to point out however, that not all urban–rural migrants return to the place they originally left. They may choose to settle in another small town or rural area instead. **Figure 3.14** illustrates both types of urban out-migration.

International Migration

International migration occurs when people cross international boundaries and take up residence in another country. Despite the fact that international migration attracts a great deal of media attention, most people in the world will never move away from the country in which they were born. Today, there are roughly 214 million international migrants, who represent just 3% of the global population. In contrast, India alone has more than 300 million internal migrants. As this example shows, internal migration affects many more people than international migration. One reason for this difference is that international migration introduces additional complexities, including citizenship status, the need for a passport and/or visa, and other costs. International migration is also more stringently regulated today than ever before.

Migration occurs on a global scale when migrants cross an ocean. This type of international migration is a relatively recent phenomenon that has grown in conjunction with European colonization and globalization. The trans-Atlantic slave trade raised global migration to a new level in terms of the sheer numbers of people involved. Beginning in the 1500s and continuing for more than three centuries, some 12 million Africans were forcibly relocated to the Americas. In the 19th and early 20th centuries, Europe experienced the greatest outpouring of individuals ever, when—as the result of political strife, famine, and other factors—approximately 20 million Europeans crossed the Atlantic Ocean between 1880 and 1914.

At the global scale a lot of attention has focused on the migration of people from developing countries to developed countries. This is an important dimension of international migration and about 35% of all international migrants move to developed countries. However, migration also occurs via another stream that is almost as large and is just as important. This stream involves migration *between* developing countries and accounts for the movement of 34% of international migrants. Adding these percentages reveals that 69% of the 214 million international migrants in the world originated in developing countries, whereas 31% of international migrants originated in developed countries.

In developed countries, the flow of city dwellers to suburbs and rural destinations tends to involve lifestyle preferences.

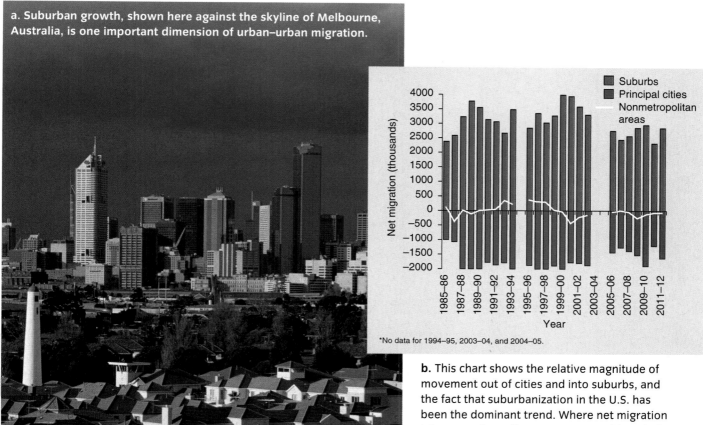

a. Suburban growth, shown here against the skyline of Melbourne, Australia, is one important dimension of urban–urban migration.

*No data for 1994–95, 2003–04, and 2004–05.

b. This chart shows the relative magnitude of movement out of cities and into suburbs, and the fact that suburbanization in the U.S. has been the dominant trend. Where net migration into nonmetropolitan areas was positive, during the early 1990s, counterurbanization was underway. (*Source:* Data from U.S. Census Bureau, 2012.)

Christopher Groenhout/Lonely Planet Images/Getty Images

Because 82% of the world population lives in developing countries, we can see that international migrants from developing countries are actually underrepresented. In contrast, developed countries are home to 18% of the global population, but migrants from developed countries account for 31% of all international migrants.

If we take a regional perspective we find that Asia, Africa, Latin America, and most Pacific Islands are sources of international migrants. Because more migrants leave these regions than enter them, they are said to have *net emigration*. Conversely, Northern America, Europe, Australia, and New Zealand are regions of *net immigration*. That is, more people

Net migration and migrant characteristics • Figure 3.15

Net migration is the difference between in-migrants and out-migrants. These figures help visualize the impact of migration on different countries, and the composition of migrant streams by gender.

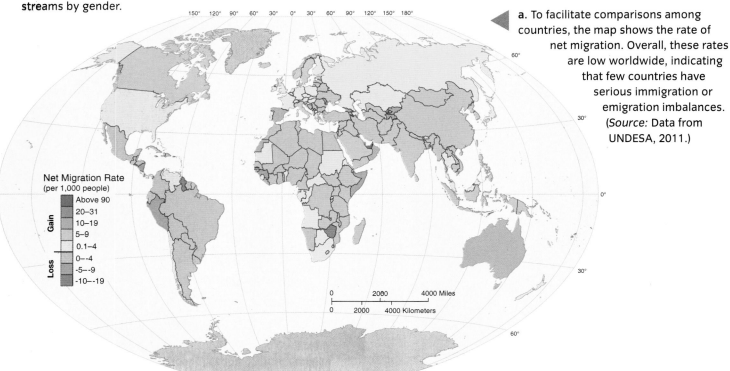

Net Migration Rate
(per 1,000 people)

Gain
- Above 90
- 20–31
- 10–19
- 5–9
- 0.1–4

Loss
- 0–-4
- -5–-9
- -10–-19

a. To facilitate comparisons among countries, the map shows the rate of net migration. Overall, these rates are low worldwide, indicating that few countries have serious immigration or emigration imbalances. (*Source:* Data from UNDESA, 2011.)

b. Expressing net migration as a count gives a better sense of the numbers of migrants involved. This table shows that Canada has a higher rate of net migration than the U.S., but the number of people Canada gains via migration is about one-fourth that of the U.S. (*Source:* Data from UNDESA, 2011.)

Country	United States	Canada	Qatar	India	Mexico	Samoa
Net migration rate	3	7	133	-1	-3	-17
Net number of migrants	4,955,000	1,098,000	857,000	-3,000,000	-1,805,000	-16,000

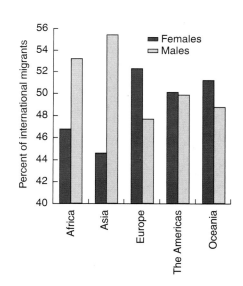

c. The percentage of women who are international migrants is increasing, but still highly variable. In the Americas, about half of all international migrants are females. In Asia women constitute just 44% of international migrants, but fewer than 25% of migrants to Qatar, the United Arab Emirates, and Saudi Arabia are women. (*Source:* Data from UNDESA, 2011.)

are admitted to these places than depart from them in a year (**Figure 3.15**).

We can get a sense of flows of people worldwide by identifying major international migration corridors (**Figure 3.16**). **Migration corridors** are the routes migrants take, show migrant sources and destinations, and can be quite durable over time. When a migration corridor develops between countries that share a border, it is likely that migrants will use some form of surface transportation (road, train, or ship) instead of air travel.

One important international migration corridor exists between the U.S. and Mexico/Latin America. Another important migration corridor has developed between Turkey and Germany, especially since the 1970s. These migrants came largely as *guest workers*, receiving temporary permits to live and work in Germany. Once their employment ended, however, many guest workers remained in Germany and subsequent *chain migrations* brought family and other members from their community or town to join them.

Migration via the Afghanistan–Iran corridor dates to the late 1800s but has regained prominence since the Soviet invasion of Afghanistan in 1979. In the following decade nearly 3 million Afghans fled to Iran, making Iran host of one of the largest **refugee** populations in the world and making Afghans the largest refugee population. Iranian government policy permitted **asylum** initially, but since the early 2000s has instead promoted repatriation—return to Afghanistan—and has

> **refugee** One who flees to another country out of concern for personal safety or to avoid persecution.
>
> **asylum** Protection from persecution granted by one country to a refugee from another country.
>
> **internally displaced persons** People forcibly driven from their homes into a different part of their country.

made it more difficult for Afghans to access services such as opening bank accounts. Refugee movements tend to be *intraregional*, or within a region. For example, the Syrian civil war has triggered the exodus of large refugee populations into neighboring Turkey, Lebanon, and Jordan since 2011.

In addition to creating refugees, the War in Iraq resulted in more than 1 million **internally displaced persons**. Recurring conflict in Colombia among different militias that make money through the drug trade or kidnappings has internally displaced more than 3 million Colombians, more than any other country. Refugees and internally displaced persons are caused by environmental degradation, droughts or other events that affect the food supply, and conflict. Armed conflict continues to be a major source of refugee movements, but discriminatory practices targeted at minority groups can also play a role.

International migration corridors • Figure 3.16

This map shows generalized migration flows between countries, not the exact routes of travel. About 15% of all international migrants in 2010 moved via these 10 corridors. (*Source:* Data from UNDESA, 2012.)

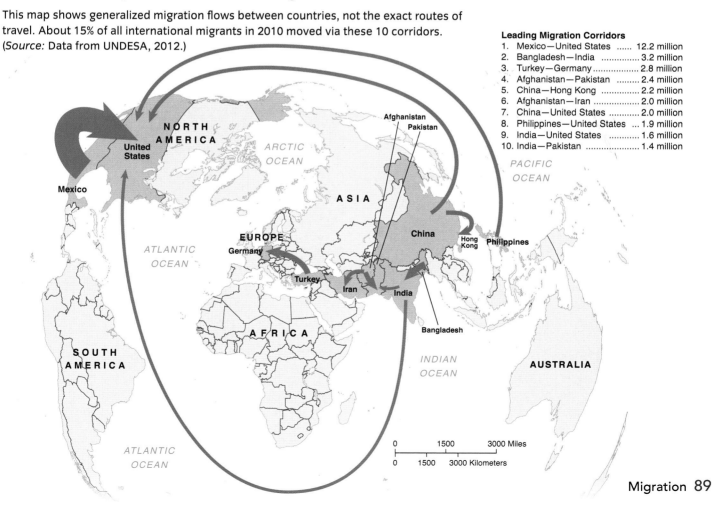

Leading Migration Corridors
1. Mexico—United States ...... 12.2 million
2. Bangladesh—India .... 3.2 million
3. Turkey—Germany .... 2.8 million
4. Afghanistan—Pakistan .... 2.4 million
5. China—Hong Kong .... 2.2 million
6. Afghanistan—Iran .... 2.0 million
7. China—United States .... 2.0 million
8. Philippines—United States ... 1.9 million
9. India—United States .... 1.6 million
10. India—Pakistan .... 1.4 million

WHAT A GEOGRAPHER SEES

Economic and Sociocultural Transnationalism

In Chapter 2 we learned that economic transnationalism or multi-nationalism involves the establishment of branch offices of a corporation in other countries. With respect to migration, however, economic transnationalism focuses on the monetary connections between an immigrant and her or his home country.

When immigrants create political, social, or family-based ties that are rooted in the values and practices of their home country and community, they forge a kind of sociocultural transnationalism. Geographers can detect different kinds of transnationalism by tracking remittances and analyzing changes in the cultural landscape.

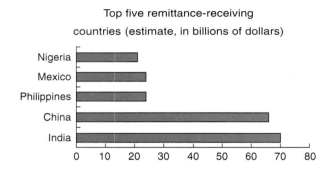

Top five remittance-receiving countries (estimate, in billions of dollars)

a. Leading remittance-receiving countries

In 2010, migrants sent approximately $440 billion in remittances. The amounts that are remitted change frequently and decline in periods of economic recession. The United States and Russia are, respectively, the leading remittance-sending countries, but India and China are the leading remittance recipients. (*Source:* Data from Ratha, Mohapatra and Silwal, 2011.)

b. Remittance inflows as a percentage of GDP

The gross domestic product expresses the value of goods and services produced in a country. Remittances are proportionally more important to the economies of developing countries. In Tajikistan, remittances are equivalent to nearly half the country's GDP. (*Source:* Data from World Bank, 2011.)

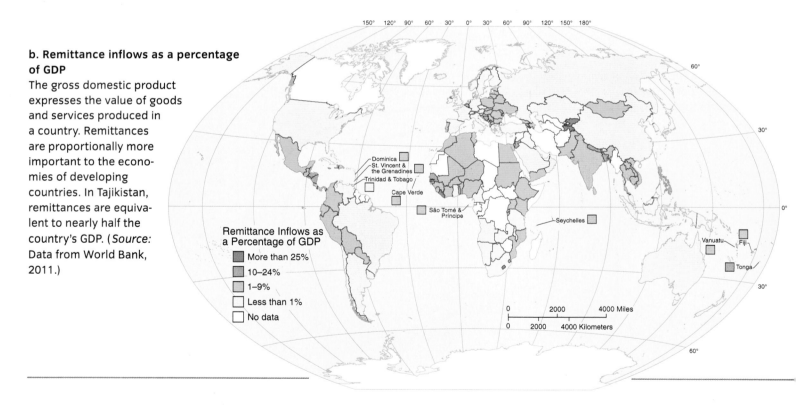

Remittance Inflows as a Percentage of GDP
- More than 25%
- 10–24%
- 1–9%
- Less than 1%
- No data

Beginning in the 1990s, a number of scholars began questioning the impact of globalization on international migration. What these scholars found is that **transnationalism** is often a key aspect of an immigrant's identity. Globalization and the greater connectivity among

> **transnationalism**
> In migration studies, the process by which immigrants develop and cultivate ties to more than one country.

places facilitate the development of transnationalism.

Transnationalism is significant because it demonstrates that migration involves a system of circulation. Ravenstein hinted at this when he noted that migrations trigger

c. Brazilian transnational landscapes in the United States
Higher wages constitute a powerful pull factor. A Brazilian bakery in Marietta, Georgia.

Photo by Alan P. Marcus. From Marcus, Alan P. 2009. (Re)Creating Places and Spaces in Two Countries: Brazilian Transnational Migration Processes. *Journal of Cultural Geography* (26) 2: 173-198.

Photo by geographer, Alan P. Marcus (taken during fieldwork June, 2007). From Marcus, Alan P. 2009. (Re)Creating Places and Spaces in Two Countries: Brazilian Transnational Migration Processes. *Journal of Cultural Geography* (26) 2: 173-198.

d. Transnational landscapes in Brazil
In the city of Piracanjuba, one of the important source communities for Brazilians in Marietta, the landscape suggests that ideas about architecture may have been influenced by Brazilians who have lived in Georgia or other parts of the U.S. South.

Think Critically

1. What are some other ways immigrants might express transnationalism?
2. Can you think of any circumstances in which a migration does not produce a counterflow?

counterflows. Perhaps the strongest evidence of these counterflows can be seen in **remittances**, the financial and non-financial resources sent by immigrants to their home countries. In other cases, however, transnationalism has influenced the cultural landscape (see *What a Geographer Sees*).

Immigration to the United States

The United States is and has been a major destination country for migrants. Twenty percent of all international migrants reside in the U.S. Like numerous other countries, the United States limits the number of immigrants that it admits. Prior to 1965, the United States set quotas for individual countries that demonstrated a preference for European immigrants. These country-specific quotas were abolished by the Immigration and Nationality Act Amendments of 1965. Since that time the United States has used category-based ceilings or limits. The four main categories used to admit immigrants are: family reunification, employment-based preferences (to attract immigrants with appropriate skills), protection for refugees, and diversity of immigrants by origin. The ceiling for family reunification is 480,000 immigrants and the ceiling for employment preference is 140,000, but because of the complexity of U.S. immigration law, including exceptions and numerical carry-overs among categories, immigrant numbers rarely match these values exactly. Nevertheless, the family reunification category is the largest and provides an important means for legal immigration into the country. Of the more than 1 million immigrants the U.S. admitted in 2011, two-thirds entered on the basis of family relations, for example, as an immediate relative, spouse, or child of a legal immigrant already in the country.

In the United States **authorized immigrants** are legal permanent residents, also called green-card holders. U.S. statistics count new arrivals and status adjusters (those already in the country) as immigrants. For example, an employer can sponsor someone who arrives on

Immigration to the United States • Figure 3.17

This chart shows the number of authorized immigrants admitted to the U.S. by region of origin since 1820. The sharp drop in immigration reflects the impact of the Depression and two world wars. The accompanying pie charts show changes in the leading countries sending immigrants to the U.S. and the diversification of immigrant origins over time. (*Source:* Data from Department of Homeland Security, 2011.)

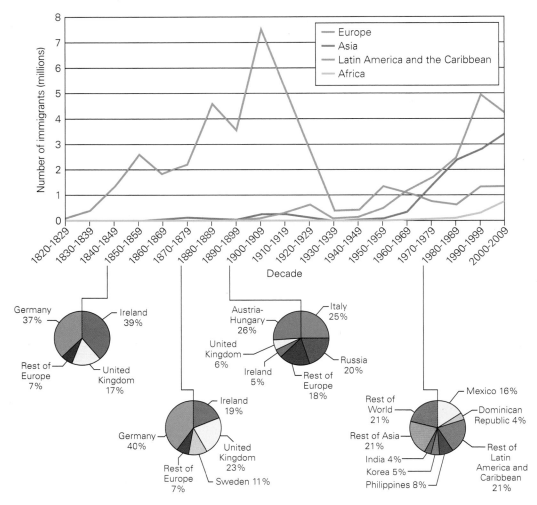

a temporary work visa for legal permanent residence. If approved, this person is counted as a status adjuster. In contrast, **unauthorized immigrants**, also called undocumented or illegal immigrants, are people who come to the United States on a temporary visa but remain in the country after their visa expires, or they cross the border without being detected. Most immigrants in the U.S. are here legally. They come mainly from Asia (41%) and Latin America (38%). This pattern differs from the historical one—from about 1750 to 1950—in which Europeans dominated the flow of immigrants to the U.S. (**Figure 3.17**).

CONCEPT CHECK

1. **How** do Ravenstein's and Lee's contributions to the study of migration differ?

2. **What** factors drive internal migration?

3. **Why** is transnationalism associated with migration, and in what ways might transnationalism be expressed?

4. **What** are the main categories on which U.S. immigration policy is based?

Summary

1 Population Fundamentals 66

- **Population geography** is the study of the spatial variations of human populations. People are unevenly distributed on the world's landmasses and tend to be concentrated in coastal lowlands.

- Two important measures of population density are **arithmetic density**, depicted here, and **physiological density**, which takes the amount of **arable land** into consideration.

Population densities • Figure 3.2

© KIM KYUNG-HOON/Reuters/Corbis

- A variety of cultural, economic, and political factors influence the patterns of birth and death around the world. The **crude birth rate (CBR)** provides one measure used to track birth-related trends in populations. Another measure with more predictive power is the **total fertility rate (TFR)**.

Globally, TFRs have fallen dramatically, and in many countries they are at or below **replacement level**.

- The **crude death rate (CDR)** measures the mortality within a population. Information about the quality of life of a population can be gleaned from its **life expectancy** and **infant mortality rate**.

2 Population Composition and Change 73

- **Population pyramids**, like this one, help show the age and gender makeup of a particular population. Population pyramids can be grouped into one of three categories: rapid population growth, slow population growth, and population decline.

Population pyramids • Figure 3.6

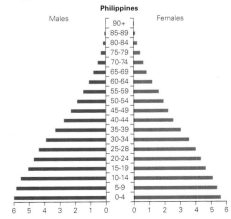

- Two important dimensions of the composition of a population include the **age-dependency ratio** and the **sex ratio**.

- Population geographers use the **rate of natural increase (RNI)** to indicate the rate at which a population grows or declines in a year. RNIs can also be used to calculate the **population doubling time** for a particular population.

- The relationship between the birth rate, death rate, and RNI forms an essential part of the **demographic transition model.** Changing patterns of infectious and chronic diseases often parallel the demographic transition. These trends are expressed in the **epidemiological transition**.

3 Population–Environment Interactions 78

- Population geography includes the study of population–environment interactions, or **population ecology**. **Neo-Malthusians** emphasize the concept of a **carrying capacity** for Earth. **Cornucopian theory** considers population growth a stimulus for technological innovations.

- In contrast to both Neo-Malthusians and cornucopians, social critics find fault with current systems of food supply and distribution. Poverty, lack of arable land, and repressive policies contribute to **food insecurity**. Chronic food insecurity has led to health problems such as stunted growth in North Korea, shown on the map.

Food insecurity • Figure 3.11

- **Epidemiological transitions** refer to the changes that occur in the patterns of disease as countries industrialize and urbanize. From the **first to the second** transition, the prevalence of epidemics declines as noncommunicable diseases increase. Emergent and resurgent infectious diseases characterize the third transition.

4 Migration 81

- **Migration** is one kind of spatial mobility. Ravenstein's principles of migration distinguished between internal and international migration, flows and counterflows, urban and rural migrants, and gender differences within migration streams.

- Deciding to move is a complicated process that usually involves weighing **push** and **pull factors**. Everett Lee's theory of migration provides a conceptual framework for understanding the factors affecting the decision to migrate.

- Most migration is internal migration. Three important drivers of internal migration are age, job opportunities, and natural amenities.

- There are two broad categories of internal migration: rural out-migration and urban out-migration. Suburban growth (see photo) is associated with urban–urban migration whereas **counterurbanization** is associated with the migration of people from metropolitan to nonmetropolitan destinations.

Urban out-migration
• Figure 3.14a

Christopher Groenhout/Lonely Planet Images/Getty Images

- Globalization has increased the potential for **international migration**, but the percentage of people who move internationally remains very small. About one-third of international migrants move from developing to developed countries, and another one-third move between developing countries.

- Tracking the origins and destinations of international migrants helps identify **migration corridors**. Migrations compelled by civil strife can lead to large numbers of **asylum** seekers, **refugees**, or **internally displaced persons**.

- The sources of immigrants to the U.S. have changed significantly over time. The country once relied on quotas that gave preference to immigrants from European countries. Today, Asian and Latin American places supply the majority of U.S. immigrants. Like most countries, the U.S. distinguishes between authorized and unauthorized immigrants.

Key Terms

- age-dependency ratio 75
- arable land 67
- arithmetic density 67
- asylum 89
- authorized immigrant 92
- carrying capacity 79
- cornucopian theory 79
- counterurbanization 86
- crude birth rate (CBR) 67
- crude death rate (CDR) 71
- demographic equation 81
- demographic transition model 77
- emigration 81
- epidemiological transition 80

- food insecurity 79
- immigration 81
- infant mortality rate 72
- internally displaced persons 89
- internal migration 82
- international migration 86
- life expectancy 72
- migration 81
- migration corridor 88
- neo-Malthusian 79
- net migration 81
- physiological density 67
- population doubling time 76
- population ecology 78

- population geography 66
- population pyramid 73
- pull factors 82
- push factors 82
- rate of natural increase (RNI) 76
- refugee 89
- remittance 91
- replacement level 67
- sex ratio 75
- total fertility rate (TFR) 67
- transnationalism 90
- unauthorized immigrant 93

Critical and Creative Thinking Questions

1. Do you think it would be feasible to establish limits on the population size or density of the world's largest cities? Why or why not?

2. Is there a relationship between the age structure of a population and crime rates? Explain your answer.

3. What would a population pyramid for a cemetery look like? Speculate on the shape of the population pyramid for Arlington National Cemetery in Virginia, where military personnel and their families are buried, and explain your reasoning.

4. What evidence does this photo provide to challenge a conventional view of age dependents?

5. Discuss how Malthusian views might affect public policy, including welfare programs.

6. If you or your family has moved, reflect on the experience and identify the specific push, pull, and personal factors as well as any intervening obstacles that came into play. If you haven't moved, find a friend who has and explore the factors that influenced his or her move.

7. Reflect on the following questions: Is the right of reproduction a basic human right? If so, do anti-natalist policies violate it?

8. What relationships might exist between education, fertility, and food security? Explain your reasoning.

David McLain/Aurora Photos, Inc.

What is happening in this picture?

A giant male figure has been carved into a chalk ridge near Cerne Abbas, England. The giant is more than 300 years old, and, though its origins are obscure, it is a recognized historic site. Conventional lore considers it an emblem of fertility.

Martin Gray/NG Image Collection

Think Critically

1. Many societies have fertility rituals. How are they similar to and different from present-day pro-natalist population control policies?
2. Can you identify some ways in which depictions of fertility vary by cultural group?
3. Do media depictions of fertility give equivalent representation to men and women?

Self-Test

(Check your answers in Appendix B.)

1. What is a population cartogram?

    a. a map that shows population density

    b. a map that shows the size of a country in proportion to its population

    c. a pie chart showing the world's population by country

    d. a graph showing population growth or decline over time

2. To calculate the physiological density of your state, you would _____.

    a. divide the area of arable land in the state by the area of arable land in the country

    b. divide the state's farming population by the area of land they own

    c. divide the area of arable land in the state by the total land area of the state

    d. divide the state's population by the area of arable land in the state

3. China's one-child policy_____.

    a. was pro-natalist

    b. was most strictly enforced in rural areas

    c. contributed to the country's steep fertility decline

    d. promoted marriage at a younger age

4. Give two examples of indirect factors that may affect fertility.

    _____

    _____

5. _____ and _____ are useful indicators of the quality of life in a population.

    a. Infant mortality rate; life expectancy

    b. Total fertility rate; life expectancy

    c. Infant mortality rate; crude death rate

    d. Total fertility rate; crude death rate

6. A high sex ratio in a population means that _____.

    a. men significantly outnumber women

    b. women significantly outnumber men

    c. there will be a lot of age-dependents

    d. the rate of natural increase will also be high

7. The population pyramid shown here _____.

   a. depicts a low sex ratio

   b. indicates that rapid population growth in the future is likely

   c. depicts a low age-dependency ratio

   d. all of the above

United Arab Emirates

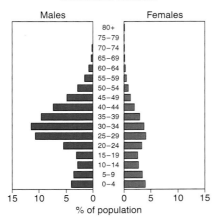

8. Which statement about the rate of natural increase (RNI) is false?

   a. The RNI can be used to calculate population doubling time.

   b. The RNI expresses the difference between births and deaths in a population.

   c. The RNI can be negative or zero.

   d. The RNI for a country today is usually 5% or higher.

9. A key component of Malthus's thought was that _____.

   a. population growth would stimulate technological innovations

   b. people would voluntarily control and lower fertility

   c. population growth increased geometrically relative to the food supply

   d. the world could not support more than 10 billion people

10. Using what you have learned about the demographic transition model, draw the lines for the birth rate and death rate on this diagram.

11. Fiji, a country located in the South Pacific Ocean to the east of Australia, has a stage 2 profile. Explain what this means according to the demographic transition model.

12. What stage of the epidemiological transition is associated with resurgent infectious diseases?

   a. stage 1   b. stage 2

   c. stage 3   d. stage 4

13. Label the four major components of Lee's conceptual framework for migration theory.

14. Net migration expresses _____.

   a. the difference between in- and out-migrants

   b. the rate of population growth

   c. the ratio of male to female migrants

   d. the value of migrant remittances

15. Which type of migration has historically been most closely linked to the growth of cities?

   a. urban-urban   b. international

   c. rural-urban   d. none of the above

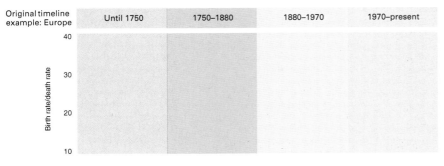

THE PLANNER ✓

Review your Chapter Planner on the chapter opener and check off your completed work.

Geographies of Language

THE LANGUAGE OF SNOWBOARDING

Have you ever heard someone talk about a sport or hobby using words that are totally unfamiliar to you? Here, a snowboarder catches some big air while performing an Indy grab off a half-pipe. *Catching air* means to go airborne, and during the *Indy grab* the snowboarder holds the toe-side edge of the snowboard. A *half-pipe* is the U-shaped track used for aerial tricks. Can you think of specialized words that you use when talking about one of your own interests? If you have noticed that your speech habits change depending on the people you are with or the circumstances you are in, then you already have some familiarity with one important aspect of language—its *situational* quality. Saying that language is situational points out another characteristic of language—its *flexibility*.

Languages change, and the changes can be tracked over time and space. Some language changes happen very quickly, from one generation to the next or even over shorter time spans. Even though you speak the same language as your parents, there are definite differences. If you have had to stop in the middle of a conversation with a parent or grandparent and explain what you mean when you use a certain word, you have experienced the flexibility of language. The meanings of words can vary over time, and how words are used can differ from one place to another.

Language provides a basis for communication, shapes peoples' identities, and reflects their relationship with place. This chapter will introduce you to different types of languages, the impacts of globalization on how languages spread and change, and aspects of dialect geography.

Photographer, Brian Mott, Southern California Collegiate Ski & Snowboard Conference, Inc (www.sccsc.com)

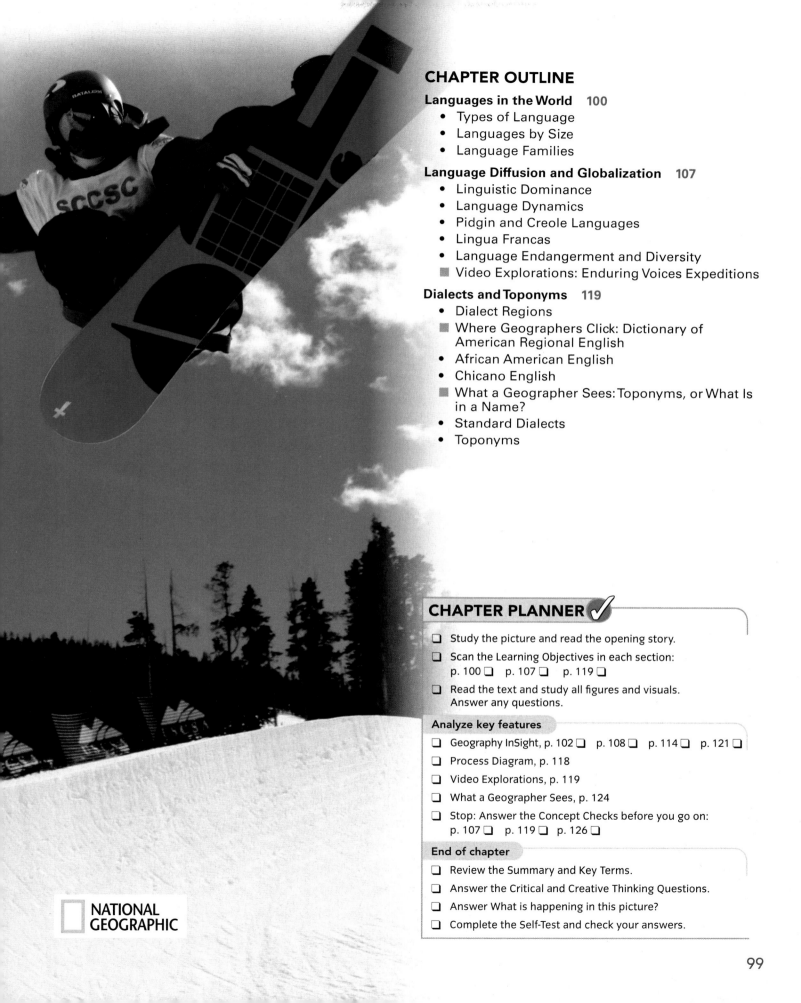

CHAPTER OUTLINE

CHAPTER PLANNER ✓

- ❏ Study the picture and read the opening story.
- ❏ Scan the Learning Objectives in each section:
  p. 100 ❏   p. 107 ❏   p. 119 ❏
- ❏ Read the text and study all figures and visuals. Answer any questions.

Analyze key features

- ❏ Geography InSight, p. 102 ❏   p. 108 ❏   p. 114 ❏   p. 121 ❏
- ❏ Process Diagram, p. 118
- ❏ Video Explorations, p. 119
- ❏ What a Geographer Sees, p. 124
- ❏ Stop: Answer the Concept Checks before you go on:
  p. 107 ❏   p. 119 ❏   p. 126 ❏

End of chapter

- ❏ Review the Summary and Key Terms.
- ❏ Answer the Critical and Creative Thinking Questions.
- ❏ Answer What is happening in this picture?
- ❏ Complete the Self-Test and check your answers.

NATIONAL GEOGRAPHIC

Languages in the World

LEARNING OBJECTIVES

1. **Define** the terms language and dialect.
2. **Distinguish** between different types of languages, including spoken, nonspoken, artificial, and natural.
3. **Identify** the pattern of large and small languages in the world today.
4. **Outline** the distribution of the major language families around the globe.

Globalization calls to mind the interconnectedness of the world, but that interconnectedness depends, in large measure, on our ability to communicate. Although we use language almost continuously throughout the day—in our speech, our thoughts, and even in our dreams—we tend to take it for granted. That is, we sometimes forget how important it is to the overall functioning of society and as a marker of who we are.

Language is a key component of culture. When two or more people speak the same language, communication occurs because the speakers know the symbols and their meanings, and how to put the symbols together to make more complicated meanings. Of course, language does not always facilitate communication; it is sometimes the source of misunderstandings.

> **language** A system of communication based on symbols that have agreed-upon meanings.
>
> **dialect** A particular variety of a language characterized by distinctive vocabulary, grammar, and/or pronunciation.

Deciding what a language is presents some complications as well. **Dialects** are not usually treated as separate languages. In addition, some languages are so similar that they have a high degree of **mutual intelligibility**. For example, people who speak Serbian can also understand Croatian, and vice versa, even though Serbian and Croatian are considered separate languages.

All human languages are capable of expressing all kinds of thought, from simple to complex. But different languages express thought in different ways. Each language has its own particular strategies for communicating, strategies that, in many cases, developed over thousands of years. These strategies include rules of grammar, specialized vocabularies, and distinctive systems of pronunciation. For example, the pronunciation of words in some of the languages of southern Africa

Linguistic differences • Figure 4.1

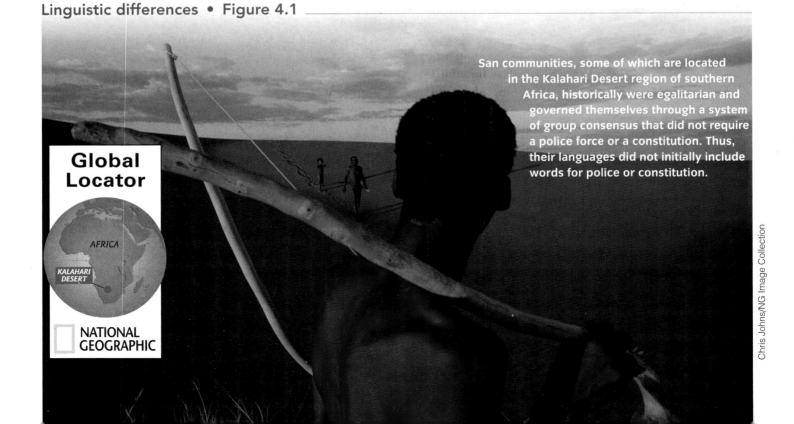

San communities, some of which are located in the Kalahari Desert region of southern Africa, historically were egalitarian and governed themselves through a system of group consensus that did not require a police force or a constitution. Thus, their languages did not initially include words for police or constitution.

Global Locator

AFRICA

KALAHARI DESERT

NATIONAL GEOGRAPHIC

Chris Johns/NG Image Collection

Justin Guariglia/NG Image Collection

arabianEye/Getty Images, Inc.

The language of greetings • Figure 4.2

Body language is highly situational and can vary from one cultural group to another. Greetings are one kind of body language. Businesspeople bow in greeting at a crosswalk in Tokyo's financial district. In Saudi Arabia a traditional greeting between male friends and relatives involves a handshake and a kiss on each cheek.

incorporates the use of click sounds. In the Hausa language, spoken in Nigeria, and in Chinese, the meaning of a word can change depending on the rise or fall in the pitch of one's voice.

Social factors influence language use and development. At one time the Japanese language did not have words for *fork* or *coffee*, but as these items entered their culture, words to express them developed. The Yiddish word *farpotchket* means "to make something worse when you were trying to fix it." There is no word for this idea in English. The absence of words in a language does not imply any inability of that language to express thought (**Figure 4.1**).

Types of Language

Although we tend to think of language as spoken and written systems of communication, certain types of language cannot be spoken, and other languages developed orally and were never written. *Sign languages* are nonspoken languages used to communicate with people whose hearing or speech is impaired. Sign languages are based on body movements, especially hand motions (signs that

stand for words and concepts) instead of sounds. Sign languages differ from country to country—there is no universal sign language. For example, a person who uses American Sign Language will not be able to communicate with someone who uses British Sign Language because they use different signs for the same words.

Sign language is one kind of *body language*—a communication system based on gestures, facial expressions, and other body movements. But sign language is also a true language, a formalized system capable of expressing all types of thought. In contrast, the body language most of us use on a daily basis consists of the gestures used in greetings, in signaling one's emotions, and in specific situations such as asking for the check in a busy restaurant (**Figure 4.2**). Unlike the gestures of sign language, these situational gestures do not make up a fully developed system of communication—they cannot communicate all kinds of thought.

Touch or *tactile language* constitutes another kind of nonspoken language. The most familiar touch language is Braille, which uses raised dots to represent letters, numbers, and other symbols. Some nonspoken languages, such

Specialized languages might use simplified pictures and symbols to express an idea, whereas tactile languages communicate via sense of touch.

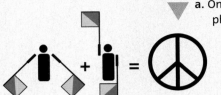

▼ **a.** One specialized language uses a semaphore alphabet consisting of colored flags held in various positions to signal different letters. The peace sign was created from the semaphore letters "n" and "d"—the first letters of the words *nuclear disarmament*. (*Source: National Geographic Magazine*, 2008.)

Steve Raymer/NG Image Collection

▲ **b.** In Malaysia a sign reminds visitors that public displays of affection are not permitted. Another specialized language has emerged to meet the needs of travelers and tourists.

c. A blind person reads a tactile-relief political map that is also in Braille. Geographic education for the visually impaired often uses textural differences to communicate spatial information.

Dominique Faget/AFP/Getty Images, Inc.

as computer programming languages, exist only in a written form. These and other *specialized languages* are designed for specific purposes, not necessarily for everyday communication among people (**Figure 4.3**).

Natural languages are those that have emerged and evolved within living or historic human communities. Languages that are intentionally constructed by people for international communication or fictional purposes are called *artificial languages*. J. R. R. Tolkien invented the Elvish languages featured in *The Lord of the Rings* trilogy. Some artificial languages have been designed for the purpose of creating a *universal language*, a language that could be understood and used by everyone in the world. The most well-known example of an artificial language is Esperanto. Invented by a Polish doctor in the late 19th century, Esperanto has a very simple and regular grammar that is intended to be much easier to learn than the grammar of natural languages. Estimates suggest that about 2 million people in 120 countries speak Esperanto today. Today it is possible to find newspapers, journals, and Bibles published in Esperanto (**Figure 4.4**).

La Esperanto-urbo • Figure 4.4

Since 2006, the German city of Herzberg am Harz has been designated "the Esperanto town." The tourist information office, shown here, greets visitors in German and Esperanto, and Esperanto is taught in schools. Esperanto versions of Facebook and Wikipedia exist, and one can tweet in Esperanto, too.

Courtesy of Zsofia Korody/Esperanto-Centro Herzberg

Languages by Size

It is generally agreed that there are about 6900 different languages in the world today. When we group the languages of the world into categories based on their estimated number of speakers, striking patterns emerge: there are a lot of small languages but just a handful of very large languages (**Figure 4.5**).

From a historical perspective, the emergence of these very large languages is a recent phenomenon that highlights an important change in the linguistic geography of the world. Their expansion has prompted some linguistic geographers to question whether the very small languages can survive, a topic we will return to later.

Language Families

To this point we have seen how languages can be classified by type or size. For geographers and linguists, however, another important system of classification involves the historical relationships among languages. For instance, do all languages derive from one source, or did multiple languages develop independently? This question remains unsettled and highly controversial. Language probably

Languages by size • Figure 4.5

Globalization and demographic change have contributed to changes in the sizes of languages.

a. Languages from very large to very small
More than half of the world's languages have fewer than 10,000 native speakers. There are, however, a few hundred languages (counted as "unknown") for which we lack reliable counts or estimates of the number of people who speak them. (*Source:* Used by permission, © SIL International ®, *Ethnologue, Languages of the World*, 16th ed., 2009.)

Size	Number of speakers	Number of languages	Percent of the world's languages	Percent of global population
Very large	100,000,000 to 999,999,999	9	0.13026	40.79696
Large	1,000,000 to 99,999,999	380	5.50007	53.29407
Medium	10,000 to 999,999	2719	39.35447	5.77057
Small	100 to 9999	3052	44.17427	0.13818
Very small	Fewer than 100	472	6.83167	0.00022
Not classified	Unknown	277	4.00926	—
TOTAL		6909	100	100

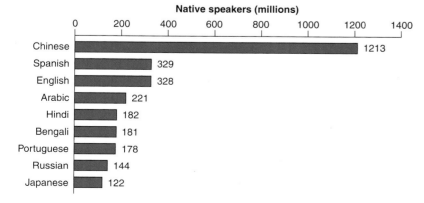

Native speakers (millions)

Chinese	1213
Spanish	329
English	328
Arabic	221
Hindi	182
Bengali	181
Portuguese	178
Russian	144
Japanese	122

b. Estimated number of native speakers
These are the nine very large languages. Hindi and Bengali are languages primarily associated with India. ▶ **How do these very large languages compare and contrast in terms of their global distribution?** (*Source:* Data from Lewis, 2009.)

Comparing language families • Figure 4.6

Language families are diverse: Some contain more than 1000 languages, whereas others may contain just a few. Thus, one way to distinguish "major" language families is to identify those that proportionally have the most languages. (*Source:* Data from Lewis, 2009.)

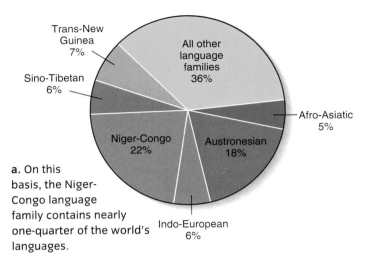

a. On this basis, the Niger-Congo language family contains nearly one-quarter of the world's languages.

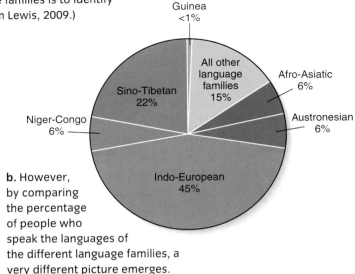

b. However, by comparing the percentage of people who speak the languages of the different language families, a very different picture emerges.

Language family	Example language(s)
Indo-European	English, Hindi, Spanish
Sino-Tibetan	Mandarin Chinese, Burmese
Afro-Asiatic	Arabic, Hebrew
Niger-Congo	Yoruba, Zulu
Austronesian	Tagalog, Bahasa Indonesia
Trans-New Guinea	Tetum

c. This table provides selected examples of languages from each of the major language families. Yoruba is spoken in Nigeria, Zulu in South Africa, Tagalog in the Philippines, and Tetum in East Timor.

existed at least 30,000 years ago or even much earlier, but we do not know its date of birth. Much of what we do know about language development comes from surviving artifacts and written texts, but there are many gaps in this historical record because most early languages were never written down. Despite these complexities, scholars continue to pursue the study of the evolution of languages and the relationships among them. Why? One major reason is that knowledge of language development contributes to our understanding of past societies, contacts among them, and patterns of human migration.

It is clear that most languages share a distant historical and genetic relationship with one or more other languages.

Terms such as **language family** and *branch* express these relationships. The world's languages have been classified into more than 90 different language families, but six are considered major language families (**Figure 4.6**).

> **language family** A collection of languages that share a common but distant ancestor.

Almost half of the world's people speak languages belonging to the Indo-European language family. In fact, of the nine largest languages shown in Figure 4.5b, all but three (Chinese, Arabic, and Japanese) are Indo-European. In later sections we will explore some of the consequences of the growth of these large languages, but we want to turn now to some facets of language distribution.

Because it is impractical to show the distribution of the world's several thousand languages on a single map, geographers instead make and use maps of the more familiar language families. Maps showing the distribution of language families raise questions about where language families originated—their **hearths**—and how they spread. For example, **Figure 4.7** shows that the Austronesian language family covers a vast maritime area from the island of Taiwan all the way to Madagascar. What would explain this kind of distribution?

> **hearth** A place or region where an innovation, idea, belief, or cultural practice begins.

Research suggests that the spread of rice cultivators and seafaring merchants played a role in the spread of Austronesian languages. In Sub-Saharan Africa, the spread of the

Niger-Congo language family occurred as Bantu farmers migrated east toward Lake Victoria about 4000 years ago and subsequently spread south.

Of the language families, the Indo-European language family has the largest number of speakers and the widest geographical distribution (refer again to Figure 4.7). Where did Indo-European languages originate? Scholars who have studied this question are usually associated with either the *Kurgan Hypothesis* or the *Anatolian Hypothesis*. To understand these hypotheses, it helps to know that most scholars agree that all Indo-European languages share a common ancestral language called *proto-Indo-European*.

The Kurgan Hypothesis proposes that the hearth of the Indo-European languages lies north of the Caspian Sea near what is now the border between Russia and Kazakhstan. This was the homeland of the Kurgan nomadic herders. These herders had domesticated the horse and began to expand beyond their hearth around 4000 BCE. Through a series of conquests they are believed to have carried proto-Indo-European to the east

and west where it replaced the local, non-Indo-European languages.

In contrast, the Anatolian Hypothesis places the hearth of the Indo-European language family in present-day Turkey and proposes that proto-Indo-European spread as Anatolian farmers expanded east across Central Asia and west into Europe. These migrations are believed to have started about 7000 BCE. The ability to produce a food surplus and support larger populations enabled these sedentary farming populations to gain numerical dominance over local hunting and gathering populations who spoke other, non-Indo-European languages. This dominance paved the way for the eventual development of the other Indo-European languages. Notice, however, that Turkish is not an Indo-European language. In the 11th century the Seljuk Turks, whose empire stretched from Central Asia, conquered Anatolia and introduced the language that would become the precursor of modern Turkish.

As we have seen, about half of the world's people speak Indo-European languages, and the language

Language families and some hearths • Figure 4.7

This map identifies the hearths of the six language families listed in boldface type in the legend. Two hearths have question marks to call attention to the debate over the origins of the Indo-European language family. The hearth of the Austronesian language family coincides with the small island of Taiwan. (*Source:* NG Maps based on *College Atlas of the World*, 2007.)

NATIONAL
GEOGRAPHIC

Major language families today
- Afro-Asiatic
- Altaic
- Austro-Asiatic
- **Austronesian**
- Dravidian
- **Indo-European**
- Japanese
- Kam-Tai
- **Niger-Congo**
- Nilo-Saharan
- **Sino-Tibetan**
- **Trans-New Guinea**
- Uralic
- Other
- *Language hearth*

Ask Yourself

Some of the patterns on this map relate to events that occurred thousands of years ago, whereas some are just a few centuries old. Identify a pattern on the map that is the result of more recent developments.

Classification of Indo-European languages • Figure 4.8

Within large language families like this one, some languages are more closely related than others. These are grouped into branches that may be further divided into subgroups or individual languages.

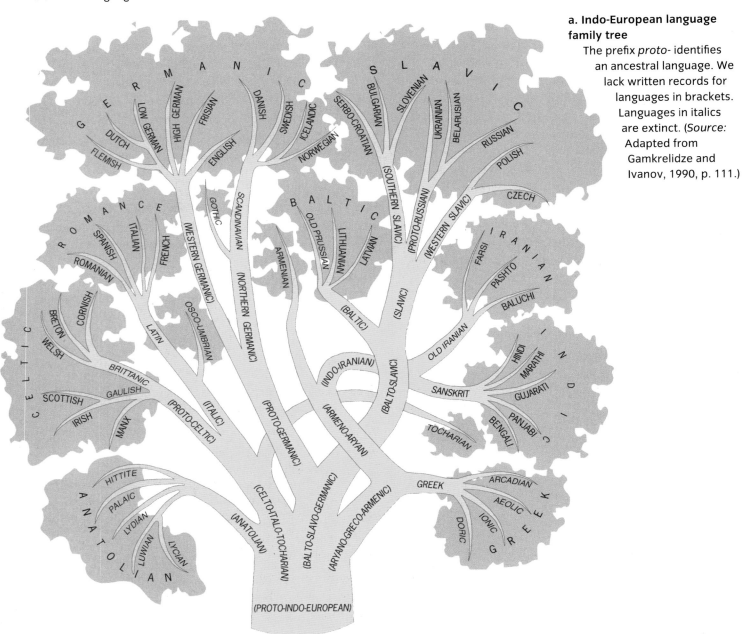

a. Indo-European language family tree

The prefix *proto-* identifies an ancestral language. We lack written records for languages in brackets. Languages in italics are extinct. (*Source:* Adapted from Gamkrelidze and Ivanov, 1990, p. 111.)

b. Language classification

One technique for classifying languages into families compares the sounds and meanings of words. This table demonstrates similarities among several Indo-European languages. The Polish word for *three* sounds like "tshay." Because Hindi is written in the Devanagari alphabet, the words here have been *transliterated* into the Latin alphabet to facilitate comparison.

Language	Term				
English	one	two	three	eye	nose
Spanish	uno	dos	tres	ojo	nariz
German	eins	zwei	drei	auge	nase
Polish	jeden	dwa	trzy	oko	nos
Hindi	eka	doe	tina	amkha	naka

family is divided into multiple branches (**Figure 4.8**). The Italic languages, more popularly referred to as Romance languages, form one branch. All of the Romance languages developed from Latin, an Italic language that became the language of the citizens of Rome in about the 6th century BCE. The subsequent rise and expansion of the Roman Empire played a major role in spreading the Latin language across much of southern and western Europe. Within the Roman Empire two classes of Latin existed: a standardized written form that came to be known as *Classical Latin* and a nonstandardized, spoken form called *Vulgar Latin*, the language of the common person. Lacking standardization, Vulgar Latin varied from place to place within the Roman Empire—that is, numerous dialects of

Vulgar Latin existed. This spatial variation in the spoken forms of Vulgar Latin contributed to the gradual evolution and emergence of the different Romance languages.

CONCEPT CHECK

1. **What** is meant by mutual intelligibility?
2. **Why** is sign language a true language?
3. **What** are the five largest languages in the world today?
4. **Where** might the Indo-European language family have originated, and how might it have spread?

Language Diffusion and Globalization

LEARNING OBJECTIVES

1. **Explain** how political, economic, and religious forces can affect the diffusion of language.
2. **Identify** factors contributing to linguistic dominance.
3. **Distinguish** among pidgin languages, creole languages, and lingua francas.
4. **Relate** the concept of language endangerment to linguistic diversity.

What social and geographic factors contribute to the spread, or diffusion, of languages? In our discussion of language families, we learned that the spread of agriculture may have facilitated the historic spread of languages. If we take a broader perspective, we can see that technology and human mobility can contribute significantly to language diffusion. Historically, ships, railroads, and other forms of transportation opened physical spaces for language diffusion, and today the Internet continues to open new virtual spaces in which language can diffuse.

Political, economic, and religious forces can also shape language diffusion. The rise of the British Empire contributed to the expansion of English. As a result of European colonization and immigration to overseas destinations, there are now more English speakers outside than inside the United Kingdom, more French speakers outside than inside France, more Spanish speakers outside than inside Spain, and more Portuguese speakers outside than inside Portugal (**Figure 4.9** on the next page).

Economic forces influence the diffusion of languages in various ways. For example, in many countries, tourism and foreign business are important sources of revenue. Being able to accommodate international tourists and conduct business in English or another European language not only creates opportunities for expanding a country's economy but also shapes language diffusion. For example, Mongolia's new English-language program seeks to make its citizens bilingual in Mongolian and English in order to attract outsourced jobs (see Chapter 10). Even on an individual level, the perception that fluency in another language will improve one's ability to land a job or earn a higher salary can influence language spread. This remains a powerful force behind the decision by many immigrants to learn the language of their new land.

Religion also influences the spread of language. Muslims whose first language is not Arabic study the Arabic language in order to be able to read the Qur'an in its original language. Historically, the diffusion of the Arabic language has been closely associated with the diffusion of Islam.

When studying language spread, linguistic geographers also consider the contexts in which a language is used. For example, in a given place one language may be used at home, another in school, and still another for business. Being aware of the different uses of languages and the spaces or settings in which they are spoken helps us understand how languages become dominant.

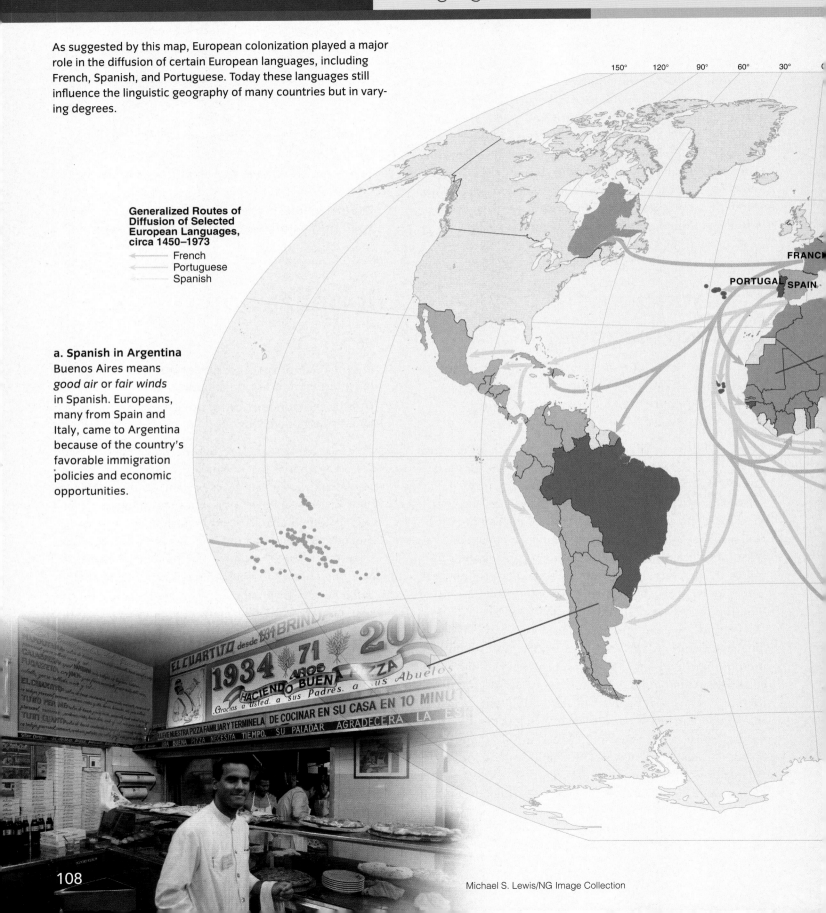

As suggested by this map, European colonization played a major role in the diffusion of certain European languages, including French, Spanish, and Portuguese. Today these languages still influence the linguistic geography of many countries but in varying degrees.

Generalized Routes of Diffusion of Selected European Languages, circa 1450–1973

- French
- Portuguese
- Spanish

a. Spanish in Argentina
Buenos Aires means *good air* or *fair winds* in Spanish. Europeans, many from Spain and Italy, came to Argentina because of the country's favorable immigration policies and economic opportunities.

FRANC
PORTUGAL SPAIN

Michael S. Lewis/NG Image Collection

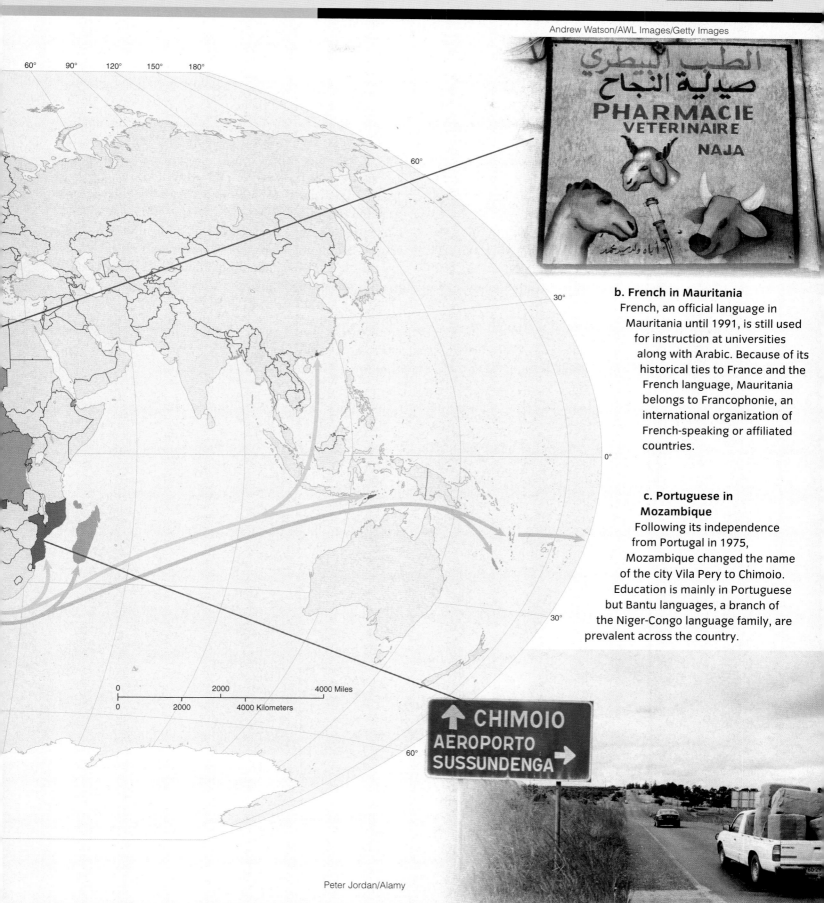

Andrew Watson/AWL Images/Getty Images

b. French in Mauritania

French, an official language in Mauritania until 1991, is still used for instruction at universities along with Arabic. Because of its historical ties to France and the French language, Mauritania belongs to Francophonie, an international organization of French-speaking or affiliated countries.

c. Portuguese in Mozambique

Following its independence from Portugal in 1975, Mozambique changed the name of the city Vila Pery to Chimoio. Education is mainly in Portuguese but Bantu languages, a branch of the Niger-Congo language family, are prevalent across the country.

Peter Jordan/Alamy

Linguistic Dominance

> **linguistic dominance**
> A situation in which one language becomes comparatively more powerful than another language.

Sheer numbers affect **linguistic dominance**, but size is not everything. Chinese, for example, with more than a billion speakers, commands the largest speech community in the world, but the geographic range of Chinese is far more restricted than that of English. On the world stage, therefore, English is considered a more dominant language than Chinese. This status shows that linguistic dominance is sometimes more a result of economic and political power than of size.

The association of a language with an independent country is also important. There are about 200 independent political states in the world but about 6900 languages. In other words, there is what we might call a *language gap*. That is, a majority of the world's languages are not directly associated with the functions of a state. Such *stateless languages* are not used for government functions and are rarely taught in schools. Although they are used in the daily lives of their speakers and are very much a part of people's identity, these uses may not confer the same kind of status on them.

Identification of an official language is often among the first acts of a newly independent country. An **official language** is one that a country formally designates for use in its political, legal, and administrative affairs. This designation is usually made in the country's constitution. A country can designate more than one official language; thus, countries can be officially unilingual, bilingual, trilingual, and so on. However, not all countries have an official language, including the United States. (see **Figure 4.10**).

Official English laws • Figure 4.10

Although the United States does not have an official language, some states have passed laws making English the official language of the state.

Mary Altaffer/AP Photo

Official English Law
No Official English Law
1981 Year Official English law was enacted
1995 Year existing Official English law was modified

a. States with an "official English" law
Thirty-one states now have some variety of "official English" law.
▶ **Supporters of these laws point out that an official English law does not ban the use of languages other than English and therefore does not have the same impact as an English-only law. Do you agree?** (*Source:* Adapted from U.S. English, Inc., 2013, www.usenglish.org.)

b. Teaching English as a second language (ESL)
This group protests cuts to ESL education. As shown here, many adult immigrants want to learn English and rely on ESL classes to do so. ▶ **If you support an official English policy, can you also support ESL instruction, or are these conflicting positions?**

Linguistic borrowing • Figure 4.11

Contact among speakers of different languages commonly results in linguistic borrowing.

▼ **a. Selected loanwords and their origins**
The list includes direct loans (e.g., *luau*) and indirect loans (e.g., *hammock*, which entered Spanish and French and then English).

Loanwords	Language
fjord, ski	Norwegian
beef, naive	French
bandit, duet	Italian
peninsula, ultimate	Latin
landscape, cruise	Dutch
glen, slogan	Scottish Gaelic
hammock, hurricane	Carib
dungarees, jungle	Hindi
caravan, candy	Persian
giraffe, sofa	Arabic
catamaran, curry	Tamil
ukulele, luau	Hawaiian
boomerang, koala	Dharuk (Australian Aboriginal)
wok, hoisin	Cantonese
karaoke, tsunami	Japanese
cola	Temne (West Africa)
okra	Igbo (West Africa)

Courtesy Alyson Greiner

b. The diffusion of ethnic food items, such as fajitas, often contributes to linguistic borrowing.

Todd Gipstein/NG Image Collection

c. The Japanese word karaoke has been borrowed into English as well as Mandarin Chinese. When pronounced, the Chinese symbols sound like *karaoke*.

International political and economic institutions such as the United Nations (UN) and the European Union (EU) can also influence linguistic dominance. Languages gain status from being selected as official languages for organizations. The UN, for example, recognizes six official languages—English, French, Spanish, Russian, Arabic, and Chinese. To avoid favoring one language over another, the EU recognizes 23 official languages, and all EU documents must be produced in each of these languages.

Language Dynamics

Languages change over time and from one place to another. As noted at the start of this chapter, snowboarders have developed a specialized vocabulary for their sport. New technologies and innovations frequently stimulate vocabulary change as words are invented to express new concepts or to name new things (e.g., *blog* or *spam*), but they can also enable new ways of using language, such as texting.

Often, vocabulary change occurs when one linguistic community borrows words from another language. These borrowed words are called **loanwords** (**Figure 4.11**).

> **loanword** A word that originates in one language and is incorporated into the vocabulary of another language.

One of the most significant forces affecting language change is human mobility or migration. Mobility can fragment linguistic communities, paving the way for new language usages to develop. The emergence of American English, Australian English, and South African English as distinct from British English provides a good example of this facet of language change.

Pidgin and Creole Languages

Just as geographic separation can create conditions favorable for linguistic change, contact between members of different speech communities can also result in language

Haitian Creole • Figure 4.12

The sign across the top of this truck reads "ice cream house." "Poze lakay" might be translated as "rest house" or even "chill out house." Haitian Creole has more than 7 million speakers mainly in Haiti, several other Caribbean countries, and the United States. This food truck is in Miami.

NATIONAL GEOGRAPHIC

pidgin language
A language that combines vocabulary and/or grammatical practices from two or more languages that have come in contact.

change. When people who speak different languages come into contact and need to communicate, they might create a **pidgin language**. This process of creating a common language by people who do not share one is known as *pidginization*. Pidgin languages typically have specialized and limited functions because they develop in response to particular circumstances.

Pidgin languages demonstrate creative and adaptive linguistic mixing. They tend to be oral languages, though some can be written, and they are rarely the first language a person learns. Pidgin languages endure as long as the contact situations in which they emerged are sustained. For example, the pidgin language Tay Boi was used for communication between the French and the Vietnamese from the 1860s to the 1950s, when Vietnam was a French colony.

What is Spanglish? There is little agreement among scholars about this. Some linguists consider Spanglish to be a pidgin language that has grown out of the contact between Spanish speakers and English speakers in the United States, in regions of Mexico adjacent to the United States border, and in Puerto Rico where Spanish and English are recognized locally as official languages. Words such as *chatear* (to chat), *lonchear* (to lunch), *mapo* (map), and *cuora* (quarter) illustrate the hybridization common in Spanglish. Other linguists contend that Spanglish is

a kind of *code switching*, or a linguistic technique in which a speaker alternates between languages during a single sentence or conversation; for example: La fiesta por mi abuelita es domingo, so I will arrive on Friday. (*The party for my grandmother is Sunday, so I will arrive on Friday.*)

We take the position that code switching is a fundamental dimension of Spanglish, and as a result, Spanglish is not as specialized and limited as most pidgins. In this respect it might be useful to think of Spanglish as intermediary between a pidgin language and a **creole language**. This is not to say, however, that pidgins always develop into creoles because they don't. Nevertheless, *creolization* describes a process of linguistic change in which the functions and use of a pidgin language expand. For example, Hawaiian Creole

creole language
A language that develops from a pidgin language and is taught as a first language.

English, which formed during the early 20th century, is based on a pidgin language that was used by the ethnically and linguistically diverse population of Hawaii. This population included native Hawaiians, Americans, and immigrant Chinese, Japanese, and Portuguese, many of whom worked on sugar and pineapple plantations. Contact among such linguistically diverse groups gave rise to Hawaiian Pigdin English, which was eventually taught to children as a first language. This practice helped to expand the language and extend its use beyond the immigrant communities, leading to the development of Hawaiian Creole English. One of the official languages in Haiti is Haitian Creole, or Kreyòl, which has its roots in the colonial period and the mixing of French with a wide variety of West African languages used by slaves (**Figure 4.12**).

Lingua Francas

As we have discussed, contact among people who speak different languages can result in the emergence and use of

lingua franca A language that is used to facilitate trade or business between people who speak different languages.

a pidgin language. Another option is to identify a **lingua franca**. The Hausa language is a lingua franca used in northern Nigeria, Niger, and neighboring regions of West Africa. Swahili is a lingua franca spoken in the East African countries of Kenya, Tanzania, Uganda, and Burundi. Russian is still used as a lingua franca in Uzbekistan, Turkmenistan, and a few other former Soviet republics. However, it is not clear how long this will last since most of these countries have identified other languages as their official languages, and some have even discouraged the use of Russian through de-Russification policies.

Today there is a growing consensus that English has become a global lingua franca. Consider the prevalent use of English in certain international contexts. For example,

English is used for communication at sea or in the air and dominates in the areas of science, medicine, technology, and international business. Every day around the world hundreds of millions of people whose first language is not English use English to communicate.

Could English eventually become a universal language through ongoing globalization? According to most experts, probably not, for two important reasons: First, as we learned in Chapter 2, globalizing forces can generate different local outcomes. The global diffusion of English provides a good example of this effect (**Figure 4.13**).

A second reason we will likely not witness the development of English as a universal language involves the spaces or domains of language use and the nature of human identity. Although English prevails in certain spaces, for example, as a language of commerce and medicine, the number of people who learn English as a second or third language exceeds the number of people who learn it as their first language. This suggests that there are spaces—households and local communities, for example—that are more resistant to the diffusion of English. Moreover, some people neither want to nor desire to speak English, preferring instead to use their first language. Nevertheless, globalization and the growth of English and other languages as very large languages are altering the geography of linguistic diversity, a topic we discuss in the next section.

English in global and local contexts • Figure 4.13

No other language has the international standing or the global reach of English. Although this diagram shows the influence of American and British English on the global spread of the language, there is not a single version of English. Rather, the va-

rieties of English that exist are highly localized. So, for example, Nigerian English differs from Pakistani English. (*Source:* Crystal, 2003, p. 107.)

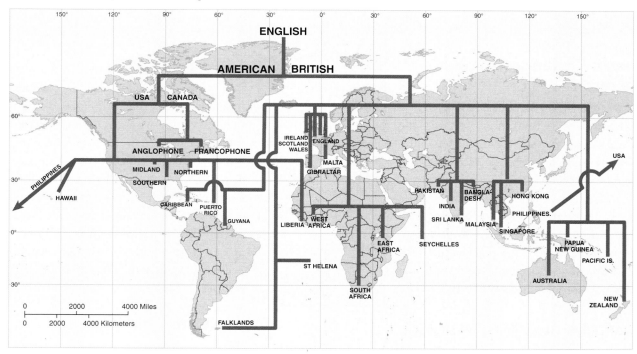

Languages in some parts of the world face serious threats of extinction. Identifying these places and languages is the first step in changing this situation.

NATIONAL GEOGRAPHIC

a. The concept of language hotspots was developed by Greg Anderson and David Harrison of the Living Tongues Institute for Endangered Languages. A language hotspot exists when three factors converge: high language endangerment, high linguistic diversity, and languages that are poorly documented. To calculate linguistic diversity, they divide the number of language families in an area by the total number of languages. (*Source:* NG Maps based on *Earth Pulse*, 2008.)

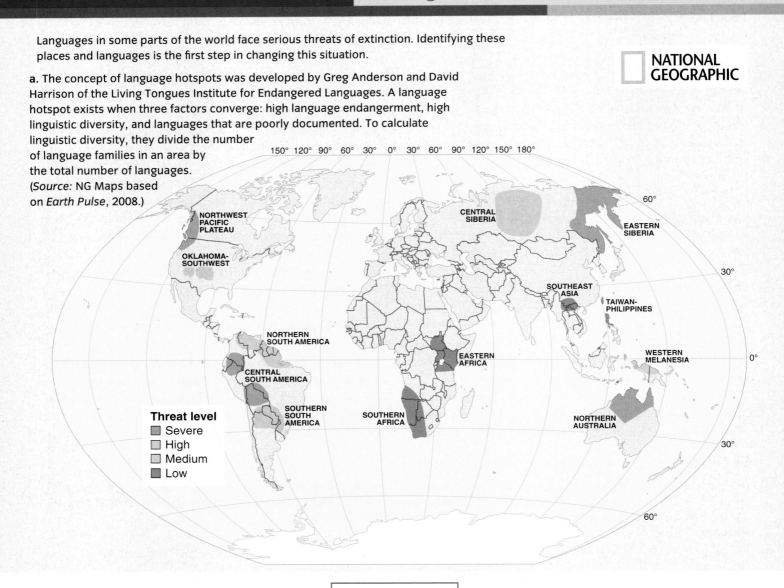

Language Endangerment and Diversity

During the 1990s, researchers began to use biological analogies when characterizing the state of languages in the world. Just as wildlife ecologists and conservation biologists use the concepts of biodiversity, endangered species, and extinction of species, language scholars speak of **linguistic diversity, endangered languages**, and **extinct** (or dead) **languages**.

Our world is now experiencing the fastest rate of language extinction ever—one language dies out approximately every two weeks.

linguistic diversity
The assortment of languages in a particular area.

endangered language A language that is no longer taught to children by their parents and is not used for everyday conversation.

extinct language
A language that has no living speakers; also called a dead language.

Some estimates suggest that as many as half of the world's languages are endangered. Many researchers fear that if this trend is not halted, we might witness a mass extinction of languages within the next 50 or 60 years. Three regions are losing languages quickly—the Americas (North America, Central America, and South America), Eastern Siberia, and Australia. Here, and in most other hotspots, the languages being lost are those spoken by the native peoples. A pioneering approach to the study of language endangerment and diversity uses the concept of *language hotspots* (**Figure 4.14**).

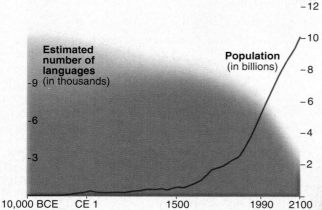

c. Researchers in Taiwan consult with Angai Kamunuana, one of 10 remaining speakers of Kanakanvu, an aboriginal language. In general, the smaller the speech community, the more urgent is the task of language preservation. Kanakanvu is related to languages believed to be the source of the Austronesian language family.

b. Globally, the historical trend is for linguistic diversity to decline as global population rises and for large languages to spread, usually at the expense of smaller languages. (*Source: College Atlas of the World,* 2007.)

Think Critically

What consequences does the extinction of a language have?

AP Photo/Wally Santana

The extinction of languages is one factor that influences the distribution and mixture of languages in the world. Mapping language hotspots thus is an important strategy for identifying those areas that possess languages that we know little about and where those languages are at risk of becoming extinct—that is, areas where research is needed.

If geographers and other experts want to know how linguistically diverse a country or region is based on the size of its population and the number of different languages spoken within its borders, they compute a **linguistic diversity index (LDI).** Values for the LDI can

linguistic diversity index (LDI) A measure that expresses the likelihood that two randomly selected individuals in a country speak different first languages.

range from 0.00 to 0.99. Countries with LDIs at or close to zero have no or very little linguistic diversity; thus, two people selected at random will probably speak the same first language. Countries with LDIs close to 1.0 possess considerable linguistic diversity, so that two randomly selected people will probably speak different first languages.

Keep in mind that the LDI does not simply reflect the number of languages spoken in a country. If it did, all countries with a large number of languages would also have high LDIs. Consider the examples of Brazil and Mexico. Brazil has nearly 200 languages, and

Mexico has nearly 300 languages, but both have very low LDIs because most of their citizens speak the predominant language—Portuguese in Brazil and Spanish in Mexico (**Figure 4.15**).

You might be wondering what happened to the hotspot in northern Australia (refer again to Figure 4.14). It does not appear on the map in Figure 4.15b because of differences in the way linguistic diversity is calculated. Remember that the LDI conveys the likelihood that two randomly selected people will speak different first languages. Aboriginal Australians constitute just 3% of the country's population, so, for the country as a whole, the LDI is quite low. A similar situation exists in New Zealand with the Maori language. Indeed, these two

Geography of the linguistic diversity index • Figure 4.15

Linguistic geographers need to know not only the number of languages in a region, but also how the number of languages relates to the country's population. For this, they use the linguistic diversity index.

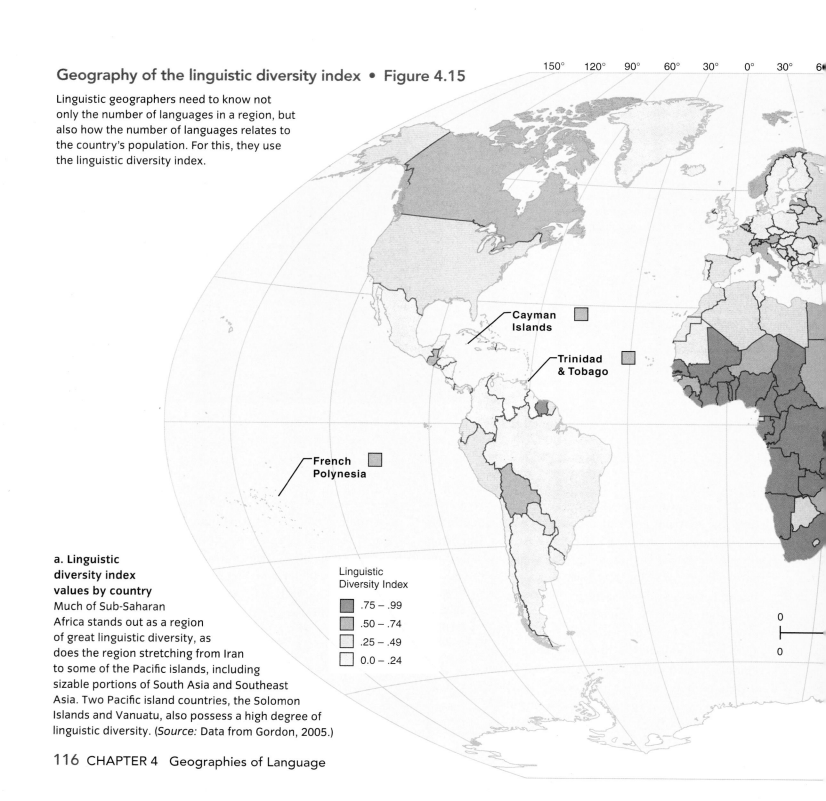

a. Linguistic diversity index values by country
Much of Sub-Saharan Africa stands out as a region of great linguistic diversity, as does the region stretching from Iran to some of the Pacific islands, including sizable portions of South Asia and Southeast Asia. Two Pacific island countries, the Solomon Islands and Vanuatu, also possess a high degree of linguistic diversity. (*Source:* Data from Gordon, 2005.)

Linguistic Diversity Index
- .75 – .99
- .50 – .74
- .25 – .49
- 0.0 – .24

countries possess minimal linguistic diversity, in dramatic contrast to the general pattern across Southeast Asia and the Pacific islands.

Other regions of low linguistic diversity include much of Mesoamerica (Mexico and Central America), South America, and Europe. The presence of nation-states—countries where the boundaries of a national group match the boundaries of the country—in Europe helps to explain the generally low LDIs in that region. European colonization is an important factor in the low LDIs in Mesoamerica and South America, as well as in Australia and New Zealand. In precolonial times, these regions possessed a diverse mixture of indigenous languages, but many of these languages have been in decline since the colonial period, and several of them

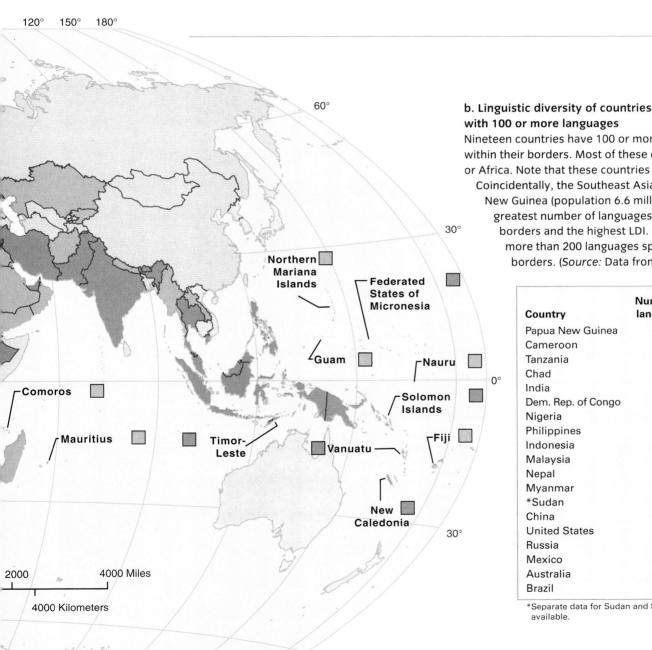

b. Linguistic diversity of countries with 100 or more languages
Nineteen countries have 100 or more languages spoken within their borders. Most of these countries are in Asia or Africa. Note that these countries are ranked by LDI. Coincidentally, the Southeast Asian country of Papua New Guinea (population 6.6 million) has both the greatest number of languages spoken within its borders and the highest LDI. Nine countries have more than 200 languages spoken within their borders. (*Source:* Data from Gordon, 2005.)

Country	Number of languages	Linguistic diversity index
Papua New Guinea	823	0.99
Cameroon	279	0.97
Tanzania	135	0.95
Chad	132	0.95
India	387	0.93
Dem. Rep. of Congo	218	0.92
Nigeria	505	0.88
Philippines	169	0.85
Indonesia	726	0.83
Malaysia	139	0.75
Nepal	120	0.69
Myanmar	107	0.64
*Sudan	134	0.56
China	201	0.48
United States	176	0.35
Russia	100	0.27
Mexico	288	0.13
Australia	235	0.13
Brazil	192	0.03

*Separate data for Sudan and South Sudan are not yet available.

THE PLANNER

Understanding language vitality and endangerment: The example of Yuchi • Figure 4.16

Language shift occurs when speakers of a language change their speech behavior—for example, by acquiring another language and altering the geography, or spaces, where their original language was used. Yuchi speakers not only learned English, but the spaces where English is used expanded as the spaces of Yuchi use contracted.

a. Pressures at different scales affect language vitality and endangerment.

National-scale pressures
- Federal removal of the Yuchi from their lands in the eastern U.S.
- Federal government policies shape Native American education and language use

Regional-scale pressures
- Railroads accelerate migration of English-speakers into area
- Oklahoma statehood in 1907 builds economic and social integration
- Yuchi and other Native American languages stigmatized

Yuchi linguistic space

Local-scale pressures
- Allotment of tribal lands fragments Yuchi settlements
- Yuchi children attend English-only boarding schools and are punished for speaking Yuchi
- Declining use of the Yuchi language among younger generations

b. A language shift occurs as Yuchi (orange) loses vitality and English (blue) grows dominant.

❶ Pre-1830s—Yuchi language vitality

Yuchi is the first language acquired and is used for all purposes—home, commerce, government, education, religion.

❷ 1830s–1940s—Yuchi language gradually becomes subordinate to English

National and regional forces confine Yuchi's linguistic space while the spaces of English use expand.

❸ Since the 1950s—Yuchi language endangerment

English dominates most linguistic spaces and Yuchi is no longer taught to children.

❹ Present day—The Yuchi attempt to revitalize their language
Renée Grounds, an instructor with the Yuchi Language Project, teaches Yuchi to children in order to build fluency and keep Yuchi language and heritage alive.

Courtesy of Renee Grounds

have become extinct. **Figure 4.16** illustrates some of the social forces that can contribute to language endangerment, using the example of the Yuchi language, a Native American language spoken in Oklahoma. Thousands once spoke it in all domains or spaces of social interaction. Since the 1800s, however, Yuchi has declined as language shift occurred, and today it has been almost entirely replaced by English. Only a handful of native Yuchi speakers remain.

For a glimpse of some of the work involved in preserving a language, see *Video Explorations*.

CONCEPT CHECK STOP

1. **How** do economic forces affect linguistic diffusion?
2. **Why** can't we simply use the size of a language to assess linguistic dominance?
3. **What** is the difference between pidginization and creolization?
4. **What** information does the linguistic diversity index provide, and why is that useful to geographers?

Video Explorations

Enduring Voices Expeditions

National Geographic

Members of the Enduring Voices Project travel to locations in northern Australia and northeastern India to record endangered languages. In addition to those shown in the video, what are some other strategies for language preservation?

Dialects and Toponyms

LEARNING OBJECTIVES

1. **Identify** the major dialect regions that exist in the United States.
2. **Distinguish** between prestige and standard dialects.
3. **Explain** what toponyms are and what information they can provide.

Beyond its function as a communication system, language also is a marker of cultural and personal identity. We identify different cultural groups around the world on the basis of their language. And on an individual level, our language—the way we speak, the words we use, our dialect—defines who we are and who we are not. Dialects, the various forms of a single language, provide important clues about the construction of linguistic boundaries and

the relationships between language and identity. In the following section we explore some facets of the dialect geography of the United States.

Dialect Regions

Although most linguistic geographers find individual differences in pronunciation fascinating, they usually concentrate their study on the spatial patterns of dialect usage. This field of study is called **dialect geography**. Hans Kurath helped pioneer the study of dialect geography in the United States beginning in the 1930s. By mapping word usage, he was able to identify **isoglosses**. He was specifically interested in the patterns of word usage along the East Coast. Kurath used interviews

> **isogloss** A line that marks a boundary of word usage.

to obtain information about the distribution of different words and expressions (**Figure 4.17**).

Some words have distinctively Northern, Midland, or Southern distributions, meaning that they are more frequently used in one of these three dialect regions (**Figure 4.18a**). The word for soft drinks displays a vivid geography. The Northern word is "soda" and the Midland word is "pop." In the past the Southern words "drink" and "cold drink" were commonly used when referring to soft drinks (**Figure 4.18b**).

The South is known for its unique vocabulary, including "y'all"—meaning "you all" (**Figure 4.18c**). Another Southern usage is saying "fixin' to" when talking about something you intend to do in the future.

Kurath's word geography • Figure 4.17

The practice of mapping word usage patterns and isoglosses was influenced by the work of linguistic geographers like Hans Kurath. (*Source:* Adapted from Kurath, 1970 [1949].)

a. This map, based on research during the 1930s and 40s, presents a word geography by showing where other terms for pancake prevailed. Because no two words have the exact same distribution, their isoglosses never exactly coincide.

b. Mapping the isoglosses of hundreds of words, as Kurath did, enabled him to see where the isoglosses clustered. Using these patterns, Kurath demarcated 18 speech areas along the East Coast and grouped them into three broad dialect regions that are still recognized today: North, Midland, and South.

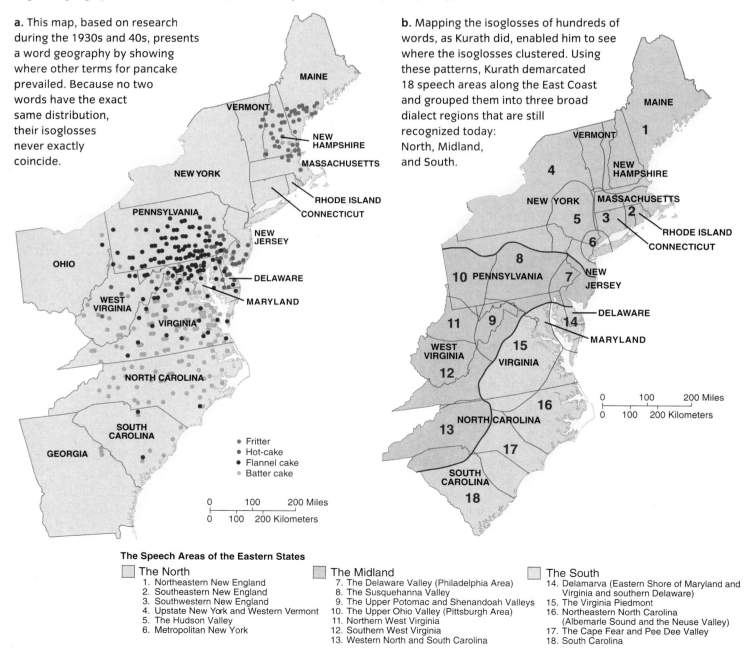

Legend (Figure 4.17a): Fritter, Hot-cake, Flannel cake, Batter cake

The Speech Areas of the Eastern States

The North
1. Northeastern New England
2. Southeastern New England
3. Southwestern New England
4. Upstate New York and Western Vermont
5. The Hudson Valley
6. Metropolitan New York

The Midland
7. The Delaware Valley (Philadelphia Area)
8. The Susquehanna Valley
9. The Upper Potomac and Shenandoah Valleys
10. The Upper Ohio Valley (Pittsburgh Area)
11. Northern West Virginia
12. Southern West Virginia
13. Western North and South Carolina

The South
14. Delamarva (Eastern Shore of Maryland and Virginia and southern Delaware)
15. The Virginia Piedmont
16. Northeastern North Carolina (Albemarle Sound and the Neuse Valley)
17. The Cape Fear and Pee Dee Valley
18. South Carolina

Geography InSight

✓ THE PLANNER

By comparing these maps we can see the extent to which selected contemporary word usage reflects the dialect regions in the country.

a. Dialect regions
This map shows major dialect regions of the United States today. (*Source:* Adapted from *National Geographic Magazine*, 2005/NG Maps.)

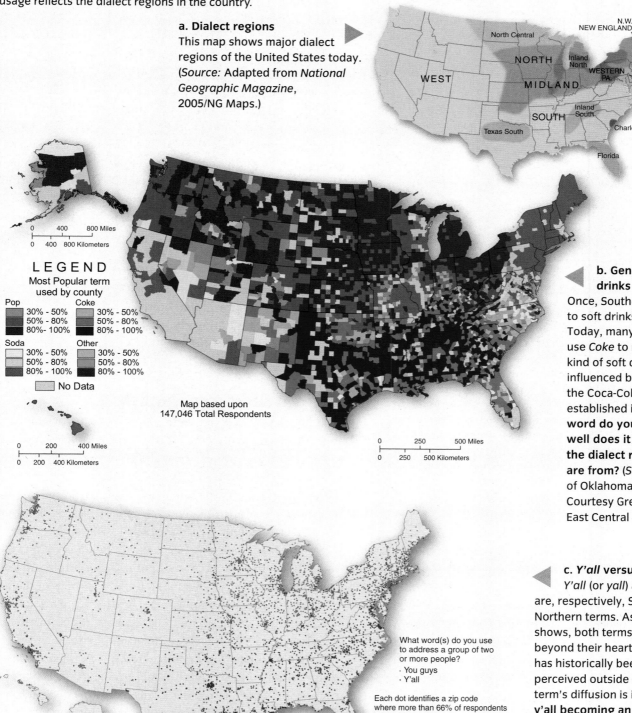

b. Generic names of soft drinks
Once, Southerners referred to soft drinks as *cold drinks*. Today, many Southerners use *Coke* to refer to any kind of soft drink, a practice influenced by the fact that the Coca-Cola Company was established in Atlanta. ► **What word do you use, and how well does it correlate with the dialect region that you are from?** (*Source:* Web Atlas of Oklahoma, www.okatlas.org. Courtesy Gregory A. Plumb, East Central University.)

c. *Y'all* versus *you guys*
Y'all (or *yall*) and *you guys* are, respectively, Southern and Northern terms. As this map shows, both terms have diffused beyond their hearths. Because *y'all* has historically been negatively perceived outside of the South, the term's diffusion is intriguing. ► **Is y'all becoming an Americanism, as some linguistic geographers have suggested?** (*Source:* Data courtesy of Bert Vaux, University of Cambridge.)

LEGEND
Most Popular term used by county

Pop
30% - 50%
50% - 80%
80% - 100%

Coke
30% - 50%
50% - 80%
80% - 100%

Soda
30% - 50%
50% - 80%
80% - 100%

Other
30% - 50%
50% - 80%
80% - 100%

No Data

Map based upon 147,046 Total Respondents

What word(s) do you use to address a group of two or more people?
· You guys
· Y'all

Each dot identifies a zip code where more than 66% of respondents selected the indicated term from a list that also included *you all, youse(e), you lot, you'uns, yin, you,* and *other.*

Dialects and Toponyms 121

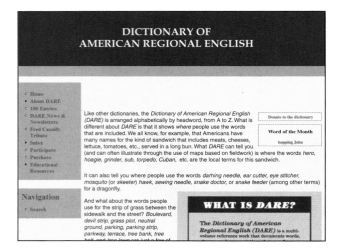
If someone asks, "Have you prepared the report?" and you reply, "I'm fixin' to," you would be using a distinctively Southern phrase.

Differences in pronunciation also help distinguish among the dialect regions in the United States. When someone speaks a dialect of our language that has a different pronunciation from our own dialect, we perceive that person as having an **accent**. Most people think that they do not speak with an accent, but the truth is that we all have an accent—we simply don't hear our own accent as an accent. In addition, in the course of our lives, each of us develops peculiarities in pronunciation—our personal accent.

One striking difference involves the pronunciation of "r" sounds. With the Northern accent, if the "r" follows a vowel, the "r" sound is lost. For example, the word *car* sounds like "cah," while the word *skirt* sounds like "skuht." The Southern accent similarly drops the "r" after vowels and between them as well (*more* sounds like "mo"). Pronunciation of "i" as if it sounded like "ah" also characterizes the Southern accent. The word *fire* sounds like "fahr" and *I'm fine* sounds like "Ahm fahn." The Southern practice of pronouncing one-syllable words as if they had two syllables, as in "thiyus" (*this*), and "wayell" (*well*), creates the Southern drawl.

Unlike either the Northern or the Southern accent, the Midland accent keeps "r" sounds after vowels. The Midland accent forms the basis of *network standard*—a way of speaking commonly utilized by TV and radio announcers with national audiences that emphasizes accent reduction through the avoidance of regionally distinctive pronunciation practices. Jay Leno has purposely acquired the network standard dialect over the course of his career. However, if you listen closely to Leno's pronunciation, you might be able tell that he is originally from the Northern dialect region by the way he drops some of his "r" sounds. (Leno was born in Boston.)

Linguistic geographers and other researchers have been gathering information on regional accents and word usage for decades. To explore this fascinating collection, see *Where Geographers Click*.

African American English

The Northern, Midland, and Southern dialect regions reflect the European origins of the settlers along the East Coast. Kurath's work, however, did not give much attention to the speech patterns of African Americans. Yet, from the 1600s into the 1800s the importation of African slaves, who spoke a wide variety of languages, greatly altered the composition of the population in the South. Consequently, many different ways of speaking developed among slave populations on plantations across the South. The origins of African American English are complex and only incompletely understood. In their communities and with one another, African American slaves began to use English differently from whites, partially as a form of linguistic resistance to their oppression. Among some African Americans, the practice of using English differently continues to this day, and African American English, also called African American Vernacular English or Black English Vernacular, constitutes another dialect of American English. Because of its emergence in the South, it shares some features with the Southern dialect, such as not pronouncing the "g" in words ending with *-ing* and dropping the "r" when it occurs between vowels.

Other pronunciation practices associated with African American English include loss of the "l" sound after vowels (*help* sounds like "hep"). When words end in two or more consonant sounds, the final consonant is often simplified (*meant* sounds like "men"). African American English also possesses some distinctive grammatical practices. One of these involves the absence of an "es" or "s" on third-person present tense verbs. Thus, instead of using "he goes"/"she goes"/"it goes," speakers of African American English say "he go"/"she go"/ "it go." Note that this grammatical practice makes English more regular. Another grammatical practice associated with African American English involves the use of the verb *to be*. *Be* is used to convey that something happens regularly: "She be workin' every day." To indicate that something is taking place at this moment, *be* is not used: "She workin' right now."

African American English possesses a distinctive vocabulary. Some scholars interpret this as a linguistic strategy that slaves used to help them communicate with one another but not be understood by their owners. In addition, many African American expressions have become very widely adopted and used. Some of these words include *jazz, funky, chill out, high-five, phat,* and *bling-bling*. Because of the international popularity of hip-hop, the vocabulary of African American English actively shapes patterns of language use not only in the United States but also around the world (**Figure 4.19**).

Although African American English emerged in the South, it has diffused widely across the country. In a large-scale movement of population called the *Great Migration*, beginning about 1916 and continuing until 1970, more than 6 million African Americans moved from the South to such Northern and Midwestern cities as New York, Philadelphia, Chicago, and Detroit. Social pressures, including residential segregation, forced many of these migrants into the inner cities, where they formed African American neighborhoods. One result of this movement is that the geography of African American English today is largely Southern, but beyond the South it is also highly urban. Of course, not all African Americans use African American English, and today some whites, Hispanics, and others have adopted aspects of African American English.

Chicano English

Kurath's work made important contributions to the study of dialect patterns in the United States in the

Brad Barket/Picture Group/©AP/Wide World Photos

Hip-hop artist Jay-Z • Figure 4.19

Shawn Carter is more popularly known by his stage name, Jay-Z, said to be derived from the word *jazzy*. The lyrics of many African American hip-hop artists illustrate highly creative linguistic practices.

1930s. Since that time, however, immigration has altered the linguistic geography of the country. *Latino* (or *Latina* for a woman) usually refers to someone who is from Latin America and has a Spanish- or Portuguese-speaking background. Although the term *Latino English* is used to identify the variety of English spoken by these people, the term is slightly misleading because there is no set of linguistic practices that members of this diverse group share.

Mexicans constitute the largest Latino population in the United States. Chicano English (the word *Chicano* derives from *Mexicano*) refers to the dialect that has emerged within that population. This dialect is frequently associated both with Mexican Americans and with Mexicans who learn English as a second language. A distinctive pronunciation in Chicano English is using an "s" sound instead of a "z" sound, so *crazy* and *his* sound like "craysee" and "hiss." Grammatically, Chicano English tends to omit the word *have* in certain instances. Instead of "I have been on campus all day" you might hear "I been on campus all day."

WHAT A GEOGRAPHER SEES

Toponyms, or What Is in a Name?

Are you aware of the political and symbolic meanings in toponyms? Geographers consider the naming of a place a fundamental way of taking possession of it and promoting unity among citizens. But renaming a place can also serve as a strategy for dispossessing people of land they have historically claimed, or for weakening a people's attachment to a place. To a geographer, toponyms are often more than mere names.

Not all toponyms reflect the past in this way, and some are interesting just for their oddity. Perhaps you have heard of Hot Coffee, Mississippi, or Truth or Consequences, New Mexico.

a. This monument commemorates the defense of Leningrad ("Lenin's City") against the Nazis in World War II. When the Soviet Union dissolved in 1991, the citizens voted to restore the pre-Soviet name, St. Petersburg. This deeply symbolic act removed the name of Lenin, founder of the Soviet Union, and re-honored Peter the Great, who helped modernize Russia.

© Chris Hammond/Alamy

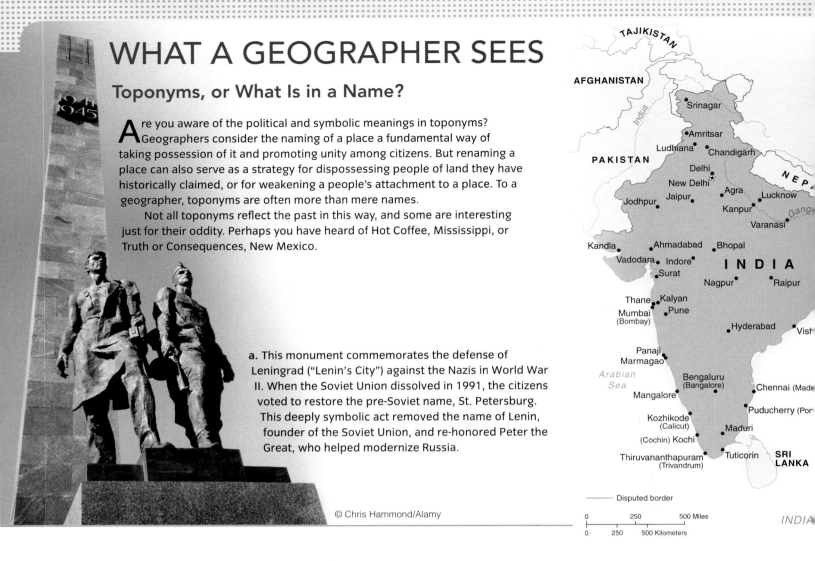

Because of the long period of contact in the borderlands between the United States and Mexico, many Spanish vocabulary words have diffused into English. You know a number of these—*enchiladas, frijoles, tortillas*—largely because of the popularity of Mexican-style food. But words such as *rodeo* and *mesa* also reflect other Spanish contributions to the English vocabulary. As with African American English, not all Mexican Americans use Chicano English.

Standard Dialects

When different dialects of a language are spoken in an area, one may be designated or become accepted as the **standard dialect**, the norm or authoritative model of language usage. You will, for example, sometimes hear references to Standard British English or Standard Russian. The selection of a standard dialect may reflect the dominance of a given way of speaking. It is more likely, however, to reflect a way of speaking that is associated with high socioeconomic or educational status or political power. Thus, the standard dialect may be perceived by some as a *prestige dialect*. A phrase, such as "the Queen's English," not only refers to the dialect that became the standard in the United Kingdom but also associates that dialect with status, power, and authority. In the United States, network standard comes the closest to being a standard dialect. Use of a standard dialect brings a consistency to the way a language is written and spoken. Standard dialects are preferred in business, government, education, and mass media, such as television and radio.

Beginning in the 1950s, government officials in China selected Northern Mandarin as the country's official language and standard dialect and have been promoting its use ever since, despite the fact that millions of Chinese use other dialects, such as Cantonese and Shanghainese. The phrase "Mandarin policy" refers to the government's active efforts to spread Northern Mandarin for the sake of national unity.

AFP Photo/Sebastian D'SOUZA/NewsCom

b. European colonization often erased local toponyms, supplanting them with the names of European kings, queens, heroes, or other familiarities. In colonial India, numerous toponyms were changed mainly by the British. Since the 1990s, however, some of India's colonial toponyms have themselves been expunged. Colonial place-names such as Bangalore, Bombay, Calcutta, among others, became Bengaluru, Mumbai, and Kolkata, respectively, as shown on this current map.

c. Like place-names, street names also have practical, symbolic, and commemorative value. They not only help us locate places, they also convey political values. Consider, for example, Independence Avenue in Washington, D.C., or the way state names have been incorporated as street names there. Street names also serve as memorials to the past. The first street to commemorate Martin Luther King, Jr., was established in Chicago in 1968. There are now more than 700 MLK streets in cities and towns across the country, most of which are in the South.

Think Critically

1. How might residents in a place express resistance to toponymic change imposed by a government or other group?
2. How might toponyms reflect spatial thinking?

©Ric Feld/AP Photo

Sometimes people mistakenly claim that using a standard dialect is the only correct or proper way to use a language. This mistake arises from not knowing how a standard dialect gets selected, and it contributes to a negative stereotyping of nonstandard dialects. For example, the Southern dialect of American English has long been negatively stereotyped. But imagine if the Southern dialect had been selected as the standard dialect—our ideas of "proper" English would be entirely different. Chicano English and African American English have been even more negatively stereotyped than the Southern dialect. Such prejudice is one of the ways in which language can be used to create and reinforce social barriers between people. When people label certain ways of speaking as "right" or "wrong," "proper" or "improper," they are making highly subjective judgments based on ignorance about how language works. Dialects represent different ways of using a language, not ways that are right or wrong.

Toponyms

As the previous discussion suggests, language use is closely associated with identity as well as social and political power. We can see this in the selection of **toponyms**, because the names given to places can make powerful statements about a group's sense of belonging in, attachment to, or control of a place (see *What a Geographer Sees*).

> **toponym** A place-name.

Geographers study toponyms not only for the insights they provide about territorial possession and political power, but also because they can provide clues about settlement history. A glance at a map of Quebec, for example, reveals Native American, French, and English-derived place-names—a reflection of its peopling. Many English-language toponyms consist of identifiable generic and specific elements. The generic element identifies the feature (mountain, city, and so on), and the specific element provides more descriptive information. In the toponym Black Mesa, *Black* is the generic element and *Mesa* is the specific element.

What do cultural groups choose to name? What can toponyms tell us about past land-use practices in a place or environmental change? Geographer J. L. Delahunty's study of yew tree toponyms in Ireland identified 70 unique place-names that contain a reference to yew trees. Examples include Youghal (yew wood) from the Irish *Eochaill* and Ture (yew) from the Irish *Iubhar*. Delahunty's research suggests a past cultural preference for yew trees, a more abundant distribution of yew trees in the past, or both.

Through the study of spatial patterns of language use, geographers make languages visible. Maps serve as a valuable tool in this respect. Maps that show isoglosses, languages used, or the distribution of language families draw out the visible dimensions of linguistic geography.

Signage, too, is important. From our gestures and dialects to our toponyms, we etch our language and our identities into our surroundings, demonstrating the interconnectedness of people, place, and environment.

Summary

1 Languages in the World 100

- **Language** gives people a voice and shapes their identity. Language is a defining element of culture. Geographers study the spatial patterns of languages and **dialects**, beginning with an understanding of **mutual intelligibility**, the kinds of languages that exist, their sizes, and relationships.

- **Language families**, such as the Indo-European language family depicted here, reflect genetic relationships among languages.

Classification of Indo-European languages • Figure 4.8

- There are 6,900 languages spoken in the world today. When these languages are classified into families, six stand out because of the large percentage of languages and speakers that they contain.

- Every language family has a **hearth**, but identifying them is complicated because of the long periods of time involved and the frequent lack of written records.

- More than half of the languages that exist today are classified as "small" or "very small" languages, but they are spoken by only a few hundred thousand people. Conversely, just nine of the world's languages are classified as "very large languages"—yet they are spoken by almost half of the world's people.

2 Language Diffusion and Globalization 107

- Technology, especially changes in transportation, and human migration influence language diffusion. In addition, the spread of language may depend on political, economic, and even religious forces.

- Contact among speakers of different languages can lead to the invention or borrowing of **loanwords** shown here, or the emergence of **pidgin languages**, **creole languages**, or **lingua francas**.

Linguistic borrowing • Figure 4.11

Courtesy Alyson Greiner

- The size of a language and the situations in which it is spoken have consequences not only for **linguistic dominance**, but also for language survival, **endangerment**, and **language extinction**. The death or extinction of languages reduces linguistic diversity. The **linguistic diversity index (LDI)** is used to express the likelihood that two randomly selected individuals in a country will speak different first languages.

- Whether recorded on maps or signs, **toponyms** (see photo) provide telling clues about our priorities, preferences, and cultural practices. Studying the events or circumstances that prompt people to change or erase toponyms also provides insight into the ways in which people etch authority and meaning into places and landscapes.

What a Geographer Sees: Toponyms, or What Is in a Name?

AFP Photo/Sebastian D'SOUZA/NewsCom

3 Dialects and Toponyms 119

- **Dialect geography** has long been a part of the spatial study of languages and frequently relies on **isoglosses** to help us understand how vocabulary usage varies from place to place.

- African American English and Chicano English are two highly dynamic and contested dialects of American English. The identification of a **standard dialect** gives an element of authority and legitimacy to one way of speaking, even though no dialect is inherently better or worse than another.

Key Terms

- accent 122
- creole language 112
- dialect 100
- dialect geography 119
- endangered language 114
- extinct language 114

- hearth 104
- isogloss 119
- language 100
- language family 104
- lingua franca 113
- linguistic diversity 114

- linguistic diversity index (LDI) 115
- linguistic dominance 110
- loanword 111
- mutual intelligibility 100

- official language 110
- pidgin language 112
- standard dialect 124
- toponym 125

Critical and Creative Thinking Questions

1. Use the accompanying photo to develop a proposal to create a tactile map of your campus or neighborhood for those who are visually impaired.

Dominique Faget/AFP/Getty Images, Inc.

2. Can you think of American English words not mentioned in this chapter that have local or regional usages? Where are they used?

3. Identify some challenges associated with counting the number of speakers of a language.

4. It has been said that network standard is a geographically neutral dialect. Do you agree? Can a dialect be socially neutral? Explain your reasoning.

5. How might governmental and educational policies prevent linguistic dominance?

6. Some scholars argue that a language must possess a literary tradition to be counted as a fully separate language. Others claim that a language should have status as an official language. What are the advantages and disadvantages of these approaches to language identification?

7. What do the toponyms where you live reveal about settlement patterns, politics, or commemoration more generally?

8. Linguistically, is the world becoming more alike or different? Explain your answer.

9. This chapter has not discussed slang. What is slang, and why is it a controversial subject? What would you say is the difference between slang and linguistic creativity? In what linguistic spaces is slang used?

What is happening in this picture?

A student writes in the Cree language in a classroom in northern Quebec, Canada. This writing system was developed in the 1830s. Shapes represent consonants and, when rotated in one of the four cardinal directions, denote vowels.

© Hemis/Alamy

Think Critically

1. What are some advantages of having a written language?
2. Are linguistic dominance and linguistic discrimination related?
3. Can linguistic dominance occur without discrimination?

Self-Test

(Check your answers in Appendix B.)

1. The Kurgan Hypothesis _____.
   a. places the hearth of the Indo-European language family north of the Caspian Sea
   b. links the origins of language families to the spread of agriculture
   c. relates linguistic dominance to economic forces
   d. rejects the idea that language families share a single ancestor

2. What is surprising about the indigenous languages of Madagascar?
   a. They incorporate the use of click sounds.
   b. They are unrelated to any other known languages.
   c. They probably diffused to Madagascar from Indonesia.
   d. None of the above is correct.

3. Accents _____.
   a. are situational, and dialects are not
   b. include distinctive vocabulary and pronunciation
   c. are mainly associated with the Southern dialect of American English
   d. can serve as markers of personal or social identity

4. An example of an artificial language intended to be universal is _____.
   a. Esperanto   c. Latin
   b. Elvish   d. body language

5. The geography of African American English _____.
   a. was once southern but is now mainly northern in its distribution
   b. was initially southern but has become increasingly urban
   c. is associated mainly with the East and West coasts
   d. has remained confined largely to the South

6. Fill in the table with the correct language family.

Language family	Example language(s)
	English, Hindi, Spanish
	Mandarin Chinese, Burmese
	Arabic, Hebrew
	Yoruba, Zulu
	Tagalog, Bahasa Indonesia
	Tetum

7. List three characteristics of African American English.

_____

_____

_____

8. Find the *false* statement about pidgin languages.

   a. They demonstrate adaptive linguistic mixing.

   b. They are the native language of people who live in multilingual communities.

   c. They are most likely to be oral languages rather than written languages.

   d. They are considered contact languages that have limited or specialized functions.

9. Creolization _____.

   a. relates to the establishment of a lingua franca

   b. describes the practice of creating and changing toponyms

   c. refers to the process by which a pidgin language develops into a first language

   d. explains the spread of the Indo-European language family around the world

10. What do the words *fajita*, *mesa*, and *rodeo* have in common?

   a. They are toponyms.

   b. They are isoglosses.

   c. They help identify speakers of Chicano English.

   d. They are loanwords.

11. This graph shows that _____.

   a. the number of languages declines as population increases

   b. the number of languages increases as population increases

   c. the number of languages and the population size are unrelated

   d. in 1500 CE the number of languages and the population were both low

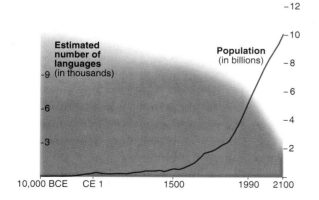

12. The linguistic diversity index expresses _____.

   a. the likelihood that two randomly selected individuals in a country will speak the same first language

   b. the ratio between the number of languages spoken in a country and the area of that country

   c. the ratio of the number of multilingual individuals in a country and the country's total population

   d. the likelihood that any randomly selected Web page will be in a language other than English

13. Why do Mexico and Brazil have such low linguistic diversity indexes (0.13 and 0.03, respectively)?

   _____

   _____

14. Find the *false* statement about language extinction.

   a. The world is experiencing the highest rate of language extinction ever.

   b. Of the world's regions, Europe is experiencing very high rates of language extinction.

   c. When speech communities are small, the potential for language extinction is usually very high.

   d. One language becomes extinct approximately every two weeks.

15. List at least one factor that has contributed to the contraction of Yuchi linguistic space at each of the three scales.

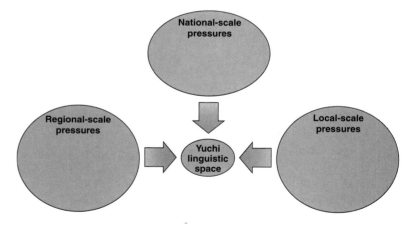

THE PLANNER ✓

Review your Chapter Planner on the chapter opener and check off your completed work.

Geographies of Religion

THE ABORIGINAL DREAMTIME

What does religion mean to you? Apart from the specific beliefs that you hold, we know that religion has a lot to do with feelings of belonging—to communities and to place. We can appreciate these aspects of belonging by considering the example of Aboriginal Australians.

The Aboriginal inhabitants of Australia share a belief in a mythic creation that they call the *Dreamtime* or *Dreaming*. At this time, Ancestral Spirits crossed the Australian continent and created physical features such as mountains, plateaus, and river valleys. By singing, the Ancestral Spirits gave names to the land, to its plants, animals, lakes, and deserts. They made the world a sacred place. But the Ancestral Spirits have not departed. They are present everywhere—in estuaries, streams, rocks, and trees.

The spiritual energies of the ancestral beings can be harnessed through the performance of certain religious rituals. Aboriginals celebrate and commemorate events in the Dreamtime through song, dance, body painting, and other forms of art. In the accompanying photo, an Aboriginal dances in a ceremony called a *corroboree*.

As this example shows, the practice of rituals builds bonds among community members and can strengthen attachments people have to certain places. Sometimes the conduct of rituals can be divisive if others do not share the same religious beliefs, or their sacred spaces overlap.

This chapter will introduce you to major world religions, including where they have grown and how they have spread. It also considers the nature of sacred space and religious landscapes.

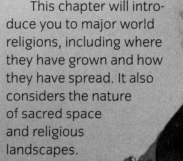

Sam Abell/NG Image Collection

NATIONAL GEOGRAPHIC

CHAPTER PLANNER ✓

- ❏ Study the picture and read the opening story.
- ❏ Scan the Learning Objectives in each section:
  p. 132 ❏ p. 140 ❏ p. 143 ❏ p. 154 ❏
- ❏ Read the text and study all visuals.
  Answer any questions.

Analyze key features

- ❏ Video Explorations, p. 132 ❏ p. 152 ❏
- ❏ Geography InSight, p. 136
- ❏ Process Diagram, p. 149
- ❏ What a Geographer Sees, p. 156
- ❏ Stop: Answer the Concept Checks before you go on:
  p. 139 ❏ p. 143 ❏ p. 153 ❏ p. 157 ❏

End of chapter

- ❏ Review the Summary and Key Terms.
- ❏ Answer the Critical and Creative Thinking Questions.
- ❏ Answer What is happening in this picture?
- ❏ Complete the Self-Test and check your answers.

Religion in Global Context

LEARNING OBJECTIVES

1. **Identify** characteristics of animistic and syncretic religions.
2. **Distinguish** between universalizing and ethnic religions.
3. **Contrast** the distributions of the Abrahamic faiths.
4. **Identify** similarities and differences among Buddhism, Hinduism, and Sikhism.

Religion is a system of beliefs and practices that help people make sense of the universe and their place in it. A religion can be very personal, or it can be highly institutionalized. Religion may involve the worship of the divine or supernatural. A religion may be **monotheistic**, **polytheistic**, or **atheistic**. However, it is important that we keep in mind that such labels yield only a simplistic way of comprehending what a religion means to its adherents. **Animistic religions**, like those of the Australian Aboriginals and many other indigenous belief systems, incorporate veneration of spirits or deities associated with natural features—rocks, mountains, trees, or rivers, for example. The environment is, in other words, an inspirited realm. Many religions are also **syncretic**—that is, they demonstrate a notable blending of beliefs and practices, usually as a result of contact between people who practice different religions. Certain African and Roman Catholic traditions became fused as a result of the African slave trade, giving rise to the syncretic religions of Santeria in Cuba and Candomblé in Brazil (**Figure 5.1**). For an introduction to Cuban Santeria, see *Video Explorations*.

> **monotheistic** The belief in or devotion to a single deity.
>
> **polytheistic** The belief in or devotion to multiple deities.
>
> **atheistic** The belief that there is no deity.

Video Explorations

Santeria

National Geographic

Santeria draws on the beliefs of West Africans, especially Yorubans, who were brought to the New World as slaves. Devotion to orishas is a fundamental aspect of Santeria, as is animal sacrifice.

A religion might also provide an explanation of the beginning of the world, or **cosmogony**. Dreamtime, discussed in the chapter opener, is a cosmogony shared by Australian Aboriginals. Cosmogonies are important because they can influence people's sense of belonging and attachment to place. Similarly, a religion may be associated with a code of behavior, morals, or ethics. For their adherents, then, religions represent or express certain truths.

Like language, religion is another facet of culture. Religion shapes the identity of a person, or an entire community.

Syncretic religion • Figure 5.1

Candomblé links worship of orishas, powerful animistic deities that manifest different qualities and energy of the divine, with Catholic saints. Candomblé recognizes a priesthood, in which the head priest is usually a woman—technically a priestess—called the *Mãe-de-Santo*, or mother of saints. Here, a Mãe-de-Santo sits in her consulting room in Bahia, Brazil.

Stephanie Maze/NG Image Collection

NATIONAL GEOGRAPHIC

Distribution of major religions • Figure 5.2

Use this chart and map to compare and contrast the sizes of the major religions and their distributions.

a. Adherents by religion and as a percentage of world population

Nearly 75% of the world's people identify with one of these four faiths: Christianity, Islam, Hinduism, and Buddhism. (*Source:* Encyclopaedia Britannica and NetLibrary, 2008.)

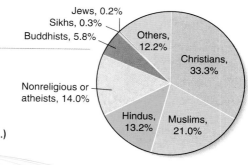

Jews, 0.2%
Sikhs, 0.3%
Buddhists, 5.8%
Others, 12.2%
Christians, 33.3%
Nonreligious or atheists, 14.0%
Hindus, 13.2%
Muslims, 21.0%

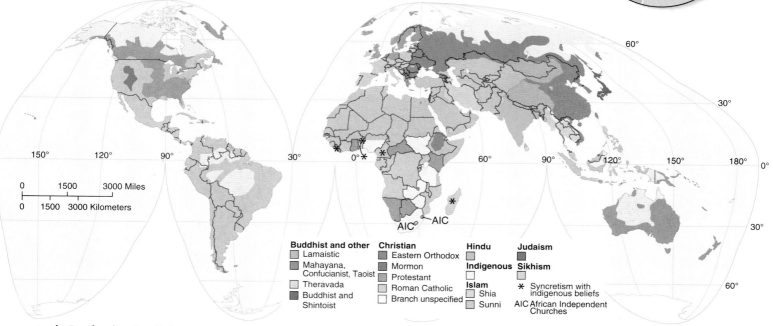

Buddhist and other
- Lamaistic
- Mahayana, Confucianist, Taoist
- Theravada
- Buddhist and Shintoist

Christian
- Eastern Orthodox
- Mormon
- Protestant
- Roman Catholic
- Branch unspecified

Hindu

Islam
- Shia
- Sunni

Indigenous

Judaism

Sikhism

* Syncretism with indigenous beliefs

AIC African Independent Churches

b. Predominant religions

Christianity's global spread stems from European conquest, colonization, and ongoing missionary work. The Middle East is a Muslim realm, but 40% of all Muslims live in the Asian countries of Indonesia, Pakistan, India, and Bangladesh. Hinduism is the largest faith in India, but the country has more than twice as many Muslims as Egypt. Buddhism is widespread across East Asia and often mixes with other religious traditions, including Confucianism, which some scholars classify as a system of ethics or a civil religion. (*Source:* NG Maps.)

NATIONAL GEOGRAPHIC

It helps people define who they are, how they behave, and how they interpret the world. Religious behavior may include the practice of **rituals** such as prayer, the maintenance of dress codes, or the celebration of religious festivals. **Piety** (or piousness) means to be deeply devoted to a religion.

Religions can be loosely grouped into two broad categories: **universalizing** and **ethnic**. Distinctions between these categories mainly involve how a religion acquires adherents or followers, and at what scale. Christianity, Islam, Buddhism, and Sikhism (a religion of northern India) are universalizing religions. Universalizing religions are closely associated with a key individual who established the religion.

Membership in ethnic religions is usually conferred by birth, and ethnic religions rarely

> **ritual** Behavior, often regularly practiced, that has personal and symbolic meaning.
>
> **universalizing religion** A belief system that is worldwide in scope, welcomes all people as potential adherents, and may also work actively to acquire converts.
>
> **ethnic religion** A belief system largely confined to the members of a single ethnic or cultural group.

use missionaries to increase the number of adherents. Ethnic religions include Judaism, Hinduism, Shintoism (a religion of Japan), and many of the belief systems of the world's indigenous peoples. Although the oldest religions in the world are ethnic religions, many of them are challenged by the growth and expansion of universalizing religions.

Globally, religion remains a profoundly influential factor in people's lives. When religious notions, symbols, and rituals infuse the political culture of an area, we refer to this as **civil religion**. For example, on the Great Seal of the United States, the Latin phrase *Annuit Cœptis* states: "He [God] has favored our undertakings." (This is visible on the back side of a dollar bill.) We will discuss civil religion in later sections, but first we need an introduction to some of the major faiths mapped in **Figure 5.2**.

Judaism, Christianity, and Islam are sometimes classified as *Abrahamic faiths*. Although the specific details differ, each of these faiths has a historical association with Abraham, who is thought to have lived in the Middle East in the 19th century BCE. In contrast, Hinduism and Buddhism are two *Vedic faiths*. The Vedas are India's oldest sacred writings and influenced the development of Hinduism. Buddhism later diverged from Hinduism. Sikhism is not exclusively Abrahamic or Vedic, but draws from both Islam and Hinduism.

Judaism

Although there are more than 13 million Jews worldwide, Israel is the only country in which a majority of the population is Jewish. Even so, the largest numbers of Jews reside in Israel and the United States, and both countries have roughly 5 million Jews each.

Abraham is considered the patriarch of the Jews, a monotheistic people who trace their origins to the Middle East. As recorded in the Torah, which is part of Judaism's sacred scripture and is sometimes referred to as the Hebrew Bible, Moses led the Jews out of slavery in Egypt.

This event is called the Exodus and constitutes a significant development in the Jewish tradition. The Torah also describes a covenant or an agreement that God made with Abraham. According to this covenant, the Jews are "chosen people" selected to uphold and abide by God's law. At Mount Sinai, in Egypt, this law was revealed to Moses. After a long desert journey the Jews settled in Canaan, the Promised Land, in what is today Israel.

Christianity

Christianity, the largest religion in the world with an estimated 2.3 billion adherents, promises forgiveness for one's sins and an eternal life in heaven through belief in Jesus and his resurrection. Most Christians share a belief in the Trinity; namely, that God is three persons in one: the Father, the Son (Jesus), and the Holy Spirit. The Bible is the holy book of Christians. Of particular importance are the Gospels, which chronicle the life of Jesus.

Since its establishment Christianity has splintered. There is not one form of Christianity; rather, many different varieties exist. As Christianity spread across Europe, it split into Western and Eastern branches. Western Christianity,

Christianity and its shift south • Figure 5.3

For many centuries, Christianity was a religion associated mainly with Europe and then with the Americas.

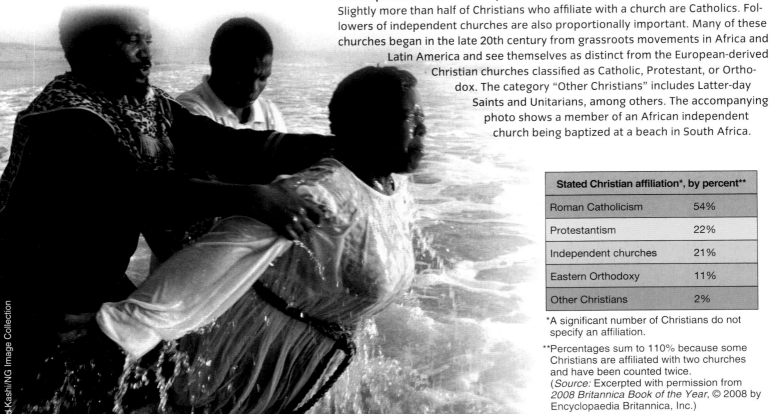

a. Composition of Christianity

Slightly more than half of Christians who affiliate with a church are Catholics. Followers of independent churches are also proportionally important. Many of these churches began in the late 20th century from grassroots movements in Africa and Latin America and see themselves as distinct from the European-derived Christian churches classified as Catholic, Protestant, or Orthodox. The category "Other Christians" includes Latter-day Saints and Unitarians, among others. The accompanying photo shows a member of an African independent church being baptized at a beach in South Africa.

Stated Christian affiliation*, by percent**	
Roman Catholicism	54%
Protestantism	22%
Independent churches	21%
Eastern Orthodoxy	11%
Other Christians	2%

*A significant number of Christians do not specify an affiliation.

**Percentages sum to 110% because some Christians are affiliated with two churches and have been counted twice.
(*Source:* Excerpted with permission from *2008 Britannica Book of the Year*, © 2008 by Encyclopaedia Britannica, Inc.)

centered on Rome and referred to as Roman Catholicism, recognized the authority of the pope. Eastern Christianity, or Eastern Orthodoxy as it came to be called, was based in Constantinople (present-day Istanbul) and did not recognize the papacy. Instead, Eastern Orthodoxy gave rise to 15 independent churches including, for example, the Greek Orthodox Church and Russian Orthodox Church. In the 16th century, Western Christianity was split by the Protestant Reformation, which took issue with Catholic practices.

The Roman Catholic, Protestant, and Eastern Orthodox branches form the three conventional branches within Christianity. About 80% of all Christians belong to one of these three branches. However, the emergence of numerous independent churches constitutes a noteworthy trend. Globally, the distribution of Christianity has changed significantly over time (**Figure 5.3**).

Islam

After Christianity, Islam is the second largest religion. More than one-fifth of the world's people call themselves Muslims. Islam is also the fastest-growing religion in the world. Geographically, Islam is the dominant religion in a belt that stretches from North Africa across the Middle East, Central Asia, and into South Asia.

Muhammad, the founder of Islam, was born in about 570 CE in Mecca, in what is now Saudi Arabia. On several occasions while meditating, Muhammad received revelations from God, whom Muslims call Allah; these revelations were communicated to him via the angel Jibril (Gabriel). Muhammad began to share with others what had been revealed to him, especially belief in the unity of Allah. He met resistance in part because of enduring polytheistic beliefs in the region.

Muslims believe that the Qur'an, Islam's holy book, records the word of God as it was revealed to Muhammad. Muslims recognize many of the people in the Old and New Testaments, including Abraham, Moses, and Jesus, for example,

b. Adherents to Christianity, 1970–2025
In the past several decades, Christianity has gained large numbers of adherents in Latin America, Africa, and Asia as a result of missionary activity, the popularity of independent churches, and population growth.
(*Source:* Data from Barrett, Johnson, and Crossing, 2005.)

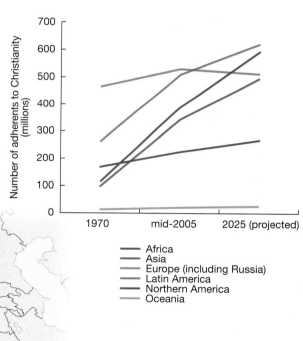

Legend:
- Africa
- Asia
- Europe (including Russia)
- Latin America
- Northern America
- Oceania

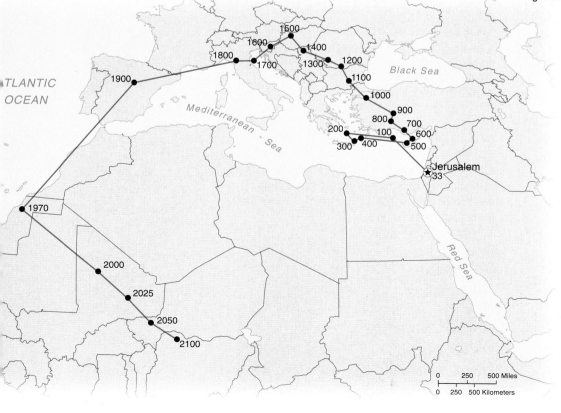

c. Christianity's global center of gravity, 33–2100 CE
An equal number of Christians live east, west, north, and south of the center of gravity. A recent study projects that the center of gravity will be located in northern Nigeria by 2100, with more than three times as many Christians living in Latin America, Africa, and Asia than in Europe and the Americas. This map shows present-day boundaries. (*Source:* Adapted from Johnson and Chung, 2004, p. 167. Wiley-Blackwell Copyright © 2004. Reprinted with permission of John Wiley & Sons Ltd.)

Geography InSight

Islam's Five Pillars of Practice • **Figure 5.4**

Islam, like many other religions, is often described as a way of life. The Five Pillars of Practice express and embody this lived dimension of the religion. Of course, being a Muslim involves more than achieving these five pillars, but they serve as major tenets of the faith.

❶ The *shahadah*, or profession of faith, in Arabic over the gateway to Topkapi Palace in Istanbul, Turkey.

❷ Muslims pray near the ticketing area of the Minneapolis-St. Paul International Airport. Muslims customarily face Mecca when they pray and kneel on a prayer rug. *Qibla*, in Arabic, means the direction of Mecca. When traveling, Muslims can use a qibla compass to determine which way to face. Alternatively, some mobile devices now come with built-in qibla compasses.

❶ Making the *shahadah*, a profession of faith expected of all Muslims. The shahadah states: There is no god but Allah, and Muhammad is his prophet.

❷ Praying five times a day. All Muslims are expected to pray before dawn, after noon, in the late afternoon, at sunset, and at night.

❸ Fasting during Ramadan, one of the months in the Islamic lunar calendar. Muslims fast from sunrise to sunset during this month in order to cleanse the body and demonstrate piety.

❹ Giving charity to the poor.

❺ Performing the *hajj*, or pilgrimage, to Mecca. All Muslims who are physically and financially capable are expected to make the hajj at least once in their life.

❸ A Muslim vendor sells food outside a mosque in Shanghai, China, during Eid al-Fitr, the festival that marks the end of Ramadan.

❹ Assembling food items donated for charity. Muslims with sufficient financial means are obligated to pay *zakat*—that is, to give 2.5% of their yearly savings for charitable purposes.

❺ The hajj is an annual pilgrimage to Mecca that Muslims participate in simultaneously. Since Islam uses a lunar calendar, the dates for the hajj, as for Ramadan, vary. Recently, the hajj has drawn more than 2 million Muslims.

but they consider Muhammad to be the final prophet of God. Islam combines faith and practice, and certain obligations are expected of all Muslims. These obligations are expressed in the Five Pillars of Practice (**Figure 5.4**).

Islam consists of two main branches, Sunnis and Shias (or Shiites). The Sunni branch is the largest and most geographically widespread branch of Islam. About 80% of all Muslims are Sunnis. No more than 15% of Muslims are Shias, although they make up a majority of the population in four countries: Iran, Iraq, Azerbaijan, and Bahrain. Other smaller branches account for the remainder of the Muslim population.

The Sunni and Shia branches emerged following Muhammad's death in 632 CE when disagreements arose about who should succeed him. Those Muslims who felt that Muhammad's immediate successor should come from within his family and favored Ali, Muhammad's cousin and son-in-law, became known as the Shias. The others, called the Sunnis, accepted someone outside Muhammad's family as the first successor. Another difference between Sunnis and Shias involves *imams*. For Sunnis, *imams* lead group prayers. For Shias, however, *Imam* is a special title reserved for a line of twelve revered and infallible spiritual leaders. Ali was the first Imam.

Hinduism

Sanatana dharma, meaning "eternal truth," is the name some Hindus use for their religion. The terms *Hindu* and, later, *Hinduism* came to be used by outsiders to refer to the people and their religion in the region that would become India. Approximately 900 million people in the world identify Hinduism as their religion, making it the largest ethnic religion in the world. Most Hindus live in South Asia, specifically India.

Hinduism includes a great diversity of religious beliefs and practices, but some common elements exist. Hindus view existence as cyclical such that souls are immortal and subject to reincarnation. The process of reincarnation brings spiritual suffering and is controlled by *karma*, the influence of past thoughts and actions. Hindus strive to attain *moksha*, or release from the cycle of death and rebirth. Moksha has been described as a state of freedom or bliss.

In the Hindu cosmogony, Brahman is the supreme spiritual source and sustainer of the universe, variously understood as an absolute and eternal force as well as a supreme being. Hinduism includes a vast number of gods and goddesses, and Hindus believe these deities express different qualities of Brahman (**Figure 5.5**).

Shiva statue • Figure 5.5

One prominent Hindu deity is Shiva, the destroyer. Located in Bengaluru, India, this statue depicts a meditating Shiva at Mount Kailash, his heavenly home. His four arms are symbolic of supreme power.

Dibyangshu Sarkar/AFP/Getty Images, Inc.

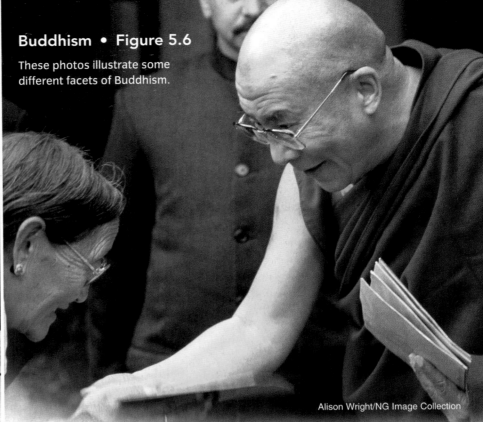

Buddhism • Figure 5.6

These photos illustrate some different facets of Buddhism.

Martin Gray/NG Image Collection

Alison Wright/NG Image Collection

a. A devotee stands in front of a statue of Buddha in Sri Lanka. In contrast to Islam, which forbids depictions of Muhammad and God, representations of the Buddha are common where Buddhism is practiced.

b. The Dalai Lama, shown here greeting Tibetans, serves as the spiritual authority of Tibet, but he has lived in exile since China invaded and occupied the region in 1959. Tibetan Buddhists believe that the Dalai Lama is the reincarnation of the bodhisattva of mercy and that when he dies his spirit will be reincarnated and enter a child.

Buddhism

Buddhism remains closely associated with East and Southeast Asia. In China, Japan, Hong Kong, Taiwan, and Singapore, Buddhism is prevalent but mixes with other local traditions, including Confucianism.

The founder of Buddhism, Siddhartha Gautama (6th century BCE), was raised a Hindu prince and lived a privileged life, sheltered from the sufferings of the sick and impoverished. Tradition maintains that at the age of 29 he witnessed these social problems and, out of compassion, gave up his life of comfort and sought to end human suffering. Siddhartha Gautama attained enlightenment while meditating. This marks his transformation into the *Buddha*, literally the *enlightened one*. After this, he began to teach and acquire disciples. His teachings are recorded in different documents, the oldest of which is the *Tripitaka*.

Buddhists believe that suffering is linked to reincarnation, and they seek to attain *nirvana*, escape from the cycle of death and rebirth. The Buddha's teachings centered on the Four Noble Truths:

1. Life brings suffering.
2. Desire causes this suffering.
3. This suffering can be overcome and nirvana can be attained.
4. Disciplining the mind and body by practicing proper thinking and behavior ends this suffering and leads to nirvana.

There are three major branches within Buddhism: Theravada, Mahayana, and Tantrayana Buddhism. Theravada means "Way of the Elders," and this form of Buddhism cultivates a monastic approach that emphasizes the study of Buddhist scripture and the practice of disciplined behavior. Meditation forms an important part of this effort. Theravada Buddhism maintains a greater presence in the island country of Sri Lanka as well as the mainland Southeast Asian countries of Thailand, Myanmar, Cambodia, and Laos. Theravada Buddhists account for fewer than 40% of all Buddhists.

Mahayana, meaning "Great Vehicle," broadened the appeal of Buddhism. Mahayana Buddhists believe that the Buddha is a compassionate deity and that Mahayana Buddhism provides a way for believers to be saved from the cycle of rebirth. Devotion to *bodhisattvas* ("Buddhas-to-be") also distin-

c. A Zen Buddhist priest meditates at the "dry landscape" garden at a Buddhist temple in Japan. Zen Buddhism developed as a movement within Mahayana Buddhism and encourages followers to cultivate the Buddha within oneself. Gardens like this aid meditation.

guishes this branch of the religion. Bodhisattvas are celestial beings that represent the qualities of the Buddha and help others achieve enlightenment. Mahayana Buddhism is most closely associated with China, Korea, Japan, and Vietnam. Slightly more than half of all Buddhists are Mahayanists.

The smallest branch of Buddhism, Tantrayana Buddhism, emerged in Tibet and spread to Mongolia. Syncretic in character, Tibetan Buddhism fused aspects of Mahayana Buddhism and native Tibetan beliefs. Indigenous influences in Mongolia have shaped the practice of Buddhism there. For many decades, however, Communist rule suppressed religious practices in both places. **Figure 5.6** illustrates some other dimensions of Buddhism.

Sikhism

Some 23 million adherents practice Sikhism, making it the smallest of the major universalizing religions. A *guru* is an inspired religious teacher, and the word *Sikh* means *disciple*. Guru Nanak (1469–1538) founded Sikhism. Sikhs believe that Guru Nanak experienced a divine revelation, after which he began teaching and establishing Sikh communities.

Sikhism emerged in northern India and bears the influences of Hinduism and Islam. For example, Sikhism teaches belief in and worship of one creator god and yet emphasizes the importance of karma. The holy book for Sikhism is the *Guru Granth Sahib*, also called the *Guru Granth*. It consists of a compilation of hymns revealed to Guru Nanak and several other gurus. Sikhs call this holy book a *guru* because they consider it to be the source of spiritual authority today.

CONCEPT CHECK STOP

1. **What** is a syncretic religion? Explain using a specific example.

2. **How** does the concept of scale relate to universalizing and ethnic religions?

3. **How** has the global geography of Christianity recently changed? Why?

4. **Where** are Buddhism and Hinduism prevalent, and how are the two faiths similar and different?

Religious Hearths and Diffusion

LEARNING OBJECTIVES

1. **Distinguish** between primary and secondary hearths.

2. **Define** diaspora.

3. **Relate** the spread of religion to different types of diffusion.

Every religion emerges in a hearth. For many adherents to a specific religion, places or sites within the hearth often acquire sacred qualities because of their association with significant events in the growth and development of the religion. Geographers recognize two categories of religious hearths: primary and secondary. *Primary hearths* are those places or regions where a wholly new religion develops. In contrast, *secondary hearths* are the places or regions where a religion fragments internally to form a new branch. Remarkably, two primary hearths, the Semitic and the Indic, have generated more religions—and more enduring religions—than any other regions (**Figure 5.7**).

Religions of the Semitic Hearth

As the birthplace of a religion, the hearth usually represents its dominant symbolic center even though the hearth may or may not be home to many of that religion's adherents. The region known historically as Palestine, and which today roughly coincides with Israel, constitutes the hearth of Judaism. However, the opportunity for Jews to live in the hearth has been much contested. The term **diaspora** developed as a specific reference to the dispersion of the Jewish population that occurred in the sixth century BCE when the Babylonians sacked Jerusalem and exiled the Jews to Babylonia, now part of Iraq. Then, following the Roman destruction of Jerusalem in 70 CE, the Jews were again expelled from Palestine. By some estimates, as many as 2 to 5 million Jews lived outside of Palestine in the first century CE, many taking residence in Europe and North Africa. Nazi atrocities committed prior to and during World War II killed 6 million Jews in Europe. These horrific events prompted many Jews to leave

> **diaspora** The scattering of a people through forced migration.

Primary hearths • Figure 5.7

Judaism, Christianity, and Islam emerged in the Semitic hearth, whereas Hinduism, Buddhism, Sikhism, and another South Asian faith, Jainism, emerged in the Indic hearth. In both the Semitic and Indic hearths, these developments played out over many centuries. ► **Why does the identification of religious hearths sometimes become a contested practice?**

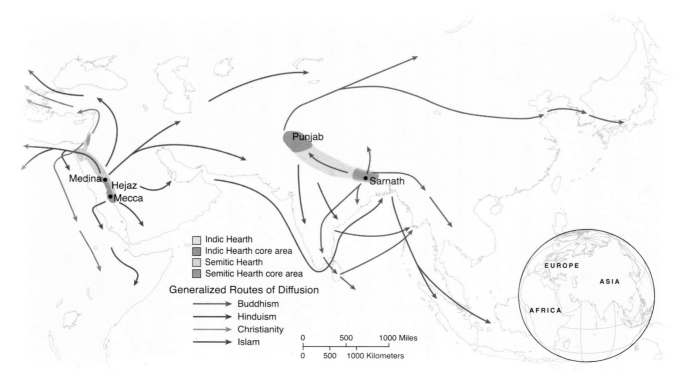

Christianity in the United States: Diffusion and fragmentation • Figure 5.8

Colonists from Europe, followed by later waves of immigrants, transferred and implanted their religious beliefs in the Americas, reshaping the religious landscape in the process.

NATIONAL GEOGRAPHIC

a. Most prevalent U.S. religious groups by county or locality

This map provides a powerful visual reminder that the label *Christianity* disguises the diversity of this religious tradition as well as the fragmentation that has affected it beyond its primary hearth. Note that important centers of Islam and Judaism are also shown. ▶ **What would be an example of a secondary hearth of Christianity in the United States?** (*Source:* NG Maps based on *College Atlas of the World*, 2007, p. 86.)

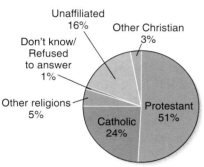

b. Religious affiliation in the United States

Globally, Catholics outnumber Protestants, but in the United States, the reverse is true. (*Source:* Data from Pew Research Center, 2008.)

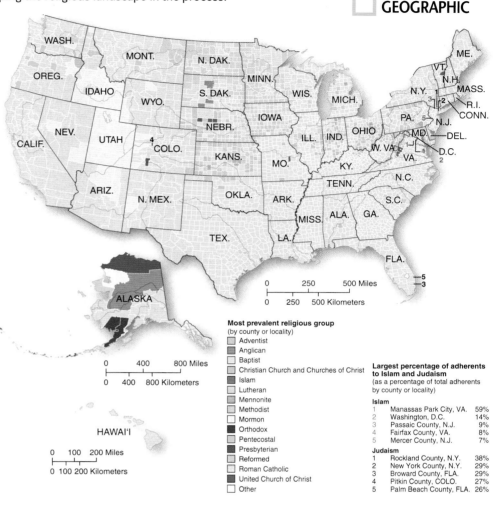

Most prevalent religious group (by county or locality)
- Adventist
- Anglican
- Baptist
- Christian Church and Churches of Christ
- Islam
- Lutheran
- Mennonite
- Methodist
- Mormon
- Orthodox
- Pentecostal
- Presbyterian
- Reformed
- Roman Catholic
- United Church of Christ
- Other

Largest percentage of adherents to Islam and Judaism (as a percentage of total adherents by county or locality)

Islam
1	Manassas Park City, VA.	59%
2	Washington, D.C.	14%
3	Passaic County, N.J.	9%
4	Fairfax County, VA.	8%
5	Mercer County, N.J.	7%

Judaism
1	Rockland County, N.Y.	38%
2	New York County, N.Y.	29%
3	Broward County, FLA.	29%
4	Pitkin County, COLO.	27%
5	Palm Beach County, FLA.	26%

Europe for Palestine and the Americas and also renewed the Jewish desire for a country of their own. Amid much controversy, in 1948 the Jewish state of Israel was carved out of land in the Middle East.

Palestine, the region of the Middle East where Jesus was born, began to teach, and gained disciples, constitutes the hearth of Christianity. Thus, Christianity and Judaism share similar but not identical hearths. At the local scale, for example, the geography of the hearth of Christianity becomes defined by those places closely associated with key events in the religion's formative period.

Contagious, relocation, and hierarchical diffusion all factored in the spread of Christianity. Jesus and the 12 disciples initially spread Christianity in contagious fashion through their personal interactions with non-Christians. Following the crucifixion of Jesus, the apostle Paul traveled as a missionary to regions bordering the Mediterranean Sea, visiting parts of Syria, Turkey, Greece, and Italy and spreading the Christian religion via relocation and contagious diffusion. In 313 CE, the Roman Emperor Constantine converted to Christianity. Subsequently, Christianity became the official religion of the Roman Empire. This development set in motion a form of hierarchical diffusion in which the religion of the emperor became the religion of the people. The rise of Christianity in cities such as Alexandria, Damascus, Constantinople, and Rome before it became established in the countryside surrounding these places shows another type of hierarchical diffusion, from large cities to smaller towns and villages. European colonialism as well as past and present missionary activity have carried Christianity far beyond its hearth, and in the process Christianity has become highly fragmented. See **Figure 5.8** for one depiction of this fragmentation.

Where Geographers CLICK

Pew Forum on Religion & Public Life: U.S. Religious Landscape Survey

Comparisons

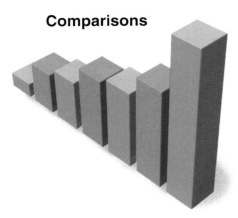

Compare the demographic characteristics, religious beliefs and practices as well as social and political views of various religious traditions in the U.S.

By clicking on the Maps tab at the Pew Forum website you can view and compare maps of the United States that show affiliation with different religious traditions. (*Source:* Pew Research Center © 2009; http://religions.pewforum.org.)

See *Where Geographers Click* to explore additional maps of religious beliefs in the United States.

Unlike Judaism and Christianity, Islam has its origins in territory that is now part of Saudi Arabia. More specifically, the Hejaz region where Mecca and Medina are situated constitutes the primary hearth of Islam. The origin and initial diffusion of Islam are closely linked to urban places. After its establishment in the 6th century, Islam spread rapidly and hierarchically, moving along established trading routes across North Africa and the Middle East. Commerce, military conquest, and scholarship contributed to the spread of Islam. Muslim scholars established libraries and academies in North Africa. By the early 8th century, Islam stretched from Spain across Central Asia and into India. Relocation diffusion was also involved. Muslim traders reached Southeast Asia in the 13th century, laying the foundation for the growth of Islam in present-day Indonesia and Malaysia.

Religions of the Indic Hearth

One of the world's oldest religions, Hinduism began to take shape some 4000 years ago. Although the hearth of Hinduism is difficult to pinpoint precisely, most scholars situate it in the Punjab, a region spanning the border between northern India and Pakistan (refer again to Figure 5.7). Unlike universalizing religions, the origin of Hinduism is generally associated with the upper classes rather than the influence of one key individual.

Hinduism diffused hierarchically and in conjunction with Sanskrit, the language of the *Vedas*. From the Punjab, Hinduism spread through the Ganges River Valley and south across the subcontinent. Relocation diffusion has carried Hinduism beyond South Asia. About 4 million Hindus live in Indonesia, mainly on the island of Bali, and about 1 million Hindus live in the United States. Smaller Hindu communities have developed a notable presence on the Caribbean island of Trinidad and in the South American countries of Suriname and Guyana. South Asian Indians were brought to these places as indentured laborers after the African slave trade ended.

Compared to Hinduism, Buddhism is a more recent faith that dates to the 6th century BCE. Siddhartha Gautama delivered his first sermon at Sarnath, near Varanasi, helping to establish the hearth of Buddhism in the eastern lowlands of the Ganges River in India. Following his enlightenment, the Buddha continued to travel and teach for more than 40 years, playing a role in the diffusion of the religion. His disciples also helped spread the religion within India. Buddhism spread through Central Asia along trade routes, entering China during the 1st century CE. In India and China, Buddhist monks frequently settled together, creating monastic communities called *sangha*. These communities often became centers of learning and continued the diffusion of Buddhism. In the 4th century CE, Buddhism diffused from China to Korea. From Korea, Buddhism spread to Japan, becoming established there in the 6th century. Buddhism was introduced to Tibet from northern India in the 7th century.

Sikhism, a third religion of the Indic hearth, dates to the 16th century CE and has its origins in the Punjab, the same region where Hinduism emerged. Compared

Sikhism and Khalistan • Figure 5.9

The creation of India and Pakistan in 1947 led to the division of the Punjab, Sikhism's hearth. Many Sikhs desire their own independent country, Khalistan, and celebrate Khalistan Day (*Vaisakhi*) as a way of expressing their religious and political commitment to this goal. This parade is in Washington, D.C.

Courtesy National Khalsa (Khalistan) Day Parade Organization.

to other universalizing religions, however, Sikhism has not spread as extensively. Nevertheless, the British colonization of South Asia contributed to the relocation diffusion of Sikhism and the emergence of diasporic Sikh communities. For example, Sikhs were recruited to work as police officers in Hong Kong, as soldiers in the British army in what is now Malaysia, and as railroad workers in East Africa, among other places (**Figure 5.9**).

CONCEPT CHECK STOP

1. **Where** are the Indic and Semitic hearths?
2. **How** is the concept of diaspora related to the geography of religion?
3. **How** has hierarchical diffusion factored in the spread of Christianity and Hinduism?

Religion, Society, and Globalization

LEARNING OBJECTIVES

1. **Discuss** the role of sacred spaces in religion.
2. **Distinguish** between modernism and religious fundamentalism.

3. **Summarize** the influence of religion on social institutions.
4. **Describe** the geography of Renewalism.

At the start of this chapter we discussed the close connection between religion and culture. Indeed, many adherents describe their religion as a "way of life." Of particular interest to geographers are the ways in which religion colors how people understand and interpret the world as well as their place in it. As geographer Roger Stump

(2008, p. 23) has observed, "religious groups do not simply exist in space; they also imagine and construct space in terms related to their faith." In the following sections, we explore some of the ways that religion shapes individual and collective views about territory, identity, and society. We begin with a consideration of sacred space.

Sacred Space

Sacred space is space that has special religious significance and meaning that makes it worthy of reverence or devotion. Sacred space includes specific places and sites that are recognized for their sanctity; however, a sacred space need not be territorially defined. The performance of religious rituals such as praying, for example, often creates a highly personal sacred space.

Ideas about sacred space can become a source of disagreement and even conflict among people. For the Mescalero Apache in New Mexico and west Texas, some sacred spaces include regions where they collect natural

Jerusalem's many sacred spaces • Figure 5.10

Jerusalem contains sites sacred to Christians, Jews, and Muslims that are in very close proximity and in some cases overlapping. What makes control of and access to these spaces so contentious is the fact that some adherents to these faiths believe that they have a unique and exclusive religious claim to them.

a. Jerusalem's Old City, the location of numerous sacred sites
The Old City is surrounded by a wall and internally partitioned into four quarters, mainly along religious lines. (*Source:* NG Maps.)

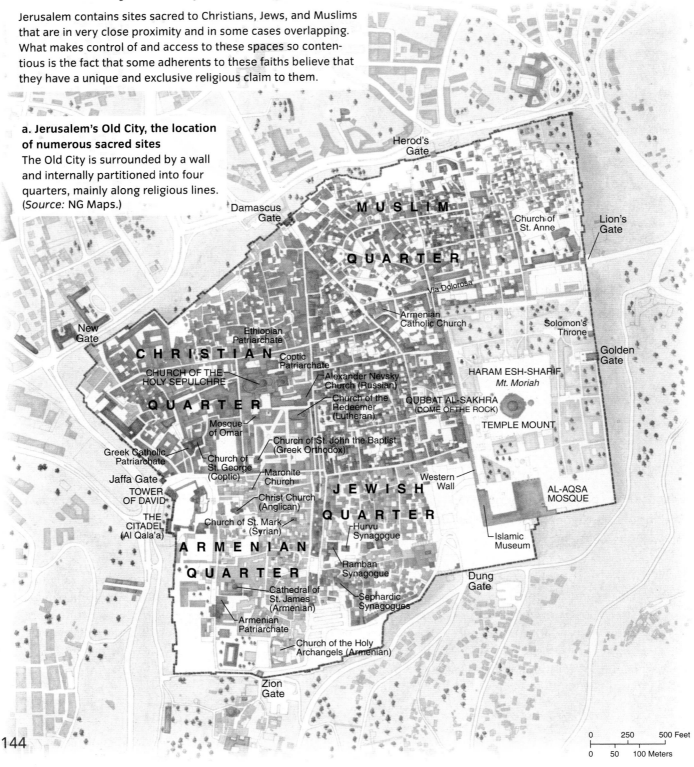

resources such as sage or mesquite fruits. When these sacred spaces exist on land that has since become federal land or highway easements, the Mescalero Apache have been charged fees, fined, or harassed for collecting these resources.

To protect their sacredness, two of the holiest cities in Islam, Mecca and Medina, are closed to non-Muslims. In an effort to resist globalization and specifically Americanization, the terrorist network al-Qaeda has argued that all of Saudi Arabia constitutes an Islamic sacred space. To al-Qaeda members, the presence of non-Muslim Americans in the country constitutes a perceived desecration of this sacred space. One of the most complex and contentious examples of sacred space involves the city of Jerusalem (**Figure 5.10**).

b. The Temple Mount, as it is known to Jews, or Haram al-Sharif—the Noble Sanctuary—to Muslims
This contested site is sacred to both groups. Muslims believe the Dome of the Rock, which sits atop the Temple Mount, marks the site from which Muhammad ascended to heaven. After Mecca and Medina, Jerusalem ranks as the third holiest site in Islam. Jews pray at the Western, or Wailing Wall, below the Dome of the Rock. For Jews, Jerusalem's Temple Mount is sacred because it housed the First and Second Temples of the Jews, which were destroyed by the Babylonians and Romans, respectively. All that remains of the Second Temple is the Western Wall.

Martin Gray/NG Image Collection

Michael Melford/NG Image Collection

c. The Church of the Holy Sepulchre
For Christians, the Church of the Holy Sepulchre marks the site of the crucifixion, burial, and resurrection of Jesus. Space within the church is heavily contested by different Christian communities, including the Greek Orthodox, Roman Catholic, Armenian, and others, and disputes among them are not uncommon.

Pilgrimage A **pilgrimage** is a journey to a sacred place or site for religious reasons. Some pilgrimages, such as the hajj for Muslims, are obligatory, whereas others are voluntary. Pilgrims conduct these journeys for a variety of reasons: to purify the soul, to demonstrate devotion, to fulfill a vow, to contemplate or gain proximity to the divine, to seek divine or supernatural assistance, to give thanks, or to perform an act of penance. Although specific reasons for and patterns of pilgrimage vary from one religion to another and even from one person to another, the geographical study of pilgrimage includes the identification of major and minor pilgrimage sites and the patterns of circulation. Major destinations can be distinguished from minor destinations on the basis of their perceived holiness, the number of pilgrims they attract, and the *catchment area*—the size and kinds of areas sending pilgrims to a particular site. Going on a pilgrimage constitutes a kind of ritual and factors prominently in many faiths (**Figure 5.11**).

Community, identity, and scale Religion can provide a strong basis for community and individual identity. In Islam the idea of a Muslim community is often expressed at different scales, from the global to the individual. The Arabic term *umma*, meaning "community of believers," refers to the worldwide population of Muslims and imagines this group of people as a community whose identity transcends doctrinal differences and geographic separation. *Dar al-Islam*, or House of Islam, usually refers to countries that are majority Muslim, but depending on the context it might also include Muslims who live in non-Muslim countries. A third scale involves the mosque. Weekly communal worship at a local mosque contributes to the sense of a shared identity among Muslims, as does planning and accumulating the resources to construct a mosque. Finally, when Muslims fast during Ramadan or when Muslim women veil themselves, the body becomes the site of an important scale of identity.

Pilgrimage in selected religions • Figure 5.11

Christians, Buddhists, and Hindus are not required to make a pilgrimage, but many adherents of these faiths do.

NATIONAL GEOGRAPHIC

Bob Edme/AP Photo

a. Pilgrimage is virtually absent in Protestantism and most pronounced in Catholicism, which possesses an elaborate network of sacred pilgrimage sites. Major destinations include the Holy Land—encompassing places such as Bethlehem and Jerusalem—as well as Rome, Italy. For many Catholics, sites associated with appearances of the Virgin Mary receive special veneration and are also major pilgrimage destinations. Most of these sites are outside Christianity's hearth. Annually, more than 6 million pilgrims flock to Lourdes, France, shown here. The basilica was built above a grotto reported to be the site of apparitions of the Virgin Mary and miracle cures.

How do other religions express a sense of community or identity at different scales?

Religion and settlement We have already seen how beliefs about sacred space can cultivate strong attachments between people and territory and can lead to competing ideas about how a particular area or site is used or who claims it. However, other distinctive associations between religious communities and territory can also develop. Diasporic religious communities—those that have become displaced from their religious hearth—provide a good example. For instance, some diasporic communities develop powerful ideas about specific territories, such that these spaces come to be perceived not only as a holy land but also as a homeland for the community of believers.

To escape persecution, the Mormons migrated beyond the frontier in the United States in the 19th century and into territory that would become Utah. There they sought to create an ideal community, a settlement that they called *Zion*, and that is known today as Salt Lake City. To the Mormon settlers, Zion represented a new Jerusalem and the start of their endeavor to build the Kingdom of God on Earth. Thus, Salt Lake City developed as a holy city for Mormons in accordance with principles established by Joseph Smith, the religion's founder. The city plan, including its square blocks, wide streets, and a designated Temple Square, linked their religious ideals with a distinctive urban form.

For the Jews, another diasporic religious community, religion and settlement have long been closely interconnected. As we have discussed, Jewish people have a special relationship with the land of Israel, which they believe was promised to Abraham and his descendants by God. Thus, they refer to this area as the Promised Land, and the desire of eventually returning to it became

b. For Buddhists, major pilgrim destinations are concentrated in the hearth area and are associated with significant events in the Buddha's life: his birthplace, his enlightenment, his first sermon, and his death. These pilgrims pray and meditate at the Bodhi Tree, or Bo Tree, where Siddhartha Gautama attained enlightenment.

c. Among Hindus, the Ganges River is revered for its energy and for its ability to sustain life and remove negative karma. A number of important pilgrimage sites have developed in close proximity to or along the banks of this river at places like this in Haridwar, where people can immerse themselves.

and continues to be an aspiration of many Jews. During the 19th century, a political movement known as *Zionism* developed. One of the goals of this movement was to create a religious and political homeland for Jews. This goal was partially realized in 1948 with the creation of the state of Israel; however, this development brought other issues to the forefront (**Figure 5.12**).

Sacred places and civil religion

We have seen that sacred sites can become powerful magnets for pilgrims and that ideas about sacred space more broadly can influence settlement patterns. But how does a place become a sacred place? The answer involves the process of **sanctification**. Because the concept of sacredness also applies in the realm of civil religion, as, for example, in the way societies venerate certain political leaders, veterans, and symbols of states such as flags, we can use civil religion to understand how sanctification occurs. Through the study of landscapes of tragedy, geographer Kenneth Foote has demonstrated how sacred sites develop and gain significance within the context of civil religion. **Figure 5.13** provides an adaptation of his explanation of sanctification.

Israeli–Palestinian conflict • Figure 5.12

This map series illustrates the emergence of Israel, a Jewish state.

a. Establishment of the state of Israel in 1948 brought the Zionist dream for a Jewish homeland, reminiscent of the Kingdom of Israel that existed in biblical times, closer to fruition. Simultaneously, however, Palestinians, a largely Muslim population living in the area, were made stateless.

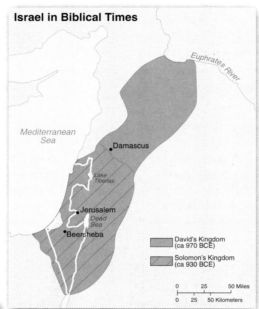

b. The Zionist dream was more fully realized in 1967 when Israel gained control of the West Bank—part of the biblical lands known as Judea and Samaria and to which Jews have a deep attachment—and access to the Western Wall in Jerusalem after the Six-Day War.

c. The political status of Jerusalem and the West Bank remains highly contested because both Palestinians and Jews feel they have legitimate claims to them. Some Jews have built settlements in the West Bank, though they are considered illegal by the United Nations. Religion is a significant factor in the Israeli-Palestinian conflict, but questions of citizenship and water rights are also involved.

Sanctification • Figure 5.13

Sanctification refers to the making of a sacred site after a significant event has occurred there. Here we consider the example of the former site of the Murrah Federal Building in Oklahoma City, which was bombed in an act of domestic terrorism in 1995. This site is today recognized as a national memorial.

© AP/Wide World Photos

❶ The event

The north side of the building in Oklahoma City is blown away by a massive truck bomb on April 19, 1995, killing 168 and injuring over 800.

Jeff Haynes/AFP//Getty Images, Inc.

❷ Informal consecration: emerging consensus and spontaneous memorials

Consecration involves public activities that set a place apart and contribute to its sacredness. Informal consecration begins as people react to the tragic event and a consensus emerges that the site is worthy of remembrance. Temporary memorials make the site hallowed.

❸ Formal consecration: official consensus for a permanent monument

An organization or other entity establishes the memorial boundaries, acquires legal right to use the land, makes plans for a permanent monument, and manages funds for the perpetual upkeep of the site. This is the Oklahoma City National Memorial, with 168 chairs (one for each victim) and a survivors' tree.

J. Pat Carter/©AP/Wide World Photos

❹ Final consecration: solemn dedication of the site

Color guard stands at the Field of Chairs during the dedication ceremony that dignifies this sacred site.

❺ Ritual commemoration

Collective memory of the event at the site is promoted through regular practices, such as an annual ceremony, or events like this Memorial Marathon.

Doug Hoke/The Oklahoman

Jerry Laizure/©AP/Wide World Photos

Tradition and Change

All religions confront the pressure to change. Indeed, as societies change economically and politically, so do people's attitudes, beliefs, and values. Of the many developments propelling such change, three deserve attention: modernism, secularization, and globalization.

Modernism refers to an intellectual movement that encourages scientific thought, the expansion of knowledge, and belief in the inevitability of progress. The roots of modernism date to the European Enlightenment of the 1700s. To some religious groups, however, modernism is perceived as dangerous because of its potential to contribute to **secularization** by reducing the scope or influence of religion. Similar concerns have been raised about globalization and its capacity to secularize society. In the early 20th century, for example, Pope Pius X formally condemned modernism because of the way it challenged basic Catholic beliefs such as the authority of the Bible. To this day, the tension between tradition and change can still be seen in the way the Vatican resists expanding women's reproductive rights and allowing women to serve as priests.

One area where Hinduism has encountered tension between tradition and change involves castes. The **caste system** refers to a hierarchical form of social stratification historically associated with Hinduism. The ancient Hindu literature known as the *Vedas* (1500–1200 BCE) contains the oldest written description of this system. The *Vedas* identify four social classes called *varnas*, ranked on the basis of purity. The caste system is hereditary, and children are born into the varna of their parents. In the past there was a strong connection between a person's varna and the occupations a person could expect to enter. Later developments introduced a fifth category of people who were considered so impure that they fell outside the varna system altogether—literally outcasts. These came to be known as the *untouchables*, and today they are called *Dalits*, meaning "the oppressed." Although the caste system has been abolished by law and is less meaningful in urban settings, it still affects social relations and interaction in rural areas (**Figure 5.14**).

Resistance to change is sometimes expressed through various kinds of fundamentalism. **Religious fundamentalism** involves an interpretation of the principles of one's faith in such a way that they come to shape all aspects of private and public life. Although the media often report on violent acts of fundamentalist groups, most fundamentalist groups do not espouse violence or terrorism. Moreover, fundamentalist movements have affected many religions, including Christianity, Hinduism, Islam, and Judaism. Christian fundamentalists consider the Bible to be infallible and to provide clear direction on political, moral, and social issues. In the United States, Christian fundamentalists oppose such practices as the teaching of evolution and the legalization of abortion.

Islamic traditionalism, or Islamism, is a movement that favors a return to or preservation of traditional, premodern Islam and resists Westernization and globalization. The al-Qaeda attacks on 9/11 specifically targeted the World Trade Center and the Pentagon

Caste system • Figure 5.14

The caste system incorporates ideas about social and spatial order. Members of a higher caste could become socially polluted just by nearness to Dalits, who were associated with jobs believed to be unclean.

a. Dalits make up about 16% of India's population, Brahmins, about 5%.

> **Think Critically**
> How could a cultural landscape such as a village reflect the caste system?

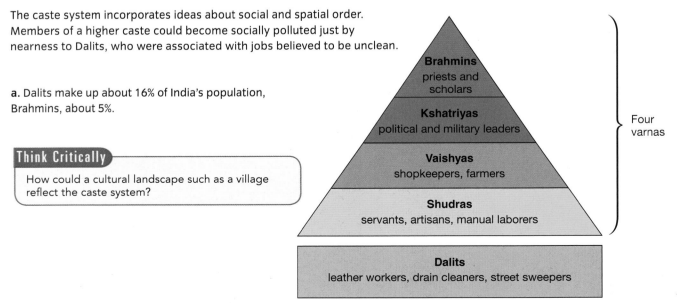

Brahmins
priests and scholars

Kshatriyas
political and military leaders

Vaishyas
shopkeepers, farmers

Shudras
servants, artisans, manual laborers

Four varnas

Dalits
leather workers, drain cleaners, street sweepers

in part because of their association with Westernization, globalization, and the perceived secularization of the world. Islamic traditionalism has existed for many years, but it is only recently that militants within this religious movement have adopted terrorism to help them accomplish their goals.

What is jihad? **Jihad** is popularly understood to mean "holy war," but a preferred translation yields the phrase "utmost struggle." This phrase has two meanings. It can be understood as a personal struggle to uphold the tenets of the faith or as a defense of Islam from threats posed by nonbelievers. In contrast to conventional Islam, some Islamic traditionalists take a very literal interpretation of this second sense, claiming that it justifies the use of terrorism as a way for Muslims to defend their faith. However, most Muslims reject this view.

Religious Law and Social Space

Religion clearly forms a significant part of the everyday functioning of society. Religion has a major presence in numerous dimensions of private and public space. Institutions such as the legal system, education, and government can reflect and be influenced by faith. These close relationships between religion and society may seem odd or unusual to most Americans, who are accustomed to the separation of church and state. Yet, in a number of states, Sunday-closing laws, or *blue laws*—laws that prohibit the sale of certain nonessential merchandise such as alcohol, tobacco, or even motor vehicles—still

exist. Blue laws derive from Sabbath-day laws that were once common in England and were designed to encourage proper observance of the day of rest.

Observance of the Sabbath is stipulated in the Ten Commandments and forms a part of the Judeo-Christian tradition but certainly is not unique to it. For Jews, the Sabbath extends from Friday to Saturday evening. As with Christians, there are variations among Jews in how the Sabbath is observed. Orthodox Jews, for example, eschew use of electricity and of motor vehicles on the Sabbath. Jewish law, called *halacah*, goes beyond the Ten Commandments and includes principles given in the Torah as well as other Jewish teachings. Dietary practices associated with keeping kosher, such as not mixing meat and milk products, stem from the divine law of the Torah.

Muslims use the term **sharia** to refer to Islamic law derived from the Qur'an, the teachings of Muhammad, and other sources. Sharia addresses different dimensions of people's lives, such as marriage, divorce, inheritance, and the status of women. Across the Muslim world many different interpretations of sharia exist. Broadly speaking, modernists see the need for sharia to be flexible and open to different interpretations in order to apply in today's society, whereas traditionalists favor narrower, more literal interpretations. Some of the strictest interpretations of sharia are associated with the Taliban, a fundamentalist movement. In Afghanistan between 1996 and 2001 and in the Swat Valley of Pakistan between 2007 and 2009, Taliban forces used sharia to justify their tyrannical control over local citizens, including prohibiting girls from attending

b. Shown here is a mass conversion to Buddhism in Mumbai, India. As it developed, the caste system sanctioned discrimination. Nowhere was this clearer than in the treatment of the Dalits, who were excluded from Hindu temples and other public facilities. Understandably, many Dalits and other lower caste Hindus have converted to Buddhism.

The status of Islamic law (sharia) in the Muslim world • Figure 5.15

This map highlights a range of perspectives on the relationship between religion and the state. According to Iran's constitution, all laws must be based on Islam. In Malaysia, Islamic law applies only to Muslims. Mauritania is an Islamic republic but does not privilege sharia in its legislation. (Data from: Stahnke and Blitt, 2005, with updates.)

☐ Constitution recognizes Islamic law as a principal basis for legislation

☐ Constitution recognizes the use of Islamic law in certain domains

☐ Constitution does not recognize Islamic law as a principal basis for legislation

★ Constitution specifically declares the state secular

Ask Yourself

1. What happens to the status of sharia at greater distances from Islam's hearth?
2. What term describes this pattern?

school. See **Figure 5.15** for a depiction of the spatial variation in the status of sharia across the Muslim world.

Globalization of Renewalism

The fastest growing branch within Christianity is **Renewalism**, a broad term that includes the Pentecostal and Charismatic movements. Examples of Pentecostal denominations include the Assemblies of God and the Church of God in Christ. Pentecostalism emphasizes interacting with and being "filled with the Holy Spirit" (Acts 2:4 NAS). For example, speaking in tongues, faith healing, and the performance of miracles are considered manifestations of the Holy Spirit. Charismatics are Catholics, Protestants, or Orthodox Christians who share a belief in the *charisms,* or gifts, of the Holy Spirit but do not belong to Pentecostal denominations. Note that Christian fundamentalists are not Renewalists and do not share the same beliefs about the gifts of the Holy Spirit.

Uncontrolled bodily movements such as speaking in tongues and altered states of consciousness, have a long historical relationship with different belief systems. For an Indonesian example, see *Video Explorations*.

Renewalists now constitute the second largest group of Christians, after Catholics. Estimates indicate that

Video Explorations

Self-Stabbing

In Bali, where Hinduism has mixed with animism, religious devotees undergo a self-stabbing ritual while in a trance. Trance states are common in the rituals of certain faiths, including Renewalism, as for example when adherents speak in tongues. In rituals of this sort, how important is place?

Megachurches • Figure 5.16

Reuters/Jo Yong-Hak/Landov LLC

Megachurches originated in the United States, but now exist on every inhabited continent. In recent decades, megachurches have grown rapidly.

a. Yoido Full Gospel Church, shown here, is a Pentecostal church in Seoul, South Korea with 800,000 members. For comparison, Lakewood Church in Houston, Texas, is the largest megachurch in the U.S. with an average weekly attendance that exceeds 43,000. However, some 7 million television viewers also watch Lakewood Church services. ▶ **What is the attraction of a megachurch?**

U.S. Region	Percentage of megachurches
Northeast	7%
Midwest	19%
South	49%
West	25%

b. In the U.S., megachurches are concentrated in the South and West. The number of megachurches in the United States has increased from about 10 in 1970 to more than 1,300 today. California, Texas, Georgia, and Florida have the megachurches with the most members. ▶ **What are some reasons for these regional patterns?** (*Source:* Bird and Thumma, 2011.)

about 26% of all Christians are Renewalists and that this proportion will increase to 30% by 2025. In 1970, by contrast, only about 6% of all Christians were Renewalists. The diffusion of Renewalism has been rapid in Latin America, Sub-Saharan Africa, and parts of Asia.

Four factors help account for the success of Renewalism. First, Renewalist missionaries have competently transcended linguistic and cultural barriers. Translating the Bible into local languages, establishing local contacts to serve as liaisons with missionaries, and encouraging local people to give testimonies in their own language have been a key part of this movement. A second and related factor is that Renewalism eschews hierarchies—anyone can receive the gift of the Holy Spirit—and has been accessible to women. Third, the emphasis on spiritual healing and personal experience with the Holy Spirit parallels beliefs about spirituality in many of the local religious traditions in Africa, Asia, and the Americas. Fourth, Renewalist churches have been quick to adopt technology and incorporate popular music. One practice that has clouded the Renewalist movement, however, is the *prosperity gospel*—the idea that one's physical and economic well-being

are direct consequences of the financial contributions a member makes to the church. Although exploitation of this sort has occurred, it should not be seen as representative of all Renewalist churches.

In the United States, so-called mainline Catholic and Protestant denominations are losing members to Renewalist churches, and **megachurches** have become very popular, especially those with Renewalist theologies (**Figure 5.16**).

> **megachurch**
> A church with 2000 or more members that follows mainline or Renewalist Christian theologies.

CONCEPT CHECK

1. **How** are pilgrimage and sacred space related?
2. **How** is Islamic traditionalism different from religious fundamentalism?
3. **What** is the role of sharia in different Muslim countries around the world?
4. **Why** has Renewalism been successful?

Religion, Nature, and Landscape

LEARNING OBJECTIVES

1. **Distinguish** among geopiety, environmental stewardship, and religious ecology.
2. **Describe** the relationship between different religions and their expression on the landscape.

What can the geography of religion reveal about nature–society relationships? One answer to this question might focus on how people interpret and view their surroundings. Religion can influence people's environmental perception. These influences, which may stem from religious doctrine, are frequently expressed in views about nature. Alternatively, we can explore the topic of nature–society relationships through a consideration of religious imprints on the land or religious landscapes.

Geopiety

Many connections exist among religion, nature, and the landscape. The Aboriginal Dreamtime discussed in the chapter opener shows that, to the Aboriginals, the Earth is imbued with holiness. A number of religious holidays (originally *holy days*) and rituals in different religions are associated with seasonal changes, including, for example harvest festivals and solstice celebrations. Similarly, the designation of sacred forests, mountains, and rivers attests to other ways in which religion and nature are linked (**Figure 5.17**).

Geographer J. K. Wright coined the term **geopiety** to reflect the religious-like reverence that people may develop for the Earth. Geographer Yi-Fu Tuan subsequently extended the definition of geopiety in order to encompass the strong attachments that people associate with both sacred and secular places. Two important points follow from this. First, a person need not be religious to experience geopiety. Second, nature can be an important dimension of civil religion. Each member of the Boy Scouts of America (BSA), for example, pledges "to do my duty to God and my country." Being reverent is also a Scout characteristic, and in their activities and service, the BSA has long cultivated a certain appreciation for and understanding of the outdoors.

Religion and Conservation • Figure 5.17

In northern Thailand, Buddhist monks have wrapped trees with saffron cloth. The Buddha also wore a saffron robe, so this action is part of a ritual that ordains the trees and makes them sacred. Some Buddhist monks ordain trees to prevent them from being logged and protect forest environments.

At what point do the connections between religion and nature provide a basis for **religious ecology**—that is, an awareness of the interdependence between people and nature? In a provocative and controversial article in 1967, the historian Lynn White, Jr. argued that Judeo-Christian views played a part in contributing to the world's ecological problems because certain biblical scriptures emphasized people's dominion over the Earth. Given the extent of environmental change the world over, it is clear that it is not possible to lay the blame for ecological problems on a specific religion.

Nevertheless, the greater legacy of White's article may be that it drew attention to the relationship between religion and the environment, and specifically the fact that religion can affect how people perceive and use the environment. Indeed, many scholars firmly agree with White (1967, p. 1204) on one point—namely, that "what people do about their ecology depends on what they think about themselves in relation to things around them." Today a number of Christians emphasize **environmental stewardship**—the idea that they should be responsible managers of the Earth and its resources; many other faiths incorporate environmental ethics as well.

Religion and Landscape

Buildings constructed for religious uses make some of the most distinctive cultural landscapes. These buildings serve important practical and symbolic purposes. The concept of the church varies in Christianity. For Protestants, the church building is not sacred, but it serves as a place for adherents to gather and worship together. For Roman Catholics and Eastern Orthodox, however, the church is a sacred place—the house of God. Mosques are the gathering places for congregational worship in Islam, and Muslims do not consider mosques sacred. Rather, they are buildings where the Muslim community assembles to hear a sermon and to pray.

Buddhists and Hindus generally do not gather for congregational worship on a specific day of the week as do Christians, Jews, and Muslims. Rather, worship tends to be more individual, though some Buddhist temples do have large halls used for instruction or other special events. Hindu temples are considered sacred spaces and, more specifically, architectural expressions of God (**Figure 5.18**). Devout Hindus usually visit a temple once a week; however, most Hindus keep a shrine in their homes for daily worship or *puja*.

Because customs associated with the disposal of the dead vary from one religion to another, an interesting and sometimes more subtle landscape expression of religion involves *deathscapes*. For example, many Christians share the practice of aligning the graves on an east-to-west axis. Some Buddhists also bury the dead in cemeteries and select specific grave sites based on their *feng shui*, how well they harmonize with the cosmic forces. Although some Christians and Muslims construct mausoleums—large tombs built to accommodate above-ground burials—Judaism requires in-ground burial of the dead.

Theravada Buddhists, Hindus, and Sikhs normally cremate the deceased. As traditionally practiced in India, cremation involves placing the body on a pyre, a large wooden structure that is set on fire. Two of the ghats—the steps down to the Ganges River in Varanasi—are used for cremation. Hindus believe that to be cremated so close to the Ganges brings *moksha*, release from the cycle of death and rebirth. For illustrations of some deathscapes, see *What a Geographer Sees* on the next page.

Hindu temple • Figure 5.18

This is an exceptional example of a Hindu temple in India's Tamil Nadu state. The innermost sanctuary contains a shrine to Lord Vishnu, the god who preserves the universe.

Michele Falzone/Getty Images, Inc.

WHAT A GEOGRAPHER SEES

Deathscapes

Necrogeographers study the cultural and spatial variations in the disposal of the dead. Often their work involves mapping data as well as reading the landscape for clues about cultural practices and their change through space and over time. Geographers see cemeteries as fascinating spaces where evidence of syncretic processes that give rise to new, hybrid forms are visible.

a. Geographer Wilbur Zelinsky mapped named cemeteries in the eastern United States to create this map of cemetery density. The dark pattern across much of Tennessee reflects a preponderance of small, family cemeteries. Low densities in Florida point to changes in the funeral industry and the rise of large, more corporate cemeteries.

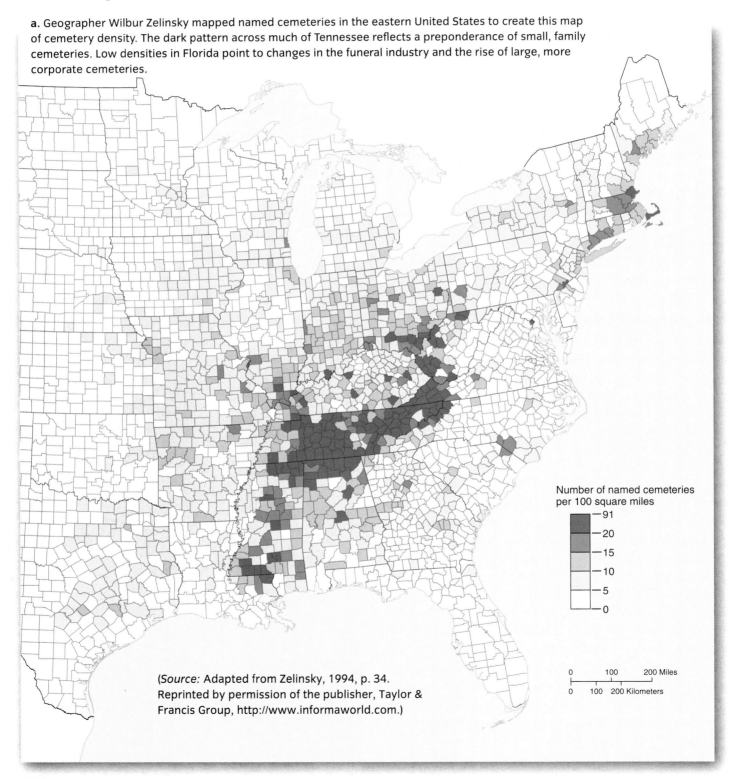

Number of named cemeteries per 100 square miles
— 91
— 20
— 15
— 10
— 5
— 0

(*Source:* Adapted from Zelinsky, 1994, p. 34. Reprinted by permission of the publisher, Taylor & Francis Group, http://www.informaworld.com.)

0   100   200 Miles
0   100   200 Kilometers

Photo courtesy of Amaury Laporte

Courtesy Alyson Greiner

b. Eklutna Cemetery in Alaska
Russian Orthodox and Native American practices fused here, as demonstrated by the spirit houses, each fronted with an Orthodox cross. In Orthodox Christianity, burial grounds are sanctified spaces and the large Orthodox cross shown here testifies to that belief.

d. A columbarium for storing cremated remains
This is a high-rise columbarium in Hong Kong. Local customs have traditionally favored in-ground burial in sites with auspicious feng shui. However, land scarcity makes such use of space economically impractical.

c. Holywell Cemetery and wildlife site in Oxford, England
In urban areas, cemeteries can provide valuable natural spaces for people as well as for flora and fauna. To promote biodiversity, this cemetery is not mowed or treated to keep grass and weeds at bay.

e. A mega-mausoleum in Los Angeles
A mausoleum provides an above-ground tomb for the dead. Historically, such tombs were reserved for social and political elites.

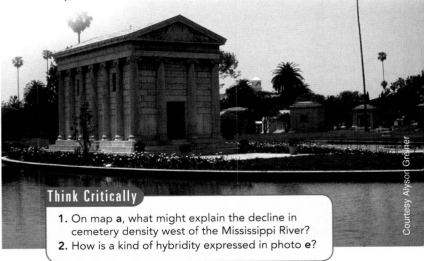

Courtesy Alyson Greiner

Think Critically

1. On map **a**, what might explain the decline in cemetery density west of the Mississippi River?
2. How is a kind of hybridity expressed in photo **e**?

CONCEPT CHECK STOP

1. **How** is geopiety expressed in religious and nonreligious contexts?
2. **How** do deathscapes reflect the beliefs of different religions?

Courtesy Aberdeen Chinese Permanent Cemetery, Hong Kong

Summary

1 Religion in Global Context   132

- **Religion** refers to the beliefs and practices that people use to understand the universe and their place in it. **Monotheistic, polytheistic,** and **atheistic** religions exist, but these terms provide at best a very rough approximation of a specific faith. Adherents of **animistic religions** believe supernatural forces and deities are present in the natural surroundings. The Candomblé religion in Brazil (see photo) is an example of a religion that is **syncretic.**

Syncretic religion • Figure 5.1

Stephanie Maze/NG Image Collection

- Religious beliefs often provide the basis for different **cosmogonies**, which may be celebrated or reenacted through **rituals**. Shared rituals help reinforce a sense of community, belonging, and identity among adherents. Such rituals can also influence individual and group behavior and make visible a person's **piety**.

- Religions can be classified as either universalizing or ethnic. **Universalizing religions** include Buddhism, Christianity, and Islam. Hinduism, Judaism, and the religions of many indigenous peoples are **ethnic religions**. **Civil religion** takes shape when certain aspects of religion become woven into the political culture of an area.

- Christianity grew out of Judaism, and Buddhism grew from Hinduism. Islam is the youngest of the Abrahamic faiths, and Sikhism developed syncretically from the blending of aspects of Hinduism and Islam. Most religions have experienced fragmentation into different branches, creating distributions that are complex and fascinating.

2 Religious Hearths and Diffusion   140

- All religions have a hearth, but the precise details of their development are not always known. Geographers distinguish between primary and secondary hearths. The Semitic and Indic primary hearths have witnessed the emergence of the world's most prevalent and influential religions.

- Geographers and other scholars identify, map, and study religious hearths because they help us to know how religions develop and change over time and across space. The geography and history of some religions, such as Judaism and Sikhism (see photo), have been shaped by **diasporas**.

Sikhism and Khalistan • Figure 5.9

Courtesy National Khalsa (Khalistan) Day Parade Organization.

- Religions are dynamic belief systems. No religion is uniform or immune to fragmentation, though some religions have fragmented more than others. In general, the spread of a religion over space is likely to increase the potential for fragmentation.

3 Religion, Society, and Globalization   143

- The identification of **sacred space** demonstrates that religion influences how people perceive and understand the world. **Pilgrimages** involve a journey to and encounter with sacred space; thus they affect patterns of human circulation and mobility. People create sacred places and sites through the process of **sanctification**. Conflict can occur when the sacred spaces of different religions overlap.

- The tension between tradition and change shapes religious beliefs and practices. **Modernism** can be perceived as a challenge to the authority of a religion or even as a form of **secularization**. Globalization and secularization are related, but globalization does not always result in secularization. Indeed, the continued importance of sacred space helps illustrate this.

- In Hinduism, the **caste system**, now abolished, highlights the tension between tradition and change. In Christianity and Islam such tensions are often expressed through **religious fundamentalism**. Since 9/11, **Islamic traditionalism** has received a great deal of attention, but fundamentalism can affect any religion. From Sabbath-day observance to **sharia**, the Abrahamic faiths in particular illustrate some ways in which religious law provides parameters for the management of social space.

- Within Christianity, **Renewalism** has grown very rapidly in the past few decades and has become a global phenomenon. **Megachurches**, such as this one, now rival mainline Protestant and Catholic churches for members.

Megachurches • Figure 5.16

Reuters/Jo Yong-Hak /LandovLLC

- Religion provides another lens through which to explore nature–society relationships including **religious ecology** and geopiety. **Geopiety** includes the reverence people may have for the Earth as well as the place attachments they develop. **Environmental stewardship** positions people as responsible managers of the Earth and its resources.

- The visible imprint of religion on the landscape varies from place to place and from one religion to another. Religious structures provide visible clues about beliefs and practices in an area. Customs for disposing of the dead also vary by religion and give rise to deathscapes, shown here.

What a Geographer Sees: Deathscapes

Courtesy Alyson Greiner

Key Terms

- animistic religion 132
- atheistic 132
- caste system 150
- civil religion 133
- cosmogony 132
- diaspora 140
- environmental stewardship 155

- ethnic religion 133
- geopiety 154
- Islamic traditionalism 150
- jihad 151
- megachurch 153
- modernism 150
- monotheistic 132
- piety 133

- pilgrimage 146
- polytheistic 132
- religion 132
- religious ecology 155
- religious fundamentalism 150
- Renewalism 152
- ritual 133

- sacred space 144
- sanctification 148
- secularization 150
- sharia 151
- syncretic religion 132
- universalizing religion 133

Critical and Creative Thinking Questions

1. Describe a religious landscape in your hometown. Discuss the forces that created it.

2. Why is Protestantism much more fragmented than Roman Catholicism? Why has Islam experienced comparatively less fragmentation than Christianity?

3. Who are the Amish and Mennonites? Do some research to learn of their origins, diffusion, and way of life.

4. View the movie *Bend It Like Beckham* and discuss its representation of Sikhism.

5. Research and then discuss the geography of cremation globally and in the United States.

6. How has the religious symbolism on graves changed over time? Test your hypothesis by visiting a cemetery to gather some data.

7. Examine a sacred religious text such as the Qur'an or Bible, and discuss how it characterizes human-environment relations.

8. What parallels can be drawn between religious practices and proper treatment of the American flag? Is this evidence of civil religion? Explain your reasoning.

9. Think about pilgrimage from the standpoint of spatial interaction. To what extent does the concept of distance decay apply? Discuss, giving specific examples.

10. Note that evidence of at least two different religious traditions is reflected in this photograph. What are they? Is this a religious landscape? Why or why not?

Courtesy National Khalsa (Khalistan) Day Parade Organization.

What is happening in this picture?

A Tibetan woman carries a prayer stone to a sacred site. Called *mani* stones, these are hand-carved and inscribed with sacred symbols or Buddhist scripture. The stone wall beside her has also been decorated with religious art.

© Steve McCurry/Magnum Photos

Think Critically

1. Can virtual pilgrimages, via the Internet, fulfill the same purpose as a personal visit to a sacred site?
2. What are some ways that religion influences gender roles?

Self-Test

(Check your answers in Appendix B.)

1. A religion that welcomes all people as potential adherents is _____.
   a. animistic
   b. syncretic
   c. universalizing
   d. ethnic

2. Civil religion _____.
   a. draws on religious law
   b. relates religion to politics
   c. promotes atheism
   d. emphasizes fundamentalism

3. Cosmogonies _____.
   a. are initiation rites
   b. stem from the natural landscape
   c. may influence environmental perception
   d. None of the above statements is correct

4. Which is *not* one of Islam's Five Pillars of Practice?
   a. completing a pilgrimage to Medina at least once
   b. making a profession of faith
   c. fasting during Ramadan
   d. praying five times a day

5. Explain the significance of this mass conversion to Buddhism that occurred in Mumbai, India.

Rajesh Nirgude/©AP/Wide World Photos

6. What happens in a secondary religious hearth?
   a. A new religion develops.
   b. A minor pilgrimage destination develops.
   c. Adherents experience a renewal or an awakening of their faith.
   d. A religion splits internally.

7. Find the *false* statement about Buddhism.
   a. Tantrayana Buddhism is closely associated with Japan.
   b. Buddhism is a universalizing religion.
   c. Mahayana Buddhists see the Buddha as a compassionate deity.
   d. Theravada Buddhism tends to be more monastic.

8. Identify the step in the process of sanctification illustrated by this photograph.

Jeff Haynes/AFP//Getty Images, Inc.

_____

9. Give an example of hierarchical diffusion in Christianity.

_____
_____

10. Zionism is important to the geography of religion because _____.
    a. it explains why and how diasporic communities form
    b. it demonstrates the spread of secularization
    c. it shows the emergence of a secondary religious hearth
    d. it illustrates the bonds between religious groups and territory

11. The emergence of Sunni and Shia branches in Islam _____.
    a. was about differences over sharia
    b. involved a dispute over Muhammad's successor
    c. was shaped by linguistic differences among Muslims
    d. was about the infallibility of the Qu'ran

12. Religious fundamentalism _____.
    a. endorses terrorism
    b. means that religious principles guide all aspects of an adherent's life
    c. is only associated with Islam
    d. All of the above statements are correct.

13. In his discussion of religious ecology, which point did Lynn White make?
    a. Any space can be a sacred space.
    b. He coined the term *geopiety*.
    c. Judeo-Christian views contributed to environmental abuse.
    d. Jihad means "utmost struggle."

14. This photo illustrates _____.
    a. geopiety
    b. syncretism
    c. resistance to change
    d. None of the above statements is correct.

Photo courtesy of Amaury Laporte

15. What is Renewalism?
    a. It is a form of secularization.
    b. It is a branch of Judaism.
    c. It refers to the spread of Islamic traditionalism.
    d. It is the fastest growing branch within Christianity.

THE PLANNER ✓

Review your Chapter Planner on the chapter opener and check off your completed work.

Geographies of Identity: Race, Ethnicity, Sexuality, and Gender

WOMEN IN COMBAT

I n 2013, the U.S. Secretary of Defense rescinded a ban excluding women from military assignments involving direct combat. Why was such a ban implemented? The answer involves long-standing social practice and ideas about gender-specific capabilities. A frequent observation was that combat is a man's domain and that women are simply too weak, both physically and emotionally, for combat. A related claim was that placing women in combat would lower the military's standards, leading to disaster on the battlefield. Women serving in combat units, it was said, would be a distraction for their male colleagues and bad for morale. Women would also require separate facilities and be expensive to accommodate.

Mounting evidence, however, contradicted these claims. Other countries had opened combat roles to women. Also, during the wars in Iraq and Afghanistan women often had to engage in direct combat in order to carry out their assignment—whether that assignment involved conducting a security patrol or driving a military vehicle. Lifting the ban against women in combat moves the military closer to a gender-neutral policy that holds women and men to the same standard. Removing the ban also gives women the opportunity to compete for more than 200,000 military jobs that were previously off-limits to them.

As this discussion shows, ideas about gender can affect people's opportunities. Gender is just one component of identity discussed in this chapter; others include race, ethnicity, and sexuality. This chapter also examines how identity shapes the places, spaces, and landscapes around us.

Scott Olson/Getty Images

CHAPTER OUTLINE

CHAPTER PLANNER ✓

- ❑ Study the picture and read the opening story.
- ❑ Scan the Learning Objectives in each section:
  p. 164 ❑   p. 168 ❑   p. 172 ❑   p. 178 ❑   p. 184 ❑
- ❑ Read the text and study all visuals.
  Answer any questions.

Analyze key features

- ❑ Process Diagram, p. 168
- ❑ Geography InSight, p. 170
- ❑ What a Geographer Sees, p. 174
- ❑ Video Explorations, p. 184
- ❑ Stop: Answer the Concept Checks before you go on:
  p. 167 ❑   p. 171 ❑   p. 177 ❑   p. 183 ❑   p. 188 ❑

End of chapter

- ❑ Review the Summary and Key Terms.
- ❑ Answer the Critical and Creative Thinking Questions.
- ❑ Answer What is happening in this picture?
- ❑ Complete the Self-Test and check your answers.

Race and Racism

LEARNING OBJECTIVES

1. **Explain** why using race as a classification system is problematic.
2. **Distinguish** between a social construction and an ideology.
3. **Contrast** the geography of the trans-Atlantic slave trade and the geography of human trafficking.

The topics of this chapter—race, ethnicity, sexuality, and gender—are among the most complex and sensitive of any discussed in this book. To ignore these topics, however, would be to overlook a crucial aspect of human geography involving the ways that different groups have modified space and place. Thus, this chapter seeks to balance a celebration of the diversity that makes the world such a rich human tapestry with an examination of some unfortunate developments, too, such as racism, ethnic conflict, and gender inequalities.

You may be wondering why such diverse topics as race, sexuality, and gender inequality are included in a single chapter. These topics have a great deal in common, especially from the standpoint of spatial inclusion and exclusion, or who is deemed to belong in a place and who is excluded from it. We will explore these points in greater detail below, but we begin by considering two basic principles about identity that will guide subsequent discussions: (1) Human identity is dynamic and contingent, and therefore cannot be easily categorized; (2) Efforts to classify people into groups tend to exaggerate the differences among people, especially visible differences.

single trait of skin color, which, to him, appeared to vary by geographic region. Some subsequent scholars insisted there were as few as three races, whereas other scholars identified 30 races or more.

These disagreements over the number of different races highlight a fundamental problem with the concept of race: the boundaries between races are always arbitrary. Geography and biology can help us understand this problem. First, physical traits in people tend to change gradually over space, like transition zones rather than sharp boundaries. Second, no two physical traits (e.g., skin color or hair type) have the same spatial distribution. Thus, both geographical and biological facts demonstrate why race is a mistaken idea. Simply stated, racial categories are subjective and arbitrary, and have no geographical or biological basis. Indeed, when people are divided into so-called races, the amount of genetic variation *within* a single race turns out to be much greater than the variation *among* the races.

The prevailing view among academics is that race is best thought of as a **social construction**—an idea or a phenomenon that does not exist in nature but is created and given meaning by people (**Figure 6.1**).

What Is Race?

Race refers to the highly influential but mistaken idea that one or more genetic traits can be used to identify distinctive and exclusive categories of people. To understand why race is a mistaken idea, we need to see how the concept developed. Initially, four major groups of people inhabiting the Earth were identified: African, American (referring to Native Americans), Asiatic, and European. The Swedish naturalist Carolus Linnaeus developed these categories in the 18th century in conjunction with his system for naming and classifying plants and animals.

Although Linnaeus called these four groups of people "varieties," his method of classification was based on the

How Has Racism Developed?

Racism includes the belief that genetic differences produce a hierarchy of peoples, from the most superior to the most inferior. Racism fuels prejudice, discrimination, and the hatred of others. It results in people being excluded and disadvantaged, as well as emotionally and physically abused. Racism can be thought of as an **ideology** that has been exploited by certain groups, such as the Nazis, at different times.

> **racism** The intolerance of people perceived to be inherently or genetically inferior.
>
> **ideology** A system of ideas, beliefs, and values that justifies the views, practices, or orientation of a group.

Constructions of race • Figure 6.1

Children born to interracial couples often come to know that race is a social construction; from firsthand experiences they learn that people, including their close friends, apply different racial identities to them. For example, U.S. President Barack Obama's mother was a Kansan of English ancestry, and his father was a Kenyan. Some people construct his racial identity as biracial while others construct it as black.

Scholars agree that events associated with the European colonization and settlement of the Americas during the 16th and 17th centuries contributed significantly to the development of racism. Historians have shown that the practice of separating whites and blacks, in particular, became emphasized in colonial Virginia around the time of Bacon's Rebellion in 1676 when poor whites and blacks formed an alliance against white elites. Bacon's Rebellion called attention to the fact that cooperation among whites and blacks could threaten elite control. Thus, racism and slavery provided mechanisms that could be used to maintain social control and power.

It was during the Enlightenment, a European intellectual movement of the late 17th and 18th centuries that probed the relationship between society, nature, and religion, that racial difference became strongly associated with inferiority. One of the more influential ideas to shape collective perceptions in Europe and European colonial outposts was that of the *great chain of being* (**Figure 6.2**).

The great chain of being contributed to an ideology of racism that helped Europeans make sense of the world, but in ways very different from the system of classification developed by Linnaeus. More specifically, the concept of the great chain of being had a far-reaching legacy that can be summarized in the following three points. First, it helped to *naturalize* the idea of human difference. The great chain of being was understood not as a social construction, but rather as a natural construction—a reflection of a God-given hierarchical ordering of the world that included human races. Second, the great chain of being supported views that emphasized the differences between people and provided a way to link those differences to ideas about genetic and intellectual inferiority as well as inequality. Third, whiteness became a standard against which others were measured.

Great chain of being • Figure 6.2

The great chain of being is based on the idea that there is a natural and ranked order of life in the world, stretching from aquatic life at the bottom up to the heavens. If the broad classes of living things were ranked, it followed that the members of those classes could be ranked as well. Visible differences including skin color were used to distinguish among different ranks and races of people.

Bonnet, 1779–83, vol. IV, p. 1. Image courtesy History of Science Collections, University of Oklahoma Libraries.

During the era of European imperialism, this ideology of racism diffused widely and was used not only to justify European dominance and colonization, but also to reinforce European power. The ideology of racism supported the idea that social inequality was a natural phenomenon and that the place for whites was at the top of the social hierarchy. In the colonies, Europeans were typically the administrators, managers, and settlers who controlled the colonized people. Residential areas in colonial towns were segregated on the basis of race (see Chapter 8). This ideology of racism helped to perpetuate slavery. Although slavery is illegal today, it still persists as one kind of human trafficking. **Human trafficking** occurs when people are forcibly and/or fraudulently recruited for work in exploitative conditions—for example, as child soldiers or prostitutes.

Historical and contemporary geographies of slavery • Figure 6.3

The enslavement of people perceived to be of a low status or class is an ancient practice known to have existed in many societies around the world. Only in the Americas, however, did a form of slavery so strongly based on visible physical difference emerge.

a. Generalized origins and destinations of African slaves
The map, with arrows resembling on- and off-ramps, shows the highway that the Atlantic Ocean became as a result of the slave trade between the 16th and 19th centuries. Brazil and the Caribbean were the leading destinations of African slaves. Two factors that sustained the trans-Atlantic slave trade were the strong demand for labor in the Americas and the increasingly common view that racial categories were natural.

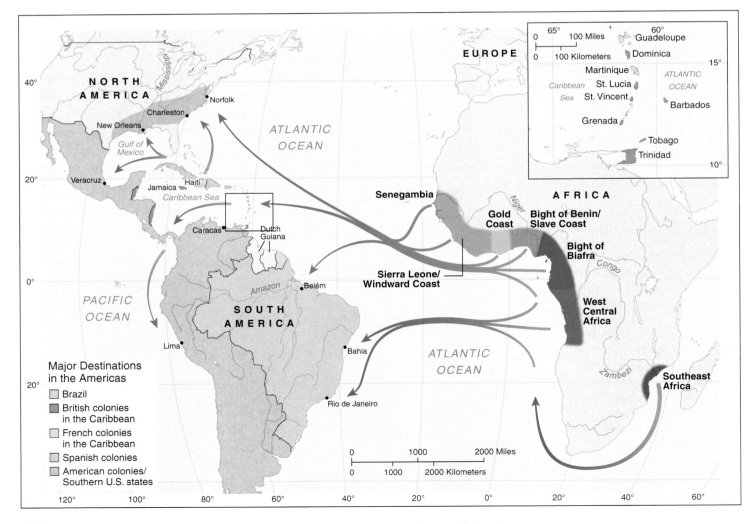

The geography of the trans-Atlantic slave trade was built on well-established routes between Africa and the Americas. Because slavery was legal for centuries, it was visible and remains so in historical documents. In contrast, the geography of human trafficking is global in scale, affecting every region of the world, but it is much less visible. Human trafficking has been called "the underside of globalization" (**Figure 6.3**).

CONCEPT CHECK

1. **What** are two principles about human identity?
2. **How** did racism become an ideology?
3. **What** factors helped sustain the trans-Atlantic slave trade?

Think Critically

1. How can children in the U.S. become victims of human trafficking?
2. How can racism contribute to human trafficking?

Kay Cherrush for the U.S. State Department

b. Bonded and forced labor

In India, this young girl and her family were trafficked and work as bonded laborers at a brick-making factory. Bonded labor means that the employer has a long-term lease for your services because of a debt that is owed. Often a family's debt is passed on from one generation to the next, creating a vicious cycle of debt slavery.

c. Estimated percentage of forced laborers, by region

Forced labor is regionally most prevalent in Asia, in part because of enduring systems of bonded labor. Perhaps 12 million people work as forced laborers worldwide—as many people as were transported to the Americas as slaves. Workers are recruited with the promise of high wages, but once employed those promises are broken and laborers are forced to work with threats of penalty or harm. (*Source:* Data from ILO, 2005.)

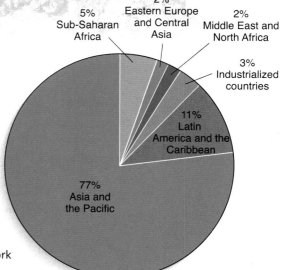

2% Eastern Europe and Central Asia
2% Middle East and North Africa
5% Sub-Saharan Africa
3% Industrialized countries
11% Latin America and the Caribbean
77% Asia and the Pacific

Race and Racism 167

Geographies of Race and Racism

LEARNING OBJECTIVES

1. **Understand** what is meant by institutional discrimination.

2. **Summarize** the relationship between race and place in Vancouver's Chinatown.

3. **Examine** the spatial consequences of the rise and fall of apartheid in South Africa.

Although academics agree that there is no biological basis for race, neither the term nor the concept has fallen out of use. Ideas about race as well as the practice of discrimination more broadly have tended to be persistent and, in some cases, institutionalized. Geographically, race and racism have influenced the spatial organization of people and their activities. In this section we examine how **institutional discrimination**, often grounded in racist views, influenced the development of two specific places: Chinatown in Vancouver, Canada, and the country of South Africa.

> **institutional discrimination**
> A situation in which the policies, practices, or laws of an organization or government disadvantage people because of their cultural differences.

Race and Place in Vancouver's Chinatown

Chinese immigrants came to the Vancouver area in the mid-1800s as gold prospectors and laborers. In a classic study, geographer Kay Anderson (1987) examined the emergence of Chinatown in Vancouver at the end of the 19th century. Her research demonstrates how attitudes about racial difference gave rise to the strong association of Chinatown with negative characteristics and how these ideas about Chinatown influenced city policies (**Figure 6.4**).

City policies in Vancouver institutionalized an ideology of racism that affected social relations between white Canadians and those of Chinese origin. Over the years, those policies have been removed or altered, and relations between the cultural groups, though not perfect, have improved. Moreover, the many contributions of the Chinese to the growth and development of Vancouver are increasingly acknowledged.

❶ Race makes place

Observable differences reinforced the perceived distance between whites mainly of European descent and Chinese, and the area where Chinese settled was called *Chinatown*. This 1907 newspaper illustration depicts Chinatown as an opium den and unsanitary place. In actuality, some Chinese operated laundries, the "business of cleanliness," according to Anderson (1987, p. 586), and Chinatown was not a center of epidemics.

RACE Chinese

Typical home of Vancouver white workingman.

A warren on Carrall Street infested by 2000 Chinese

Global Locator

British Columbia, Canada

NATIONAL GEOGRAPHIC

Ask Yourself

How did language factor in the making of the place of Chinatown?

The interaction between race and place • Figure 6.4

Cultural difference

Including such characteristics as appearance, language, religion, and other customs

One of the key contributions of Kay Anderson's research on Vancouver's Chinatown from the 1880s to the 1920s is her demonstration of the mutually reinforcing processes of how race makes place and place makes race. Today, Vancouver's Chinatown is widely perceived to be a popular destination and downtown attraction.

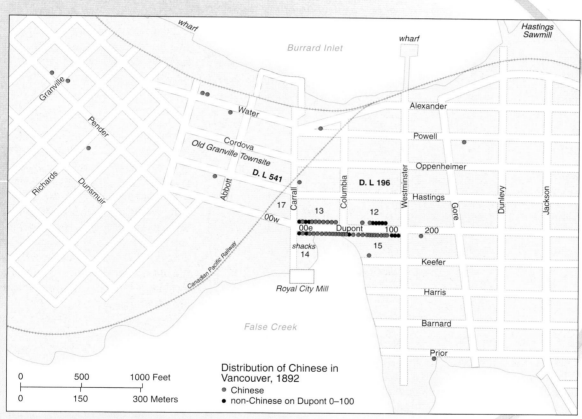

Distribution of Chinese in Vancouver, 1892
- Chinese
- non-Chinese on Dupont 0–100

(*Source:* Redrawn from Anderson, 1987, p. 588, Taylor & Francis, Ltd., http://www.informaworld.com.)

PLACE
Chinatown

Institutional discrimination

Examples of some anti-Chinese city practices:
- Restricting locations of Chinese-operated laundries.
- Treating Chinatown like a factory, a place needing frequent inspection because of its perception as a public nuisance.
- Targeting Chinese residences or buildings deemed unsanitary for destruction.

❷ Place makes race

The stigmatization of Chinatown as a socially troubled area influenced the actions of Vancouver's civic leaders, who sought to contain and control Chinatown's "problems" through city rules and regulations. To say that place makes race means that perceptions of Chinatown reinforced racialized views of the Chinese as a different breed of people who needed to be spatially separated and monitored.

In theory, apartheid was to produce a society that was segregated on a racial and territorial basis. Every racial group was to have its own geographic space. Underscoring all of this was the myth of racial purity, a myth shared by many Afrikaner Nationalists. Physical separation of the races would therefore protect their racial purity and enable each group to pursue its separate cultural and economic development. In reality, however, no group had the same access to or control of resources as white South Africans did.

a. Grand apartheid
Designed as a comprehensive system, apartheid operated on two spatial scales. At the national scale there was *grand apartheid*, intended to separate population groups territorially. Legislation authorized the creation of black homelands, called Bantustans.
▶ **Can you give some reasons to explain the location and distribution of these homelands?** (*Source:* CIA, 1979.)

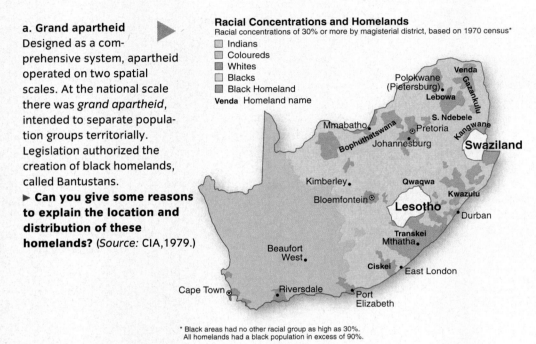

Racial Concentrations and Homelands
Racial concentrations of 30% or more by magisterial district, based on 1970 census*

- Indians
- Coloureds
- Whites
- Blacks
- Black Homeland
- **Venda** Homeland name

* Black areas had no other racial group as high as 30%.
All homelands had a black population in excess of 90%.

b. Petty apartheid
Petty apartheid operated at the individual scale and resulted in segregated public facilities, including restrooms, drinking fountains, schools, and beaches.

c. Townships
Achieving complete physical segregation in cities proved to be complicated and unreasonable because of labor needs. Many blacks were employed by whites as housekeepers, while many others worked in construction. Therefore, black residential areas, called *townships*, formed on the outer edges of South African cities. Still in existence, these townships are, in effect, slums.

Institutional discrimination can take place at any scale, and one of the most extensive forms of it was implemented throughout the country of South Africa in the decades following World War II. As the civil rights movement gathered momentum in the United States and the push to end segregation spread, events in South Africa moved that country in the opposite direction and led to the implementation of apartheid. The word **apartheid**, meaning *apartness*, refers to the government-sponsored policy of racial segregation and discrimination that came to define South Africa and regulated the social relations and opportunities of its people.

Geographies of Apartheid

Southern Africa was already home to numerous different African cultural groups when Dutch settlers arrived in Cape Town in 1652. These settlers called themselves *Boers*, from a Dutch term meaning *farmer*. Today, persons of Dutch descent living in South Africa usually call themselves *Afrikaners* (from *Afrikaans*, the name of the Dutch-derived language they speak).

Toward the end of the 18th century, however, a number of British settlers had also moved into the area. To avoid British rule, most of the Boers eventually migrated away from the Cape Town vicinity and took control of lands in the interior. Beginning in the middle part of the 19th century, the British shipped Indian laborers from their colonies in South Asia to the area around Durban to work on the sugar plantations. In South Africa the term *coloured* (retaining the British spelling) came to identify a person of mixed ancestry who did not fit either

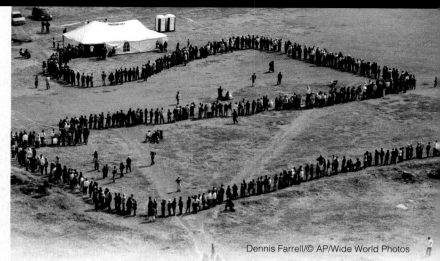

Dennis Farrell/© AP/Wide World Photos

David Turnley/©Corbis

Tomasz Tomaszewski/NG Image Collection

d. Waiting to vote in post-apartheid free elections
In 1991 the legal framework of apartheid was repealed. Three years later all South African adults were allowed to vote in national elections for the first time ever, creating long lines at polling stations such as this one. Nelson Mandela, a key figure in the anti-apartheid movement, was elected president.

Population group	Percent unemployed
Black/African	30%
Coloured	23%
Indian/Asian	11%
White	5%

e. Apartheid's deep legacy
South Africa continues to implement programs to reduce poverty, but unemployment—especially among blacks—remains very high. (*Source: Statistics South Africa*, 2012.)

the African, Asian Indian, or European racial categories. This categorization was different from that in the United States, where the term *colored* was mainly used to refer to blacks.

When South Africa achieved independence in 1910, it formalized a system of white minority rule. At the time, the population composition of the country was about 69% black, 20% white, 8% coloured, and 3% Asian. Then, in 1948, the Afrikaner Nationalist Party gained power. One of the main components of its platform was *baaskap*, a term meaning to keep blacks in their place. According to many Afrikaners, previous governments had not done enough to segregate the races. Apartheid, then, was the mechanism to help achieve baaskap, and it became official state policy in

1948. See **Figure 6.5** to learn more about how apartheid altered South Africa's human geography.

CONCEPT CHECK 🛑 STOP

1. **How** can racism or discrimination become institutionalized?

2. **What** role did cultural difference play in the making of Vancouver's Chinatown?

3. **How** might institutional discrimination alter the spatial arrangement of a city or country?

What Is Ethnicity?

LEARNING OBJECTIVES

1. **Summarize** the relationship between ethnicity and othering.
2. **Identify** different components of ethnicity.
3. **Identify** a regional pattern associated with use of the terms *race* and *ethnicity* on censuses.
4. **Explain** the concept of discourse.

The word *ethnicity* stems from the Greek *ethnos*, meaning people. In a broad sense, ethnicity involves the formation and maintenance of individual and collective identities. Therefore, we take the terms *ethnicity* and *ethnic identity* to mean the same thing, and we will use the terms synonymously. Ethnicity is another complex concept, but it becomes a little easier to comprehend when we emphasize two fundamental points about it. First, ethnicity is about people constructing a sense of social belonging. Second, this process of belonging involves **othering**—the act of differentiating between individuals and groups such that distinctions are made between "me" and "you" and between "us" and "them."

Defining and Characterizing Ethnicity

ethnicity The personal and behavioral basis of an individual's identity that generates a sense of social belonging.

ethnic group People who share a collective identity that may derive from common ancestry, history, language, or religion, and who have a conscious sense of belonging to that group.

Understanding **ethnicity** provides a starting point for identifying and studying **ethnic groups**. Although the terms *nationality* and *ethnic group* are closely related, they are not synonymous. *Nationality* expresses a person's affiliation with a country, usually in terms of citizenship.

When speaking of ethnicity, geographers recognize that it has different facets. For example, ethnicity has internal, personal components as well as external, behavioral components. A personal component of ethnicity includes who we think and feel we are. This sense of identity may or may not stem from a person's ancestry. A person whose father is Peruvian and whose mother is Japanese, for example, might consider herself to be ethnically Japanese, ethnically Peruvian, some mixture of both, or none of these. In this way, ethnicity is subjective.

One's ethnic identity also depends on how an individual's identity has formed over time. At times in a person's life, an individual may choose to embrace or reject an ethnic identity. In addition, the process of ascription can strongly influence one's identity. **Ascription** occurs when people assign a certain quality or identity to others, or to themselves (called *self-ascription*). A person's ethnic identity derives from processes of ascription and self-ascription. For example, when a Turkish man named Bülent married Leyla, a Kurd, the Turkish community that Bülent belonged to did not approve of the marriage and ascribed to him a Kurdish identity. Bülent has since developed a strong affinity with the Kurdish community to the point that he considers himself a Kurd and is accepted as one by the Kurdish community. Ethnicity is, therefore, flexible and contingent on the circumstances and people that shape our lives.

In addition to personal components of ethnicity, there are also behavioral components. These typically include practices that mark who we are, such as language, religious beliefs, and customary traditions associated with dietary preferences, styles of dress, dance, music, or art. But it is often the case that the personal and behavioral components of ethnicity are mutually reinforcing. In other words, one's sense of ethnic identity can depend on or be defined by the practice of certain customs (**Figure 6.6**).

Another aspect of ethnicity relates to indigenous or native peoples and their identity. There is no agreed-upon definition of indigenous peoples, but three characteristics are commonly cited: (1) ancestral ties to pre-colonial or pre-settler societies; hence indigenous peoples are sometimes called *first peoples*; (2) self-identification of and acceptance by others as a member of an indigenous group; and (3) status in society as a nondominant (e.g., numerically, economically, or politically) group. Thus, indigenous peoples are ethnic groups, but they may prefer to identify themselves by different names, such as aboriginals, tribes, or native peoples. Moreover, their sense of identity is also highly contingent as demonstrated in the following quote:

> [W]hen we are introduced to a man in the village of Mishongnovi on Second Mesa in Arizona . . . we are told his name and that he is a member of the Coyote Clan. When he goes on business to the nearby town of Window Rock, capital of the Navajo Nation, he specifies that he is a Hopi; at a lecture he delivers in Chicago he claims to be Native American and at the Palais Wilson in Geneva,

Ethnicity and ancestry • Figure 6.6

Ethnicity has visible and invisible aspects. Depending on the person, one's ethnic identity may or may not be strongly tied to ancestry.

a. A couple prepares to eat pho, a Vietnamese soup made with rice noodles, beef or chicken, chili peppers, bean sprouts, and different herbs. ▶ **To what extent are your food preferences an expression of your ethnicity?**

b. Bolivian president Evo Morales takes part in a purification ritual prior to his formal inauguration. Morales (center) is an Aymara Indian and Bolivia's first indigenous president. ▶ **What components of ethnicity are visible here?**

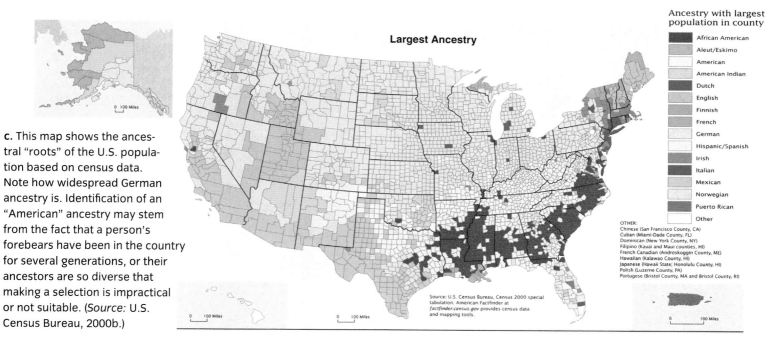

Largest Ancestry

Ancestry with largest population in county

- African American
- Aleut/Eskimo
- American
- American Indian
- Dutch
- English
- Finnish
- French
- German
- Hispanic/Spanish
- Irish
- Italian
- Mexican
- Norwegian
- Puerto Rican
- Other

OTHER:
Chinese (San Francisco County, CA)
Cuban (Miami-Dade County, FL)
Dominican (New York County, NY)
Filipino (Kauai and Maui counties, HI)
French Canadian (Androskoggin County, ME)
Hawaiian (Kalawao County, HI)
Japanese (Hawaii State; Honolulu County, HI)
Polish (Luzerne County, PA)
Portugese (Bristol County, MA and Bristol County, RI)

Source: U.S. Census Bureau, Census 2000 special tabulation. American Factfinder at *factfinder.census.gov* provides census data and mapping tools.

c. This map shows the ancestral "roots" of the U.S. population based on census data. Note how widespread German ancestry is. Identification of an "American" ancestry may stem from the fact that a person's forebears have been in the country for several generations, or their ancestors are so diverse that making a selection is impractical or not suitable. (*Source:* U.S. Census Bureau, 2000b.)

as he sits between a Dayak woman from Kalimantan, Indonesia, and an Ogiek man from Kenya while attending an international human rights conference, he identifies himself, and is identified by others, as indigenous. (Levi and Maybury-Lewis, 2010, p. 4)

Ethnicity, Race, and Censuses

Like race, ethnicity is a subjective social construction that defies the use of fixed categories that neatly divide and classify people. Although collecting data on ethnicity proves to be extremely difficult, many governments insist on identifying

different ethnic or racial groups and enumerating them. During the apartheid era in South Africa, government officials required this enumeration so that they could maintain social and political control. In countries such as Brazil, Canada, the United Kingdom, and the United States, such enumerations help to identify minority groups and prevent discrimination. For example, the U.S. Equal Credit Opportunity Act is a civil rights law requiring the collection of information about the ethnic or racial identity of loan applicants as a way to monitor fairness in lending practices.

WHAT A GEOGRAPHER SEES

U.S. Census Geography

Many geographers use U.S. Census Bureau data in their work. Effective use of this information requires knowledge of the geographic areas for which data are reported. These areas include the following scales: national, state, county (or parish or borough), census tract, and city block. We will start at the state scale and use California as an example.

a. California counties
We'll look at Los Angeles County, home to 9.8 million people, or approximately 27% of the state's population.

b. Census tracts of Los Angeles County
Counties are divided into census tracts. Los Angeles County has some 2000 census tracts. The size of a census tract varies, but each contains, on average, 4000 people.

c. Census tracts near downtown LA
Every census tract is assigned a unique number. Census tract 2132.01 is located in the area known as Koreatown. (*Source:* U.S. Census Bureau, 2000c.)

Even though many countries collect data in order to chart ethnic or racial affiliation, there is considerable spatial variation in the use of terms such as *ethnicity* and *race* around the world. The sociologist Ann Morning has produced a fascinating study of the geographic differences in the terminology and meaning of words, including *ethnicity*, *race*, *indigenous group*, and *nationality* on official censuses. Her study reveals that most countries do enumerate their populations on the basis of some form of national, ancestral, or ethnic identity. The most common

term used in such questions is *ethnicity*. "More specifically," Morning explains, "census usage of *race* is found almost entirely in the former slaveholding societies of the Western Hemisphere and their territories" (Morning, 2008, p. 248).

Globally, the United States is one of a small number of countries that use the term *race* on its census form. Before examining the implications of this practice, let's first consider the role of the U.S. Census Bureau, and how census data is gathered and reported.

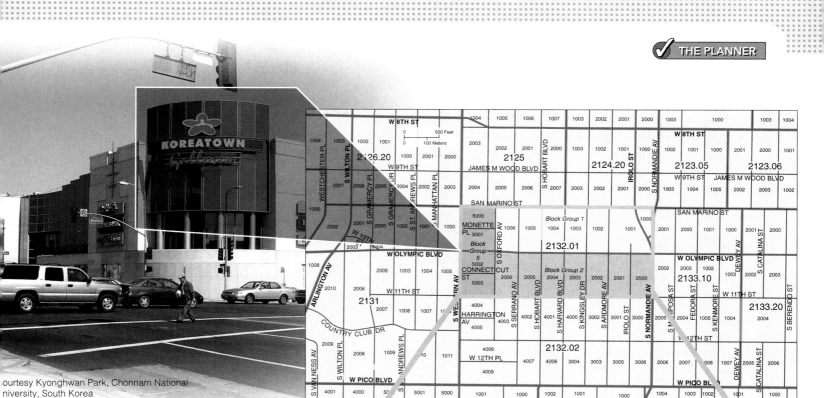

courtesy Kyonghwan Park, Chonnam National
University, South Korea

d. Census tracts, block groups, and blocks

Each census tract consists of one or more
block groups. There are three block groups
in census tract 2132.01. Block groups
are subdivided into blocks, the smallest
geographic unit for which census data are
reported. The Koreatown Galleria, shown
here, is located in Block Group 5, block 5002.
(*Source:* U.S. Census Bureau, 2000a.)

e. Census tract data

This table shows the population composition
of census tract 2132.01, by race and ethnicity.
(*Source:* U.S. Census Bureau, 2010a.)

Total population	4,198	100.0%
Hispanic or Latino (of any race)	2,116	50.4
Not Hispanic or Latino	2,082	49.6
One race	**4,050**	**96.5**
White	901	21.5
Black or African American	136	3.2
American Indian and Alaska Native	14	0.3
Asian	1,807	43.0
Native Hawaiian and Other Pacific Islander	1	0.0
Some other race	1,191	28.4
Two or more races	**148**	**3.5**

Think Critically

1. Why is the scale of the block group needed?
2. Why are census data not reported for blocks?

The United States Census Bureau is the government
agency responsible for enumerating the country's population. A crucial reason for the census is to ensure proper
political representation (see Chapter 7) and to plan for
the provision of public services. The Census Bureau collects a wide range of data about the population and the
economy, such as age, education, household size, employment, and commuting patterns. This information is valuable to different agencies and organizations. For example,
school districts consult census data to learn about the
diversity of their students. Human geographers and other
researchers greatly appreciate the volume and variety of
data collected by the Census Bureau. Indeed, many geographical studies would not be possible without U.S. Census data. The phrase, *U.S. Census geography* refers to the
different units or scales for which census data is collected
and presented. For an introduction to U.S. Census geography, see *What a Geographer Sees.*

In the United States the Office of Management and Budget (OMB) is charged with the supervision of federal agencies, including the Census Bureau. In 1977 the OMB issued Directive 15, which mandated that all federal agencies use uniform procedures for collecting racial and ethnic data. Directive 15 recognized a single ethnic category—Hispanic—and four racial categories: American Indian or Alaska Native, Asian or Pacific Islander, Black, and White. OMB added a fifth racial category, Native Hawaiian or Other Pacific Islander, in 1997. These categories are still in use on census forms today (**Figure 6.7**).

Why would the U.S. Census Bureau collect data on one ethnicity but multiple races? One answer is that this

Prevalent ethnicities • Figure 6.7

Responses to the accompanying census questions about race and ethnicity were tallied to generate the pie charts and map.

b. U.S. population composition from two perspectives

The pie chart on the left shows Hispanic and non-Hispanic origin for the population. The pie chart on the right shows the count and percentage of those who selected just one racial category. (*Source:* Data from U.S. Census Bureau, 2010a.)

a. U.S. census form questions on race

The U.S. Census form is sent to all households every 10 years. Note that Hispanic origin is represented as something other than race. (*Source:* Adapted from U.S. Census Bureau.)

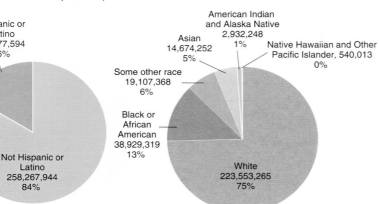

Hispanic or Latino 50,477,594 16%

Not Hispanic or Latino 258,267,944 84%

American Indian and Alaska Native 2,932,248 1%

Asian 14,674,252 5%

Native Hawaiian and Other Pacific Islander, 540,013 0%

Some other race 19,107,368 6%

Black or African American 38,929,319 13%

White 223,553,265 75%

NOTE: Please answer BOTH the question about Hispanic origin and the question about race. For this census, Hispanic orgins are not races.

Is Person 1 of Hispanic, Latino, or Spanish origin?

☐ No, not of Hispanic, Latino, or Spanish orgin
☐ Yes, Mexican, Mexican Am., Chicano
☐ Yes, Puerto Rican
☐ Yes, Cuban
☐ Yes, another Hispanic, Latino, or Spanish origin— *Print origin, for example, Argentinean, Colombian, Dominican, Nicaraguan, Salvadoran, Spaniard, and so on.* ↘

What is Person 1's race? Mark ☒ One or more boxes.

☐ White
☐ Black, African Am., or Negro
☐ American Indian or Alaska Native — *Print name of enrolled or principal tribe.* ↘

☐ Asian Indian   ☐ Japanese   ☐ Native Hawaiian
☐ Chinese   ☐ Korean   ☐ Guamanian or Chamorro
☐ Filipino   ☐ Vietnamese   ☐ Samoan
☐ Other Asian — *Print race, for example, Hmong, Laotian, Thai, Pakistani, Cambodian, and so on.* ↘   ☐ Other Pacific Islander — *Print race, for example, Fijian, Tongan, and so on.* ↘

☐ Some other race — *Print race.* ↘

c. Leading minority group, by county

White, non-Hispanic is the majority population group. Excluding that data enables us to map and see the distribution of minority groups. California, Hawaii, New Mexico, Texas, Washington, D. C., and Puerto Rico are *majority-minority*, meaning that more than half of the population is minority. (*Source:* Suchan *et al.*, 2007.)

American Indian and Alaska Native
Asian
Black
Hispanic
Pacific Islander
Two or More Races

Non-Hispanic Some Other Race group was not the most common in any county; Pacific Islander was most common in Kalawao County, HI

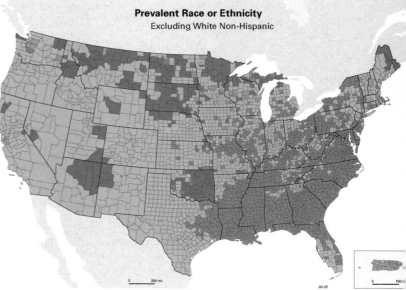

Prevalent Race or Ethnicity
Excluding White Non-Hispanic

American FactFinder

This is an online resource provided by the U.S. Census Bureau. You can use this website to view and create maps of different kinds of census data. From the main page, click on Guided Search and follow the steps.

S. Meltzer/PhotoLink/Photodisc/Getty Images, Inc.

discourse
Communication that provides insight on social values, attitudes, priorities, and ways of understanding the world.

practice represents an artifact of the guidelines established by Directive 15. A more critical response, however, involves the role of **discourse**. For example, a conversation is a kind of a discourse, and the language that we use—or fail to use—reveals the meanings we give to places, people, and events. Institutions, including legal systems and entities such as the U.S. Census Bureau, also create discourses.

The way in which the U.S. Census gathers information about race and ethnicity is part of a broader discourse of identity that has developed around two important issues. The first issue is that the Census Bureau assumes a person's race can be objectively defined. The second and related point is that the U.S. Census uses ethnicity in a way that does not capture the sense of social belonging that ethnicity involves. In other words, according to the Census Bureau one's membership in a racial or ethnic group is still based on skin color (for example, white or black) and ancestry (for example, Chinese or Native Hawaiian). Bear in mind that these issues are contrary to some of the main characteristics of race and ethnicity already presented in this chapter.

The discourse of the U.S. Census, then, reinforces and legitimizes certain ways of thinking about race and ethnicity even though they may be misleading or inconsistent. In fact, the U.S. Census has often been inconsistent in its classification of the population by ethnicity and race. Some scholars have argued, for example, that the census has been anchored to a discourse that draws on a binary vision created by the categories of "white" and "nonwhite." The "nonwhites" are further subdivided into blacks, American Indians, Chinese, Asian Indians, and so on, but "white" remains a singular category that is not subdivided.

The Census Bureau clearly plays an influential role in shaping a discourse of identity in the United States. Specifically, it contributes to the erroneous assumption that race is real. The Bureau's actions and policies carry authority because it is the key institution charged with enumerating and classifying people. According to Kenneth Prewitt, former director of the Census Bureau, "[T]he public face of America's official racial classification is its census" (Prewitt, 2005, p. 6). Thus, it is instructive to critically appraise the procedures the Census Bureau uses so that we are better informed users of its data.

You can explore some census data through the Census Bureau's website. A good place to start is with their data access tool called FactFinder. For more information on this see *Where Geographers Click*.

CONCEPT CHECK 🛑 STOP

1. **How** does ethnicity differ from nationality?
2. **What** characteristics help define indigenous peoples?
3. **What** geographic units are used to provide census data below the county level?
4. **How** and why does the U.S. Census contribute to a discourse of identity?

Ethnicity in the Landscape

LEARNING OBJECTIVES

1. **Identify** three models of ethnic interaction.
2. **Distinguish** between ethnic islands, ethnic neighborhoods, and ethnoburbs.
3. **Explain** symbolic ethnicity.
4. **Explain** the reasons for ethnic conflict and violence in Sudan.
5. **Define** environmental justice.

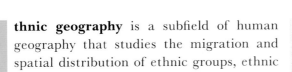

Ethnic geography is a subfield of human geography that studies the migration and spatial distribution of ethnic groups, ethnic interaction and networks, and the various expressions or imprints of ethnicity in the landscape. The study of such ethnic imprints, or **ethnoscapes**, has traditionally focused on identifying and documenting distinctive examples of material culture including religious buildings, community centers, murals, and ethnic restaurants.

> **ethnoscape**
> A cultural landscape that reveals or expresses aspects of the identity of an ethnic group.

Lately, the study of ethnic imprints has broadened to include radio and television stations that cater to particular ethnic groups, as well as Internet sites that support ethnic communities.

Ethnic Interaction and Globalization

In the United States, the study of ethnic geography, and specifically ethnic interaction, tends to overlap with studies of immigration. Scholars have developed different models to depict and help explain ethnic interaction. Three of these models—*assimilation*, *pluralism*, and *heterolocalism*—have been the most influential. Of these, the assimilation model is the oldest and dates to the early 20th century. Pluralism is nearly as old but did not gain currency until the 1960s. The model of heterolocalism is the most recent and was first proposed in 1998.

For a long time much scholarship on ethnic groups conducted by geographers, historians, and social scientists was shaped by the assimilation model. Assimilation describes the outcome of interactions between members of an ethnic group and outsiders. More specifically, **assimilation** refers to the gradual loss of the cultural traits, beliefs, and practices that distinguish immigrant ethnic groups and their members. The assimilation model promotes the view of society as a melting pot. The **pluralism** model, by contrast, builds on the premise that members of immigrant ethnic groups resist pressures to assimilate and retain those traits, beliefs, and practices that make them distinctive. The pluralism model gives rise to the tossed salad metaphor for society, and geographically to the idea of *ethnic enclaves*—spatially distinct areas with a notable concentration of members of an ethnic group.

In a groundbreaking study, geographer Wilbur Zelinsky and the sociologist Barrett Lee coined the term *heterolocal*, literally meaning *different place*, and argued that globalization had so fundamentally altered the patterns and consequences of ethnic interaction that a new model was needed (Zelinsky and Lee, 1998). The concept of **heterolocalism** means that members of an ethnic group maintain their sense of shared identity even though they are residentially dispersed.

Zelinsky and Lee (1998) identified four characteristics crucial for the development of heterolocalism. These are: (1) an immigrant population that, upon arrival, clusters only minimally if at all; (2) the conduct of social activities (shopping, employment, entertainment, residence) in separate, nonoverlapping areas; (3) the persistence of a sense of identity as a community because of technological advances, such as the Internet, or what Zelinsky and Lee (1998, p. 285) call "community without propinquity;" and (4) a history tied to the processes of late-20th-century globalization. Cartographically, what would a heterolocal community look like? See **Figure 6.8**.

Ethnic settlements Geographers have identified several different kinds of ethnic settlements, and three of the more common types are ethnic islands, ethnic neighborhoods, and ethnoburbs. **Ethnic islands** are associated with rural areas. In the United States they vary in size from smaller than a county to multicounty regions that may

Heterolocalism • Figure 6.8

Some 40,000 Vietnamese live in and around Washington, D.C., but at the level of the census tract nowhere do they make up more than 18% of the population. By contrast, they accounted for less than 1% of the population in most census tracts. In this shopping center catering to Vietnamese clientele in Falls Church, Virginia, the clock tower resembles one in Saigon and the yellow flag is the flag of the former South Vietnam.

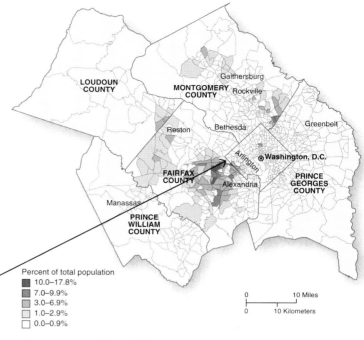

Percent of total population
- 10.0–17.8%
- 7.0–9.9%
- 3.0–6.9%
- 1.0–2.9%
- 0.0–0.9%

(*Source:* Airriess, 2007, p. 302.)

Compliments of Eden Center

Ethnic islands • Figure 6.9

The Hopi and Navajo Reservations (population approximately 7000 and 174,000, respectively) are ethnic islands and enclaves in the U.S. When mapped, we can see that they also form enclaves of each other.

extend into several states. Ethnic islands and ethnic neighborhoods are sometimes called *enclaves*. (An enclave is a unit that is nested within another unit). In terms of population ethnic islands may have fewer than 100 residents or several thousand (**Figure 6.9**).

In contrast to ethnic islands, **ethnic neighborhoods** develop in urban areas but may vary in scale from a few city blocks to sizable districts within a city. Such places as Chinatown and Little Italy are examples of ethnic neighborhoods. A *ghetto* is a type of ethnic neighborhood. The first ghettos were involuntary settlements created in the Middle Ages when Jews were forced to live in one district of the city. In the United States, the term *ghetto* refers to inner-city neighborhoods with predominantly African American populations. As impoverished and economically marginalized areas, ghettos—like Chinatowns—have historically been racially stigmatized spaces.

Ethnoburbs are multiethnic suburban settlements associated mainly with large metropolitan areas. Two forces play a role in the formation of ethnoburbs: economic globalization and social stratification. Greater economic globalization and changes in immigration policies have diversified the pool of new immigrants to the United States and contributed to the multiethnic composition of ethnoburbs. Also, many of these immigrants are well educated and work in jobs that are linked to highly globalized sectors of the economy, including international trade and banking. Some of these immigrants even shuttle frequently between the United States and their country of origin, maintaining global as well as local social networks. Significantly, ethnoburbs are mosaics. In contrast to ethnic neighborhoods, ethnoburbs function as both commercial and residential areas. Moreover, the population within ethnoburbs is not only ethnically diverse, but it is also economically stratified, with low-skill, low-wage workers as well as more affluent residents.

> **ethnoburb**
> A multiethnic residential, commercial, or mixed suburban cluster in which a single ethnic group is unlikely to form a majority of the population.

Ethnic groups and location quotients When geographers want to know how the proportional presence of an ethnic group in a region compares to the proportional presence of that same ethnic group in the country, they use the **location quotient**. The location quotient (LQ) can be calculated using the following formula:

$$LQ = \frac{\text{(Population of ethnic group in an area/Total population of that area)}}{\text{(National population of ethnic group/National population)}}$$

The numerator expresses the percentage of an ethnic group in a given area such as a county or state. The denominator expresses the national percentage of that same ethnic group. Dividing these two percentages yields the location quotient. If the location quotient equals one, then the percentage of the ethnic group in the state matches the percentage of the ethnic group nationally. When the location quotient is greater than one, the ethnic group is overrepresented in that area. When the location quotient is less than one, the ethnic group is said to be underrepresented in comparison to the national percentage (**Figure 6.10**).

Location quotients • Figure 6.10

Calculating and mapping location quotients help reveal the spatial variation in patterns of ethnic group concentration.

a. The table presents population data for Australia and its indigenous populations, the Aboriginals and Torres Strait Islanders. Nationally, they constitute just 2.5% of the population, and only in the Northern Territory do they make up more than one-quarter of the population. (*Source:* Australian Bureau of Statistics, 2009.)

Australian state or territory	Indigenous population*	Total population*	Percentage indigenous	Location quotient for indigenous populations
New South Wales	152,685	6,816,087	2.24%	0.90
Victoria	33,517	5,126,540	0.65%	0.26
Queensland	144,885	4,090,908	3.54%	1.42
South Australia	28,055	1,567,888	1.79%	0.72
Western Australia	70,966	2,059,381	3.45%	1.38
Tasmania	18,415	489,951	3.76%	1.50
Northern Territory	64,005	210,627	30.39%	12.16
Australian Capital Territory	4,282	334,119	1.28%	0.51
Australia	517,043	20,697,880	2.50%	

* Numbers are estimates.

b. Where are Australia's indigenous peoples over- and underrepresented? If you noticed that the location quotient for the Northern Territory is well above all the other values, then you have discovered one of the limitations of this measure. Although the location quotient can be less than one, it can never be lower than zero. This means that the location quotient is not as effective at capturing the degree of underrepresentation of a particular group.

Other Ethnic Imprints

On a spectrum of visibility, ethnic imprints may be subtle, highly visible, or virtually anywhere between these two possibilities. For example, Joseph Sciorra (1989) used yard shrines and sidewalk altars as markers of Italian American residences in New York City. Ethnic radio and television are other examples of ethnic imprints. Since 1998 Asian Indians in the United States with access to satellite television have been able to tune into Zee TV, a station based in India which broadcasts in Hindi and other Indian languages.

Ethnic restaurants are one of the most visible ethnic imprints, but even within this category a great deal of variation exists. For example, Chinese and Mexican restaurants are widespread in the United States, but in the United Kingdom Indian and Chinese restaurants are more prevalent. Why do you suppose that Pakistani, Bangladeshi, Filipino, or Nigerian restaurants are less common even in countries with diverse immigrant populations?

Public festivals also provide a highly visible expression of ethnicity and identity. In the Crown Heights neighborhood of Brooklyn, for example, immigrants from several of the Caribbean Islands hold a yearly festival they call the West Indian Carnival. Like Mardi Gras, Carnival developed as a pre-Lenten celebration in which participants design and wear elaborate costumes. Carnival was originally a winter festival held indoors, but in Brooklyn today it takes place outdoors on Labor Day and attracts more than 3 million visitors. Some now refer to the festival as the "Labor Day Carnival."

To some observers, festivals are at best contrived and staged examples of ethnicity that generate business and tourist revenue. But this interpretation neglects to consider the complexity of ethnic identity and the role of **symbolic ethnicity**—the way in which a collection of symbols imparts meaning and identity to members of an ethnic group. These symbols can be thought of as expressions of ethnicity and often include such things as flags, music, styles of dress, and cuisine.

Participation in or attendance at festivals such as Carnival, then, is a component of symbolic ethnicity and may in fact be very meaningful in terms of reaffirming a sense of belonging individually and collectively. Ethnic geographers agree that it is important to study the evolution of different traditions such as Carnival in order to understand how they have changed over time and what they mean in the context of symbolic ethnicity, rather than simply dismiss them as contrived or inauthentic (**Figure 6.11**).

Symbolic ethnicity • Figure 6.11

Participants in the annual Carnival parade in Crown Heights, Brooklyn, an area with a sizable population of immigrants from the Caribbean. As a way of experiencing and enjoying traditions associated with an ethnic group, symbolic ethnicity often involves performance. Making and parading in elaborate costumes has long been a part of Carnival.

Ethnic Conflict

No discussion of ethnicity would be complete without a consideration of ethnic conflict. The phrase *ethnic conflict* is commonly used to characterize conflicts, including the crisis in Darfur (a region portrayed as troubled by ethnic and tribal rivalries), the breakup of Yugoslavia (described as a product of historical ethnic animosities among the Croats, Serbs, Bosnians, and others), and the unrest in Sri Lanka (cited as an ethnic conflict between Sinhalese and Tamils).

Many human geographers, however, find the label *ethnic conflict* to be problematic because it tends to suggest a single cause for conflict: ethnic difference or ethnic hatred. Most conflicts, however, have multiple causes such as political exclusion, disputes over land or access to other resources. Events in Darfur, a large and very ethnically diverse region in western Sudan, provide a good example of the complex and multifaceted nature of conflict.

Conflict in Sudan • Figure 6.12

Conflict in Darfur has destroyed hundreds of villages, raised the death toll to nearly 500,000, and displaced some 2.5 million people. South Sudan gained its independence from Sudan in 2011. ▶ **Using the map as a guide, how might oil also be a factor in Darfur?**

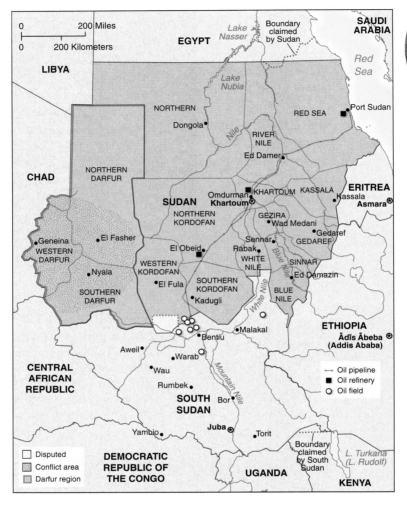

The origins of the conflict in Darfur are rooted in events that have changed the relationship between sedentary farmers and nomadic pastoralists. In Darfur (meaning land of the Fur people), the Fur, Masalit, and Zaghawa are sedentary farmers often of African descent, whereas the pastoralists are mainly Arab-descended. All of these groups are Muslim, and historically, disputes among them were settled through indigenous systems of mediation. Only recently has the conflict in Darfur become charged with ethnic and racial overtones.

Political and economic factors have strongly shaped events in Darfur. Compared to other regions in Sudan, Darfur is much less developed. For decades, the government in Khartoum has done little to change this or give Darfuris a voice in political affairs. This neglect contributed to the formation of a number of regional political movements in Darfur, some seeking self-determination.

In 2003, two of these militias led a rebellion in the region. In response, the government sent its forces into Darfur. The government also provided support and equipment to separate militias known as the *janjaweed* (a word for armed men riding horses or camels). The janjaweed is called an "Arab militia" because its members have been recruited from pastoral communities that are Arab or Arabic-speaking. The janjaweed have forcibly removed the Fur, Masalit, and Zaghawa from the area through **ethnic cleansing**. Most tragically, the janjaweed have targeted civilian populations, committed atrocities against them, and created a humanitarian crisis in the region (**Figure 6.12**).

Proximity to environmental burdens • Figure 6.13

Certain large industrial facilities (called toxic release facilities or TRIs) are required to report to the Environmental Protection Agency amounts of toxins they emit into the air. Data from the San Francisco Bay Area shows that some ethnic groups are more likely than others to live near such a facility. (*Source: Pastor et al., 2007.*)

a. Population by race/ethnicity and proximity to a toxic release facility

Notice how the composition of population groups changes with increasing distance from the toxic release facility.

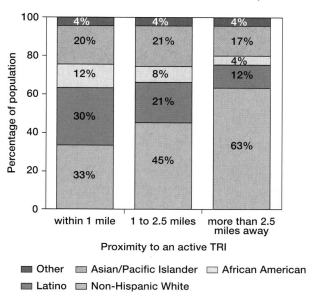

b. Households within one mile of a toxic release facility by income, race/ethnicity

Compare this graph to the one in (a). ▶ **What do these data suggest in terms of the distribution of environmental burdens in the San Francisco Bay area and the interconnectedness of geography, race or ethnicity, and income? What other factors need to be considered?**

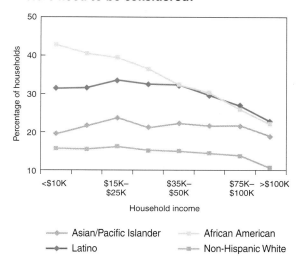

Environmental Justice

Another factor that can contribute to tension among ethnic groups is the lack of equity in the distribution of hazardous sites or facilities. *Equity* means without favoritism or bias. The movement for environmental justice originated in the 1980s amid a growing awareness that certain groups had little involvement in decisions that affected the locations of toxic waste sites, industrial hazards, and other undesirable uses of land. According to the U.S. Environmental Protection Agency, "**Environmental justice** is the fair treatment and meaningful involvement of all people regardless of race, color, national origin, or income with respect to the development, implementation, and enforcement of environmental laws, regulations, and policies." Since 1994 all federal agencies have adopted the principle of environmental justice.

At the global scale, the disposal of toxic waste, including electronic or e-waste generated from discarded computers, TVs, and other electronic devices, is a major area of concern for advocates of environmental justice. Considerable volumes of contaminated waste are exported,

sometimes illegally, to developing countries for recycling or disposal. When the recycling or disposal is not effectively regulated, however, workers can be exposed to dangerous acids and environmental contamination can occur.

Environmental justice and its counterpart environmental injustice are inherently geographical because they involve understanding what groups of people and which places are disproportionately burdened by exposure to environmental hazards (see **Figure 6.13**).

CONCEPT CHECK

1. **What** is heterolocalism?
2. **How** is globalization related to the formation of ethnoburbs?
3. **What** can a location quotient tell us?
4. **Why** is "ethnic conflict" a sometimes problematic label?
5. **How** can geography inform the study of environmental justice?

Sexuality and Gender

LEARNING OBJECTIVES

1. **Distinguish** between sexuality and gender.
2. **Explain** how ideas about sexuality can affect the use of space.
3. **Explore** the geographical variation in gender roles and gender gaps.

Two other important facets of identity are **sexuality** and **gender**. Both are social constructions; however, the distinction between the sexes has been based on a dichotomy once thought to be exclusive. Biologically, females have two X chromosomes and males have one X and one Y chromosome. But we now know that human biology is not always this straightforward. For example, some individuals inherit only one X chromosome (XO), or an extra X or Y chromosome (XXY or XYY, respectively). None of these chromosome patterns fits either the female (XX) or male (XY) categories. Thus, it is clear that human sexuality cannot be reduced to a simple binary or twofold classification of individuals into females and males. Moreover, the problems of classifying people according to their chromosomal makeup resemble the problems we mentioned earlier of attempting to classify people into separate and distinct racial categories.

> **sexuality** A basis for personal and social identity that stems from sexual orientation, attitudes, desires, and practices.
>
> **gender** The cultural or social characteristics society associates with being female or male.

The term **gender role** conveys the idea that there are certain social expectations, responsibilities, or rights associated with femininity and masculinity. Notice how a dominant discourse in society privileges a binary view about sexuality and gender. This discourse specifically reinforces the thinking that there should be a correspondence between the two. In other words, society expects that a person who is female will behave in ways that reinforce and reflect a female gender role and a feminine identity. However, a person's sexual identity may or may not be related to her or his biological or chromosomal makeup. **Transgendered** persons, for example, do not identify with the gender assigned them at birth (see *Video Explorations*).

Video Explorations

Taboo Sexuality: Eunuchs

National Geographic

A eunuch is a castrated male, but in India the term *eunuch* or, more commonly, *hijra* also encompasses people who are born male but identify as women. Thus, eunuchs are referred to as a third sex or third gender in India. Paradoxically, they are considered to be endowed with spiritual powers, yet they are also discriminated against. The video highlights a group of eunuchs in their struggle to make a life in India, where society privileges the conventional view that the existence of two genders, male and female, is "normal."

Sexuality, Identity, and Space

As individuals, our identity may be shaped as much by our sexuality as by our gender, ethnicity, ancestry, and other unique biographical details. Until the late 1970s, however, geographers ignored the ways in which sexuality contributed to identity, promoting instead the fiction that the world could best be understood through approaches that privileged a **heterosexual norm**—a binary vision of the sexes based on clearly defined masculine and feminine gender roles. Today a number of geographers study the ways in which diverse sexualities influence the configuration and use of space.

The relationship between sexuality and space makes sense if we think about how language is often used to describe sexuality. For example, we talk about gays and lesbians as "coming out." The heterosexual norm promotes the idea that those who are not heterosexual are socially deviant and need to suppress, ignore, or hide their identity and occupy or use different social spaces. This norm has geographic ramifications because it can affect certain kinds of space, including **public space**. Sometimes the enforcement of heterosexual norms turns public space into space that is actually not public. One of the clearest examples of this involves the conflict over the issue of gays in the military. Instead of allowing gays and lesbians to be open about their identity, the U.S. military adopted and implemented the "don't ask/don't tell" policy from 1993 until 2011. In practice, it meant that gays and lesbians were not allowed to speak about their sexual orientation. The policy effectively imposed limitations on free speech in a public space.

> **public space** A kind of commons; a space intended to be open and accessible to anyone.

During the 1950s and 1960s, police sometimes raided private establishments frequented by gay, lesbian, and transgendered individuals. In these instances the police monitored private spaces in the name of public decency. Local statutes against solicitation, public lewdness, or vagrancy, for example, were used to justify arresting the patrons of gay bars. This kind of harassment and institutional discrimination worked to forge a sense of shared identity among gay, lesbian, bisexual, and transgendered individuals and to launch the gay rights movement following the Stonewall Rebellion in New York City in 1969. The Stonewall Rebellion occurred when customers at the Stonewall Inn, a gay bar, resisted and fought against police during a raid of the bar. These events helped geographers and other scholars realize that sexuality can often influence a person's political identity (**Figure 6.14**).

Geography and Gender

Janet Townsend, a geographer at the University of Durham, provided one of the most succinct statements about the relationship between geography and gender when she observed that "gender matters to geography and geography matters to gender at all places and scales" (1991, p. 25). She went on to explain that a thorough understanding of a particular place must involve an examination of the ways in which gender intersects with and affects the lives and activities of people in that place. One way to accomplish this is to consider the spatial variation in gender roles.

Same-sex marriage • Figure 6.14

The status of same-sex marriage and other legal alternatives such as domestic partnerships and civil unions demonstrates the politically charged nature of sexuality. Most U.S. states have both a law and a constitutional amendment that define marriage as the union of a man and a woman and, in effect, prohibit same-sex marriage. Same-sex marriage is legal in nine states and the District of Columbia. (*Source:* Data from Vestal, 2009; HRC 2010a; HRC 2010b, with updates.)

Gender roles vary geographically and can influence the division of labor. In rural Tanzania, for example, men are expected to be the main economic providers and women the caretakers of families. In contrast, different gender roles in Ghana ensure that women manage a wide variety of activities, including wholesaling and retailing in urban markets. Significantly, gender roles can change over time. In the United States, for example, gender roles changed during World War II as more women began working outside of the home in factories and in jobs once considered "men's work."

The factors that influence gender roles are numerous but include ideas (sometimes mistaken) about the skills women and men possess, as well as attitudes about empowerment and who should have decision-making authority. The mass media and other religious, educational, political, and corporate institutions strongly reinforce gender roles. Even in the United States, enduring and deep-seated views about gender roles have been persistent.

Consider, for example, the underrepresentation of women in science and engineering, or the arguments against permitting women to engage in combat as mentioned in the chapter opener.

Elsewhere, long-standing customary practices within families and communities continue to shape gender roles. Some Muslim and Hindu women, for example, observe *purdah*, which refers to the practice of wearing clothes that cover all of the body. Purdah also includes the practice of socially segregating women and men. Purdah developed not only as a means of ensuring that women were not seen by men unrelated to them, but also as a way of defining acceptable behavior and gender roles. For example, in Saudi Arabia, women are not permitted to drive and, if traveling alone, they must have permission from a male relative to board an airplane. Moreover, in Saudi Arabia, segregation of men and women is sanctioned by law. This has given rise to banks that have

Gender gap index and gender disparities • Figure 6.15

These images illustrate geographical differences in gender equality.

a. Sweden has the narrowest gender gap (0.81), and Yemen has the widest (0.45). To calculate the index, male and female enrollments in school are examined, as are labor participation rates. ▶ **How might you explain the large gender gap index for Japan?**
(*Source:* 2007 Gender Gap Heatmap. *The Global Gender Gap Report.* © World Economic Forum. Available online at http://www.weforum.org/pdf/gender-gap/2007_heatmap.pdf.)

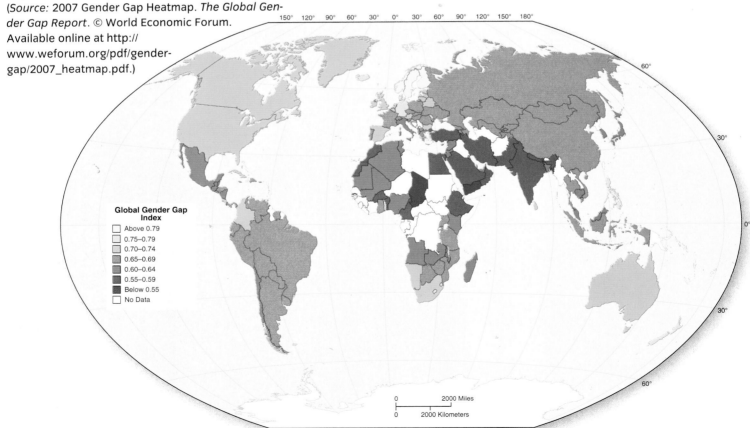

Global Gender Gap Index
- Above 0.79
- 0.75–0.79
- 0.70–0.74
- 0.65–0.69
- 0.60–0.64
- 0.55–0.59
- Below 0.55
- No Data

separate branches for women, segregated universities, and segregated workplaces. Because of this segregation, it has only been within the past 20 years that Saudi women have been able to pursue careers in such fields as architecture and journalism.

Gender roles do not always result in men and women working in separate spheres or spaces, however. In Tamil Nadu, India, for example, both men and women work in agriculture and participate in the same activities. However, men spend comparatively more time plowing the fields, whereas women spend more time selecting seeds, weeding, and preparing crops for storage.

The persistence of gender roles can contribute to the development of stereotypes about what constitutes "men's work" or "women's work." When such stereotypes develop, they can create social barriers that constrain the opportunities available and contribute to a

gender gap
A disparity between men and women in their opportunities, rights, benefits, behavior, or attitudes.

gender gap. Many researchers pay close attention to gender gaps because they are good indicators of gender-based inequalities. For example, even though women constitute 40% of the global labor force, they earn just 25% of the income generated in the world. As a whole, women are less likely to work in salaried jobs, and when they do, they do not earn as much as men, creating a gender gap in wages.

One way of examining the gender gap is to use the gender gap index—a measure developed in 2006 to help assess how effective different countries have been at closing the gender gap. The index is based on a mixture of economic, political, educational, and health-related data. Countries that have a value close to one have a narrow gender gap (a value of one would indicate gender equality rather than a gender gap), while countries with values close to zero have a wide gender gap (**Figure 6.15**).

Pavel Rahman/©AP/Wide World Photos

Hassan Ammar/©AP/Wide World Photos

b. Bangladeshi women carry a banner proclaiming "gender equality needs equal rights to property and resources." In parts of Asia, women cannot inherit property, but they can inherit debt.

c. In Saudi Arabia, women can own cars, but they cannot drive them. In a remarkable protest against the ban in 1990, women drove cars in Riyadh. In commemoration of that day, this woman takes advantage of a loophole in the law and drives an ATV.

d. In a list of values ordered from low to high, the median is the value in the middle; half of the values are higher than it, and half of the values are lower than it. Based on median income data for the U.S., shown here, a persistent income gap not only separates men from women but also separates blacks and Hispanics, both male and female, from other racial groups. In 2007, the highest median income for women (among Asians) was still below the lowest median income for men (among Hispanics). (*Source:* U.S. Census Bureau, 2010b.)

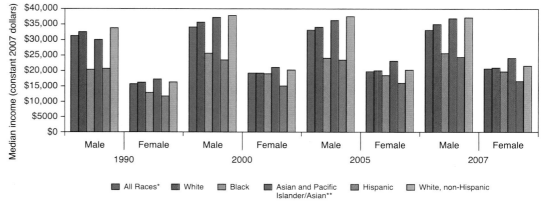

*Includes other races not shown separately

**Years 2005 and 2007 show data for Asians alone

The presence of a gender gap matters because it points to the institutionalization of status differences between women and men in society. Status is a way of socially ranking and valuing certain types of knowledge and skills that people possess. Status takes on a geographic dimension when it affects how the spaces and places of home, school, and work are organized and controlled. We continue our discussion of geography and gender in several other chapters, including Development, Industry, and Agriculture.

CONCEPT CHECK STOP

1. **What** are the limitations of binary views of sexuality and gender?

2. **How** can norms about sexuality affect public space?

3. **Why** is an understanding of gender important to the study of geography?

Summary

1 **Race and Racism 164**

- The concept of **race** developed as a way to classify people into biologically distinct groups, or races. On a genetic basis, however, humans are so similar that identifying distinct racial categories is an entirely arbitrary exercise. Because nature does not provide a basis for classifying people into racial categories, race is best thought of as a **social construction**.

- **Racism** is rooted in perceptions that people who are different from us are inferior to us. During the Enlightenment in Europe, a complex **ideology** of racism developed in conjunction with ideas about the great chain of being, shown here. **Human trafficking** is also tied to perceptions of human difference and represents an enduring form of slavery.

Great chain of being • Figure 6.2

Bonnet, 1779-83, vol. IV, p. 1. Image courtesy History of Science Collections, University of Oklahoma Libraries.

2 **Geographies of Race and Racism 168**

- **Institutional discrimination** disadvantages people because of their cultural differences. Geographers recognize that institutional discrimination and racism can have a significant impact on the spatial functioning and configuration of cities and countries.

- In certain instances, ideas about race and place mutually reinforce one another and can lead to institutional discrimination, racism, or both.

- From 1948 to 1991, **apartheid**, a system of racial segregation, was official policy in South Africa. Apartheid affected the use of space not only at the national scale but also, as the photo shows, at the individual scale.

The rise and fall of apartheid • Figure 6.5

David Turnley/©Corbis

3 What Is Ethnicity? 172

- **Ethnicity** refers to the personal and behavioral basis of an individual's identity, which generates a sense of social belonging among members of an **ethnic group**. As illustrated in the photo, the preparation of food and the kinds of foods consumed might be two personal components of ethnicity. Others might include language, religion, or styles of dress or music. An individual's ethnicity is contingent and flexible, and stems from processes of **othering** and **ascription**.

Ethnicity and ancestry • Figure 6.6

© Photo Resource Hawaii/Alamy

- Many countries use their censuses to collect data about the ethnicity of their citizens. Geographically, use of the term *race* on census forms is most commonly associated with the Americas, prompting interest in how census questions contribute to **discourses** of identity.

4 Ethnicity in the Landscape 178

- **Ethnic geography** includes the study of **ethnoscapes**. In the study of ethnic interaction, three models have prevailed: the **assimilation** model, the **pluralism** model, and the **heterolocalism** model. Heterolocalism occurs when members of an ethnic group who, upon arriving in a place, disperse or cluster minimally while maintaining a sense

of ethnic identity, such as the Vietnamese in metropolitan Washington, D.C. (See map.)

Heterolocalism • Figure 6.8

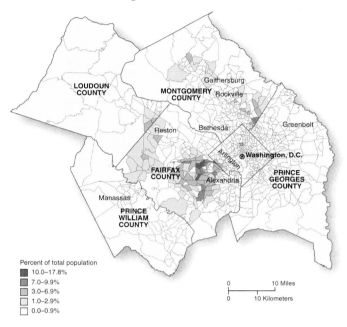

Percent of total population
- 10.0–17.8%
- 7.0–9.9%
- 3.0–6.9%
- 1.0–2.9%
- 0.0–0.9%

- When studying ethnic settlements, geographers distinguish among **ethnic islands**, **ethnic neighborhoods**, and **ethnoburbs**.

- The **location quotient** is a measure that helps to determine how the presence of an ethnic group in a region compares to that same group's presence nationally.

- Ethnic imprints provide landscape expressions of the presence of ethnic groups. Ethnic festivals are one kind of ethnic imprint and help to shed light on the ways in which **symbolic ethnicity** shapes the identity of an individual or a group.

- Ethnic tension may be a factor that contributes to ethnic conflict, but few conflicts can be explained solely on the basis of ethnic strife, even when **ethnic cleansing** occurs.

- Concern about the inequitable exposure to environmental hazards associated with the locations of toxic waste sites and toxic release facilities prompted the **environmental justice** movement.

5 Sexuality and Gender 184

- Convention teaches us that there are only two sexes: females and males. On a biological basis, however, human **sexuality** is similar to race in that it cannot always be made to fit into separate categories. These points remind us that a person's identity—whether sexual, ethnic, or gendered—is not biologically determined, nor is it fixed.

- The configuration and use of space tend to reflect dominant beliefs about **gender** and sexuality. In addition, ideas about sexuality have important geographical and political implications.

- Globally, a **heterosexual norm** prevails. This norm is rooted in a binary vision of the sexes based on clearly defined masculine and feminine gender roles. Persons who identify themselves as **transgendered** challenge such norms and illustrate the complexity of human identity.

- Geographically, **gender roles** vary from place to place, can affect the organization of space as well as the use of **public space**, and can lead to gender-based inequalities in terms of access to resources. Such inequalities help perpetuate a **gender gap** that many women, including those shown here, hope to narrow and eventually eliminate.

Gender gap index and gender disparities • Figure 6.15

Pavel Rahman/©AP/Wide World Photos

Key Terms

- apartheid 170
- ascription 172
- assimilation 178
- discourse 177
- environmental justice 183
- ethnic cleansing 182
- ethnic geography 178
- ethnic group 172

- ethnic island 178
- ethnic neighborhood 179
- ethnicity 172
- ethnoburb 180
- ethnoscape 178
- gender 184
- gender gap 187
- gender role 184

- heterolocalism 178
- heterosexual norm 184
- human trafficking 166
- ideology 164
- institutional discrimination 168
- location quotient 180
- othering 172

- pluralism 178
- public space 185
- race 164
- racism 164
- sexuality 184
- social construction 164
- symbolic ethnicity 181
- transgender 184

Critical and Creative Thinking Questions

1. Use the U.S. Census Bureau website and the map shown here to identify the census tract, block group, and block where you live. Describe the ethnic composition of your census tract or several census tracts in your county.

2. Use the U.S. Census Bureau website to find the population data for your state and county and then calculate the state and county location quotients for one or two ethnic groups of your choice. What geographical observations can you make about your findings?

3. Do some additional reading on ghettos and Indian reservations. How are they similar and different?

4. Some scholars have argued that in the United States one discourse about wilderness is that it is an ideal promoted by and for white people to the exclusion of people of color. What evidence can you provide for or against this position?

5. Do some fieldwork in your community. What ethnic imprints can you identify? What spatial patterns do you notice, and how might you account for them?

6. Cities with sizable gay communities are increasingly promoting them as a kind of alternative ethnic space and another tourist attraction. What are the implications of this for the gay communities?

7. Some scholars argue that gender segregation and strongly defined gender roles are empowering for women. Do you agree? Why or why not?

8. If poor people move into an area where a toxic waste site is located, has environmental injustice occurred? Explain your reasoning.

What is happening in this picture?

In Papua New Guinea, Huli men participating in certain ceremonies wear elaborate wigs constructed from their hair and adorned with feathers from birds. Boys who want to become warriors in Huli society are segregated from women and learn the art of beautifying their hair.

Tim Laman/NG Image Collection

Think Critically

1. What are the implications of this for our understanding of masculinity, gender roles, and geography?
2. Do you think there is a relationship between the visibility of an ethnic group and the cohesiveness of its members?

Self-Test

(Check your answers in Appendix B.)

1. Which of the following is *not* associated with the historical development of a European ideology of racism?

   a. the great chain of being

   b. the view that nature is ordered hierarchically

   c. skin color

   d. overlapping racial categories

2. _____ exists when policies, practices, or laws disadvantage people because of their differences.

   a. Ideology

   b. Institutional discrimination

   c. Interaction between race and place

   d. Apartheid

3. Which statement about apartheid is *false*?

   a. It contributed to the impoverishment of many South Africans.

   b. It was implemented at different scales.

   c. It contributed to the development of Bantustans.

   d. It was most effectively implemented in urban areas.

4. The phrase "the underside of globalization" is a reference to _____ .

   a. human trafficking

   b. the widening gender gap

   c. institutional discrimination

   d. environmental injustice

5. What types of census geography are shown here?

   a. census tracts and census groups

   b. block groups and census blocks

   c. census areas and census tracts

   d. counties and block groups

6. Briefly explain the fundamental problem with the concept of race:

   _____

   _____

7. _____ occurs when people assign a specific quality or identity to others.

   a. Othering

   b. Racism

   c. Ascription

   d. Social construction

8. Which characteristic of ethnicity does this photo illustrate?

   a. Ethnicity is subjective.

   b. Ethnicity is inherited.

   c. Ethnicity is expressed behaviorally.

   d. Ethnicity is fixed.

Dado Galdieri/©AP/Wide World Photos

9. As discussed in the chapter, the U.S. Census is unusual because _____ .

   a. its questions are discourse-free

   b. it separates race from ethnicity

   c. it is conducted every year

   d. each state conducts a separate census

10. Provided sufficient corroborating evidence, this chart might indicate _____ .

    a. an ethnic enclave

    b. a ghetto

    c. environmental injustice

    d. pluralism

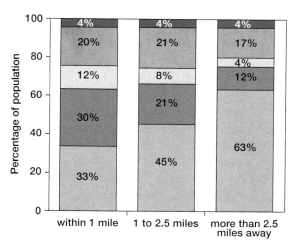

Proximity to an active TRI

- ▪ Other ▨ Asian/Pacific Islander ▫ African American
- ▨ Latino ▨ Non-Hispanic White

11. Which is *not* a characteristic of heterolocalism?

    a. community without propinquity

    b. living in one area but shopping in another

    c. globalization

    d. ethnic enclaves of immigrant communities

12. Which is *not* a characteristic of an ethnoburb?

    a. It is mainly a commercial space.

    b. It is ethnically diverse.

    c. It is socially stratified.

    d. It forms in a suburban location.

13. Which statement about Darfur is *false*?

    a. It is a region where ethnic cleansing has occurred.

    b. It is rich in oil.

    c. The conflict there has only recently become charged with ethnic hatred.

    d. Disputes in the region were customarily settled via mediation.

14. The social expectation that certain kinds of work are "men's work" is a good example of _____ .

    a. a gender gap

    b. a heterosexual norm

    c. a gender role

    d. All of the above statements are correct.

15. Purdah _____ .

    a. refers to the practice of socially segregating women and men

    b. refers to the practice, among certain women, of wearing clothes that cover the entire body

    c. may affect public as well as private space

    d. All of the above statements are correct.

THE PLANNER ✓

Review your Chapter Planner on the chapter opener and check off your completed work.

Political Geographies

VOTING PRACTICES AROUND THE WORLD

What would you think if the legal voting age in the United States were 16 instead of 18? Would it have encouraged you to become more involved in political issues at a younger age? Does it surprise you to hear that a few countries including Austria, Argentina, Brazil, Cuba, Ecuador, and Nicaragua permit 16-year-olds to vote in national elections? In most countries, 18 is the legal voting age, although there are a handful of countries where one has to be 21 to vote.

As these examples show, election practices vary in intriguing ways around the world. Some countries have election weeks instead of an election day. In India, for example, election officials operate some 900,000 polling stations across the country. Voting takes place over several days, and in places (see photo) voting machines are transported on elephant. Until recently, voters in the Philippines wrote the candidates' names on the ballot, but such a practice requires that voters be literate (and have a good memory). Alternatively, many countries design ballots so that those who cannot read or write may still cast a vote for each of the political parties. Some ballots show photographs of the different candidates.

Thinking about the variations from one country to another in terms of voting and electoral practices is just one dimension of political geography. We will say more about electoral geography later in the chapter; first we want to introduce you to the development of our political map, its states, and contemporary geopolitics.

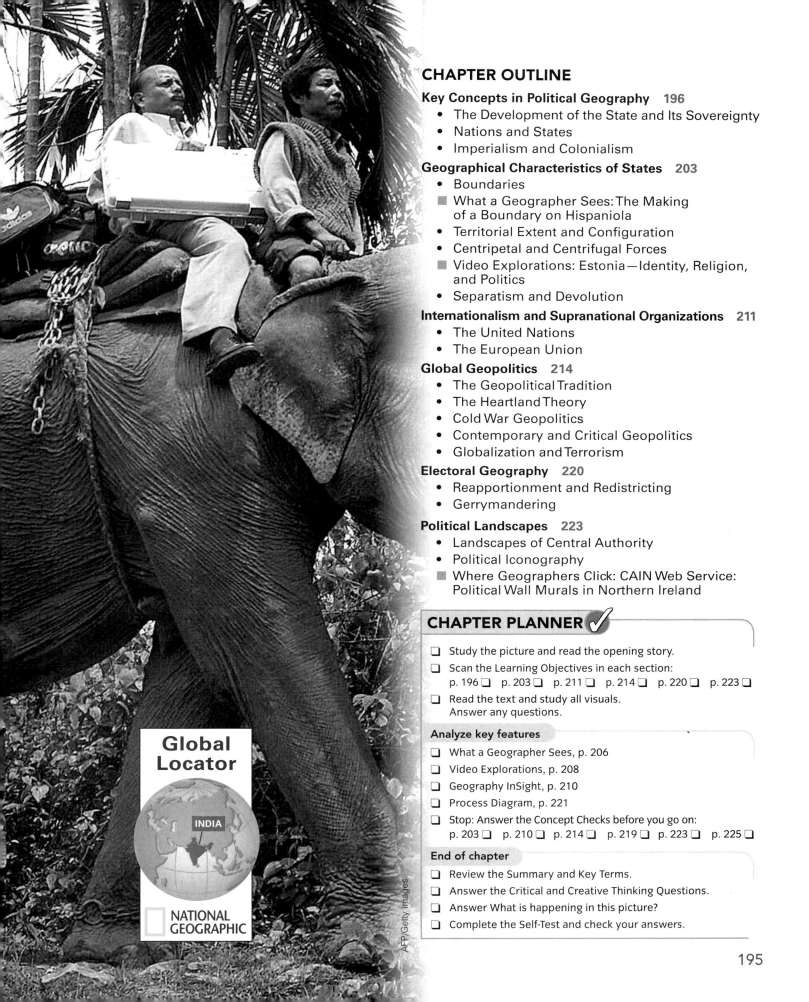

CHAPTER OUTLINE

CHAPTER PLANNER ✓

- ☐ Study the picture and read the opening story.
- ☐ Scan the Learning Objectives in each section:
  p. 196 ☐   p. 203 ☐   p. 211 ☐   p. 214 ☐   p. 220 ☐   p. 223 ☐
- ☐ Read the text and study all visuals. Answer any questions.

Analyze key features

- ☐ What a Geographer Sees, p. 206
- ☐ Video Explorations, p. 208
- ☐ Geography InSight, p. 210
- ☐ Process Diagram, p. 221
- ☐ Stop: Answer the Concept Checks before you go on:
  p. 203 ☐   p. 210 ☐   p. 214 ☐   p. 219 ☐   p. 223 ☐   p. 225 ☐

End of chapter

- ☐ Review the Summary and Key Terms.
- ☐ Answer the Critical and Creative Thinking Questions.
- ☐ Answer What is happening in this picture?
- ☐ Complete the Self-Test and check your answers.

Global Locator

INDIA

NATIONAL GEOGRAPHIC

AFP/Getty Images

Key Concepts in Political Geography

LEARNING OBJECTIVES

1. **Define** sovereignty.
2. **Distinguish** between a state and a nation.
3. **Identify** some of the impacts of colonialism on the political geography of Africa.

 t is sometimes said that **political geography** exists because people are territorial. Most political geographers consider human **territoriality** to be more than an instinctive, biological response. Instead, they see it as a complex form of behavior that is shaped by diverse social and cultural factors related to human identity.

Territoriality can be expressed by individuals and by groups. The concept of personal space helps us understand territoriality on an individual level. Personal space is

> **political geography** The study of the spatial aspects of political affairs.
>
> **territoriality** Strong attachment to or defensive control of a place or an area.

Political map of the world • Figure 7.1

The 195 countries shown on this map provide one powerful expression of human territoriality. The use of such territorially defined political units has become the dominant mode of political organization around the world only within the past four centuries. Throughout most of human history, people organized themselves in different ways, for example, according to class, kinship, or as subjects owing allegiance to a king, an emperor, or other ruler. (*Source:* NG Maps.)

the space around our bodies that we consider to be an extension of ourselves and therefore "our space." People differ a great deal in terms of how expansive their personal space is but are likely to feel uncomfortable when others encroach on it. The presence of political states (countries) that are connected with a specific territory shows that territoriality exists among groups of people (**Figure 7.1**).

The Development of the State and Its Sovereignty

How did the political map of the world come about? Although the answer to this question goes beyond the scope of this chapter, the question points to one of the key concepts in political geography: the development of the state. The practice of using territory as a basis for political organization stems from ideas about **sovereignty** that gained prominence following the Peace of Westphalia in 1648. This peace settlement included a series of treaties signed at the end of the Thirty Years' War, a long religious and territorial conflict in Europe. Since the mid-17th century, then, sovereignty has meant that states are distinct territorial units, that

> **sovereignty**
> Supreme authority of a state over its own affairs and freedom from control by outside forces.

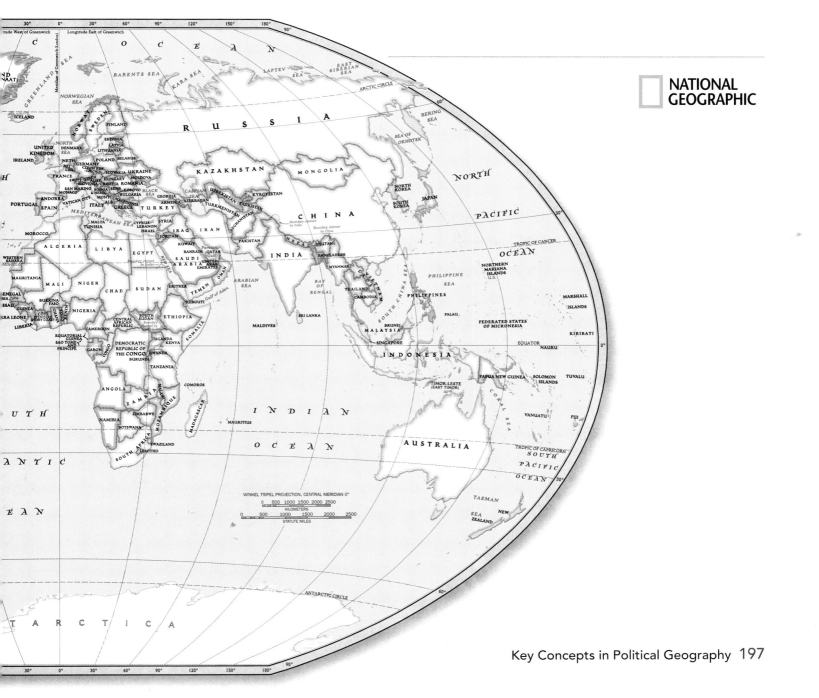

one state has no business interfering in the affairs of another state, and that states are expected to recognize the existence of other states.

For political geographers, the terms *state* and *country* mean the same thing; *state* is considered a more formal term. Therefore, a **state** exists when the following four conditions are met:

1. It consists of a specific territory with defined boundaries.
2. Its territory includes a permanent population.
3. It is recognized as a state by other states.
4. It has a government with supreme authority over its domestic and international affairs.

> **state** An internationally recognized political unit with a permanently populated territory, defined boundaries, and a government with sovereignty over its domestic and international affairs.

Sovereignty is a fundamental aspect of statehood, but even though we have carefully defined sovereignty, the fact of the matter is that people, acting on behalf of states, use it to suit their own purposes. Thus, questions of sovereignty can become a basis for political disputes. For example, different perspectives exist concerning the status of Taiwan. The origins of this dispute date to the 1940s, when civil war broke out between the Communists and Nationalists in China. Following the war, the People's Republic of China was established. In defeat, the Nationalists retreated to Taiwan in 1949. Since that time, China and Taiwan have developed very different economic and political systems. Although the Taiwanese

A divided state • Figure 7.2

The Republic of Cyprus gained its independence from Britain in 1960.

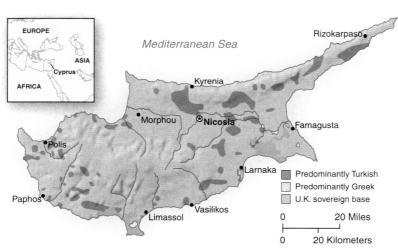

a. Ethnic distribution, 1970
The country's independence, however, did not heal the rifts that had developed between Greek Cypriots (78% of the population) and Turkish Cypriots (18% of the population). A degree of residential separation already existed between these groups by the 1970s.

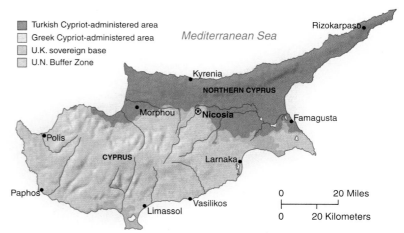

b. Division of Cyprus
After a coup in 1974 led by some Greek Cypriots seeking unification with Greece, Turkey invaded the northern third of the island. Partition followed (compare to **a**), with the United Nations maintaining a buffer zone. Thousands of people were internally displaced. The Turkish Republic of North Cyprus was established in 1983, but only Turkey has recognized it.

have never declared their independence from China, the government of Taiwan represents itself as the Republic of China—a continuation of the government that existed in China before its civil war.

The Chinese government asserts sovereignty over Taiwan and considers the island to be its twenty-third province, but it does not control the island's political affairs. Thus, it can be said that Taiwan has de facto (actual) sovereignty because it manages its own affairs, but Taiwan lacks de jure (legal) sovereignty because the international community does not recognize it as a full-fledged state.

Different conceptions of sovereignty also make a simple question like "how many states are there?" more complicated than it may seem. We might reasonably ask whether Cyprus, a sovereign state divided since the 1970s between a Turkish-dominated North and a Greek-dominated South, should be counted as one state or two (**Figure 7.2**).

Nations and States

Thus far we have talked about states, but we have said very little about the people within them, especially those who see themselves as belonging to a **nation**. What gives a nation its shared sense of identity? Often it is a mixture of various historical, cultural, economic, or political circumstances. Certainly the Palestinian nation has been shaped by its long struggle to gain independence and statehood, among other factors. For the French-speaking Québécois in

> **nation** A sizable group of people with shared political aspirations whose collective identity is rooted in a common history, heritage, and attachment to a specific territory.

Stefanos Kouratzis/AFP/Getty Images, Inc.

▲ **c. Nicosia divided**
When Cyprus was divided, so was the capital city, Nicosia. Ledra Street, shown here, was blocked to prevent movement between the Turkish and Greek Cypriot parts of the city.

d. Potential resolution
In April 2008, Ledra Street was reopened in a symbolic move to build support for reunification of the island. Like sovereignty, the issue of which states are counted as states involves some subjectivity.

Canada, a shared language and experience as a minority group have shaped their national identity.

In popular usage, the terms *nation* and *state* are frequently used interchangeably, but political geographers and other scholars are careful to note that the terms are not synonymous. Simply stated, a nation refers to a people and a state refers to a political unit. *Nationalism*, then, is the expression of loyalty to and pride in a nation, whereas *patriotism* is the expression of love for and devotion to one's state.

In a **multinational state**, the population consists of two or more nations. Most countries in the world are multinational states, including, for example, Brazil, Canada, China, Indonesia, Mexico, Nigeria, Spain, Sudan, and the United Kingdom. A **nation-state** exists when the boundaries of a nation coincide with the boundaries of the state and the people share a sense of political unity. A narrow understanding of the nation-state concept means that a nation-state possesses a fairly homogeneous population. For example, Icelanders make up 94%

of the population of Iceland, and Japanese account for 99% of the population of Japan. But very few of the states in the world meet this strict definition of nation-state. Thus, a broader understanding of the nation-state concept helps us see that even a multinational state can develop an identity as a nation-state by socially, economically, and politically integrating its people. Let's consider the United States. Because of its Native American nations, such as the Chickasaw Nation and the Navajo Nation among others, the United States is multinational in terms of its population composition. Nevertheless, the United States functions as a nation-state through the creation of a political identity that sees the American nation and the state of the United States as identical and indivisible.

For a variety of political, economic, and social reasons, some multinational states are simply not able to successfully integrate the nations inside their borders. This is demonstrated by, among other events, the collapse of three multinational states in the 1990s: the Union of Soviet Socialist

The breakup of a multinational state • Figure 7.3

Some factors contributing to the fall of the Soviet Union were economic crises such as food shortages, poor industrial performance, German reunification, and the related fall of communism in eastern Europe. When Russia declared its sovereignty in 1990, that act significantly undermined the political legitimacy of the Soviet Union. Home to a diverse population, the Soviet Union fractured largely along internal political and national lines as 15 new states came into existence in 1991. (*Source:* NG Maps.)

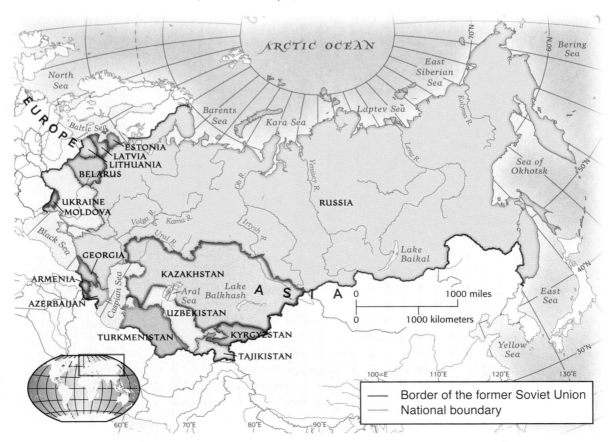

Republics (U.S.S.R.), Yugoslavia, and Czechoslovakia. Since 1991, 24 new states have been created from the breakup of these three states. The splitting up of the U.S.S.R. alone accounted for 15 of these new states, of which Russia is the largest (see **Figure 7.3**).

Imperialism and Colonialism

The dual processes of **imperialism** and **colonialism** have contributed to the creation of many of the world's multinational states largely because gaining access to and control of additional territory usually brings different national groups into contact. Imperialism and colonialism are closely connected, though the terms are not necessarily interchangeable.

States use imperialism and colonialism as strategies to extend their power over other lands and peoples. In the 15th century, news of Portu-

> **imperialism** One state's exercise of direct or indirect control over the affairs of another political society.
>
> **colonialism** A form of imperialism in which a state takes possession of a foreign territory, occupies it, and governs it.

guese explorations along the coast of Africa, and Portuguese and Spanish ventures in the Americas, prompted the Netherlands, Britain, and France to seek additional territory beyond their borders. Other European states such as Belgium, Germany, and Italy followed suit, and European colonies were eventually established in Africa, Asia, the Americas, and the Pacific. Although most of the colonies in the Americas had gained independence by 1825, sizable portions of Africa and Asia were still controlled by Europeans in 1914. With colonies on every continent (except Antarctica), the British created the largest colonial empire in history. France built the second most extensive empire, assembling colonies across West Africa, Southeast Asia, and the Pacific. The establishment of European colonies in Africa provides a stark example of one of the largest land grabs in history, often referred to as the "scramble for Africa."

a. As the rupture occurred, the boundaries of the internal Soviet republics became the boundaries of the newly independent states. For example, the Uzbek Soviet Socialist Republic became the new state of Uzbekistan. Tellingly, the names of these new states, like the names of the republics before them, evoke the diverse human mosaic that the Soviet Union was—for embedded in each is also the name of a prominent ethnic group: the Russians, Uzbeks, Tajiks, and so on.

b. In 2008, the Georgian military attacked locations in South Ossetia ostensibly to protect Georgians living in the region, and the Russians responded by sending troops into the region. The photo shows Georgians protesting this intervention outside the Russian Embassy in Paris. Expressions of Georgian nationalism have at times invoked the idea of a homogeneous nation-state and alienated other national groups in the country by claiming that "Georgia is for Georgians."

Remy de la Mauviniere/©AP/Wide World Photos

c. Banners carried by Latvian nationalists reveal their enduring opposition to Russia and Russian dominance associated with the former Soviet Union. Significantly, however, about 30% of the Latvian population is Russian. In fact, all of the states created in the breakup of the Soviet Union are themselves multinational.

Mindaugas Kulbis/©AP/Wide World Photos

Colonial legacies in Africa • Figure 7.4

Colonialism transformed Africa. Among other impacts, it gave rise to a number of multinational and landlocked states, shaped new political identities, and built new road, rail, and trade networks.

▼ a. Africa in 1914

The political map of Africa, as we know it today, began to take shape during the colonial period, and the first major boundary-making exercise by colonial powers took place in conjunction with the 1884–1885 Berlin Conference. (*Source:* NG Maps.)

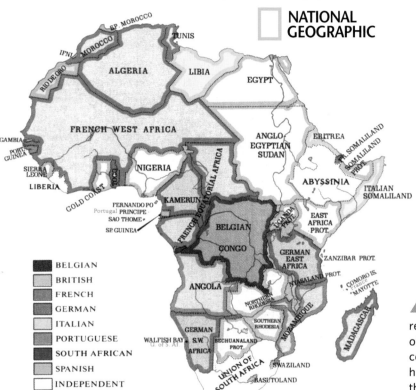

NATIONAL GEOGRAPHIC

- ■ BELGIAN
- ☐ BRITISH
- ■ FRENCH
- ■ GERMAN
- ☐ ITALIAN
- ■ PORTUGUESE
- ■ SOUTH AFRICAN
- ■ SPANISH
- ☐ INDEPENDENT

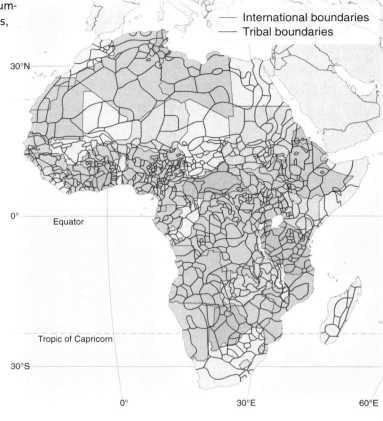

— International boundaries
— Tribal boundaries

▲ b. Africa's states and one depiction of its cultural groups

The present-day boundaries of African states more closely resemble those of the European colonies than they do the boundaries of the African peoples. But notice that this statement implies that a country should be a nation-state, in the strict sense of the term. The human diversity of the world, glimpsed via this map of Africa, suggests that the idea of creating homogeneous nation-states is impractical, if not impossible. (*Source:* Based on Murdock, 1959.)

▼ c. Rwandan refugees and a refugee camp

In some places, like Rwanda, European colonialists stoked animosities between local groups that have continued to the present. Rwanda descended into a horrific civil war in the 1990s. In 1994, approximately 250,000 refugees entered neighboring Tanzania in just 24 hours, prompting the establishment of substantial refugee camps. The adoption of a new constitution in 2003 ensuring a balance of power between Hutus and Tutsis has helped stabilize the country, but there are still thousands of refugees scattered across the region.

UNHCR/C. Sattleberger

The Berlin Conference, held in 1884–1885, began the process of formalizing modern political boundaries in Africa. Representatives from the leading European powers, as well as the United States and Russia, met to discuss the partitioning of the African continent. Not a single African was present at the conference. In a boardroom in Berlin, Europeans made decisions about their control of territory in Africa almost as if they were playing a game of Monopoly in which the object was to control the most (and most valuable) land.

Boundaries separating British, French, Belgian, Portuguese, Spanish, Italian, and German spheres of influence in Africa were superimposed. That is, they were often drawn as straight lines with little awareness of or concern for the different ethnic groups living there. In East Africa, for example, the Somali people lived in lands that were partitioned between the British, French, and Italians. In numerous other instances tens and sometimes hundreds of different ethnic groups were combined in a single colony.

Each of the European powers administered its colonies in different ways, but a guiding philosophy of managing colonies was rooted in the racist belief that Africans were inferior. Sometimes colonial administrators used ethnic differences to create animosities between certain Africans. In Rwanda, for example, the Germans and later the Belgians exploited differences between Tutsis and Hutus. The Belgians showed favoritism to the Tutsis, however, allowing some of the men to attend school and rewarding them with jobs handling the day-to-day affairs of the colony. In 1962, following a Hutu rebellion, the Belgians granted independence to Rwanda, which came into existence as a multinational state with a population that was seriously divided (**Figure 7.4**).

Before and after World War II there was a surge in efforts by Africans and other colonized peoples to attain independence and achieve **self-determination**, the ability to choose their own political status. Globally, colonialism fell out of favor. On the continent of Africa, for example, some 32 former colonies gained their independence between 1960 and 1970. Even though European colonialism was waning, the framework for the political organization of space that exists today was cemented because the newly independent countries often retained their colonial boundaries.

CONCEPT CHECK

1. **How** did the concept of sovereignty change after the Peace of Westphalia?
2. **What** are the four criteria that define a state?
3. **What** is a legacy of the Berlin Conference?

Geographical Characteristics of States
LEARNING OBJECTIVES

1. **Explain** how boundaries affect access to resources.
2. **Compare** and contrast centripetal and centrifugal forces.
3. **Identify** two systems of internal spatial organization.
4. **Define** devolution.

E arlier, in our discussion of Africa, we touched on boundaries and the role they played in transforming the political spaces of the African continent. Boundaries are regulatory devices that not only sanction territorial possession, but also help identify the contents—the people, natural resources, and territory—of states. In this section, we first examine different types of boundaries, visualizing the ways boundaries simultaneously secure, divide, and configure political space. Then, in subsequent sections, we consider other forces that affect the spatial functioning of states such as pressures of political integration or belonging, and political separation.

Exclusive economic zones • Figure 7.5

EEZs extend up to 200 nautical miles from shore, as shown for Australia. Coastal and island states have a reduced form of sovereignty—the "sovereign right"—to manage the resources in the waters and on the ocean floor in that area within their exclusive economic zones. This contrasts with their territorial seas, where they have full sovereignty. Note that Australia is one of several countries that assert sovereignty over part of Antarctica. (*Source:* © Commonwealth of Australia [Geoscience Australia] 2009. Based upon an original drawing by Geoscience Australia 2009.)

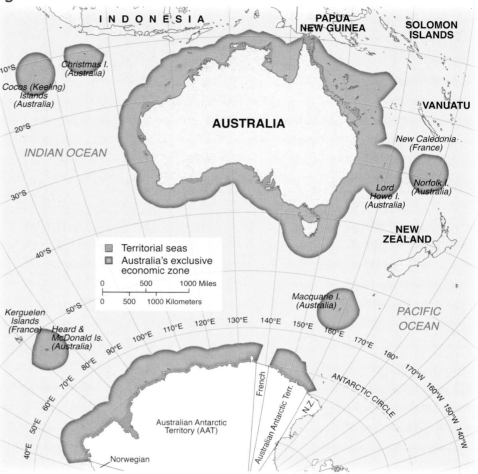

Boundaries

Every state consists of a defined territory marked by at least one **boundary**. We tend to think of boundaries as lines that stretch horizontally through space—the way we see them on maps—but boundaries are better understood as having a vertical extent, dividing the airspace above the ground and the rocks and resources below ground. The boundaries of coastal states extend offshore. The waters enclosed by these boundaries are considered part of the territory of the state and are called **territorial seas**. By international convention, territorial seas rarely exceed 19 km (12 mi). Over the past several decades, desire for rights to marine resources has led to the development of *exclusive economic zones* (EEZs) for coastal and island states (**Figure 7.5**).

> **boundary**
> A vertical plane, usually represented as a line on a map, that fixes the territory of a state.

By convention, boundaries are defined in legal documents, are drawn or delimited on maps, and may also be demarcated on the ground with signs, posts, fences, or other markers. Not all boundaries are marked or demarcated on the ground. A boundary might not be demarcated because it is disputed. This is the case with portions of the boundary between India and China. Sometimes even boundaries that are not disputed are not demarcated as, for example, in lightly populated areas, such as the high-altitude zones along the Andes Mountains between Chile and Argentina.

All political boundaries are human creations, but they often make use of physical features. A *physiographic boundary* follows a natural feature, such as a river or mountain range. For example, the boundary between Bulgaria and Romania follows the Danube River for much of its length. In mountainous areas, physiographic boundaries usually follow the crest, the line connecting the highest points. When a river is used, the boundary may be placed along one bank, in the middle of the river, or along the deepest part of the river channel. One problem with using rivers as boundaries is the potential for a river to substantially shift its course (**Figure 7.6**).

Fixing a boundary • Figure 7.6

We expect boundaries to be fixed or stable, but rivers are dynamic. This variability was a long-standing problem between El Paso, Texas, and Ciudad Juarez, Mexico, where the Rio Grande (called the Rio Bravo in Mexico) separates the two countries. The issue was finally resolved in the 1960s when a portion of the river was canalized—forced to flow in a concrete-lined channel in order to keep it from changing course and causing people to find themselves on the other side of the political boundary.

Image courtesy of photographer Scott Cutler

United States

Mexico

Canalized portion of the Rio Grande

Geometric boundaries are drawn as straight lines and sometimes follow lines of latitude or longitude. As we have discussed, the concentration of geometric boundaries in Africa stems from the Berlin Conference. West of the Great Lakes, the boundary between the United States and Canada follows the 49th parallel, and the straight line between Alaska and the Yukon Territory follows the 141st meridian.

Ethnographic boundaries may be based on one or more cultural traits such as religion, language, or ethnicity. In South Asia, the boundary drawn between India and Pakistan was conceived as an ethnographic boundary separating Hindus from Muslims. Linguistic boundaries are common in Europe. For example, the boundary between Spain and Portugal is linguistic, as is the boundary separating Bulgaria from Greece.

A *relic boundary* is one that used to exist but is no longer recognized as an official boundary and, therefore, is no longer formally defined or delimited. Relic boundaries result from changes in the ways that geographic space is administered over time. Perhaps the most familiar example is the Great Wall of China (**Figure 7.7**)

Relic boundary • Figure 7.7

Dean Conger/NG Image Collection

NATIONAL GEOGRAPHIC

This section of the Great Wall of China, located about 40 miles from Beijing, dates to the 15th century, but other parts of it were constructed at various times between the 7th century BCE and the 16th century CE to protect the Chinese Empire from intrusions by nomadic peoples. The impressive structure served not only as a boundary but also as a fortification.

WHAT A GEOGRAPHER SEES

The Making of a Boundary on Hispaniola

Politically, the Caribbean island of Hispaniola is occupied by two states: the Dominican Republic on the east and Haiti on the west. Spain asserted a claim to the island following the voyages of Christopher Columbus, but the island later came under French control. Although Haiti and the Dominican Republic achieved independence, respectively, in 1804 and 1844, disputes developed over the location of the boundary.

Courtesy Dr. Jack Child, American University

a. This map shows the present location of the international boundary, which dates from a 1929 agreement negotiated between Haiti and the Dominican Republic. Prior to this agreement, however, the location of the boundary was a source of contention. (*Source:* NG Maps.)

b. At the turn of the 20th century, the Dominican Republic recognized a very different boundary. When the Dominican Republic issued this stamp in 1900, it provoked a political crisis. As you can see, the Dominican Republic had pushed the boundary significantly to the west and claimed possession of about three-fourths of the island, much to the consternation of the Haitian government as well as Haitians living in the disputed area. The Dominican Republic eventually relinquished its claims, paving the way for the 1929 treaty.

NASA/Goddard Space Flight Center Scientific Visualization Studio

c. This satellite image shows a portion of the international boundary on Hispaniola. The Dominican Republic appears on the right and is greener. ► **Can you spot the boundary?**

Global Locator

HISPANIOLA

NATIONAL GEOGRAPHIC

Think Critically

1. What might cause such a striking difference between the two countries, as shown in image **c**?
2. How is the boundary an ethnographic boundary?

The 10 largest states in the world Table 7.1		
State	**Area (sq km)**	**Area (sq mi)**
Russian Federation	17,098,242	6,601,665
Canada	9,984,670	3,855,101
United States	9,826,675	3,794,099
China	9,596,961	3,705,406
Brazil	8,514,877	3,287,611
Australia	7,741,220	2,988,901
India	3,287,263	1,269,219
Argentina	2,780,400	1,073,518
Kazakhstan	2,724,900	1,052,089
Algeria	2,381,741	919,595
(*Source:* Data from CIA, 2009.)		

Many boundaries have complex origins and in reality often reflect a consideration of multiple factors, including competing political concerns (see *What a Geographer Sees*).

Territorial Extent and Configuration

States come in a variety of shapes and sizes (refer again to Figure 7.1). The smallest state in the world, Vatican City, covers just 44 hectares (109 acres) within the city of Rome. It is a *microstate*, a political state that is extremely small in total land area. At the opposite extreme, Russia is the largest state in the world, more than one and a half times the size of the United States (see **Table 7.1**). Antarctica is the only landmass that is not part of any state, though some countries have claims to parts of it (refer again to Figure 7.5).

On the basis of their shape, states can be classified as compact, elongated, prorupt, fragmented, or perforated. **Figure 7.8** illustrates these shapes.

A rupture in the territory of a state may result in the creation of an **enclave** or an **exclave**. Vatican City is not only a microstate, it is also an enclave state because it is completely surrounded by territory belonging to Italy. As shown in Figure 7.8, Lesotho perforates the territory of South Africa, making Lesotho an enclave state. Look again at Figure 7.8. Is Swaziland also an enclave state? Strictly speaking, the answer

enclave Territory completely surrounded by another state but not controlled by it.

exclave Territory that is separated from the state to which it belongs by the intervening territory of another state.

Shape	Territorial configuration	Selected examples (with simple outline maps)
Compact	Somewhat circular	MACEDONIA
Elongated	Long and often narrow	VIETNAM
Prorupt	Includes a projection or panhandle	NAMIBIA
Fragmented	Divided into two or more parts	PHILIPPINES
Perforated	Interrupted or penetrated by an intervening state or states	SWAZILAND LESOTHO SOUTH AFRICA

Shapes of states • Figure 7.8

Geographers recognize five basic shapes of states, but sometimes a state exhibits characteristics of more than one of these shapes. For example, Vietnam is both elongated and, because of offshore islands, it is also fragmented. South Africa has two perforations and is prorupt. For political geographers, awareness of the configuration of a state's territory, the nature of its topography, the characteristics of its boundaries, and its relations with its neighbors are just some factors that affect the security of a state.

is no since Swaziland shares a border with the states of South Africa and Mozambique and is not completely surrounded by another state. For this reason, Swaziland constitutes a kind of semi-enclave with respect to South Africa.

In North America, the territory of Canada intervenes to make Alaska an exclave of the United States. In southern Spain, the narrow peninsula of Gibraltar (the location of the picturesque Rock of Gibraltar) is a self-governing British territory. Because Gibraltar is a peninsula and is not surrounded by Spanish territory, it constitutes a semi-enclave with respect to Spain and an exclave with respect to the United Kingdom. As a general rule, all perforated states have enclaves or semi-enclaves, but not all fragmented states have exclaves. Can you explain why?

For administrative purposes, states are divided internally into territorial subdivisions that are variously called regions, provinces, districts, states, or cantons. How the central government interacts with its territorial subdivisions varies from country to country. Globally, two systems of government have emerged: the federal and the unitary systems. A state organized according to the *federal system* distributes some power to its territorial subdivisions so that they have the authority to develop and implement their own laws and policies. This authority is granted by and detailed in the constitution of the state. Therefore, in a federal system the constitution guarantees a decentralization of governmental authority.

In contrast, the *unitary system* concentrates power in the central government instead of distributing some of it among its territorial subdivisions. Decision making and policy development are therefore more centralized in a unitary state. China is a unitary state, as are Pakistan, Turkey, Ghana, Kenya, and Peru. Examples of federal states include Australia, the United States, Brazil, India, Mexico, and Russia. While it existed, the Soviet Union was also a federal state. However, under the control of the Communist Party decision making in the Soviet Union was highly centralized. As we have seen, when the Soviet Union fractured apart, some lines that had previously served as internal, administrative boundaries within the Soviet Union suddenly became international boundaries. See *Video Explorations* to understand some of the other consequences of this political change.

Centripetal and Centrifugal Forces

Whether unitary or federal, all states must deal with forces that can affect their unity. Political geographers distinguish between two kinds of such forces: centripetal and centrifugal.

Video Explorations

Estonia—Identity, Religion, and Politics

National Geographic

The video introduces the Setu people of southeastern Estonia and explores the impact of political change on them and their local landscapes.

The events on 9/11 are considered a **centripetal force** for the United States because they contributed to a collective sense of being under attack and to a shared sense of grief. The cultural diversity of some states, where different groups struggle for access to resources, can be a **centrifugal force**, especially if one group feels that it is not treated equally. In addition to cultural diversity, economic disparities within a country's population can have a centrifugal effect. Similarly, a serious economic downturn can erode people's support for the government. Government policies that exclude one or more groups of people or diminish their political voice can contribute to rebellions or insurgencies.

Centripetal forces include certain policies and practices of governmental and nongovernmental institutions. Schools as well as the armed forces inculcate patriotism and build support for a state. Even international athletic competitions can unite a country's people.

> **centripetal force**
> An event or a circumstance that helps bind together the social and political fabric of a state.
>
> **centrifugal force**
> An event or a circumstance that weakens a state's social and political fabric.

Writing in 1940 when World War II was underway, the political geographer Richard Hartshorne drew attention to the importance of centripetal forces and specifically the value of the raison d'être, or reason for being.

A *raison d'être* is the idea, belief, or purpose that justifies the existence of a state. It is also the most significant centripetal force. The raison d'être for Pakistan was to create a Muslim-majority state in South Asia. The raison d'être for Israel was to create a homeland for the Jews. The absence of a raison d'être can be equally detrimental for the cohesiveness of a state. Yugoslavia was created as a multinational state whose citizens were separated by linguistic and religious differences and who did not share a raison d'être. The dictatorial rule of President Tito (from 1953 to 1980) held its diverse peoples together. After Tito's death, the country broke apart largely along ethnic, religious, and linguistic lines.

Whether a specific event is a centripetal or centrifugal force depends on one's perspective and may even change over time. For example, the 1989 reunification of Germany was widely perceived as a powerful centripetal force when it happened. However, the challenges of bridging the social divide between East and West Germans and the financial burden of reunification have, for a number of citizens, contributed to a greater awareness of the centrifugal forces associated with reunification.

It is impossible to list all of the kinds of centripetal and centrifugal forces. Depending on the situation, religion might be a centripetal force in one instance but highly divisive in another instance. The same can be said for issues involving language, immigration, election results, and national identity (**Figure 7.9**).

Separatism and Devolution

States change over time, and so do the centripetal and centrifugal forces that affect them. The stability of a state depends on how effectively it manages these forces. Even very stable states continually face challenges to their unity. **Separatism**, the desire of a nation to break apart from its state, is one of these challenges. A nation's sense of identity and the perception that it is different from other groups in the state can contribute to separatist sentiment. Separatism is closely connected with calls for greater *autonomy*, or self-government. When a state transfers some power to a self-identified community within it, the process is called **devolution**. Devolution is one mechanism that states use to help accommodate separatist pressures.

Centrifugal and centripetal forces in Serbia • Figure 7.9

Kosovo is a region in the country of Serbia. The population of Kosovo consists of an Albanian majority and a Serb minority. Kosovo's declaration of independence from Serbia in 2008 has had both centrifugal and centripetal consequences: centrifugal in that it has challenged the unity of the Serbian state, but centripetal in that it has renewed Serb attachment to the region.

a. With a sign proclaiming "Kosovo is Serbia," protestors march in opposition to Kosovo's declaration of independence.

b. A Kosovar Albanian teacher shows her class the Kosovo flag.

AFP/Getty Images, Inc.

Bela Szandelszky/©AP/Wide World Photos

Geography InSight

Café para todos? A model of integration in multinational Spain • Figure 7.10   ✓ THE PLANNER

From the late 1930s until 1975, Spain was ruled by the dictator Francisco Franco. His idea of nationalism followed the idea of the nation-state strictly. He banned the use of the Euskera and Catalan languages and forbade the use of national symbols such as the Basque and Catalan flags. Franco's treatment of both groups fortified their national identity. It also contributed to the formation of Euskadi Ta Azkatasuna, or ETA, a Basque group that has often resorted to terrorism. How has Spain integrated these nations since?

a. Spain ratified a new constitution in 1978 that recognized the unity of the Spanish nation but also guaranteed autonomy to the "nationalities and regions integrated in it." This has been called the "café para todos" (*coffee for all*) model. The constitution fashioned the autonomous communities system and paved the way for the creation of the country's 17 autonomous regions (see map). As autonomous regions, the Basque Country and Catalonia control their own police forces, education, health care, and other services.

b. Basque separatists at a rally carrying a banner with a map of the Basque region. Note that there is a Basque population in southwestern France and that part of France is included in the territory referred to as "Greater Basque Country." In 2008, the Basque government advanced a proposal for Basque self-determination—a sign that some Basques desire separation from Spain. The proposal was overturned by the Spanish government.

c. Catalans carry placards that read "som una nació" (*we are a nation*) and Catalan flags. The 2006 Catalan Charter devolved additional power to Catalonia in immigration, taxation, and transportation. One of the wealthiest regions in Spain, Catalonia has often used its economic importance as a bargaining chip for additional autonomy. In 2013, Catalonia's parliament passed a symbolic declaration of sovereignty.

Spain is a multinational state (population 47 million) that has confronted separatist movements led by two of its nations: the Basques (population about 2.2 million), and the Catalans (population about 7.4 million). The national identity of the Basques stems in part from their language, called Euskera, and a shared history as a self-governing people. Catalan nationalism derives from similar factors, including the Catalan language and a tradition of autonomy. See **Figure 7.10** to learn more about these movements and how Spain has dealt with them.

CONCEPT CHECK   STOP

1. **Why** is the vertical extent of a boundary significant?
2. **How** might a state's shape contribute to centrifugal or centripetal forces?
3. **What** are the main differences between unitary and federal systems of government?
4. **How** have devolution and multinationalism shaped Spain's political geography?

Internationalism and Supranational Organizations

LEARNING OBJECTIVES

1. **Explain** how internationalism and supranational organizations are related.
2. **Distinguish** between the General Assembly and the Security Council of the United Nations.
3. **Summarize** the key events leading to the establishment of the European Union.

Although separatism is a potentially destabilizing force, it is in some ways countered by the spread of **internationalism**, the development of close political and economic relations among states. The growth of supranational political organizations provides the clearest expression of internationalism. A **supranational organization** consists of multiple states that agree to work together for a common economic, military, cultural, or political purpose, or a combination of several of these. The United Nations (UN) is a supranational organization promoting global peace and security. The Association of Southeast Asian Nations (ASEAN), the Commonwealth of Independent States (CIS), and the European Union (EU) are other supranational organizations whose member states cooperate for political and economic purposes. The North Atlantic Treaty Organization (NATO) is a military alliance including several North American and European countries. Each of the supranational organizations mentioned here—indeed most of the supranational organizations that exist today—were formed after World War II.

The benefits of membership in a supranational organization vary depending on the purpose of the organization but typically include improved political security or enhanced trading opportunities. Membership in a supranational organization, however, has a cost, and that cost is associated with the loss of a portion of a state's sovereignty. The existence of supranational organizations introduces a tension between internationalism and sovereignty. Therefore the benefits of membership need to be perceived as outweighing any sacrifices to a state's sovereignty. Participation in a supranational organization indicates a willingness to be a team player—to support the decisions and policies of the organization rather than to take actions that support only the goals of one's own state.

The United Nations

The **United Nations (UN)** was founded in 1945 as a supranational organization charged with promoting peace in the world. The mission of the UN includes building and sustaining cooperative relations among states and, when conflict arises, using diplomacy to negotiate peaceful solutions. The experience of two devastating world wars plus the desire to avoid a third one contributed to international support for an organization like the UN. Almost every country in the world is represented in this organization. At present, Vatican City does not have full membership but is an observer state because of its expressed desire to remain neutral on certain issues. Although Kosovo declared its independence in 2008, this Balkan territory's status remains disputed, and it is not a member of the UN. (This explains why there are 193 members of the UN but 195 sovereign states in the world.)

Headquartered in New York City, the UN has many different constituent parts. We can distinguish between specialized agencies and principal organs. Some specialized UN agencies include the World Health Organization and the Food and Agriculture Organization. The Security Council, General Assembly, and International Court of Justice (ICJ) are principal organs of the UN. Located in the Hague, Netherlands, the ICJ resolves international legal disputes. The General Assembly, which consists of all members of the UN, controls its budget and oversees the activities of the other branches of the organization.

The UN Security Council and peacekeeping operations • Figure 7.11

Two dimensions of the UN are highlighted here: the composition of the Security Council and peacekeeping operations.

The Horseshoe Table
(Seating is in alphabetical order by country name.)

Associated Press

Permanent members
(China, France, Russia,
United Kingdom, United States)

Nonpermanent members
(elected by the General Assembly
and serve for two years)

African

Asian

Latin American

West European and Other

East European

a. The composition of the Security Council
The UN Charter is vague on how equitable geographic representation of nonpermanent members should be achieved. In practice, seats are allocated according to the regional groups shown. The "other" in the West European group includes Australia and New Zealand.

b. UN peacekeepers at work
UN peacekeepers, or "blue helmets," patrol the Israel–Lebanon border to maintain security in this region. Other peacekeepers monitor elections or provide humanitarian assistance. The UN does not have an army. Rather, UN members contribute their own military personnel for peacekeeping operations.

The real power for the day-to-day maintenance of international peace and security lies with the Security Council. Depending on the situation, the Security Council might recommend sanctions against a country or might recommend that peacekeeping forces be deployed. In order for recommendations made by the Security Council to be acted upon, there must be nine affirmative votes from nonpermanent members and unanimous support from the permanent members. In 2003, for example, the United States and the United Kingdom sought UN support for the invasion of Iraq to overthrow Saddam Hussein. UN support was not forthcoming because three members of the Security Council —China, France, and Russia—opposed it. **Figure 7.11** provides an overview of the Security Council.

The European Union

Whereas the UN is a supranational organization that is global in scale and focuses primarily on issues of international security and well-being, the **European Union (EU)** is regional in scale and came into existence in order to enhance economic cooperation in western Europe. Five important developments contributed to the establishment of the EU:

1. Creation, in 1944, of Benelux, an association made up of Belgium, the Netherlands, and Luxembourg. These three small western European countries realized that economically they could lower their costs of production if they cooperated with one another to remove tariffs and ease restrictions on the movement of goods among them.

2. Implementation of the Marshall Plan following World War II, which stimulated the rebuilding of Europe and encouraged regional cooperation.

3. Establishment of the separate European Coal and Steel Community (ECSC) in 1952. The ECSC worked to remove barriers on the movement of coal and steel. The Benelux countries joined France, West Germany, and Italy as members of the ECSC.

4. Acceptance of the Treaty of Rome in 1957, which created the European Economic Community (EEC),

sometimes also called the Common Market. The Treaty of Rome committed its signatories to still greater economic union, through the creation of a single common market to enable the unrestricted movement of goods, people, services, and capital among them. The six countries that belonged to the ECSC were also founding members of the EEC.

5. Implementation of the Treaty of Brussels, or "Merger Treaty," in 1967. This treaty amended the Treaty of Rome and provided a framework for political cooperation, including a European parliament. To reflect its broader mission, the EEC was renamed the European Community (EC).

The Treaty of Rome incorporated the idea that the EEC would attract other countries sharing the same economic and political ideals. By 1981, six other countries had become members. Then, in 1992, these 12 member countries signed the Treaty of European Unity (also called the Maastricht Treaty) in the Netherlands. From this point forward, the term *European Union* has been used as the name of the supranational organization. Since 1993 the EU has admitted another 15 countries as members, expanding its membership to a total of 27 countries (**Figure 7.12**).

Since 2009, the euro zone crisis has raised concerns about the viability of monetary union. This crisis has affected some of the EU's geographically peripheral members, including Greece, Ireland, Portugal, Spain, Italy, and Cyprus. Italy and Spain have, respectively, the third and fourth largest economies in the euro zone, so they are not peripheral economically.

Two major factors have contributed to the euro zone crisis: (1) high government debt levels (also called

EU members and the euro zone • Figure 7.12

The EU now has a population of 504 million and a gross domestic product of nearly $16 trillion, making it a leading economic power. Major progress toward monetary union occurred in 1999 when the EU adopted a single currency, the euro. The 17 countries that have since replaced their currency with the euro collectively form a region known as the euro zone. ▶ **Why is membership in the EU more widespread than the euro zone? Why has use of the euro expanded to nonmembers?**

sovereign debt), and (2) banking system vulnerabilities involving insufficient assets to cover defaults on loans. Both factors are seen as stemming from problems with the implementation of monetary union. In short, monetary union was achieved within the euro zone, but banking or fiscal union was not. The absence of a system for dealing with banking system crises illustrates this lack of integration.

The euro zone crisis has triggered deep recession, high unemployment, bailouts, and tough austerity measures in the affected countries. *Austerity* refers to actions that reduce government spending and raise taxes. In order to prevent similar crises in the future, the EU has approved a fiscal compact requiring that member states have a balanced budget. Other proposed changes are that the European Central Bank will have the authority to monitor the health of euro zone banks, not unlike the Federal Reserve System in the United States.

The extent of supranational cooperation among EU members is unprecedented, but not without controversy. The United Kingdom, for example, does not use the euro and opposed the fiscal compact. Still, in notable ways, the EU resembles a state. It has a central bank, a parliament, a flag, and a national anthem. It has also developed a constitution, though it has not been ratified. These developments have led scholars to ask whether the EU represents a new kind of supranational state.

CONCEPT CHECK

1. **What** are some costs and benefits associated with membership in a supranational organization?
2. **What** votes are required for Security Council action?
3. **What** caused the euro zone crisis?

Global Geopolitics

LEARNING OBJECTIVES

1. **Define** geopolitics.
2. **Summarize** the heartland theory.
3. **Distinguish** between Cold War geopolitics and contemporary geopolitics.
4. **Explain** how globalization can influence the diffusion of terrorism.

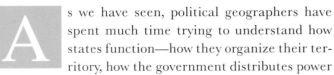

As we have seen, political geographers have spent much time trying to understand how states function—how they organize their territory, how the government distributes power to different territorial units within the state, and how states forge supranational organizations. Over the years political geographers have proposed different theories concerning the development of the state and the nature of political power. In this section we examine a few of the most important schools of thought or traditions within political geography.

The Geopolitical Tradition

As traditionally practiced, **geopolitics** has focused on the ways in which states acquire power, the relations among states, and the formulation of strategic foreign policy. Geopolitics, one branch of political geography, has its roots in the work of the German scholar Friedrich Ratzel (1844–1904). Ratzel, a zoologist by training, became interested in political geography and in 1897 developed his *Theory of the Organic State*, which

> **geopolitics**
> The study of the relations among geography, states, and world power.

compared the growth of a state to the growth of an organism. Ratzel theorized that, like organisms, states needed sustenance in the form of resources and room to grow. Ratzel used the term *Lebensraum*—literally "living space"—to describe these needs.

The theory of the organic state draws a strong connection between the natural environment and the power of a state, as demonstrated by the idea that states develop and grow stronger through the addition of new territories. Ratzel's theory provides an example of the environmental determinism (see Chapter 1) that informed early geopolitical thought. It also shows the influence of Charles Darwin's ideas. Ratzel was familiar with Darwin's work, and the theory of the organic state placed importance on the concept of competition. According to Ratzel's theory, states competed with one another for resources and space, as do members of the animal world.

Ratzel never used his theory to guide foreign policy, but others did. Ratzel's ideas were adopted by Rudolf Kjellen (1864–1922), a Swedish professor and the person who actually coined the term *geopolitics*. Kjellen used Ratzel's ideas to argue that only large states would endure and that foreign policy should support the creation of a large state. Kjellen's work was translated into German and was used by the Nazis in the 1930s to support their goal of strengthening and enlarging the German state. As a result, German geopolitics was, for several decades, tainted by its connections with the Nazis.

The Heartland Theory

Halford Mackinder (1861–1947), a British geographer and member of parliament, contributed another geopolitical theory called the *heartland theory*. To understand this theory, it helps to know that Mackinder linked geopolitical stability with maintenance of a balance of power among states. Thus, if the balance of power was upset, a state or a combination of states could become *the* dominant world power. How might the balance of power be upset? It was not through control of the seas, Mackinder theorized, but rather through control of the large Eurasian landmass. In the interior of Eurasia was a region free from the danger of being attacked from the sea. Mackinder called this area the *geographical pivot*; later he referred to it as the **heartland** (**Figure 7.13**).

Mackinder's heartland • Figure 7.13

According to Mackinder, the heartland, shown here, possessed the best combination of strategic geographic factors for world domination. An icy, inaccessible northern coast, desert and mountain barriers, and a European frontier that could be closed by land power made the heartland citadel-like. In Mackinder's view, whoever dominated the heartland would be able to defeat any sea power. (*Source:* Based on Mackinder, 1904.)

Think Critically

What is strategic about the pattern of river drainage within the heartland?

Cold War geopolitical configuration • Figure 7.14

The bipolar configuration during the Cold War pitted the capitalist West (the United States and its allies) against the Communist East (the Soviet Union and its allies). However, important military and ideological battles during the Cold War were waged in some unaligned states in an attempt to gain influence there. Note that the map shows 1980 political boundaries. (*Source:* Huntington, 1996. Adapted with the permission of Simon & Schuster, Inc.)

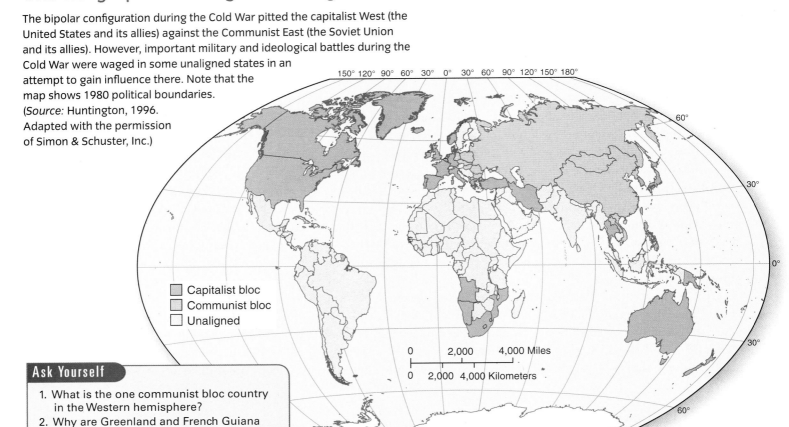

Capitalist bloc
Communist bloc
Unaligned

Ask Yourself

1. What is the one communist bloc country in the Western hemisphere?
2. Why are Greenland and French Guiana associated with the capitalist bloc? (Refer back to Figure 7.1.)

Mackinder's heartland theory also contains some elements of environmental determinism. Although he was aware of nonenvironmental factors, such as economic strength and transportation networks, Mackinder considered the territorial basis of states to be crucial to geopolitical power. In his words, "the [physical] geographical quantities in the calculation [of balance of power] are more measurable and more nearly constant than the human" (Mackinder 1942 [1919], p. 192). Although the heartland theory oversimplified global geopolitics, it anticipated Russia's rise to power and encouraged scrutiny of the Soviet Union and its policies.

Cold War Geopolitics

After World War II, relations between the United States and the Soviet Union cooled significantly. The term **Cold War** describes the hostility and rivalry that existed between the United States and the Soviet Union from the mid-1940s to the late 1980s. The race to build nuclear weapons was one expression of the rivalry between these superpowers. Geopolitically, the Cold War created a *bipolar world*—that is, a world divided into two opposing groups (**Figure 7.14**).

During the Cold War, the foreign policy of the United States was heavily influenced by the theory that if one country became Communist, other countries in the region would do the same and thus enable Communist domination of the world. Called the *domino theory*, this philosophy was used to justify the American policy of *containment*—the effort to limit the spread or influence of a hostile power or an ideology. One of the reasons the United States became involved in the Vietnam War was to prevent or "contain" the spread of communism in Asia.

Contemporary and Critical Geopolitics

The end of the Cold War in the early 1990s brought an end to the bipolar capitalist–Communist geopolitical configuration of the world. However, many political geographers maintain that there is still a bipolar configuration of the world that consists of a Global North and a Global South, separated on the basis of levels of development and wealth. We explore the basis for a North–South divide in greater detail in Chapter 9. Here, we focus on two other prevalent schools of thought. The first draws on the ideas of political scientist Samuel Huntington and his book, *Clash of Civilizations and the Remaking of the World Order*, published in 1996. In this book Huntington argues that instead of two opposing groups, there is a global configuration that is *multipolar* and consists of several groups or "civilizations." Using the terms *tribe, ethnic group, nation, civilization* as indicators of scale, Huntington argues that a civilization is the largest scale from which meaningful personal identity is derived. In his view, religion is the most important component that gives a civilization its identity, even more so than language or ancestry.

Therefore, future conflict will result from the clash of these civilizations—in other words, cultural conflict, and the locations of this conflict will occur on fault lines. In this sense, a *fault line* is a place where civilizations meet, either within a country or along international boundaries (**Figure 7.15**).

This civilization-based view of geopolitics still privileges a geopolitical view of the world that sees strong bonds between people and territory. But a second school of thought sees a very different world order in which globalization enables *deterritorialization*, a loosening of ties between people and place. The modern state has its roots in the concepts of territoriality and sovereignty, but globalization—especially greater human mobility and technological integration—may facilitate deterritorialization. Members of a nation may be extremely geographically dispersed but can maintain close ties, even virtual communities, through

Huntington's "civilizations" • Figure 7.15

Huntington theorizes that geopolitics since the 1990s has been shaped more by factors affecting cultural identity—especially religion—than by the ideological differences that fueled the Cold War. Compare this map to Figure 7.14. His civilizations are, however, very broad categories that may give a false impression of unity when there is none or it is only weakly developed. Critics ask, for example, can we really speak of a single African or Islamic civilization today? (*Source:* Huntington, 1996. Adapted with the permission of Simon & Schuster, Inc.)

Technological integration • Figure 7.16

Iranian university exchange students in Rome join in a global protest against the outcome of Iran's presidential election in June 2009. This woman carries a photo showing government security personnel beating an Iranian protester in Tehran. Internet platforms including Twitter and YouTube became sites of political resistance for many Iranians around the world and were used to coordinate this global protest.

the use of technologies such as e-mail, social media, and cell phones. Therefore, a community's identity may be sustained in spite of its detachment from a specific territory (**Figure 7.16**).

Globalization and Terrorism

Terrorism is not new and has been used as a political tactic by individuals, groups, and even states. Most terrorist activities are perpetrated by individuals or small groups, but state-sponsored terrorism remains an important part of global affairs. A state can sponsor terrorism in

> **terrorism** The threat or use of violence in order to inculcate fear, gain influence, and/ or advance a specific cause or conviction.

several ways. It might provide a refuge for terrorists, help train them, provide them with weapons or equipment, share intelligence with them, or support them financially. A state might also be directly involved in designing terrorist activities. The U.S. Department of State currently recognizes four state sponsors of terrorism: Cuba, Iran, Sudan, and Syria.

There are four broad and often overlapping categories of terrorism: revolutionary, separatist, single-issue, and religious. Revolutionary terrorism seeks regime change. For example, the Algerian terrorist group Front de Libération Nationale (FLN) fought against French colonial rule from 1954 to 1962. Separatist terrorism may be perpetrated by groups seeking autonomy or independence, such as the Basque group ETA. Use of terrorism by individuals or groups to advance a specific cause, such as animal rights or environmental values, constitutes single-issue terrorism.

Al-Qaeda is a major terrorist organization whose motives are both revolutionary and religious. When al-Qaeda was formed by Osama bin Laden in 1988, its revolutionary cause was initially directed against the Soviet Union, whose troops had invaded Afghanistan and occupied the capital city. Gradually, bin Laden fused this revolutionary cause with a religious one as well: the waging of a holy war against the invaders.

The revolutionary and religious goals of al-Qaeda remain central to its mission of establishing a Pan-Islamic Caliphate—a Muslim-controlled state that encompasses the Islamic community extending from Spain to Indonesia. A related aspect of al-Qaeda's mission involves forcing Westerners to leave Muslim countries. Al-Qaeda gained global attention with its attacks on the World Trade Center and Pentagon on September 11, 2001.

Membership in al-Qaeda is not precisely known but may include as many as several thousand people. Its members come from countries around the world, giving it a global presence. Even so, al-Qaeda functions as a decentralized and geographically dispersed network of affiliated groups rather than a centralized organization. Al-Qaeda operates through local cells that are directed by a group of leaders. The cells consist of small groups of individuals usually tasked with specific activities such as planning or carrying out an attack. Communications between cell members are carefully managed so that members of one cell do not know the nature of the work, identity, or location of members of another

Terrorist activities • Figure 7.17

These graphs show trends in terrorism over time. (*Source:* National Consortium for the Study of Terrorism and Responses to Terrorism (START). 2012. Global Terrorism Database. Retrieved from http://www.start.umd.edu/gtd.)

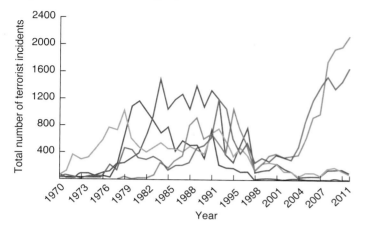

Central America, Caribbean
South America
South Asia
Western Europe
Middle East, North Africa

a. The graph shows the number of terrorist incidents by region. Terrorist activity related to the status of Northern Ireland, the Basque Country, and the French island of Corsica in the Mediterranean Sea helps explain the spike in western Europe in the 1970s.

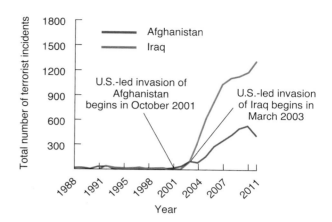

b. The Taliban has been responsible for most of the terrorist attacks in Afghanistan, whereas al-Qaeda and affiliated groups are leading perpetrators of terrorism in Iraq. Attacks in Iraq often target government facilities, police, and civilians. In Afghanistan, they target the troops and military facilities.

cell. Thus, effective counterterrorism against the al-Qaeda cells in one country is likely to have no effect on its cells in other countries. The killing of bin Laden in 2011 dealt a major blow to al-Qaeda's operations in Afghanistan and Pakistan, but al-Qaeda affiliates in the Arabian Peninsula, North Africa, and elsewhere continue to operate.

Some experts consider the development of these decentralized networks to be a strategy that has been facilitated by globalization. Advances in communications and Internet technologies have made it easier, faster, and less expensive to share information. Moreover, the Internet has helped open up new spaces via Facebook and Twitter that terrorist groups can use to spread threats or recruit members.

Other terrorist experts argue that terrorism today is an expression of resistance to globalization, and specifically the global diffusion of Western values associated with modernism (see Chapter 5). As evidence, these experts cite the rise in terrorist activity in places such as Afghanistan and Iraq since the U.S.-led invasions (**Figure 7.17**).

Instability can also facilitate the spread of terrorism. The Arab Spring—a reference to the protests and uprisings against governments across the Middle East and North Africa since 2010—is paradoxically linked both to pro-democracy movements and civil unrest. Al-Qaeda has taken advantage of this unrest. For example, after Libyan dictator Qaddafi was overthrown, numerous Tuareg (nomadic herders) who had served in the Libyan military returned to Mali. A rebellion that they staged was gradually infiltrated by al-Qaeda members.

CONCEPT CHECK STOP

1. **How** has geopolitical thinking changed over time?

2. **How** does the environment factor in the heartland theory?

3. **What** political concerns shaped Cold War geopolitics?

4. **How** has the geography of terrorism changed over time?

Electoral Geography

LEARNING OBJECTIVES

1. **Define** electoral system.
2. **Distinguish** between reapportionment and redistricting.
3. **Explain** gerrymandering.

In a representative democracy, voters elect legislators whose duty is to develop and implement public policy on behalf of their constituents. The set of procedures used to convert the votes cast in an election into the seats won by a party or candidate is referred to as an **electoral system**. *Electoral geographers* study the spatial aspects of electoral systems, voting districts, and election results.

Several different electoral systems are used in the world, but they can be classified into two main systems: the majority-plurality system and the proportional system. With *majority-plurality representation* (also called geographic representation), the person who receives a majority or plurality of the votes is elected and represents all of the voters in an electoral district. Majority-plurality systems create single-member electoral districts that are territorially defined. In general, the majority-plurality system is commonly associated with countries that have two dominant political parties, as in the United States.

In contrast, with *proportional representation* (also called party-political representation) multiple representatives can be elected. When proportional representation is used, voters choose from among political parties rather than individual candidates. After the votes are tallied, legislative seats are divided on a proportional basis. For example, a party receiving 30% of the votes would receive 30% of the legislative seats. The proportional system is widely used in Europe.

Reapportionment and Redistricting

reapportionment
The process of allocating legislative seats among voting districts so that each legislator represents approximately the same number of people.

For majority-plurality representation to be equitable, voting districts should have approximately the same number of people. **Reapportionment** becomes necessary because, over time, the population of a state can change. For example, in the U.S. House of Representatives, there are 435 seats for congressional representatives, and according to the U.S. Constitution, these seats must be apportioned or divided as equitably as possible among the 50 states according to their population. Indeed, the U.S. Constitution requires that the government conduct a census of the population every 10 years. Because of demographic change between 2000 and 2010, New York lost two legislative seats while Texas gained four in the reapportionment that took place following the 2010 U.S. Census.

Reapportionment is often followed by **redistricting** (**Figure 7.18**). Three criteria, established by the Supreme Court, guide the redistricting process. Congressional districts: (1) are to have equal population; (2) are to be contiguous and compact; and (3) are to respect the boundaries of other administrative units such as counties or parishes. Redistricting is the responsibility of each state and is usually carried out by the state legislature. As a result, redistricting often becomes a contentious exercise that is influenced by party politics.

redistricting
Redrawing the boundaries of voting districts usually as a result of population change.

Gerrymandering

Reapportionment and redistricting are intended to ensure equal representation on the basis of population in the House of Representatives. They are also supposed to treat political parties, as well as racial and ethnic minorities, equally. But legislators are well aware that how the boundaries of congressional districts are drawn can influence the outcome of elections. As a result, the redistricting process regularly raises concerns about **gerrymandering**.

Electoral geographers recognize two basic gerrymandering techniques: excess vote gerrymandering

gerrymandering
The process of manipulating voting district boundaries to give an advantage to a particular political party or group.

Reapportionment and redistricting in the United States • Figure 7.18

Every state is divided into congressional districts, with each represented by a single congressperson. To ensure equality among a state's districts, each representative is to speak for an equal number of people. If the population of a voting district changes, redistricting may become necessary to create districts of equal population. Arizona provides a good example of the reapportionment and redistricting processes.

❶ Congressional districts based on 2000 census
The map shows the eight congressional districts that were created following the 2000 census. They had equal populations of 641,329 people at the time.

❷ Population growth and reapportionment
By the 2010 census, Arizona's population had increased 25%, to 6,392,017. As a result of this growth, the state gained one House seat through reapportionment. The population growth was unequally distributed among the districts, as shown in the table. (*Source:* Data from Arizona Independent Redistricting Commission.)

The eight 2000 congressional districts	Their unequal populations in the 2010 census
1	774,310
2	972,839
3	707,919
4	698,314
5	656,833
6	971,733
7	855,769
8	754,300
Total	6,392,017

❸ Redistricting
Because the state's population growth was spatially uneven, Arizona needed to redistrict. Each of the newly created congressional districts contained 710,224 people. Each congressional district has the same number of people but a different ethnic mix. These pie charts show how the voting age population varies in four of the districts. (*Source:* Data from Arizona Independent Redistricting Commission.)

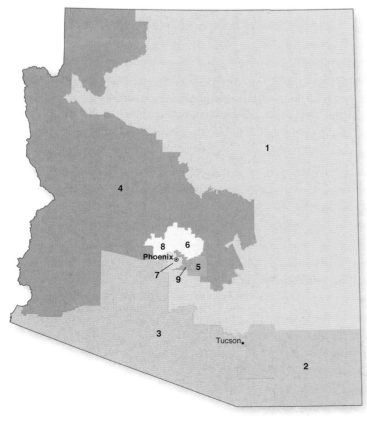

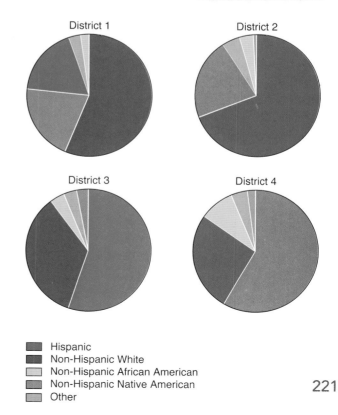

District 1   District 2

District 3   District 4

- Hispanic
- Non-Hispanic White
- Non-Hispanic African American
- Non-Hispanic Native American
- Other

Gerrymandering in Texas • Figure 7.19

These maps show the Twenty-third Congressional District of Texas in 2002, 2004, and 2006.

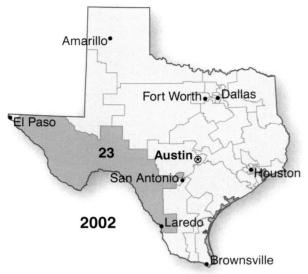

a. In 2002, the Twenty-third Congressional District was a majority-minority district (55% Hispanic, 45% non-Hispanic). Its voting age population of Hispanics was also over 50%. That year, a Republican candidate narrowly defeated a Democrat in the election for district representative.

b. Texas broke from the practice of redistricting once every 10 years and redistricted in 2003. By 2004, with redistricting completed, the Twenty-third District had been redrawn in such a way, shown here, that the district remained 55% Hispanic but the voting age population of Hispanics dropped to 46% and created a district much more likely to elect a Republican. Lawsuits challenged the constitutionality of these actions.

c. In a decision issued in 2006, the Supreme Court upheld the state's calendar for redistricting, but found that the Twenty-third District was gerrymandered to dilute the power of the Hispanic vote. The Supreme Court ordered a further redistricting to correct this problem, leading to the creation of a district with a voting age population that was 57% Hispanic.

Ask Yourself

Based on the map in part **c** and the events described here, what can you surmise about the composition of the voting age population in the green area south of San Antonio?

and wasted vote gerrymandering. The *excess vote technique* creates a few electoral districts in which support for the opposition forms a strong majority. In these districts, excess voting occurs because many more votes are cast than are needed to win the election. Although the opposition wins overwhelmingly in these few districts, it does not secure majority control overall, and may lose seats in other districts. In contrast, the *wasted vote technique* disperses support for the opposition so that the opposition loses by a slim margin, say, 45–55%, or 40–60%. "Wasted votes" are the votes recorded for the losing candidate. When the support for the opposition draws heavily from racial or ethnic minorities, it is easy to see how these two gerrymandering techniques make it possible to create voting districts that diminish the effectiveness of the minority vote.

To try to prevent this from happening, the Voting Rights Act was amended in two important ways in the 1980s. First, it prohibited gerrymandering that dilutes minority voting power. Second, it stipulated that there may be some circumstances in which it is necessary to create voting districts that concentrate the strength of a specific minority group. This last change supported the creation of *majority-minority districts* (districts where minority group members form the majority) in order to improve minority representation. See **Figure 7.19** for an example of gerrymandering involving a majority-minority district.

CONCEPT CHECK

1. **What** is the difference between majority-plurality representation and proportional representation?
2. **Why** are reapportionment and redistricting necessary?
3. **When** does redistricting become gerrymandering?

Political Landscapes

LEARNING OBJECTIVES

1. **Explain** what a landscape of central authority is.
2. **Distinguish** between security landscapes and landscapes of governance.
3. **Define** political iconography.

How do political affairs shape political landscapes? In what ways are cultural landscapes used to convey political power? How and why do certain landscapes, both cultural and natural, become the focus of intense political disputes? These are just some of the questions that help guide the study of political landscapes.

Landscapes of Central Authority

States exercise their political control through government. In turn, the policies, agencies, and laws of government affect the look of cities and towns as well as the countryside. When governments fund the design and construction of infrastructure including railroads, sewage, irrigation, or power facilities, they are creating landscapes of central authority. If you drive on a U.S. interstate to get to school or work, that interstate is part of a transportation network and landscape of central authority created by the federal government largely as a result of the 1956 Federal Highway Act. We can also see the stamp of central authority in the landscape of Egypt's Aswan High Dam, a major source of hydroelectric power for the entire country.

Landscapes of central authority are important because they contribute to the process of state-building. For example, they may help connect different parts of a country while reinforcing the power and significance of the central government.

Security landscapes in the West Bank • Figure 7.20

The separation barrier is a concrete wall, some 600 km (400 mi) long, that Israel has built in the West Bank. To some Israelis, the barrier provides security from Palestinian suicide bombings; to Palestinians, it is Israel's way of annexing territory. In an advisory opinion in 2004, the International Court of Justice found the barrier contrary to international law.

a. Here the barrier separates the Israeli town of Matan (foreground) from the Palestinian town of Hableh.

b. The barrier, 8 m (25 ft) high, divides the town of Abu Dis.

Menahem Kahana/AFP/Getty Images, Inc.

Lefteris Pitarakis/©AP/Wide World Photos

West Bank

Security landscapes Boundaries establish the limits of a state's jurisdiction and, in effect, the limits of a state's political authority. Many demarcated boundaries are **security landscapes**—a specific type of political landscape created to protect the territory, people, facilities, and infrastructure of a state. Security cameras, metal detectors, and gated entrances are some measures intended to deter terrorist attacks and, in the event of one, minimize the damage and loss of life (**Figure 7.20**).

Landscapes of governance The imprint of central authority can also be revealed through an examination of legal policies. Laws can encourage or discourage certain human behaviors, which, in turn, may lead to the creation of distinctive landscapes of governance. Farm policy can influence agricultural practices. In Europe, where it is too cool to cultivate sugarcane, the sugar beet crop is an important source of sugar. Without sizable EU subsidies, however, sugar beet production would not be as widespread in Europe as it presently is, nor would the EU continue to be a net sugar exporter.

Landscapes of governance are also created when systems of land survey are commissioned by a government prior to the settlement of an area. Many other kinds of laws affect the landscape as well. Inheritance laws requiring that land be divided among all children, rather than passing to the oldest child, can result in fragmented landholdings. When governments change the laws and regulations in order to encourage particular businesses or industries to locate in an area, landscape change is likely to occur. The establishment of national parks and forests signals the impact of laws that protect, preserve, or regulate the use of the natural environment.

Political Iconography

Landscapes are not only affected by governmental laws and policies, but are also coded with political meaning. Examples of **political iconography** include flags, statues or images of political or military leaders, national anthems, war memorials, and symbols of political parties. These symbols come to represent certain ideals, such as freedom or democracy, and help build a shared sense of identity (*Where Geographers Click* and **Figure 7.21**).

> **political iconography** An image, object, or symbol that conveys a political message.

Where Geographers CLICK

 THE PLANNER

CAIN Web Service: Political Wall Murals in Northern Ireland

©Cain (cain.ulster.ac.uk)

Search for murals on the CAIN web service to learn more about political iconography and the conflict in Northern Ireland by exploring the murals that mark and demarcate the region's public spaces. There is a great deal to explore here. You might begin by following the link to **The Bogside Artists**.

Political iconography • Figure 7.21

U.S. Marines placed an American flag on a statue of Saddam Hussein in Baghdad in 2003. The Marines then helped topple the statue. The power of political iconography derives from the way it becomes part of the shared vocabulary of some groups but not others. ▶ **How do you think Americans interpreted this image? Why is it provocative to many Middle Easterners?**

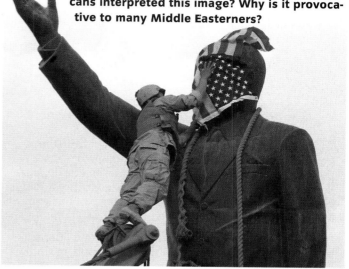

Ramzi Haidar/AFP//Getty Images, Inc.

CONCEPT CHECK STOP

1. **What** functions do landscapes of central authority serve?
2. **How** are landscapes of governance significant?
3. **How** is political iconography related to nationalism?

 THE PLANNER

Summary

1 Key Concepts in Political Geography 196

- **Political geography** is a branch of human geography that focuses on the spatial aspects of political affairs and is heavily influenced by human **territoriality**, which can transform an open space into a divided or closed one, as shown here in Cyprus.

- An important turning point in the development of the **state** occurred during the middle of the 17th century, when ideas about **sovereignty** became strongly linked to specific units of territory.

A divided state • Figure 7.2

Petros Karadjias/©AP/Wide World Photos

- When there is congruence between the boundaries of a **nation** and the boundaries of a state, a **nation-state** exists. Importantly, a **multinational state** can function as a nation-state if the different national groups are effectively integrated.

- Sizable portions of the globe have been shaped by **imperialism** and **colonialism**. These processes are especially visible on the contemporary map of Africa; they created an enduring framework for the political organization of African space even as Africans achieved **self-determination** and independence.

2 Geographical Characteristics of States 203

- The geographical characteristics of states include the **boundaries**, the character and configuration of a state's territory and **territorial seas**, the internal spatial organization of the state, and any **centripetal** or **centrifugal forces**. The shape of a state as well as the presence of **enclaves** and **exclaves** can influence a state's political affairs.

- For administrative purposes, states are divided internally into smaller units such as provinces or districts. In a federal system of government, the state distributes power to its territorial subdivisions; in a unitary system the power of the state is concentrated in the central government.

- Depending on the circumstances, nationalism can be a centripetal or centrifugal force. The map that is shown here, for example, can be seen as an expression of both nationalism and **separatism**.

A model of integration in multinational Spain • Figure 7.10

Alvaro Barrientos/©AP/Wide World Photos

3 Internationalism and Supranational Organizations 211

- **Internationalism** can lead to the formation of **supranational organizations** such that multiple states agree to work together for common economic, military, political, or other purposes.

- The **United Nations** is a supranational political organization that is global in scale and promotes international peace and security. Protecting civilians and maintaining regional stability, as shown here, are just some of the kinds of peacekeeping operations the UN provides. The **European Union**, in contrast, began as an economic organization and operates on a regional scale.

UN Security Council and peacekeeping operations • Figure 7.11

Associated Press

4 Global Geopolitics 214

- How states acquire and deploy their power are important dimensions of **geopolitics**. The theory of the organic state and the heartland theory were two early and influential geopolitical theories. According to the heartland theory, the Eurasian landmass, shown here, provided a territorial basis for a state or allied states to become the dominant world power.

Mackinder's heartland • Figure 7.13

- During the **Cold War**, the geopolitical configuration of the world was divided into two opposing groups: the capitalist West and the Communist East. The end of the Cold War has led some scholars to argue that the geopolitical configuration of the world has become multipolar.

- Most acts of **terrorism** can be classified into one of four categories, but it is often the case that terrorism is used for multiple purposes. An important geographical dimension of terrorist networks today is that they have a global reach but work through highly decentralized and localized cells.

5 Electoral Geography 220

- Electoral geography is the study of the spatial aspects of electoral systems, voting districts, and election results. Two main types of **electoral systems** exist: the majority-plurality system and the proportional system.

- In the United States, **reapportionment** and **redistricting** are electoral processes designed to ensure equal representation. Over time, shifts in population similar to those recorded here, create imbalances in the system of representation and underscore the necessity of redistricting. Redistricting often raises concerns about **gerrymandering**.

Reapportionment and redistricting in the United States • Figure 7.18

The eight 2000 congressional districts	Their unequal populations in the 2010 census
1	774,310
2	972,839
3	707,919
4	698,314
5	656,833
6	971,733
7	855,769
8	754,300
Total	6,392,017

6 Political Landscapes 223

- Political landscapes can be thought of as a visual expression of political affairs. Landscapes of central authority are political landscapes that are the result of policies and programs implemented by the central or federal government.

- **Security landscapes** reflect a state's concern about its people, borders, and territory. But the construction of prominent security landscapes such as the one shown here can also be seen as a provocative political act.

Security landscapes in the West Bank • Figure 7.20

Menahem Kahana/AFP/Getty Images, Inc.

- Landscapes of governance reveal the impact of certain laws on the landscape. **Political iconography** refers to the use of symbols to convey political messages.

Key Terms

- boundary 204
- centrifugal force 208
- centripetal force 208
- Cold War 216
- colonialism 201
- devolution 209
- electoral system 220
- enclave 207
- European Union (EU) 212
- exclave 207
- geopolitics 214

- gerrymandering 220
- heartland 215
- imperialism 201
- internationalism 211
- multinational state 200
- nation 199
- nation-state 200
- political geography 196
- political iconography 224
- reapportionment 220
- redistricting 220

- security landscape 224
- self-determination 203
- separatism 209
- sovereignty 197
- state 198
- supranational organization 211
- territorial seas 204
- territoriality 196
- terrorism 218
- United Nations (UN) 211

Critical and Creative Thinking Questions

1. Will Internet voting ever replace the use of traditional polling places? What geographic and political conditions would be most conducive to such change?

2. List some advantages and disadvantages of majority-plurality and proportional representation systems.

3. Do some fieldwork in the area where you live and identify a relic boundary. What processes led to the creation of that boundary?

4. Not all ethnic groups are nations. Why?

5. Under what circumstances might devolution become a centrifugal force?

6. A political geographer might argue that the Berlin Conference was an exercise in gerrymandering. Explain what is meant by this statement and take a position on it.

7. What similarities and differences are there between the division of Germany after World War II and the division of Cyprus?

8. Review the geographic composition of the UN Security Council, shown in the diagram. Does it need reform? Why or why not?

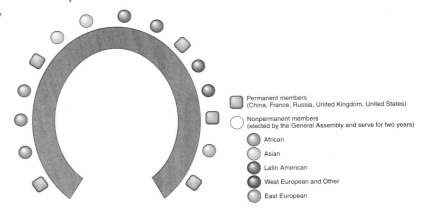

Permanent members
(China, France, Russia, United Kingdom, United States)

Nonpermanent members
(elected by the General Assembly and serve for two years)

African
Asian
Latin American
West European and Other
East European

What is happening in this picture?

Kuwaiti women line up to vote. Kuwait's constitution, drafted in 1962, contained an electoral law that prevented women's political participation. In 2005, that law was amended to allow women the right to vote and run for election, but in accordance with Islamic law, polling places must be segregated.

Yasser Al-Zayyat/AFP/Getty Images, Inc.

Think Critically

1. Worldwide, what circumstances or developments have facilitated the spread of women's right to vote?
2. In any society, why has giving women the right to vote tended to be controversial?

Self-Test

(Check your answers in Appendix B.)

1. A _____ exists when the boundaries of a nation match the boundaries of the state.
   a. multinational state   c. state
   b. nation   d. nation-state

2. The Berlin Conference is associated with all of the following *except* _____.
   a. the granting of self-determination
   b. the creation of geometric boundaries
   c. the creation of multinational states
   d. the political map of Africa today

3. The areas where coastal states have the right to manage ocean resources are called _____.
   a. territorial seas   c. exclusive economic zones
   b. boundary waters   d. offshore waters

4. One of the causes of the euro zone crisis is _____.
   a. that fiscal union in euro zone countries was achieved too quickly
   b. the Arab Spring
   c. vulnerabilities in the banking system of euro zone countries
   d. the failure of all EU members to adopt the euro

5. A(n) _____ shape is most likely to be considered an efficient way of organizing territory.

   a. fragmented   c. elongate

   b. compact   d. prorupt

6. Use the accompanying map to describe the territorial configuration of South Africa.

   _____

   _____

7. Which characteristic below is usually considered a centripetal force?

   a. a multinational population

   b. a raison d'être

   c. an exclave

   d. an elongate shape

8. The transfer of power from a state to a self-identified community within it is called _____.

   a. self-determination   c. separatism

   b. autonomy   d. devolution

9. In Europe, the first collaborative trading agreement and important forerunner of the EU was _____.

   a. the Treaty of Rome

   b. the Treaty of European Unity

   c. Benelux

   d. the European Coal and Steel Community

10. According to the heartland theory, world power was based on _____.

   a. land power   c. air power

   b. sea power   d. nuclear weapons

11. This diagram depicts what kind of geopolitical configuration of the world?

   a. unipolar   c. multipolar

   b. bipolar   d. deterritorialized

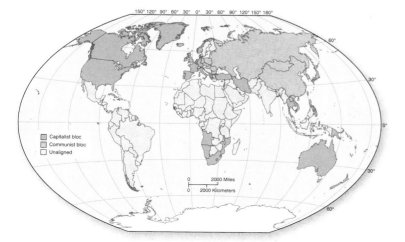

12. Countries that have more than two dominant political parties are most likely to have an electoral system based on _____.

   a. proportional representation

   b. majority-plurality representation

   c. federal representation

   d. unitary representation

13. The type of gerrymandering that creates voting districts where the opposition loses by a slim margin is called the _____.

   a. excess vote technique

   b. dilution technique

   c. wasted vote technique

   d. majority-minority technique

14. National parks provide landscape evidence of _____.

   a. centrifugal forces

   b. the imprint of central authority

   c. security landscapes

   d. devolution

15. This image provides a good example of _____.

   a. imperialism   c. a geometric boundary

   b. a relic boundary   d. political iconography

Courtesy Dr. Jack Child, American University

THE PLANNER ✓

Review your Chapter Planner on the chapter opener and check off your completed work.

8 Urban Geographies

BUILDING A SUSTAINABLE CITY

Can you imagine a city without privately-owned cars, trucks, and SUVs parked along the sides of streets or in front of stores? Would you like to live in a city that encourages walking and reliance on public transportation such as clean energy buses or personal rapid transit vehicles, shown here? These are some of the features of Masdar City, a sustainable city that is under construction in the United Arab Emirates.

Masdar City incorporates innovative traditional and state of the art design principles in order to show that we can build successful sustainable cities. Renewable energy will power Masdar City. Streets will be oriented to take advantage of the cooling effects of local wind patterns and breezes. The streets will also be narrower to benefit from the shade of adjacent buildings. Solar energy, wind energy, and the conversion of waste products into energy will supply the city's electricity. All wastewater will be treated and used in landscape management.

Approximately 40,000 people will live in Masdar City when construction is completed, and it will be a center for the development of advanced green technology. If we can create environmentally sustainable cities, what would it take to transform our cities into places that provide greater social equity—for example, in the form of adequate housing and jobs for all their residents? With this question in mind, this chapter seeks to introduce you to the geography of cities, their structure, and the processes that shape them.

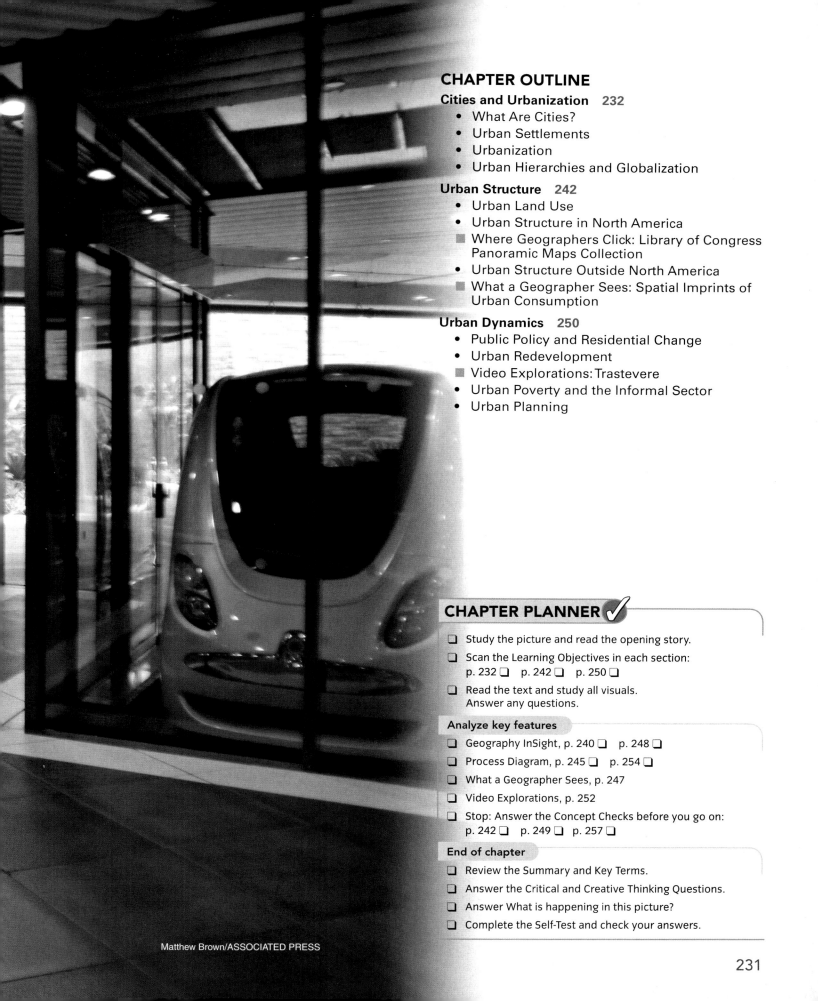

CHAPTER OUTLINE

CHAPTER PLANNER ✓

- ☐ Study the picture and read the opening story.
- ☐ Scan the Learning Objectives in each section:
  p. 232 ☐   p. 242 ☐   p. 250 ☐
- ☐ Read the text and study all visuals.
  Answer any questions.

Analyze key features

- ☐ Geography InSight, p. 240 ☐   p. 248 ☐
- ☐ Process Diagram, p. 245 ☐   p. 254 ☐
- ☐ What a Geographer Sees, p. 247
- ☐ Video Explorations, p. 252
- ☐ Stop: Answer the Concept Checks before you go on:
  p. 242 ☐   p. 249 ☐   p. 257 ☐

End of chapter

- ☐ Review the Summary and Key Terms.
- ☐ Answer the Critical and Creative Thinking Questions.
- ☐ Answer What is happening in this picture?
- ☐ Complete the Self-Test and check your answers.

Matthew Brown/ASSOCIATED PRESS

Cities and Urbanization

LEARNING OBJECTIVES

1. **Explain** what is meant by functional complexity.
2. **Summarize** trends in global urbanization.
3. **Distinguish** between urban primacy and urban hierarchy.
4. **Explain** central place theory.

L ove them or hate them, cities are a defining feature of our world and a driving force in the global economy. As hubs of activity, cities are constantly changing, and yet their role as important gateways endures. Globally, the pace of urbanization over the past 60 years has been swift, and more than half of the world's people now live in cities. But just what is a city, what does it mean to be urban, and how is the global urban network configured?

What Are Cities?

Someone from Tokyo, a city of 37 million people, probably has ideas about what a city is that are very different from those of someone from Stillwater, Oklahoma, a city of about 50,000 people. When asked about the differences between the two places, Japanese students from Tokyo who attend Oklahoma State University in Stillwater mention Stillwater's small population. To these students Stillwater feels empty, yet they find it difficult to get around because they do not have cars. They point out that even with the congestion in Tokyo it is still easier to go places because of the city's extensive subway system. Conversely, Stillwater natives who have visited Tokyo say that they were surprised by how densely packed Tokyo is—with people and high-rises—but that they enjoyed Tokyo's nightlife. These students also recall being shocked to learn that many families in Tokyo live in apartments no bigger than their dorm rooms. Clearly, Stillwater and Tokyo are both cities, but as these divergent views show, the cities function as different kinds of **central places** and they serve contrasting **hinterlands** (**Figure 8.1**).

In spite of their diversity, cities share six basic characteristics. (1) Cities possess dense concentrations of people. (2) Cities, unlike rural settlements, are distinguished by **functional complexity**. (3) Cities are centers of institutional power

> **central place**
> A settlement that provides goods and services for its residents and its surrounding trade or market area.
>
> **hinterland**
> The trade area served by a central place.
>
> **functional complexity** The ability of a town or city to support sizable concentrations of people who earn their living from specialized, nonfarming activities.

Cities as central places • Figure 8.1

Tokyo, Japan, and Stillwater, Oklahoma, are very different kinds of central places not only because of their settlement histories but also because of the population and the specialized activities they support.

a. Tokyo, for example, is heavily involved in international trade, banking, and industry.

b. Stillwater, by contrast, is a small city whose largest employer is a university.

Justin Guariglia/NG Image Collection

©Alyson Greiner

Urban settlements in the landscape • Figure 8.2

These images show aspects of the urban setting of Connecticut's capital, Hartford.

a. This map shows Hartford in relation to the urbanized and metropolitan areas surrounding it.

b. Hartford's CBD, shown in this photo, has been a center of the insurance industry since the mid-19th century, but the city now competes with surrounding suburbs to attract and retain jobs.

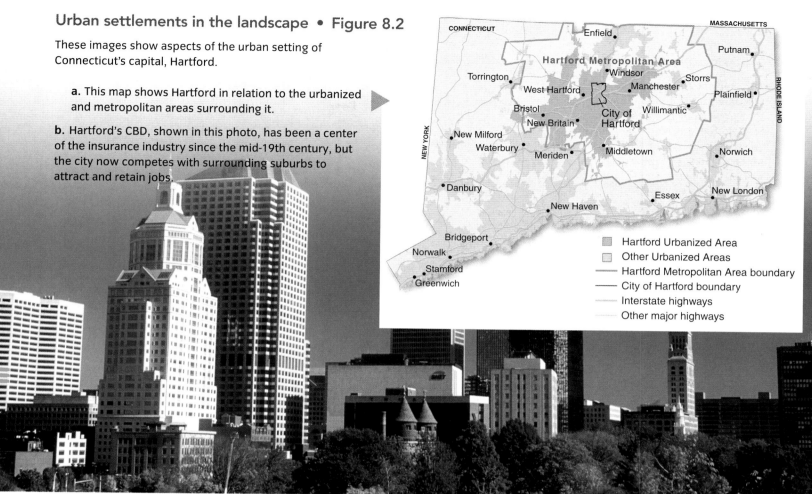

© Andre Jenny/Alamy

associated with the business, governmental, or cultural activities of that place. (4) Cities are dynamic, human-created environments that possess complex patterns of specialized land use (for example, residential, industrial, public, and private). (5) Cities are linked, via trade, transportation, or communication, to other urban and rural places. (6) As places, cities are full of contradictions. They are hubs of creativity, opportunity, and hope but are simultaneously also places of poverty, deprivation, and despair.

Urban Settlements

What constitutes an urban settlement? There is no simple answer to this question in part because different countries use the term *urban* to mean different things. Some countries define urban on the basis of a minimum population size. For example, in Australia the minimum population for an urban settlement is 1000. In Japan, however, to be designated urban a settlement must have 50,000 or more people. The U.S. Census Bureau considers a territory urban if it has a residential population of at least 2500 and a population density of at least 1000 people per square mile.

In other places the term *urban* refers to certain territories or administrative divisions. For example, New Caledonia (a French territory located in the southwest Pacific near Australia) designates its capital city as urban. Still other countries examine both the population size and the kinds of employment patterns, reserving the term *urban* for those places where the majority of the residents have nonagricultural jobs.

Most cities have boundaries (city limits) that are legally defined. The area enclosed by these boundaries is referred to as the **central city**. The part of the downtown where major office and retail activities are clustered constitutes the **central business district** (CBD), whereas the **suburbs** are the built-up areas that surround the central city. In everyday usage the term **urbanized area** refers to land that has been developed for commercial, residential, or industrial purposes. The U.S. Census Bureau uses a more formal definition of urbanized area that refers to territory—usually the central city plus adjacent suburbs—that has at least 50,000 people and a population density of 1000 people or more per square mile (**Figure 8.2**).

Megalopolis • Figure 8.3

This map shows the growth of Megalopolis since 1950. Although the term *megalopolis* originally referred to the urban corridor stretching between Boston and Washington, D.C., unless capitalized, it now describes any coalescing metropolitan areas such as Tokyo and Yokohama in Japan or Rio de Janeiro and São Paulo in Brazil. (*Source:* Adapted from Morrill, 2006.)

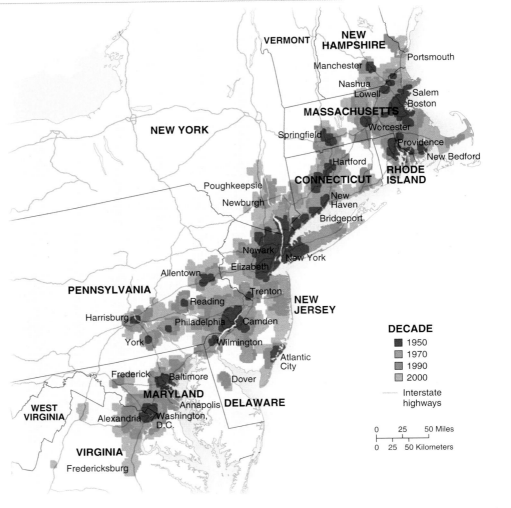

Ask Yourself

1. What cities now mark the endpoints of Megalopolis?
2. By 2000, Megalopolis had three distinct cores. Where were they?

In contrast, a **metropolitan area** encompasses a large population center (50,000 people minimum) and the adjacent zones that are socially and economically connected to it, such as the places sending commuters into the city. The boundaries of urbanized areas follow those of U.S. Census blocks or block groups (see Chapter 6) because they are used to calculate population densities. The boundaries of metropolitan areas, however, follow local government units such as counties, or in the case of certain New England states, towns. Finally, a **megalopolis**, or conurbation, is a massive urban complex created by converging metropolitan areas (**Figure 8.3**).

Urbanization

Urbanization refers to the processes that concentrate people in urban places. When geographers measure urbanization, they can use one of two methods: the level of

urbanization or the rate of urban growth. Urban geographers and other analysts use both measures to compare trends in urbanization in one country or region to another. The **level of urbanization** indicates the percentage of people living in urban places in some defined area (e.g., a county or a country). An area is considered urbanized if 50% or more of the population resides in urban places. The **rate of urban growth** refers to the annual percentage increase in an urban population. Geographers consider urban growth rates between 2% and 4% to be high.

Globally, the percentage of people living in urban places has increased dramatically over time: from 13% in 1900 to 29% in 1950. Today more than 50% of the world's people are urbanites. This level of urbanization represents a significant new moment in the geography and history of our world and underscores the importance of cities as systems of social organization. Current estimates indicate that by 2050, approximately 70% of the global population will be urban.

In general, developed countries tend to have higher levels of urbanization than developing countries. The level of urbanization is about 78% among developed countries and about 47% among developing countries (**Figure 8.4**).

Between 1970 and 2011, the urban growth rate of the world averaged 2.4% and the number of people living in cities increased from 1.4 to 3.6 billion. The rate of urban growth for the world has since slowed considerably and is now about 1.8%. Even so, the developing regions of the world are projected to have the highest rates of urban growth for the next two decades. Between 2011 and 2030, for example, the rate of urban growth in developing regions is estimated to be approximately 2.0%, with a population doubling time of 35 years. This compares to a projected urban growth rate of 0.5% in developed regions.

Levels of urbanization • Figure 8.4

This figure presents historical and geographical patterns of urbanization.

a. The world reached a new milestone—an urban transition—in 2008, with half of the global population living in urban areas. Most of these urban residents live in towns and cities with fewer than 1 million people. (*Source:* Adapted from Kaplan, Wheeler, and Holloway, 2008. Reprinted with permission of John Wiley & Sons, Inc.)

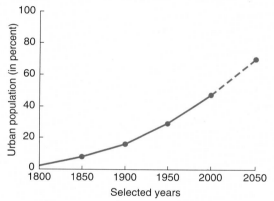

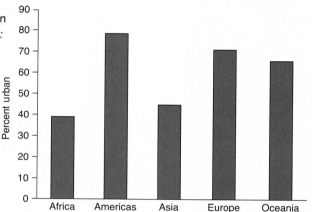

b. When levels of urbanization are charted and mapped, we can see the unevenness of urbanization around the world. Although there is great variation from country to country, Africa and Asia are the least urbanized of the populated continents in the world.

(*Source:* Data from Population Reference Bureau, 2011.)

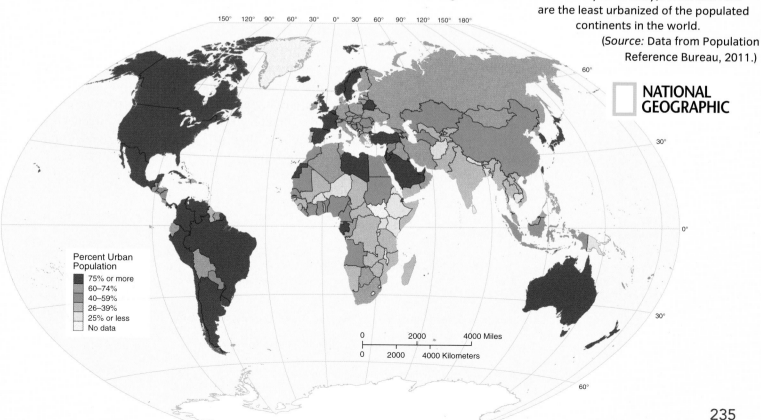

Percent Urban Population
- 75% or more
- 60–74%
- 40–59%
- 26–39%
- 25% or less
- No data

NATIONAL GEOGRAPHIC

These rates of urban growth highlight three important trends in global patterns of urbanization. First, most of the population growth in the world is occurring in urban places. Second, most of this urban growth will take place in developing regions. Third, in general, rural populations in developed regions of the world are declining while the urban populations are growing slowly.

Urban growth usually is the result of numerous interrelated factors. For example, demographic characteristics of urban populations have a bearing on natural population growth. Similarly, urban growth is connected to the processes of migration and globalization. The movement of people from rural to urban areas has had a major influence on urban growth, but migration from one urban area to another is also important, as we learned in Chapter 3. Globalization can create economic opportunities that affect migration patterns. Likewise, government policies and business practices can create incentives for urban growth. Even other geographical attributes of an urban area such as its climate, accessibility, and amenities can influence its growth. These factors are summarized in **Table 8.1**.

Urbanization, development, and megacities

Cities have been a part of our world for about 6000 years. By studying historic urban sites, scholars have identified two circumstances considered necessary for the emergence of cities: (1) development of an agricultural system that enabled the production and storage of a food surplus; and (2) a system of social organization dominated by an elite, nonfarming social class. Both of these circumstances were conducive to the transformation of agricultural settlements into more functionally complex places.

The circumstances that contributed to the emergence of the world's first cities are still relevant to discussions of contemporary cities, but additional considerations come into play. One way to recognize these other factors is to reflect on the geographic patterns of urbanization shown in **Figure 8.4b**. For example, why do more developed countries tend to have higher levels of urbanization and lower rates of urban growth? The answer to this question relates to social and technological changes associated with the Industrial Revolution that began in western Europe during the mid-18th century (Chapter 3). As industrialization and mechanization spread, fewer people were needed to work the land. In turn, jobs at factories and industries in the growing cities drew rural residents from the countryside to the cities, fueling urbanization.

Since the Industrial Revolution, the regions of the world that were the first to industrialize, primarily the countries in western Europe and North America, also were the first to urbanize most extensively. Industrialization and urbanization contributed to the economic growth of these regions. The use of steel frames and electric elevators enabled the construction of skyscrapers and transformed the appearance of these cities.

For most of the 20th century, the largest cities in the world were geographically concentrated in the more developed regions of Europe and North America. After 1975, however, that pattern began to change as a result of rapid urbanization and the growth of **megacities** (**Figure 8.5**).

> **megacity** A city with 10 million or more residents.

When ignored or poorly managed, rapid urbanization can be accompanied by a host of problems, including unemployment, the development of slums or shantytowns, traffic congestion, and pollution. We discuss these issues later in the chapter, but first we need to introduce primacy, a condition that affects the spatial distribution of people among cities.

Factors that influence urban growth   Table 8.1

- Geographic location (e.g., accessibility to markets, natural resources, other cities)

- Industrialization and globalization

- Demographic trends (e.g., rural-to-urban migration, natural population increase, urban-to-urban migration)

- Policies promoting economic growth (e.g., improved transportation and communication infrastructure)

- Improved services and amenities (e.g., public transportation, urban parks, public safety)

Urban growth and megacities • Figure 8.5

These charts show the remarkable growth in the world's urban population and megacities. All population numbers are for the urbanized area.

 a. Urban population by size of city in 1975 and 2011
Compare these charts to see how much the urban population has increased and to see the rising share of the urban population that lives in megacities. (*Source:* Data from UNDESA, 2008 and 2012.)

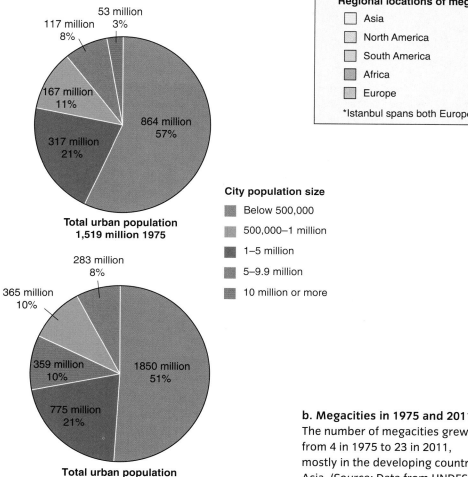

Total urban population 1,519 million 1975

City population size
- Below 500,000
- 500,000–1 million
- 1–5 million
- 5–9.9 million
- 10 million or more

Total urban population 3,632 million 2011

1975		2011	
Megacity	**Population (millions)**	**Megacity**	**Population (millions)**
1. Tokyo, Japan	26.6	1. Tokyo, Japan	37.2
2. New York, USA	15.9	2. Delhi, India	22.7
3. Shanghai, China	11.4	3. Mexico City, Mexico	20.4
4. Mexico City, Mexico	10.7	4. New York, USA	20.4
		5. Shanghai, China	20.2
		6. São Paulo, Brazil	19.9
		7. Mumbai, India	19.7
		8. Beijing, China	15.6
		9. Dhaka, Bangladesh	15.4
		10. Kolkata, India	14.4
		11. Karachi, Pakistan	13.9
		12. Buenos Aires, Argentina	13.5
		13. Los Angeles, USA	13.4
		14. Rio de Janeiro, Brazil	12.0
		15. Manila, Philippines	11.9
		16. Moscow, Russia	11.6
		17. Osaka-Kobe, Japan	11.5
		18. Istanbul, Turkey*	11.3
		19. Lagos, Nigeria	11.2
		20. Cairo, Egypt	10.8
		21. Guangzhou, China	10.8
		22. Shenzhen, China	10.6
		23. Paris, France	10.6

Regional locations of megacities
- Asia
- North America
- South America
- Africa
- Europe

*Istanbul spans both Europe and Asia.

b. Megacities in 1975 and 2011
The number of megacities grew from 4 in 1975 to 23 in 2011, mostly in the developing countries of Asia. (*Source:* Data from UNDESA, 2012.)

Urban primacy Urban growth in the developing world is more likely to give rise to **primate cities** than urban growth elsewhere. For example, Mexico City has a population in excess of 20 million, whereas the second largest city in the country, Guadalajara, has a population of about 4 million. Thailand provides an even more extreme example. With a population of 6.9 million, Bangkok is more than 9 times the size of Samut Prakan (population 700,000), Thailand's next largest city.

Primate cities can become islands of growth and contribute to uneven development within a country. Like magnets, these cities attract factories and businesses, which in turn attract more people. Most primate cities are also

> **primate city** A city that has a population two or more times the population of the second largest city in the country.

Urban primacy • Figure 8.6

Functions of cities and their size shape the development of primate cities.

Historical/Political	Largest city is also the capital city Colonial or ex-colonial status Policy favoritism toward a specific city A unitary state with a free enterprise economy
Economic	Agricultural orientation Low level of economic development High concentration of wealth among elites and large gap between the rich and the poor Economic favoritism toward a specific city

James P. Blair/NG Image Collectic

a. Conditions associated with urban primacy
Most urban geographers agree that primacy is more likely to develop under certain conditions, including but not limited to those identified in the table. (*Source:* Mutlu, 1989.)

b. Buenos Aires, Argentina
With a population of 13.8 million, Buenos Aires is Argentina's capital city and primate city. ▶ **Why is experience as a colony often associated with urban primacy?**

capital cities; thus, they function as the main political and administrative center of the country. Similarly, primate cities tend to attract more cultural and educational resources. Urban primacy, then, involves more than the size of a city's population; it also includes the concentration of political, economic, and cultural functions within a city.

Some countries in the developing world, such as China and India, do not have primate cities. Moreover, primate cities are not unique to the developing world. Several European capitals, including London, Paris, Vienna, and Athens, are also primate cities. In Australia primacy exists at the state level rather than the national level. Within the state of New South Wales, for example, the primate city of Sydney is more than eight times the size of Newcastle. See **Figure 8.6** for an overview of conditions associated with primacy.

Urban Hierarchies and Globalization

As we have seen, a variety of different types of urban settlements or central places exists. In addition, the size of the hinterland is directly related to the size of the central place. For example, a village will have a much smaller hinterland than a city. The relationship between a central place and its hinterland is important because it indicates that a hierarchy of central places exists, and this, in turn, can affect their distribution. The first geographer to detect

and analyze regularities in the system of central places was Walter Christaller. His ideas were formulated in the 1930s and provide the basis for central place theory—one of the fundamental theories in urban geography.

Central place theory Christaller developed two concepts—range and threshold—to help explain the emergence of a hierarchy of central places. Both concepts relate to the provision of goods or services. The **range** is the maximum distance a consumer will travel for a particular good or service. Consumers are willing to travel longer distances to obtain luxury items or to make special purchases—to find the perfect wedding dress, for example, or to see their favorite band—but will not travel very far to buy a gallon of milk or mail a package.

If the range establishes the size of a market area, the threshold indicates what goods and services are likely to be available. In order to supply a particular good, a central place must have an adequate consumer base. The **threshold**, then, is the smallest number of consumers required to profitably supply a certain good or service. More specialized goods and services require larger thresholds. This helps explain why rare book and map stores and brain surgeons are found in larger cities. Thus, goods that have a large range and threshold are *high-order goods*. *Low-order goods* are those that we need frequently, such as groceries, and have a small range and threshold.

The **urban hierarchy**, therefore, consists of a ranked series of central places. At the top of the hierarchy are central places such as New York, Tokyo, and London that supply all of the basic necessities as well as the most specialized goods and services. Next, moving down the urban hierarchy, are the smaller cities, towns, and villages that, respectively, offer fewer goods and have smaller market areas. Hamlets, the central places characterized by the smallest thresholds and ranges, occupy the bottom of the hierarchy.

By focusing on the relationship between threshold and range, Christaller detected regularities in the distribution of central places and wondered whether it might be possible to predict the spatial arrangement of central places. Thus, **central place theory** posits that market forces account for the distribution of central places in an area, and that the optimal spatial arrangement of central places creates hexagonally shaped trade areas.

Christaller built his theory using three important assumptions:

1. The landscape consists of a uniform, flat surface.
2. The population is evenly distributed across this landscape.
3. As consumers, these people would always purchase the goods and services they need from the central place closest to them.

Christaller realized that these conditions would influence the shape of market areas. If there were no other central places in the area competing for consumers, the shape of the market area would be circular. But Christaller was not examining just one central place. Rather, he sought to understand the effects of multiple central places of different sizes in the urban hierarchy. Therefore, he theorized that the optimal shape of the market area would instead be hexagonal because market areas would be split between competing central places.

Christaller's work confirmed the interdependence of central places—that the size, retail functions, and location of one central place depend on the characteristics of other central places (**Figure 8.7**).

Spatial arrangement of central places • Figure 8.7

These diagrams show how central place theory accounts for the distribution of central places and how that distribution reflects an urban hierarchy.

a. Optimal market areas
Following Christaller's assumption that people would travel to the nearest central place, market areas, usually circular, become hexagonal when there are other central places of the same rank in the area and to prevent gaps. (*Source:* Adapted from Hartshorn, 1992. Reprinted with permission of John Wiley & Sons, Inc.)

b. Nested hexagons
The idealized hierarchy of central places, as theorized by Christaller, yields a lattice of central places. Within this lattice, smaller central places occur most frequently and are closest together. In contrast, larger central places are more widely spaced. (*Source:* Adapted from Hartshorn, 1992. Reprinted with permission of John Wiley & Sons, Inc.)

● City ▲ Town ● Village

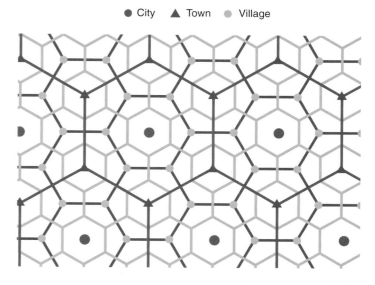

Geography InSight
Food deserts • Figure 8.8  THE PLANNER

Following central place theory, groceries are low-order goods because they are widely available. Food deserts develop when supermarkets close or do not locate in certain areas; thus, they stem from location decisions and reduce access to nutritious and affordable food. Let's consider the Canadian city of London, Ontario (population 350,000).

a. These maps show how supermarkets and their surrounding service areas (here defined as places within a 15-minute walk from the supermarket), became more suburban. ▶ **Identify a food desert that had emerged by 2005. How does the existence of a food desert challenge a basic tenet of central place theory?**

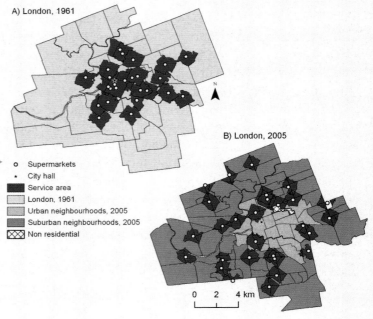

A) London, 1961

B) London, 2005

- ○ Supermarkets
- * City hall
- ■ Service area
- □ London, 1961
- Urban neighbourhoods, 2005
- Suburban neighbourhoods, 2005
- ⊠ Non residential

0   2   4 km

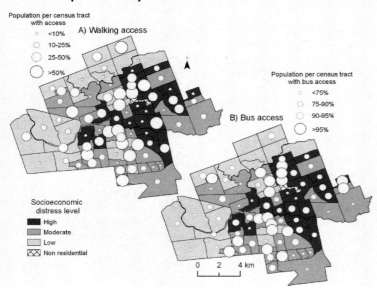

Population per census tract with access

A) Walking access
- <10%
- 10-25%
- 25-50%
- >50%

Population per census tract with bus access
- <75%
- 75-90%
- 90-95%
- >95%

B) Bus access

Socioeconomic distress level
- ■ High
- Moderate
- Low
- ⊠ Non residential

0   2   4 km

b. Socioeconomic distress is a composite measure derived from unemployment, poverty, and other data. Darker colors show higher socioeconomic distress, and smaller circles indicate poorer access to supermarkets. ▶ **Notice that areas with both high and low socioeconomic distress have poor access to supermarkets. What does this suggest about supermarket profitability?** (*Source:* Figures 8.8a and b from Larsen and Gilliland, 2008.)

Central place theory prompted hundreds of studies of the spatial arrangement of urban settlements and continues to serve as a starting point for discussions about the geographies of marketing areas. Central place theory also provides insights on the geography of urban **food deserts** (**Figure 8.8**).

> **food desert** An area characterized by a lack of affordable, fresh, and nutritious foods.

World cities and networks Urban geographers have documented transformations in the world's urban system because of globalization. Specifically, they have witnessed the growth and dominance of **world cities**. World cities tend to be large but are not necessarily megacities

> **world city** A principal center of global economic power that significantly influences the world's business.

because city size is not always an indicator of global influence or power. What *is* different about world cities is the way they have developed into command centers or nodes that greatly influence the flow of information, goods, and capital throughout the global urban system. Two related factors help explain the rise of world cities. One factor has been the growth of multinational corporations and the concentration of their headquarters in certain cities. The second factor involves the increasing importance of advanced professional services such as banking, insurance, advertising, and legal services, and the concentration of these operations in certain cities.

Some urban geographers think of world cities as the top tier in the hierarchy of urban places proposed by Christaller; other urban geographers, however, contend that world cities function so differently from other cities that traditional conceptualizations of the urban system need to be revised to emphasize global linkages. Therefore, the global urban system consists of hierarchies that can be understood as vertical relationships connecting central places *and* a global system of networked central places, linked through horizontal flows and connections. In other words, Christaller's model falls short when urban geographers use it to analyze or model the global urban system. Recall, for example, that in Christaller's model the market areas of central places in the same rank do not overlap. Today, however, overlapping market areas are common in part because people in the hinterland of one city can transact business—often electronically—with people in another city of the same urban rank on the other side of the world. The term **hinterworlds** conveys the idea that the area served by a world city potentially includes the entire globe, not just the territory adjacent to a specific city.

Most urban geographers agree that London, New York, and Tokyo are world cities. Identifying other world cities is challenging because experts can use many different criteria for evaluation and they disagree about which criteria are most important (**Figure 8.9**).

World cities • Figure 8.9

Studying the characteristics of world cities helps explain how they develop and differ from one another.

a. Selected indicators of world cities

▶ **How are primate cities and world cities alike? How are they different?**

Key indicators of world cities

1. Recognized center of political power and influence, often because of the concentration of government or institutional functions, e.g., United Nations, International Monetary Fund.

2. Major site of knowledge and information production from public and private sources, e.g., government documents, university studies, and leading business or financial companies.

3. Strong integration in the global economy.

4. High volume of interactions with other world cities.

5. Presence of a major international airport.

6. Major provider of advanced professional services such as accounting, financial services, insurance, and law.

7. State of the art telecommunications technologies and infrastructure, e.g., fiber optics, wireless networking.

8. Presence of a highly skilled, mobile, and multicultural labor pool.

9. Heavy reliance on a two-tiered structure of personnel in businesses and corporations that consists of an elite class associated with service sector jobs, e.g., financial managers, and an underclass associated with low or unskilled jobs, e.g., janitorial staff.

10. High-profile reputation as a center for arts and entertainment.

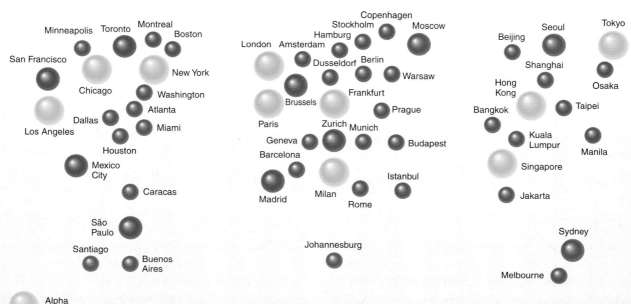

Alpha world cities

Beta world cities

Gamma world cities

b. This map presents one classification of world cities based on the geographies of dominant firms in four sectors: accounting, advertising, banking, and legal services. Alpha world cities had the greatest overall dominance in those sectors, followed by Beta world cities and then Gamma world cities.

▶ **If world cities reflect globalization, what message does this map convey?**

(*Source:* Beaverstock, Taylor, and Smith, 1999.)

Why are some large cities not world cities? The answer, according to urban geographer John Rennie Short (2004), involves four factors: poverty, social collapse, avoidance of risk by managers of global firms, and exclusion from or resistance to globalization. These factors work to repel investment and exclude cities from the global economy. For example, large cities that have high poverty rates often cannot afford to build the high-tech infrastructure necessary to support advanced professional services and consequently do not attract corporate headquarters. Social tensions including ethnic conflict and political corruption can also adversely affect business development. Similarly, the publication by businesses and corporations of risk ratings for different countries also deters investment. Cities located in high-risk countries are likely to be overlooked by business managers trying to identify new locations for their firms. Lastly, exclusion from the global economy or resistance to globalization might reflect different political perspectives and help explain why cities such as Kolkata (Calcutta) or Tehran are not world cities.

CONCEPT CHECK

1. **How** are the concepts of functional complexity and hinterlands related?
2. **How** has the geography of the largest cities changed since 1975?
3. **What** impact does a primate city have on the urban hierarchy?
4. **How** do world cities challenge central place theory?

Urban Structure

LEARNING OBJECTIVES

1. **Explain** what a bid-rent curve is.
2. **Identify** and explain four models of urban structure for North American cities.
3. **Account** for differences in the urban form of eastern and western European cities.
4. **Describe** the characteristics of a hybrid city.

Now that we are familiar with some of the global dimensions of urbanization and the interdependence of central places, we can take a closer look at the spatial configuration of cities. This involves a consideration of the forces affecting how urban land is used and how these patterns of land use change over time. We examine different models of urban structure to help visualize these patterns and processes.

Urban Land Use

Three important processes that affect the structure of cities are centralization, decentralization (also called suburbanization), and agglomeration. **Centralization** refers to forces that draw people and businesses into the downtown or central city. **Decentralization** has the opposite effect and draws people and businesses out of the central city, often into suburbs. Suburbanization can limit the territorial growth of cities, and the relocation of stores and businesses from the central city to the suburbs can reduce a city's tax base.

Agglomeration, or the clustering of like or unlike activities in an area, shapes both central city and suburban locations. For example, the agglomeration of different businesses such as hotels, restaurants, and conference space makes central cities desirable convention sites and acts as a centralizing force. In contrast, suburbs grow as residential agglomerations but also become sites for the agglomeration of similar business services such as data processing or product research.

Cities are also characterized by **functional zonation**. When geographers study land use in cities, they recognize three primary categories—residential, commercial, and industrial land use—and they seek to identify and understand the different forces that influence land-use patterns.

> **functional zonation**
> The division of a city into areas or zones that share similar activities and land use.

Land values and land use • Figure 8.10

Bid-rent curves depict changes in land value and land use across urban space, and help to visualize functional zonation.

a. Traditional bid-rent curves

Retailing activities that benefit from pedestrian flow or businesses such as mailing services that need to be close to their clients are willing to pay more for highly accessible, central locations. (*Source:* Adapted from Hartshorn, 1992. Reprinted with permission of John Wiley & Sons, Inc.)

b. Bid-rent curves and varying accessibility

This graph hints at the complexity of urban land values and shows that suburban locations that are highly accessible tend to be associated with higher land values. ▶ **What is the general relationship between land value and land-use density?** (*Source:* Adapted from Hartshorn, 1992. Reprinted with permission of John Wiley & Sons, Inc.)

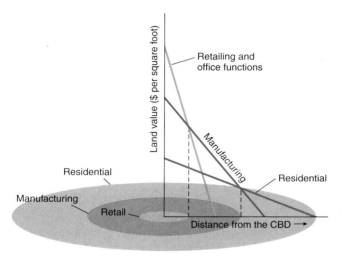

Dominant land use

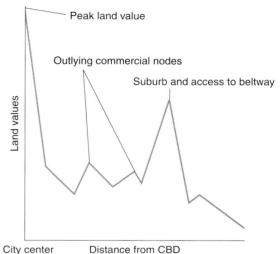

The value of land is one economic force that has a strong influence on land use in cities. Land values reflect, among other considerations, the accessibility and desirability of a particular site. Of course, these considerations vary from one enterprise to another, but as a rule, the more accessible or desirable a site is, the more expensive it is. Bid-rent curves help to visualize these economic forces. A **bid-rent curve** shows the amount a bidder (a business or individual, for example) is willing to pay for land relative to the distance from the central business district (CBD) (**Figure 8.10**).

Sometimes institutional forces have a major impact on urban land-use patterns. If left alone, market forces tend to inhibit certain activities. For example, high land-use values can exclude hospitals, schools, and parks. By intervening,

> **zoning** Laws that regulate land use and development.

city, state, or national governments can alter market forces and change land-use patterns. **Zoning** is another institutional force that directly affects urban land use. City councils, for example, can limit specific kinds of land use to certain parts of the city, concentrating factories or warehouses in particular areas.

Urban geographers have long been interested in the spatial organization of cities and have developed models to describe their internal structure. Each of these models is

a generalization and a simplification of the complexity of real cities. Nevertheless, these models help us understand the diverse forces that affect cities.

Urban Structure in North America

A number of models of urban structure were developed specifically through the study of U.S. cities. In this section we examine four of those models in chronological order and, in the process, show how the models have become more sophisticated.

Concentric zone and sector models In 1925, the sociologist Ernest Burgess produced the **concentric zone model**, one of the first models of urban spatial structure, based on his study of Chicago. He developed an ecological interpretation of urban growth and argued that in cities, as in the natural environment, groups competed for space and resources. These processes contributed to a sorting of social groups along economic and ethnic lines such that communities came to occupy distinctive niches or zones of urban space. Upward mobility, the arrival of new immigrants, or changes in land use or land value triggered the movement of people from one zone to another in a process he called *succession*. The concentric zone model shaped scholarly thinking about the structure of cities for many years, but critics point out that the model is overly simplistic and does not adequately account for the impact of transportation on urban form.

In 1939, the economist Homer Hoyt proposed the **sector model** to describe the land-use patterns and spatial structure of cities. This model places greater emphasis on the role of transportation and incorporates Hoyt's observation that the location of high-income groups influences the direction of a city's growth. New high-class neighborhoods tend to be built along the outer edges of cities. This sets in motion a process of succession called *filtering*. As Kenneth Jackson, an expert in urban history, concisely explains, **filtering** is "the sequential reuse of housing by progressively lower income households" (1985, p. 285). **Figure 8.11** compares and contrasts the sector and concentric zone models.

Multiple nuclei and urban realms models In 1945, two geographers, Chauncy Harris and Edward Ullman, proposed the **multiple nuclei model** as an alternative way of understanding the urban spatial structure of North American cities. Harris and Ullman observed that cities often had multiple cores, or nuclei, rather than a single core (the CBD). Specific nuclei varied from city to city but might include a harbor area, government district, university, or manufacturing areas. In turn, these multiple nuclei influenced the patterns of land use in the city.

Together, the concentric zone model, sector model, and multiple nuclei model constitute the three traditional models used to describe the internal structure of a North American city. None of these models, however, accounts for the impact of the automobile on the evolving spatial arrange-

Early models of North American cities • Figure 8.11

Early studies of U.S. cities gave rise to these two, now classic, models of urban structure.

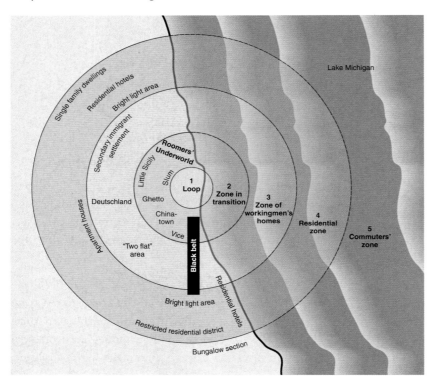

a. Burgess's concentric zone model
Similar patterns of land use develop around the CBD in rings, or in the case of Chicago, concentric arcs because of the city's lakefront location. Nonresidential land use occurs primarily in the Loop, the local name for the CBD, and spreads into the zone in transition, which is also the destination of newly arrived immigrants. (*Source:* Based on Burgess, 1925.)

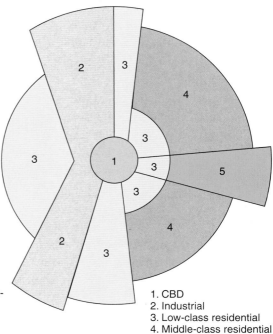

b. Hoyt's sector model
Transportation influences the development of industrial sectors, which follow rail or river routes, for example, but high-income residential sectors also tend to grow in proximity to the fastest transportation routes. Filtering occurs as the well-to-do move into new homes and their vacated homes become available or "filter down" to middle-income households. Middle-income homes also filter down to low-income households. (*Source:* Adapted from Harris and Ullman, 1945, p. 13.)

1. CBD
2. Industrial
3. Low-class residential
4. Middle-class residential
5. High-class residential

How changes in transportation influence urban form • Figure 8.12

In 1970, geographer John Adams related stages in the development of transportation to changes in the residential structure of cities. Although he concentrated on the Midwest, his stages are broadly applicable to other parts of the country. Because of changes in city shape since 1970, urban geographers have added a fifth stage. (*Source:* Adapted from Hartshorn, 1992. Reprinted with permission of John Wiley & Sons, Inc.)

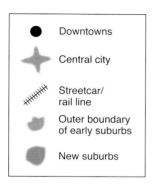

- ● Downtowns
- ✦ Central city
- ╫╫╫ Streetcar/ rail line
- Outer boundary of early suburbs
- New suburbs

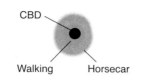

CBD

Walking   Horsecar

① Walking/horsecar era
Prior to the 1880s, urban residential form was compact.

② Electric streetcar era
With streetcars, and in some cities, subway systems, more people could live farther from their place of work. Streetcar networks were widespread in American cities between about 1880 and 1920 and influenced a star-like urban form.

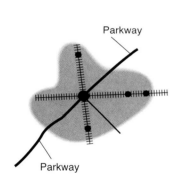

Parkway

Parkway

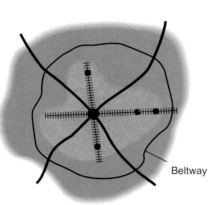

Beltway

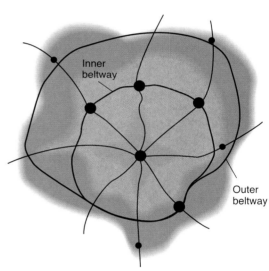

Inner beltway

Outer beltway

③ Recreational auto era
Wealthier Americans who purchased cars gained greater mobility between the 1920s and the 1940s and helped open new suburbs in areas not serviced by streetcars.

④ Freeway era
Since World War II, *automobility* has continued to propel urban decentralization.

⑤ Outer beltway era
A survey of urban experts ranked outer beltways serving edge cities as one of the major factors shaping American cities now and in the years to come.

ment of cities. For that, geographers needed yet another model, one that emphasized process more than form.

In 1964, the geographer James Vance developed the **urban realms model**. This model was based largely on his observations of San Francisco, where the suburbs had become self-sufficient centers. Each suburb was a new *urban realm*—an independent entity with its own downtown or commercial center. Vance's model recognizes the importance of the automobile in the evolu-

edge cities
Suburban clusters with office, retail, entertainment, and residential space that are often located at major highway interchanges.

tion of the spatial form of the city. It also acknowledges that these new suburban downtowns, linked by beltways or ring roads, frequently rival the traditional CBD for commercial and retail trade. Because these suburban downtowns resemble cities and have grown on the edges of the traditional city, they are often referred to as **edge cities**.

The emergence of edge cities indicates that transportation has a major impact on the shape of cities. **Figure 8.12** depicts, in a general way,

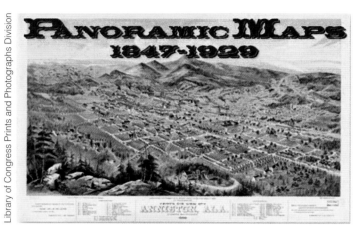
the relationship between changes in transportation, urban form, and the residential structure of North American cities.

For another method of visualizing urban street and settlement patterns, see *Where Geographers Click*.

Urban Structure Outside North America

Thus far the models we have discussed have been developed in conjunction with studies of North American cities. In Europe, cities have a very different look and configuration. Moreover, there are notable differences between cities in western and eastern Europe because of eastern Europe's long association with socialism. After examining European cities we discuss colonial cities and Islamic cities.

European cities Several of Europe's cities retain medieval characteristics, including remnants of a surrounding city wall, a historic core consisting of a church, marketplace, and dense concentration of buildings, an irregular street pattern, and a low central city skyline. Western European cities have retained a different spatial form because of the

interplay of various kinds of economic, institutional, and sociocultural forces. More specifically, the following six centralizing tendencies have been especially influential:

1. Cities are pedestrian- and bicycle-friendly, and parts of the central city may even be closed to vehicular traffic.
2. Private transportation is expensive. Individuals pay more for vehicles (in the base cost of a vehicle, taxes, and registration) and for the gas to operate them.
3. Public transportation is widely accessible and affordable.
4. Private home ownership is not as widespread in part because house prices are higher and because 5- or 10-year mortgages are customary (as opposed to 30-year mortgages).
5. Public sentiment has favored the preservation of historic buildings and structures and resisted urban redevelopment.
6. Central cities have long been highly desirable and stable residential locations.

After World War II and until the fall of communism in 1989, cities across eastern Europe and the Soviet Union were influenced by political and economic systems different from those in western Europe. Such "socialist cities," as they were sometimes called, developed a distinctive urban form. One crucial difference is that because the land and economy were controlled by the state, there was no bidding process for land. Large, residential "housing estates" consisting of numerous apartment buildings were often built near factories and on the margins of the city (**Figure 8.13**).

Soviet-era housing estates • Figure 8.13

These apartment blocks on the outskirts of Tallinn, Estonia, stand in contrast to the city's medieval skyline. They illustrate that the attributes of socialist cities were sometimes grafted onto preexisting cities.

Cotton Coulson/NG Image Collectic

WHAT A GEOGRAPHER SEES

Spatial Imprints of Urban Consumption

The urban landscape of Warsaw has changed dramatically since 1989, following the shift in Poland from a socialist to a market economy.

a. Europlex

The first map shows that prior to 1989 this was the site of a public park with a nearby movie theater. A mall, multiplex theater, and adjacent office building have since been constructed. (*Source:* Kreja, 2006.)

Before 1989

Today

b. Galeria Mokotów

Compare these maps to see the transformation of this former industrial site into a huge commercial complex. When first opened in 2000, this was one of the largest shopping centers in Poland. (*Source:* Kreja, 2006.)

Before 1989

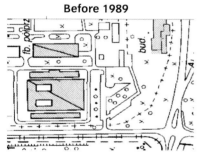

Today

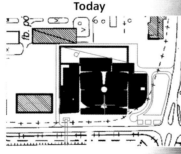

Think Critically

1. What happens to a bid-rent curve in a socialist city?
2. What are some implications of the changes captured in these photos and maps for public space?

Compared to cities in the West, retail and commercial land use in the socialist city was much more limited, but there were sizable plazas and parks for public use. Since the fall of communism, the urban landscapes in the former Soviet Union and eastern Europe have experienced major transformations, many of which are tied to globalization (see *What a Geographer Sees*).

Colonial cities The establishment of European colonies in Latin America, Southeast Asia, and Africa has had an enduring impact on the urban fabric of these regions. Depending on the needs of the colonizing power, colonial cities functioned as administrative, economic, and/or military centers. In some cases colonial cities were built near or even grafted onto an extant indigenous city or urban

Geography InSight

THE PLANNER

Accra, capital and largest city of Ghana, is a hybrid city. It has three central business districts (CBDs)—local, national, and global. Their development is linked to both historical and contemporary forces. (*Source:* Grant and Nijman, 2002.)

Makola Market

Thomas Cockrem/Alamy

Global Locator

AFRICA
GHANA
Accra

NATIONAL GEOGRAPHIC

Near Cantonments Road

Olivier Asselin/Alamy

c. Global CBD
- exhibits a ribbon-like configuration along certain major thoroughfares
- includes subsidiaries of foreign firms and headquarters of Ghanaian multinational firms
- has a growing concentration of shops and amenities for the well-to-do

a. Local CBD
- includes indigenous markets and small-scale retailing that serves a local clientele and adjacent residential areas
- has been a chief destination of rural migrants

Kwame Nkrumah Motorway

0   0.5   1.0 Mile
0   0.5   1.0 Kilometer

Achimota Road

Kotoka International Airport

Winneba Road

Global CBD

Ring Road Central

Independence Avenue

Kwame Nkrumah Ave.

Aboose-Okai Road

Ring Road West

Local CBD

Cantonments Road

Kinbu Road

Market St.

Labadi Road

National CBD

Gulf of Guinea

Supreme Court Building

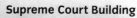

Eitan Simanor/Alamy

b. National CBD
- corresponds to the CBD established when Ghana was a British colony
- includes a mix of domestic and some older foreign firms as well as government functions

settlement. In other cases entirely new cities were built. Significantly, colonial cities were defined by social segregation, in which European residential and commercial districts were spatially separated from African market areas and residential districts.

Like all cities, however, these former colonial cities are constantly changing under the pressures of urban growth

hybrid city
A city that exhibits a mixture of indigenous, colonial, and globalizing influences.

and globalization. Consequently, some geographers now prefer the term **hybrid city**. A good example of a hybrid African city is Accra, Ghana (see **Figure 8.14**).

Islamic cities Is there such a thing as an Islamic city—one with an urban structure influenced by Islam? If we seek a specific type of city such that similar land-use patterns are replicated in all cities that were influenced by Islam, then the answer is no. In fact, many so-called Islamic cities have several features in common with the medieval cities of Europe: notably, a religious center (anchored by a cathedral in Europe and a mosque in Islamic cities), a central marketplace (called a *suq* in Islamic cities), residential quarters based on ethnicity or occupation, an irregular street pattern, and a surrounding defensive wall.

If, however, we shift our focus from form to process and acknowledge that Islam did (and still does) influence ideas about urban social relations, then we have a basis for identifying an Islamic city, though some urban experts prefer to speak of "traditional" Islamic cities. As an example, consider the *umma*, the global community of Muslims (see Chapter 5). An Islamic city is one that helps to link the local Muslim community with the international Muslim community. For example, geographer Michael Bonine (1990) has shown that some cities in Morocco are oriented according to the *qibla*, the sacred direction of Mecca. Another feature of some traditional Islamic cities that reveals the influence of Islam on social relations involves an emphasis on privacy and private space. This aspect has been expressed in the landscape through the construction of L-shaped entranceways, front doors that are offset rather than directly across from each other, and the absence of street-level windows (**Figure 8.15**).

Many of the cities in North Africa, the Middle East, Central Asia, and Indonesia bear evidence of the influence of Islam, but to identify an Islamic city requires that we consider how Islam shapes urban social relations. Thus, even though the design of the futuristic Masdar City, mentioned at the start of this chapter, will incorporate some

Islamic influence on the urban landscape • Figure 8.15

In Jeddah, Saudi Arabia, Islamic law places importance on maintaining visual privacy. Latticed balconies not only create private domestic spaces but also provide a kind of curtain such that women, who would be expected to be veiled when in public, can see out but cannot be seen by outsiders.

Julian Nieman/Alamy

elements of medieval urban form and is being built in a Muslim country, it would be premature to call it an Islamic city until we better understand how it works.

CONCEPT CHECK STOP

1. **How** is urban land use related to land value?

2. **How** do the models of North American cities account for the impact of transportation?

3. **How** and why has urban land use in eastern European cities changed since 1989?

4. **Why** might hybrid cities be considered an effect of globalization?

Urban Dynamics

LEARNING OBJECTIVES

1. **Distinguish** between redlining and blockbusting.
2. **Define** sprawl and explain how it is measured.
3. **Summarize** the process of slum formation.
4. **Identify** the main goals of new urbanism.

C ities are dynamic entities that change in response to the decisions made by individuals, groups, institutions, as well as circumstances brought about by nature. Previously, we discussed such topics as the importance of transportation to urban form and structure, and touched on the influence of social relations on urban space. Here we explore in greater detail additional causes and consequences of urban transformation, including residential change, urban redevelopment, and slum formation.

Public Policy and Residential Change

Certain public policies adopted by U.S. government agencies such as the Federal Housing Administration (FHA) and the Veterans' Administration (VA), as well as actions by realtors, have contributed to the decentralization of American cities and the transformation of residential areas. The FHA was created to revitalize home construction and to expand home ownership during the Depression when many Americans had defaulted on their loans and lost their homes because of bank foreclosures. The FHA developed a new loan program in which the federal government guaranteed the full value of home loans (mortgages). Such FHA-insured loans significantly reduced the risk to private banks and lenders on home loans and lowered down payments, making it possible for more people to purchase homes. In the 1940s similar loan programs were implemented by the VA and helped thousands of returning soldiers finance homes.

The FHA and the VA did not agree to back every home loan. Instead, the agencies adopted a rating system and used it to map and classify neighborhoods considered to be financial risks. Neighborhoods were given one of four grades, from best to hazardous. Those neighborhoods that appeared crowded, had older, deteriorating housing stock, were close to industrial or commercial areas, or were transitioning socially or economically received low grades on the assumption that the value of the property would decline. FHA neighborhood appraisers were specifically taught to "investigate areas surrounding the location to determine whether or not incompatible racial and social groups are present, to the end that an intelligent prediction may be made regarding the possibility or probability of the location being invaded by such groups" (*Federal Housing Administration*, 1936). The use of this discriminatory rating system became known as **redlining**.

FHA and VA loans also supported the purchase of freestanding homes on larger lots, not row houses. Thus, these policies sustained the construction of homes on city peripheries. According to urban historian Kenneth Jackson (1985), between 1930 and 1960 the city of St. Louis received one-fifth the number of FHA loans that suburbanizing St. Louis County received.

Segregation was simultaneously enforced through the actions of realtors, especially those who encouraged **blockbusting**. For example, realtors, who stood to profit on the sale of the affected properties, drew on racial prejudices to promote the perception among white residents that a "black invasion" of their neighborhood was underway and that property values in the neighborhood would decline. In some instances, all of the properties on a block were put up for sale as whites sought to leave the area. Blockbusting and redlining contributed to *white flight*, the departure of whites from downtown neighborhoods to the suburbs. For example, between 1930 and 1960 the population of St. Louis dropped from 822,000 to 750,000 (and to 318,000 today). Based on housing patterns, St. Louis had become one of the most segregated U.S. cities by 1980. These practices enforced a pattern of residential change and segregation that is often still visible today (**Figure 8.16**).

> **redlining** The biased practice of refusing to offer home loans in neighborhoods judged to be a financial risk without considering an individual's financial qualifications.

> **blockbusting** Using scare tactics and panic selling to promote the rapid transition of a neighborhood from one ethnic or racial group to another.

Urban Redevelopment

By the 1940s the tenements and apartments in many inner-city residential areas were aging and physically deteriorat-

Segregated St. Louis • Figure 8.16

The St. Louis metropolitan area crosses the Mississippi River and incorporates parts of neighboring Illinois. This maps show a portion of the metropolitan area, centered on the city of St. Louis (compare to locator map). Notice the separation of racial/ethnic groups at the census tract level. (*Source:* Data from U.S. Census Bureau.)

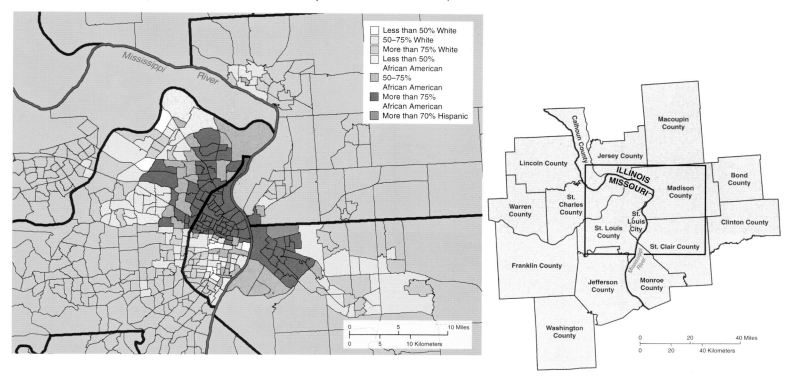

Legend:
- Less than 50% White
- 50–75% White
- More than 75% White
- Less than 50% African American
- 50–75% African American
- More than 75% African American
- More than 70% Hispanic

ing. To local city officials, the presence of this impaired and dilapidated housing stock was a form of urban blight. Local officials sought federal assistance in attempting to solve the problem of blight, and this set in motion a new kind of change referred to as **urban redevelopment**—the process of renovating an area of a city, often by completely destroying dilapidated structures and rebuilding on the site.

Using provisions in the Federal Housing Act of 1949, the government can take possession of city property that has

> **eminent domain**
> The authority of a government to take private property when doing so serves the public's interests.

been classified as "blighted." The procedure typically involves the use of **eminent domain**. When eminent domain is invoked, the government must pay the private owner the market value of the property. Blight removal is considered to serve the public by improving the quality of the housing stock. After the government obtains the rights to the property, the buildings or structures on it are bulldozed. The property can then be sold or leased to developers for the eventual construction of hospitals, hotels, stadiums, convention centers, and other facilities.

Urban redevelopment solved the problem of blight, but it created other problems in the process. Urban redevelopment displaced people and broke up long-standing neighborhoods. To counter these adverse effects, the government financed a number of public housing projects. In the 1950s and 1960s, inner-city public housing took the form of high-rise apartments. These apartments were initially celebrated as an innovative solution to the problem of blight but were soon heavily criticized. Elderly residents and families with young children have different needs, but these were not adequately considered in the design of this public housing, which reflected a "one size fits all" vision. In addition, they created pockets where poverty was concentrated. Because of their shortcomings, many of these multistory public housing projects have since been torn down and replaced with smaller multifamily housing units in a variety of styles for residents with a mix of different incomes.

Gentrification Blight removal was one strategy used to redevelop neighborhoods in the inner city. A different approach involves rehabilitating the structures instead of bulldozing them. **Gentrification** occurs when more

Before and after gentrification • Figure 8.17

Gentrification refashions the urban landscape in ways that are often visually and aesthetically appealing. But if we only focus on landscape change, such as that shown in these photos of Bricktown, Oklahoma City, we lose sight of the fact that gentrification can result in the displacement of lower-income individuals who can no longer afford to live in the gentrified districts.

Courtesy Greater Oklahoma City Chamber

Courtesy Greater Oklahoma City Chamber

affluent people purchase deteriorated buildings in low-income neighborhoods in order to restore or renovate them. Gentrification addresses the problem of blight and can act as a centralizing force by drawing middle-income residents and retail establishments catering to them, into the inner city. Those who favor a lifestyle different from that of the typical suburbanite—artists, do-it-yourselfers, gays and lesbians, and others—often help propel gentrification. The results of gentrification are hotly contested, however. Supporters of gentrification maintain that it raises property values, but opponents argue that gentrification is a form of economic exploitation of the urban poor (**Figure 8.17**).

For another look at how gentrification transforms urban space and competing perspectives about those changes, see *Video Explorations*.

Sprawl Like gentrification, sprawl is a process that transforms urban landscapes. **Sprawl** occurs when the rate at which land is urbanized greatly exceeds the rate of population growth in a given period of time. To urbanize land means to develop it for residential, commercial, or industrial purposes. Thus, sprawl rapidly extends the footprint of urban space and leads to low-density land use in the form of strip mall development, office parks, and single-family residential subdivisions. Sprawl is closely associated with the growth of *exurbs*, low-density residential developments built beyond suburbs and edge cities in rural areas (**Figure 8.18**).

Sprawl has a number of economic and environmental costs. It is costly because it results in uneven, checkerboard patterns of development. The costs of extending water, electricity, ambulance, and other services to these developments can be very high, particularly if all infrastructures must be newly built. Such costs are usually passed along to the public in the form of additional taxes to fund the development and to the homeowners, who pay higher prices for their homes and often higher rates on basic utilities.

Sprawl carries development beyond the areas that are served by public transportation. Because residential areas are often separated from commercial areas (refer again to Figure 8.18), sprawl contributes to a dependency on automo-

Video Explorations
Trastevere

National Geographic

Trastevere, a neighborhood in Rome, Italy, has undergone much recent development and change. Residents and local business owners comment on the changes.

Suburban sprawl in Phoenix • Figure 8.18

Tyrone Turner/© National Geographic Image Collection

A wide variety of economic, political, social, and geographic forces contribute to sprawl. These might include such things as rising household incomes, municipal decisions on the construc-tion of roads, population growth, and the presence of open, undeveloped land. Even divorce and the shift away from multi-generational households can affect sprawl.

biles. Moreover, sprawl, and the spread of urbanized land in general, increase the area covered by impervious surfaces. More asphalt and concrete surfaces speed water runoff and alter drainage patterns.

In the Sunbelt states of Arizona, California, Florida, and Nevada, high rates of in-migration from other parts of the country fueled rapid population growth in the early and mid-2000s, driving urban and exurban growth and sprawl. In Arizona, ranches have been sold for residential development. One effect of the collapse of the housing market in 2007–2008 was to stop sprawl, particularly in cities such as Las Vegas and Phoenix. A number of scholars anticipate a reversal in this trend as the housing market recovers. Sprawl has received a great deal of attention in the United States, but it can affect any city and raises important questions about how cities manage their growth. We will return to some of these issues in the section on urban planning, but first we need to examine the urban dynamics of poverty.

Urban Poverty and the Informal Sector

Urban poverty is a serious global problem. Broadly speaking, urban poverty is associated with four conditions: (1) increasing costs of basic necessities (food, water, electricity, transportation); (2) a widening gap between the money a person earns and the price of renting a dwelling; (3) joblessness or irregular employment; and (4) a failure to recognize the magnitude of urban poverty and/or the inability to allocate sufficient funds to address it.

In the United States, the geography of urban poverty has changed significantly since 2000. Until that time, urban poverty was concentrated in the central cities of the country's major metropolitan areas. Since 2000, the suburbanization of poverty has been underway. There are two primary reasons for this change. The first reason involves decentralization, including the ongoing relocation of people and businesses away from the urban core and into suburbs and edge cities. The second reason relates to economic challenges created by two recessions, beginning in 2001 and 2007, respectively, and the subsequent housing crisis. There are now more poor people in U.S. suburbs than central cities. Sunbelt and Midwestern cities have seen especially rapid growth in urban poverty. Nationwide, the number of poor people in the U.S. grew from 34 million to 46 million between 2000 and 2011.

The highest levels of urban poverty, as measured by the number and percentage of urban poor, exist in the developing world. There, the urban poor are highly visible in part because of the extensive **slums** or shantytowns that have grown up in and on the outskirts of the region's cities. Approximately 1.2 billion people live in slums. Asia has the greatest number of urban poor, more than 500 million, but Sub-Saharan Africa has the highest proportion of urban residents who live in slums—62%.

> **slum** An area of a city characterized by overcrowding, makeshift or dilapidated housing, and little or no access to basic infrastructure and services such as clean water and waste disposal.

Slum formation • Figure 8.19

Declining agricultural yields and/or environmental degradation
A Cambodian farmer

Thomas J. Abercrombie/NG Image Collection

Conflict and human displacement
Conflict migrants in Sri Lanka receive aid.

Pritt Veslind/NG Image Collection

Rapid urbanization remains closely associated with slum formation. Greater potential for slums to form exists when city governments have not planned for such rapid urbanization or lack the resources to do so. Slums provide a visual and spatial expression of differential access to resources and power. This diagram largely emphasizes slum formation in the developing world, but slums exist in developed countries as well.

① Preconditions — Migration into cities and/or urban population growth — **② Rapid urbanization** — Increased demand for housing, jobs, urban infrastructure

Employment Prospects
Migrant workers in China listen to a prospective employer and check the postings for jobs.

© epa european pressphoto agency b.v./Alamy

In a different sense, however, the urban poor are also highly invisible. High percentages of the urban poor, especially in the developing world, work in the informal sector or economy. The **informal sector** consists of the retail, manufacturing, and service activities that operate on a small scale and without government regulation or oversight. The informal sector is not taxed and is not measured or monitored in formal or official statistics kept by governments. The informal sector exists in part because the formal economy cannot provide employment for all of the city residents. Informal sectors operate in both developed and developing countries, but they are more pronounced in developing countries. Countless different jobs exist in the informal sector, but two examples include working as street vendors selling food or beverages and washing windshields of vehicles in city traffic.

Slums demonstrate the existence of an informal housing sector. Indeed, slums are a kind of *informal set-*

Favela Morumbi,
São Paulo, Brazil

Alexandre Meneghini/©AP/Wide World Photos

Maria Stenzel/NG Image Collection

3
Other factors
driving slum
formation

Crowding; rundown
or improvised housing
on undesirable or hazardous
land; lack of services
(clean water, sanitation)

4
Slum
formation

Inner-city slum, Camden, New Jersey

Michael Nichols/NG Image Collection

Makeshift dwellings in the Tanah Abang slum,
Jakarta, Indonesia

tlement in that they are unplanned and often develop as a result of transactions that do not follow procedures established by city or national governments. Not all slums are illegal, however. In fact, rental agreements and land tenure practices may be rooted in local customary law. Often different systems of land management coexist, and these different practices can complicate the ability to manage land use in and around a city, affecting slum development. When slums do develop illegally,

as for example when people build shelters on property without the consent of the landowner, they are more accurately termed *squatter settlements*. Slums and informal settlements more generally are referred to as *favelas* in Brazil, *gecedondus* in Turkey, and *kampungs* in Malaysia.

No single cause triggers the formation of slums. Rather, slum formation is the result of myriad factors including economic, social, and institutional decisions. To better understand slum formation, see **Figure 8.19**.

Slum alleviation According to a recent estimate, it would cost between $60 and $70 billion to upgrade the slum dwellings of 100 million people. Although this sounds like a lot of money, government officials know all too well that the continued existence of slums costs a city and country far more because slums incur significant social, political, and economic costs as well.

A failed approach to slum alleviation is eviction. Forcing people out of slums and destroying their dwellings never solves the problem of slum development. Rather, it simply displaces it. Thus, there is no simple solution for alleviating slums. There is, however, one approach to slum alleviation that has a consistently strong record of success: community-driven projects that involve slum dwellers as agents of change. One of the most successful of these projects creates community-managed savings groups for **microfinancing**. Community members are encouraged to save some money—no matter how little—every day. The savings are pooled and used to improve the conditions of their dwellings or neighborhood, sometimes with additional financial assistance from governmental and nongovernmental organizations (**Figure 8.20**).

> **microfinancing**
> Providing access to credit and other financial services for low-income individuals or groups.

Urban Planning

Slum alleviation and upgrading draw on the principles of urban planning, for urban planners seek to improve the physical and social conditions in towns and cities.

Women's savings group, India • Figure 8.20

Slum dwellers do not have the same access to lending and credit programs that higher-income individuals do. Obtaining credit can be additionally challenging for women because of discrimination. These women in Daspar slum, Kolkata, have benefited from microfinancing initiatives which, in turn, contribute to slum improvement projects.

Mukherjee/Demotix/Corbis

The scope of **urban planning** is broad and includes designing efficient systems of transportation, working with developers to coordinate housing construction in order to meet the needs of a city, providing facilities and open spaces for public use and recreation, and ensuring that different parts of a city are served by a safe water supply, schools, ambulance and fire service, and trash collection.

Many urban geographers pursue careers in planning, and those who do often work for local governments in city or county planning departments. Perhaps no other issue better illustrates the connection between planning and government functions than zoning. Planners use and recognize many different kinds of zoning, but three broad categories include zoning for residential, commercial, or industrial purposes. Zoning regulates the development of cities and this makes it an intensely political activity that sometimes pits homeowners against developers, or individual interests against the collective interests of corporations and local governments. How would you feel, for example, if a decision were made to change the zoning classification of a parcel of land near your home from residential to commercial so that a hotel or shopping center might be built? Planners are usually involved in both the development and enforcement of zoning codes.

The theory behind zoning today differs considerably from the zoning theory of just a few decades ago. In the past, zoning theory was guided by a greater emphasis on the creation of exclusive zones that permitted just one type of land use in a district. As a result, residential areas were completely separated from commercial and industrial areas. These areas were further partitioned so that, for example, in residential zones, apartment districts were separated from those with single-family houses. Critics have pointed out that exclusive zoning increased the need for and reliance on cars, and today zoning codes can more easily accommodate a mixture of land uses.

In the 1990s a new urban planning movement developed called neotraditional town planning or **new urbanism**. Proponents of new urbanism argue that too often urban planning has failed to consider the environmental impact of planning decisions, resulting in suburban sprawl, the loss of affordable housing, and the demise of cohesive urban neighborhoods. New urbanism has two main goals: to prevent sprawl and to create walkable neighborhoods.

A primary strategy used to achieve these goals involves **mixed-use development**—the combination of

New urbanist neighborhood, Celebration, Florida • Figure 8.21

At the neighborhood scale, three attributes of new urbanism are emphasized: compactness, walkability, and mixed-use development with diverse house styles. These are not the fronts but the backs of the houses. ▶ **How does situating the garage on a back alley promote walkability within a neighborhood?**

Preston Mack/Stringer/Getty Images News/Getty Image

different types of land use within a particular neighborhood. For example, retail land use can be integrated with residential land use and transportation corridors by including shops and grocery stores that are within walking distance. Other strategies include using smaller lot sizes for residences and clustered development on them. Instead of building on the entire lot, clustered development encourages use of just part of a lot (**Figure 8.21**).

CONCEPT CHECK STOP

1. **How** has public policy in the United States affected residential change?
2. **What** are some environmental costs of sprawl?
3. **How** does the informal sector relate to slums?
4. **What** approach to zoning does new urbanism promote?

✓ THE PLANNER

Summary

1 Cities and Urbanization 232

- Cities are concentrations of large numbers of people who earn their living through nonagricultural pursuits. Cities function as **central places** serving their **hinterlands** in a system of commercial exchange. **Functional complexity** is a defining characteristic of cities.

- **Central cities** are legally defined and bounded, and possess an identifiable **central business district (CBD)**. There is no standardized definition of the term *urban*; however, an **urbanized area** includes land converted to commercial, residential, or industrial uses. When **metropolitan areas** coalesce, a **megalopolis** can form.

- Two measures of **urbanization** include the **level of urbanization** and the **rate of urban growth**. Globally, higher levels of urbanization tend to be associated with higher levels of industrialization. The geography of **megacities**, however, illustrates the rapid rates of urbanization occurring in parts of the developing world. The development of **primate cities**, though not unknown in the developed world, is more commonly associated with developing countries.

- The concepts of **range** and **threshold** help explain the **urban hierarchy**. **Central place theory** advances the idea that market forces contribute to the development of an idealized lattice of central places, shown here.

Spatial arrangement of central places • Figure 8.7

● City ▲ Town ● Village

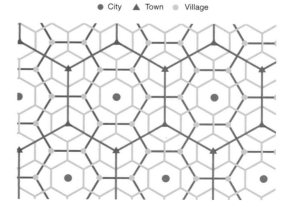

- The identification of **food deserts** and the emergence of **world cities** and **hinterworlds** highlight the complexities of the urban hierarchy.

2 Urban Structure 242

- The internal spatial organization of cities varies from one region of the world to another and is affected by **centralization, decentralization,** and **agglomeration**. Urban models and **bid-rent curves** help to visualize the **functional zonation** of cities.

- Several different models have been proposed to describe and explain the diverse forces that have helped structure the cities of North America. The **concentric zone model** and **sector model**, respectively, identify the processes of succession and **filtering** as key to understanding urban land-use patterns. Both models describe the land-use patterns in a city with a single CBD, in contrast to the **multiple nuclei model** and **urban realms model**. Changing transportation practices and the emergence of **edge cities** are two developments that have altered the spatial configuration of numerous cities.

- The geography of urban structure in cities outside of North America is just as complex. Western European cities have been shaped by a number of centralizing forces. Since 1989 the urban landscapes of eastern European cities have been dramatically transformed by capitalism and globalization, as shown here.

What a Geographer Sees: Spatial Imprints of Urban Consumption

Courtesy Karina Kreja

- Elsewhere, colonialism has influenced urban form, and many colonial cities are, in effect, **hybrid cities**. Throughout the Muslim world many cities bear the influence of Islam but in diverse ways. An orientation toward Mecca as well as design elements that reflect concern with private space and privacy are associated with traditional Islamic cities.

3 Urban Dynamics 250

- Cities are dynamic entities. Thus, understanding how and why they change remains essential to the work of urban geographers. Much recent change in American cities is related to policies that contributed to racially discriminatory practices including **redlining** and **blockbusting**.

- **Urban redevelopment** efforts target blight but also transform the look and socioeconomic makeup of cities. **Eminent domain** is a mechanism that facilitates urban redevelopment. **Gentrification** is a form of urban redevelopment that typically upgrades dilapidated buildings instead of razing them. Although gentrification may help counter the effects of **sprawl**, depicted here, gentrification has other social costs.

Suburban sprawl in Phoenix • Figure 8.18

Tyrone Turner/© NationalGeographic Image Collection

- Urban poverty is a serious global problem made spatially visible through the existence of **slums** but economically invisible through the operation of the **informal sector**. Understanding slum formation constitutes an important first step toward slum alleviation. **Microfinancing** has become an increasingly popular way for slum dwellers to plan and implement slum upgrading projects.

- **Urban planning** involves gauging the future needs of a city and developing ways to prepare for and accommodate them. Making decisions about **zoning** is one important aspect of urban planning. **New urbanism** challenges conventional zoning regulations and promotes **mixed-use developments** instead.

Key Terms

Critical and Creative Thinking Questions

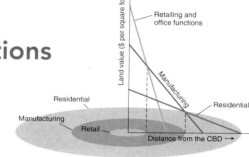

1. Select a city and do some fieldwork to evaluate the extent to which the concentric zone, sector, and multiple nuclei models apply. What other methods could you use to make this evaluation?

2. What informal economies exist in the United States?

3. Which cities have hosted the Olympics in the past five years? Ten years? Are cities that host the Olympics world cities? Explain and provide an assessment of the patterns you observe.

4. Watch the movie *Slumdog Millionaire* and evaluate its depiction of Mumbai's slums.

5. Should capitalism be considered a driver of slum formation? Explain your reasoning.

6. How can bid-rent theory, modeled here, help explain sprawl?

7. Watch *The End of Suburbia* (available on DVD). Evaluate its presentation of issues in urban geography.

8. What measures can be taken to reduce the social impact of gentrification?

9. Do you think that women and men experience cities differently, and can urban spaces be made to work well for all people? Why or why not?

What is happening in this picture?

Rickshaw pullers move through the streets of Kolkata, India. Rickshaw pullers provide an affordable means of transportation around the clock as well as year-round. Unlike cars and buses, rickshaw pullers can still navigate inundated streets during the monsoon rains. But city officials consider rickshaw pullers a reason for traffic congestion and have proposed banning them.

Think Critically
1. What does this photo suggest are some other causes of traffic congestion?
2. Could rickshaws be considered a sustainable form of urban transportation? Why or why not?

Self-Test

(Check your answers in Appendix B.)

1. Cities share all of the following characteristics *except* _____.
   a. functional complexity
   b. edge cities
   c. hinterlands
   d. accessibility

2. A city with 10 million or more inhabitants is a _____.
   a. metropolitan area
   b. megalopolis
   c. metroplex
   d. megacity

3. A significant aspect of the geography of megacities is that _____.
   a. they are increasingly associated with the developing world
   b. they are home to a majority of the world's people
   c. most of them are also world cities
   d. they originated in Asia and then spread to Europe and North America

4. A concept that helps explain why some small towns lack fast-food restaurants is _____.
   a. threshold
   b. range
   c. decentralization
   d. urban food deserts

5. Explain how this photo illustrates the concept of agglomeration.

   _____

   _____

   _____

Cotton Coulson/NG Image Collection

6. The development of edge cities is most closely associated with the _____ model.
   a. concentric zone
   b. urban realms
   c. sector
   d. multiple nuclei

7. _____ occurs when financial institutions grade urban areas on the quality of their housing or ethnic composition and use the ratings to refuse home loans.
   a. Blockbusting
   b. Urban redevelopment
   c. Redlining
   d. Eminent domain

8. These photos illustrate the process of _____.
   a. urban sprawl
   b. gentrification
   c. filtering
   d. zoning

Courtesy Greater Oklahoma City Chamber

Courtesy Greater Oklahoma City Chamber

9. From the end of World War II until 1989, probably the most significant factor shaping urban form in East European and Soviet cities was _____.

a. the development of large parks

b. state control of the urban land markets

c. the emphasis on manufacturing and industry

d. the absence of slums

10. What do American suburbs and colonial cities have in common?

a. large housing estates

b. similar patterns of industrial land use

c. a history of residential segregation

d. low levels of population growth

11. Identify at least three urban processes that have contributed to this scene.

_____

_____

_____

Tyrone Turner/© National Geographic Image Collection

12. Which statement about primate cities is FALSE?

a. Primate cities are unique to the developing world.

b. Primate cities are associated with uneven economic development.

c. Primate cities can exist at the national or state/provincial level within a country.

d. Primate cities may result from historical forces.

13. Some large cities are not world cities because of their _____.

a. language differences

b. remote location

c. political corruption

d. bid-rent curves

14. The term _____ conveys the idea that a city's influence may extend well beyond its formal boundaries.

a. urbanized area

b. megalopolis

c. megacity

d. metropolitan area

15. Of the following items, which one best explains the reason for hexagonal hinterlands in central place theory?

a. bid-rent curves

b. nearby central places of the same rank

c. land-use values

d. the assumption of a uniform surface

THE PLANNER ✓

Review your Chapter Planner on the chapter opener and check off your completed work.

Geographies of Development

BHUTAN'S QUEST FOR GROSS NATIONAL HAPPINESS

Imagine your own Shangri-la—that is, an idyllic place. What place on Earth, if any, comes closest to matching that? Did the country of Bhutan come to mind? Most likely it did not, although in recent years this small mountainous state nestled between India and China has occasionally been described as a Shangri-la. This designation has less to do with Bhutan's striving to be a perfect place and more to do with its physical setting and its ideology of development.

Until the early 1970s, Bhutan was among the world's most impoverished countries. Then, King Jigme Singye Wangchuck conceived a development strategy that would balance economic growth with environmental protection, Bhutanese cultural traditions, and democratic governance. He envisioned a path to development that, in his words, would bring "gross national happiness."

Bhutan has since invested heavily in education and health care. In the early 1980s, Bhutan had an adult literacy rate of 23% and an infant mortality rate of 163. Today, adult literacy approaches 60%, and infant mortality has dropped to 47. The accompanying photo shows traditional Bhutanese homes with solar panels.

Although Bhutan may not be a Shangri-la and still has room to improve the social well-being of its people, its example is instructive because it highlights a concerted effort to achieve development in a way that is environmentally sustainable and socially conscious.

This chapter covers different facets of development such as ways of measuring and mapping development and income inequality. It also introduces the major approaches that have shaped development efforts.

EyesWideOpen/Getty Images

CHAPTER PLANNER ✓

- ❑ Study the picture and read the opening story.
- ❑ Scan the Learning Objectives in each section:
  p. 264 ❑   p. 277 ❑   p. 282 ❑
- ❑ Read the text and study all figures and visuals. Answer any questions.

Analyze key features

- ❑ Geography InSight, p. 276
- ❑ Process Diagram, p. 283
- ❑ What a Geographer Sees, p. 288
- ❑ Video Explorations, p. 290
- ❑ Stop: Answer the Concept Checks before you go on:
  p. 277 ❑   p. 282 ❑   p. 290 ❑

End of chapter

- ❑ Review the Summary and Key Terms.
- ❑ Answer the Critical and Creative Thinking Questions.
- ❑ Answer What is happening in this picture?
- ❑ Complete the Self-Test and check your answers.

What Is Development?

LEARNING OBJECTIVES

1. **Explain** what development is.
2. **Distinguish** between development indicators and indexes.
3. **Contrast** the HDI, IHDI, and GII.
4. **Identify** geographic and institutional factors that can affect development.

One of the axioms of **development** is that, no matter how it is measured, it is geographically uneven. Human geographers study the differences in development from one place or region to another as well as the social and environmental consequences of development.

> **development**
> Processes that bring about changes in economic prosperity and the quality of life.

When comparing countries or regions on the basis of their levels of development, different terms and classifications are used including high-, middle-, and low-income countries, or more developed and less developed countries. The terms *First World* and *Third World* are problematic because they reinforce a view that less developed countries are intrinsically inferior. Today, most development practitioners use the terms *developed* and *developing*. These terms are not strictly defined, but general usage recognizes Australia, New Zealand, Japan, Europe, Canada, and the United States as developed. Although not entirely geographically accurate, the terms *Global North* and *Global South* also refer, respectively, to developed and developing regions. Similarly, the phrase *global North-South divide* expresses the imbalance in development that separates richer and poorer regions of the world.

The study of development is always a **normative** project. The term *normative* refers to the establishment of standards, or norms, to help measure the quality of life and economic prosperity of groups of people. Conventional views of development are strongly associated with normative ideas of progress, advancement, and social betterment. Consequently, *development* usually implies improvement in one or more of the following: a society's economic, social, or environmental conditions. Development experts recognize, however, that a gain in one area, such as economic growth, may have adverse consequences in another area, such as the environment. For this reason, whether development can be called an improvement depends on the situation.

The global economic system depends on human, financial, and natural resources. This raises questions about the relationship among the economy, development, and the environment. Broadly speaking, there are two perspectives on this: conventional and sustainable. *Conventional development* favors economic and social gains but gives scant attention to the impact of these gains on resource use, consumption, or the state of the environment. In contrast, *sustainable development* favors economic and social gains achieved in ways that do not compromise natural resources or the state of the environment for future generations.

These viewpoints aside, what are the conditions or indicators that social scientists and others use to measure or gauge development? They recognize different types of indicators and group them into the following three categories: economic, sociodemographic, and environmental. When two or more indicators are combined, the result is called an *index*. Whereas indexes are most often used for country-level or international data, indicators can also describe very small areas.

Economic Indicators

We can use many different **economic indicators** to gauge development, from levels of debt to trade imbalances to the kinds of consumer goods that people purchase. In this section, we focus on three of the most basic economic indicators: gross national income, gross domestic product per capita, and poverty.

The most common measure of economic development historically has been the **gross national income (GNI)**, formerly known as the gross national product. The GNI expresses the total monetary value of goods and services produced in a year by a country, whether those operations are located within the country or abroad. For example, if a Canadian company operates a plant in India, the profits that plant earns are counted in Canada's GNI. Similarly, the income earnings of Canadians living abroad are counted in the GNI for Canada. In contrast, the **gross domestic product (GDP)** expresses the total monetary value of goods and services produced *within* a country's geographic borders. In the previous example, the profits of the Canadian-owned plant operating in India would contribute to India's GDP.

Economic development • Figure 9.1

These images help visualize different levels of economic development at global, national, and local scales.

a. Gross national income per capita, globally
Many development agencies use the specific values shown in the map key to distinguish the most from the least economically developed countries. Note that the middle income category is subdivided into upper- and lower-middle income groups. (*Source:* Data from World Bank, 2013.)

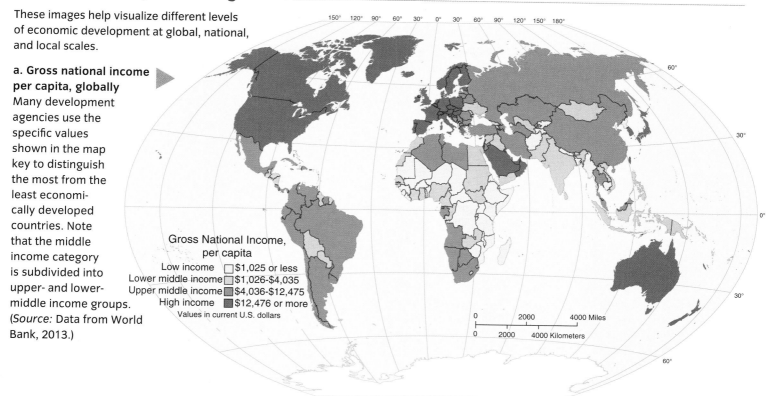

Gross National Income, per capita

Low income	$1,025 or less
Lower middle income	$1,026-$4,035
Upper middle income	$4,036-$12,475
High income	$12,476 or more

Values in current U.S. dollars

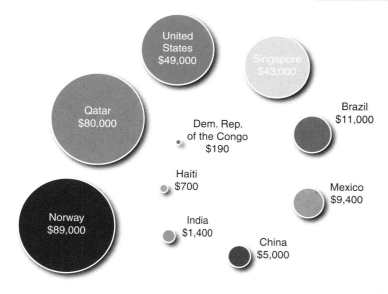

United States $49,000

Singapore $43,000

Qatar $80,000

Dem. Rep. of the Congo $190

Brazil $11,000

Haiti $700

Mexico $9,400

Norway $89,000

India $1,400

China $5,000

b. Gross national income per capita, by selected country
These proportional circles help compare the values for selected countries. (*Source:* Data from World Bank, 2013.)

Behrouz Mehri/AFP/Getty Images

c. Vehicles on a Pakistani highway
In general, car ownership increases as a country develops economically. In Pakistan, which has one of the lowest rates of car ownership in the world, one occasionally sees mule-drawn carts on the highway.

To express these data on a per person basis, we divide the GNI or GDP in a given year by the total population in the same year. This yields, respectively, the GNI per capita or GDP per capita. These values are useful for comparing countries that have different population sizes. Of these, the GNI per capita is regularly used to classify countries into low-, middle-, and high-income categories (**Figure 9.1**).

The GNI and GDP have long been used as measures of economic development. It is common practice to refer to the GDP when making claims about a country's overall wealth. However, it is important to recognize that both of these indicators have three significant limitations. First, these indicators only reflect the monetary value of official receipts generated by the formal economy. They do not capture the value of goods and services produced through the informal economy, a key dimension of the economies of developing countries (see Chapter 8). Second, neither the GDP nor GNI provides information on the evenness or unevenness of distribution of wealth within a country. Third, the GDP and GNI do not take into consideration the social or environmental

GDP per capita • Figure 9.2

These graphs show change in GDP per capita by region and for selected countries. More steeply sloped lines indicate a faster rate of growth or decline.

NATIONAL GEOGRAPHIC

a. Despite some declines, every region has experienced overall growth since 1980, and some regions have grown more rapidly than others. These data are reported in "constant 2005 international dollars" to show that they have been adjusted to remove distortions caused by inflation, using 2005 as a baseline year. (*Source:* Data from World Bank, 2013.)

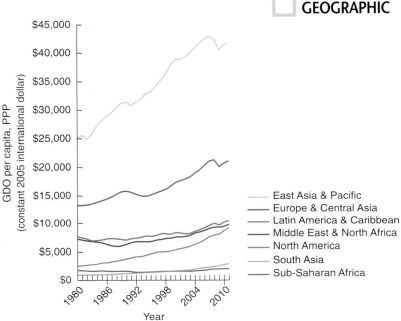

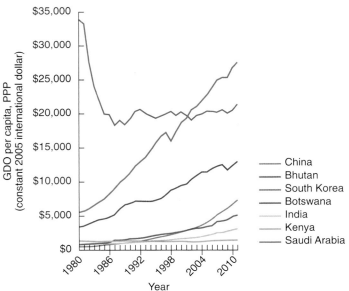

b. This graph records South Korea's phenomenal economic growth before and after the 1998 Asian financial crisis. It also shows the precipitous decline in Saudi Arabia triggered by an oil glut in the early 1980s. Bhutan (recall the chapter opener) and China have also experienced significant per capita GDP growth. (*Source:* Data from World Bank, 2013.)

Ask Yourself

1. What region experienced the sharpest decline in per capita GDP between 1980 and 1988?
2. What region has had the smallest growth in GDP per capita since 1980?

costs associated with the consumption of resources used in the production of the various goods and services. On the other hand, if we keep these limitations in mind, we can use GDP data to track economic growth or decline over time.

To facilitate international comparisons, it is common to show values in purchasing power parity. In its most basic form, **purchasing power parity (PPP)** is an exchange rate used to compare output, income, or prices among countries with different currencies. PPP is based on the idea that the price of a good or service in one country should equal the price of that same good or service in another country when it is converted to a common currency. PPP is merely a unit indicating that a bottle of water in Cairo is equivalent to a bottle of water in Paris, even though the local prices for bottled water may be substantially different. If you are wondering why PPPs are used instead of currency exchange rates, the answer is that currency exchange rates can fluctuate tremendously from day to day. When a value is expressed in PPP it may also be accompanied by the term "international dollar." This is just a way of indicating how much a U.S. dollar can buy in any other country. Look at **Figure 9.2** to see how GDP per capita has changed since the 1980s.

> **poverty** Insufficient income to purchase the basic necessities of food, clothing, and shelter.
>
> **poverty line** The specific income amount social scientists and others use to separate the poor from the nonpoor.
>
> **poverty rate** The percentage of the population below the poverty line.

Another issue related to development is **poverty**—an extremely complex phenomenon that rarely has a single cause. Poverty is both an economic and social condition because it affects income as well as other facets of well-being, such as education and health. There are several economic indicators of poverty, including the poverty line and the poverty rate. In the United States, the government identifies **poverty lines** for different household units. For example, in 2012, the poverty line for a family of four with two children under the age of 18 was $23,283. The **poverty rate** is the most common measure used to express the occurrence or incidence of poverty. The recession has increased poverty in the U.S. to levels not seen since the 1960s. Approximately 49 million Americans live in poverty, giving the United States a poverty rate of about 16%.

Because living standards and perceptions of poverty vary, individual countries often develop their own benchmarks for poverty. This practice makes comparisons of poverty among countries surprisingly difficult. In an attempt to solve this problem the World Bank, which provides financial and other forms of assistance to developing countries, has established two international poverty lines that distinguish between extreme poverty and moderate poverty: the $1.25/day (PPP) line and the $2/day (PPP) line, respectively.

Globally, 2.6 billion people live on less than $2 a day. Approximately 1.3 billion people live in extreme poverty. The geography of extreme poverty has changed since the 1980s. Significantly, the number of people living in extreme poverty dropped 36% between 1981 and 2008. Much of this success results from dramatic economic growth and rising prosperity in East Asia and the Pacific—specifically in China, where the poverty rate has dropped from 84% to 13%. For a depiction of the prevalence of extreme poverty, see **Figure 9.3** on the next page.

Sociodemographic Indicators

People are the most important resource a country has, as it is they who determine the use of the other resources—natural, manufactured, and creative. Thus, having a healthy, literate, and educated populace is an essential step toward successful development. **Sociodemographic indicators** provide information about the welfare of a population, including, for example, data on the prevalence of disease or the levels of literacy and education.

Sociodemographic indicators are complex and interrelated. For example, nutrition can impact health, which in turn, can affect the ability to work. Hunger and malnourishment are widespread issues that have the gravest consequences for children. Malnourishment affects nearly one-quarter of children under the age of five in developing countries. Other sociodemographic indicators include life expectancies and infant mortality rates (Chapter 3). Of the various sociodemographic indicators, infant mortality rates are considered the most telling

A geography of extreme poverty • Figure 9.3

This chart and the accompanying map provide a look at the changes in extreme poverty over time and its present distribution.

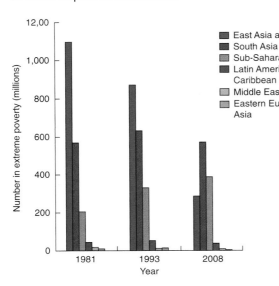

a. The greatest reductions in extreme poverty have come in East Asia, largely in conjunction with China's economic growth. In contrast, Sub-Saharan Africa has seen increases in extreme poverty. (*Source:* Data from World Bank, 2013).

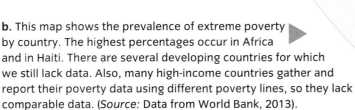

b. This map shows the prevalence of extreme poverty by country. The highest percentages occur in Africa and in Haiti. There are several developing countries for which we still lack data. Also, many high-income countries gather and report their poverty data using different poverty lines, so they lack comparable data. (*Source:* Data from World Bank, 2013).

Share of population living on less than $1.25 a day
- 50% or more
- 25.0–49.9%
- 10.0–24.9%
- 2.0–9.9%
- Less than 2.0%
- No data

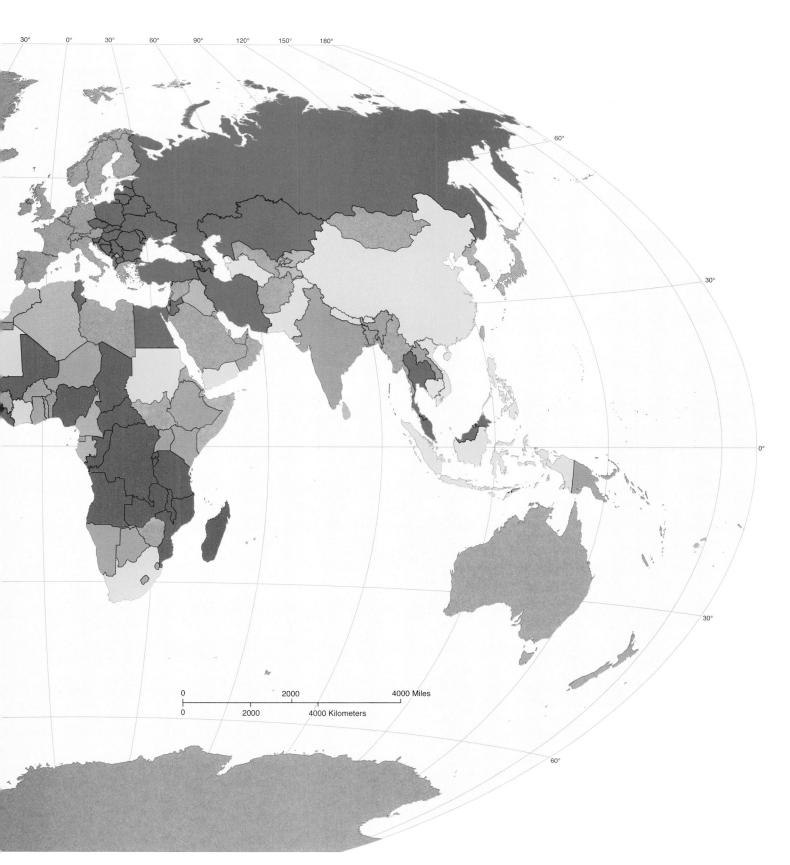

Infant mortality rates • Figure 9.4

Infant mortality rates and access to skilled health personnel are sociodemographic indicators.

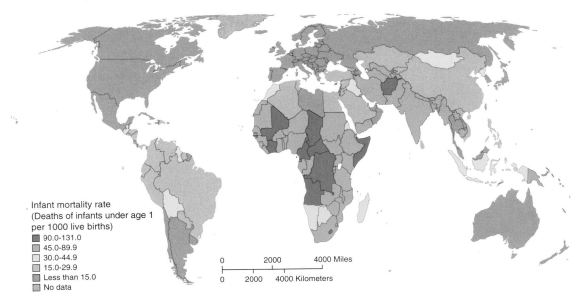

Infant mortality rate
(Deaths of infants under age 1
per 1000 live births)
- 90.0-131.0
- 45.0-89.9
- 30.0-44.9
- 15.0-29.9
- Less than 15.0
- No data

0   2000   4000 Miles

0   2000   4000 Kilometers

a. Infectious diseases and malnourishment rank as leading causes of high infant mortality rates but medical care before, during, and after the delivery of a child is also crucial.
▶ **How does this map compare to the one in Figure 9.1?** (*Source:* Data from Population Reference Bureau, 2011.)

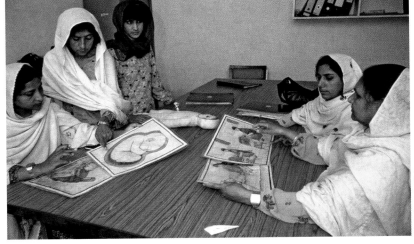

Neil Cooper/Alamy

b. Midwives in Indonesia receive training on resuscitating infants. Studies suggest that small measures, such as improved access to skilled midwives, can significantly reduce infant mortality rates.

because they so tragically highlight lost potential in a country's human resources (**Figure 9.4**).

Environmental Indicators

Compared to economic and sociodemographic indicators, the use of **environmental indicators** is a more recent phenomenon. Their development and use stem largely from the 1992 United Nations Conference on Environment and Development. Also known as the Earth Summit, this conference was held in Rio de Janeiro and grew out of widespread concern about the extent of global environmental problems, such as pollution and loss of biodiversity. The conference focused on making environmentally sustainable development a priority for all countries, rich and poor alike.

Agenda 21, the action plan that resulted from the Earth Summit, encouraged governments and other agencies to develop indicators that could be used to assess sustainable development. Since that time, hundreds of different indicators have been developed. Examples of environmental indicators include frequency of environmental hazards such as flooding, drought, and earthquakes; loss of biodiversity; and access to safe, potable water (**Figure 9.5**).

Development and Gender-Related Indexes

To what extent can the study of development be reduced to a consideration of one or more different indicators? Many development practitioners take the position that indicators alone are insufficient to gauge changes in development because development encompasses much more than just an increase in income, a rise in GDP per capita, or access to a safe water supply. Consequently, geographers and others are interested in combining a number of economic, sociodemographic, and environmental indicators in order to create development indexes. These indexes provide a broader, more inclusive

Access to clean water • Figure 9.5

Most Americans take for granted access to piped, safe water and do not think much about the source of it, but in parts of the developing world collection and consumption of untreated surface water is common.

National Geographic

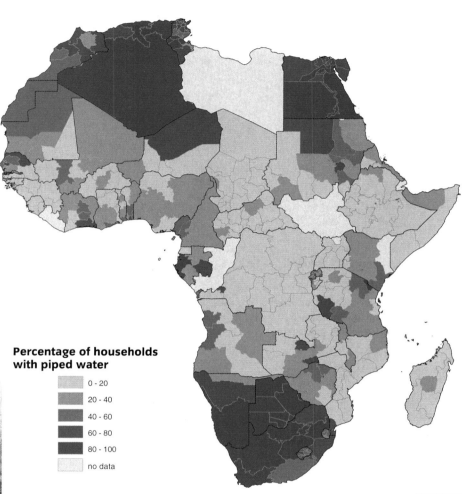

Percentage of households with piped water

- 0 - 20
- 20 - 40
- 40 - 60
- 60 - 80
- 80 - 100
- no data

Sources: Demographic and Health Surveys (DHS) and UNICEF Multiple Indicator Cluster Surveys (MICS)

CIESIN
Columbia University

a. Percentage of households with piped water in Africa
This map shows that there are numerous districts in Africa where most households lack piped water. (*Source:* CIESIN Columbia University, © 2006 The Trustees of Columbia University in the City of New York.)

b. The burden of water collection often falls to women and children, as shown here in Uganda. Consumption of untreated water is linked to diarrhea and other diseases.

What Is Development? 271

assessment of a country's development. No index is perfect or provides a universal solution to the complex issue of development. Rather, indexes serve as tools to help make decisions about human and environmental resource management. This section discusses three of these indexes: the human development index, the inequality-adjusted human development index, and the gender inequality index.

Created in 1990, the **human development index (HDI)** has since been adopted by the United Nations Development Programme (UNDP), the entity charged with measuring development worldwide and proposing strategies for improving it. Every year the UNDP produces the *Human Development Report*, a summary assessment of development in the world. In the words of Mahbub ul Haq, a Pakistani economist and one of the founders of UNDP:

> Human development is about . . . creating an environment in which people can develop their full potential and lead

productive, creative lives in accord with their needs and interests. People are the real wealth of nations. Development is thus about expanding the choices people have to lead lives that they value. And it is thus about much more than economic growth, which is only a means—if a very important one—of enlarging people's choices. (UNDP, *The Human Development Concept*)

The HDI was the first development measure to incorporate information about the standard of living, health, and education of a country's people in a single statistic. The HDI has evolved over the years. Until recently, the HDI was based on the GDP (PPP) per capita, life expectancy, the adult literacy rate, and the total enrollment in education as a percentage of the total school-age population. As a result of changes made in 2010, however, the HDI is now based on GNI (PPP), life expectancy, the average years of schooling for adults, and the expected years of schooling for children given present enrollment

Human development index • Figure 9.6

The HDI integrates country-based data about income, education, and life expectancy to generate a measurement of human development. The IHDI is the HDI adjusted to account for inequality, which exists in varying degrees in every country.

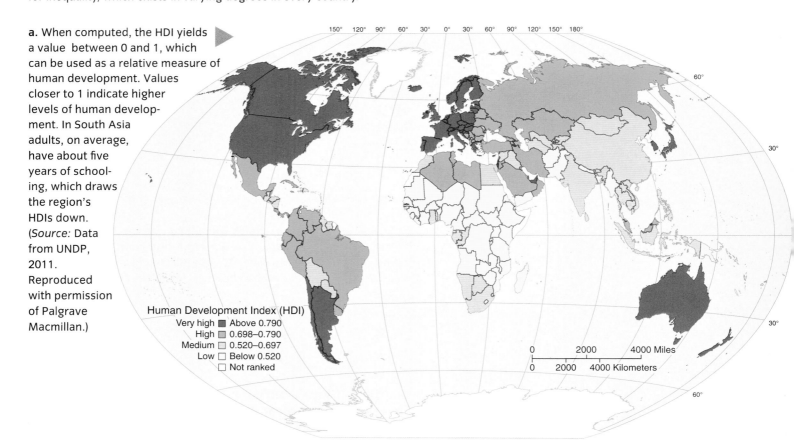

a. When computed, the HDI yields a value between 0 and 1, which can be used as a relative measure of human development. Values closer to 1 indicate higher levels of human development. In South Asia adults, on average, have about five years of schooling, which draws the region's HDIs down. (*Source:* Data from UNDP, 2011. Reproduced with permission of Palgrave Macmillan.)

Human Development Index (HDI)
Very high ■ Above 0.790
High ■ 0.698–0.790
Medium □ 0.520–0.697
Low □ Below 0.520
□ Not ranked

trends. Different factors prompted this change. In part because it includes remittances, GNI was considered more suitable than GDP. Also, significant increases in literacy rates worldwide mean that they are less useful for discerning differences in human development.

These changes are not the only ones that have helped improve the HDI. One significant criticism of the HDI has centered on its failure to account for inequality. This led to the creation of the **inequality-adjusted HDI (IHDI)**. The IHDI applies a reduction to the HDI based on the inequality of access to income, health care, and education. Thus, the IHDI may give a better indication of actual circumstances. **Figure 9.6** explains the HDI and IHDI in greater detail.

Prompted by the realization that development is not gender neutral—that the impacts of development affect women and men differently—the UNDP has called for the "engendering of development" since 1995. As stated in the *Human Development Report* for that year, "human development, if not engendered, is endangered." That is, if human development centers on improving and expanding people's choices, then the options, opportunities, and rights of women and men must be considered a crucial component of a society's overall development.

The UNDP has used a number of gender-related indexes over the years, but has recently introduced a new one, the **gender inequality index (GII)**. In effect, the GII combines aspects of earlier gender-related indexes. The need for the gender inequality index stems from two related issues. The first is that gender inequality deprives societies of the full potential of their people. The second is that women confront significant disadvantages, even discrimination, in areas such as education, employment, and medical care, as we discussed in Chapter 6. These disparities, or gender gaps, affect the qualities of women's lives, diminish their basic freedoms, and impair social and economic development. Thus, the GII provides a measure of inequalities that affect women.

Country	Human development index (HDI)	GNI per capita (in PPP)
Cuba	0.776	$5,400
Botswana	0.633	$13,000

b. A high GNI per capita does not necessarily correspond to a high HDI. In general, Cubans have high life expectancies, good access to education, and a government-financed health care system that provides coverage to all citizens. Despite its mineral resource wealth, Botswana has one of the lowest life expectancies of any country and low levels of education. (*Source:* Data from UNDP, 2011. Reproduced with permission of Palgrave Macmillan.)

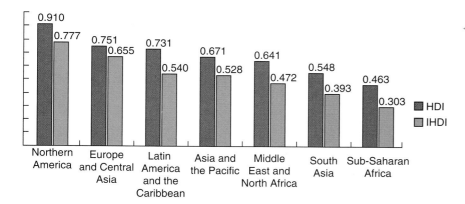

c. This chart compares the HDI and IHDI by world region. Equal values would indicate full equality. The closer the bars, the lower the inequality. (*Source:* Data from UNDP, 2011. Reproduced with permission of Palgrave Macmillan.)

Gender inequality index • Figure 9.7

The gender inequality index helps make international comparisons and see regional trends in gender disparity. These images explore the GII and some of the indicators on which it is based.

a. Values for the GII are mapped by country. In contrast to the HDI and IHDI, values closer to 1 indicate greater gender inequality. In Sub-Saharan Africa, very high maternal mortality and adolescent fertility rates plus low percentages of women with high school education contribute to high gender inequality. (*Source:* Data from UNDP, 2011. Reproduced with permission of Palgrave Macmillan.)

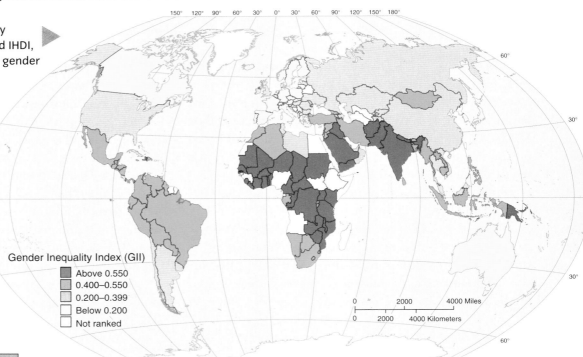

Country	Adolescent fertility rate
South Korea	2.3
Libya	3.2
Italy	6.7
China	8.4
Uzbekistan	13.8
Canada	14.0
Ireland	17.5
United Kingdom	29.6
United States	41.2
Egypt	46.6
Chile	58.3
Mexico	70.6
Ecuador	82.8
India	86.3
Honduras	93.1
Iraq	98.0
Nepal	103.4
Uganda	149.9
Angola	171.1
Niger	207.1

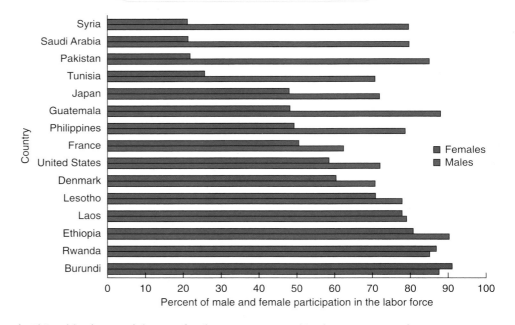

b. This table shows adolescent fertility rates for selected countries. These rates tend to echo marriage patterns. Even though age at marriage has risen, women tend to be younger than men at marriage and in rural parts of developing regions they often marry as adolescents. ▶ **How might adolescent fertility affect subsequent life choices?** (*Source:* Data from UNDP, 2011. Reproduced with permission of Palgrave Macmillan.)

c. This chart compares the percent of women and men in the labor force for different countries. In the East African countries of Rwanda and Burundi, the percentage of women in the labor force exceeds that of men. Across much of the Middle East and North Africa, women's participation in the labor force is very low. (*Source:* Data from UNDP, 2011. Reproduced with permission of Palgrave Macmillan.)

Like the HDI, the GII is derived from several different measures. These include level of education, participation in the labor force, share of seats held in national parliament, and two reproductive health-related components. One of these components is the adolescent fertility rate, defined as the number of births to adolescent women (aged 15–19) per 1000 adolescent women. Adolescent fertility is known to have higher risks and to strongly shape other decisions that women make about education and work. The second health component included in the GII is maternal mortality, or the ratio of maternal deaths to live births in a year, per 100,000 live births. Maternal mortality expresses the risks associated with pregnancy. **Figure 9.7** provides an overview of the GII. Also see *Where Geographers Click*.

Environment and Development

Thus far we have examined a variety of different indicators and indexes that help to measure development, but what causes these different levels of development? The 18th-century economist Adam Smith suggested that the physical geography of an area influenced its economic growth and development. Similarly, during the 19th and early 20th centuries, geographers who held environmentally deterministic views argued that geographic factors explained why some countries were economically advanced and others were not.

Today, however, one explanation is that differences in development are the result of many diverse and interconnected conditions that fall into two broad categories: geographic conditions and institutional conditions. Thus, a more complete understanding of the development experience of a country or region calls for a consideration of its

geographical endowment. Some significant components of a country's geographic endowment are shown in **Table 9.1**. In Sub-Saharan Africa, a combination of difficult or adverse conditions works to complicate the development process. For example, a number of countries are landlocked, have poor soils, and have a heavy disease burden associated with both malaria and HIV/AIDS.

Selected geographic conditions that may affect development Table 9.1	
Situational	Landlocked state Small, isolated island state Limited natural resource base
Transport	Distant from major markets Population distant from coasts or navigable rivers Large population living in mountainous areas
Agroclimatic	Low and/or highly variable rainfall Poor or depleted soils
Health/disease	High prevalence of tropical diseases High prevalence of HIV/AIDS
Disaster vulnerability	High susceptibility to natural disasters (e.g., hurricanes, earthquakes, floods) Large population living in disaster-vulnerable regions

Geography InSight

THE PLANNER

The Central American country of Costa Rica is a little smaller than the state of West Virginia and has a population of 4.7 million. In the early 1980s, it was a poor and heavily indebted country. Today, it ranks among the countries with a high HDI. Although not the only contributing factor, tourism oriented around the country's unique biodiversity played an important role in transforming the country's development and making a name for Costa Rica as a tourism destination.

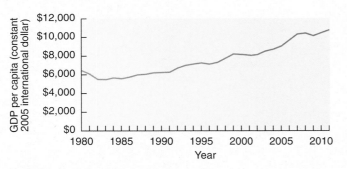

Global Locator

COSTA RICA

NATIONAL GEOGRAPHIC

a. This chart shows the change in GDP per capita since 1980. Estimates suggest that tourism contributes about 7% to Costa Rica's GDP. (*Source:* Data from World Bank, 2013.)

Costa Rica at a glance	
GNI per capita	$14,500
International tourists per year	2,196,000
Tourist receipts	$2,009,000,000
Tourist receipts as a percent of export earnings	23%
Land area protected (park or conservation area)	25%

Think Critically

1. Can mass tourism contribute to sustainable development?
2. What are some other ways that tourism can benefit or hinder development?

b. This table shows that Costa Rica is a middle-income country where tourist receipts make up the equivalent of nearly one-quarter of its exports. Situated between the Caribbean Sea and Pacific Ocean, Costa Rica possesses great biodiversity.

Danita Delimont/Alamy

c. Tourists walk across a bridge in a Costa Rican rainforest. Tourism—including ecotourism—contributes to development by generating foreign exchange, increasing income, and providing jobs that are directly and indirectly related to tourism. At ecotourist sites, a portion of visitor fees are used for conservation efforts.

d. These cruise ships are docked in Costa Rica. Mass tourism may generate more foreign exchange, but it also increases leakage, the loss of profit to foreign entities such as tour operators or resort developers, and has a greater environmental impact.

Geographic conditions, however, are just one part of the development picture. Institutional conditions also have a bearing on development. For example, authoritarian rule can stifle debate about human and environmental well-being, and corruption can result in mismanagement of financial or natural resources. Similarly, discrimination against ethnic or minority groups can marginalize or entirely exclude them from access to public services, such as education or health care. We should realize that linkages also exist between geographic and institutional conditions. In some cases, the development process itself can lead to increased vulnerability to natural disasters. Rapid urbanization, for example, can lead to the construction of housing developments on unstable slopes or in floodplains.

On the other hand, many developing countries are increasingly turning to tourism as a strategy to promote their unique geographic endowment and improve social and economic development in the process. In some cases countries have specifically promoted ecotourism—tourism that supports environmental conservation and minimally affects the environment. Just how does tourism contribute to development, and what impacts does it have on the environment? We can begin to answer these questions by considering the example of Costa Rica (**Figure 9.8**).

CONCEPT CHECK STOP

1. **Why** is development a normative project?
2. **What** is the difference between GNI and GDP?
3. **What** indicators are used to generate the HDI?
4. **What** is a situational condition that may affect development?

Development and Income Inequality

LEARNING OBJECTIVES

1. **Distinguish** between income distribution and income inequality.
2. **Describe** techniques for measuring and mapping income inequality.
3. **Identify** factors that can affect income distribution.
4. **Summarize** opposing views on the relationship between globalization and income inequality.

H ave you ever thought about how income is distributed among the employees of a company or between men and women? Did you know that in the United States a woman earns just 77 cents for every dollar earned by a man? Unless income is equally distributed, there is a gap between those who earn more and those who earn less. We have already explored some dimensions of the geography of poverty, but tracking **income distribution** and **income inequality** is also important. Although it is possible to use the average income of a country to get an overall picture of the presence or absence of poverty, information about income distribution and income inequality is more revealing because this kind of data shows the share of the income held by the richest and poorest groups.

income distribution How income is divided among different groups or individuals.

income inequality A ratio of the earnings of the richest to the earnings of the poorest.

Development geographers examine income distribution and income inequality at different scales and between different clusters of countries. The **Organisation for Economic Co-operation and Development (OECD)** is one such cluster. Established in 1961, the OECD was created to enhance development by promoting economic growth and improving the standard of living of its member

Thirty countries belong to the OECD. With a few exceptions, such as Mexico and Turkey, OECD members are very wealthy, industrialized countries. Thus, the OECD is sometimes called the "rich country club of the world." ▶ **How does the planned**

expansion of OECD membership challenge the global North–South divide mentioned at the start of the chapter? (*Source:* Data from OECD, 2008.)

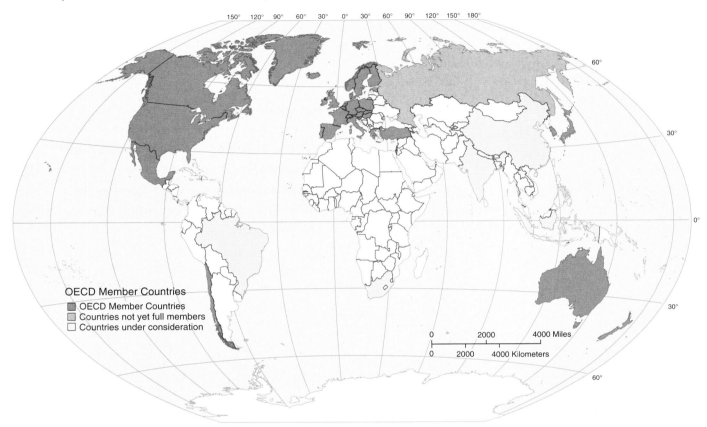

OECD Member Countries
- ■ OECD Member Countries
- ▨ Countries not yet full members
- □ Countries under consideration

countries. Since that time, its mission has expanded to include financial and other forms of assistance for developing countries that are not OECD members (**Figure 9.9**).

The Gap Between the Rich and the Poor

At the global scale, income inequality is very high. One of the most comprehensive studies of income distribution to date shows the concentration of large shares of income among the elites who form a minority of the population. This phenomenon has a *champagne-glass effect* on the pattern of income distribution (**Figure 9.10**).

Is income inequality increasing or decreasing? No clear consensus exists within the research community about these trends, in part because there is considerable variation in the quality and availability of the data to

measure this and also because it depends on the period of time as well as the countries being examined. Studies of eastern and central Europe show that income inequality increased by more than 40% between 1970 and 2000. The transition from communism to capitalism helps explain this increase.

In the United States there is also evidence that income inequality has been rising. The Occupy Wall Street movement, which lasted from September 2011 to February 2012, grew in part as a protest against the role of the U.S. financial industry in the 2008 economic crisis, corporate greed, and increasing economic inequality. The slogan, "we are the 99%" that the movement adopted was specifically a reference to the gap between the very rich 1% of the population and everyone else. The release of a report by the nonpartisan Congressional Budget Office in October 2011 on the distribution

Global income inequality • Figure 9.10

This series of graphs examines income distribution and inequality first at the global scale and then at the regional scale. Household surveys conducted by the various countries, usually as a part of their population census, provide the data on income.

a. This chart depicts the distribution of income in five classes, from the richest to the poorest, of the world's people. In 2007, the most recent year for which comparable data exist, the richest 20% of the world's population held 70% of the income in the world. Conversely, the poorest 20% held a mere 2% of global income, creating the champagne-glass effect. (*Source:* Adapted from UNDP, 2005, Fig. 1.16, p. 37.)

b. The widest gap exists in Africa, but sizable divides separate the richest and poorest groups in the various world regions and the OECD. Income inequality is powerfully captured through juxtapositions, such as that shown in this photo of a homeless man, his belongings in tow, in front of the U.S. Treasury Department. (*Source:* Data from Dikhanov, 2005.)

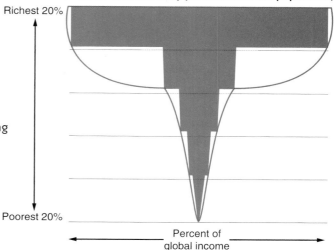

World income distributed by percentiles of the population, 2000

Richest 20%

Poorest 20%

Percent of global income

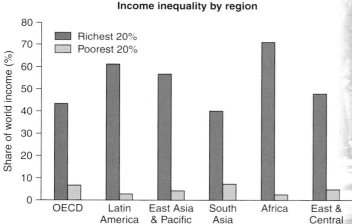

Income inequality by region

- Richest 20%
- Poorest 20%

Share of world income (%): OECD, Latin America, East Asia & Pacific, South Asia, Africa, East & Central Europe

Marcy Nighswander/©AP/Wide World Photos

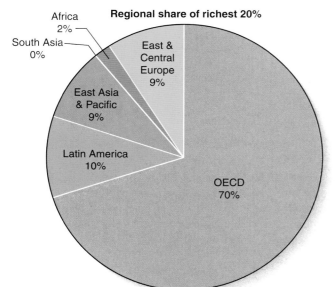

Regional share of richest 20%

- Africa 2%
- South Asia 0%
- East & Central Europe 9%
- East Asia & Pacific 9%
- Latin America 10%
- OECD 70%

c. No other group of countries in the world has such a large share of the global income as the OECD countries do. For every $100 held by the richest 20% of the world's population, $70 of those are in OECD countries; $28 are split among the regions of Latin America, East Asia and the Pacific, and eastern and central Europe; and $2 are in Africa. (*Source:* Data from Dikhanov, 2005.)

of household income gave momentum to the Occupy Wall Street movement. The first page of this report stated that, "For the 1 percent of the population with the highest income, average real after-tax household income grew by 275% between 1979 and 2007" (Congressional Budget Office, 2011). However, no other income group experienced an increase of more than 65% in the same time period, and the poorest saw their household income increase by just 18%.

Globally, one fact about income distribution remains clear: there are a few very, very wealthy individuals but several billion people who live in poverty. According to one analysis, the incomes of the 500 richest people in the world exceed the incomes of 400 million others. For some, this is evidence enough that we should be concerned about the patterns of income inequality.

When geographers measure income inequality, one statistic they often use is the Gini coefficient. Values for the Gini coefficient range between 0 and 100; the closer to 0, the more equally income is distributed, and the closer to 100, the more unequally income is distributed. The lowest Gini coefficients recorded in the world are 24.7 and 24.9, for Denmark and Japan, respectively. For the world as a whole, the Gini coefficient is 67. The United States has a Gini coefficient of 40.8, Brazil's is 59.3, and Namibia's is 70.7. This latter figure indicates that there is greater income inequality within Namibia than there is in the world. In fact, the richest 20% in Namibia hold nearly 80% of the country's income. On this basis, Namibia proves the exception rather than the rule because globally the trend is that greater income inequality exists between countries rather than within them. **Figure 9.11** explains how Gini coefficients are derived and shows their global variation.

Factors Affecting Income Distribution

There is no consensus on the causes of income inequality. What analysts do agree on is that multiple, often interrelated factors affect the equality or inequality of income distribution. The factors affecting income distribution can be grouped into four categories: individual, social, policy-related, and historical. Broadly speaking, what all of these factors have in common is that they contribute to

Measuring and mapping income inequality • Figure 9.11

The Gini coefficient helps compare income inequality among countries. Because the Gini coefficient is derived from Lorenz curves, we discuss them first.

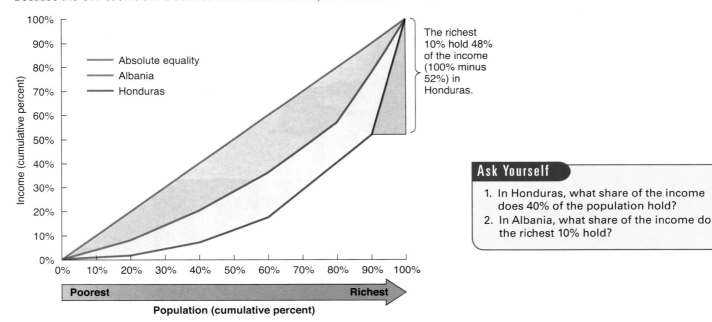

The richest 10% hold 48% of the income (100% minus 52%) in Honduras.

Ask Yourself

1. In Honduras, what share of the income does 40% of the population hold?
2. In Albania, what share of the income do the richest 10% hold?

a. Lorenz curves disclose income inequality within countries
Economist Max Lorenz developed this method to show the relationship between a country's income and population, broken into deciles (groups of 10%). The red curve is a baseline showing an idealized equal-income distribution (10% of the people have 10% of the income, 50% of the people have 50% of the income, etc.). The other curves graph examples for two countries. The "lower" a country's Lorenz curve, the more unequal its income distribution. Thus, Honduras has greater income inequality than Albania. (*Source:* Data from World Bank, 2013.)

circumstances that affect the ability of people to earn or to save money.

Individual factors that affect income distribution include the skills and abilities each one of us possesses as well as the attitudes we have about work and leisure. *Social factors* refer to conditions or circumstances within society at large that introduce different kinds of pressures. For example, the social pressure to be successful can affect the distribution of income. Even within different kinds of employment, the social expectations related to work can vary tremendously. The age of a country's work force is also an important social factor.

Policy-related factors are numerous and often reveal the priorities of a particular country or society. These include policies affecting taxation, international trade, labor, immigration, and education. Some scholars point to the decline in unionism as one factor associated with an increase in income inequality in the United States. *Historical factors* are often closely connected with social and policy-related factors and include events that have had a significant impact on the structure of a country's society and economy. Slavery, colonization, warfare, and internal unrest are some examples of

historical factors that can affect income distribution. There is considerable income inequality in Latin America, a region long affected by both slavery and colonization. In Brazil, for example, the richest 10% of the population holds almost half of the income while the poorest 10% holds less than 1% of the income.

Globalization and Income Distribution

Many geographers and others are asking questions about the impact of globalization on the distribution of income. To what extent has globalization been the world's great equalizer? There are two very different schools of thought on this: a trickle-down theory and the theory of the widening gap between the rich and the poor.

Proponents of the trickle-down theory of globalization argue that income convergence or equality follows trade. Historically, they point to the convergence in incomes between the United States and Europe that occurred in the late 19th century as trade expanded. In other words, trade is essential because it leads to specialization, increased

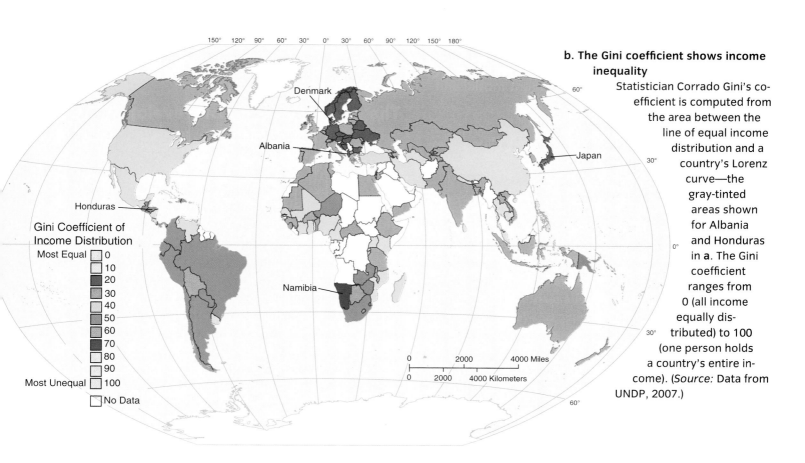

b. The Gini coefficient shows income inequality

Statistician Corrado Gini's coefficient is computed from the area between the line of equal income distribution and a country's Lorenz curve—the gray-tinted areas shown for Albania and Honduras in **a**. The Gini coefficient ranges from 0 (all income equally distributed) to 100 (one person holds a country's entire income). (*Source:* Data from UNDP, 2007.)

Gini Coefficient of Income Distribution

Most Equal ☐ 0
☐ 10
☐ 20
☐ 30
☐ 40
☐ 50
☐ 60
☐ 70
☐ 80
☐ 90
Most Unequal ☐ 100
☐ No Data

competition, and rising prosperity. For these trickle-down effects to occur, barriers to trade need to be removed.

In contrast, proponents of the theory of the widening gap between the rich and the poor argue that globalization works against a level playing field. Instead, it creates a higher demand for skilled workers, placing a premium on those with a college education or graduate degree. The more skilled the labor force, the higher the earning potential of that labor force. Those who lack the skills and education are more likely to find themselves left behind, unable to gain access to or compete for jobs. In some circumstances, globalization can create unemployment, which in turn, affects the distribution of income.

No matter which school of thought you subscribe to, the degree of income inequality in a country can have a number of serious consequences for development. First, income inequality is associated with a higher incidence of poverty, which in turn, can deter investment and development. Second, income inequality can exacerbate tensions between the rich and the poor, upsetting the political and social stability of a country. This unrest can derail economic growth and development. Third, and perhaps most importantly, when high income inequality coincides with unemployment, countries squander valuable human resources that could be used for the betterment of the society and economy.

CONCEPT CHECK

1. **What** does the phrase *champagne-glass effect* mean in the context of income distribution?
2. **What** does a Lorenz curve show?
3. **What** factors have affected income inequality in Latin America?
4. **Which** perspective on the relationship between globalization and income inequality was part of the ideology of the Occupy Wall Street movement?

Development Theory

LEARNING OBJECTIVES

1. **Contrast** the classical development model and dependency theory.
2. **Summarize** world-system theory.
3. **Explain** the relationship between neoliberalism and structural adjustment.
4. **Identify** four principles that have shaped poverty-reduction theory.

Anyone who studies the geography of development quickly realizes that the opportunities an individual has in life are very strongly tied to the level of development and the distribution of income within the country in which he or she is born and raised. Simply stated, someone born in a Sub-Saharan African country today is more likely to live in extreme poverty, to live a shorter life, and to be less educated than someone born in a country in another part of the world. This reality challenges development practitioners to think about ways of raising standards of living around the world and improving the quality of life. In this section, we examine some of the different theories and models of development.

The Classical Model of Development

In 1960, the economic historian Walt W. Rostow proposed a five-stage model of development—also known as Rostow's Stages of Development—that is now considered to be the **classical model of development**. Rostow placed a heavy emphasis on economic growth, which he considered to be a direct product of the structure of a country's economy. In other words, less developed countries had agricultural economies and, as development occurred, the structure of the economy changed to emphasize manufacturing and then service industries, such as health care and education. The stimulus for economic growth, in his view, was investment (**Figure 9.12**).

Rostow's model has suffered three major criticisms. First, the model assumes that every country begins the process of development from the same starting point. But has Peru, for example, faced the same conditions as the United Kingdom? Critics note that Rostow's model does

Classical model of development • Figure 9.12

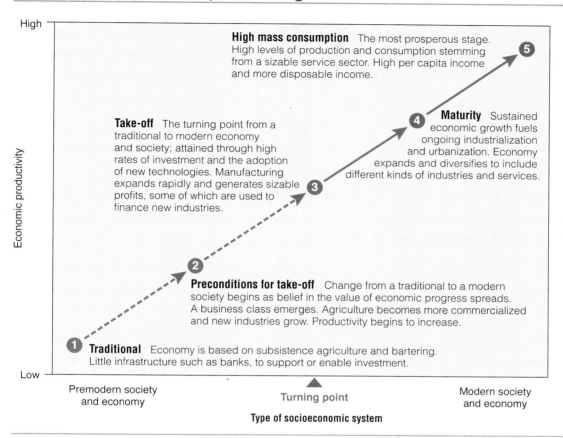

Rostow envisioned five stages of development that would transform a country with a traditional or premodern socioeconomic system into one with a highly modern society and economy. Rostow set forth these ideas in his book titled, *The Stages of Economic Growth: A Non-Communist Manifesto.*

not effectively account for such economic differences. A second criticism of Rostow's model is that it works from a very narrow understanding of development with a singular focus on a pattern of linear economic growth. The model fails to consider that receipt of monetary aid from another country might stimulate economic growth in the short term but can also result in high levels of debt that stifle economic growth over the long term. Finally, the third major criticism of the model is that it is strongly Eurocentric in the way it envisions that development will yield a technologically advanced and modernized Western society. Moreover, Rostow's model assumes that what worked for the West will necessarily work for non-Western countries as well.

Dependency Theory

Rostow's Stages of Development were so controversial that several alternative theories of development were proposed. In the 1960s and 1970s, a school of thought known as **dependency theory** gained prominence.

Dependency theorists argued that development might be better understood as a relational process rather than a series of stages, and that this process was linked to international trade.

Studying the system of international trade revealed the existence of two kinds of states: dominant and dependent. *Dominant states* are the most developed countries—the industrialized states of Europe, North America, and Japan—that command the economic resources and power to shape the policies and practices of international trade. *Dependent states* lack these economic resources and power. They represent the developing countries.

Dependency is, therefore, a condition that stems from patterns of international trade and results in underdevelopment, or low levels of development. According to dependency theorists, for example, the development of Europe resulted in the dependency and underdevelopment of Africa and Latin America. Contrary to Rostow's model, as Europe grew more developed and richer, development in Africa and

Latin America was stymied. Dependency theorists argue that imperialism played a crucial role in this process because it helped shape a pattern of international relations built on a system of domination and dependency. Some dependency theorists argue that today's multinational corporations also create dependency (**Figure 9.13**). Dependency theory has also been heavily criticized for encouraging a simplistic view of international relations, for neglecting to consider the role of local politics and social classes in shaping development, and for treating dependency as a natural outcome of international relations.

World-System Theory

For some development experts, **world-system theory** provides a more theoretically informed body of ideas explaining dependency and underdevelopment. World-system theory has its origins in the work of sociologist Immanuel Wallerstein and his book, *The Modern World-System*, the first volume of which was published in 1974. Unlike the early dependency theorists, who saw the international system of trade as the cause of underdevelopment, Wallerstein argued that the capitalist world-system caused dependency and underdevelopment. There was not a First World or Third World in Wallerstein's view; rather there was one world connected by and through the network of capitalism—in effect, a world economy. This is what he meant by the term *world-system*. Wallerstein traced the emergence of the capitalist world-system to 16th century Europe and argued that during the 20th century the system became fully global, with capitalist markets reaching and integrating all parts of the world.

According to world-system theory, the operation of capitalism gives rise to a specific kind of international division of labor that, in turn, creates a geographic hierarchy of interdependent states or regions. Wallerstein's world-system consisted of core states, semiperipheral areas, and peripheral areas. The term *international division of labor* refers to the assignment of different tasks of production to different regions of the world. For example, Wallerstein showed that *core states* are militarily strong, share a highly-skilled labor force, and possess a diversified economy based on a system of production that relies on high inputs of capital per person. In contrast, *peripheral regions* possess a less-skilled labor force and a more labor-intensive system of production. Peripheral regions tend to be colonies rather than full-fledged states (or have a history as a colony), are politically weak, and usually lack diversified economies. Positioned in between core and periphery are the *semiperipheral regions*, which have some capital-intensive manufacturing and economic diversification. They are likely to be core states that are in decline or once peripheral regions that are now on the rise (**Figure 9.14**).

Dependency theory • Figure 9.13

Dependency can develop through imperial dominance or financial–technological dominance.

Imperial dependency

Defense ← **Dominant states** → Manufacture of finished goods

Trade in merchandise

Exports

Military protection

Timber • Ores • Cotton

Resource exports

Merchandise imports

Dependent states

- Failure to diversify economy
- External relations dominate economic and military affairs

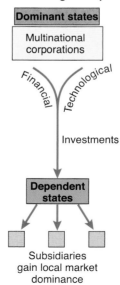

Financial–technological dependency

Dominant states

Multinational corporations

Financial — Technological

Investments

Dependent states

Subsidiaries gain local market dominance

- Failure to diversify economy
- Inability to compete with multinational dominance

The world-system then and now • Figure 9.14

Wallerstein's world-system consisted of a core, semiperiphery, periphery, and external arenas.

a. This map shows the world-system in 1900, following his descriptions. The external arenas represented the most isolated places, detached from the workings of capitalism but likely to become part of the periphery as capitalism expanded. (*Source:* NG Maps.)

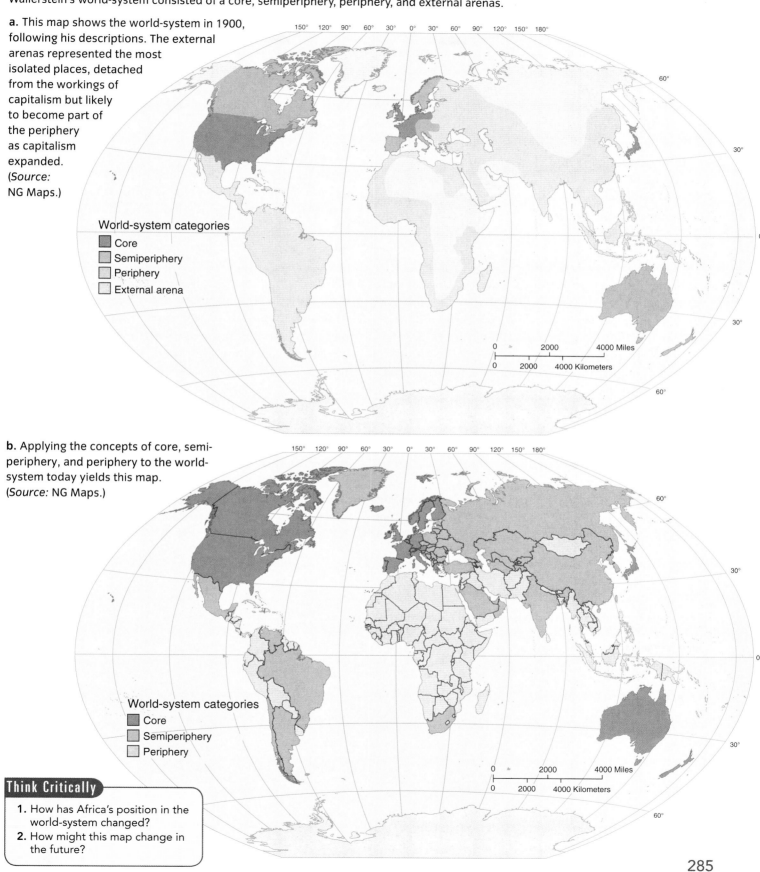

World-system categories
- Core
- Semiperiphery
- Periphery
- External arena

b. Applying the concepts of core, semiperiphery, and periphery to the world-system today yields this map. (*Source:* NG Maps.)

World-system categories
- Core
- Semiperiphery
- Periphery

Think Critically

1. How has Africa's position in the world-system changed?
2. How might this map change in the future?

Wallerstein argued that the operation of capitalism creates a system of unequal exchange in which core states dominate the semiperiphery and periphery, and semiperipheral areas dominate the periphery. Core states profit tremendously from this relationship, accumulating more capital and more wealth. Some of this capital is used to finance the development of new technologies that reinforce the competitive advantage of core states. World-system theory recognizes that the relations between the core, periphery, and semiperiphery are always dynamic but that the efficient operation of capitalism demands and depends upon the existence of spatial variation in the labor force and specifically an international division of labor.

The Neoliberal Model of Development

By the end of the 1970s, Rostow's Stages of Development model had been dismissed and world-system theory had come under fire by some critics for its Marxist-influenced critique of capitalism. In the 1980s, many development experts turned to an alternative paradigm, or school of thought, that was strongly anchored to the idea that capitalism could in fact drive development, rather than underdevelopment, as long as appropriate reforms were implemented to allow economic competition and free markets to flourish. This theory of development is called *neoliberalism* or the *neoliberal model of development*.

Liberalism refers to a political and economic theory associated with the thought and writings of people such as Jean-Jacques Rousseau, Thomas Jefferson, and Adam Smith. Liberalism promotes political equality through the development of laws and rights that are universally applicable. It emphasizes the protection of human rights, property rights, and individual freedom. Economically, liberalism favors a free, unregulated market and the removal of barriers to the movement of goods, services, and capital. The term **neoliberalism** refers to the revival and application of the theory of liberalism during the late 20th century.

Structural adjustment programs From a neoliberal standpoint then, the causes of underdevelopment did not stem from flaws with capitalism, as world-system theorists argued. Rather, underdevelopment was an indication that poorly conceived political and economic policies were impeding the efficient operation of capitalism and preventing economic growth. Thus, underdevelopment could be solved with **structural adjustment programs (SAPs)**. That is, the economies of developing countries needed to be completely overhauled—to have their economic structure adjusted—following the principles of neoliberalism. The actual process of structural adjustment involves many economic changes, but these can be grouped into two broad categories: market reforms and deregulation. Some specific examples of mechanisms to bring about structural adjustment are listed in **Table 9.2**.

> **structural adjustment program (SAP)** A country-specific economic policy based on neoliberal principles intended to promote economic growth and development.

Economic reforms associated with structural adjustment Table 9.2	
Market reforms	**Deregulation**
Reduce budget deficits and inflation	Reduce role of state in economic affairs
Meet debt-payment schedule	Privatize state-owned enterprises
Promote exports	Reduce government spending on public services
Reduce tariffs	Liberalize labor laws
Devalue currency	Liberalize foreign investment regulations

Structural adjustment programs became the cornerstone of the neoliberal development model during the 1980s and 1990s, and they influenced the policies of the International Monetary Fund (IMF) and the World Bank. These international financial institutions are independent agencies within the United Nations system. IMF programs help countries avoid financial crises and develop sufficient exports to pay for imported goods. A main function of the World Bank is to foster long-term development by providing loans or other technical assistance to developing countries.

By the end of the 1980s, SAPs accounted for nearly one-quarter of loans provided by the World Bank. Within another decade, SAPs had been developed or implemented in almost every developing country. Many observers agree that SAPs helped to curb the high rates of inflation and reduce the budget deficits in a number of countries. Others take the position that neoliberalism in general and structural adjustment in particular caused more harm than good because they have adversely affected the poorest individuals.

Criticisms of structural adjustment Since the early 1980s, both neoliberalism and structural adjustment have been heavily criticized. Much of this criticism has centered on the following five points. First, because SAPs call for reduced government spending and cuts in public services, health care systems are often negatively impacted. Clinics that receive government funding may be forced to reduce their hours, lay off personnel, or stop providing certain services. Alternatively, without government funding these facilities may be forced to charge user fees for certain services, making it even more difficult for the poorest individuals to afford health care. Second, and related to the previous point, SAPs encourage the removal of agricultural subsidies as another way of reducing government spending. Usually the removal of subsidies raises the price of foodstuffs, with the most severe consequences for those who are most impoverished.

A third criticism of SAPs is that they often recommend the devaluation of the local currency. One of the effects of currency devaluation is to raise the price of all imported goods, whether it is medicine, equipment, or consumer goods. Fourth, SAPs promote the development of exports. Thus, developing countries often fall back on the troublesome pattern of exporting an agricultural or mineral commodity instead of diversifying their economies. Fifth, SAPs are a form of external involvement by the World Bank and IMF in the internal affairs of states. Specifically, the World Bank and IMF used various criteria (e.g., currency devaluation) as conditions that had to be met before either institution would provide aid or loans. Joseph Stiglitz, the former chief economist at the World Bank, has become one of the leading critics of structural adjustment.

Poverty-Reduction Theory and Millennium Development

For many development experts, structural adjustment and neoliberalism were too narrowly focused on economic growth and did not give enough consideration to improvements in the quality of people's lives. Would the 21st century be another century marked by extensive poverty? The sheer number of people living in extreme poverty worldwide and the prospect that most of the population growth in coming years will be in developing countries prompted yet another paradigm shift in development theory. Since 1999, **poverty-reduction theory** has been the focal point of present development theory, particularly as advanced by the World Bank and IMF. Small area mapping has become an important tool geographers use for reducing poverty (see *What a Geographer Sees* on the next page).

poverty-reduction theory A development theory focused specifically on lowering the incidence of poverty in a developing country.

Poverty-reduction strategies have often been developed in concert with the Millennium Development Goals. The *Millennium Development Goals* (MDGs) were conceived in September 2000 when the leaders of the countries that are members of the United Nations convened the Millennium Summit in New York City. At this meeting, they recognized that every country shares the responsibility of helping attain economic and social development, and that the United Nations must play a fundamental role in this process. As a step in that direction, the United Nations adopted eight MDGs and

WHAT A GEOGRAPHER SEES

Poverty Mapping

Poverty is etched in both landscapes and statistics. It is also highly variable from place to place, so understanding its spatial distribution at various scales helps governments and aid organizations to manage it. Madagascar is a good example, as Earth's fourth-largest island (see locator map) and one of its poorest countries.

1. Population and terrain of Madagascar

Outside of urban areas, some of the highest population densities occur in the highland regions. (*Source:* NG Maps.)

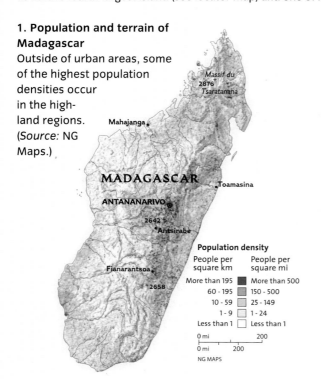

Population density

People per square km	People per square mi
More than 195	More than 500
60 - 195	150 - 500
10 - 59	25 - 149
1 - 9	1 - 24
Less than 1	Less than 1

0 mi   200
0 mi   200
NG MAPS

2. Distribution of Madagascar's poverty

Poverty can be expressed in consumption patterns, such as spending. This lets geographers use census data and household-expenditure surveys to create *small area estimation maps* that reveal poverty at administrative or municipal scales. The maps here show Madagascar's poverty at three scales—provincial, district, and commune.

2a. Madagascar's poverty mapped at the provincial level

Poverty ranges from 33% to 82%, and in every province, the highest poverty rates are in rural areas. (*Source:* Paternostro *et al.*, 2001. Permission granted by World Bank Publications.)

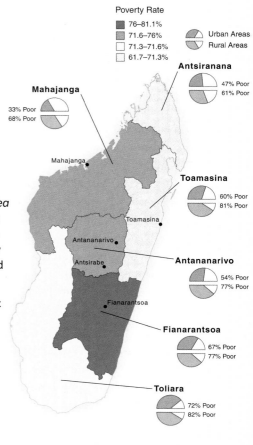

Poverty Rate

76–81.1%
71.6–76%
71.3–71.6%
61.7–71.3%

Urban Areas
Rural Areas

Antsiranana
47% Poor
61% Poor

Mahajanga
33% Poor
68% Poor

Toamasina
60% Poor
81% Poor

Antananarivo
54% Poor
77% Poor

Fianarantsoa
67% Poor
77% Poor

Toliara
72% Poor
82% Poor

3.
Rural poverty stems from factors such as low agricultural yields, and is compounded by water availability. Compare this map to the population density map to see that some of the most densely settled areas also have low water availability. Compare this map to the map in **2a** to see that water availability is lowest in Toliara, the province with the highest rural poverty. (*Source:* NG Maps.)

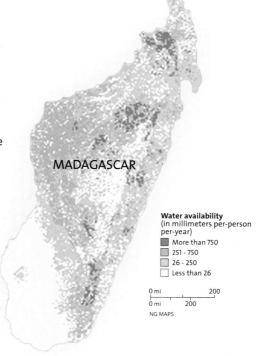

Water availability
(in millimeters per-person per-year)

More than 750
251 - 750
26 - 250
Less than 26

0 mi   200
0 mi   200
NG MAPS

2b. Madagascar's poverty mapped at the district level
The island's poverty rate is 70%, and districts are colored to show whether they are above or below that rate. Compare the patterns on this map to the patterns on map **2a**.

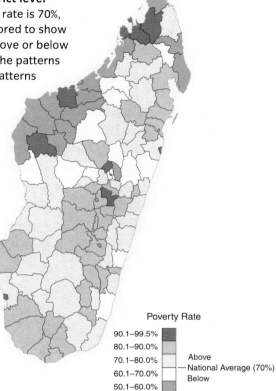

2c. Madagascar's poverty mapped at the commune level
This map details the spatial variation of poverty that is not visible at larger scales. The circled area shows that a high-poverty commune can be nearly surrounded by communes having lower poverty rates—a pocket of poverty that could be missed if relief administrators rely on data mapped at provincial or district scales. District boundaries are shown for comparative purposes. (*Source:* Mistiaen *et al.*, 2002. Permission granted by World Bank Publications.)

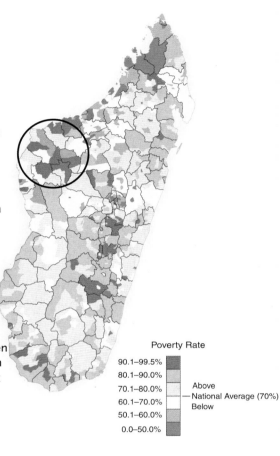

Poverty Rate
90.1–99.5%
80.1–90.0%
70.1–80.0%
60.1–70.0%
50.1–60.0%
0.0–50.0%

Above
— National Average (70%)
Below

Poverty Rate
90.1–99.5%
80.1–90.0%
70.1–80.0%
60.1–70.0%
50.1–60.0%
0.0–50.0%

Above
— National Average (70%)
Below

Global Locator

AFRICA

MADAGASCAR

NATIONAL GEOGRAPHIC

3a. Most rural Madagascar households cultivate wet rice, requiring a reliable water supply.

3b. Deforestation and soil erosion, in addition to long distances to markets and a poor transportation network, create additional economic challenges.

IFAD Photo by Robert Grossman

IFAD Photo by Horst Wagner

Think Critically

1. What different geographies of poverty do the maps in **2** present?
2. How does the geography of poverty vary by scale?

identified the year 2015 as the target date for achieving them. They aim to:

1. Eradicate extreme poverty and hunger;
2. Achieve universal primary education;
3. Promote gender equality and empower women;
4. Reduce child mortality;
5. Improve maternal health;
6. Combat HIV/AIDS, malaria, and other diseases;
7. Ensure environmental sustainability;
8. Create a global partnership for development,

Each of the MDGs consist of several more specific sub-targets. For example, a specific sub-target in the area of poverty is to cut in half the number living in extreme poverty. As noted earlier, the substantial reductions of poverty in East Asia mean that this sub-target was met in 2010, well before the planned deadline.

Poverty reduction is fundamental to achieving the MDGs. The theory of poverty reduction grows out of four key principles of development. The first principle is that because poverty is a complex, multifaceted problem, reducing poverty requires a comprehensive approach—one that balances concern for economic growth with improvements in social and environmental well-being. The second principle is that both the action plan for poverty reduction and the desired goals need to come from the developing country instead of being imposed by external institutions. The third principle follows from the first two in that successful strategies for development require effective partnerships between domestic and external agencies. Lastly, the fourth principle is that in order to be sustainable, development and poverty reduction demand a long-term perspective.

Albania became one of the first countries to link its poverty-reduction strategy to the MDGs. The country has already met its goal to cut poverty in half but is struggling to reduce unemployment levels. We should note that Albanian development experts have also been tracking personal perceptions of poverty as a way of more fully understanding the nature of the poverty problem. Compared to other countries, Albanians are more likely to avoid paying income tax, which adversely impacts government revenue. However, simply raising the tax rate or increasing the penalties on tax evasion may not be the best approach to building such confidence. Recognizing and understanding unique local circumstances such as this are important parts of

Video Explorations

Solar Cooking

Karyn D. Ellis, courtesy Solar Cookers International, www.solarcookers.org

A stove powered by the Sun is making a big difference in impoverished communities. Solar stoves are a great energy saver, providing an alternative to traditional fuels. Solar Cookers International, a Californian nonprofit, supports this technology that could save the lives of women and children around the world. The group trains families to use this simple stove and use it as a sustainable way to purify water using a wax-based gauge called a *wabi*.

poverty-reduction theory. Of course, large institutions such as the World Bank and IMF are not the only ones involved in poverty reduction and human development. Indeed, many nonprofit organizations play an important role too, especially through their efforts at the local level. As an example, see *Video Explorations*.

CONCEPT CHECK STOP

1. **Why** has the classical model of development been criticized?
2. **What** makes world-system theory a geographic theory?
3. **What** kinds of reforms are associated with structural adjustment programs?
4. **How** is poverty-reduction theory different from neoliberalism?

Summary

1 What Is Development? 264

- **Development** refers to processes that bring about changes in economic and social well-being with the goals of improving peoples lives and ending **poverty** and deprivation. Development is **normative** because it involves setting standards and measuring achievements compared to those standards.

- Many different indicators are used to measure development and these indicators are commonly grouped into three categories: economic, sociodemographic, and environmental. Common **economic indicators** include the **gross national income (GNI)**, **gross domestic product (GDP)**, **poverty lines**, and **poverty rates**. **Sociodemographic indicators** provide information about the welfare of a population. **Environmental indicators** provide a means to assess sustainable development.

- Development indexes are created by combining several indicators into a single measure. The **human development index (HDI)**, mapped here, incorporates information on the wealth, health, and education of a population. Discounting the HDI to account for inequality yields the **inequality-adjusted human development index** (IHDI).

Human development index • Figure 9.6

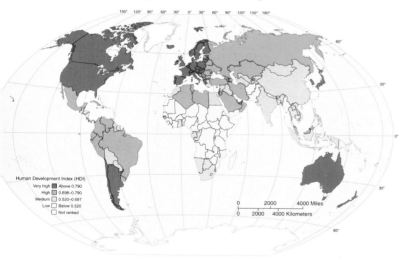

- The **gender inequality index (GII)** is based on indicators relating to women's reproductive health, political participation, and participation in the labor force. No country has full gender equality, but persistent gender disparities not only affect women's health and well-being, they also impede social and economic development.

- One important difference between an indicator and an index is that indicators can be used for very small areas but indexes are typically used with country-level or international data. Indicators and indexes also point to the ways in which geographic and institutional conditions can impact development.

2 Development and Income Inequality 277

- The study of development necessarily involves examining the spatial variation in poverty with techniques such as poverty mapping. It also raises important questions about **income distribution** within a population and **income inequality**, or the extent of the gap between the rich and the poor.

- Geographers frequently use Lorenz curves, shown here, and Gini coefficients to assess income distribution and income inequality. Individual, social, policy-related, and historical factors can affect the distribution of income.

Measuring and mapping income inequality • Figure 9.11

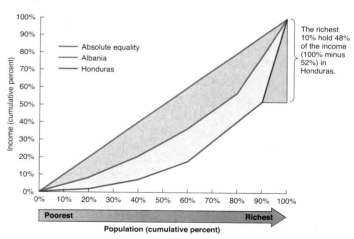

- Views on the effect that globalization has on income distribution fall mainly into two camps: the trickle-down theory of globalization and the theory of the widening gap between the rich and the poor.

3 Development Theory 282

- Development theory has been strongly shaped by five main models. Rostow's Stages of Development has become the **classical model of development**. **Dependency theory** focuses on development as a relational process rather than a series of stages. Wallerstein's **world-system theory** highlights the influence capitalism has on the emergence of global core-periphery patterns, and uneven development (see map).

- The neoliberal model of development emphasizes economic growth through **structural adjustment.** The intellectual roots of **neoliberalism** derive from the theory of **liberalism**, which promotes free trade and unregulated markets. Today, a dominant approach to development applies **poverty-reduction theory** to achieve the Millennium Development Goals.

The world-system then and now • Figure 9.14

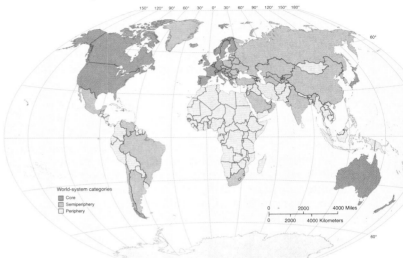

Key Terms

- classical model of development 282
- dependency 283
- dependency theory 283
- development 264
- economic indicator 264
- environmental indicator 270
- gender inequality index (GII) 273
- gross domestic product (GDP) 264
- gross national income (GNI) 264

- human development index (HDI) 272
- income distribution 277
- income inequality 277
- inequality-adjusted HDI (IHDI) 273
- liberalism 286
- neoliberalism 286
- normative 264
- Organisation for Economic Co-operation and Development (OECD) 277

- poverty 267
- poverty line 267
- poverty rate 267
- poverty-reduction theory 287
- purchasing power parity (PPP) 267
- sociodemographic indicator 267
- structural adjustment program (SAP) 286
- world-system theory 284

Critical and Creative Thinking Questions

1. Do the people and governments of developed countries have a moral and financial obligation to improve the life chances of people in developing countries? Explain your thinking.

2. In 1969, the Commission on International Development recommended that developed countries should commit 0.7% of their GNI to foreign aid by 1975. Few countries have done this. The United States contributes about 0.2% of its GNI to foreign aid. Although the United States contributes more money to foreign aid than any other country, as a proportion of its GNI, the aid disbursed is still very low. Should the United States raise its contribution to meet the goal of 0.7% of its GNI? Defend your position.

3. What are some advantages and disadvantages of a country providing foreign aid to another?

4. A nongovernmental organization (NGO) is a nonprofit organization providing humanitarian assistance and development work around the world. CARE and Oxfam are two examples of NGOs. Do some research to establish how they are similar and different from one another.

5. Review the theories about development. To what extent do they reflect either "top-down" or "bottom-up" approaches to development and why is that significant?

6. Choose two of the low-income countries from the map in Figure 9.1 and contrast them using the criteria in Table 9.1, shown here. Provide specific data to illustrate the contrasts.

Selected geographic conditions that may affect development   Table 9.1

Situational	Landlocked state Small, isolated island state Limited natural resource base
Transport	Distant from major markets Population distant from coasts or navigable rivers Large population living in mountainous areas
Agroclimatic	Low and/or highly variable rainfall Poor or depleted soils
Health disease	High prevalence of tropical diseases High prevalence of HIV/AIDS
Disaster vulnerability	High susceptibility to natural disasters (e.g., hurricanes, earthquakes, floods) Large population living in disaster-vulnerable regions

7. Using data from the U. S. Census Bureau website, work with a classmate to construct a Lorenz curve for your state and then interpret the curve.

8. Working individually and using data from the U.S. Census Bureau or your state's website, find or compute the poverty rate for your state. How does it compare to the national poverty rate? Using what you learned about location quotients in Chapter 6, can you calculate a location quotient for your state using the poverty data?

What is happening in this picture?

In Rajasthan, India, a sign points the way to public toilets and shows that women are charged a fee to use them but men are not. Keep in mind that census results show that more than half of the households in India do not have toilets, making reliance on public toilets all the more urgent.

Bernd Jonkmanns/laif/Redux

Think Critically

1. What does the availability of toilets, public or private, have to do with development?
2. Is development a right or a need?

Self-Test

(Check your answers in Appendix B.)

1. The global North-South divide refers to _____.

   a. the separation between conventional versus sustainable development perspectives

   b. the separation between liberal and neoliberal development initiatives

   c. the separation between developed and developing countries and regions

   d. the separation between regions of poverty and extreme poverty

2. The difference between the GNI and GDP is that _____.

   a. the GNI cannot be calculated per capita

   b. the GNI includes the value of goods produced abroad

   c. the GNI is limited to the value of goods produced within a country's borders

   d. the GNI provides information about the value of goods produced in the informal sector

3. An example of a sociodemographic indicator is the _____.

   a. infant mortality rate

   b. poverty rate

   c. vulnerability to drought

   d. poverty line

4. Which of the following statements about poverty is *false*?

   a. Every country may have a slightly different poverty line.

   b. The poverty rate tells us how far below the poverty line a country's poor are.

   c. Extreme poverty has been reduced in East Asia and the Pacific since the 1980s.

   d. There are different economic indicators of poverty.

5. An important reason for creating and using the GII was _____.

   a. to be able to penalize countries for poor performance on them

   b. the realization that men often earn more than women

   c. to be able to reward countries for strong performance on them

   d. the realization that development does not always proceed in gender-neutral ways

6. The example of Costa Rica shows ___.

   a. that tourism can contribute to development

   b. the applications of poverty mapping

   c. the impact of neoliberalism

   d. the example of an environmental indicator

7. Environmental indicators _____.

   a. were part of the first development index, the HDI

   b. can be used to measure pollution but probably not access to clean water

   c. reflect the growing concern for assessing sustainable development

   d. always include data on two or more environmental problems or concerns

8. As discussed in the chapter, factors affecting development can be grouped into two broad categories. What are they?

   a. indexes and indicators

   b. conventional and sustainable

   c. historical and individual

   d. geographic and institutional

9. The OECD _____.

   a. is a branch of the World Bank

   b. still reflects the global North-South divide through its membership

   c. is an international organization that aids developing countries

   d. has no notable income inequality on the part of its members

10. This chart shows that _____.

    a. the richest 20% of the world's people hold most of the world's income

    b. the share of income held by the poorest 20% of the world's people is increasing

    c. globally, income levels are rising rapidly

    d. none of the above

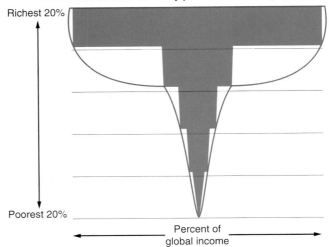

World income distributed by percentiles of the population, 2000

Richest 20%

Poorest 20%

Percent of global income

11. A _____ curve, shown here, helps visualize the relationship between a country's income and population.

    a. Gini

    b. normative

    c. dependency

    d. Lorenz

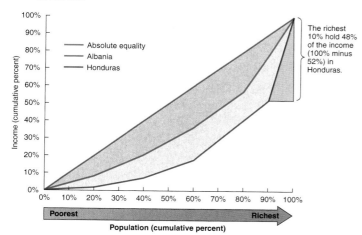

12. Which of the following is *least* likely to affect income distribution?

    a. peer pressure to be successful

    b. individual credit ratings

    c. the age of a workforce

    d. tax laws

13. According to the classical model of development, illustrated in this diagram, the turning point coincides with which stage?

    a. take-off

    b. maturity

    c. preconditions for take-off

    d. high mass consumption

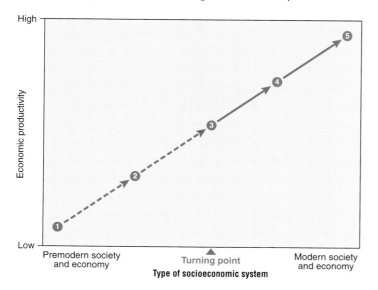

14. Which statement best summarizes world-system theory?

    a. Development involves investment that leads to mass consumption.

    b. Development involves core dominance of the periphery.

    c. Development creates conditions of dependency before mass consumption.

    d. Development requires belief in the value of economic progress.

15. Which of the following pairs is *incorrectly* matched?

    a. poverty-reduction theory – Millennium Development Goals

    b. neoliberalism – structural adjustment

    c. dependency theory – currency devaluation

    d. world-system theory – international division of labor

THE PLANNER

Review your Chapter Planner on the chapter opener and check off your completed work.

Changing Geographies of Industry and Services

GEOGRAPHY AND INDUSTRY

Have you ever been inside a factory or visited a call center, a facility that handles large volumes of calls? These are very different operations, but they are both components of our industrial landscape.

Today, industrial activities are more footloose than they were in the past. For example, for one hundred years the British company Dunlop Slazenger operated a factory that produced tennis balls. In the early 2000s, the Dunlop Slazenger factory closed, and the company moved its operations to the Philippines, shown here. Since that time, the Philippines has also become a major call center hub, employing more people at call centers today than India does. Just recently some American banking and financial services companies decided to shift some of their jobs from the United States to call centers in the Philippines.

Industries move their operations for many reasons, among them lower costs. The Dunlop Slazenger factory moved into an export-processing zone and the call center operations from the United States moved into a special economic zone in the Philippines. Both zones provide tax holidays for industries doing business there. They also provide access to a pool of low-wage workers who are not permitted to strike.

From the production of tennis balls to the staffing of call centers, the geography of industry increasingly relies on parts, labor, and knowledge from countries around the world. This chapter examines the spatial patterns of industry and services, and how and why these patterns have changed.

Romeo Ranoco/Reuters/Landov LLC

CHAPTER PLANNER ✓

- ❏ Study the picture and read the opening story.
- ❏ Scan the Learning Objectives in each section:
  p. 298 ❏   p. 303 ❏   p. 309 ❏   p. 316 ❏
- ❏ Read the text and study all visuals.
  Answer any questions.

Analyze key features

- ❏ What a Geographer Sees, p. 306
- ❏ Process Diagram, p. 315
- ❏ Video Explorations p. 317
- ❏ Geography InSight, p. 318
- ❏ Stop: Answer the Concept Checks before you go on:
  p. 303 ❏   p. 309 ❏   p. 314 ❏   p. 321 ❏

End of chapter

- ❏ Review the Summary and Key Terms.
- ❏ Answer the Critical and Creative Thinking Questions.
- ❏ Answer What is happening in this picture?
- ❏ Complete the Self-Test and check your answers.

Types of Industry

LEARNING OBJECTIVES

1. **Distinguish** between primary, secondary, and tertiary industries.

2. **Explain** staple theory.

3. **Summarize** the origins and diffusion of the Industrial Revolution.

What is the difference between industry and manufacturing? Although the terms are broadly synonymous, we should recognize the distinctions between them. For human geographers, economists, and others, *industry* refers to distinct groups of economic activities (e.g., the electronics industry or the automotive industry), whereas *manufacturing* is one kind of industrial activity that involves the physical or chemical transformation of materials into new products.

Industrial activities can be grouped into one of three broad categories: **primary, secondary,** and **tertiary industries** (**Figure 10.1**). The following sections explore primary and secondary industries. We will return to tertiary industry later in the chapter when we discuss services.

> **primary industry**
> Industry that extracts natural resources from the Earth.
>
> **secondary industry**
> Industry that assembles, processes, or converts raw or semiprocessed materials into fuels or finished goods.
>
> **tertiary industry**
> Industry that provides services, usually in the form of nontangible goods, to other businesses and/ or consumers.

Primary Industry

All primary industries extract natural resources. These extracted but unprocessed natural resources are referred to as *primary products*. When people assign economic value to these resources and trade them, they become *commodities*. This is another dimension of the process of commodification that we discussed in Chapter 2. Because resources are unevenly distributed, trade in commodities has become an enormously important part of the global economy. In addition, reliance on commodities has consequences for the kinds of industries established in a place.

Staple theory How do commodities affect the economic development of a country or region? This question was independently explored by two Canadian scholars, W. A. Mackintosh and Harold Innis, beginning in the 1920s. Their work generated a collection of ideas referred to as staple theory. A *staple* is a primary product that dominates the exports of an economy. **Staple theory** posits that the resource geography of an area shapes its economic system through linkages. Broadly speaking, **linkages** refer to the other economic activities that emerge in conjunction with a specific primary industry.

There are three types of linkages: forward, backward, and demand. *Forward linkages* process the staple resource. Sawmills are forward linkages associated with logging wood, the primary or staple product. *Backward linkages*, by contrast, consist of the economic activities that help access or extract the staple. These could include saw blade manufacturers or engineering firms that develop road or other transportation routes. *Demand linkages* refer to the demand for and purchase of consumer goods, especially by workers as the production of a staple commodity stimulates the accumulation of income. In the logging example, demand linkages include consumer demand for furniture.

As Mackintosh and Innis showed, the economic consequences of staple production vary at different geographic scales. At a local scale, the economic system of the staple-producing area is shaped by the natural resources. At a regional or even global scale, however, the staple-producing area functions as a hinterland economy that supplies commodities to more powerful economic centers. Interestingly, Mackintosh and Innis came to different conclusions about the impact of staples on long-term economic development. Mackintosh held the view that the development of a staple-based economy would enable subsequent industrial development, whereas Innis took the position that reliance on staples inhibited economic growth and contributed to staple or commodity dependence.

There are many reasons for these different interpretations. One that is particularly significant involves the geographic impact of forward and backward linkages.

For example, Innis believed that linkages frequently fail to stimulate growth in the local economy. Australia during the late 19th and early 20th centuries provides a good example. One of Australia's staples was wool, but forward linkages to textile processing did not develop there. Instead, mills in England processed the wool. Similarly, backward linkages in Australia were also weak because equipment to shear the animals was imported from England and not supplied locally.

A number of scholars argue that a high degree of commodity dependence—a characteristic of many developing countries—lends support to Innis's interpretation. Until the mid-1980s most of the world's developing regions were heavily dependent on exports of primary products.

Types of industry • Figure 10.1

NATIONAL GEOGRAPHIC

We can group industries according to broadly similar economic activities, as shown here.

a. Primary industry
The logging that cleared this swath of forest in British Columbia, Canada is an example of a primary industry. Primary industries include other extractive activities such as fishing and mining.

Stephen Sharnoff/NG Image Collection

c. Tertiary industry
This waiter works at an Indonesian hotel. Tertiary industry includes hotel and restaurant businesses.

b. Secondary industry
This steel mill in the Ukraine manufactures pipes for oil and gas companies. The worker grinds the ends of these freshly made steel sections before they are pressed into the desired forms.

Vincent Mundy/Bloomberg via Getty Images

Alison Wright/NG Image Collection

Commodity dependence From an economic standpoint heavy reliance on commodities is problematic for three reasons. First, commodity prices are volatile and fluctuate a great deal over time. As an example, the average price of an ounce of gold dropped below $300 in 2001, rose to $700 in 2007, and topped $1600 in 2013. A second and related problem with commodities is that when compared to the prices of manufactured goods, the prices of commodities do not rise as rapidly over the long term. Third, and as we have seen, heavy reliance on commodities is often associated with lack of economic diversification.

The term *commodity-dependent developing countries* (CDDC) is used to refer to those countries that have a heavy reliance on the export of primary commodities. Different measures of commodity dependence exist. For example, commodity dependence could be expressed as the ratio of the value of commodity exports to a country's gross domestic product, or GDP (see Chapter 9). Alternatively, commodity dependence could be expressed as the percentage of a country's total exports from the four leading commodities exported as shown in **Figure 10.2**.

Secondary Industry

Secondary industries assemble, process, or manufacture raw or semiprocessed materials into useful products, fuels, or finished goods. Sometimes a distinction is made between heavy and light manufacturing. *Heavy manufacturing* refers to the fabrication of items such as steel, nuclear fuel, chemical products, or petroleum as well as durable goods such as motor vehicles, refrigerators, and military equipment. *Light manufacturing* includes activities related to the assembly of clothing or small appliances such as irons or light fixtures as well as the manufacture of food products, beverages, or medical instruments.

For a neat collection of maps depicting different primary and secondary industries, see *Where Geographers Click*.

The Industrial Revolution The geography of secondary industry has been dramatically shaped by technological innovations—especially since the Industrial Revolution. The term **Industrial Revolution** refers to the fundamental changes in technology and systems of production that began in England in the late 18th century. The phrase *system of production* refers to the dominant ways of organizing and coordinating the manufacture of goods. Prior to the Industrial Revolution, manufacturing was largely characterized by small-scale craft production of

ceramics, cloth, and metal goods. The labor was provided by members of a household or community, giving rise to the term *cottage industries*. With the onset of the Industrial Revolution, cottage industries in England gave way to factories, which were then an innovative way of organizing labor. The Industrial Revolution first affected textile production and then metal working.

Two major developments helped spur the Industrial Revolution. The first involved greater access to capital, much of which was generated by England's commanding position in the system of global trade and its control over resources in its colonies. The second major development involved not one but a series of technological innovations that worked to raise output. Some of these innovations improved agricultural production, whereas others improved the processing of raw materials such as cotton. For example, the spinning jenny—a device that twists cotton fibers into thread—was developed in 1764. Another crucial innovation was the development of the steam engine by James Watt in 1769.

Resources such as coal and iron ore influenced the geography of industrialization in England because factories were initially located near energy sources, especially coalfields. Workers moved to live near the factories in urban places, and transportation networks that funneled raw

Primary commodity dependence among developing countries • Figure 10.2

Countries where the four major commodities account for 60% or more of the exports have high commodity dependence. Commodity fuel dependence is high in the Middle East and Africa. (*Source:* Adapted from UNCTAD, 2008, p. 51.)

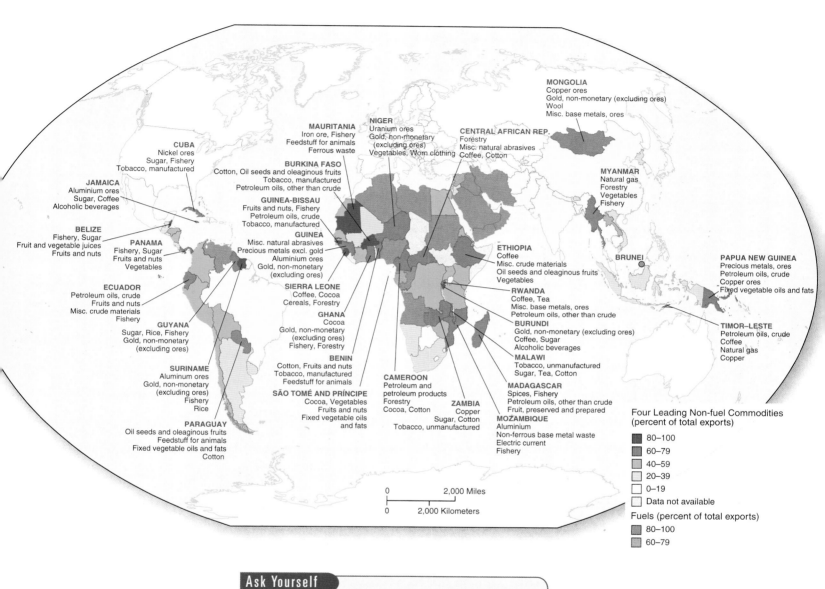

MONGOLIA
Copper ores
Gold, non-monetary (excluding ores)
Wool
Misc. base metals, ores

MAURITANIA
Iron ore, Fishery
Feedstuff for animals
Ferrous waste

NIGER
Uranium ores
Gold, non-monetary
(excluding ores)
Vegetables, Worn clothing

CENTRAL AFRICAN REP.
Forestry
Misc. natural abrasives
Coffee, Cotton

CUBA
Nickel ores
Sugar, Fishery
Tobacco, manufactured

BURKINA FASO
Cotton, Oil seeds and oleaginous fruits
Tobacco, manufactured
Petroleum oils, other than crude

MYANMAR
Natural gas
Forestry
Vegetables
Fishery

JAMAICA
Aluminium ores
Sugar, Coffee
Alcoholic beverages

GUINEA-BISSAU
Fruits and nuts, Fishery
Petroleum oils, crude
Tobacco, manufactured

BELIZE
Fishery, Sugar
Fruit and vegetable juices
Fruits and nuts

PANAMA
Fishery, Sugar
Fruits and nuts
Vegetables

GUINEA
Misc. natural abrasives
Precious metals excl. gold
Aluminium ores
Gold, non-monetary
(excluding ores)

ETHIOPIA
Coffee
Misc. crude materials
Oil seeds and oleaginous fruits
Vegetables

BRUNEI

PAPUA NEW GUINEA
Precious metals, ores
Petroleum oils, crude
Copper ores
Fixed vegetable oils and fats

ECUADOR
Petroleum oils, crude
Fruits and nuts
Misc. crude materials
Fishery

SIERRA LEONE
Coffee, Cocoa
Cereals, Forestry

RWANDA
Coffee, Tea
Misc. base metals, ores
Petroleum oils, other than crude

GUYANA
Sugar, Rice, Fishery
Gold, non-monetary
(excluding ores)

GHANA
Cocoa
Gold, non-monetary
(excluding ores)
Fishery, Forestry

BURUNDI
Gold, non-monetary (excluding ores)
Coffee, Sugar
Alcoholic beverages

TIMOR–LESTE
Petroleum oils, crude
Coffee
Natural gas
Copper

SURINAME
Aluminum ores
Gold, non-monetary
(excluding ores)
Fishery
Rice

BENIN
Cotton, Fruits and nuts
Tobacco, manufactured
Feedstuff for animals

MALAWI
Tobacco, unmanufactured
Sugar, Tea, Cotton

SÃO TOMÉ AND PRÍNCIPE
Cocoa, Vegetables
Fruits and nuts
Fixed vegetable oils
and fats

CAMEROON
Petroleum and
petroleum products
Forestry
Cocoa, Cotton

MADAGASCAR
Spices, Fishery
Petroleum oils, other than crude
Fruit, preserved and prepared

ZAMBIA
Copper
Sugar, Cotton
Tobacco, unmanufactured

MOZAMBIQUE
Aluminium
Non-ferrous base metal waste
Electric current
Fishery

PARAGUAY
Oil seeds and oleaginous fruits
Feedstuff for animals
Fixed vegetable oils and fats
Cotton

Four Leading Non-fuel Commodities
(percent of total exports)
- 80–100
- 60–79
- 40–59
- 20–39
- 0–19
- Data not available

Fuels (percent of total exports)
- 80–100
- 60–79

0 ___ 2,000 Miles
0 ___ 2,000 Kilometers

Ask Yourself

What do many of the countries with high dependence on agricultural products also have in common?

Industrialization in historical perspective • Figure 10.3

The uneven diffusion of the Industrial Revolution contributed to core-periphery patterns of development.

a. When the Industrial Revolution began to unfold, household cottage and craft industries generated most of the manufactured goods. This chart shows that as the Industrial Revolution spread in core countries and mechanization transformed the scale and system of production, manufacturing in the countries of the periphery declined. (*Source:* Bairoch, 1982, p. 275.) ▼

Year	Percent of global manufacturing production	
	Peripheral countries	Core countries
1750	73.0	27.0
1800	67.7	32.3
1860	36.6	63.4
1900	11.0	89.0
1953	6.5	93.5
1980	12.0	88.0

b. This chart compares GDP per capita, often used to gauge the level of industrialization in a country, for core and periphery countries before and after the Industrial Revolution. (*Source:* Data from Maddison, 2003.) ▼

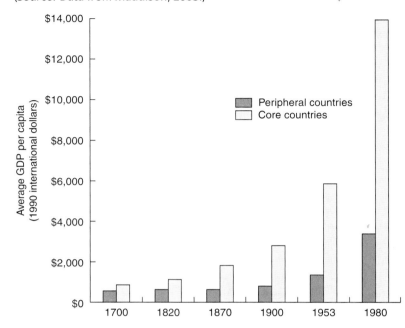

materials to the factories and finished goods to markets grew denser. Thus, industrialization has been strongly associated with urbanization.

Diffusion of the Industrial Revolution The global diffusion of the system of production associated with the Industrial Revolution has occurred slowly and in three general phases. During the first phase, which ran from roughly 1760 to 1880, the Industrial Revolution diffused to Belgium, the Netherlands, France, Germany, and the United States. The second phase, spanning the years 1880 to 1950, carried the Industrial Revolution to Russia, Japan, and Canada among other primarily Western places, especially British dominions. During this time, some industrial centers developed in places that were still predominantly agricultural, including Shanghai, China; Bombay, India; Monterrey, Mexico; and São Paulo, Brazil. The third phase, which began in the 1950s and is still underway, has

seen the continued industrialization of countries affected by phase two and the industrialization of Israel and several Pacific Rim countries.

Diffusion of the Industrial Revolution has been highly uneven not only at the global scale but also within individual countries. As a result, *core-periphery patterns* of industrialization and development are often discernible. Within the United States, for example, manufacturing initially concentrated within New England, making it a core area of secondary industry focused on textile mills, while the South, a cotton-supplying region, functioned as the commodity-supplying periphery. As we discussed in Chapter 9 in conjunction with world-system theory, the emergence of the global core associated with Western Europe, North America, Russia, and Japan is strongly associated with patterns of trade and industrialization. **Figure 10.3** provides two ways of envisioning the impact of the Industrial Revolution on global core-periphery patterns.

1. **How** are primary and secondary industries different?

2. **How** does staple theory address economic development?

3. **How** did the diffusion of industrialization demonstrate a core-periphery pattern?

Evolution of Manufacturing in the Core

LEARNING OBJECTIVES

1. **Identify** two groups of factors that can influence the location of manufacturing.

2. **Outline** the development of Fordism.

3. **Contrast** Fordist and flexible systems of production.

4. **Distinguish** between outsourcing and offshoring.

ince the Industrial Revolution there has been considerable change in the geography of manufacturing. This section explores the broad trends that have characterized manufacturing in the core—those regions that constitute the developed world.

Factors Affecting the Location of Manufacturing

What is the optimal location of a particular factory? Usually the answer involves a consideration of the costs and benefits of different sites and situations. See **Table 10.1** for a description of some of these factors.

Through the first and second phases of the Industrial Revolution, decisions about where to locate factories were strongly influenced by the cost of transporting raw materials. To minimize these costs, iron and steel mills were located close to the coalfields and iron ore deposits. For many firms today, having access to the market so that finished goods can readily be distributed and sold has taken on greater significance in decisions about factory location. Manufactured goods typically cost more to transport, mainly because such goods are often bulk-gaining.

Site and situation factors in industrial location Table 10.1	
Site factors	**Situation factors**
Labor costs and availability	Proximity to the market
Land availability, accessibility, value, and taxes	Transportation options and costs
Energy costs (e.g., oil, electricity)	Agglomeration effects
Local environmental regulations	Political policies (e.g., right-to-work laws)
Local amenities or tax advantages	Other (e.g., proximity to schools for families of employees)

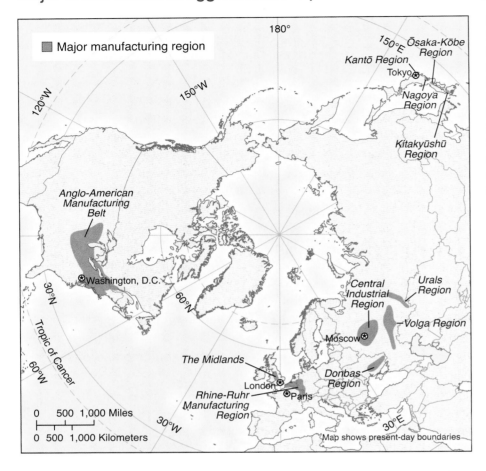

Historically speaking, proximity to raw materials, a good transportation network, and dense concentrations of people help explain the emergence of these major centers of manufacturing. Because of its limited resource base, Japan has been significantly more dependent on imported raw materials. In the planned economy of the former Soviet Union, decisions about industrial development and production were made in Moscow.

▶ **What transportation network grew in conjunction with industrialization?**

That is, they are heavier than the component parts that compose them, and they take up larger volumes (e.g., televisions). Thus, access to the market can help minimize transportation costs.

Another important factor that can affect a firm's profitability involves **agglomeration**. In addition to labor, firms need inputs such as equipment, which they acquire from other enterprises called suppliers. Firms can achieve cost savings by locating in urban areas that have a sizable pool of skilled labor and also house needed suppliers. Such savings are called *agglomeration economies*. Sometimes, however, urban growth can result in increased taxes or increased transportation costs because of congestion, creating *agglomeration diseconomies*.

agglomeration
The spatial clustering of people and economic activities, especially industries that are related or interdependent, in a place.

Deciding where to locate an industry is not simply a matter of listing the site and situational factors. Rather, it also involves analyzing and predicting how the contingencies of a place may change (Chapter 1). See **Figure 10.4** for a map of the major manufacturing centers that developed in the core.

Fordism

To varying degrees, firms in each of the urban-industrial agglomerations depicted in Figure 10.6 used systems of factory production that were influenced by the ideas of F. W. Taylor and Henry Ford. Taylor was a mechanical engineer whose book *The Principles of Scientific Management* (1911) promoted the division of labor into the most elemental tasks. Scientific management, now called **Taylorism**, involved studying the tasks performed by workers, timing the workers, and, if necessary, altering their movements in order to minimize wasted effort. Taylor did not want workers to think about what they were doing because he considered that a distraction and potential waste of time.

Ford, who was familiar with Taylor's ideas, is credited with developing a moving assembly line to mass produce automobiles at his Highland Park factory in 1913. Using a production process based on interchangeable parts, clear divisions of labor, and product standardization, the assembly line cut in half the time to produce a single car. The word **Fordism**, then, refers to a system of industrial production designed for mass production and influenced by the principles of scientific management.

The impact of Fordism on the evolution of manufacturing can hardly be overstated. The implementation of Fordist principles had three major consequences. First, Fordism contributed significantly to the de-skilling of labor. Whereas early factories employed craftspeople who were experts in their particular specialty such as metal fabrication, the fragmentation of production into a series of tasks for the assembly line meant that factory workers did not need to be craft experts any longer.

A second and related consequence of Fordism is that it reinforced the existence of a rigid social hierarchy between the workers and the managers. In fact, the spread of Fordism, especially in the United States, is closely associated with the unionization of the labor force. Third, Fordism contributed to the rise of multinational corporations (MNCs). The Ford Motor Company grew to become a MNC over time, establishing factories and assembly plants in the United Kingdom, France, Denmark, and other countries. Today it has operations in more than 100 countries. As we discussed in Chapter 2, tens of thousands of MNCs exist today.

Fordist Production

The moving assembly line is not only efficient, it is also very productive. There are, however, three major weaknesses. One is that it requires a regular and steady supply of inputs at the scale of the assembly line and also at the scale of the company. For example, if a machine on the assembly line malfunctions, the entire operation has to be halted. Likewise, should the company fail to receive adequate quantities of steel, assembly-line production will be affected. A second weakness is that, in order to be successful, Fordism relies on a mass market that can consume the goods that are produced. In terms of the history of manufacturing, Fordism helped to connect mass production with mass consumption. This relationship is summed up by the saying, "Everything we produce has already been sold." The problem with this approach is that it assumes unlimited growth in both production and sales. A third weakness of Fordism is that assembly-line work can be extremely boring for the employees, resulting in high rates of worker turnover.

If you were a manager of a company using a Fordist system of production, what would you do to address these weaknesses? Most likely you would find ways to stabilize the system. Although the specific strategies that were used varied from industry to industry, some common practices emerged. These include purchasing large quantities of stock and storing it in warehouses so that the manufacturer always has a supply of necessary inputs. Another strategy to stabilize the system of Fordist production was to vigilantly maintain and service the equipment on the assembly lines in order to prevent breakdowns. Because labor is also a major input, having a reliable workforce was essential. High wages and long-term labor contracts were used to minimize employee turnover, as were *collective agreements*—contracts between unions and management stipulating employment practices and employee benefits.

For many business managers, vertically integrating the company was another solution. **Vertical integration** occurs when a company controls two or more stages in the production or distribution of a commodity either directly or through contractual arrangements. Thus, vertical integration is a strategy of extending a company's ownership and control "up" the supply stream and/or "down" the distribution stream of a good or service in order to lessen the company's vulnerability. The Ford Motor Company became vertically integrated early in the 20th century, especially in an upstream direction. The facilities Ford constructed at the River Rouge plant in Michigan provide an excellent example of vertical integration (**Figure 10.5**).

Vertical integration • Figure 10.5

By the 1940s, Ford owned mines, quarries, and forests in different states and built facilities at the River Rouge plant to manufacture iron, steel, tires, glass, and lumber used in the production of cars. These massive coal and ore bins are a testament to the vast scale of Ford's operations made possible by vertical integration.

Everett Collection/SuperStock

As Fordist systems of production developed, they became closely associated with producer-driven commodity chains, which also have important limitations. A **commodity chain** (also called a production chain or value-added chain) is the linked sequence of operations from the design to the production and distribution of a good. *Producer-driven commodity chains* are associated with large, vertically integrated MNCs, and they influence decisions about production. These decisions are made months in advance of the actual production, and they are communicated in a top-down fashion through the MNC to the manufacturers as well as the distributors and retailers. Because these decisions have to be made so far in advance, they may not reflect actual consumer demand when a product is finally manufactured. To better understand the geographical dimensions of commodity chains, see *What a Geographer Sees*.

By the 1950s, Fordist systems prevailed in the industrial regions of the core but were most extensively

WHAT A GEOGRAPHER SEES

A Commodity Chain

A commodity chain can be thought of as a network that connects the different steps in the production of a good, from information and resource gathering to the manufacture, distribution, and marketing of it. Every manufacturing operation makes use of one or more commodity chains, and such networks are increasingly globalized. Here we present a commodity chain for fur garments, which is strongly anchored to the northern hemisphere.

Procurement	Manufacturing	Distribution and Retail

Fur Trapping → Fur Farming → Fur Auctions → Initial Processing (Fur dressing and dyeing) → Fur Garment Manufacture → Marketing and Sales

a. Globalization can affect any part of a commodity chain. Historical centers for the dressing and dyeing of fur included Paris, London, Leipzig (Germany), Montreal, and St. Louis. This map shows that the manufacturing of fur garments has globalized and shifted east.

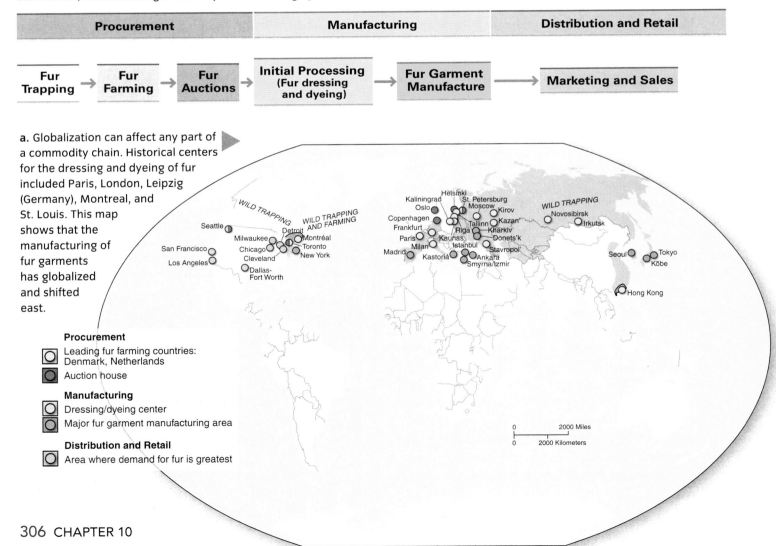

Procurement
- Leading fur farming countries: Denmark, Netherlands
- Auction house

Manufacturing
- Dressing/dyeing center
- Major fur garment manufacturing area

Distribution and Retail
- Area where demand for fur is greatest

developed in North America and Western Europe. Firms and employees benefited from rising profits and wages during a boom that lasted nearly 20 years. The *crisis of Fordism* marks the end of that boom and specifically refers to the declining productivity and competitiveness of firms. Two major developments contributed to the crisis of Fordism: (1) the energy crisis of the 1970s, which increased manufacturing and transportation costs, and (2) improvements in computers and electronics, which began to transform industrial practices. Together, these two developments showed that Fordism is a highly inflexible system of production that does not easily or rapidly adjust to changing economic or market conditions. Indeed, some of the financial troubles of the U.S. auto industry today stem from its inability to shift quickly to the production of more fuel-efficient vehicles and hybrid technologies as the price of oil increased in the mid-2000s.

Peter Foerster/dpa /Landov LLC

✓ THE PLANNER

◀ **b.** Global sourcing of fur dates to at least the 1600s, but since World War II, Europe has become a major center of fur farming. The photo shows a mink farm in Germany.

c. Fur garments are a status symbol for some and a contested commodity for others. The fur industry describes itself as a "responsible industry." Some experts consider the eastward shift of fur manufacturing to be partially the result of animal rights campaigns. ▼

Paul Chesley/NG Image Collection

Mike Theiler/Getty Images, Inc.

Think Critically

1. How and in what way is responsibility a component of the global commodity chain?
2. How would a commodity chain for an automobile manufacturer differ from this one?

307

In Japan, however, Fordism developed differently. Unlike the United States with its large domestic market, manufacturing and production in Japan had to be adapted to a much smaller market. Many of these adaptations originated in the automobile industry and specifically within the Japanese company Toyota, where **flexible production** was pioneered. Flexible, or lean, production uses information technologies such as computer networking, high-tech sensors, and automation technology to make the production of goods more responsive to market conditions and therefore more efficient. In contrast to Fordism, flexible production relies on *consumer-driven commodity chains* in which consumer demand shapes the amount and kind of products produced.

Table 10.2 highlights some of the major differences between Fordism and flexible production. Even the assembly-line system had its limitations. In the United States, each model of car required a completely different assembly line. This was not the case in Japan, however, where a single assembly line could produce different models, depending on specific market conditions. Flexible production is also based on the idea that workers should be empowered to think, troubleshoot, and perform multiple work responsibilities. One of the mottoes of flexible production is to promote the continuous improvement of the product. Thus, workers and managers need to communicate and collaborate on a frequent basis.

Two strategies that have been crucial to the success of flexible production are just-in-time delivery and outsourcing. **Just-in-time delivery** refers to how a company manages its inventory and obtains the materials, components, or supplies it needs. Supplies are ordered in smaller quantities on an as-needed basis. Just-in-time delivery enables a company to match production quantities to actual customer demand without the need for or costs of maintaining large warehouses and inventory stockpiles. By **outsourcing,** a company subcontracts a business activity that was previously performed in-house (such as the manufacture of a part, packaging, or customer support) to another firm. Outsourcing can be thought of as a kind of vertical disintegration. Many business processes (sometimes called *back-office functions*) such as data entry, bookkeeping, and other administrative, legal, or information technology (IT) operations are outsourced. Except for strategic planning, virtually all internal company operations are subject to outsourcing (**Figure 10.6**).

It is important to note that outsourcing always involves another firm, or subcontractor, and this firm may be located in the same country as the company or abroad (i.e., offshore, as shown in Figure 10.6). **Offshoring** is the transfer of an internal or outsourced business activity from a domestic to an international location. Nike, for example, offshores the manufacture of its footwear to factories located in Southeast Asia and China, while Dell offshores the manufacture of its desktop computers to Taiwan. Offshoring has shaped the globalization of industry and is so important to the geography of manufacturing today that we will return to it in the next section.

Major contrasts between Fordism and flexible production Table 10.2	
Fordism	**Flexible production**
Maximize inventory held in warehouses	Minimize inventory; no need for warehouses
Vertical integration	Outsourcing
Producer-driven commodity chain	Consumer-driven commodity chain
Highly standardized product design	Made-to-order product design
Strongly hierarchical management style	Flat management style
Minimally skilled labor	Multiskilled labor
Large labor force	Smaller and more efficient labor force

Business process outsourcing • Figure 10.6

Aijaz Rahi/©AP/Wide World Photos

These employees work in Hewlett-Packard's business process outsourcing center in Bangalore, India. Reasons for outsourcing vary depending on the type of business, but generally companies outsource in order to streamline their business operations. This includes achieving reductions in the cost of utilities, labor, rent, or personnel and resource management. ▶ **Are there other reasons, not listed here, for outsourcing?**

CONCEPT CHECK STOP

1. **How** did the leading urban-industrial agglomerations of the core develop?
2. **Why** is Fordism associated with vertical integration?
3. **How** are the two types of commodity chains different?
4. **What** are examples of activities that might be outsourced?

Evolution of Manufacturing Beyond the Core

LEARNING OBJECTIVES

1. **Discuss** the rise of the Asian NIEs.
2. **Explain** what an export-processing zone is.
3. **Distinguish** between a maquiladora and a special economic zone.

M anufacturing transforms a product and adds value to it. One way to measure industrial output is to use the **manufacturing value added (MVA)**. We can calculate this by taking the cost of the finished product and subtracting from it the cost of purchased inputs necessary to produce it such as fuel, electricity, and the cost of other parts or materials.

By the 1970s, an important two-stage shift in the geography of manufacturing was beginning to unfold. The first stage involved a shift *within* the core as Japan experienced rapid growth in its MVA and began to rival in output centers of manufacturing in Europe and the United States. The second stage involved the rise in importance of manufacturing centers in certain semiperipheral areas in Asia in conjunction with the third phase of the diffusion of the Industrial Revolution. We can visualize this by comparing the value added in manufacturing among regions (**Figure 10.7**).

Percentage of global manufacturing (MVA) • Figure 10.7

Developing economies generate about one-third of the global MVA. That proportion is expected to increase as more manufacturing shifts to developing countries. Manufacturing is drawn to these places by cheaper labor, large markets, and good transportation and communication systems. (*Source:* Data from UNIDO, 2011.)

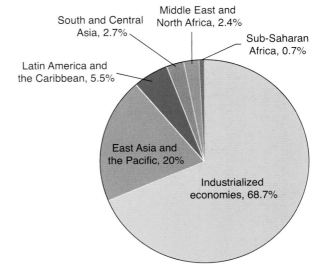

South and Central Asia, 2.7%
Middle East and North Africa, 2.4%
Sub-Saharan Africa, 0.7%
Latin America and the Caribbean, 5.5%
East Asia and the Pacific, 20%
Industrialized economies, 68.7%

Between the 1960s and 1980s, the NIEs had high rates of growth in manufacturing output—often in excess of 10%. In addition, manufacturing shifted to the production of higher technology goods.

a. First-and second-tier Asian NIEs
First-tier NIEs showed substantial growth and productivity in manufacturing in the 1970s. Second-tier NIEs experienced similar growth a decade later.
► **How did the diffusion of industrialization play out differently in Asia than in Europe a century earlier?**

Newly Industrialized Economies

Japan's manufacturing success was paralleled by rapid economic growth, improved living standards, and reductions in poverty. The country became an example for others to emulate. Indeed, by the 1970s four other East Asian centers were showing signs of substantial growth and productivity in manufacturing. These **newly industrialized economies (NIEs)**, sometimes referred to as the Four Asian Tigers, are Hong Kong, Singapore, South Korea, and Taiwan. A second tier of Asian NIEs began to emerge as important centers of manufacturing in the 1980s. This tier includes Indonesia, Malaysia, the Philippines, and Thailand.

The economic transformation of the NIEs is related to three major factors: (1) government-supported initiatives to increase manufacturing productivity and improve trade; (2) a gradual shift from low-skill, labor-intensive industries to higher value-added technology-intensive industries such as the manufacture of computer components and scientific instruments; and (3) the presence of a skilled labor force. In most of the NIEs, growth in the textile/apparel industry helped fuel the initial production of manufactured goods for export, though its importance has diminished over the years (**Figure 10.8**).

The NIEs increasingly compete against one another to attract manufacturing. The production of hard disk drives for computers provides a good example. During the 1990s the leading manufacturers of hard disk drives—multinational corporations such as Seagate, Western Digital, Maxtor, and Hitachi—had opened manufacturing facilities in Singapore. However, by 1996 Seagate had established

	Apparel as a percentage of total exports		
Region/Country	1980	1990	2000
Hong Kong	25.4	18.7	12.0
South Korea	17.0	12.4	2.9
Taiwan	12.3	5.8	2.0
Indonesia	2.4	10.3	7.8
Malaysia	1.2	4.5	2.3
Thailand	4.2	12.2	5.5
Philippines	4.9	8.4	6.9

b. Initial growth through textiles/apparel
Notice the geographic pattern that distinguishes first-tier NIEs, which experienced significant declines in the 1980s, from the second-tier NIEs, whose declines are more recent. (*Source:* Gereffi and Memedovic, 2003, table 2.)

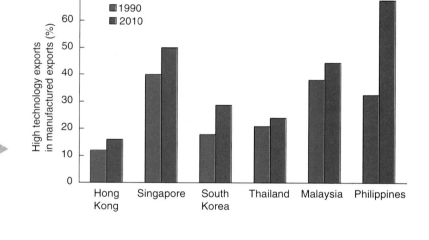

c. Shift to high-tech manufacturing
The production and export of high-tech goods is on the rise in most NIEs. The Philippines has expanded rapidly into electronics, including the manufacture of cell phone chips. (*Source:* Data from World Bank, 2013.)

two major plants for the production of hard disk drives and their components in Thailand. Shortly thereafter, Western Digital relocated its manufacturing operations to Thailand and Malaysia. Singapore remains an important center for the design and development of hard disk drives, but the actual manufacture of these devices has become even more diffuse. Although not classified as an NIE, China has experienced rapid growth in the production of high-technology products as well and appears to be following a similar path in its efforts to upgrade industrially.

Export-Processing Zones

Some of the manufacturing growth in the semiperiphery and periphery is attributed to government policies encouraging the creation of export-processing zones such as the one in the Philippines described at the start of this chapter. An **export-processing zone** (EPZ), also called a free-trade zone, is an industrial area that operates according to different policies than the rest of the country in which it is located in order to attract and support export-oriented production. For example, an EPZ may be a duty-free zone or may have simplified customs and/or tax regulations. EPZs also provide access to transportation and communication networks. As an additional incentive to firms, trade union activity in EPZs is often prohibited or closely monitored.

EPZs vary in size, but most usually cover about half a square mile (1.3 km²) and are fenced. EPZs are not unique to the developing world, however the geography of manufacturing in the periphery and semiperiphery has been strongly

Maquiladoras are workshops, but their exteriors rarely reveal the nature of the work performed inside.

a. Located in Tijuana, across the border from San Diego, this U.S.-owned maquiladora manufactures medical devices. Of the border cities, Tijuana has the largest number of maquiladoras.

b. These women make wire harnesses for automobiles at a maquiladora. Maquiladoras have increased the participation of women in the workforce, but they have also been associated with the discriminatory practice of making pregnancy tests a condition of hire.

©John Gibbins/San Diego Union-Tribune/Zuma Press/Alamy.

Joe Raedle/Newsmakers/Getty Images, Inc.

influenced by the explosive growth in the number of EPZs. Between 1975 and 2006, for example, the number of EPZs increased from 79 to 3,500, and EPZs now employ some 66 million people, two-thirds of whom are in China. EPZs have drawn more women into the workforce, and in a number of EPZs, women make up a strong majority of the labor force.

EPZs have been promoted as a strategy for helping countries industrialize. They help attract foreign investment and trade, can enable the production of new, nontraditional exports, and can generate jobs. EPZs, however, have also been criticized. From a geographic standpoint, they can exacerbate uneven development by concentrating resources and infrastructure in them, to the neglect of other regions. From a labor standpoint, EPZs vary considerably in their practices and treatment of workers. On the one hand, studies indicate that workers benefit from the ability to earn bonuses. Similarly, worker pay, though it is low by Western standards, is often higher than that provided by other jobs outside of the EPZ. On the other hand, some factories in EPZs have been likened to sweatshops where labor is severely exploited. For example, low wages, long hours, and the failure of firms to pay workers for their overtime have contributed to labor unrest at factories located in EPZs in Bangladesh.

Maquiladoras A *maquiladora*, or *maquila*, is a manufacturing plant, often foreign-owned, that receives duty-free imported materials, assembles or processes them, and then exports them. A maquiladora can be thought of as an EPZ that consists of a single factory. Historically, maquiladoras have been associated with Mexico, but today the term *maquiladora* is sometimes used to describe similar assembly-for-export plants in other parts of Latin America and the Caribbean.

In Mexico, maquiladoras were part of a government-based strategy to alleviate unemployment in the states along the border with the United States and to disperse some of the industry away from the region around Mexico City. Following the implementation of the North American Free Trade Agreement (NAFTA) by the United States, Canada, and Mexico in 1994, the number of maquiladoras in Mexico surged. The reasons for this surge include geographic proximity to the American market, low wages in Mexico, and a growing U.S. economy. Maquiladoras are responsible for most of Mexico's manufacturing output, and are an increasingly important component of manufacturing in Central America as well. Geographically, maquiladoras are most heavily concentrated along the U.S.-Mexico border (**Figure 10.9**).

The economic benefits of maquiladoras are not limited to Mexico and Central America. Maquiladoras help keep U.S. goods competitive because of the lower costs of production. Because maquiladoras use many U.S. components and generate income for American companies, they benefit the U.S. economy as well. But maquiladoras are not without controversy. Their workers are paid very low wages. Although minimum wage varies by location and skill level in Mexico, nonprofessional workers earn the equivalent of just over $5 a day. Also, maquiladoras can be significant sources of water and air pollution because of less stringent environmental regulations in Mexico and Central America.

Special economic zones Special economic zones (SEZs) are export-processing zones established in China as part of a national policy to create a more open, market-oriented economy. When this policy was first implemented in 1979, the creation of such "islands" of capitalism within communist China represented a massive change in the economic functioning of the country. Therefore, SEZs were developed on an experimental basis. To restrict the spread and influence of capitalism, SEZs were initially created in just four cities (**Figure 10.10**).

Like other export-processing zones, China's SEZs were conceived as a tool to attract foreign investment with a variety of incentives, including tax holidays, exemptions from customs duties on imported and exported goods, and reduced rates on the lease of land or buildings.

Two characteristics of SEZs differentiate them from other export-processing zones. The first is their size. As a whole, SEZs tend to be larger than EPZs. For example, the Shenzhen SEZ covers about 126 square miles (328 km²)—nearly twice the size of Washington, D.C. The second characteristic is that they tend to be more comprehensively conceived. That is, in addition to the production of goods for export, other economic facets of the SEZs are promoted such as research and development as well as tourism. Arguably, China has made a concerted effort to use SEZs to generate both forward and backward linkages.

Few scholars dispute the overall success of China's SEZs. Between 1980 and 1988, for example, Shenzhen's exports as a percentage of all exports from Guangdong Province grew from less than 1% to nearly 25%. As a result of this and similar success in other SEZs, China has continued to transform its economy in a variety of

ways. In 1984 the country "opened" 14 cities to foreign investment, enabling the creation of multiple SEZs within them. These open areas have since been extended geographically to include major delta, peninsular, and island zones, as well as interior locations (refer again to Figure 10.10). Numerous other countries in Asia and Latin America have recently made plans to create their own SEZs.

Offshoring

The establishment of export-processing zones is linked to the offshoring of certain aspects of manufacturing to developing regions. We can better comprehend why semiperipheral and peripheral areas have become popular locations

China's special economic zones
• Figure 10.10

Zhuhai, Shenzhen, Shantou, and Xiamen were the first SEZs. Hainan Island was then added as a fifth SEZ. Until recently, the geography of China's SEZs and open areas has been predominantly coastal. (*Source:* Based on Dicken, 2003, fig. 6.10 and Phillips and Yeh, 1990, fig. 9.4.)

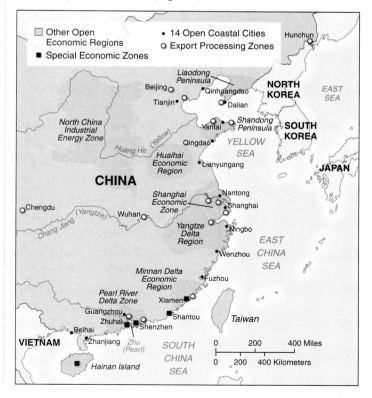

How manufacturing value added changes across the commodity chain • Figure 10.11

Value added in manufacturing and the required skill level of the workers increase as the work performed changes from assembly to the creation of brand-name designs such as Levi's jeans, and research and development. Places that have export-processing zones and large pools of low-skilled labor tend to be especially attractive to low value-added types of manufacturing. (*Source:* Adapted from Dedrick and Kraemer, 1998, fig. 5.2. By permission of Oxford University Press, Inc.)

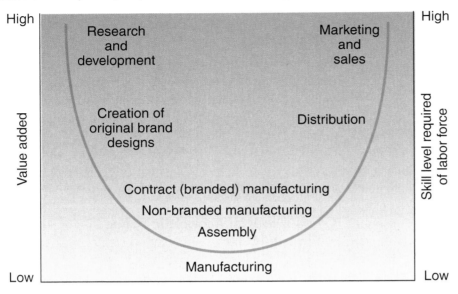

for offshore manufacturing when we consider the relationship between different types of manufacturing and the value they add to the finished product (**Figure 10.11**).

It is easier to comprehend the extent and impact of offshoring when we realize that companies such as Nike, Reebok, Ikea, and The Gap do not own any manufacturing plants. Rather, these companies create original brand designs, and they offshore and subcontract the production of their goods mainly to manufacturing plants in developing countries in a process called contract or branded manufacturing. By some estimates, Nike subcontracts 61% of its product manufacturing to Southeast Asian countries and 38% to China. Foxconn, a Taiwanese manufacturer, subcontracts work for Apple, Sony, and other companies. Sometimes subcontractors outsource work they have agreed to perform to sub-subcontractors, or lower-tier subcontractors. A tragic garment factory fire in Bangladesh drew attention to this practice and revealed that the lower-tier subcontractors were not held to the same workplace safety standards expected of the subcontractor.

Propelled by multinational corporations, offshoring has had three important geographic consequences. First, it has given manufacturing a much more global character

because different operations—from the supply of materials and components to the assembly, production, and sale of final products—now take place in countries other than the one in which a firm is based. Second, it has contributed to a *new* international division of labor such that certain kinds of manufacturing and product assembly are increasingly handled by countries in peripheral and semiperipheral regions. The term *new* is used to draw a contrast with the old or historical division of labor associated with commodity extraction in the semiperiphery and periphery and manufacturing in the core (see Chapter 9). Third, offshoring has impacted the geography of profit captured from manufacturing (**Figure 10.12**).

CONCEPT CHECK

1. **How** have the Asian NIEs been able to increase their MVA?

2. **Where** have export-processing zones tended to concentrate?

3. **How** has the creation of globalized commodity chains affected the maquiladora industry in Mexico?

Manufacturing value added and profit captured in an iPad Figure 10.12

PROCESS DIAGRAM

All purchased inputs for an iPad total $316. Subtracting that amount from the cost of the finished product, $499, generates a MVA of $183. Where is that MVA produced? Where are the profits returned?

Molly Riley/Reuters/Newscom

① Design and development
Apple, based in the United States, is responsible for the development of the product, the brand design, marketing, and distribution. The company also makes decisions about where manufacturing occurs.

② Manufacturing value added (MVA)
Apple outsources the manufacture of certain components to numerous companies, including Samsung (South Korea) and Toshiba (Japan). South Korea creates most of the MVA because the most expensive components are manufactured there. (*Source:* Data from Kraemer, Linden, and Dedrick, 2011.)

Country	Component or process	Estimated cost ($)
South Korea	Display and touchscreen	127
Taiwan	Battery	32
Japan	Memory	31
USA	Processor	23
Other purchased inputs		103
Total		316

③ Profit captured
Notice how the geographic distribution of profit differs from the gegography of MVA. Because the Taiwanese firm, Foxconn, owns the factories in China that assemble the iPad, the small profit that China makes stems mainly from wages. (*Source:* Data from Kraemer, Linden, and Dedrick, 2011.)

Country	Role	Profit ($)
USA	Brand design, distribution, retail	162
South Korea	Original part supplier	34
China	Pre–installation processing/ assembly	8
Japan	Original part supplier	7
Taiwan	Original part supplier	7
Other	Manufacturing	20
Total profit captured		238

④ Total profit captured, by role in commodity chain
Most profits are returned to Apple, but about a third are distributed among offshore manufacturers. (*Source:* Data from Kraemer, Linden, and Dedrick, 2011.)

Bloomberg via Getty Images

U.S. manufacturing — 5%

Apple, Inc. design and marketing — 63%

Offshore manufacturing — 32%

AP Photo/Apple

Evolution of Manufacturing Beyond the Core **315**

Services

LEARNING OBJECTIVES

1. **Define** deindustrialization.
2. **Identify** different categories of services.
3. **Characterize** a postindustrial society.
4. **Explain** the development of technopoles.

As we have learned, tertiary industry is the service-providing industry. For example, banking and transportation are services needed by businesses and consumers. Thus, another term for tertiary industry is *services*. Sometimes the terms *primary*, *secondary*, and *tertiary* are also used to refer to sectors of the economy. When people speak of the structural makeup of an economy, they are referring to how each sector contributes to GDP and whether each sector is gaining or losing jobs. Recently, the service sector has grown rapidly. This section explores this structural change, different types of services, and the emergence of postindustrial societies.

Trends in manufacturing • Figure 10.13

MVA is falling in industrialized countries and rising in less developed countries as they become more industrialized. (*Source:* Data from UNIDO, 2009.)

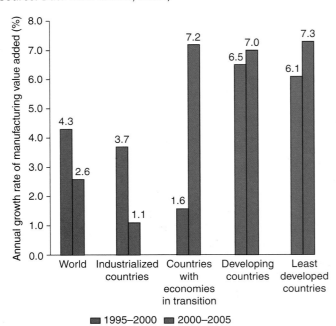

■ 1995–2000 ■ 2000–2005

Deindustrialization, Globalization, and Growth in Services

The growth of the service sector is perhaps best understood in conjunction with changes in manufacturing. The crisis of Fordism marked a period of structural change within the core industrialized countries that involved declines in manufacturing employment. But these declines do not mean that the core industrialized countries have lost their global dominance in manufacturing, whether that dominance is measured by the value added in dollars or by a percentage of global manufacturing value added. As we have seen, industrialized countries still generate nearly 70% of global MVA. The geography of *growth* in MVA, however, has shifted significantly in recent decades (**Figure 10.13**).

Job losses in manufacturing in core countries raise questions about the causes and consequences of **deindustrialization**. Three broad explanations help account for deindustrialization: (1) greater productivity gains from manufacturing than from services; (2) changing resource endowments; and (3) economic globalization. We will discuss each of these in turn.

> **deindustrialization**
> The long-term decline in industrial employment.

According to the first explanation, productivity gains in manufacturing outpace productivity gains in services, and this triggers deindustrialization. Think of the gains in productivity of the systems of flexible production we discussed earlier in the chapter in which one assembly line can manufacture several different models of vehicles. Now contrast this example with one of a lawyer who has to learn the details of each specific case and client.

These differences in productivity are also related to the adoption of technology to perform automated tasks. In contrast to manufacturing, fewer job tasks in the service sector can be mechanized. Thus, productivity gains in manufacturing not only enhance industrialization, they also trigger deindustrialization.

A second explanation of deindustrialization draws on the significance of changing resource endowments. By resource endowments we mean not only the natural resources, but also the infrastructure in a place and the skills and education of its workforce. When resource endowments change, a firm in another country may be able to take advantage of lower costs of production and, as a consequence, gain a comparative advantage in the manufacture of a good (**Figure 10.14**).

A third and related explanation of deindustrialization involves economic globalization and the new international division of labor that has shifted manufacturing jobs to

Deindustrialization and service sector growth • Figure 10.14

Deindustrialization has affected factories from Pennsylvania to Illinois, a region now dubbed the "Rust Belt."

a. The Bethlehem Steel mill in Pennsylvania closed when the U.S. steel industry experienced substantial declines between the 1960s and 1980s and lost its comparative advantage, in part because it was unable to compete with more efficient steel manufacturers in Japan and Korea.

b. A casino has opened at the site of the former steel mill, promising to revitalize the city of Bethlehem and highlighting the process of structural change in the local economy. ▶ **How do you think the wages and skills of the casino employees might compare to those of steel mill workers?**

Matt Rourke/©AP/Wide World Photos

Rick Smith/©AP/Wide World Photos

developing regions. Globalization and the increased trade that it has fostered have helped to diffuse manufacturing in some places and contribute to deindustrialization in other places. The closing of the Dunlop Slazenger factory in the United Kingdom and the relocation of its operations to the Philippines, as mentioned in the chapter opener, provides a good example of these interconnected processes. For a different example of the nature of structural change, see *Video Explorations*.

Historically, a common trend in the structural change of an economy has been for the primary sector to be the most important sector initially, followed by growth in industry and expansion of the service sector. What causes the service sector to expand? Lifestyle changes that come with increased income play an important role. Because we desire different kinds of entertainment and specialized health care, services emerge to meet these demands.

Types of Services

As our discussion of deindustrialization, structural change, and service sector expansion shows, the types of jobs and patterns of employment are more heterogeneous than ever. Just what kinds of economic activities does the service sector include?

Video Explorations

Essaouira, Morocco

National Geographic

As fishing opportunities in Essaouira decline, its economy is increasingly focused on tourism.

You already have a general idea of some of the kinds of jobs that are service sector jobs, but you may not realize just how diverse the service sector is. Thus far we have taken an expansive view of service industries. However, many geographers and other scholars point out that important distinctions can be made between different kinds of service activities, including **quaternary** and **quinary services**. When we identify quaternary and quinary services, it becomes necessary to adopt a narrower view of tertiary activities that associates them with the provision of domestic and quasi-domestic services, as shown in **Figure 10.15**.

What kind of job do you plan to have after you graduate? Will it be a job in the primary, secondary, or tertiary sector? It is very likely that you will work in the services since that is the sector of the economy with the most jobs in the United States. More than 75% of all U.S. jobs are service sector jobs, and that percentage is expected to increase in the coming years. During the recession, the U.S. economy saw employment increase in education and health-care related services and contract in manufacturing. Today just 9% of the U.S. workforce is employed in manufacturing, compared to about 23% in 1940.

Geography InSight

Categories of services
• Figure 10.15

THE PLANNER

The diversity of service activities has prompted the identification of different categories of services.

TERTIARY INDUSTRY

Categories of services

Domestic/Quasi-domestic	Information processing/Managerial	Human/Societal capacity building
Tertiary	*Quaternary*	*Quinary*
Restaurants and hotels Hair salons Dry cleaning Retail Repair and maintenance of household goods	Transportation Communication Real estate Insurance Finance Management — *Advanced professional services*: Advertising, Legal services, Investment banking, Consulting	Education Medical care Engineering Research and development Government Recreation and fine arts

© Ramin Talaie/Corbis

a. Tertiary services
Retail services are quasi-domestic tertiary services geared toward consumers. Here a barista prepares a beverage.

© winhorse/iStockphoto

Ron Chapple/Taxi/ Getty Images

b. Quaternary services
Quaternary services, such as package transport, help improve business efficency. Advanced professional services, including legal services, are a subset of quaternary services that require specialized expertise.

Steve Debenport/E+/ Getty Images

c. Quinary services
Quinary services produce knowledge and enhance quality of life. The photo shows a senior scientist conducting research.

Ask Yourself

To which category of services do accountants belong? What about not-for-profit organizations such as Doctors Without Borders?

Growth in the service sector has been accompanied by a concentration of women in service-related jobs, and efforts to promote gender mainstreaming.

a. These pie charts show the proportional growth in the service sector from 1970 to 2011. The geography of employment in the service sector, however, remains highly uneven. Today, nearly three-quarters of the labor force in developed countries is employed in services, yet in developing countries service jobs employ just over one-third of the labor force. (*Source:* Data from USAID, 2000; ILO, 2012.)

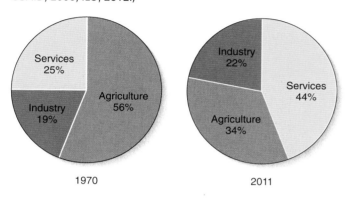

1970   2011

b. Globally, men are more concentrated in industry-related jobs and women are more concentrated in the services and agriculture. (*Source:* Data from ILO, 2012.)

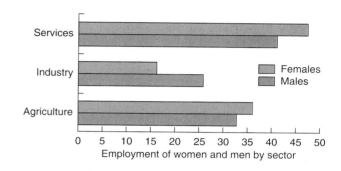

Services, Gender, and Postindustrial Society

The service sector has expanded rapidly in the United States and worldwide. When the world's countries are ranked by the share of their GDP derived from services, the United States comes out at the top. Remarkably, services account for 80% of the U.S. GDP. In general, services constitute a higher percentage of the GDP (approximately 71%) in developed countries compared to about 55% of the GDP in developing countries.

Today, the global economic structure is quite different than it was 40 years ago. Globally, the percentage of people employed in services worldwide has nearly doubled since 1970, and the service sector now employs a higher percentage of the world's people than agriculture (**Figure 10.16**). Improvements in technology and communication, including lower costs for sending and receiving data internationally, have contributed in very significant ways to the spread of services worldwide.

Service sector growth has also had a major impact on the employment of women. Even though women form a significant part of the labor force in EPZs and maquiladoras, on a global scale neither agriculture nor industry has as feminized a labor force as the service sector does. There are numerous countries where women account for 75% or more of the employment in services and a kind of gendered

occupational segregation exists. In order to level the playing field, the various divisions of the United Nations have supported gender mainstreaming for more than a decade. The aim of gender mainstreaming is to promote the equitable participation of women and men in all types of jobs.

Growth in the service sector not only points to important changes in employment patterns, but is also associated with the emergence of **postindustrial societies**. There are five main characteristics of postindustrial societies: (1) high levels of urbanization; (2) dominance of the service sector, especially in total employment; (3) prevalence of "white-collar" workers (professionals and highly skilled specialists) in the labor force; (4) an infrastructure heavily based on information and communication technology (ICT) such as computer software, networks, and satellites; and (5) a knowledge-based economy. In a *knowledge-based economy* expertise, know-how, and resourceful ideas drive innovation and create value. Knowledge is a productive asset that rivals traditional productive assets such as land or labor. If Fordist mass production was the dominant system of production in developed countries from World War II until the 1980s, then the ICT system prevails in postindustrial societies. Fordist production systems based on linear processes have been supplanted by networked systems driven by high-tech innovations.

Technopoles • Figure 10.17

The locations and characteristics of technopoles point to the rise of knowledge-based economies.

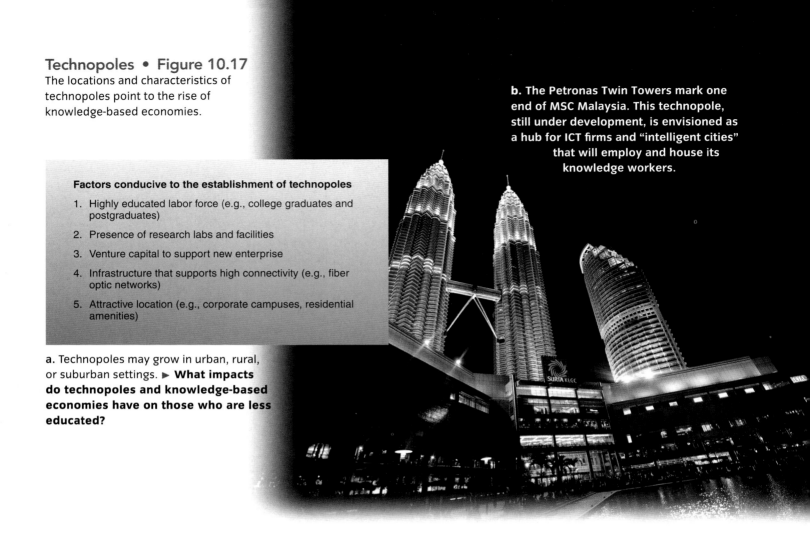

b. The Petronas Twin Towers mark one end of MSC Malaysia. This technopole, still under development, is envisioned as a hub for ICT firms and "intelligent cities" that will employ and house its knowledge workers.

Factors conducive to the establishment of technopoles

1. Highly educated labor force (e.g., college graduates and postgraduates)
2. Presence of research labs and facilities
3. Venture capital to support new enterprise
4. Infrastructure that supports high connectivity (e.g., fiber optic networks)
5. Attractive location (e.g., corporate campuses, residential amenities)

a. Technopoles may grow in urban, rural, or suburban settings. ▶ **What impacts do technopoles and knowledge-based economies have on those who are less educated?**

One of the best indicators of a knowledge-based economy is the amount spent on research and development (R&D). High-income countries spend three or more times as much money on R&D as do middle- and low-income countries. Funds for R&D are provided by a mix of private firms, nonprofit organizations, and government agencies. One of the landscape expressions of R&D is the **technopole**—an area with a cluster of firms conducting research, design, development, and/or manufacturing in high-tech industries such as wireless communications, integrated circuitry, or software development. California's Silicon Valley, which began to develop as a technopole in the 1950s, is the recognized prototype. Google, Intel, Hewlett-Packard, and numerous other ICT firms have their headquarters in the Silicon Valley.

Technopoles provide a good example of the agglomeration that is associated with high-tech industries. Manuel Castells, a sociologist who has written several books on the information revolution, gives three reasons for the development of technopoles: reindustrialization, regional development, and synergy. The first two reasons are closely related. In an area that has experienced job loss, creation of a technopole can provide a source of employment. Similarly, as nodes of economic activity, technopoles can rejuvenate regional economies. In some cases, technopoles are specifically used as a strategy for urban and economic development. By synergy, Castells refers to the benefits achieved through cross-fertilization. Technopoles can be thought of as "incubators of innovation" that capitalize on agglomeration and the reduced transaction costs that agglomeration brings. As shown in **Figure 10.17**, several factors are conducive to the establishment of technopoles.

Spatially, technopoles usually begin as a collection of nodes that, over time, grow along transportation routes. The Research Triangle in North Carolina has coalesced around the cities of Raleigh, Durham, Chapel Hill, and the several highways and interstates that serve the area. Silicon Fen has developed around Cambridge, England; Sweden has its Wireless Valley outside Stockholm; and the

Sophia Antipolis technopole has grown between Nice and Cannes in France.

Although technopoles are not unique to the developed world, their presence in semiperipheral and peripheral countries is often the result of planned government initiatives. Since 1999 the government of the State of Karnatka, India, has promoted the development of an IT Corridor on the outskirts of Bangalore; it is now called the Silicon Valley of India. Similarly, the city of Hyderabad, also in India, has supported the creation of Hi-Tec City (Hyderabad Information Technology and Engineering Consultancy), sometimes referred to as "Cyberabad."

Other technopoles include the MSC (Multimedia Super Corridor) in Malaysia, and the emerging Smart City in Cairo.

CONCEPT CHECK

1. **How** are industrialization and deindustrialization interconnected?
2. **What** is the dominant system of production in postindustrial societies?
3. **Where** are technopoles likely to develop?

Summary

1 Types of Industry 298

- Human geographers recognize the existence of three types of industry. **Primary industry,** shown here, is extractive; **secondary industry** includes manufacturing and is transformative; and **tertiary industry** provides services to consumers or other businesses.

Types of industry • Figure 10.1

Stephen Sharnoff/NG Image Collection

- **Staple theory** explores the relationship between primary industry, the creation of **linkages,** the economic development of a region or country, and commodity dependence. In the developing world, commodity dependence has weakened since the 1980s but remains a serious problem for many countries.

- The **Industrial Revolution** refers to interrelated changes in technology and changes in the system of production of goods that began in England in the late 18th century. Greater access to capital combined with technological innovations helped unleash the Industrial Revolution. Geographically, the diffusion of the Industrial Revolution has been highly uneven at local, national, and global scales.

2 Evolution of Manufacturing in the Core 303

- A key aspect of the geography of manufacturing includes identifying the optimal location for firms. Consequently, geographers examine the costs and benefits of diverse site and situation factors. They also try to understand how such factors may change over time and what the consequences might be for their firm.

- The diffusion of the Industrial Revolution and **agglomeration** help explain the emergence of the major centers of manufacturing in the core prior to the 1970s. Within the core, **Fordism** and **Taylorism** strongly influenced the systems of production in North America and Western Europe. Between the 1930s and the 1970s, **vertical integration** developed in concert with producer-driven **commodity chains** geared toward the mass production of standardized goods for mass consumption, sometimes involving vast scales of production (see photo).

Vertical integration • Figure 10.5

Everett Collection/SuperStock

- **Flexible production**, a system pioneered in Japan, contributed to the crisis of Fordism in the 1970s and played a major role in reshaping the geography of manufacturing with the use of **just-in-time delivery** and **outsourcing**.

- Outsourcing may or may not involve **offshoring**, but the occurrence of offshoring is significant for the globalization of manufacturing.

3 Evolution of Manufacturing Beyond the Core   309

- By the 1980s, remarkable gains in industrial output had been achieved by the **newly industrialized economies (NIEs)** in Asia.

- The practice of offshoring and the existence of **export-processing zones**, including maquiladoras (see photo), have helped diffuse manufacturing into semiperipheral and peripheral areas to a greater extent than ever before. This diffusion has contributed to the growth of transnational supply chains and has resulted in a new international division of labor.

Maquiladoras and manufacturing • Figure 10.9

©John Gibbins/San Diego Union-Tribune/Zuma Press/Alamy.

4 Services   316

- Recent structural change in the core industrialized countries involves **deindustrialization** and the expansion of the service sector. Industrialization and deindustrialization are complicated and interconnected processes.

- The service industries are so diverse that it is helpful to distinguish among **tertiary**, **quaternary**, and **quinary services**.

- Globally, the percentage of people employed in the service sector has nearly doubled since the 1970s. Tertiary industries have a high concentration of women, more so than either primary or secondary industries. Gender mainstreaming constitutes one effort to address these occupational disparities.

- The emergence of a knowledge-based economy built around information and communication technologies and **technopoles**, such as the one shown here, indicates the ongoing importance of technological advances to structural, and specifically the emergence of **postindustrial societies**.

Technopoles • Figure 10.17

AFP/Saeed Khan/Getty Images, Inc.

Key Terms

- agglomeration 304
- commodity chain 306
- deindustrialization 316
- export-processing zone (EPZ) 311
- flexible production 308
- Fordism 305

- Industrial Revolution 300
- just-in-time delivery 308
- linkage 298
- manufacturing value added (MVA) 309
- newly industrialized economy (NIE) 310

- offshoring 308
- outsourcing 308
- postindustrial society 319
- primary industry 298
- quaternary service 318
- quinary service 318
- secondary industry 298

- staple theory 298
- Taylorism 304
- technopole 320
- tertiary industry 298
- vertical integration 305

Critical and Creative Thinking Questions

1. Staple theory has been criticized for being environmentally and technologically deterministic. Explain the rationale for these criticisms.

2. Review the two different methods for measuring commodity dependence in the first section of this chapter "Types of Industry." Discuss the advantages and disadvantages of each.

3. Identify an industrial firm in your area and do some research to explain what it produces and why it located where it did.

4. In 1942, the economist Joseph Schumpeter used the term *creative destruction* to explain that innovation drives competition and economic growth, but ironically, also unravels the status quo as old business practices and technology give way to newer ones. Why is the concept of creative destruction significant, and how is it relevant to the geography of industry and services?

5. What is a "right-to-work" state, and do you live in one? Has right-to-work legislation affected industry in your region?

6. To what extent does specialization in the provision of services resemble Fordism? Justify your response.

7. In addition to research and development expenditures, what other national data might be used to identify a knowledge-based economy?

8. The greater participation of women in the workforce, like the example in the photo, might be considered both advantageous and problematic for women. Why?

Joe Raedle/Newsmakers/Getty Images, Inc.

What is happening in this picture?

These women break up and carry rocks at a construction site in India. In parts of South and Southeast Asia, women and men work alongside one another in construction, though most laborers are male.

Think Critically

1. What does this photo suggest about the geography of gender mainstreaming?
2. What factors contribute to the gendering of certain occupations?

Blaine Harrington III/Alamy

Self-Test

(Check your answers in Appendix B.)

1. Identify two service activities associated with each category and write them in the appropriate boxes

TERTIARY INDUSTRY

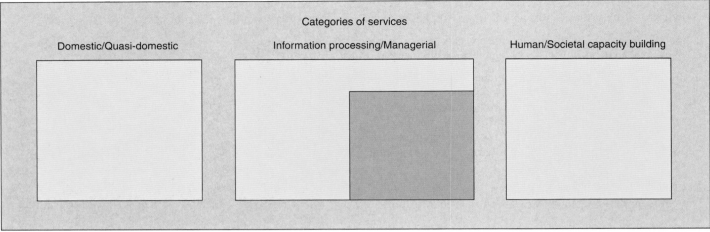

2. What kind of activity is advanced professional services?

a. primary

b. secondary

c. quaternary

d. quinary

3. The construction of railroad lines to supply a steel mill with iron ore and coal provides an example of _____ linkages.

a. forward

b. backward

c. demand

d. industrial

4. Staple theory _____.

a. explains the growth of export-processing zones

b. uses natural resources to explain an area's economic development

c. relates secondary industry to Fordism and Taylorism

d. accounts for the growth of services

5. _____ is considered to be the hearth of the Industrial Revolution.

a. England

b. Germany

c. The United States

d. Belgium

6. Identify the characteristic below that is associated with a Fordist system of production.

a. multiskilled labor

b. little inventory

c. producer-driven commodity chain

d. flat management style

7. Manufacturing value added (MVA) is defined as _____.

a. the cost of the finished product

b. the sum of all inputs used to make a product

c. the value gained by putting a brand name on a manufactured good

d. the cost of the finished product minus the cost of all inputs used to make it

8. Using your knowledge of MVA, place these labels on the diagram: research and development; distribution; contract manufacturing; marketing and sales; assembly; creation of original brand designs.

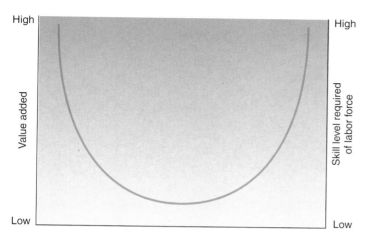

Stage in the commodity chain

9. _____ is a second-tier newly industrialized economy.
   a. Thailand
   b. Hong Kong
   c. Singapore
   d. Taiwan

10. Location in the global periphery and simplified tax regulations are characteristics of _____.
    a. outsourcing
    b. export-processing zones
    c. multinational corporations
    d. commodity dependence

11. Briefly identify three factors that help explain the rise of the Asian NIEs as important centers of manufacturing.

_____

_____

_____

12. Explain the difference between outsourcing and offshoring.

_____

_____

_____

_____

13. Use these images to explain what geographers mean by structural change.

_____

_____

_____

Matt Rourke,©AP/Wide World Photos

Rick Smith/©AP/Wide World Photos

14. Which statement about offshoring is *false*?
    a. Offshoring originated with China's special economic zones.
    b. Offshoring has affected the global character of manufacturing.
    c. Offshoring has affected the geography of profit from the sale of manufactured goods.
    d. Offshoring is associated with a new international division of labor.

15. As discussed in the chapter, which of the following is *not* one of the reasons given to explain the development of technopoles?
    a. synergy among local businesses
    b. a need to reindustrialize
    c. a desire to promote regional development
    d. structural change associated with deindustrialization

THE PLANNER ✓

Review your Chapter Planner on the chapter opener and check off your completed work.

Agricultural Geographies

AGRICULTURE AND FAIR TRADE

Do you think coffee is expensive? Over the past two decades, the price of coffee has fluctuated erratically, falling to record lows in some years with devastating effects on coffee producers, most of whom are small farmers. In fact, about 25 million small farmers grow and harvest nearly three-fourths of the world's coffee.

Even though it is not unusual for Americans to pay as much as $25 for a pound of specialty Ethiopian coffee, most of the small coffee farmers in Ethiopia and the sorters, like the women shown here, remain impover-ished and earn less than $10 a week. In contrast, coffee pur-chasers such as Kraft and Nestlé earn large profits generated from coffee sales.

Enter Fair Trade—a social movement and trading partnership committed to helping farmers whose situation has worsened rather than improved as a result of global trade. In these partnerships, companies agree to pay higher, stable prices to farmers along with an additional premium for investing in social projects. In return, farmers organize cooperatives, provide safe working conditions, reinvest in community development, and adopt sustainable practices. Fair Trade products must meet other criteria and be certified.

As this example shows, agriculture is closely connect-ed with trade, globalization, and community development. One of the goals of this chapter is to help you understand agriculture in local and global contexts, beginning with the origins of agriculture. We also examine different agricultural practices, followed by a discussion of sustainability and globalization.

Global
Locator

ETHIOPIA

NATIONAL
GEOGRAPHIC

CHAPTER OUTLINE

CHAPTER PLANNER ✓

- ❑ Study the picture and read the opening story.
- ❑ Scan the Learning Objectives in each section:
  p. 328 ❑   p. 335 ❑   p. 346 ❑
- ❑ Read the text and study all visuals.
  Answer any questions.

Analyze key features

- ❑ Video Explorations, p. 329
- ❑ Process Diagram, p. 330 ❑   p. 336 ❑
- ❑ Geography InSight, p. 332 ❑   p. 343 ❑
- ❑ What a Geographer Sees, p. 346
- ❑ Stop: Answer the Concept Checks before you go on:
  p. 334 ❑   p. 345 ❑   p. 350 ❑

End of chapter

- ❑ Review the Summary and Key Terms.
- ❑ Answer the Critical and Creative Thinking Questions.
- ❑ Answer What is happening in this picture?
- ❑ Complete the Self-Test and check your answers.

Agriculture: Origins and Revolutions

LEARNING OBJECTIVES

1. **Identify** the hearths of agriculture.
2. **Distinguish** among the first, second, and third agricultural revolutions.
3. **Contrast** the Green Revolution and the Gene Revolution.

 lthough we seldom think about it, our lifestyle is intimately connected with and highly dependent on **agriculture**, especially the ability to produce, process, and transport agricultural commodities. Agriculture involves the ongoing process of **domestication**—selecting plants or animals for specific characteristics and influencing their reproduction. Domestication not only makes plants and animals visibly or behaviorally distinct from their wild ancestors but also increases the interdependence between people and the domesticate. Domestication reflects human agency.

> **agriculture** Activities centered on cultivating domesticated crops and livestock in order to procure food and fiber for human use or consumption.

Until very recently, agriculture employed the highest percentage of people worldwide. As we saw in Chapter 10, the service sector now employs the highest percentage of people—about 44% of the world's workforce. In comparison, the agricultural sector employs approximately 34% of the world's workforce.

This decline in the share of agricultural employment is a testament to the ongoing urbanization of our world as well as the mechanization and industrialization of agriculture. Even so, employment in the agricultural sector differs vastly from one region and country to another. Although women have been involved in agriculture since it began, certain trends increasingly point to a new feminization of agriculture (**Figure 11.1**).

Origins of Agriculture

Hunting and gathering is the oldest method of obtaining food, and historically all people obtained their food this way. Most hunters and gatherers moved frequently in pursuit of game and seasonally available plants, although some groups that relied heavily on fishing might settle permanently in one location. Strictly speaking, however, hunters and gatherers are not classified as agriculturalists because they use wild rather than domesticated plants and animals.

> **hunting and gathering** Hunting wild animals, fishing, and gathering wild plants for food.

A geography of employment in agriculture • Figure 11.1

Agricultural employment varies by region and gender.

a. Employment in agriculture by region
Agriculture employs a higher percentage of people in Sub-Saharan Africa than in any other world region. For example, in Tanzania, Rwanda, and Ethiopia the share of the labor force employed in agriculture exceeds 80%. (*Source:* Data from ILO, 2012.)

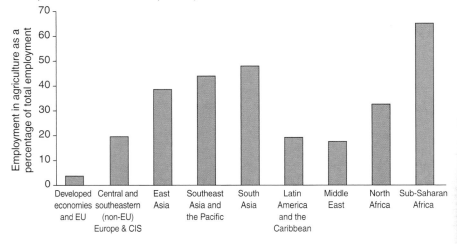

b. Gender and agriculture
Women, like these threshing millet in Niger, produce a majority of the food in developing countries. The new feminization of agriculture in these regions stems in part from the migration of men into cities for work, the increase in households headed by women, and the willingness of women to perform tasks once assigned to their children so that their children can attend school.

Finbarr O'Reilly/Landov LLC

As a way of life, hunting and gathering is in decline because of the dominance of settled agriculture and its close association with the modern state and global economy. Today hunting and gathering is confined to peripheral areas, where it is practiced by small numbers of people including, among others, the San of southern Africa, some Aboriginals in the interior of Australia, and the Moken of Myanmar (see *Video Explorations)*. The notion that hunters and gatherers live on the brink of starvation is a popular misconception; numerous studies have shown that hunters and gatherers are generally well nourished. Historically, the transition from hunting and gathering to farming marks the first of three sweeping revolutions that have transformed the world.

The First and Second Agricultural Revolutions

The development of agriculture constitutes the **first agricultural revolution**, which began with the domestication of plants and animals some 11,000 years ago. Most geographers agree that agriculture was independently invented at different locations and at different times (**Figure 11.2**).

Video Explorations

Moken

National Geographic

This video provides an introduction to the Moken people of Myanmar (Burma), sometimes called hunters and gatherers of the sea.

Hearths of agriculture • Figure 11.2

The map shows the five hearths of agricultural innovation and three secondary centers. They are secondary centers because it is not clear if diffusion of crops and food production practices contributed to the origins of agriculture in these locations or if people independently developed agriculture there.

Eastern United States 2500 BCE
Sunflower and other local plants

Mesoamerica 3500 BCE
Corn, beans, squash, turkey

Western Amazonia

Andean Highlands 3500 BCE
Potatoes, manioc, llama

Fertile Crescent 8500 BCE–8000 BCE
Wheat, barley, sheep, goat

China 7500 BCE
Millet, Chinese cabbage, pig

Sub-Saharan Africa

New Guinea

■ Hearths of agricultural innovation and selected domesticates

■ Secondary centers of agriculture

0   2000 Miles
0   2000 Kilometers

Four-course crop rotation • Figure 11.3

This system, introduced to England from Holland in the 18th century, is based on a four-year planting regime. This crop cycle balances the planting of food crops with feed crops and incorporates legumes that enrich the soil. By removing the need for a fallow period, this practice also enables higher agricultural yields. Many variations on this system exist today.

Course 1 Small grain crop

In the first year a small grain, such as wheat, barley, rye, or oats is planted and provides a marketable crop.

Course 2 Root crop

Fields planted to small grain crops are susceptible to weeds. Thus, in the second year root crops, such as turnips, are planted in rows that can be hoed to remove weeds. Turnips also provide feed for livestock.

dem10/iStockphoto

Elena Elisseeva/ iStockphoto

The roots of the **second agricultural revolution** can be traced to new agricultural practices in western Europe. During the Middle Ages the adoption of two innovations, both of which likely originated in China, significantly raised farming yields. The first was the introduction of a curved metal plate used to make the moldboard plow, which enabled farmers to turn over heavy soils. The second was the use of the horse collar. Prior to the collar's introduction, farmers used oxen—much slower animals.

During the 17th and 18th centuries a modification in the technique of **crop rotation** helped boost farm yields. Traditional agricultural practice involved planting the same crop in a field each year, which reduced soil fertility; as a result, farmers were forced to periodically leave their fields uncultivated, or *fallow*, so that the soil could recover. The **four-course system** eliminated the fallow period entirely (**Figure 11.3**).

In addition, as a result of the Industrial Revolution, more horse-drawn equipment was developed, while other

crop rotation
Growing a sequence of different crops in the same field in order to maintain soil fertility and health.

tools improved the efficiency of farm practices. For example, Jethro Tull's seed drill placed seed directly into small holes. Before the seed drill, farmers often planted seeds by tossing handfuls of them into a field.

The Third Agricultural Revolution

Technological innovations and scientific farming techniques developed in the 20th century form the basis for the **third agricultural revolution.** More specifically, the third agricultural revolution includes extensive mechanization, heavy reliance on irrigation and chemical applications, and biotechnology. The third agricultural revolution is still in progress.

The internal combustion engine, developed in the late 19th century and improved during the 20th century, paved the way for the greater mechanization of agriculture, as gas and diesel engine tractors were more powerful and maneuverable than those powered by steam engines. Beginning in the United States, the tractor contributed to the transformation of agriculture in at least three significant ways. First, tractors reduced the number of laborers required for a

Course 3 Small grain crop

Barley is planted in the third year, providing another marketable crop.

Mlenny/iStockphoto

Course 4 Legume

A forage legume, such as clover, is planted in the fourth year. Legumes boost soil fertility by converting atmospheric nitrogen into a form more useful for plants. Livestock are grazed on the clover and their manure, also nitrogen rich, helps fertilize the soil.

Rachel Dunn/iStockphoto

particular task and simultaneously improved the efficiency and productivity of farming. Second, the tractor helped bring more land into cultivation. Third, tractors facilitated the shift to **monoculture**, leading to a substantial alteration of environments and landscapes. Similar impacts have occurred elsewhere as adoption and use of tractors continue.

> **monoculture**
> Planting a single crop in a field, often over a large area.

Scientific farming, another hallmark of the third agricultural revolution, relies on technology and synthetic chemicals to promote crop growth, deter crop disease, prevent weeds, or solve other agricultural challenges. Although irrigation has long been practiced, improved irrigation technologies have facilitated the spread of crops into areas once considered too dry for them. Since the 1960s, for example, the amount of irrigated land in the world has more than doubled. Although use of chemical fertilizers and pesticides has increased yields, our dependence on them has significant ecological costs—including pollution and greater reliance on petroleum, which is used to apply and manufacture many of them.

Agricultural biotechnology, or agro-biotech, is an additional facet of the third agricultural revolution. Broadly speaking, **agro-biotech** seeks to improve the quality and yield of crops and livestock through the use of such techniques as cross-breeding, hybridization, and, more recently, genetic engineering. The impact of agro-biotech developments on agriculture can best be understood by distinguishing between the **Green Revolution** and the **Gene Revolution**. In this context, *green* refers to the expansion of productive agriculture, not to the adoption of organic or eco-friendly practices in the way we popularly use the term today.

There are two fundamental differences between the Green Revolution and the Gene Revolution. The first is that innovations associated with the Green Revolution,

> **Green Revolution**
> The dramatic increase in grain production between 1965 and 1985 in Asia and Latin America from high-yielding, fertilizer- and irrigation-dependent varieties of wheat, rice, and corn.
>
> **Gene Revolution**
> The shift, since the 1980s, to greater private and corporate involvement in and control of the research, development, intellectual property rights, and genetic engineering of highly specialized agricultural products, especially crop varieties.

The Green Revolution
• **Figure 11.4**

The Green Revolution grew out of an effort to alleviate world hunger. In the 1950s, scientists in Mexico developed a high-yield strain of wheat responsive to fertilizer and irrigation. High-yielding seed varieties were exported to India and Pakistan in the 1960s; in less than a decade, wheat production nearly doubled in both countries.

Narinder Nanu/AFP/Getty Images, Inc.

b. This farmer in the Punjab region of India examines his wheat crop.

a. This chart shows changes in the nature of agricultural production in India, Pakistan, and other developing countries in Asia. The Green Revolution introduced a new system of agriculture dependent on irrigation, heavy inputs of synthetic fertilizers, greater mechanization, and the monoculture of wheat or rice. (*Source:* Adapted from Borlaug and Dowswell, 2004.)

Year	Area irrigated in million hectares (acres)	Fertilizer nutrient use (million tons)	Tractors (millions)
1961	87 (215)	2	0.2
1970	106 (262)	10	0.5
1980	129 (319)	29	2.0
1990	158 (390)	54	3.4
2000	175 (432)	70	4.8

c. Government policies encouraged farmers to adopt this new system. These policies were implemented in India.

Selected government policies implemented in India
• A minimum support price for wheat and rice: If the market price of the grain fell below this price, the government reimbursed the farmer the difference. This policy lessened the financial risk of adopting high-yielding strains.
• Subsidies for synthetic fertilizer
• Subsidies on electricity, which is necessary to power well pumps for irrigation
• Increased opportunities for agricultural loans and credit-based purchases of various supplies (seeds, fertilizer, pesticides) and equipment

such as high-yielding varieties, were shared with governments and agencies in developing countries, whereas genetically engineered crops produced during the Gene Revolution have been protected by patents. The second difference is that the Gene Revolution is more closely associated with multinational corporations and the spread of global capitalism. See **Figure 11.4** for a visual depiction of other facets of the Green Revolution.

The Green Revolution staved off famine in Asia and enabled India to become self-sufficient in grain production. However, yields have begun to level off, raising concerns about future food security. Will advances associated with the Gene Revolution help extend the gains of the Green Revolution? This is a contentious issue, in part because it leads many critics to question the motives for and consequences of the Gene Revolution. For

d. The Green Revolution has diffused unevenly. Worldwide, wheat, rice, and corn production have been strongly affected. Africa, which depends on other cereal crops, remains least affected by the Green Revolution. Within Asia and Latin America, areas with reliable rainfall and where irrigation is possible have benefited the most. (*Source:* Data from FAOSTAT, 2013.)

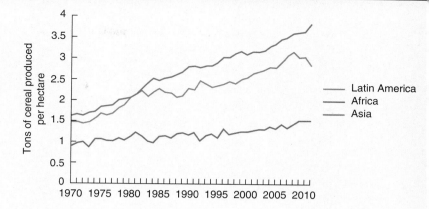

e. The Green Revolution has also brought about some problems. Farmers' debt has risen, groundwater has been overexploited, soil fertility has declined, and fertilizer and pesticide residues have built up in the environment. Open water sources in the area, like the one shown here, can be contaminated when fields are sprayed with pesticides.

Bloomberg via Getty Images

example, whose interests are served when the genetic makeup of crops is protected by patents? Monsanto, an agro-biotech multinational, acquired the company that developed *terminator seeds*—seeds that produce sterile plants so that farmers have to purchase new seeds from Monsanto each year. Monsanto has not marketed these seeds because of public outcry, but the example is instructive nonetheless.

As we have seen, genetic engineering is an important part of the Gene Revolution. More specifically, genes with the code for certain traits, such as drought tolerance or stronger stalks, are transferred from one organism to another. Part of the controversy of this kind of genetic engineering centers on the role and level of human involvement or interference. Genetic engineers transfer genes from animals or even viruses to crops rather than allowing these

GM cropping • Figure 11.5

Genetically modified (GM) crops can be made more resistant to weeds, pests, and disease, and sometimes have higher nutritional value than traditional crops.

a. The number of countries planting GM crops climbed from 6 in 1996, the first year they were introduced, to 25 in 2008. GM varieties are used to plant about 40% of the total acreage sown to soybeans, maize (corn), cotton, and canola. (*Source:* Data from ISAAA, 2008.)

Biotech Cropland, 2008 (in million hectares)

- More than 10
- 2.5–10
- 0.5–2.49
- 0.1–0.49
- Less than 0.1
- Data not available

NATIONAL GEOGRAPHIC

b. GM crops remain controversial because they mix genes from different organisms. Also, some GM foods are marketed without labeling to indicate that they have been genetically modified. This protest is in London.

Think Critically

What factors might influence a farmer's decision to plant GM crops?

Graeme Robertson/Getty Images, Inc.

transfers to occur naturally. Plants and animals changed as a result of biotechnology are referred to as *transgenic* or *genetically modified organisms* (GMOs). Proponents of this kind of genetic engineering consider it a viable means of overcoming environmental problems and generating more reliable yields. Opponents raise questions about the actual effectiveness of GMOs, the safety of GMOs for human health, and the long-term ecological consequences of genetic engineering (**Figure 11.5**).

CONCEPT CHECK   **STOP**

1. **How** do geographers distinguish between hearths of agriculture and secondary centers of agricultural innovation?

2. **What** agricultural advances led to the changeover from the first to the second to the third agricultural revolutions?

3. **What** is the controversy around the Gene Revolution?

Agricultural Systems

LEARNING OBJECTIVES

1. **Distinguish** between subsistence and commercial systems of agriculture.
2. **Discuss** the distribution of the four types of subsistence agriculture.
3. **Provide** examples of specialization in different types of commercial agriculture.
4. **Summarize** the von Thünen model.

W e might think of agriculture as a system of food production and thus a strategy for human survival. A *system* is a set of interacting components that functions as a unit. Food-producing systems include the land, the inputs (e.g., labor, machinery, fertilizer), the outputs or commodities that are produced, the consumers, and the various flows among the different components (e.g., migrant farm laborers to available jobs, of seeds to farmers, or of grain to food processors).

There are different ways of categorizing agricultural systems. Some experts prefer to distinguish between **subsistence agriculture** and **commercial agriculture**. **Figure 11.6** describes some of the differences between these systems and maps several of the world's major agricultural systems that are discussed in greater detail in the following sections.

subsistence agriculture A farming system that is largely independent of purchased inputs and in which outputs are typically used or consumed by farmers and their family or extended family.

commercial agriculture A farming system that relies heavily on purchased inputs and in which products are sold for use or consumption away from the farm.

The world's major agricultural systems • Figure 11.6

These images show the characteristics and distribution of different systems of agriculture.

a. The table distinguishes between subsistence and commercial systems of agriculture. This categorization is useful as long as we remember that the different types of agriculture form a continuum marked by a great many variations.

The continuum of agricultural systems		
	Subsistence	**Commercial**
Farm size	small	large
Agricultural activity	diverse	specialized
Scale of consumption	household, local	national, international
Land tenure	communal, private	private, corporate
Purchased inputs	low	high
Contract farming	infrequent	frequent
Vertical integration	low	high
Proportion of output sold	minority	majority or all

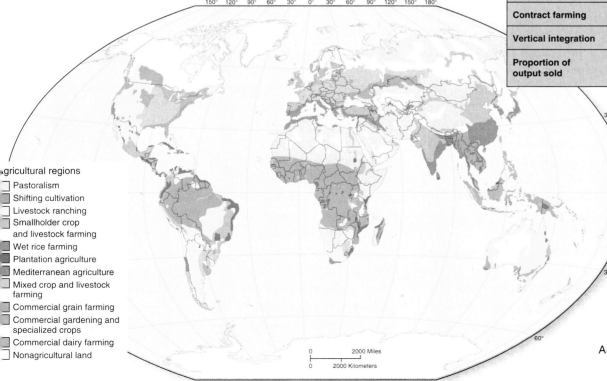

Agricultural regions
- Pastoralism
- Shifting cultivation
- Livestock ranching
- Smallholder crop and livestock farming
- Wet rice farming
- Plantation agriculture
- Mediterranean agriculture
- Mixed crop and livestock farming
- Commercial grain farming
- Commercial gardening and specialized crops
- Commercial dairy farming
- Nonagricultural land

b. Hundreds of different agricultural systems exist around the world, but this map depicts just a fraction of them. For instance, urban agriculture is not included on the map. Keep in mind that even though some areas share similar agricultural systems, local agricultural practices may vary considerably because of different policies, climate patterns, or traditions. (*Source:* Adapted from Hammond, 2004, p. 31.)

Shifting cultivation • Figure 11.7

Shifting cultivation is associated with rainforest zones, in both lowland and upland regions of the humid tropics. The cultivated land is usually owned or controlled by local families or by an entire village. Although the total area of land controlled by a village can be sizable, individual fields are small, perhaps 5 acres (2 ha).

1 Selecting a site
Farmers consider family needs, ecological conditions, past successes or failures in the area, and other factors when choosing a site.

2 Clearing a field
Using a "slash-and-burn" technique, farmers kill the trees by cutting into them and removing a ring of bark from each. They then burn the trees and undergrowth, sometimes selectively retaining those that provide a resource or serve an important function, such as preventing soil erosion. The residual ash adds nutrients and improves the soil.

3 Planting
Fields may include a single crop, have patches planted to different crops, or may be intercropped. If intercropped, tall, sturdy, or broadleaved crops provide support, shade, and even protection from heavy rains for lower growing crops and reduce the need for weeding.

© David R. Frazier Photolibrary, Inc. / Alamy

A farmer sows seed in a smoldering field in Indonesia.

Photo from Marco Schmidt 2006. Pflanzenvielfalt in Burkina Faso-Analyse, Modellierung und Dokumentation. With permission of the author.

Corn grows amid diverse trees in Burkina Faso.

Subsistence Agriculture

Worldwide, millions of people earn their living through subsistence agriculture. This system is especially prevalent in Africa, much of Asia, and parts of Central and South America. There is a stunning array of subsistence agricultural practices around the world. Here, we will consider a few of them so that you may better understand some of the constraints and opportunities that subsistence agriculturalists face. From the many different of types of subsistence agriculture, we will focus on four, each of which is suited to a different climate, environment, and land type.

> **shifting cultivation**
> An agricultural system that uses fire to clear vegetation in order to create fields for crops; it is based on a cycle of land rotation that includes fallow periods.

Shifting cultivation Also known as *swidden* or *slash-and-burn agriculture*, **shifting cultivation** has been practiced for thousands of years in the tropical and subtropical regions of Southeast Asia, Central and South America, and Africa. Shifting cultivation has different local names: *milpa* in Central America, *ladang* in Indonesia and Malaysia, *roca* in Brazil, and *chitimene* in some African countries, including Zambia and Zimbabwe. Some shifting cultivators plant two or more crops in a field at the same time—a strategy known as **intercropping** (**Figure 11.7**).

Agricultural experts are divided over the impact that shifting cultivation has on tropical deforestation, in part because they interpret deforestation in different ways. For example, deforestation is commonly understood to include both permanent and temporary forest removal; a view that magnifies the role of shifting cultivation in deforestation. In the Amazon, however, the expansion of other agricultural systems, including cattle ranches and soybean plantations, is hastening the permanent destruction of tropical rainforests on an unprecedented scale.

Ask Yourself

Why is shifting cultivation called a system of land rotation rather than crop rotation?

4 Harvesting

The harvest cycle depends on the crops that are planted. Intercropping may extend the harvest as different crops reach maturity at different times and may lessen the impact if one crop fails. As soil fertility declines, usually in about two to four years, yields begin to diminish.

©2008 by William Robichaud

Swidden rice field after harvest in central Laos.

5 Fallowing the land

The field is fallowed in order to regain fertility. The length of the fallow period—5, 7, 10, or more years—depends on local conditions. A single family will have several fields in different phases: Some ready to be fallowed, others about mid-way through the fallow cycle, and still others soon to be cleared for cultivation.

In Thailand, previously cleared forest regrows in the background.

©Dr. Jack D. Ives

Shifting cultivation can be sustainably practiced, but under certain conditions it can adversely affect the environment, or fail. Conditions that shorten the fallow period present a serious problem because they inhibit the ability of the soils to regain their fertility. An increase in the number of households engaged in shifting cultivation or loss of land to urbanization or highways can shorten the fallow period and affect the sustainability of the system.

When faced with such pressures, one strategy used by shifting cultivators to maintain adequate yields and improve the soil involves **agroforestry**, or the purposeful integration of trees with crops and/or livestock in the same field simultaneously or sequentially, one after the other. Many shifting cultivators now increasingly "manage the fallows" by planting species that help restore the soil's fertility or provide another resource, such as a fruit crop.

Pastoralism Domesticated livestock form the centerpiece of **pastoralism**. Pastoralists favor reindeer in the cold lands, and camels, cattle, goats, or sheep in arid regions. Because of their importance as a resource, the livestock are rarely killed and consumed for their meat. Consequently, in varying degrees pastoralists trade with, and rely on, settled farmers for cereal crops, fruits, and vegetables. Pastoralism is well adapted to arid and semiarid regions.

> **pastoralism** An agricultural system in which animal husbandry based on open grazing of herd animals is the sole or dominant farming activity.

Mobility is an important dimension of pastoralism, since pastures cannot support livestock herds year-round. **Transhumance**—moving herds on a seasonal basis to new pastures or water sources—is a common practice, but the nature and frequency of mobility varies among pastoralists.

Often the women and children may not move with the animals; instead, they will settle and farm small plots of land in areas where rainfall or access to water is more reliable (**Figure 11.8**).

Is pastoral life incompatible with modernization? Some government officials claim that the mobility of pastoralists interferes with government programs such as population censuses, the provision of schools or basic medical care, and the establishment of protected areas and reserves. Increasingly, pastoral groups are pressured to take up sedentary agriculture in permanent settlements or seek non-agricultural occupations. For example, since the breakup of the Soviet Union, land privatization in Kyrgyzstan has limited pastoralists' access to pastures.

Wet rice farming

Where rice is the primary crop and staple food, **wet rice farming** constitutes a prime example of **intensive agriculture**. In the world's most densely populated regions, the amount of land owned or worked by a family may be only 3 or 4 acres (1–2 ha), sometimes even smaller. In these circumstances, wet rice farming also constitutes a form of **smallholder agriculture**. Farmers cultivate wet rice in coastal lowlands, deltas, and river valleys (**Figure 11.9**).

> **wet rice farming** Rice cultivation in a flooded field.
>
> **intensive agriculture** An agricultural system characterized by high inputs, such as labor, capital, or equipment, per unit area of land.
>
> **smallholder agriculture** A farming system characterized by small farms in which the household is the main scale of agricultural production and consumption.

In order to produce yields sufficient to provide for a family, the land must be intensively worked year-round. Following the harvest, the paddy may be prepared for planting a second time. The technique of **double cropping**—completing the cycle from planting to harvesting on the same field twice in one year—is common. Where a humid winter aids the cultivation cycle, as in southeastern China, rice is double cropped. In drier areas, farmers double crop by growing rice in the summer and wheat or barley during the winter.

Asia produces and consumes most of the rice in the world, and wet rice production benefited from the Green Revolution. Leading rice exporters include Thailand, Vietnam, India, and the United States, but rice production in the United States differs vastly from that in these other countries because it is not a smallholder system. In addition, rice production is highly mechanized in all stages in Japan, Korea, Taiwan, and the United States.

Smallholder crop and livestock farming

In those places in Asia where conditions are not conducive to wet rice farming, **smallholder crop and livestock farming** prevails. This system also occurs in other parts of the developing world, but the specific combination of crop types and livestock varies significantly from one place to another because of different socioeconomic,

NATIONAL GEOGRAPHIC

Pastoralism • Figure 11.8

Mobility is a key part of pastoralism.

a. Yak herders in India practice vertical transhumance—moving their herds into mountain pastures in the summer and into lowland pastures in the winter. In Nigeria, the Fulani practice horizontal transhumance, moving their cattle north to avoid the brunt of the wet season. They return south in the dry season.

Steve Winter/NG Image Collection

b. Governmental policies can cause pastoralism to break down. The creation of wildlife conservation areas in Tanzania has reduced the rangelands and mobility of Maasai herders like the one shown here.

Randy Olson/NG Image Collection

Wet rice farming • Figure 11.9

Wet rice cultivation begins as seeds are sown in planting beds. In one to two months the seedlings will be ready for transplanting, and the wet field where the rice seedlings will grow to maturity—the paddy—is plowed.

a. Wet rice cultivation takes place on hillside terraces in Longsheng, China. In smallholder wet rice systems, most rice is consumed by the members of the household but any surplus rice is sold. Households also typically keep some pigs or poultry and cultivate small plots for vegetables.

b. Women in Vietnam transplant rice seedlings into a field that has been flooded with water. Workers apply large amounts of fertilizer, manually weed and harvest the rice, and after harvesting, thresh it. Women contribute half or more of the labor through their work transplanting, weeding, harvesting, and threshing.

climatic, and soil conditions. Crop cultivation generally revolves around a grain crop, a tuber or root crop, legumes, and some vegetable crops. Many households also keep different kinds of livestock but in small numbers—for example, a single cow and a few pigs or chickens.

Across the drier parts of Asia corn and wheat are common grains, sweet potatoes a key root crop, and cattle and pigs the main livestock. In the Middle East and North Africa,

farmers cultivate wheat as the staple grain, barley primarily as animal feed, and legumes such as lentils and chickpeas. Sheep, goats, and cattle are important livestock. Corn, millet, and sorghum are common grains cultivated in Africa south of the Sahara. Cassava, a tuber, is also widely cultivated there. In contrast to wet rice cultivation, smallholder crop and livestock farmers apply fewer inputs of fertilizer and irrigated water, and do not double crop (**Figure 11.10**).

Smallholder crop and livestock farming • Figure 11.10

Lynn Johnson/NG Image Collection

Smallholder agriculture is highly diverse.

b. A Nigerian woman carries her baby and cassava home from the field. The root crop is a staple starch across Sub-Saharan Africa.

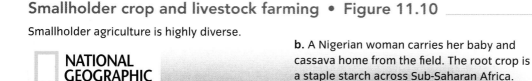

a. A smallholder farm in the Andes Mountains of Peru. Smallholders are more likely to depend on rainfall than on irrigation.

Commercial Agriculture

Commercial farmers and their families are not the primary users or consumers of the agricultural goods they produce. Rather, they sell their farm products to food-processing companies. Commercial agriculture is one part of the large industry of food production often referred to as **agribusiness**. One of the hallmarks of agribusiness is *vertical integration*—when a company controls two or more stages in the production or distribution of a commodity directly or through contractual arrangements (see Chapter 10).

> **agribusiness**
> The interconnected industry of food production involving farmers, processors, distributors, and retailers.

A number of food processors, such as Tyson, Kraft, and Kellogg's, have become household names. These companies consider commercial farmers to be their suppliers and negotiate contracts with them in order to secure the beef, poultry, wheat, corn, or other products they need for processing into the packaged meats, soups, cereals, and other items for consumers. In commercial agriculture, food-processing companies serve as an intermediary between producers and consumers.

As you read about some of the different types of commercial agriculture in this section, think about the impact they have had on landscape change, how they have altered social relations, and to what extent conventional ideas about the importance of physical proximity to market matter today.

Plantation agriculture Plantations have long been associated with the production of high-value **cash crops**, such as coffee, tea, palm oil, and sugar, that are sold on the international market. As we discussed in Chapter 10, many developing countries have become highly dependent on the export of staple commodities, including cash crops, because they contribute significantly to the national economy. Cotton, for example, ranks as the most valuable fiber crop. Plantations are not the sole source of the world's so-called plantation crops, however. Smallholder farmers also cultivate a number of these crops, including cacao, coffee, and coconuts among others (**Figure 11.11**).

> **plantation** A large estate in tropical or subtropical areas that specializes in the production of a cash crop.

The Portuguese established the first plantations in Africa in the 15th century. These plantations used slave labor to produce sugarcane. Relying on unskilled or semiskilled labor to plant, harvest, and process the

Plantation agriculture • Figure 11.11

Historically, plantations were established near the coast or serviced by rail lines in order to facilitate the export of plantation commodities.

a. A sugar plantation near Durban, South Africa
It is presently more cost-effective to burn the vegetation that remains once the sugarcane is harvested, though such burning is contested by environmentalists.

b. Modest housing for tea plantation workers in Malaysia
Work conditions at plantations are demanding, sometimes dangerous, and the pay is low. ▶ **Why are the houses virtually identical?**

James P. Blair/NG Image Collection

Stuart Forster/Alamy

farm commodities remains a defining feature of plantation agriculture today. Indeed, the plantation system perpetuates a **dual society** consisting of two distinct social classes—the upper-class plantation managers and the lower-class laborers.

In addition, the plantations are frequently owned by multinational corporations, a number of which are headquartered in Europe or North America. One example is the fruit company Dole. It is headquartered in California, operates plantations in the Philippines and Costa Rica, owns and runs a cannery in Thailand, and has cold-storage facilities in Chile. These pockets of commercial agriculture in developing countries also foster a **dual economy**, with large-scale, export-oriented agriculture operating alongside smallholder agriculture.

Commercial gardening, specialized crops, and Mediterranean agriculture

Geographically, com-

> **commercial gardening** The intensive production of nontropical fruits, vegetables, and flowers for sale off the farm.

mercial gardening zones developed just beyond the built-up areas of towns and cities and supplied urban residents with fresh produce. Historically, farmers located near the markets to minimize the problem of spoilage, and local products were destined for local consumption. However, well-developed transportation networks and long-distance trucking industries mean that fresh produce can now be shipped from farm to market over hundreds of miles in a matter of hours.

Since World War II, a form of commercial gardening known as **truck farming** has emerged in the United States. Important crops produced on truck farms include tomatoes, lettuce, melons, broccoli, onions, and strawberries. Most of these farms are large, specialize in the production of one commodity, are distant from the markets they serve, and rely on migrant farm laborers during the harvest season. Although product shipment involves large-capacity trucks, this is not the source of the term *truck farming*. Rather, one of the meanings of the word *truck* is "vegetables grown for market." Truck farming is heavily concentrated in the southeastern United States, but numerous other zones of specialized crop production exist, including parts of Maine and Idaho where potatoes are produced, and the Caucasus (located between Europe and Asia)

Mediterranean agriculture • Figure 11.12

Sheep graze in between the grape vines, an illustration of one facet of the integration of livestock and vine crops in Portugal. The sheep keep the vineyard weeded, provide manure, and can be trained to avoid eating the grape vines.

where such crops as cabbage, onions, and eggplant are farmed.

The lands surrounding the Mediterranean Sea constitute the hearth of **Mediterranean agriculture**. In its traditional form, Mediterranean agriculture was a kind of agroforestry centered on the integrated cultivation of livestock, a grain crop, and a tree or vine crop. Olives, grapes, and citrus fruits are strongly associated with regions of Mediterranean agriculture, but, as with commercial gardening, Mediterranean agriculture has been affected by specialization. This is especially the case in the Central Valley of California and in the region surrounding Valparaiso, Chile, which increasingly focus on the production of specialized crops. Around the Mediterranean Sea, wheat remains a principal grain crop, and some farms still manage livestock; however, tree and vine crops, especially olives and grapes, provide the most valuable commodities (**Figure 11.12**). Seasonal demand for work on these farms in Europe draws many farm laborers from Romania, Bulgaria, and Albania as well as North Africa. Migrant labor has long been crucial to agricultural harvesting in the Central Valley of California as well.

Commercial dairy farming Commercial **dairy farming** is an intensive and heavily mechanized form of agriculture. Fresh milk production relies on automatic milking machines, vacuum systems, and pipelines to move the milk into refrigerated storage tanks before it is transferred to tank trucks for shipment to milk-processing plants. In spite of the mechanization, dairy farming requires constant vigilance. The cows need to be milked twice a day and have their nutrition closely monitored, or they will not produce the desired quality or volume of milk.

The geography of fluid milk production has evolved in connection with the rise of cities. Because milk is perishable, it initially had to be consumed on the farm or made into another, less perishable dairy product such as cheese. Dairy farming areas on the outskirts of cities that supply fluid milk constitute the *milkshed*. Improvements in transportation and refrigeration now enable dairy farms producing milk to locate farther from cities, expanding the milkshed. California has been the largest fluid milk-producing state in the United States since the early 1990s, a development closely associated with the emergence of *dry-lot dairies* that facilitate high-volume production (**Figure 11.13**).

Mixed crop and livestock farming As historically practiced, **mixed crop and livestock farming** was an integrated system that involved

> **commercial dairy farming**
> The management of cattle for producing and marketing milk, butter, cheese, or other milk by-products.

> **factory farm**
> A farm that houses huge quantities of livestock or poultry in buildings, dry-lot dairies, or feedlots.
>
> **feedlot** Confined space used for the controlled feeding of animals.

raising crops to feed livestock. The animal products were then sold off the farm, generating most of the farm's revenue. This type of farming once defined an extensive part of Europe, stretching from France across central Europe and into Russia, where corn, barley, and oats were grown as feed crops for beef cattle and hogs. Across the Corn Belt of the United States (from central Ohio to eastern Nebraska), corn and soybeans were raised to feed cattle and hogs.

Agricultural specialization continues to transform these practices, however. In Europe, some regions once associated with mixed crop and livestock farming in countries including Germany, France, and Poland now concentrate on producing high-value oilseed crops such as canola. Specialization in the Corn Belt has involved two main trends. One trend emphasizes cash-grain farming of corn and soybeans in rotation, with corn planted one year and soybeans the next year. There are different ways to define *cash-grain farms* (also called commercial grain farms) but the distinction is usually based on revenue, with grain sales accounting for 50% or more of farm products sold. The second trend involves specialized hog production on **factory farms**, also known as concentrated animal feeding operations (CAFOs). **Feedlots** have become emblematic of factory farms. The dry-lot dairies mentioned in the previous section are a type of feedlot developed for dairy cattle. **Figure 11.14** illustrates some of the changes affecting the Corn Belt.

Ric Francis/©AP/Wide World Photos

Dairy farming and milk production • Figure 11.13

Globally, dry-lot dairying is the exception rather than the rule.

a. A California dry-lot dairy, like this one, contains no pasture and holds some 600 dairy cows on open lots, often with sun shades. In contrast, dairy farms in the Upper Midwest typically maintain about 70 pasture-fed dairy cows.

b. Regionally, the three main centers of milk production are in Europe, South Asia, and Northern America. More than half of the milk produced in South Asia comes from water buffalo. (*Source:* Data from FAOSTAT, 2010.)

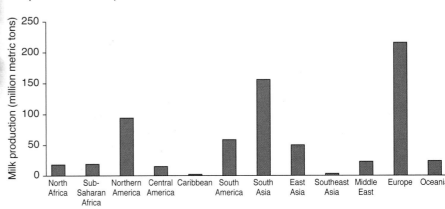

Many Corn Belt farms do still integrate the production of corn, soybeans, and hogs. However, changes in farming practices in the region are underway.

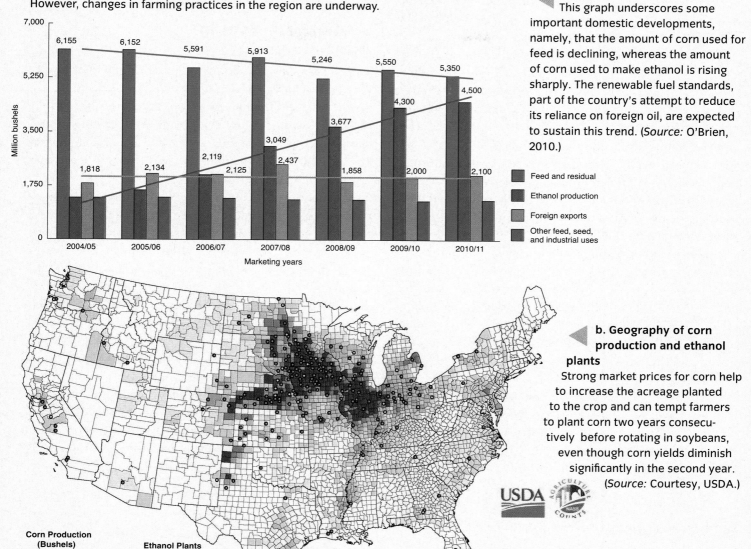

a. Trends in U.S. corn use
This graph underscores some important domestic developments, namely, that the amount of corn used for feed is declining, whereas the amount of corn used to make ethanol is rising sharply. The renewable fuel standards, part of the country's attempt to reduce its reliance on foreign oil, are expected to sustain this trend. (*Source:* O'Brien, 2010.)

Chart: Million bushels vs. Marketing years (2004/05 – 2010/11)

Legend:
- Feed and residual
- Ethanol production
- Foreign exports
- Other feed, seed, and industrial uses

Values shown: 6,155; 1,818 (2004/05); 6,152; 2,134 (2005/06); 5,591; 2,119; 2,125 (2006/07); 5,913; 3,049; 2,437 (2007/08); 5,246; 3,677; 1,858 (2008/09); 5,550; 4,300; 2,000 (2009/10); 5,350; 4,500; 2,100 (2010/11)

b. Geography of corn production and ethanol plants
Strong market prices for corn help to increase the acreage planted to the crop and can tempt farmers to plant corn two years consecutively before rotating in soybeans, even though corn yields diminish significantly in the second year. (*Source:* Courtesy, USDA.)

Corn Production (Bushels)
- Not Estimated
- < 1,000,000
- 1,000,000 - 4,999,999
- 5,000,000 - 9,999,999
- 10,000,000 - 14,999,999
- 15,000,000 - 19,999,999
- 20,000,000 +

Ethanol Plants
- Construction
- Producing
- Not producing

U.S. Department of Agriculture, National Agricultural Statistics Service

USDA

Mike Stewart/©AP/Wide World Photos

c. Hog CAFO near Milan, Missouri
Hog farms are distinguishable by long, rectangular buildings that are grouped together and adjacent to a lagoon, which holds the waste from the hog houses. Since the 1990s, the Corn Belt has lost hog farms to North Carolina and Oklahoma, in part the result of lower labor and production costs, and economies of scale. Some of the largest hog farms can produce in excess of 200,000 hogs per year.

lagoon

lagoon

Commercial grain farming and livestock ranching The staple item of most people's diets is the grain of a cereal grass. Common grains include wheat, rice, corn, barley, oats, millet, and sorghum. These grains not only feed people and animals, they frequently have industrial uses as well. **Commercial grain farming** is closely associated with temperate grassland environments. Monoculture prevails, with farms covering large areas of flat to gently rolling land that is planted to a single crop.

> **commercial grain farming** Agriculture involving the large-scale, highly mechanized cultivation of grain.

Some of these farms can top 2000 acres (800 ha). This type of large-scale grain farming has been made possible because of mechanization. Indeed, commercial grain farming remains heavily dependent on fossil fuels used in the production of fertilizers and in the gas consumed in working the fields.

Lands that are unsuitable for more valuable agricultural uses—for example, in arid and semiarid regions—tend to be used for **livestock ranching**. Ranchers have fixed places of residence and graze their livestock on the open range or on fenced land. The rangelands used cover sizable areas. Historically, these regions have been distant from the centers of demand—the cities and towns. Getting the animals to slaughterhouses required that they be herded long distances overland to railroads. Both commercial grain

> **livestock ranching** A form of agriculture devoted to raising large numbers of cattle or sheep for sale to meat processors.

farming and livestock ranching are considered examples of **extensive agriculture** (**Figure 11.15**).

> **extensive agriculture** An agricultural system characterized by low inputs of labor, capital, or equipment per unit area of land.

Spatial Variations in Agriculture

Thus far we have examined the practice and distribution of different types of agriculture, but land-use decisions are another aspect of the geography of agriculture that interest many scholars. More specifically, is it possible to predict what crops will be grown or how land on a commercial farm will be used if we know where the farm is located in relation to the market?

One of the people who initiated the study of this question was Johann Heinrich von Thünen (1783–1850), a farmer, scholar, and estate owner who lived in northern Germany. Over years of traveling from his property to towns in the region, he observed that agricultural practices and crops changed as he got farther away from the marketplace. He used these observations to devise a model, the **von Thünen model**, to account for spatial variations in commercial agriculture.

To simplify the complexity of real-world conditions, von Thünen assumed that the quality of the land is the same everywhere. Following the economic principle that land-use decisions are profit-maximizing decisions, he reasoned that transportation costs determine how farmers can make the most profitable use of their land (**Figure 11.16**).

Extensive agriculture • Figure 11.15

Extensive agriculture often involves large farms or ranches.

a. Wheat being harvested in Saskatchewan, Canada
In the Southern Plains wheat is harvested in early summer. In the Northern Plains wheat is harvested at the end of the summer. Crews of laborers and "custom cutters" with combines move across the wheat belt to take advantage of these seasonal differences.

Peter Carroll/Alamy

b. Sheep grazing in Wanaka, New Zealand
In New Zealand, more than 40% of the farmland in the country is devoted to sheep raising, and the country remains the world's leading exporter of mutton.

Todd Gipstein/NG Image Collection

The von Thünen model • Figure 11.16

Farmers located near the market or city have low transportation costs and can afford to engage in more intensive agriculture than farmers farther away, creating rings of agricultural land use. The forestry ring provides one exception to this pattern. Timber, still needed for fuel and building in von Thünen's time, is a less intensive, low-value good that would not be profitable if transported long distances. ▶ **What accounts for our ability to profitably transport timber over longer distances today? What does the diagram suggest about how terrain might influence land use?** (*Source:* Adapted from Chisholm, 1968.)

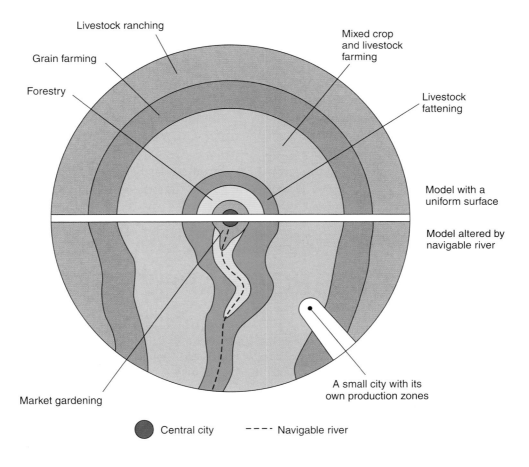

Livestock ranching

Grain farming

Forestry

Mixed crop and livestock farming

Livestock fattening

Model with a uniform surface

Model altered by navigable river

A small city with its own production zones

Market gardening

● Central city   ---- Navigable river

Although von Thünen's model may seem oversimplified, its principles still have relevance and help us explore such questions as what economic forces make it possible for cut flowers from South America to be shipped to Miami and sold in other U.S. cities, and how does globalization affect the geography of intensive agriculture? Taking a different approach, Arild Angelsen, a scientist with the Center for International Forestry Research, has used von Thünen's model to examine the relationship between profitable land use and tropical deforestation. Angelsen shows that land used for agriculture—for example, beef cattle production—generates more profit than land that is forested. Thus, economic considerations can drive tropical deforestation and influence decisions about land use.

CONCEPT CHECK

1. **What** is meant by the continuum of agricultural systems?

2. **How** is mobility a factor in shifting cultivation and nomadic pastoralism?

3. **Where** have plantations tended to locate and why?

4. **How** does von Thünen's model account for spatial variations in intensive and extensive agriculture?

Agriculture, the Environment, and Globalization

LEARNING OBJECTIVES

1. **Define** desertification and salinization.
2. **Distinguish** between sustainable agriculture and organic agriculture.
3. **Explain** how agriculture has been affected by globalization.
4. **Summarize** the causes of recent global food crises.

A griculture and the environment are intimately interconnected. Soil or climatic conditions in an area can influence decisions about what to grow or how to use the land. At the same time, the practice of agriculture can have a significant impact on the environment. Since the first agricultural revolution, clearing forests and draining wetlands have been common strategies for increasing the acreage devoted to cropland.

Human actions as well as changes in climate can contribute to **desertification**. Overgrazing damages vegetation, while poor crop management depletes the soil's fertility. Both of these practices can create environments that are unable to sustain the herds or crops that they once did.

> **desertification**
> The creation of desert-like conditions in nondesert areas through human and/or environmental causes.

Irrigation can have a detrimental effect on the environment, even though it is usually thought of as a strategy for expanding agriculture. If irrigation draws on groundwater aquifers, water usage has to be monitored so that the aquifer is not depleted. In soils that

WHAT A GEOGRAPHER SEES

The Shrinking Aral Sea

For more than 40 years, water has been diverted from the rivers that feed the Aral Sea in Central Asia to irrigate land for cotton and rice production. As a result, the lake has lost more than 60% of its water and has shrunk from over 65,000 sq km (25,000 sq mi) to less than half that size. In the process, the sea has been transformed from a fresh to saltwater environment.

a. A rusted boat is left high and dry. An increase in the lake's salt concentration from 10% to more than 23% has devastated fish populations. Camel breeding has replaced fishing as a primary source of local income.
▶ **Is the level of human involvement or interference with nature here different from the human involvement in the making of GMOs? Why or why not?**

© Aurora Photos/Alamy

Global Locator

ARAL SEA

ASIA

NATIONAL GEOGRAPHIC

drain poorly, irrigation can lead to waterlogging and crop death. When irrigation is used in arid and semiarid regions where evaporation rates are high, **salinization** becomes an issue and can result in decreased productivity (see *What a Geographer Sees*).

Applications of chemical fertilizers, herbicides, pesticides, and fungicides also have an impact on the environment. The production of fertilizers such as ammonia uses large amounts of energy. In addition, runoff from fields treated with other chemicals used in commercial farming can pollute surface water and groundwater supplies.

salinization The accumulation of salts on or in the soil.

sustainable agriculture Farming practices that carefully manage natural resources and minimize adverse effects on the environment while maintaining farm profits.

result, there is growing interest in **sustainable agriculture**. Examples of sustainable farming practices include measures taken to conserve soil and water resources, such as contour plowing, strip cropping, and the establishment of filter or buffer strips. *Contour plowing* follows the slopes in a field, rather than cutting across them. *Strip cropping* alternates the planting of row crops, such as cotton, with bands of sod crops, such as alfalfa or soybeans. *Filter strips* or *buffer strips* are belts of vegetation that surround fields and act to prevent runoff.

No-till farming also encourages sustainable land use. *No-till farming* avoids agitating the soil with tractor-drawn implements that remove weeds, mix in fertilizers, or shape the soil for seeding—all of which can lead to erosion. Crop rotations that help prevent disease or pest problems, and actions taken to reduce reliance on fossil fuels, especially petroleum, are also sustainable practices.

Sustainable Agriculture

The environmental impacts of agriculture, especially large-scale commercial agriculture, have prompted experts to question its ability to provide for future generations. As a

b. Satellite images illustrate the lake's reduction from 2000 to 2009 and relative to the shoreline in 1960. Soil from the exposed lake beds feeds salt particles and pesticide residues into dust storms. The resulting pollution has been linked to respiratory problems for those who live in the region. The lake's increased salinity reduces crop yields in the fields that are irrigated with the diverted water.

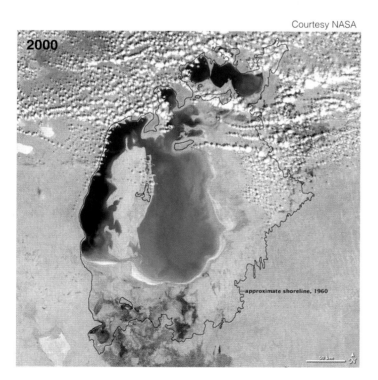

Courtesy NASA

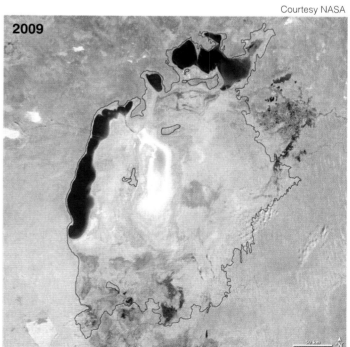

Courtesy NASA

Precision agriculture employs technologies such as the global positioning system (GPS) and aerial imagery to measure and map the spatial variation in environmental conditions within a field. Soil fertility is rarely uniform across an agricultural field, for example. Mapping the site-specific soil conditions reveals the geography of soil nutrients in a field. This information can then be used to calibrate farm machinery to apply fertilizer at variable rates, releasing more in those areas where the soil is deficient in nutrients. Precision agriculture can also be used to manage pesticide applications, determine the best sowing density, and more accurately predict crop yields. In that they are closely tied to effective soil and field management, certain precision agriculture techniques can support sustainable practices. It should be noted, however, that some experts

> **organic agriculture**
> A farming system that promotes sustainable and biodiverse ecosystems and relies on natural ecological processes and cycles, as opposed to synthetic inputs such as pesticides.

contest the association of precision agriculture with sustainability, in part because precision agriculture often uses synthetic chemicals that require large amounts of energy to manufacture.

Another expression of concern about the sustainability of agriculture involves the growing demand for **organic agriculture**. Organic agriculture accounts for a very small share of all agricultural products sold; however it is the fastest growing sector of agriculture today. Globally, Australia, Argentina, and Brazil have the largest areas under organic management, but the highest percentages of organic land are consistently found in Europe. This is partly the result of agricultural policies in Europe that have subsidized organic farming. At present, most of the organic farm products from Africa and Latin America are exported (**Figure 11.17**).

Sustainable agricultural practices • Figure 11.17

Sustainable agriculture is associated with organic farming and a variety of conservation techniques.

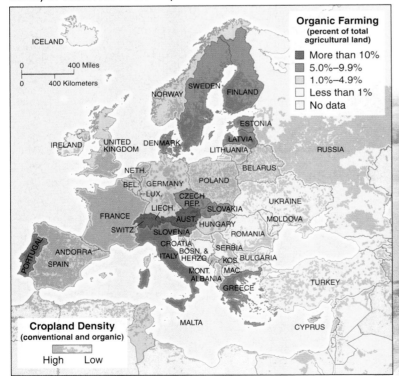

Cropland Density (conventional and organic)
High   Low

Organic Farming (percent of total agricultural land)
- More than 10%
- 5.0%–9.9%
- 1.0%–4.9%
- Less than 1%
- No data

▲ **a. Organic farming in Europe**
Nearly 25% of all organically managed land is in Europe. Tiny Liechtenstein boasts the highest proportion—29%—of its agricultural land used for organic farming, followed by Austria and Switzerland with 13% and 11%, respectively. ▶ **What other regional patterns are evident on the map?** (*Source:* NG Maps, based on Willer and Yussefi, 2007 and Ramankutty *et al.*, 2008.)

b. Soil conservation techniques
Contour plowing and strip cropping in southwest Wisconsin create a distinctive agricultural landscape. Green strips of alfalfa hay alternate with the taller strips of corn. The alfalfa crop slows runoff and helps prevent erosion. ▼

MARK FALLANDER/ASSOCIATED PRESS

NATIONAL GEOGRAPHIC

Globalization and Agriculture

Our ability to purchase grapes from Chile, tea from Sri Lanka, or apples from New Zealand at grocery stores here in the United States is certainly one expression of the globalization of agriculture. Although globalization brings increased trade and access to a greater variety of agricultural products, it is also clear that the globalization of agriculture creates significant challenges, especially for poorer countries. We can glimpse this problem through the workings of the World Trade Organization (WTO), discussed briefly in Chapter 2.

The WTO seeks to make trade freer through the removal of tariffs and other policies that distort the market. Although the least developed countries have been given longer time frames to dismantle trade barriers, it is still reasonable to ask how a smaller and much poorer country such as Jamaica can compete with a country like the United States in terms of producing and selling its agricultural goods. One particular issue that creates an unlevel playing field and that the WTO has been slow to address involves government subsidies to farmers. Poorer countries cannot provide such subsidies. Thus, their farmers bear a higher share of the production costs, and this translates into higher prices for their agricultural products. Many trade experts have argued that domestic subsidies create severe market distortions and prevent free trade in agricultural goods.

The globalization of agriculture also affects diets. Patterns of food consumption are changing as the availability of processed foods increases. Asian diets, specifically those of the urban and middle classes, are becoming westernized and are contributing to a **nutrition transition**—a shift characterized by a decline in the consumption of rice and an increase in meat, wheat-based food products, and convenience foods. Although Asian diets now include a greater variety of foodstuffs, many of these items also have more fats and refined sugars, with the potential for adverse health consequences including obesity and diabetes. To find and view maps of caloric consumption by country, region, and for the world, see *Where Geographers Click*.

Over the past decade, developing countries in East and Southeast Asia, Latin America, and Africa have also witnessed the rapid spread of supermarkets. This *supermarket revolution* affects the way that fruits and

Where Geographers CLICK

Food and Agriculture Organization

Udo Weitz/Bloomberg via Getty Images

The Food and Agriculture Organization maintains data about food balance (expressed in caloric consumption per person per day), as well as information on crop and livestock production in their FAOSTAT database. From the FAOSTAT website, open the database and click on "Browse data" to select data and view maps.

vegetables are grown and sold throughout world. Although supermarkets can lower food prices for consumers, small retailers often cannot compete with them. In addition, supermarket chains are often just as likely to source their products from distant rather than local suppliers, with negative consequences for the local agricultural sector.

Agriculture and resource use • Figure 11.18

Agriculture both consumes and produces resources.

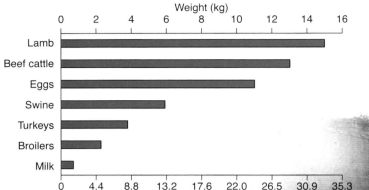

a. Amount of grain needed to produce 1 kilogram (2.2 pounds) of meat or other animal product

Livestock are inefficient producers of protein and, as shown by this graph, must consume inordinate amounts of grain to generate adequate weight gain to produce meat. ▶ **Should our agricultural practices change in times of food crisis, so that grain that is processed into feed for animals could be used instead to feed people?** (*Source:* Data from USDA, 2001.)

Paul Kaldjian

b. Urban agriculture

In Istanbul, Turkey, spaces devoted to urban agriculture are called *bostans*. These bostans are next to the old city walls. Urban agriculture can be an important mechanism for improving nutrition and access to fresh produce among the urban poor.

Global Food Crises

Food prices worldwide spiked in 2008, setting in motion a **global food crisis**. Although not as severe, the world experienced another food crisis in 2011 and food prices remain near record high levels. What has caused these crises? The answer involves a mix of diverse factors affecting grain markets.

Droughts and other weather events in major grain-producing countries have affected production. High oil prices have increased costs of fertilizers and fuel. Another contributing factor involves increased production of **biofuels**, especially the use of corn to produce ethanol. Although biofuels are renewable and reduce reliance on fossil fuels, farmlands and crops must be diverted away from food production to generate biofuels. At the same time, rising consumer demand for meat products in conjunction with the nutrition transition discussed earlier has increased pressure on the grain market. When food prices rise, the poor—who spend a

biofuel Fuel derived from renewable biological material, such as plant matter.

disproportionate share of their income on food—suffer the most. Such food crises raise questions not only about the efficiency of certain agricultural practices but also about strategies that might help people reduce their vulnerability to them. One practice that could help improve future food security at the household level is **urban agriculture**—the use of vacant lots, rooftops, balconies, or other spaces to raise food for the household or neighborhood (**Figure 11.18**).

CONCEPT CHECK

1. **How** are desertification and salinization related to changes in the Aral Sea?
2. **What** are some specific techniques associated with sustainable agriculture?
3. **Why** might the globalization of agriculture be considered a mixed blessing?
4. **How** are meat production and consumption related to grain supply?

Summary

1 Agriculture: Origins and Revolutions 328

- **Agriculture** is an economic activity centered on the purposeful tending of crops and livestock in order to procure food and fiber for human use or consumption. Prior to the development of agriculture, people subsisted by **hunting and gathering**, which still forms the basis of some livelihoods today.

- Three agricultural revolutions have transformed human geographies, including both social and environmental dynamics. The rise of farming about 11,000 years ago, made possible by the domestication of plants and animals in at least five hearths and numerous secondary centers, shown here, marked the **first agricultural revolution**.

Hearths of agriculture • Figure 11.2

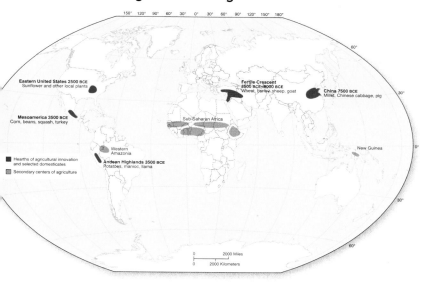

- The **second agricultural revolution** began in Europe during the Middle Ages and was prolonged because of developments during the Industrial Revolution. Innovations that made the second agricultural revolution possible include the development of the moldboard plow, the horse collar, and the **four-course system** of **crop rotation**.

- The **third agricultural revolution** began in the 20th century and is still underway. It is associated with a shift toward monoculture, greater reliance on chemical applications, and **agro-biotech** practices.

- The **Green Revolution** and the **Gene Revolution** are both associated with the third agricultural revolution. The Green Revolution involved increased grain production in certain developing regions as a result of high-yielding, fertilizer- and irrigation-dependent varieties of wheat, rice, and corn. The Gene Revolution is marked by the shift toward greater control of the research, development, intellectual property rights, and genetic engineering of highly specialized agricultural products.

2 Agricultural Systems 335

- Many different types of agriculture are practiced in the world, and they can be placed along a continuum from **subsistence agriculture** to **commercial agriculture**. In **smallholder agriculture** the scale of production is geared to the household.

- There are four major types of subsistence agriculture. **Shifting cultivation** and **pastoralism** support low population densities. **Wet rice farming**, which prevails in more humid parts of Asia, and **smallholder crop and livestock farming**, which takes place in regions too dry to support wet farming, are both forms of **intensive agriculture**.

- Today, commercial agriculture is one component in an interconnected system of food production that involves farmers, processors, distributors, and retailers. Vertical integration has become a defining feature of **agribusiness** and has led to greater involvement of corporations in farming. Corporations increasingly participate in the technical aspects of crop and stock management, as well as processing agricultural products and moving them to market.

- Specialization has had a strong impact on commercial agriculture. **Plantation** agriculture is practiced in tropical and subtropical areas and has a strong presence in developing regions. **Commercial gardening** is a kind of **truck farming** and is increasingly associated with large, specialized farms. **Mediterranean agriculture** is closely associated with the production of tree and vine crops. Within the United States, dry-lot dairies have altered the geography of **commercial dairy farming**. **Factory farms** and **feedlots** are changing farming practices in **mixed crop and livestock farming** regions. **Commercial grain farming** occurs in the temperate grassland regions of North and South America, Australia, and eastern Europe and Russia. The practice of **livestock ranching**, a type of extensive agriculture, tends to be spatially associated with regions that are drier and/or more remote from major markets, as in New Zealand (see photo).

Extensive agriculture • Figure 11.15

Todd Gipstein/NG Image Collection

- The **von Thünen model** helps to depict the relationship between location, or nearness to the market, and how land is used for commercial agriculture.

3 Agriculture, the Environment, and Globalization 346

- All types of agriculture transform the environment. The nature and extent of the impact on the environment differs from place to place and from farmer to farmer. Soil degradation and the impacts of climate change are serious issues that all farmers confront. **Desertification**, whether caused by human or climatic factors, can prohibit the practice of agriculture. Irrigation can lead to **salinization**.

- **Sustainable agriculture** and **organic agriculture** have developed in response to concerns about the adverse impacts that commercial farming can have on the environment. Although **precision agriculture** was not developed strictly for reasons of sustainability, some aspects of it support the careful management of resources.

- Globalization has had an impact on food consumption and agricultural practices around the world. Many cities in the developing world are experiencing a **nutrition transition** as Western, high-fat foods are gaining popularity. Westernized diets are becoming increasingly popular in Asia, placing greater demands on wheat production. Developing countries in Asia, Latin America, and Africa have also seen a rapid rise in supermarkets over the past decade, which has had important consequences for local farmers and retailers.

- Unseasonable droughts in grain-producing nations, rising oil prices, the conversion to **biofuels**, and changing dietary patterns around the globe contributed to the **global food crisis** experienced in 2008 and again in 2011. These events contributed to an increase in food prices, and had a significant impact on producers and consumers around the world.

- **Urban agriculture**, glimpsed here, could help improve future food security at the scale of the household.

Agriculture and resource use • Figure 11.18

Paul Kaldjian

Key Terms

- agribusiness 340
- agriculture 328
- agro-biotech 331
- agroforestry 337
- biofuel 350
- cash crop 340
- commercial agriculture 335
- commercial dairy farming 342
- commercial gardening 341
- commercial grain farming 344
- crop rotation 330
- desertification 346
- domestication 328
- double cropping 338
- dual economy 341
- dual society 341
- extensive agriculture 344

- factory farm 342
- feedlot 342
- first agricultural revolution 329
- four-course system 330
- Gene Revolution 331
- global food crisis 350
- Green Revolution 331
- hunting and gathering 328
- intensive agriculture 338
- intercropping 336
- livestock ranching 344
- Mediterranean agriculture 341
- mixed crop and livestock farming 342
- monoculture 331
- nutrition transition 349
- organic agriculture 348
- pastoralism 337

- plantation 340
- precision agriculture 348
- salinization 347
- second agricultural revolution 330
- shifting cultivation 336
- smallholder agriculture 338
- smallholder crop and livestock farming 338
- subsistence agriculture 335
- sustainable agriculture 347
- third agricultural revolution 330
- transhumance 337
- truck farming 341
- urban agriculture 350
- von Thünen model 344
- wet rice farming 338

Critical and Creative Thinking Questions

1. What is slow food? It might be said that slow food is fundamentally about the relationship between people and place. Do you agree? Does slow food provide a viable mechanism for eliminating global hunger?

2. How does the Fair Trade movement reflect a concern with moral geographies?

3. How has the diffusion and popularity of pizza affected the geography of dairy products?

4. What kind of evidence would a diffusionist use to support the theory that agriculture developed only once and spread from that location around the world?

5. How did European colonization affect global patterns of agriculture?

6. What is aquaculture, and should we consider it a type of agriculture? Explain your answer.

7. Will there be a fourth agricultural revolution, and if so, what might it involve?

8. Using this map, how do you explain the presence of producing ethanol plants (refineries) in counties where the production of corn is low?

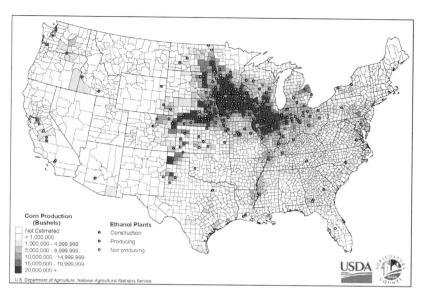

What is happening in this picture?

The photograph shows Tamil women plucking tea leaves in Sri Lanka. Pluckers take new growth from the top, wedging leaves between thumb and forefinger before placing them in a basket.

Think Critically

1. What type of agriculture is this woman involved in?
2. In what ways might increased mechanization help her? In what ways might it have a negative impact on her life?
3. What impact might the use of biotechnology have on the harvest, the workers, and the environment?

© hadynyah/iStockphoto

Self-Test

(Check your answers in Appendix B.)

1. In most of Africa south of the Sahara, the percentage of farmers exceeds _____%. In developed economies it is about _____%.

   a. 90; 10

   b. 35; 15

   c. 60; 5

   d. 50; 25

2. One misconception about hunting and gathering is that _____.

   a. its historical decline was due to a reduction in wild animals and plant resources

   b. hunters and gatherers were close to starvation

   c. it declined as agriculture began to develop about 11,000 years ago

   d. it is still practiced in some parts of the world

3. _____ was introduced during the first agricultural revolution. The second agricultural revolution included the development of _____. The third agricultural revolution involves _____.

   a. Domestication; four-course crop rotation; biotechnology

   b. Seed propagation; fertilizers; scientific farming

   c. The horse collar; the seed drill; mechanization

   d. Crop rotation; the internal combustion engine; organic agriculture

4. List three characteristics of subsistence agriculture.

   _____

   _____

   _____

5. Identify the type of agriculture and mobility pattern depicted in this photograph.

   _____

Steve Winter/NG Image Collection

6. Swidden is another name for _____.

   a. shifting cultivation

   b. intercropping

   c. crop rotation

   d. subsistence farming

7. Intensive wet rice farming often employs a system of _____.

   a. buffer strips

   b. agroforestry

   c. monoculture

   d. double cropping

8. _____ perpetuates a dual economy.

   a. Truck farming

   b. Plantation agriculture

   c. Livestock ranching

   d. Mediterranean agriculture

9. The image shows _____.

   a. double cropping

   b. intercropping

   c. precision agriculture

   d. strip cropping

MARK FALLANDER/ASSOCIATED PRESS

10. Place the following labels on this diagram of the von Thünen model.

   a. Dairy farming

   b. Grain farming

   c. Mixed crop and livestock farming

   d. Livestock ranching

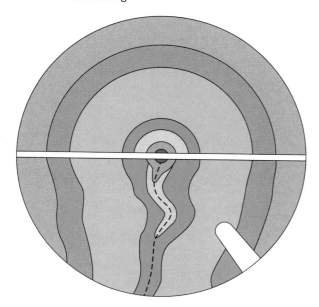

11. Mediterranean agriculture has had an important association with _____.

   a. dry-lot dairies

   b. plantations

   c. agroforestry

   d. organic agriculture

12. This photograph shows _____.

   a. a desalinization plant in Central Asia

   b. a dry-lot dairy in California

   c. specialized hog production in the Corn Belt

   d. none of the above

Mike Stewart/©AP/Wide World Photos

13. _____ caused the Aral Sea to _____ and its salinity to _____.

   a. Drought; shrink in size; fluctuate

   b. Irrigation; shrink in size; increase

   c. A series of wet years; increase in size; decrease

   d. Altered drainage patterns; increase in size; stay about the same.

14. Which is *not* a major milk-producing region?

   a. East Asia

   b. South Asia

   c. Europe

   d. Northern America

15. Find the *false* statement about the globalization of agriculture.

   a. The globalization of agriculture is linked with a nutrition transition.

   b. The globalization of agriculture is resisted by the WTO.

   c. The globalization of agriculture is associated with specialization.

   d. The globalization of agriculture is related to the supermarket revolution.

THE PLANNER ✓

Review your Chapter Planner on the chapter opener and check off your completed work.

Environmental Challenges

THE INUIT AND ARCTIC ENVIRONMENTAL CHANGE

Have you heard of the Inuit? They are one of several indigenous peoples who have long inhabited the Arctic and sub-Arctic regions of the globe and have adapted to its extremely cold conditions. These adaptations stem from their detailed environmental knowledge about the thickness of the ice, where cracks are likely to form in the ice, and animal migration patterns.

Recently, however, notable changes in local environmental conditions have occurred. The ice thaws earlier in the spring and some waters are no longer freezing at all. Instead of hunting by dog sled or snowmobile, some Inuit must hunt by boat. But this requires dragging their boat over melting ice to reach open water. Walking on melting ice, as shown in photo, is treacherous. The disappearance of sea ice has also exposed areas of the coast to erosion and flooding.

For the Inuit, these environmental changes mean that they must travel farther to reach hunting grounds. And, lately, the poor quality of the snow has complicated their ability to build their hunting shelters. The historical record, which shows that over the past century temperatures in the Arctic have risen at nearly twice the rate for the world, supports Inuit observations.

Environmental change and the relationships between the Inuit and the environment are complex and interconnected. Environmental challenges, the title of this chapter, captures this complexity, as we study in greater detail the human–environment interactions we introduced in Chapter 1.

Gilles Mingasson/Getty Images

CHAPTER OUTLINE

CHAPTER PLANNER ✓

- ❏ Study the picture and read the opening story.
- ❏ Scan the Learning Objectives in each section:
  p. 358 ❏   p. 362 ❏   p. 370 ❏   p. 376 ❏
- ❏ Read the text and study all visuals.
  Answer any questions.

Analyze key features

- ❏ Geography InSight, p. 366
- ❏ Process Diagram, p. 368
- ❏ Video Explorations, p. 375 ❏   p. 382 ❏
- ❏ What a Geographer Sees, p. 379
- ❏ Stop: Answer the Concept Checks before you go on:
  p. 361 ❏   p. 370 ❏   p. 375 ❏   p. 382 ❏

End of chapter

- ❏ Review the Summary and Key Terms.
- ❏ Answer the Critical and Creative Thinking Questions.
- ❏ Answer What is happening in this picture?
- ❏ Complete the Self-Test and check your answers.

Ecosystems

LEARNING OBJECTIVES

1. **Define** ecosystem.
2. **Distinguish** between human and natural causes of environmental degradation.
3. **Identify** examples of common property and open-access resources.

When you use the word *environment*, do you mean just the natural world? Limiting the word in this way is a common practice in popular usage. As we discussed in Chapter 1, human geographers and environmental scientists, however, usually take a broader view. For them, the **environment** refers to one's surroundings—that is, all of the biotic (living) and abiotic (nonliving) factors with which people, animals, and other organisms coexist.

Since the 1930s scholars have used the ecosystem concept to study the interactions between different components of the environment. **Ecosystems** can be defined at a variety of scales. The Earth, for example, is an ecosystem; so are oceans, deserts, tropical rainforests, estuaries, grasslands, and even the neighborhood pond (**Figure 12.1**). Among academics, the general consensus is that the complexity of an ecosystem derives from its **biodiversity**, or the variety of species contained within it. On this basis, tropical ecosystems are considered some of the most complex. Although scientists may attempt to study a single ecosystem

ecosystem The living organisms, their physical environment, and the flows of energy and nutrients cycling through them.

as though it could be isolated, the fact is that all ecosystems are interconnected. Together, these interconnected ecosystems constitute the **biosphere**—the zone of the Earth, extending from the soil and waters to the lower parts of the atmosphere, that supports and includes living organisms.

Ecological Concepts

To capture the interconnectedness of people and the environment, the biologist Garrett Hardin (1985, p. 471) used the maxim "we can never do merely one thing." With this simple expression he helped codify what is sometimes called the **First Law of Ecology**. He hoped that drawing attention to this fundamental principle would lead not just to additional study of the environment but also to greater concern for and awareness of the consequences of human actions.

Since the late 1980s another expression of the interdependence and interconnectedness of nature and society has emerged. It involves the concept of natural capital. The term *capital* refers to assets derived from human creativity (e.g., financial assets or knowledge). In contrast, **natural capital** refers to the goods and services provided by nature. Natural capital includes four component parts: (1) the renewable

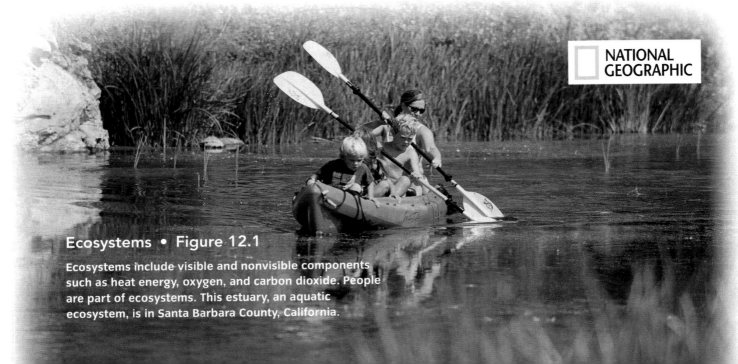

Ecosystems • Figure 12.1

Ecosystems include visible and nonvisible components such as heat energy, oxygen, and carbon dioxide. People are part of ecosystems. This estuary, an aquatic ecosystem, is in Santa Barbara County, California.

Unsustainable and sustainable harvests • Figure 12.2

Fish stocks and forest resources are renewable if they are sustainably harvested.

◀ **a.** Tuna caught off the coast of Turkey. In the Mediterranean Sea, recent catches of the endangered Bluefin tuna—a prized fish for sushi—have been more than three times the established sustainable yield. Nearly one-third of the world's harvested fish stocks are overfished.

Oliver Berg/dpa/Landov LLC

b. To promote responsible forest management, the international Forest Stewardship Council (FSC) certifies wood harvested from forests that are sustainably managed. Compliance with guidelines in order to obtain FSC certification is voluntary.

resources, (2) the nonrenewable resources, (3) the Earth's biodiversity, and (4) the ecosystems. The first three of these components constitute the goods or stocks of natural resources, whereas the fourth component illustrates the importance of services or processes provided by the natural world. These include the cycling of nutrients through ecosystems and processes such as photosynthesis. Without natural capital there would be no life on Earth. Moreover, natural capital makes possible the functioning of the economy, which is based on human use of natural resources.

There are two different types of natural resources, nonrenewable and renewable, and both types can be depleted. **Nonrenewable resources** are considered finite because they are not self-replenishing or they take very long periods of time to do so. **Renewable resources** are replenished naturally or through human intervention, such as planting trees. The quantities of nonrenewable resources are fixed—once they are used they are gone forever. In theory, human use could entirely exhaust these nonrenewable resources; however, economic depletion usually precedes and in effect prevents total resource depletion. *Economic depletion* occurs

when the cost of extracting the resource exceeds the economic value of it. As a rule, economic depletion exists when 80% of the resource has been extracted. The concept of economic depletion is related to expected future revenue and is an important business concern.

The concept of economic depletion can be applied to renewable resources as well, but scholars usually apply the concept of sustainable yield instead. *Sustainable yield* refers to the maximum quantity of a resource that can be harvested or used without impairing its ability to renew or replenish itself. One problem with this concept, however, is that it is often applied on a species-specific basis without considering the impacts that harvesting a particular species may have on the ecosystem. That is, a yield of a particular species that is determined to be sustainable may still have significant consequences for the functioning of its ecosystem. For this reason, some scholars prefer the term *ecologically sustainable yield*, which takes a systems view of the impact of extracting or harvesting renewable resources. See **Figure 12.2** for contrasting approaches to resource extraction.

Environmental Degradation

To degrade something is to impair one or more of its physical properties. The leaching, or draining, of minerals or nutrients from soil—for example, by rain—is a form of natural environmental degradation. In popular usage, however, environmental degradation is understood to be *anthropogenic*, or caused by human activities. Defining environmental degradation is no simple task, largely because the perception of what constitutes environmental degradation varies from one group to another and even from one person to another.

It is also helpful to note that human activities can directly or indirectly trigger environmental degradation. When crude oil is spilled on land or in water, toxins in it pose a direct risk to people and wildlife. Road construction in mountainous regions of the tropics can cause unstable slopes. Government policies that support road construction but do not consider its environmental impacts can indirectly trigger environmental degradation.

If we think about degradation from the standpoint of sustainability and ecologically sustainable yields, it is possible to offer a broad definition of the term that draws on three major conditions. **Environmental degradation** occurs when one or more of these conditions are met: (1) when a resource is used at a rate faster than its rate of replenishment, (2) when human activities impair the long-term productivity or biodiversity of a location, or (3) when concentrations of pollutants exceed recognized standards for maximum allowable levels.

One limitation of this definition of environmental degradation is that it fails to acknowledge that some human activities are beneficial for the environment.

Therefore, geographers Piers Blaikie and Harold Brookfield (1987) have proposed another way of conceptualizing degradation. In their view a more complete assessment of environmental degradation should add together all degrading processes, both natural and human, and then subtract from this total all natural replenishment and all of the ways in which human activities have contributed to environmental restoration. See **Figure 12.3** for one example of environmental restoration.

Common Property Resources

Common property resources (CPRs) include community forests, pastures, and fishing grounds. Worldwide, many of the landless—those people who do not own individual units of land—depend on common property resources to obtain necessities such as firewood, food items, and pasture grasses for livestock (**Figure 12.4**). Common property resources differ from **open-access resources**. The air we breathe, the open seas, solar energy, national parks, and outer space are open-access resources. There may or may not be any rules controlling the use of open-access resources.

An issue that has long fascinated researchers involves the relationship between common property resources and environmental degradation. The most famous essay on this subject remains "The Tragedy of the Commons," written by

> **common property resources** Natural resources, equipment, or facilities that are shared by a well-defined community of users.
>
> **open-access resources** Goods that no single person can claim exclusive right to and that are available to everyone.

Riverine wetland restoration • Figure 12.3

Awareness of environmental degradation sometimes overlooks human impacts that benefit the environment.

a. Intrusive woody vegetation along the Central Platte River in Nebraska degraded the wetland habitat and clogged the river channel.

b. Restoration work removed the intrusive vegetation to re-create a wetland environment. Migratory waterfowl, some of which are endangered, use the islands and sandbars in the river to roost.

Common property resources in Africa • Figure 12.4

These photos illustrate two types of common property resources.

Danielle Lema Ngono/CIFOR

a. Women in Cameroon collect nontimber forest products
Common property in forests includes timber and nontimber forest resources such as berries, seeds, leaves, and oils.

Keren Su/Getty Images, Inc.

b. Maasai pastoralist in Tanzania
Historically, the Maasai have managed their pasturelands as common property resources. Since the 1980s, however, their pastures have been subdivided into individual ranches—in effect enclosing the commons. ▶ **What consequences might such change bring?**

Garrett Hardin and published in 1968. Hardin focused his essay on this question: Does pursuit of self-interest contribute to the public good? To answer this question, Hardin used the example of a community pasture open to all. In this scenario, the costs of keeping a large herd on the commons are shared by all of the herders, but the profits are not. Instead, profits from the sale of an animal accrue to the individual herder. Thus, it is clearly in every herder's self-interest to maximize her or his use of the commons, but if every herder does this the commons will be destroyed by overgrazing. The tragedy, according to Hardin, is that "Freedom in a commons brings ruin to all" (1968, p. 1244).

Hardin argued that private property provided only a partial solution to the problem of the tragedy of the commons. He felt that individual ownership of land would prevent environmental degradation of it but would do nothing to solve the problem of air pollution because the atmosphere cannot be divided into individually owned units. For Hardin, this meant that government policies, including taxes and regulations, were also necessary to prevent the tragedy of the commons.

The most significant flaw in Hardin's work was his mistaken assumption that common property resources lacked rules governing their use and that they are the same as open-access resources. As we have discussed, common property resources are used and managed in accordance with the established laws or customary practices within

a particular community. Moreover, with common property resources, the community of users is clearly defined and is exclusive. That is, not just anyone can use common property resources. It is also the case that the usage rights granted to different members of the community vary. For example, rights of use can vary depending on one's age, gender, and/or social status.

Scholars now realize that traditional or indigenous knowledge (see Chapter 2) plays a major role in the management of common property resources. Fishers in the Torres Strait north of Australia, for example, stop fishing when they notice the size of their catches declining. In Canada, the Cree do not hunt for waterfowl during the breeding season. These and other practices serve as checks to prevent destruction of the commons. Not every system of common property resource management is successful, but successful examples raise important questions about some of the premises of Hardin's argument.

CONCEPT CHECK   STOP

1. **Do** ecosystems have boundaries?
2. **How** is economic depletion related to environmental degradation?
3. **Why** is it important to distinguish between common property and open-access resources?

Nonrenewable Energy Resources

LEARNING OBJECTIVES

1. **Identify** important regional variations in the distribution of global oil reserves.
2. **Explain** the reasons for the production booms in the U.S. oil and gas industry.
3. **Evaluate** the challenges of extracting and using coal.
4. **Cite** specific factors that have shaped the geography of nuclear energy use.

N onrenewable energy resources include fossil fuels and uranium. **Fossil fuels** derive from the buried remains of plants and animals that lived millions of years ago. Over time, sand and other sediments covered these deposits while heat and pressure gradually transformed them into coal, oil, or natural gas. Burning fossil fuels for energy contributes to global warming, an issue we take up later in the chapter. Sources of renewable energy include solar, wind, water, geothermal, and biomass (from wood products or waste products). As the pie chart in **Figure 12.5** shows, the world depends very heavily on nonrenewable energy sources.

Oil and Natural Gas

Oil, also referred to as *crude oil* or, more broadly, *petroleum*, is often found near or together with natural gas. Though nonrenewable, oil and natural gas are versatile energy resources for industrialized countries that have the necessary infrastructure to store, process, and transport them. From water bottles to cell phones, most of our plastic products are made from oil, as are cosmetics and even some pharmaceuticals. Both oil and natural gas can be used as fuels, to heat buildings, and to generate electricity, although natural gas produces less air pollution and less carbon dioxide when burned. Using oil not only contributes to air pollution, it also carries the risk of oil spills that cause water pollution and contaminate the environment, issues we return to later in the chapter.

With nonrenewable resources the term *proved* (or *proven*) reserves expresses the estimated quantity of a resource that could be extracted in the future given present financial, technological, and geological conditions. Proved reserves are not fixed; they change as a result of consumption, discoveries of additional resources, or advances in the process of recovering resources. Global and U.S. proved oil and natural gas reserves have increased because of new discoveries and technologies.

We should bear in mind that, in spite of their name, proved reserves are always estimated amounts. Despite technological advances, there is no way to know for certain how much oil the Earth contains. Even if we did know how much oil or natural gas exists, there is no assurance that we would be able to recover it. **Figure 12.6** highlights the geography of proved oil reserves.

How long will the world's current oil reserves last? The *reserves-to-production ratio* (or R/P ratio) provides one

Global energy consumption by fuel • Figure 12.5

As this chart shows, almost 90% of the energy consumed comes from fossil fuels. (*Source:* Data from BP, 2012.)

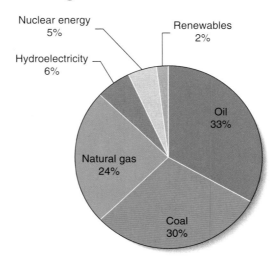

Nuclear energy
5%

Renewables
2%

Hydroelectricity
6%

Oil
33%

Natural gas
24%

Coal
30%

Oil reserves • Figure 12.6

Proved oil reserves are dynamic and unevenly distributed.

a. The countries with the largest proved oil reserves

Venezuela has surpassed Saudi Arabia to have the largest proved oil reserves. Canada's reserves include oil sands. Instead of being drilled, oil sands are mined in open pits. The product first recovered is bitumen, a much lower grade of crude oil that must be upgraded before it can be refined. (*Source:* Data from BP, 2012.)

Country	Proved oil reserves (billions of barrels)	Percent of world reserves
Venezuela	297	17.9
Saudi Arabia	265	16.1
Canada	175	10.6
Iran	151	9.1
Iraq	143	8.7
Kuwait	102	6.1
United Arab Emirates	98	5.9
Russia	88	5.3
Libya	47	2.9
Nigeria	37	2.3
United States	31	1.9
Kazakhstan	30	1.8
Qatar	25	1.5
China	15	0.9

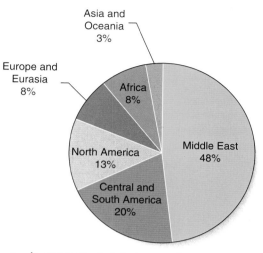

b. Percent of global proved reserves, by region

The Middle East has by far the largest share of proved oil reserves, but that percentage has declined from over 60% to 48% as proved oil reserves have increased in the Americas. (*Source:* Data from BP, 2012.)

estimate. Dividing the total remaining global reserves by the annual rate of oil production gives the R/P ratio in years. The R/P ratio for the world is 41.6. Thus, at the present rate of production and barring substantial new discoveries, the world's oil will last a little more than four decades.

According to some oil industry experts, another important concern is the time at which the world will pass the point of peak oil production. The concept of *peak oil* was first developed in the 1950s by the geologist M. King Hubbert, who argued that resource extraction tends to follow a bell-shaped curve in which production tends to rise rapidly at first, reaches a peak, and then declines rapidly. In his view, the rate of production declines following the peak because resource extraction becomes more costly.

As with most complex questions, there is no clear consensus on when the world will reach peak oil production. Indeed, a number of experts have challenged Hubbert's work. They disagree with his assertion that oil production necessarily declines at a steady and rapid rate, and that oil production is mainly shaped by resource constraints. Rather, they contend that a variety of factors such as global oil demand and politics affect oil production.

For us, Hubbert's work on peak oil is significant because he drew attention to a foreseeable *energy transition*. In other words, he recognized that oil production would decline and that this would compel people to use a different energy source. He also thought that an energy transition would have serious consequences for the global economy unless people anticipated it and were prepared for it. Does the increasing use of electric buses and gas-electric hybrid vehicles mark the onset of an energy transition?

Oil production and consumption The Persian Gulf countries, with their massive oil reserves, are major oil producers. The Organization of the Petroleum Exporting Countries (OPEC) also influences oil production. OPEC was formed in 1960 in an attempt to counter the dominance of the oil market by a few Western (mainly American and British) oil companies. OPEC seeks to coordinate oil production among its members. It does this by functioning as a *cartel*, an organization that controls the supply of a commodity and therefore its demand and price (see Chapter 2). The first sign of OPEC's international influence came in 1973 during the Arab Oil Embargo when it restricted the movement of oil tankers to ports in Europe and the United States, triggering the first major spike in oil prices. See **Figure 12.7** to learn more about OPEC and oil production.

Much of the success of a cartel depends on the ability of its members to coordinate their production. OPEC has long used oil production quotas to regulate the supply of crude oil but has had a difficult time enforcing them. When the price of crude oil is high, for example, greater temptation exists for a country to cheat and exceed its quota in order to earn higher revenues.

OPEC and patterns of oil production • Figure 12.7

These images show the composition of OPEC, events affecting oil prices, and oil production by OPEC and non-OPEC countries.

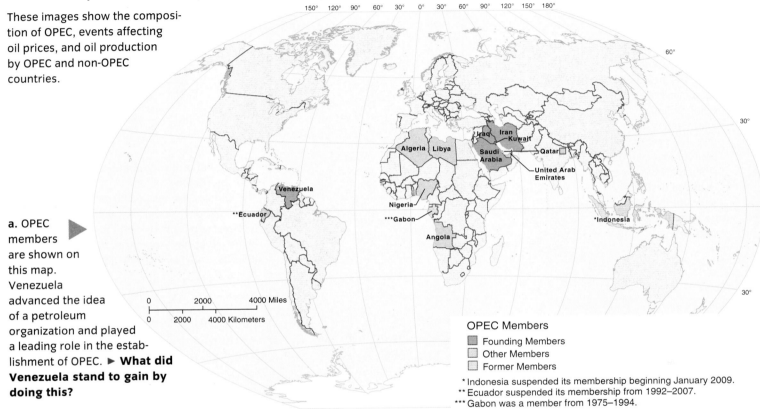

a. OPEC members are shown on this map. Venezuela advanced the idea of a petroleum organization and played a leading role in the establishment of OPEC. ▶ **What did Venezuela stand to gain by doing this?**

OPEC Members

- ▇ Founding Members
- ▢ Other Members
- ▢ Former Members

* Indonesia suspended its membership beginning January 2009.
** Ecuador suspended its membership from 1992–2007.
*** Gabon was a member from 1975–1994.

b. This graph shows changes in the price of a barrel of oil. High oil prices usually mean high prices at the gas pump. Notice that many events labeled on this graph directly involve OPEC countries. Thus, OPEC's oil production policies influence and are influenced by regional and global affairs. (*Source:* Data from Energy Information Administration, 2013a.)

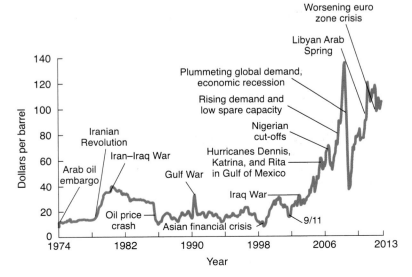

c. This graph shows oil production over time. OPEC produces about 43% of the world's oil; however, analysts predict OPEC's share of of global production to approach 50% by 2030. (*Source:* Data from Energy Information Administration, 2009 and 2013b.)

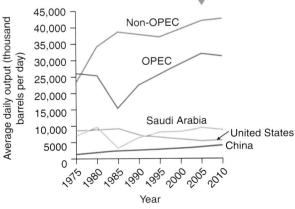

Significant geographic disparities exist in the patterns of production and consumption of oil. For example, the United States ranks third as a global oil producer, but it has by far the greatest thirst for oil of any country in the world. The United States consumes more than two times what China, the second leading consumer, uses. On a daily basis, the United States uses more than 19 million barrels of oil (one barrel equals 42 gallons). In contrast, Saudi Arabia, the world's leading oil producer, drops out of the list of the top five consumers of oil. Japan, also a leading consumer of oil, has only limited oil reserves and must import almost all of its oil (**Figure 12.8**).

Industrialized countries account for a disproportionate share of the daily global consumption of oil. In one day the world consumes in excess of 87 million barrels of oil. More than half of that total is consumed by the 30 wealthiest and most industrialized countries of the world each day. However, some analysts contend that oil consumption in these countries has peaked and that demand for oil in the coming years will be driven by energy needs in developing countries. As evidence they cite the following trends.

For decades the United States and Japan were the two leading consumers of oil in the world. In about 2003, however, China overtook Japan and moved into second place and in 2007 India moved into fourth place. Most striking is the rate at which oil use in China and India has increased. Between 1997 and 2010 oil consumption in China more than doubled, and in India it grew 84%. By comparison, oil consumption increased 19% for the world as a whole. In Japan, however, oil use dropped 22% over the same time period, in part because of government policies designed to reduce the country's dependence on oil.

Oil and natural gas from shale

In the United States, oil and natural gas production are experiencing a boom. To understand this boom it helps to distinguish between *conventional* and *unconventional* oil and natural gas. These terms are not firmly defined, but in general conventional oil and natural gas are pumped directly from the ground, whereas unconventional oil and natural gas require other extraction techniques and are therefore more costly. Oil extracted from tar sands as well as oil and natural gas extracted from *shale* and other formations are considered unconventional resources. *Shale* refers to a type of sedimentary rock that can trap oil and natural gas.

Geologists have long known about the presence of oil and gas in shale, but it is only recently that events have converged to make extractions from shale economically feasible. Two developments have been crucial to the shale oil and gas boom: persistently high prices for crude oil in excess of $80 per barrel, and improved extraction techniques that combine horizontal drilling with hydraulic fracturing, or *fracking*. Fracking uses high pressure pumps to force a mix of sand, water, and chemicals into a horizontally drilled well. This procedure causes fractures in the shale that permit the oil or gas to flow up the well.

The benefits of horizontal drilling and fracking were realized in the 1990s with highly successful natural gas extraction from the Barnett Shale in Texas. Since about 2004 well drilling and production have boomed across the Bakken Shale in North Dakota (a source of shale oil), the Marcellus Shale in New York, Pennsylvania, West Virginia, and Ohio (a source of natural gas), and the Eagle Ford Shale (a source of shale oil) in Texas.

Shale oil and natural gas production is not without controversy, however. A single well may require several

Oil production and consumption • Figure 12.8

National variation among major oil producers, exporters, and consumers
These average daily volumes show that five leading consumer nations account for 45% of global oil consumption. The United States consumes about twice as much oil as it produces and exports very little.
(*Source:* Data from BP, 2008 and EIA, 2010.)

Ask Yourself

1. What are the five leading oil producers?
2. What are the five leading oil consumers?

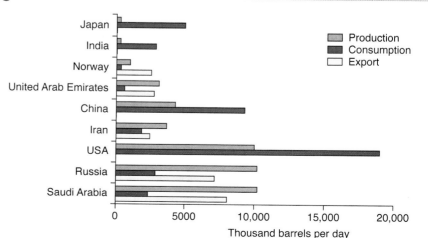

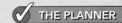
Shale oil and natural gas production are booming. Forecasts show that the United States will surpass Saudi Arabia to become the leading oil producer. These images highlight some of the consequences of these developments.

a. Shale formations are referred to as *plays*. This map shows the location of active shale plays in the contiguous United States. Shale oil extracted from the Bakken Shale Play has made North Dakota the second leading oil-producing state, after Texas.

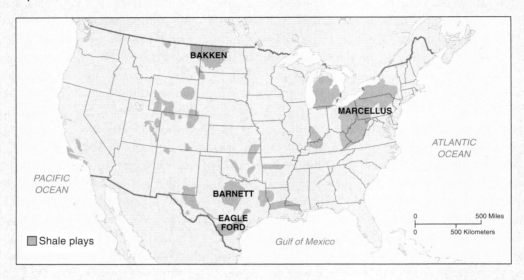

b. This oil rig stands above the Eagle Ford Shale Play in South Texas. Here and across the country this oil boom is taking place on private property, and hundreds of rigs like this have been constructed.

© Zuma Press, Inc./Alamy

© Zuma Press, Inc./Alamy

c. The devices on the left are frack pumps needed for pressurized pumping. Some concerns have been raised about the amount of chemicals used in the injection water, and that the wastewater generated by fracking could seep into groundwater and contaminate household water supplies.

© Zuma Press, Inc./Alamy

d. This once defunct railroad spur in South Texas has grown into a major railroad yard. Trains bring sand and pipes in and, until pipelines are constructed, haul oil out.

million gallons of water during the fracking process. Much of the water that is used for fracking is recovered, but it is a form of wastewater and contains chemicals that are dangerous to people and the environment. See **Figure 12.9** for other impacts of shale oil and natural gas production.

Coal

The coal mined and extracted today derives from the woody, partially decomposed remains of plants and trees that accumulated in swampy environments some 300 to 400 million years ago. Coal seams or deposits formed over millions of years as this plant matter was covered by other sediment and then compacted under very high pressure.

Coal distribution and consumption
Coal is the most abundant and the most geographically widespread of the fossil fuels. More than 70 countries have workable coal reserves. In rank order, the three countries with the most sizable proved coal reserves are the United States, Russia, and China. Forecasts indicate that global coal reserves will last 112 years at the current rate of production.

Unlike oil and natural gas, people have used coal as a source of fuel for thousands of years. Coal, which was burned to heat water and generate steam power, also literally fueled the Industrial Revolution. After oil, coal is the second most widely consumed fossil fuel in the world today. Whereas oil is used mainly for transportation and heating, coal is the leading fuel used in generating electricity (by coal-burning power plants). Coal is also one of the key ingredients needed to produce steel.

China is heavily dependent on coal, and is by far the number one coal producer and consumer in the world today. In 2011, for example, China consumed more than three and a half times as much coal as the United States, the second largest coal consumer in the world. The amount of coal China consumes each day is equivalent to about 37 million barrels of oil. This figure is nearly four times the amount of oil China presently uses in one day.

The challenges of coal Although coal is the most abundant of the fossil fuels, extracting and using the resource present a number of serious environmental and social challenges. Coal burns far less cleanly than the other fossil fuels and contributes to air pollution, smog, and **acid rain**. Coal combustion emits sulfur dioxide and nitrogen oxide. These compounds interact with water, oxygen, and other chemicals in the atmosphere to form acidic substances that fall to the Earth in rain and snow, as acid rain. You may have noticed that coal-burning power plants and other factories often have tall smokestacks. These smokestacks release pollutants higher in the atmosphere so that they are carried by the wind. Thus, acid rain becomes a *transboundary* problem. That is, the effects of acid rain may be "exported" to other communities, sometimes to different countries (**Figure 12.10**).

> **acid rain**
> Precipitation that, primarily because of human activities, is significantly more acidic than normal and can harm aquatic and terrestrial ecosystems.

Acidity of precipitation • Figure 12.10

The pH expresses the measured acidity of water or another solution. On the pH scale, values below 7 are acidic, and the lower the value, the greater the acidity. Unpolluted rainwater has a pH of about 5.6. (*Source:* Map courtesy National Atmospheric Deposition Program, with data from Moran, 2007.)

Ask Yourself
1. What is the main cause of acid rain in the eastern United States?
2. What is the main cause of acid rain in the western United States?

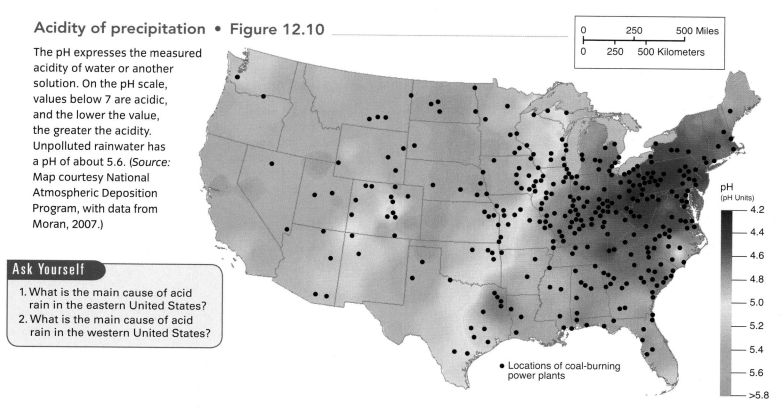

pH (pH Units)
— 4.2
— 4.4
— 4.6
— 4.8
— 5.0
— 5.2
— 5.4
— 5.6
— >5.8

• Locations of coal-burning power plants

PROCESS DIAGRAM

Understanding mountaintop removal • Figure 12.11

Mountaintop removal is a controversial mining method. Although it profitably produces vast tonnages of coal, it also contributes to massive landscape change and alters local and regional watersheds.

NATIONAL GEOGRAPHIC

Dragline

Melissa Farlow/NG Image Collection

Troy Fleece/©AP/Wide World Photos

1 **Removing mountaintops**
First, all vegetation is removed from the area to be mined. Then explosives loosen thick rock above the coal (called overburden), and mammoth draglines scoop the overburden into large trucks.

2 **Filling valleys**
The trucks haul the overburden and dump it in nearby valleys. These "valley fills" are unstable, slide-prone, and can leach toxic metals into streams and alter drainage patterns. These changes not only affect the environment but also can have serious consequences for people who live in the area.

Melissa Farlow/NG Image Collection

Melissa Farlow/NG Image Collection

3 **Mining the coal**
Large front loaders scoop coal from the exposed seam, pouring it into trucks that haul it to loading docks, where the coal is transferred to railroad cars or river barges.

5 **Reshaping the land**
The law allows mining companies to reshape land into a gently rolling surface instead of restoring mountaintops to their original contour. Sometimes entirely new uses of the mined site are created. Here a golf course was built on a mine site where the mountaintop was removed.

4 **Rehabilitating the site**
Former mining site being hydroseeded (sown with a watery mixture of seeds, fertilizer, and mulch) to establish vegetation that will retain the soil and reduce erosion. The plants that are sown are not necessarily native to the site or region and sometimes have difficulty becoming established.

Melissa Farlow/NG Image Collection

Melissa Farlow/NG Image Collection

The combustion of coal also releases mercury into the air. Atmospheric processes such as precipitation deposit mercury on land or in water. Once the mercury is in lakes and streams it can build up in the tissue of fish and enter the food chain. Scrubbers and special procedures for high-temperature mercury capture are some of the technologies that help reduce mercury and other pollutants from coal-fired power plants. When the Environmental Protection Agency issued the Clean Air Mercury Rule in 2005, the United States took an important step toward becoming the first country to regulate the emissions from utility companies.

Not only does the burning of coal present serious environmental challenges, so does the extraction of coal. The most controversial method of coal mining involves mountaintop removal (MTR); the controversy stems from the scale and impact of the operations involved in MTR.

The use of MTR as a coal extraction method dates to the 1970s. In the United States, federal regulation of MTR officially began in 1977 with passage of the Surface Mining Control and Reclamation Act. This law requires that mining companies restore land that has been surface mined unless they have been granted an exception. Not all countries have such laws, however, and it is usually much cheaper for a mining company if it does not have to restore the site. **Figure 12.11** depicts the steps in MTR.

Nuclear Energy

Nuclear energy, produced from uranium, is one of the most controversial energy sources, even though its use is comparatively small (**Figure 12.12**). Uranium is a naturally occurring radioactive element that is found in certain mineral ores. It is not a fossil fuel but is a nonrenewable resource and the basic fuel supply for nuclear energy and nuclear weapons. At the present rate of consumption, uranium reserves are expected to last about another 100 years.

Uranium is used primarily to generate nuclear energy, which heats water to produce steam that turns turbines and generates electricity. The ability to harness nuclear energy dates to the 1940s—a time when much nuclear energy research focused on producing the atomic bomb. In 1957 the International Atomic Energy Association, an organization promoting peaceful uses of nuclear energy, was formed. Commercial development of nuclear energy followed rapidly in the 1950s and 1960s.

Nuclear energy constitutes a small fraction—about 5%—of the energy consumed worldwide (refer again to Figure 12.5). There are fewer than 450 operating nuclear power plants in the world today. Although the United States has more operating nuclear power plants than any other country, less than 20% of its electricity comes from nuclear energy. France is exceptional in that nuclear power supplies 78% of its electricity. Globally, the geography of nuclear power plants is highly uneven and strongly associated with the most industrialized countries. There are three main reasons for this pattern. First, the ability to harness and control the production of nuclear energy as well as its waste materials requires specialized knowledge and expertise. Second, there are very high costs (of up to several billion

Nuclear energy controversy • Figure 12.12

The Fukushima Daiichi nuclear accident was caused by a massive offshore earthquake which triggered a tsunami that shut down the power supply and prevented proper cooling of the facility. Many Japanese are questioning the viability of the country's reliance on nuclear energy.

a. This photo shows an explosion at the Fukushima Daiichi nuclear power plant. The power plant had been built to withstand a tsunami about 20 feet high, but not a nearly 50-foot high one like the one that struck the facility.

b. Protesters meet police at an anti-nuclear protest in Japan following the Fukushima Daiichi accident. After the accident, the Japanese government shut down all of its nuclear power plants, but the government may reverse that decision.

dollars) involved in building nuclear reactors. Third, nuclear power plants also require a substantial supporting infrastructure including power generators, appropriate sites for waste storage or management, and other facilities.

Because it does not rely on fossil fuels, nuclear energy is sometimes heralded as an alternative energy source. We should note, however, that most experts do not consider use of nuclear energy a substitute or replacement for oil since most of the oil consumed is used for transportation, not electricity generation. Nevertheless, the use of nuclear energy to produce electricity presents a number of advantages. One advantage is that nuclear fuel can be stockpiled and stored for long periods of time. It is not practical to do this with coal, oil, or natural gas. In addition, on a per-weight basis, uranium generates more electricity than do the fossil fuels. If less uranium is needed, some experts argue, the disturbance to the landscape caused by mining it will be significantly less than the disturbance caused by mining coal. Other advantages of nuclear power include low air pollution and very low emissions of carbon dioxide.

One disadvantage of nuclear power is that it is expensive to develop. The accident at the Fukishima Dai-ichi nuclear power plant in Japan, the worst since the Chernobyl nuclear plant disaster in Ukraine in 1986, refocused attention on the disadvantages of nuclear energy (see again Figure 12.12). Radiation leakage is a major concern with all nuclear power plants, and following the Fukishima Daiichi accident more than 100,000 people had to evacuate their homes to avoid exposure to radiation. Concerns still linger about radiation contamination of soils and food.

Another disadvantage of nuclear energy is that it generates radioactive waste. The safe handling of these waste materials has become a major issue and is central to the ongoing debate about nuclear power. Some nuclear energy proponents recommend the long-term storage of these wastes underground in areas that have very stable rock structures, while others prefer recycling nuclear waste, which results in much lower volumes of radioactive waste. Although Germany plans to shut down all of its nuclear reactors within the next decade, China has some 30 nuclear reactors under construction. Japan, however, remains deeply divided on the use of nuclear energy.

CONCEPT CHECK   STOP

1. **How** does the distribution of oil reserves compare and contrast with geographical patterns in the consumption of oil?
2. **Why** was OPEC formed, and what challenges does it face?
3. **Why** is mountaintop removal controversial?
4. **What** are the advantages and disadvantages of nuclear energy?

Renewable Energy Resources

LEARNING OBJECTIVES

1. **Explain** what biomass energy is.
2. **Assess** the sustainability of hydropower.
3. **Identify** barriers associated with the wider adoption of renewable energy resources.
4. **Distinguish** between direct and indirect uses of geothermal energy.

 When we think about different systems of energy production around the world, it is useful to distinguish between commercial and noncommercial energy. Commercial energy has historically been produced largely from fossil fuels, nuclear fuel, or large-scale hydropower facilities. Consumers access and purchase commercial energy through a networked infrastructure such as an electric grid. Commercial energy is often used or consumed a long way from its original source or where it was refined, whereas noncommercial energy is produced and consumed locally or regionally—for instance, at the village or household level. Thus, noncommercial energy can be thought of as "off-grid" energy.

On a daily basis, noncommercial energy satisfies the energy needs of hundreds of millions of people across rural areas throughout much of the developing world. Although considerable data exist on the supply and consumption of commercial energy, much less information is available about the regional geographies of noncommercial energy. One measure that suggests the extent of noncommercial energy use is the population without electricity. About one-quarter of the world's people live without electricity.

Renewable energy, also called *alternative energy*, has, until very recently, been largely a component of noncommercial energy. In fact, the only renewable fuel type that is a major source of commercial energy is water—that is, hydropower (refer again to Figure 12.5). It is important to note that most of the energy that is generated from hydropower comes from large-scale facilities (with dams that are more than 15 meters or 50 feet high) such as the Three Gorges Dam in China or the Grand Coulee Dam in Washington State. Today, however, these massive facilities are considered to have such substantial environmental impacts that they are excluded from the category of renewable energy. **New renewables**, therefore, include biomass, tidal, solar, wind, and geothermal energy as well as small-scale hydropower.

Biomass Energy

Biomass, the organic matter in an ecosystem, is an important source of energy worldwide. More specifically, **biomass energy** is obtained from plant matter and/or animal wastes. Common sources of biomass energy include wood, charcoal, crop residues such as plant stalks or coconut shells, and cattle manure. Even though fossil fuels ultimately derive from the buried remains of plants, they are not counted as a source of biomass energy because of the chemical changes in their makeup that have occurred over lengthy periods of time. Unlike fossil fuels, biomass energy is renewable as long as the resource that supplies it is sustainably managed.

There are two methods for harnessing the energy from biomass: direct and indirect. The direct method is to burn unprocessed biomass and use the energy released for cooking or heating. The indirect method involves converting the biomass into a gas (biogas) or liquid fuel (biofuel), with the help of naturally occurring microbes. Methane, a biogas, can be used for cooking, heating, or lighting. Liquid ethanol, a biofuel that can be obtained from the residues of certain crops, notably corn and sugarcane, can be used to power certain vehicles. Biodiesel can be manufactured from vegetable oils, including used cooking oils (**Figure 12.13**).

Biomass is the leading type of renewable energy used worldwide. A large part of the global demand for biomass stems from its use as fuel for cooking. Indeed, more than 3 billion people prepare and cook their foods with the heat generated by burning fuelwood, dung, or various crop residues. Of these, fuelwood remains the principal source of biomass energy in many developing countries. Recent estimates indicate that fuelwood is the dominant source of energy in more than 90% of rural households in Sub-Saharan Africa.

Biodiesel • Figure 12.13

This gas station near Los Angeles offers a biodiesel fuel. Whereas most developed countries including the United States have generally been slow to adopt biofuels, Brazil has been using sugarcane to generate ethanol as a fuel for cars and light trucks since the 1970s.

Peter Bennett/Ambient Images/Alamy

A serious problem associated with reliance on fuelwood, however, is that it can intensify pressures on local forest resources. From a socioeconomic standpoint, the time spent collecting fuelwood, a task most often relegated to women and girls, can interfere with their education or opportunities to earn additional income. Also, burning fuelwood is a major source of indoor air pollution and has been linked to tuberculosis, lung disease, cataracts, and other ailments. Across the developing world, indoor air pollution poses the greatest threat to women and children because they are most likely to spend long hours working inside and in poorly ventilated rooms. To address this problem, both governmental and nongovernmental organizations are increasingly promoting improved ventilation systems.

Biogas digester • Figure 12.14

In the Causcasus, a Georgian villager tends to her biogas digester. Biogas digesters are specially designed tanks that are usually placed in the ground and have an above-ground opening. People simply add biomass such as crop residues or animal waste to the digester, which facilitates the conversion of the biomass into a biogas that can be used as a household fuel supply for cooking and lighting. Collecting livestock and poultry waste in biogas digesters instead of discharging them into streams helps prevent water pollution.

Reuters/David Mdzinarishvili/Landov LLC

Another type of technology that enables people to make use of biomass—most commonly dung and vegetable matter—is a *biogas* or *methane digester*. Although biogas digesters have been around for centuries, they have attracted more attention lately because of their household and environmental benefits. Biogas digesters are fairly easy to build, can be used by rural and urban dwellers alike, and can be built to supply energy at the industrial or household scale (**Figure 12.14**).

Hydropower

Hydropower is a nonpolluting, renewable source of energy. Less than one-third of the world's economically viable hydropower potential has been tapped. The countries or regions with the greatest hydropower potential include China, Russia, Sub-Saharan Africa, Southeast Asia, and Central and South America. On a per-person basis, mountainous Nepal has one of the highest hydropower potentials in the world. Hydropower ranks a distant fourth after oil, coal, and natural gas as a source of electricity. Large hydropower facilities produce about 15% of the world's electricity. As we have seen, in most industrialized countries, use of hydropower to generate electricity constitutes a small part of the overall energy picture. However, a few countries, including Norway, Brazil, and Argentina, obtain most of their electricity from hydropower.

Globally, the heyday of large dam construction occurred between the 1930s and 1970s. At the time, many development experts believed that these massive facilities would help solve the problem of uneven economic development by improving food security, lessening import dependence, and providing jobs. More dams were approved for construction during the 1970s than in any other decade. Although they have provided numerous benefits, such as a year-round water supply for irrigation, large dams have not solved the problem of uneven development and have contributed to a host of environmental problems.

Large dams fragment rivers and alter the ecosystems of river basins. According to a report of the World Commission on Dams, "Large dams generally have a range of extensive impacts on rivers, watersheds and aquatic ecosystems—these impacts are more negative than positive and, in many cases, have led to irreversible loss of species and ecosystems" (WCD, 2000, p. xxxi). Beyond the impact on the physical environment, large dam construction also has major consequences for people, including forced resettlement or loss of livelihood (**Figure 12.15**).

Hydropower production • Figure 12.15

Hydropower production is a small part of the global energy picture, but is very important in many local contexts.

a. Leading hydropower producers

The leading producers account for nearly half of the world's hydroelectricity production. (*Source:* Data from Energy Information Administration, 2008.)

Producer	Percent of world total
China	14.4%
Canada	12.0%
Brazil	11.5%
United States	9.7%
Russia	5.8%
Norway	3.9%
India	3.8%
Japan	2.8%
Venezuela	2.7%
Sweden	2.0%

b. The world's largest dam

The massive Three Gorges Dam on the Chang Jiang (Yangtze) River in China provides flood control and has boosted China's production of hydropower, but construction of the dam also forced the relocation of more than 1 million people and has altered the river's water quality and ecosystems.

Wen Zhenxiao/Xinhua/Landov LLC

Today, small hydropower (SHP) is favored as a more sustainable alternative. By definition, SHP includes those facilities that generate fewer than 10 megawatts of electricity. Depending on specific river and site characteristics, the electricity generated from SHP facilities can serve a local community or a single household. Like the use of biomass, the development of SHP holds promise as another mechanism that can spread rural electrification in developing areas.

Solar and Wind Energy

Energy from the sun can be harnessed in two ways: passively and actively. *Passive solar collection* uses the design of a building and its materials to capture sunlight. In the northern hemisphere, for example, south-facing windows are advantageous for passive solar collection. *Active solar collection* uses different devices including solar panels, mirrors, or photovoltaic cells to capture, store, or use the sun's energy. Photovoltaic (PV) cells enable the conversion of sunlight directly into electricity. In other systems the sun's energy warms a liquid such as water. Solar hot water heaters work on this principle. Prompted by electricity shortages, Cape Town, South Africa, has implemented a city by-law that encourages households to install solar water heaters.

Technological and financial barriers have limited our ability to maximize use of this form of renewable energy. Solar energy systems tend to be expensive to install, and at present it can take from 5 to 15 years to recoup these costs. Nevertheless, growth in the solar energy sector has been rapid in recent years, with most of the installed capacity making use of PV cells. Many states now offer incentives for solar installations. Like hydropower, one of the major advantages of solar and wind power is that they are emission free.

The sun is the ultimate source of wind power. Winds are created through the uneven heating of the Earth's surface by the sun. Wind turbines harness the energy from moving air and convert it to electricity. The precursor to the wind turbine was the windmill, a device used in Europe from the 1200s to grind grain and pump water. Electricity can be generated from a single turbine or multiple turbines. Most commercial uses of wind power now involve the construction of *wind farms*, clusters of turbines in an area.

At present, wind power contributes only minimally to the world's energy supply. Denmark provides one important exception to this trend—in recent years wind power has supplied approximately 20% of the country's electricity. No other country comes close to this figure. For example, in the United States wind power produces a little more than 2% of the country's electricity. Nevertheless, the wind energy industry is growing very rapidly. New turbine installations in 2012 increased the world's wind power capacity by 20%. Two factors contributing to the popularity of wind energy are concerns about energy security associated with reliance on oil imports and concerns about climate change (**Figure 12.16**).

Geothermal Energy

Geothermal energy comes from the interior of the Earth. High pressures combined with the slow radioactive decay of elements in the Earth's core produce vast amounts of heat. The surrounding rock materials absorb this heat such that the materials closest to the Earth's core are the hottest. In some places, such as Iceland, which is situated along a rift in the Earth's surface, it is possible to find extremely hot rock material and water near the Earth's surface. At some locations, for example, underground waters about 3 km (2 mi) deep have temperatures in excess of 150 degrees Celsius (300 degrees Fahrenheit).

Geothermal energy is harnessed by drilling deep wells in order to tap into reservoirs of heated groundwater. This hot water can then be used as a direct source of heat for homes and other buildings. More than 80% of Iceland's residences are heated geothermally with piped hot water.

Installed wind power capacity • Figure 12.16

The geographic centers of the wind energy industry have traditionally included western Europe and the United States. Today, however, the wind energy industry is becoming more globalized and has literally moved offshore. (*Source:* Data from EIA, 2013c.)

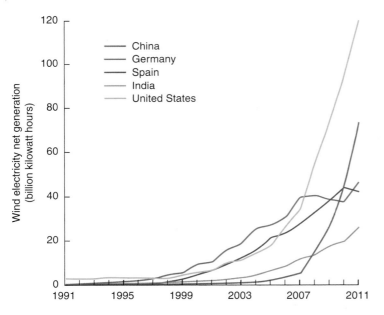

Geothermal energy • Figure 12.17

Geothermal energy warms this outdoor spa in Iceland and powers the energy plant in the background. Geothermal energy supplies 25% of Iceland's power—far more than any other country.

NATIONAL GEOGRAPHIC

© Hemis/Alamy

If the hot water is converted to steam, it can be used indirectly to rotate turbines and generate electricity. At present, most of the existing capacity for geothermal power generation is confined to a handful of countries, including the United States (especially the western states), the Philippines, Mexico, Italy, Indonesia, Japan, Iceland, and New Zealand (**Figure 12.17**).

You don't have to live in Iceland to benefit from geothermal energy. The development of geothermal technologies means that it is possible to have geothermal systems installed in homes and businesses. These systems take advantage of the fact that, below the frost line, the Earth maintains a steady temperature of about 50°F and this natural energy can be used to heat or cool buildings. Many types of renewable energy exist, but different barriers have slowed adoption of them. For another perspective on this topic, see *Video Explorations*.

CONCEPT CHECK

1. **What** are some environmental and social issues related to the use of fuelwood?

2. **Why** are large-scale hydropower facilities not considered renewable sources of energy?

3. **What** developments help explain the popularity of wind energy?

4. **How** is geothermal energy produced and harnessed?

Video Explorations

Alternative Energy

National Geographic

This video clip reviews several different forms of alternative energy; specifically wind power, solar energy, and biomass fermentation. It explores the current uses of each alternative energy form in the United States and interviews several alternative energy advocates. It also discusses why alternative energy use remains low in the United States.

Global Environmental Change

LEARNING OBJECTIVES

1. **Distinguish** between the greenhouse effect and global warming.
2. **Relate** land-use and land-cover change to sustainability.
3. **Explain** the significance of the Kyoto Protocol and the Copenhagen Accord.

As we saw in the previous section, important strides are being made in the adoption and use of renewable forms of energy. Collectively, however, we still have a long way to go before we can end our addiction to fossil fuels. In this final section we examine the relationship between human activities and global environmental change.

The Greenhouse Effect and Global Warming

Academics and nonacademics alike regularly use the term *greenhouse effect* to explain how the Earth's atmosphere works. Unfortunately, the term is slightly misleading. A greenhouse receives incoming solar radiation that warms the inside air. This warm air is then trapped within the greenhouse by the glass windows and doors that enclose it. The atmosphere—that thin gaseous layer that surrounds the Earth—works in a different manner. Recall that the atmosphere consists of nitrogen (78%), followed by oxygen (21%) and a combination of other gases. It is some of these other gases, including water vapor, carbon dioxide, methane, nitrous oxide, and hydrochlorofluorocarbons (HCFCs), that are

> **greenhouse effect** A natural process, involving solar radiation and atmospheric gases, that helps to warm the Earth.

greenhouse gases. **Figure 12.18** provides a simplified depiction of the **greenhouse effect**.

The greenhouse effect is a naturally occurring process that helps enable life on Earth. The concern about the greenhouse effect, however, centers on the increasing concentrations of greenhouse gases in the atmosphere because of certain human activities. Let's consider carbon dioxide (CO_2). Burning fossil fuels and plant matter releases CO_2 into the atmosphere. Considerable historical data confirm that the atmospheric concentrations of CO_2

The greenhouse effect • Figure 12.18

Solar radiation passes through the atmosphere and warms the Earth. As the Earth's surface warms, it emits heat, some of which passes into space and some of which is "trapped" or absorbed by molecules of water vapor, carbon dioxide, methane, and other greenhouse gases. The heat that these gases emit warms the atmosphere.

have increased sharply since the Industrial Revolution. Given that there is no known natural process or source that could account for this increase in CO_2, scientists attribute the rise in CO_2 concentrations to human activities, primarily the burning of fossil fuels (**Figure 12.19**).

Like CO_2, atmospheric concentrations of methane and nitrous oxide have also increased significantly since the Industrial Revolution. These increases, too, are tied to human activities. Worldwide, the human activity responsible for releasing the greatest amounts of methane into the atmosphere is livestock production. Ruminant livestock such as cattle, sheep, and goats produce methane during digestion. Nearly 30% of the methane from human activities comes from livestock. Wet rice farming (see Chapter 11) is another important source of methane because the processes of anaerobic (without oxygen) decay that occur in the flooded fields produce methane. In addition, methane can leak into the atmosphere when we drill gas wells, transport natural gas through pipelines, or use gas dryers. Methane can be used as a clean-burning fuel, but there is presently no practical way to harness the methane produced by livestock or agricultural processes.

Anthropogenic sources of nitrous oxide include agriculture—specifically, the application of nitrogen fertilizers. Under certain soil and moisture conditions, the natural

Atmospheric concentrations of carbon dioxide • Figure 12.19

Global emissions of CO_2 have more than doubled since 1970. This graph shows that combustion of gas, liquid, and solid forms of fossil fuels generates most of these emissions. Land-use change—especially deforestation—also raises CO_2 levels because forests help remove CO_2 from the atmosphere. (*Source:* Boden, Marland, and Andres, 2012.)

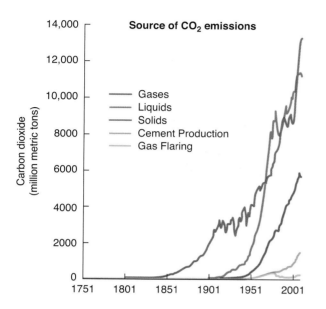

melting of snow and ice and rising global average sea level" (IPCC 2007, p. 30). Based on temperature records that date to the 1850s, scientists recorded the warmest surface temperatures between 1995 and 2006. Over an even longer perspective, the data convey a similar message about global warming: the past 50 years were warmer than any other 50-year period in 1,300 years (**Figure 12.20**).

As noted at the start of the chapter, changes to the Arctic sea ice are having consequences for local people such as the Inuit. However, global warming has the potential to affect the continental ice sheets in Greenland and West Antarctica. These ice sheets are so substantial that if they melt they will cause sea level to rise. Even a 1-meter (3-foot) rise in sea level means that low-lying coastal areas around the globe will be flooded, or put at risk of hazards caused by storm surges or erosion, with additional costs to maintain infrastructure and protect people or property in these areas.

Rising global temperatures also have consequences for ecosystems. Some species of plants, trees, and amphibians among others, may be endangered by significantly warmer temperatures. Climate models indicate that precipitation patterns would also be affected by global warming, raising questions about the impact on agriculture.

bacterial action that occurs in the presence of these fertilizers can result in the formation of nitrous oxide. Energy use is another major source of nitrous oxide. Motor vehicles emit nitrous oxide; this is the leading anthropogenic source of it in the United States. Coal-fired power plants are also an important source of nitrous oxide.

Unlike the other greenhouse gases, HCFCs do not occur naturally. Rather, they are synthesized specifically for human use. HCFCs are used as coolants in refrigerators and air conditioners. The manufacture of HCFCs is now being phased out around the world.

The consensus among most scientists is that our activities have amplified the greenhouse effect and have contributed to **global warming**. According to the Intergovernmental Panel on Climate Change, "Warming of the climate system is unequivocal, as is now evident from observations of increases in global average air and ocean temperatures, widespread

> **global warming**
> A rise in global temperatures primarily attributed to human activities that have increased concentrations of greenhouse gases in the atmosphere.

Global annual surface temperatures • Figure 12.20

Fluctuations in global temperatures are normal and in any single year are the result of a variety of natural and human factors including solar radiation and greenhouse gases. Climate scientists focus on long-term trends, such as the upward trend in temperatures since the 1960s, shown here. (*Source:* Berg and Hager, 2009. Reprinted with permission of John Wiley & Sons, Inc.)

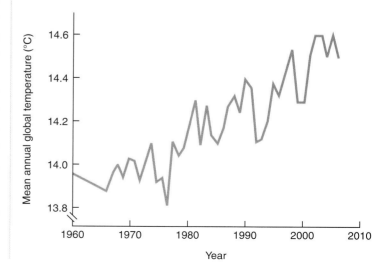

Leading carbon dioxide emitters • Figure 12.21

Contrast these charts to see how the leading CO_2 emitters change when these emissions are calculated on a percentage and per capita basis.

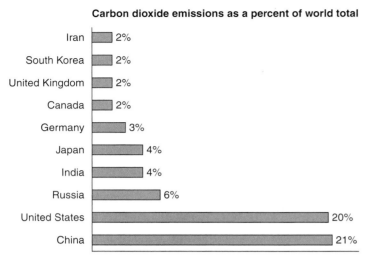

Carbon dioxide emissions as a percent of world total

Iran	2%
South Korea	2%
United Kingdom	2%
Canada	2%
Germany	3%
Japan	4%
India	4%
Russia	6%
United States	20%
China	21%

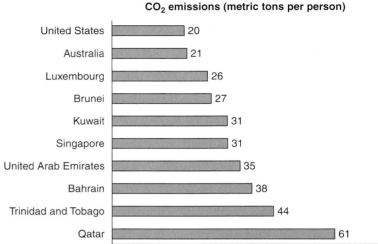

CO_2 emissions (metric tons per person)

United States	20
Australia	21
Luxembourg	26
Brunei	27
Kuwait	31
Singapore	31
United Arab Emirates	35
Bahrain	38
Trinidad and Tobago	44
Qatar	61

a. China is now the world's leading emitter of CO_2. Collectively, China and the United States are responsible for 41% of the world's CO_2 emissions. (*Source:* Data from Energy Information Administration, 2008.)

b. Emissions for Qatar, Trinidad and Tobago, Bahrain, the United Arab Emirates, Kuwait, and Brunei are a result of burning waste gas at natural gas wells. In the other countries, high CO_2 emissions stem from fossil fuel consumption for power and industry. (*Source:* Data from Energy Information Administration, 2008.)

In arid and semiarid regions, for example, problems of water scarcity may worsen, and droughts may become more frequent. For human geographers and others, global warming raises numerous environmental and ethical questions. As an example, Pacific Island countries contribute less than 1% of the world's carbon dioxide emissions, yet will be among the first places affected by climate change, especially because many of the islands face inundation and erosion from rising sea levels.

Carbon dioxide factors prominently in studies of global warming not only because atmospheric concentrations of it have increased so markedly, but also because it stays in the atmosphere a long time. Globally, the geography of CO_2 emission is highly uneven. The richest and most industrialized countries in the world account for nearly half of the CO_2 emissions. In contrast, the countries of Sub-Saharan Africa generate less than 3% of the world's CO_2 emissions. The two greatest CO_2 emitters are China and the United States (**Figure 12.21**).

In the past several years the term **carbon footprint**—the amount of CO_2 emitted as a result of human activity—has gained currency. The carbon footprints of developed countries as well as China and India swamp those of the least developed countries. In an effort to reduce its greenhouse gas emissions, California is implementing a *cap-and-trade*

program. The *cap* refers to company limits or allowances on greenhouse gases. To meet the cap, which is reduced over time, companies can reduce their emissions and/or buy (trade) allowances from other companies.

Land-use and Land-cover Change

Scientists recognize that another key factor affecting global climate patterns is **land-use and land-cover change** (LULCC). Some examples of LULCC include the conversion of woodlands to agricultural fields, the drainage of wetlands to construct shopping centers, the expansion of paved surfaces as cities grow, desertification caused by overgrazing, or water withdrawals that drastically alter a river's flow. Not all LULCC is human-induced.

> **land-use and land-cover change** An interdisciplinary approach to studying human–environment interactions based on an awareness of the linkages between ecosystem processes and social conditions.

Drought or other natural stresses can affect the ability of vegetation to regenerate and alter local or regional biodiversity. Under certain conditions, human activity and natural fluctuations in weather or climate patterns may coincide and intensify LULCC. Changes in the Louisiana coastal zone provide an instructive example (see *What a Geographer Sees*).

WHAT A GEOGRAPHER SEES

Environmental Change

About half of the coastal wetlands in the United States are located along the shores the Gulf of Mexico. These wetlands not only provide habitats for a wide variety of aquatic and terrestrial species, they also help buffer storm surges, protect against erosion, improve water quality, and offer numerous opportunities for tourism and recreation. But these coastal wetlands continually face impacts that are both natural and human-induced. One result is the significant loss of land along the Louisiana coast. What has happened to cause this land-cover change?

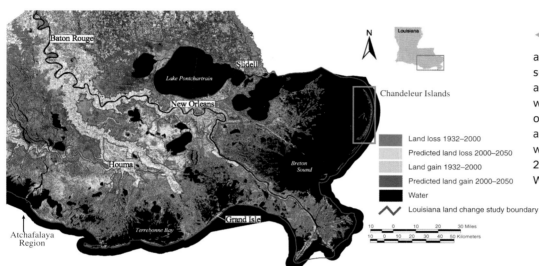

Land loss 1932–2000
Predicted land loss 2000–2050
Land gain 1932–2000
Predicted land gain 2000–2050
Water
Louisiana land change study boundary

a. Changing coastline

With the help of remote sensing and GIS, geographers and other scientists have identified where as well as how much of Louisiana's coastal wetlands have been lost to the Gulf of Mexico. Between 1932 and 2000, an area about the size of Delaware washed away, and between 2000 and 2050 an area about ten times the size of Washington, D.C. is expected to be lost.

b. Natural causes of coastal change

These satellite images show the effects that hurricanes Ivan and Katrina had on the northern half of Chandeleur barrier islands. Tropical storms can drastically reconfigure coastal landscapes.

US. Department of the Inteior/U.S.Geological Survey

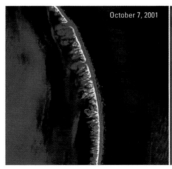
October 7, 2001

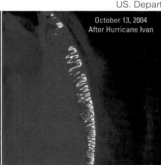
October 13, 2004
After Hurricane Ivan

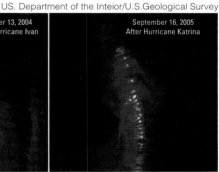
September 16, 2005
After Hurricane Katrina

U.S. Geological Survey, National Wetlands Research Center, Layette, LA

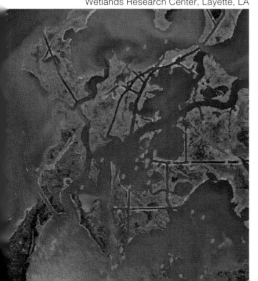

c. Human-induced coastal impacts

Oil and gas production from both on- and offshore wells is a mainstay of Louisiana's economy. Many well sites in the coastal zones are not accessible by roads; consequently, numerous channels have been built through the wetlands. In this image of the Atchafalaya region the channels are the straight or nearly straight waterways. Note the spatial association between the channels and the locations of well sites (in purple). (*Source:* Lyles and Namwamba, 2005.)

Think Critically

1. Why is channel construction in this coastal zone linked to environmental degradation? What would environmental restoration here involve?
2. What impacts on land use, land cover, and livelihoods has the BP oil spill of 2010 had?

LULCC has implications not only for conditions at the local, national, and global scales, but also for sustainability. For geographers, LULCC fits squarely within the tradition, discussed in Chapter 1, that emphasizes the view of the Earth as a dynamic, integrated system.

In the tropical rainforests of the Brazilian Amazon, for example, deforestation has been a major aspect of LULCC, especially since the 1980s. Rainforest clearance often results in warmer temperatures and drier conditions because less water evaporates or cycles from the

Land-use and land-cover change in the Brazilian Amazon • Figure 12.22

Satellite imagery and maps reveal the extent of deforestation in Amazonia.

a. Key forces propelling this deforestation include population growth and resettlement, logging, farm and ranch development, and road construction. Brazil has become a major beef exporter, and cattle ranching continues to spread into previously forested areas. Soybean farms are also increasingly common. (*Source:* NG Maps based on *Earth Pulse* 2008.)

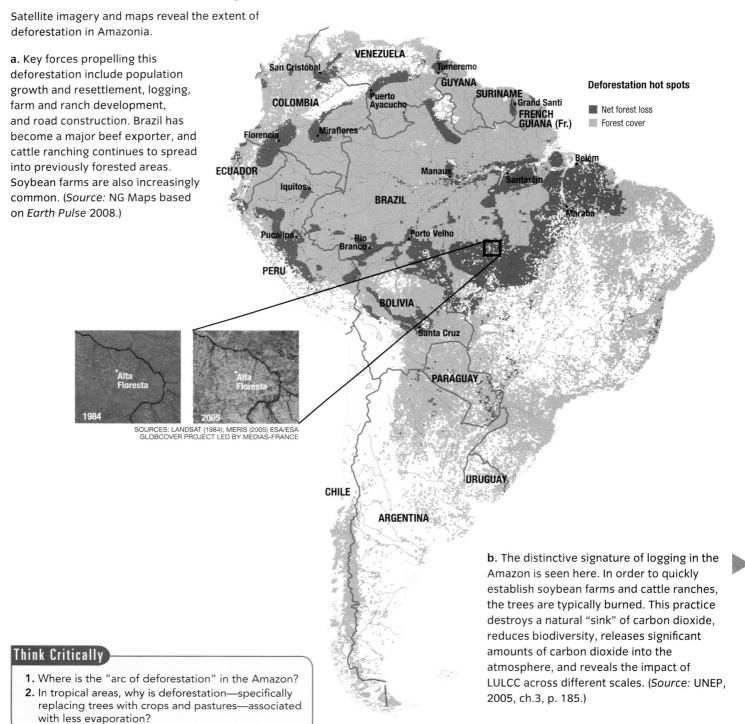

SOURCES: LANDSAT (1984); MERIS (2005) ESA/ESA GLOBCOVER PROJECT LED BY MEDIAS-FRANCE

b. The distinctive signature of logging in the Amazon is seen here. In order to quickly establish soybean farms and cattle ranches, the trees are typically burned. This practice destroys a natural "sink" of carbon dioxide, reduces biodiversity, releases significant amounts of carbon dioxide into the atmosphere, and reveals the impact of LULCC across different scales. (*Source:* UNEP, 2005, ch.3, p. 185.)

Think Critically

1. Where is the "arc of deforestation" in the Amazon?
2. In tropical areas, why is deforestation—specifically replacing trees with crops and pastures—associated with less evaporation?

vegetation into the atmosphere. These conditions have consequences for cloud formation and, in turn, precipitation patterns. When these changes are coupled with an awareness of economic and demographic factors influencing human behavior, such as job availability and migration, we can more fully understand how and why changes in land management occur. **Figure 12.22** depicts some of these changes.

Targeting Greenhouse Gas Reduction

For more than 150 years the developed countries have contributed disproportionately to the atmospheric concentrations of carbon dioxide and many other anthropogenic greenhouse gases. Consequently, many experts argue that these same countries are obliged to acknowledge the long historical trajectory of their contribution to greenhouse gases and to implement measures to stabilize or reduce their greenhouse gas emissions. See *Where Geographers Click* for access to a website that tracks different environmental trends.

One international agreement that marks an important step toward improved management of greenhouse gases is the **Kyoto Protocol**. A key aspect of the Kyoto Protocol is the commitment of a large number of developed countries to reducing their greenhouse gas emissions 5% below their 1990 levels by 2012. The treaty was adopted in 1997 and went into effect in 2005. It has been ratified by 191 countries and the European Union. This number, however, does not include the United States. Some legislators oppose the Kyoto Protocol and argue that it would harm U.S. economic interests.

The first phase of the Kyoto Protocol expired in 2012, and many observers expected the Copenhagen Climate Change Summit in 2009 to generate the successor to the Kyoto Protocol. It did not; the result instead was the Copenhagen Accord. The Accord is an important achievement that is now supported by about 120 countries, many of which have pledged to reduce their emissions. Nevertheless, three weaknesses of the Accord deserve mentioning. First, the Accord is not a legally binding global agreement. Second, no specific emission-reduction targets were established for developed countries. Third, no specific target for the reductions in global emissions was identified (e.g., cutting global emissions in half by 2050).

With the Copenhagen Accord, the global community has acknowledged the importance of regulating activities that affect global warming. The challenge is to achieve a consensus on specific targets and to find ways to actually meet those targets. To learn how carbon farming can help manage greenhouse gases, see *Video Explorations*.

Video Explorations

 THE PLANNER

Carbon Farming

National Geographic

Each year farmers release huge amounts of carbon dioxide into the atmosphere when they plow their fields. This video describes new plowing techniques that help farmers keep the carbon in the soil.

CONCEPT CHECK STOP

1. **How** is the greenhouse effect related to global warming?

2. **How** can human activities and natural processes affect local and global climate patterns?

3. **What** prompted the Kyoto Protocol and Copenhagen Summit, and what have they achieved?

Summary

1 Ecosystems 358

- An **ecosystem** includes the living organisms, their physical **environment**, and the flows of energy and nutrients cycling through them. Ecosystems exist at a variety of scales, from a local estuary such as the one shown here, to a desert that spans several countries. The Earth's interconnected ecosystems constitute the **biosphere**.

Ecosystems • Figure 12.1

Rich Reid/NG Image Collection

- The **First Law of Ecology** expresses the principle that the environment is an interconnected web that includes people, and that human actions have environmental consequences.

- The environment is also a form of **natural capital**, which includes its **nonrenewable** and **renewable resources**. When assessing **environmental degradation**, a more complete picture considers both beneficial and detrimental processes.

- Another way of classifying resources distinguishes between **common property** and **open-access resources**. The idea of the tragedy of the commons, as presented by Garrett Hardin, was based on some incorrect assumptions about common property resources but raised provocative questions about resource management and environmental degradation.

2 Nonrenewable Energy Resources 362

- **Fossil fuels** are nonrenewable resources and include oil, natural gas, and coal. The world is heavily dependent on fossil fuels, especially oil, a versatile and valuable energy resource.

- Most of the proved oil reserves are concentrated in the Middle East. The single greatest consumer of the world's oil is the United States. In the United States, oil and natural gas production from shale formations is changing the energy landscape.

- Coal, the most abundant of fossil fuels, presents a number of environmental challenges when extracted and used. Mountaintop removal, depicted here, remains a controversial technique, and burning coal is linked to mercury pollution and **acid rain**.

Understanding mountaintop removal • Figure 12.11

Troy Fleece/©AP/Wide World Photos

- Though not a fossil fuel, uranium is a nonrenewable resource used to produce nuclear energy. Worldwide, nuclear energy constitutes a minor part of the energy picture. The controversy over nuclear energy stems from concerns about its safety.

3 Renewable Energy Resources 370

- Renewable energy resources have long been used noncommercially but are an increasingly important component of commercial energy as well. **New renewables** are energy resources such as biomass, small-scale hydropower, solar, wind, and geothermal energy.

- Globally, the most-used source of renewable energy is **biomass energy**, specifically fuelwood for cooking. Biogas digesters built for household, village, or industrial operations provide an ecologically sustainable energy alternative and can help relieve pressure on forests for fuelwood.

- Most of the world's hydropower resources remain untapped. Because of the way large dams such as the Three Gorges Dam (see photo) fragment habitat and ecosystems, their sustainability has been questioned.

Hydropower production • Figure 12.15

Wen Zhenxiao/Xinhua/Landov LLC

- The sun provides solar energy and through the uneven heating of the Earth's surface also creates wind energy. At present, both forms of energy contribute minimally to the world's energy supply but are gaining popularity as emission-free sources of energy. The Earth's core generates **geothermal energy** that can be used to heat or cool buildings.

4 Global Environmental Change   376

- The **greenhouse effect**, depicted here, enables life on Earth but also is associated with global climate change.

The greenhouse effect • Figure 12.18

- Most climate scientists agree that human activities have increased atmospheric concentrations of greenhouse gases, thereby contributing to **global warming**.

- The concept of a **carbon footprint** provides one means of expressing the amount of carbon dioxide emissions from human activities. **Land-use and land-cover change** also plays an important role in global environmental change.

- The **Kyoto Protocol** and the Copenhagen Accord are international agreements aimed at achieving reductions in emissions of greenhouse gases.

Key Terms

Critical and Creative Thinking Questions

1. Some ecologists have compared the Earth to an island ecosystem. What are the strengths and weaknesses of this analogy?

2. In what ways are the concepts of regions and ecosystems similar to and different from one another?

3. Do you agree with the statement that national parks are open-access resources? Is the Internet a common property or an open-access resource? Defend your answers.

4. The coal industry has been promoting the use of "clean coal." Do some research on this and assess the extent to which clean coal lives up to its name.

5. Use this photo to develop three or four questions that a land-use and land-cover change scientist might ask about mountaintop removal.

6. Use a carbon footprint calculator, such as the one hosted by the University of California at Berkeley, to calculate your personal carbon footprint. What could you do to reduce the size of your footprint? Are you willing to change your lifestyle to do so?

7. What is carbon sequestration? Do some research on it and evaluate its viability as a solution to the challenge of carbon emissions.

8. What are some major environmental consequences of globalization?

9. Give some reasons to explain the slow development and adoption of alternative energy uses for transportation.

Melissa Farlow/NG Image Collection

What is happening in this picture?

© pixzzle/iStockphoto

This is a green, or living wall on a building in southern Europe. The plants grow in hydroponic pots, without soil. Instead, nutrients dissolved in water provide the necessary food for the plants to live.

NATIONAL GEOGRAPHIC

Think Critically

1. What are the environmental benefits of green walls?
2. Are there other benefits or disadvantages of green walls?

Self-Test

(Check your answers in Appendix B.)

1. The term _____ refers to the zone of life on Earth.
   a. ecosystem
   b. biosphere
   c. environment
   d. biomass

2. Natural capital includes all of the following except _____.
   a. the greenhouse effect
   b. photosynthesis
   c. fossil fuels
   d. hydrochlorofluorocarbons (HCFCs)

3. Economic depletion of a mineral means that _____.
   a. the cost of extracting the mineral exceeds the economic value of it
   b. the value of a mineral has peaked and is declining rapidly
   c. the mineral has lost all value as a commodity
   d. the mineral has been completely exhausted

4. _____ are natural resources that are shared by a well-defined community of users.
   a. Open-access resources
   b. Degraded resources
   c. Common property resources
   d. Renewable resources

5. A flaw in Hardin's argument on "The Tragedy of the Commons" is its failure to _____.
   a. acknowledge the existence of customary rules
   b. see the commons as a scarce resource
   c. incorporate the First Law of Ecology
   d. specify where the commons was located

6. Which of the following is *not* associated with the production of oil and natural gas from shale _____.
   a. horizontal drilling
   b. high rates of water use
   c. high crude oil prices
   d. decreased demand for oil

7. As discussed in the chapter, this sequence of before and after photos relates to environmental degradation through the idea of _____ .

U.S. Fish and Wildlife Service - Nebraska Partners for Fish and Wildlife Program photo

   a. natural degrading processes
   b. human interference
   c. natural reproduction
   d. environmental restoration

8. The leading consumer of oil in the world is _____, but the leading carbon dioxide emitter is _____.
   a. Japan; Singapore
   b. Saudi Arabia; Russia
   c. the United States; China
   d. China; Saudi Arabia

9. Of the fossil fuels, the one that burns the least cleanly is _____.

   a. oil

   b. natural gas

   c. coal

   d. uranium

10. Using the photo of mountaintop removal, identify the step shown here and explain why it is controversial.

Melissa Farlow/NG Image Collection

11. List three problems associated with large-scale hydropower facilities:

   _____, _____, and _____.

12. What is the leading type of renewable energy used worldwide?

   a. oil

   b. coal

   c. biomass

   d. hydropower

13. The rise in atmospheric concentrations of carbon dioxide since the Industrial Revolution is primarily attributed to _____.

   a. the widespread application of fertilizers

   b. natural causes

   c. wet rice farming

   d. the burning of fossil fuels

14. The term _____ refers to the amount of carbon dioxide emitted as a result of human activity.

   a. carbon footprint

   b. greenhouse effect

   c. global warming

   d. emissions allowance

15. What has happened here and why?

NASA Earth Observatory

THE PLANNER

Review your Chapter Planner on the chapter opener and check off your completed work.

When we want to see what the Earth looks like, we use a globe or a digital version of a globe as found in GoogleEarth, for example. Globes are scale models of the Earth that help us see places, regions, or other features in geographic context. Much of the usefulness of globes stems from their faithful depiction of the relative shapes and areas of landmasses, as well as distances and directions from one point to another. The small scale of a globe limits the amount of detail that can be shown, although digital globes more easily allow us to change scale by zooming in and out. Even as digital globes have helped make globes less bulky, maps, whether in digital or paper form, provide a practical alternative to depicting the Earth's geography.

The process of converting the Earth's spherical properties into flat map or planimetric form is called *map projection*. Imagine trying to flatten the peel of an orange. Flattening it will cause it to tear, deforming the spherical surface in the process. In analogous fashion, projecting a map introduces the problem of *distortion*, or the misrepresentation of the spatial and geometric properties of the Earth. Another way to think about distortion on map projections is to consider what happens to the *graticule*, the imaginary grid consisting of lines of latitude that parallel the Equator and meridians of longitude that converge at the poles (**Figure A.1**).

Understanding the process of map projections becomes a little easier if we visualize the kind of surface that is used when transforming the spherical Earth into a map. For example, if you wrap a transparent globe with a piece of paper so that it forms a cylinder around the globe and then place a light source nearby, the graticule and outlines of landmasses will be projected onto

The graticule or geographical grid • Figure A.1

On a sphere, lines of latitude (parallels) and lines of longitude (meridians) intersect at right angles, and lines of latitude become shorter closer to the poles. Even an inexperienced map user can make observations about map distortion by thinking about how closely the graticule on a particular map resembles the graticule on a globe.

the paper. You can use a similar approach and project the features of the globe onto a cone-shaped piece of paper or a flat piece of paper. Use of these different surfaces, respectively, gives rise to three broad families of map projections: *cylindrical*, *conic*, and *planar* (**Figure A.2**).

Map projection families • Figure A.2

CYLINDRICAL   CONIC   PLANAR

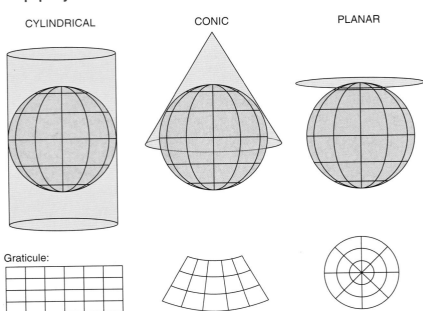

Graticule:

One method of classifying map projections is based on the kind of projection surface used. Cylinders, cones, and planes are the three conventional surfaces. For each surface, the corresponding effect on the graticule is also shown. (*Source:* Adapted from A. H. Robinson, R. D. Sale, J. L. Morrison, and P. C. Muehrcke, 1984. *Elements of Cartography*. 5th ed. NY: John Wiley & Sons. Reproduced with permission of John Wiley & Sons, Inc.)

Projections and patterns of distortion • Figure A.3

A standard line represents a line of contact between the projection surface and the globe. Tangent relationships use a single standard line, whereas secant relationships use two standard lines. The darker the color in this illustration, the greater the distortion. (*Source:* Adapted from A. H. Robinson, R. D. Sale, J. L. Morrison, and P. C. Muehrcke, 1984. *Elements of Cartography.* 5th ed. NY: John Wiley & Sons. Reproduced with permission of John Wiley & Sons, Inc.)

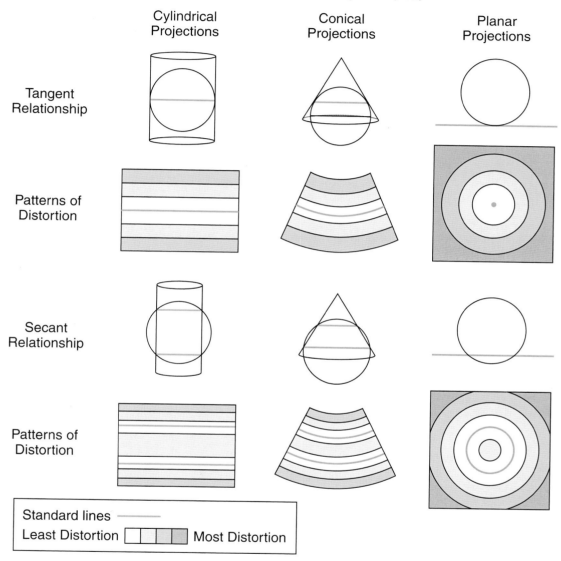

When making cylindrical or conic projections, we can wrap the paper so that it touches the globe along a single line and creates a *tangent* relationship. In the case of a planar projection, the paper is tangent to the globe at a single point. However, we can also envision situations in which the paper cuts through the globe along two lines, creating a *secant* relationship of the projection surface to the globe. The way in which the paper touches the globe matters because it affects the patterns of distortion on the map projection. More specifically, the line or lines of contact between the surface and the globe in the tangent and secant examples are known as *standard lines;* along these lines the map is true to scale and distortion is minimized. These tangent and secant relationships, as well as their patterns of distortion, are shown in **Figure A.3**.

Of course, today it is much more efficient to use computers and projection programs to make map projections instead of transparent globes and a light source. Even with the use of more sophisticated technologies, it is still impossible to represent the spherical Earth on a flat surface without some distortion. Moreover, no single map projection is perfect for all mapping needs. When deciding which map projection to use, cartographers (people who design and create maps) and geographers consider where distortion on a map is minimized and more specifically, the effect a map projection has on geometric and spatial properties such as area, shape, scale, and direction. It is practical, then, to know about a slightly different classification system that groups map projections according to similar properties. Here we focus on a fourfold classification consisting of *equal-area*, *conformal*, *azimuthal*, and a broad category of *other* map projections.

Conformal Projections

In the context of map projections, *conformal* means to show small areas in their correct form or shape, and conformal projections are sometimes described as shape-preserving. Strictly speaking, however, the property of conformality (being conformal) applies to points and the angles about them. This property makes conformal projections useful for showing the relief or topography of an area. A projection that maintains angles and shapes and that is well suited to mapping regions in the middle latitudes with a predominantly east-to-west extent is the Lambert conformal conic projection with two standard parallels (**Figure A.4**).

In order to maintain proper angles and shapes, however, conformal projections sacrifice the property of size. This is because maintaining certain angular relationships when converting a spherical to a flat form requires that some distances be stretched or compressed, and such alterations affect the sizes of regions. Thus, conformal projections cannot also show large areas in their proper relative sizes. This characteristic is especially noticeable on the Mercator projection, a projection that is both conformal and cylindrical.

In 1569, the Flemish cartographer Gerardus Mercator (1512–1594) created the map projection that now bears his name. He specifically devised this projection as a navigational aid for mariners. The value of Mercator's projection stems from the fact that any straight line drawn between two places on the map is a line of constant compass bearing, or a *rhumb line*. On a Mercator projection, the rhumb line always crosses lines of longitude at the same or constant angle.

The Mercator projection is a cylindrical projection that is often developed with a standard parallel along the Equator. Cartographers needing a conformal map of equatorial regions often select the Mercator projection because distortion is minimized there. However, since the Mercator projection is conformal, the correct representation of sizes of regions is sacrificed for the correct representation of angular relationships. This is most visible in the high-latitude zones where the meridians, instead of converging toward the poles, remain far apart (**Figure A.5**).

Lambert conformal conic projection • Figure A.4

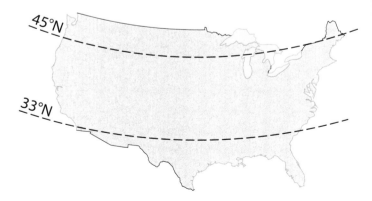

This projection is frequently used for representing the coterminous United States. The standard lines or more specifically here, the standard parallels, are at 33° and 45° north latitude.

Mercator projection • Figure A.5

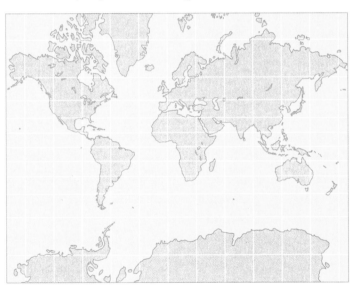

Rhumb lines always appear as straight lines on the Mercator projection, so navigators measure the angle between their planned route and a meridian to identify the compass bearing or direction of travel. Relative sizes of areas especially in the higher latitudes, however, are exaggerated. Despite what the Mercator projection shows, Greenland is just one-eighth the size of South America. (*Source:* NG Maps.)

Examples of equal-area world map projections • Figure A.6

a. Molleweide projection
Developed in the early 19th century, this projection represents the globe as an oval or, technically, an ellipse. (*Source:* NG Maps.)

b. Eckert IV projection
To preserve area on this and the Molleweide projection, the parallels are not equally spaced. As a result, shapes in the low latitudes appear stretched. (*Source:* NG Maps.)

Equal-Area Projections

As its name suggests, an equal-area projection (sometimes also called an equivalent projection) is one that shows mapped regions in their true relative sizes. As we have discussed, no map can be both conformal and equal-area. Therefore, if you need a map of the world that shows landmasses and oceans in their correct proportions, it is advisable to select an equal-area projection. However, for a long time and mainly out of complacency, the Mercator projection was widely used as a reference map of the world in classrooms, in the media, and in books and atlases, even though it was not designed to be used for such purposes.

Repeated use of the Mercator and similar cylindrical projections in popular books and media inadvertently reinforces the notion that such maps provide a reliable representation of what the Earth looks like, when, in fact, this is far from the case. Look again at the Mercator projection in Figure A.5. Where are the North and South Poles? What shape does the Mercator projection give to the Earth?

In the late 1980s, the Map Projections Committee of the American Cartographic Association issued a formal resolution urging book and map publishers to stop using the Mercator projection and other rectangular world maps as general-purpose or basic reference maps because of their considerable distortion. Two equal-area projections recommended, among other suitable alternatives, were the Molleweide projection and the Eckert IV projection (**Figure A.6**).

Briefly, then, equal-area projections facilitate areal comparisons, enabling us to visually compare the extent of countries, continents, or bodies of water, for example. Similarly, we should choose an equal-area map projection when mapping densities (e.g., popu-lation density or livestock density) or if we have other area-based data, such as the percentage of land area in a country planted to a certain kind of crop. To varying degrees, conformal projections distort size dimensions, and equal-area maps distort shapes. Compare and contrast the projections in Figures A.5 and A.6.

Azimuthal Projections

Azimuthal projections are planar projections created from either a tangent or secant relationship between the plane used as the projection surface and the globe. To understand the properties of azimuthal projections, it helps to know about great circles. A *great circle* is formed by the intersection of a sphere with a flat surface or plane that passes through the center of the sphere. All great circles divide the Earth into two hemispheres, and each line of longitude is one-half of a great circle. An *azimuth* is a line of direction, and every great circle forms what is called a *true azimuth*. That is, if you begin at one point along a great circle and follow its path around the Earth and return to your starting point, then you have followed a true azimuth.

Great circles have significance for distances as well. More specifically, the shortest distance over the Earth between any two locations follows the arc of a great circle between them. On an azimuthal map projection, great circles that pass through the center point of the projection show as straight lines. This makes sense if we think about what happens to the graticule when we create an azimuthal projection with the plane tangent to the Earth at either the North or South Pole: Lines of longitude (parts of great circles) are represented as straight lines extending from the center (refer again to Figure A.2).

Examples of azimuthal projections • Figure A.7

a. Gnomonic projection
Great circles show as straight lines on these projections. Since rhumb lines on Mercator projections are not great circle routes and do not identify the shortest distances, navigators consult both of these projections when determining their routes.

b. Azimuthal equidistant projection
Both distances and directions are true from the center point to any other point on these projections. Thus, they are favored when mapping seismic waves, the vibrations caused by earthquakes. (*Source:* NG Maps.)

c. Orthographic projection
These projections provide a hemispheric perspective of the globe. Distortion occurs along the edges. The global locators used in this book provide examples of orthographic projections. (*Source:* NG Maps.)

There are numerous different kinds of azimuthal projections. Three of them are the gnomonic projection, the azimuthal equidistant projection, and the orthographic projection. You can think of a gnomonic projection as one created by placing a light source at the center of a transparent globe and projecting the sphere onto a tangent plane. Gnomonic projections are particularly useful for navigation because they show great circles as straight lines anywhere on the map, not just from the center point.

When projecting a map it is not possible to preserve scale or map distances properly everywhere, but distances can be preserved between certain points or along specific lines. An important property of azimuthal equidistant map projections is that distances are correct from the center point to any other point on the map. A third kind of azimuthal projection, called an orthographic projection, gives a hemispheric view of the Earth as if observed from a location far above it. Illustrations of these different azimuthal projections are shown in **Figure A.7**.

Other Projections

There are so many other kinds of projections that, for simplicity, we have grouped them into this very broad and inclusive category. We discuss three examples as a way of highlighting some of the diversity within this grouping. Two of these examples illustrate different types of interrupted projections, and the third illustrates a compromise projection.

Technically speaking, all maps are interrupted because they show the Earth as having edges instead of showing it as the continuous surface that it is. When cartographers and map projection experts speak of interrupted map projections, however, they are referring to the practice of breaking up either the oceans or the landmasses in order to highlight the other.

The Interrupted Goode Homolosine projection is an equal-area projection that interrupts the oceans so that land areas can be emphasized. The Dymaxion map projection created by R. Buckminster Fuller (1895–1983) also interrupts the oceans (**Figure A.8**).

The Winkel Tripel projection, a projection used throughout this book, provides a third example of yet another kind of projection. In contrast to the Dymaxion map and the Interrupted Goode Homolosine projections, the Winkel Tripel projection is not classified as an interrupted projection. It is, however, usually described as a *compromise projection*. This is to say that the map projection strikes a balance between aesthetics and distortion (**Figure A.9**).

Examples of interrupted projections • Figure A.8

a. Interrupted Goode Homolosine projection
This equal-area projection, with its elliptical polar zones, is partly based on the Molleweide projection. The continuity of the oceans is sacrificed to highlight land areas. (*Source:* NG Maps.)

b. Dymaxion map projection
R. Buckminster Fuller was an inventor. His unique map projection defies the conventional practice of orienting maps so that north is at the top and emphasizes the near connectedness of the Earth's land areas. This projection modestly distorts land areas and shapes. (*Source:* NG Maps.)

Winkel Tripel projection • Figure A.9

The shapes of the landmasses on this compromise projection very closely resemble how they look on a globe, while the distortion of areas is kept to a minimum. This projection is used on most of the world maps in this book. (*Source:* NG Maps.)

Self-Tests

Chapter 1
1. d; 2. b; 3. d; 4. d; 5. a; 6. b; 7. c; 8. b; 9. d; 10. c; 11. d; 12. a; 13. c; 14. a; 15. c

Chapter 2
1. Possible answers include: capitalism, technological advances, reduced business costs, international trade and investments, and policies supporting globalization; 2. a; 3. a; 4. d; 5. c; 6. a; 7. It contributed to the view that members of a folk culture were less civilized and usually excluded elites; 8. d; 9. a; 10. d; 11. c; 12. Acupuncture diffused with Buddhism; via trade; within the medical profession and via Chinese immigrants; 13. b; 14. d; 15. b

Chapter 3
1. b; 2. d; 3. c; 4. economic conditions such as a recession, and social circumstances such as level of education; 5. a; 6. a; 7. c; 8. d; 9. c; 10. See Figure 3.9.; 11. Fiji has a high birth rate, low death rate, and high rate of natural increase; 12. c; 13. See Figure 3.12; 14. a; 15. c

Chapter 4
1. a; 2. c; 3. d; 4. a; 5. b; 6. See Figure 4.6c; 7. Answers may vary. Some possible answers: omission of "l" between vowels; omission of "r" between vowels; use of "be" to indicate a regular activity; 8. b; 9. c; 10. d; 11. a; 12. a; 13. Their low LDIs are a legacy of European colonization, which caused the extinction of many indigenous peoples and their languages, and led to the diffusion of Spanish and Portuguese; 14. b; 15. See Figure 4.16

Chapter 5
1. c; 2. b; 3. c; 4. a; 5. It illustrates a reaction to the caste system, a legacy of Hinduism; 6. d; 7. a; 8. informal consecration; 9. Answers may vary and might include Christianity's spread from large cities to smaller settlements and rural areas; 10. d; 11. b; 12. b; 13. c; 14. b; 15. d

Chapter 6
1. d; 2. b; 3. d; 4. a; 5. b; 6. There is no biological basis for exclusive racial categories; 7. c; 8. c; 9. b; 10. c; 11. d; 12. a; 13. b; 14. c; 15. d

Chapter 7
1. d; 2. a; 3. c; 4. c; 5. b; 6. It is prorupt and perforated; 7. b; 8. d; 9. c; 10. a; 11. b; 12. a; 13. c; 14. b; 15. d

Chapter 8
1. b; 2. d; 3. a; 4. a; 5. Answers will vary depending on what part of the image the student focuses on but should include mention of the clustering of activities (residential and religious). More thorough answers will incorporate reference to clusters of like and unlike activities; 6. b; 7. c; 8. b; 9. b; 10. c; 11. Possible answers include sprawl, decentralization, single-use zoning; 12. a; 13. c; 14. d; 15. b

Chapter 9
1. c; 2. b; 3. a; 4. b; 5. d; 6. a; 7. c; 8. d; 9. c; 10. a; 11. d; 12. b; 13. a; 14. b; 15. c

Chapter 10
1. See Figure 10.15; 2. c; 3. b; 4. b; 5. a; 6. c; 7. d; 8. See Figure 10.11; 9. a; 10. b; 11. Answers should include mention of government initiatives to increase manufacturing productivity, the shift from labor-intensive to technology-intensive industries, and presence of a skilled labor force; 12. Outsourcing subcontracts an in-house business activity to another firm, whereas offshoring moves a business activity to a foreign country; 13. Answers should include a discussion of the shift from secondary to tertiary industries (service sector jobs) as measured by employment in them; 14. a; 15. d

Chapter 11
1. c; 2. b; 3. a; 4. See Figure 11.6a; 5. nomadic herding and vertical transhumance; 6. a; 7. d; 8. b; 9. d; 10. See Figure 11.16; 11. c; 12. c; 13. b; 14. a; 15. b

Chapter 12
1. b; 2. d; 3. a; 4. c; 5. a; 6. d; 7. d; 8. c; 9. c; 10. Step 2, (valley fill) and see Figure 12.11. Controversy relates to scale and impact of operations; 11. habitat fragmentation, species loss, forced resettlement; 12. c; 13. d; 14. a; 15. Image shows a signature of logging in the Amazon to clear land for soybean farms or cattle ranches.

Ask Yourself

Chapter 1
p. 7, Fig. 1.1: 1. To show they overlap; 2. For example, via the study of hazards. p. 21, WAGS: 1. Graphic scale; 2. On a map, perspective is from directly overhead.

Chapter 2
p. 41, Fig. 2.4: about 5%; about 45%

Chapter 3
p. 76, Fig. 3.8: 1. Much of Sub-Saharan Africa and parts of the Middle East; 2. Russia and parts of Europe; 3. Sub-Saharan Africa, Middle East, Central, South, and Southeast Asia, Latin America.

Chapter 4
p. 105, Fig. 4.7: The Indo-European language family spread to North and South America, Africa, and Australia as a result of colonization.

Chapter 5
p. 152, Fig. 5.15: 1. Sharia has less influence on legislation with greater distance from Islam's hearth; 2. core-periphery pattern.

Chapter 6
p. 168, Fig. 6.4: Language differences contributed to the separation of different culture groups and language was also used to construct negative characterizations of Chinatown. p. 176, Fig. 6.7: African Americans are the prevalent minority group in much of the Southeast and East Coast. Asians are the prevalent minority group in portions of the upper Midwest, New England, the Pacific Northwest, and the West Coast.

Chapter 7

p. 196, Fig. 7.1: **1.** An advantage is being able to see all the countries and a disadvantage is the loss of detail on small countries and islands; **2.** French Guiana, Greenland, Western Sahara, Northern Mariana Islands, American Samoa, and French Polynesia. p. 215, Fig. 7.14: **1.** Cuba; **2.** Greenland is territory of Denmark and French Guiana is territory of France. p. 222, Fig. 7.19: It has a significant Hispanic population.

Chapter 8

p. 234, Fig. 8.3: **1.** Portsmouth, Maine and Fredericksburg, Virginia; **2.** The area around Boston from Rhode Island to New Hampshire, the area around New York from Springfield, Massachusetts to Wilmington, Delaware, and the area around Washington, D.C. from Fredericksburg, Virginia to north and east of Baltimore, Maryland.

Chapter 9

p. 266, Fig. 9.2: **1.** Middle East and North Africa; **2.** Sub-Saharan Africa. p. 280, Fig. 9.11: **1.** About 5%; **2.** About 22% (100% minus 78%).

Chapter 10

p. 301, Fig. 10.2: They have a high rate of poverty and a history of colonization. p. 318, Fig. 10.15: Quaternary; quinary.

Chapter 11

p. 331, Fig. 11.3: Course 2–Root crop. p. 336, Fig. 11.7: Because land is rotated in and out of cultivation depending on its fertility.

Chapter 12

p. 365, Fig. 12.8: **1.** Saudi Arabia, Russia, USA, China, Iran; **2.** USA, China, Japan, India, Russia. p. 367, Fig. 12.10: **1.** Coal-burning power plants; **2.** Motor vehicle exhaust.

Glossary

accent Differences in pronunciation among speakers of a language.

acid rain Precipitation that, primarily because of human activities, is significantly more acidic than normal and can harm aquatic and terrestrial ecosystems.

actor–network theory A body of thought that emphasizes that humans and nonhumans are linked together in a dynamic set of relations that, in turn, influence human behavior.

acupuncture An ancient form of traditional Chinese medicine that promotes healing through the insertion of needles into the body at specific points.

age-dependency ratio The number of people under the age of 15 and over the age of 65 as a proportion of the working-age population.

agglomeration The spatial clustering of people and economic activities, especially industries that are related or interdependent, in a place.

agribusiness The interconnected industry of food production involving farmers, processors, distributors, and retailers.

agriculture Activities centered on cultivating domesticated crops and livestock in order to procure food and fiber for human use or consumption.

agro-biotech (short for agricultural biotechnology) One facet of the third agricultural revolution that seeks to improve the quality and yield of crops and livestock using techniques such as cross-breeding, hybridization, and, more recently, genetic engineering.

agroforestry The purposeful integration of trees with crops and/or livestock in the same field simultaneously or sequentially.

allopathic medicine Medical practice that seeks to cure or prevent ailments with procedures and medicines that have typically been evaluated in clinical trials.

Americanization The diffusion of American brands, values, and attitudes throughout the world.

animistic religion A system of beliefs and practices that incorporates veneration of spirits or deities associated with natural features such as mountains, trees, or rivers.

apartheid In South Africa, the government-sponsored policy of racial segregation and discrimination that regulated the social relations and opportunities of its population from 1948 to 1991.

arable land Land that can be used for agriculture.

arithmetic density The number of people per unit area of land.

ascription A process that occurs when people assign a certain quality or identity to others, or to themselves.

assimilation A model of ethnic interaction that describes the gradual loss of the cultural traits, beliefs, and practices that distinguish immigrant ethnic groups and their members.

asylum Protection from persecution granted by one country to a refugee from another country.

atheistic The belief that there is no deity.

authorized immigrant In the United States, a legal permanent resident who is sometimes also called a green-card holder.

bid-rent curve A graph that shows the amount a bidder (e.g., a business or individual) is willing to pay for land relative to the distance of that land from the central business district.

biodiversity The variety of species contained within an ecosystem.

biofuel Fuel derived from renewable biological material, such as plant matter.

biomass energy Energy that is obtained from plant matter and/or animal wastes.

biosphere The zone of the Earth, extending from the soil and waters to the lower parts of the atmosphere, that supports and includes living organisms.

blockbusting Using scare tactics and panic selling to promote the rapid transition of a neighborhood from one ethnic or racial group to another.

boundary A vertical plane, usually represented as a line on a map, that fixes the territory of a state.

capital Financial, social, intellectual, or other assets that are derived from human creativity and are used to create goods and services.

carbon footprint The amount of carbon dioxide emitted as a result of human activity.

carrying capacity The number of people the Earth can support at a comfortable standard of living given current technology and habits of resource use.

cartel Entity consisting of individuals or businesses that control the production or sale of a commodity or group of commodities—often worldwide.

cash crop Broadly, any high-value crop that is sold for profit; historically, traditional cash crops are coffee, tea, tobacco, cocoa, rubber, and sugar—nonfood crops that have been closely associated with plantation agriculture.

caste system A hierarchical form of social stratification historically associated with Hinduism.

central business district (CBD) The part of the downtown where major office and retail activities are clustered.

central city The area enclosed by the legal boundaries of a city.

central place A settlement that provides goods and services for its residents and its surrounding trade or market area.

central place theory A theory developed by Walter Christaller that posits that market forces account for the distribution of central places in an area, and that the optimal spatial arrangement of central places creates hexagonally shaped trade areas.

centralization Forces that draw people and businesses into the downtown or central city.

centrifugal force An event or a circumstance that weakens a state's social and political fabric.

centripetal force An event or a circumstance that helps bind together the social and political fabric of a state.

civil religion A set of beliefs and practices that takes shape when religious notions, symbols, and rituals infuse the political culture of an area, as for example when people share the collective belief that a country's constitution is sacred.

classical model of development An accounting of economic development that was formulated by Walt W. Rostow as a series of five stages through which countries pass as they are transformed, by economic investment, from a traditional to a modern society.

Cold War The hostility and rivalry that existed between the United States and the Soviet Union from the mid-1940s to the late 1980s.

colonialism A form of imperialism in which a state takes possession of a foreign territory, occupies it, and governs it.

commercial agriculture A farming system that relies heavily on purchased inputs and in which products are sold for use or consumption away from the farm.

commercial dairy farming The management of cattle for producing and marketing milk, butter, cheese, or other milk by-products.

commercial gardening The intensive production of nontropical fruits, vegetables, and flowers for sale off the farm.

commercial grain farming Agriculture involving the large-scale, highly mechanized cultivation of grain.

commodification The conversion of an object, a concept, or a procedure once not available for purchase into a good or service that can be bought or sold.

commodity chain (also a production chain or value-added chain) The linked sequence of operations from the design to the production and distribution of a good.

common property resource Natural resources, equipment, or facilities that are shared by a well-defined community of users.

complementarity A situation in which one place or region can supply the demand for resources or goods in another place or region.

concentric zone model A description of urban structure that was created by Ernest Burgess and emphasizes the development of circular rings of similar land use around the central city, each occupied by different ethnic and socioeconomic groups.

conflict diamonds (also blood diamonds) Diamonds sold to finance wars or terrorist activities.

consumption Broadly defined, the use of goods to satisfy human needs and desires.

cornucopian theory A theory positing that human ingenuity will result in innovations that make it possible to expand the food supply.

cosmogony A set of beliefs that provides an explanation of the beginning of the world.

counterurbanization The deconcentration of population in an area that occurs as people move from metropolitan to nonmetropolitan areas.

creole language A language that develops from a pidgin language and is taught as a first language.

crop rotation Growing a sequence of different crops in the same field in order to maintain soil fertility and health.

crude birth rate (CBR) The annual number of births per 1000 people.

crude death rate (CDR) The annual number of deaths per 1000 people.

cultural ecology A subfield within human geography that studies the relationship between people and the natural environment.

cultural geography A branch of human geography that emphasizes human beliefs and activities and how they vary spatially, utilize the environment, and change the landscape.

cultural landscape The collection of structures, fields, or other features that result from human transformation of the natural environment; any landscape created or modified by people.

culture A social creation consisting of shared beliefs and practices that are dynamic rather than fixed, and a complex system that is shaped by people and, in turn, influences them.

decentralization In urban geography, forces that draw people and businesses out of the central city, often into suburbs. In political geography, a process whereby a state transfers functions or authority from the central government to lower-level internal subdivisions.

deindustrialization The long-term decline in industrial employment.

demographic equation A technique for measuring population change in a region over a specified period of time by adding population growth through natural increase and net migration to the population at the start of the time period being examined.

demographic transition model A simplified representation of a common demographic shift from high birth and death rates to low birth and death rates over time and in conjunction with urbanization and industrialization.

dependency In development studies, a condition that stems from patterns of international trade and results in underdevelopment, or low levels of development among states that lack the resources to command or control the system of trade.

dependency theory A theory that relates disparities in levels of development to relations between dominant and dependent states in the system of international trade.

desertification The creation of desert-like conditions in nondesert areas through human and/or environmental causes.

development Processes that bring about changes in economic prosperity and the quality of life.

devolution A kind of decentralization whereby a state transfers some power to a self-defined community, such as one of its national groups.

dialect A particular variety of a language characterized by distinctive vocabulary, grammar, and/or pronunciation.

dialect geography The study of the spatial patterns of dialect usage.

diaspora The scattering of a people through forced migration.

diffusionism A belief, associated with the rationality doctrine and cultural superiority, that the spread of Western science, technology, and practices to non-Westerners (deemed inferior) would enable them to advance socially and economically.

discourse Communication that provides insight on social values, attitudes, priorities, and ways of understanding the world.

dissonance The quality of being inconsistent; within heritage studies the idea that the meaning and value of heritage vary from group to group.

distance decay The tapering off of a process, pattern, or event over a distance.

distribution The arrangement of phenomena on or near the Earth's surface.

domestication An ongoing process of selecting plants or animals for specific characteristics and influencing their reproduction in ways that make them visibly and/or behaviorally distinct from their wild ancestors.

double cropping Completing the cycle from planting to harvesting on the same field twice in one year.

dual economy An economy in which two production systems operate virtually independently from one another, as for example when large-scale export-oriented agriculture exists alongside smallholder agriculture.

dual society A society that is sharply divided into two social classes such as upper-class plantation managers and lower-class plantation laborers.

economic indicator A value or measure that can be used to gauge development, such as gross national income, gross domestic product per capita, or incidence of poverty.

ecosystem The living organisms, their physical environment, and the flows of energy and nutrients cycling through them.

edge cities Suburban clusters with office, retail, entertainment, and residential space that are often located at major highway interchanges.

electoral system The set of procedures used to convert the votes cast in an election into the seats won by a party or candidate.

emigration The out-migration or departure of people from a location.

eminent domain The authority of a government to take private property when doing so serves the public's interests.

enclave In political geography, territory completely surrounded by another state but not controlled by it. In ethnic geography, spatially distinct areas with a notable concentration of members of an ethnic group.

endangered language A language that is no longer taught to children by their parents and is not used for everyday conversation.

environment All of the biotic (living) and abiotic (nonliving) factors with which people, animals, and other organisms coexist.

environmental degradation The result of human or natural processes that impair the Earth's physical properties or ecosystems.

environmental determinism A theory maintaining that natural factors control the development of human physiological and mental qualities.

environmental indicator A value or measure that provides information about the state of the environment such as levels of pollution or loss of biodiversity.

environmental justice A social movement and an approach to public policy that is concerned with analyzing and managing the impacts of environmental hazards so that no people are disproportionately burdened by exposure to such hazards because of their race, ethnicity, national origin, income, gender, or disability.

environmental stewardship The view that people should be responsible managers of the Earth and its resources.

epidemiological transition Broadly, a notable shift in disease prevalence and mortality patterns associated with lifestyle and/or environmental changes.

ethnic cleansing The forced removal of an ethnic group from an area.

ethnic geography A subfield of human geography that studies the migration and spatial distribution of ethnic groups, ethnic interaction and networks, and the various expressions or imprints of ethnicity in the landscape.

ethnic group People who share a collective identity that may derive from common ancestry, history, language, or religion, and who have a conscious sense of belonging to that group.

ethnic island A pattern of settlement, quite variable in size and population, formed by some ethnic groups in rural areas.

ethnic neighborhood A pattern of settlement formed by some ethnic groups in urban areas.

ethnic religion A belief system largely confined to the members of a single ethnic or cultural group.

ethnicity The personal and behavioral basis of an individual's identity that generates a sense of social belonging.

ethnoburb A multiethnic residential, commercial, or mixed suburban cluster in which a single ethnic group is unlikely to form a majority of the population.

ethnoscape A cultural landscape that reveals or expresses aspects of the identity of an ethnic group.

European Union (EU) A supranational organization that has enlarged considerably since its establishment in western Europe and is characterized by a significant degree of both economic and political integration among its members.

exclave Territory that is separated from the state to which it belongs by the intervening territory of another state.

export-processing zone (EPZ) (also free-trade zone) An industrial area that operates according to different policies than the rest of the country in which it is located in order to attract and support export-oriented production.

extensive agriculture An agricultural system characterized by low inputs of labor, capital, or equipment per unit area of land.

extinct language A language that has no living speakers; also called a dead language.

factory farm A farm that houses huge quantities of livestock or poultry in buildings, dry-lot dairies, or feedlots.

feedlot Confined space used for the controlled feeding of animals.

feng shui The Chinese art and science of situating settlements or designing cultural landscapes in order to harmonize the cosmic forces of nature with the built environment.

filtering In urban geography, the process whereby home ownership in a neighborhood gradually transitions from high- to middle- to lower-income households over time.

first agricultural revolution The rise of agriculture, which began with the domestication of plants and animals some 11,000 years ago.

First Law of Ecology The axiom that people and the environment are intimately interconnected such that any single human action has multiple consequences.

flexible production (also lean production) A system of industrial production that uses information technologies such as computer networking, high-tech sensors, and automation technology to make the production of goods more responsive to market conditions and therefore more efficient.

food desert An area characterized by a lack of affordable, fresh, and nutritious foods.

food insecurity A situation in which people do not have physical or financial access to basic foodstuffs.

Fordism A system of industrial production designed for mass production and influenced by the principles of scientific management.

foreign direct investment (FDI) The transfer of monetary resources by a multinational corporation from its home country abroad in order to finance its overseas business activities.

formal region An area that possesses one or more unifying physical or cultural traits.

fossil fuel Nonrenewable energy resources that derive from the buried remains of plants and animals that lived millions of years ago.

four-course system A system of crop rotation that is based on a four-year planting regime that removes a fallow period, balances the planting of food crops with feed crops, and incorporates legumes that enrich the soil.

functional complexity The ability of a town or city to support sizable concentrations of people who earn their living from specialized, nonfarming activities.

functional region An area that is unified by a specific economic, political, or social activity and possesses at least one node.

functional zonation The division of a city into areas or zones that share similar activities and land use.

gender The cultural or social characteristics society associates with being female or male.

gender gap A disparity between men and women in their opportunities, rights, benefits, behavior, or attitudes.

gender inequality index (GII) A measure that shows the differential impacts of development on women and men. The GII is calculated from data on gender differences in levels of education, participation in the labor force, share of seats held in national parliament, as well as information on adolescent fertility and maternal mortality.

gender role The association of certain social expectations, responsibilities, or rights with femininity and masculinity.

Gene Revolution The shift, since the 1980s, to greater private and corporate involvement in and control of the research, development, intellectual property rights, and genetic engineering of highly specialized agricultural products, especially crop varieties.

gentrification A process of urban residential change that occurs when more affluent people purchase deteriorated buildings in low-income neighborhoods in order to restore or renovate them.

geographic information systems (GIS) A combination of hardware and software that enables the input, management, analysis, and visualization of georeferenced (location-based) data.

geographic scale Broadly, a way of depicting, in reduced form, all or part of the world, or a level of analysis used in a specific project or study.

geopiety The religious-like reverence that people may develop for the Earth.

geopolitics The study of the relations among geography, states, and world power.

geothermal energy The use of heat from within the Earth as a source of energy.

gerrymandering The process of manipulating voting district boundaries to give an advantage to a particular political party or group.

global food crisis A protracted condition of food insecurity worldwide in scope or significance.

global positioning system (GPS) A constellation of artificial satellites, radio signals, and receivers used to determine the absolute location of people, places, or features on Earth.

global warming A rise in global temperatures primarily attributed to human activities that have increased concentrations of greenhouse gases in the atmosphere.

globalization The greater interconnectedness and interdependence of people and places around the world.

glocalization The idea that global and local forces interact and that both are changed in the process.

greenhouse effect A natural process, involving solar radiation and atmospheric gases, that helps to warm the Earth.

Green Revolution The dramatic increase in grain production between 1965 and 1985 in Asia and Latin America from high-yielding, fertilizer- and irrigation-dependent varieties of wheat, rice, and corn.

gross domestic product (GDP) The total monetary value of goods and services produced within a country's geographic borders in a year.

gross national income (GNI) The total monetary value of goods and services produced in a year by a country, whether those operations are located within the country or abroad.

haka A collective, ritual dance of the New Zealand Maori and other Polynesian peoples.

hearth A place or region where an innovation, idea, belief, or cultural practice begins.

heartland Generally, any area of vital interest to a state; according to Halford Mackinder's heartland theory, a region possessing the best combination of strategic geographic factors for world domination, specifically the interior of the Eurasian landmass.

heritage Property transmitted to an heir or, more broadly, any contemporary use of the past.

heritage industry Enterprises, such as museums, monuments, and historical and archaeological sites that manage or market the past.

heterolocalism A reflection of the impact of globalization on ethnic interaction such that members of an ethnic group maintain their sense of shared identity even though they are residentially dispersed.

heterosexual norm The conventional, binary division of the sexes based on clearly defined masculine and feminine gender roles.

hinterland The trade area served by a central place.

hinterworld The idea that the trade area served by a world city potentially includes the entire globe because of increased opportunities for spatial interaction.

holistic approach Within traditional medicine, a manner of understanding health such that it encompasses all aspects—physical, mental, social, and spiritual—of a person's life.

horizontal expansion In the context of globalization, the increase in international connections among places via rapid flows of goods, people, and ideas.

human development index (HDI) The first development measure or index to incorporate information about the wealth, health, and education of a country's people in a single statistic. The HDI has been refined over the years and is based on the GNI per capita, life expectancy, and both average and expected years of education.

human geography A branch of geography centered on the study of people, places, spatial variation in human activities, and the relationship between people and the environment.

human trafficking The forcible and/or fraudulent recruitment of people for work in exploitative conditions, for example, as child soldiers or prostitutes.

hunting and gathering Hunting wild animals, fishing, and gathering wild plants for food.

hybrid city A city that exhibits a mixture of indigenous, colonial, and globalizing influences.

ideology A system of ideas, beliefs, and values that justifies the views, practices, or orientation of a group.

immigration The in-migration or arrival of people at a location.

imperialism One state's exercise of direct or indirect control over the affairs of another political society.

income distribution How income is divided among different groups or individuals.

income inequality A ratio of the earnings of the richest to the earnings of the poorest. More broadly, the unequal distribution of income in a society.

Industrial Revolution Fundamental changes in technology and systems of production that began in England in the late 18th century and transformed manufacturing from small-scale craft to factory-based production.

inequality-adjusted HDI (IHDI) A development index that is derived by applying a reduction to the HDI based on inequality of access to income, health care, and education in a country and may give a better indication of actual circumstances than the HDI.

infant mortality rate The number of deaths of infants under one year of age per 1000 live births.

informal sector The retail, manufacturing, and service activities that operate on a small scale, without government regulation or oversight, and that are not measured or recorded in formal or official statistics.

institutional discrimination A situation in which the policies, practices, or laws of an organization or government disadvantage people because of their cultural differences.

intensive agriculture An agricultural system characterized by high inputs, such as labor, capital, or equipment, per unit area of land.

intercropping The strategy of planting two or more crops in a field at the same time.

internal migration Migration within a country, from one county, state, or region to another.

internally displaced persons People forcibly driven from their homes into a different part of their country.

international migration Movement across an international boundary in order to take up long-term or permanent residence in another country.

internationalism The development of close political and economic relations among states.

intervening opportunity A situation in which a different location can provide a desired good more economically than another location.

Islamic traditionalism (or Islamism) A movement that favors a return to or preservation of traditional, premodern Islam and resists Westernization and globalization.

isogloss A line that marks a boundary of word usage.

jihad A term that is popularly understood to mean "holy war" but is preferably translated as "utmost struggle" and refers to a personal struggle to uphold the tenets of Islam.

just-in-time delivery An inventory management strategy associated with flexible production in which supplies are ordered on an as-needed basis instead of being stockpiled.

Kyoto Protocol An international agreement since 1997 designed to reduce greenhouse gas emissions by binding the industrialized countries that have ratified it to specific emission targets.

land-use and land-cover change (LULCC) An interdisciplinary approach to studying human–environment interactions based on an awareness of the linkages between ecosystem processes and social conditions.

language A system of communication based on symbols that have agreed-upon meanings.

language family A collection of languages that share a common but distant ancestor.

level of urbanization The percentage of people living in urban places in some defined area (e.g., a county or a country).

liberalism An 18th-century political and economic theory that emphasizes the protection of human rights, property rights, and individual freedom. Economically, liberalism favors a free, unregulated market and the removal of barriers to the movement of goods, services, and capital.

life expectancy The average length of time from birth that a person is expected to live given current death rates.

lingua franca A language that is used to facilitate trade or business between people who speak different languages.

linguistic diversity The assortment of languages in a particular area.

linguistic diversity index (LDI) A measure that expresses the likelihood that two randomly selected individuals in a country speak different first languages.

linguistic dominance A situation in which one language becomes comparatively more powerful than another language.

linkage Narrowly, an economic activity that emerges in conjunction with a specific primary industry, such as blade manufacturers that supply the lumber industry. More broadly, the interconnections that develop among businesses.

livestock ranching A form of agriculture devoted to raising large numbers of cattle or sheep for sale to meat processors.

loanword A word that originates in one language and is incorporated into the vocabulary of another language.

local culture The practices, attitudes, and preferences held in common by the members of a community in a particular place.

local knowledge The collective wisdom of a community that derives from the everyday activities of its members.

location quotient A measure that can be used to show how the proportional presence of an ethnic group in a region compares to the proportional presence of that same ethnic group in the country.

manufacturing value added (MVA) A measure of industrial output calculated by taking the cost of the finished product and subtracting from it the cost of purchased inputs necessary to produce it, such as fuel, electricity, and the cost of other parts or materials.

material culture The tangible and visible artifacts, implements, and structures created by people such as dwellings, musical instruments, and tools.

Mediterranean agriculture As historically practiced, a form of agroforestry that integrated cultivation of livestock, a grain crop, and a tree or vine crop, and that is today increasingly affected by specialization.

megachurch A church with 2000 or more members that follows mainline or Renewalist Christian theologies.

megacity A city with 10 million or more residents.

megalopolis (also conurbation) A massive urban complex created as a result of converging metropolitan areas.

metropolitan area A large population center (50,000 people minimum) and the adjacent zones that are socially and economically connected to it, such as the places from which people commute.

microfinancing Providing access to credit and other financial services for low-income individuals or groups.

migration Movement from one territorial or administrative unit to another associated with long-term or permanent change in residence.

migration corridor A route migrants take that is often durable over time and helps identify migration flows.

mixed crop and livestock farming A farming system in various stages of evolution worldwide from an integrated system based on raising crops to feed livestock and selling the animal products off the farm to a more specialized emphasis on cash grain production.

mixed-use development An approach to urban design that combines different types of land use within a particular neighborhood or district.

modernism An intellectual movement that has roots in the European Enlightenment of the 1700s and encourages scientific thought, the expansion of knowledge, and belief in the inevitability of progress.

monoculture Planting a single crop in a field, often over a large area.

monotheistic The belief in or devotion to a single deity.

multinational corporation (MNC) (also a transnational corporation, or TNC) A company that owns offices or production facilities in one or more countries.

multinational state A state whose population consists of two or more nations.

multiple nuclei model An accounting of urban spatial structure that was developed by Chauncy Harris and Edward Ullman and that relates land-use patterns to the influence of two or more cores, as opposed to a single core represented by the central business district.

mutual intelligibility The ability of speakers of different but related languages to understand one another.

mystical ecology The interrelationship between an awareness of cosmic forces and human use of the environment.

nation A sizable group of people with shared political aspirations whose collective identity is rooted in a common history, heritage, and attachment to a specific territory.

nation-state In a narrow sense, a political entity in which the boundaries of a nation coincide with the boundaries of the state and the people share a sense of political unity. More broadly, a state whose population possesses a shared political identity that sees the nation and the state as the same.

natural capital The goods and services provided by nature, including renewable resources, nonrenewable resources, Earth's biodiversity, and its ecosystems.

nature In one sense, the physical environment that is external to people, but also a social construction derived from ideas that people have about the physical environment.

nature–culture dualism A conceptual framework that separates nature from culture (nature is not culture, and vice versa) and is rejected by many scholars today.

neo-Malthusian Someone who shares the same general views of Thomas Malthus and argues that, since the world's resources are limited, there is also a natural limit to the number of people the Earth can support at a comfortable standard of living.

neoliberalism The revival and application of the theory of liberalism, especially since the late 20th century.

neolocalism A renewed interest in sustaining and promoting the uniqueness of a place.

net migration A measure of migration-based population change in a place; calculated as the number of immigrants minus the number of emigrants.

new renewable Energy sources that include biomass, tidal, solar, wind, and geothermal energy as well as small-scale hydropower facilities but exclude large hydropower facilities because of their significant environmental impacts.

new urbanism (also neotraditional town planning) An urban planning movement that developed in the 1990s around the two main goals of preventing sprawl and creating walkable neighborhoods.

newly industrialized economies (NIEs) Economies in which rapid growth, improved living standards, and reductions in poverty have been achieved in East Asia first by Hong Kong, Singapore, South Korea, and Taiwan, and more recently by Indonesia, Malaysia, the Philippines, and Thailand.

nonmaterial culture The oral traditions, behavioral practices, and other nontangible components of a cultural group's way of life, including recipes, songs, or philosophies.

nonrenewable resource A resource that is considered finite because it is not self-replenishing or takes a very long period of time to do so.

normative In reference to development, the establishment of standards, or norms, to help measure the quality of life and economic prosperity of groups of people.

nutrition transition A change in patterns of food consumption toward an increasingly Westernized diet consisting of more meat, wheat-based food products, and convenience foods.

official language A language that a country formally designates, usually in its constitution, for use in political, legal, and administrative affairs.

offshoring A kind of outsourcing that moves a business activity to another country.

open-access resource Goods that no single person can claim exclusive right to and that are available to everyone.

organic agriculture A farming system that promotes sustainable and biodiverse ecosystems and relies on natural ecological processes and cycles, as opposed to synthetic inputs such as pesticides.

Organization for Economic Co-operation and Development (OECD) An organization founded in 1961 to enhance development by promoting economic growth among its member countries. Most members have historically been the very wealthy, industrialized countries.

othering The act of differentiating between individuals and groups such that distinctions are made between "me" and "you," and between "us" and "them."

outsourcing A business practice whereby a company subcontracts an activity that was previously performed in-house (such as the manufacture of a part, packaging, or customer support) to another firm.

pastoralism An agricultural system in which animal husbandry based on open grazing of herd animals is the sole or dominant farming activity.

perceptual region An area that people perceive to exist because they identify with it, have an attachment to it, or imagine it in a certain way.

personal approach Within traditional medicine, a manner of understanding health in which it is possible for two people to have the same symptoms but receive different treatments because of their different individual circumstances.

physiological density The number of people per unit area of arable land.

pidgin language A language that combines vocabulary and/or grammatical practices from two or more languages that have come in contact.

piety (or piousness) A state of deep devotion to a religion.

pilgrimage A journey to a sacred place or site for religious reasons.

place A locality distinguished by specific physical and social characteristics.

placelessness The loss of the unique character of different places and the increasing standardization of places and cultural landscapes that is often attributed to the diffusion of popular culture.

plantation A large estate in tropical or subtropical areas that specializes in the production of a cash crop.

pluralism A model of ethnic interaction that characterizes members of immigrant ethnic groups as resisting pressures to assimilate and retaining those traits, beliefs, and practices that make them distinctive.

political ecology An offshoot of cultural ecology that studies how economic forces and competition for power influence human behavior, especially decisions and attitudes involving the environment.

political geography The study of the spatial aspects of political affairs.

political iconography An image, object, or symbol that conveys a political message.

polytheistic The belief in or devotion to multiple deities.

popular culture The practices, attitudes, and preferences held in common by large numbers of people and considered to be mainstream.

population doubling time The number of years it takes a population to double; calculated by dividing the number 70 by the rate of natural increase.

population ecology The study of the impacts populations have on their environments as well as the ways in which environmental conditions affect people and their livelihoods.

population geography The study of spatial variations among populations and population–environment interactions.

population pyramid A bar graph that shows the age and gender composition of a population.

possibilism A theory that people use their creativity to decide how to respond to the conditions or constraints of a particular natural environment.

postindustrial society A society characterized by high levels of urbanization, dominance of the service sector especially in total employment, prevalence of skilled professionals in the labor force, infrastructure that is heavily based on information and communication technology, and a knowledge-based economy.

poverty Insufficient income to purchase the basic necessities of food, clothing, and shelter.

poverty line The specific income amount social scientists and others use to separate the poor from the nonpoor.

poverty rate The percentage of the population below the poverty line.

poverty-reduction theory A development theory focused specifically on lowering the incidence of poverty in a developing country.

precision agriculture The application of technologies such as the global positioning system (GPS) and aerial imagery to measure and map the spatial variation in environmental conditions within a field, and the related use of this information to calibrate machinery for site-specific applications of fertilizers or pesticides, for example.

primary industry Industry that extracts natural resources from the Earth.

primate city A city that has a population two or more times the population of the second largest city in the country.

public space A kind of commons; a space intended to be open and accessible to anyone.

pull factors Favorable conditions or attributes of a place that attract migrants.

purchasing power parity (PPP) An exchange rate that is used to compare output, income, or prices among countries with different currencies and that is based on the idea that the price of a good or service in one country should equal the price of that same good or service in another country when it is converted to a common currency.

push factors Unfavorable conditions or attributes of a place that encourage migration.

qanat A system of water supply that uses shaft and tunnel technology to tap underground water resources.

quaternary service Within the tertiary sector or tertiary industry, a category of service activities associated with the provision of services to other businesses and consumers; includes information processing, management, and advanced professional services.

quinary service Within the tertiary sector or tertiary industry, a category of service activities associated with enhancing human and societal capacities for development through the production of new knowledge and innovations.

race The mistaken idea that one or more genetic traits can be used to identify distinctive and exclusive categories of people; hence, race is today understood to be a social construction.

racism The intolerance of people perceived to be inherently or genetically inferior.

range The maximum distance a consumer will travel for a particular good or service.

raster data A grid-based format for storing location-based data in a geographic information system in which each equally-sized cell or pixel contains a value that represents geographic data such as land cover or elevation.

rate of natural increase (RNI) The percentage of annual growth in a population excluding migration.

rate of urban growth The annual percentage increase in an urban population.

rationality doctrine The attitude and belief that Europeans were rational and non-Europeans, especially colonized peoples, were irrational.

reapportionment The process of allocating legislative seats among voting districts so that each legislator represents approximately the same number of people.

redistricting Redrawing the boundaries of voting districts usually as a result of population change.

redlining The biased practice of refusing to offer home loans in neighborhoods judged to be a financial risk without considering an individual's financial qualifications.

refugee One who flees to another country out of concern for personal safety or to avoid persecution.

regional analysis The study of the cultural, economic, political, physical, or other factors that contribute to the distinctiveness of geographical areas.

religion A system of beliefs and practices that help people make sense of the universe and their place in it.

religious ecology The interdependence between people, their religious beliefs and practices, and nature.

religious fundamentalism An interpretation of the principles of one's faith in such a way that they come to shape all aspects of one's private and public life.

remittance The cash, goods, or other in-kind transfers sent by immigrants to family members or relatives in their home countries.

remote sensing A means of acquiring information about something that is located at a distance from you or the sensing device, such as a satellite.

renewable resource A resource that is replenished naturally or through human intervention.

Renewalism A branch of Christianity that includes the Pentecostal and Charismatic movements.

replacement level The fertility rate necessary for a population to replace itself.

ritual Behavior, often regularly practiced, that has personal and symbolic meaning.

sacred space An area that has special religious significance or meaning that makes it worthy of reverence or devotion.

salinization The accumulation of salts on or in the soil.

sanctification The process by which people come to associate a place or site with sacredness; the making of a sacred site.

second agricultural revolution A fundamental change involving the adoption of new agricultural practices in western Europe, such as the moldboard plow and the horse collar, beginning in the Middle Ages.

secondary industry Industry that assembles, processes, or converts raw or semiprocessed materials into fuels or finished goods.

sector model An accounting of urban spatial structure that was developed by Homer Hoyt and that relates the formation of sectors or wedges of similar land use to transportation factors and the influence of high-income groups.

secularization A process that reduces the scope or influence of religion.

security landscape A type of political landscape created to protect the territory, people, facilities, and infrastructure of a state.

self-determination The ability of people in a territory to choose their own political status.

separatism The desire of a nation or other group to break apart from its state.

sex ratio The proportion of males to females in a population.

sexuality A basis for personal and social identity that stems from sexual orientation, attitudes, desires, and practices.

sharia Islamic law derived from the Qur'an, the teachings of Muhammad, and other sources.

shifting cultivation An agricultural system that uses fire to clear vegetation in order to create fields for crops; it is based on a cycle of land rotation that includes fallow periods.

site The physical characteristics of a place, such as its topography, vegetation, and water resources.

situation The geographic context of a place, including its political, economic, social, or other characteristics.

slum An area of a city characterized by overcrowding, makeshift or dilapidated housing, and little or no access to basic infrastructure and services such as clean water and waste disposal.

smallholder agriculture A farming system characterized by small farms in which the household is the main scale of agricultural production and consumption.

smallholder crop and livestock farming An agricultural system that is based on the management of a combination of plants and livestock that varies significantly from one region to another.

social capital The social ties, networks, institutions, and trust that members of a group use to achieve mutual benefits.

social construction An idea or a phenomenon that does not exist in nature but is created and given meaning by people.

sociodemographic indicator A value or measure that provides information about the welfare of a population, such as data on the prevalence of disease or the levels of literacy and education.

sovereignty Supreme authority of a state over its own affairs and freedom from control by outside forces.

space A bounded (absolute) or unbounded (relative) area. Absolute space can be precisely measured; relative space is shaped by contingency.

spatial association The degree to which two or more phenomena share similar distributions.

spatial diffusion The movement of a phenomenon, such as an innovation, information, or an epidemic, across space and over time.

spatial interaction The connections and relations that develop among places and regions as a result of the movement or flow of people, goods, or information.

spatial variation Changes in the distribution of a phenomenon from one place or area to another.

sprawl A process that occurs when the rate at which land is urbanized greatly exceeds the rate of population growth in a given period of time, leading to the spread of low-density land use.

standard dialect The designation of a specific dialect as the norm or authoritative model of language usage.

staple theory A system of ideas developed by W. A. Mackintosh and Harold Innis that posits that the commodities of an area shape its economic system by triggering the formation of related industries.

state An internationally recognized political unit with a permanently populated territory, defined boundaries, and a government with sovereignty over its domestic and international affairs.

structural adjustment program (SAP) A country-specific economic policy based on neoliberal principles intended to promote economic growth and development.

subsistence agriculture A farming system that is largely independent of purchased inputs and in which outputs are typically used or consumed by farmers and their family or extended family.

suburb The built-up area that surrounds or lies beyond the central city.

supranational organization A political entity created when multiple states agree to work together for a common economic, military, cultural, or political purpose, or a combination of several of these.

sustainable agriculture Farming practices that carefully manage natural resources and minimize adverse effects on the environment while maintaining farm profits.

sustainable development An approach to resource use and management that meets economic and social needs without compromising the resources for future generations.

symbolic ethnicity The way in which a collection of symbols (e.g., flags, music, dress styles) imparts meaning and identity to members of an ethnic group.

syncretic religion A religion that demonstrates a notable blending of beliefs and practices, usually as a result of contact between people who practice different religions.

Taylorism (also scientific management) A philosophy about industrial production that was developed by F. W. Taylor and that promotes the division of labor into the most elemental tasks for greatest efficiency.

technopole An area with a cluster of firms conducting research, design, development, and/or production in high-tech industries.

territorial seas The waters that are enclosed by the boundaries of a coastal state and that are considered part of the territory of that state.

territoriality Strong attachment to or defensive control of a place or an area.

terrorism The threat or use of violence in order to inculcate fear, gain influence, and/or advance a specific cause or conviction.

tertiary industry Industry that provides services, usually in the form of nontangible goods, to other businesses and/or consumers.

tertiary service Within the tertiary sector or tertiary industry, a category of service activities associated with the provision of domestic and quasi-domestic services.

third agricultural revolution A fundamental change in agriculture associated with technological innovations and scientific farming techniques developed in the 20th century including extensive mechanization, heavy reliance on irrigation and chemical applications, and biotechnology.

threshold The smallest number of consumers required to profitably supply a certain good or service.

time–space convergence The process by which places seem to become closer together in both time and space as a result of innovations in transportation and communication that weaken the barrier or friction of distance.

toponym A place-name.

total fertility rate (TFR) The average number of children a woman is expected to have during her childbearing years (between the ages of 15 and 49), given current birth rates.

traditional medicine Medical practices, derived from a society's long-established health-related knowledge and beliefs, that are used to maintain or restore well-being.

transferability The cost of moving a good and the ability of the good to withstand that cost.

transgender A term describing someone who does not identify with the gender assigned them at birth.

transhumance Moving herds on a seasonal basis to new pastures or water sources.

transnationalism In migration studies, the process by which immigrants develop and cultivate ties to more than one country.

truck farming A form of commercial gardening centered on the specialized production of fruits and vegetables for market.

unauthorized immigrant Also called an undocumented or illegal immigrant in the United States; person who enters a country on a temporary visa but remains in the country after their visa expires, or who crosses the border without being detected.

United Nations (UN) A supranational organization founded in 1945 for the purpose of promoting international peace and security.

universalizing religion A belief system that is worldwide in scope, welcomes all people as potential adherents, and may also work actively to acquire converts.

urban agriculture The use of vacant lots, rooftops, balconies, or other urban spaces to raise food for metropolitan households or neighborhoods.

urban hierarchy A series of central places ranked on the basis of their threshold, range, and market area.

urban planning A field of study broadly concerned with improving the physical and social conditions in towns and cities through the wise use and management of urban space.

urban realms model An accounting of urban structure that was developed by James Vance and that emphasizes the influential effects of suburbanization on the evolution of urban form.

urban redevelopment The process of renovating an area of a city, often by completely destroying dilapidated structures and rebuilding on the site.

urbanization Processes that concentrate people in urban places.

urbanized area Less formally, land that has been developed for commercial, residential, or industrial purposes. According to the U.S. Census Bureau, the territory, usually the central city plus adjacent suburbs, that has at least 50,000 people and a population density of 1000 people or more per square mile.

vector data A format for storing location-based data in a geographic information system that uses latitude and longitude coordinates to represent geographic features with points, lines, and other complex shapes.

vernacular architecture The common structures—dwellings, buildings, barns, churches, and so on—associated with a particular place, time, and community.

vertical expansion In the context of globalization, the deepening of connections between places through the development of policies, such as trade agreements that formalize and strengthen those linkages.

vertical integration A strategy of extending a company's ownership and control "up" the supply stream and/or "down" the distribution stream of a good or service in order to lessen the company's vulnerability to disruptions and stabilize the system of production.

von Thünen model A model that relates transportation costs to agricultural land-use decisions and yields a concentric ring pattern showing progressively more extensive forms of agriculture practiced at greater distances from the city or market.

wet rice farming Rice cultivation in a flooded field.

world (or global) heritage Sites perceived to have outstanding universal value for all of humanity.

world city A principal center of global economic power that significantly influences the world's business.

world-system theory A body of ideas that was developed by Immanuel Wallerstein and that links dependency and underdevelopment to capitalism and its role in creating an international division of labor that shapes relations between core, semiperipheral, and peripheral regions of the world.

zoning Laws that regulate land use and development.

Chapter 1

Adams, B. J., Huyck, C. K., Mansouri, B., Eguchi, R. T., and Shinozuka, M. 2004. Application of High-Resolution Optical Satellite Imagery for Post-Earthquake Damage Assessment: The 2003 Boumerdes (Algeria) and Bam (Iran) Earthquakes. *Research Progress and Accomplishments 2003–2004*. Buffalo, NY: Multidisciplinary Center for Earthquake Engineering Research, University at Buffalo.

Agnew, J., Livingstone, D. N., and Rogers, A., eds. 1996. *Human Geography: An Essential Anthology*. Oxford: Blackwell.

Bauman, K. J., and Graf, N. L. 2003. Educational Attainment: 2000. Census 2000 Brief. Washington, DC: U.S. Census Bureau. Available online at: http://www.census.gov/prod/2003pubs/c2kbr-24.pdf.

Blaut, J. M. 1961. Space and Process. *Professional Geographer* 13(4): 1–7.

Block, R., and Bernasco, W. 2008. Finding a Serial Burglar's Home Using Distance Decay and Conditional Origin-Destination Patterns: A Test of Empirical Bayes Journey-to-Crime Estimation in The Hague. Unpublished manuscript available online at: http://www.aic.gov.au/en/events/seminars/2008/rblock.aspx.

Castree, N. 2001. Socializing Nature: Theory, Practice, and Politics. In *Social Nature: Theory, Practice and Politics*, eds. N. Castree and B. Braun, 1–21. Malden, MA: Blackwell.

College Atlas of the World. 2007. Washington, DC: National Geographic.

Cronon, W. 1995. The Trouble with Wilderness; or, Getting Back to the Wrong Nature. In *Uncommon Ground: Rethinking the Human Place in Nature*, ed. W. Cronon, 69–90. New York: W. W. Norton & Co.

Cutter, S. L., Holm, D., and Clark, L. 1996. The Role of Geographic Scale in Monitoring Environmental Justice. *Risk Analysis* 16(4): 517–526.

DeFries, R. H., Hansen, M., Townshend, J. R. G., Janetos, A. C., and Loveland, T. R. 2000. A New Global 1 km Data Set of Percent Tree Cover Derived from Remote Sensing. *Global Change Biology* 6: 247–254.

DeGroote, J. P., Sugumaran, R., Brend, S. M., Tucker, B. J., and Bartholomay, L. C. 2008. Landscape, Demographic, Entomological, and Climatic Associations with Human Disease Incidence of West Nile Virus in the State of Iowa, USA. *International Journal of Health Geographics* 7: 19. Available online at: http://www.ij-healthgeographics.com/content/7/1/19.

Dobson, J. E., and Fisher, P. F. 2003. Geoslavery. *IEEE Technology and Society Magazine* (Spring): 47–52.

Downs, R. M. 1997. The Geographic Eye: Seeing Through GIS? *Transactions in GIS* 2(2): 111–121.

ESRI. 2008. *GIS Best Practices: Essays on Geography and GIS*. Redlands, CA: ESRI.

Fenneman, N. M. 1919. The Circumference of Geography. *Annals of the Association of American Geographers* 9: 3–11.

Foucault, M. 1977. *Discipline & Punish: The Birth of the Prison*. Trans. by Alan Sheridan. New York: Vintage Books.

Gaile, G. L., and Willmott, C. J., eds. 2003. *Geography in America at the Dawn of the 21st Century*. New York: Oxford University Press.

Goodchild, M. F. 2004. The Validity and Usefulness of Laws in Geographic Information Science and Geography. *Annals of the Association of American Geographers* 94(2): 300–303.

Greiner, A. L., Wikle, T. A., and Spencer, J. 2000. *Where Geography Can Take You: An Interactive CD-ROM*. Stillwater, OK: Department of Geography.

Grossner, K. E., Goodchild, M., and Clarke, K. 2008. Defining a Digital Earth System. *Transactions in GIS* 12(1): 145–160.

Holdsworth, D. W. 1997. Landscape and Archives as Text. In *Understanding Ordinary Landscapes*, eds. P. Groth and T. W. Bressi, 44–55. New Haven, CT: Yale University Press.

Hubbard, P., Kitchin, R., Bartley, B., and Fuller, D. 2002. *Thinking Geographically: Space, Theory and Contemporary Human Geography*. London: Continuum.

Jackson, P. 1989. *Maps of Meaning: An Introduction to Cultural Geography*. London: Unwin Hyman.

Johnston, R. J., Gregory, D., Pratt, G., and Watts, M., eds. 2000. *The Dictionary of Human Geography*. 4th ed. Malden, MA: Blackwell.

Jordan, T. G. 1992. The Concept and Method. In *Regional Studies: The Interplay of Land and People*, ed. G. E. Lich, 9–24. College Station: Texas A&M University Press.

Kwan, M.-P. 1999. Gender, the Home-Work Link, and Space-Time Patterns of Nonemployment Activities. *Economic Geography* 75(4): 370–394.

Kwan, M.-P. 2000a. Interactive Geovisualization of Activity-Travel Patterns Using Three-Dimensional Geographical Information Systems: A Methodological Exploration with a Large Data Set. *Transport Research Part C* 8: 185–203.

Kwan, M.-P. 2000b. Gender Differences in Space-Time Constraints. *Area* 32(2): 45–56.

Kwan, M.-P. 2002. Feminist Visualization: Re-envisioning GIS as a Method in Feminist Geographic Research. *Annals of the Association of American Geographers* 94(2): 645–661.

Kwan, M.-P. 2008. From Oral Histories to Visual Narratives: Re-presenting the Post-September 11 Experiences of the Muslim Women in the USA. *Social & Cultural Geography* 9(6): 653–669.

Marston, S. A. 2000. The Social Construction of Scale. *Progress in Human Geography* 24(2): 219–242.

Minot, N., Baulch, B., and Epprecht, M. 2003. *Poverty and Inequality in Vietnam: Spatial Patterns and Geographical Determinants*. Washington, DC: International Food Policy Research Institute (IFPRI) and Institute of Development Studies.

Mitchell, D. 1995. There's No Such Thing as Culture: Towards a Reconceptualization of the Idea of Culture in Geography. *Transactions of the Institute of British Geographers* NS, 20(1): 102–116.

Mitchell, D. 2000. *Cultural Geography: A Critical Introduction*. Malden, MA: Blackwell.

Plumwood, V. 2006. The Concept of a Cultural Landscape: Nature, Culture, and Agency in the Land. *Ethics & Environment* 11(2): 115–150.

Robbins, P. 2004. *Political Ecology: A Critical Introduction*. Malden, MA: Blackwell.

Robbins, P. 2007. *Lawn People: How Grasses, Weeds, and Chemicals Make Us Who We Are*. Philadelphia: Temple University Press.

Sauer, C. O. 1963 [1925]. The Morphology of Landscape. In *Land and Life: A Selection from the Writings of Carl Ortwin Sauer*, ed. J. Leighley, 315–350. Berkeley: University of California Press.

Shuurman, N. 2000. Trouble in the Heartland: GIS and Its Critics in the 1990s. *Progress in Human Geography* 24(4): 569–590.

Sui, D. Z. 2004. Tobler's First Law of Geography: A Big Idea for a Small World? *Annals of the Association of American Geographers* 94(2): 269–277.

Sunderlin, W., Dewi, S., and Puntodewo, A. 2008. Poverty and Forests: Multi-Country Analysis of Spatial Association and Proposed Policy Solutions. *CIFOR Occasional Paper 47*, rev. ed. Bogor Barat, Indonesia: Center for International Forestry Research.

Taaffe, E. J. 1997. Spatial Organization and Interdependence. In *Ten Geographic Ideas that Changed the World*, ed. S. Hanson, 145–162. Piscataway, NJ: Rutgers University Press.

Thrift, N. 2003. Space: The Fundamental Stuff of Human Geography. In *Key Concepts in Geography*, eds. S. Holloway, S. P. Rice, and G. Valentine, 95–108. London: Sage Publications.

Tobler, W. 1970. A Computer Movie Simulating Urban Growth in the Detroit Region. *Economic Geography* 46(June supplement): 234–240.

Tobler, W. 2004. On the First Law of Geography: A Reply. *Annals of the Association of American Geographers* 94(2): 304–310.

Ullman, E. L. 1954. Geography as Spatial Interaction. *Annals of the Association of American Geographers* 43: 54–69.

Wiehe, S. E., Carroll, A. E., Liu, G. C., Haberkorn, K. L., Hoch, S. C., Wilson, J. S., and Fortenberry, J. D. 2008. Using GPS-Enabled Cell Phones to Track the Travel Patterns of Adolescents. *International Journal of Health Geographics* 7 (22). Available online at: http://www.ij-healthgeographics.com/content/7/1/22.

Chapter 2

Alanen, A. R. 1988. Architecture and Landscapes in Colombia: The Viability of the Vernacular. *Journal of Popular Culture* 22(1): 99–119.

Alvarez, M. 2008. Striking a Global Pose: Considerations for Working with Folk and Traditional Cultures in the 21st Century. Issues in Folk Arts and Traditional Culture Working Paper Series, The Fund for Folk Culture. Available online at: http://www.folkculture.org/AboutOurWork/ResearchandPublications/tabid/67/Default.aspx.

Appadurai, A. 1997. *Modernity at Large: Cultural Dimensions of Globalization*. Minneapolis: University of Minnesota Press.

Basser, S. 1999. Acupuncture: A History. *The Scientific Review of Alternative Medicine* 3(1): 34–41.

Blaut, J. 1987. Diffusionism: A Uniformitarian Critique. *Annals of the Association of American Geographers* 77: 30–47.

Bowers, J. Z. 1973. Acupuncture. *Proceedings of the American Philosophical Society* 117(3): 143–151.

Cressy, G. B. 1958. Qanats, Karez, and Foggaras. *Geographical Review* 48(1): 27–44.

Foster, G. M. 1953. What Is Folk Culture? *American Anthropologist* 55: 159–173.

Giddens, A. 2000. *Runaway World: How Globalization Is Reshaping Our Lives*. New York: Routledge.

Graff, T. O., and Ashton, D. 1993. Spatial Diffusion of Wal-Mart: Contagious and Reverse Hierarchical Diffusion. *Professional Geographer* 46(1): 19–29.

Graham, B., Ashworth, G. J., and Tunbridge, J. E. 2000. *A Geography of Heritage: Power, Culture & Economy*. London: Arnold.

Hinrichs, T. H. 1998. New Geographies of Chinese Medicine. *Osiris* 2nd Series 13: 287–325.

Holson, L. M. 2005. The Feng Shui Kingdom. *New York Times*, April 25.

Holton, R. 2000. Globalization's Cultural Consequences. *Annals of the American Academy of Political and Social Science* 570: 140–152.

Jackson, P. 1999. Commodity Cultures: The Traffic in Things. *Transactions of the Institute of British Geographers* NS 24(1): 95–108.

Jordan, T. G., and Kaups, M. 1987. Folk Architecture in Cultural and Ecological Context. *Geographical Review* 77: 52–75.

Knapp, R. G. 1999. *China's Living Houses: Folk Beliefs, Symbols, and Household Ornamentation*. Honolulu: University of Hawaii Press.

KPMG. 2006. *The Global Gems and Jewellery Industry. Vision 2015: Transforming for Growth*. Mumbai: GJEPC-KPMG.

Kunstler, J. H. 1993. *The Geography of Nowhere: The Rise and Decline of America's Man-Made Landscape*. NY: Simon & Schuster.

Lightfoot, D. L. 2000. The Origin and Diffusion of Qanats in Arabia: New Evidence from the Northern and Southern Peninsula. *The Geographical Journal* 166(3): 215–226.

Lowenthal, D. 1975. Past Time, Present Place: Landscape and Memory. *Geographical Review* 65: 1–36.

Mikesell, M. W. 1978. Tradition and Innovation in Cultural Geography. *Annals of the Association of American Geographers* 68: 1–16.

Mintz, S. W. 1953. The Folk-Urban Continuum and the Rural Proletarian Community. *The American Journal of Sociology* 59: 136–143.

Mitchell, D. 1995. There's No Such Thing as Culture: Towards a Reconceptualization of the Idea of Culture in Geography. *Transactions of the Institute of British Geographers* NS 20: 102–116.

Oliver, P., ed. 1997. *Encyclopedia of Vernacular Architecture of the World*. 3 vols. Cambridge: Cambridge University Press.

Parsons, J. J. 1991. Giant American Bamboo in the Vernacular Architecture of Colombia and Ecuador. *Geographical Review* 81(2): 131–152.

Pieterse, J. N. 2009. *Globalization and Culture: Global Mélange*. 2nd ed. Lanham, MD: Rowman & Littlefield.

Pocock, D. 1997. Some Reflections on World Heritage. *Area* 29(3): 260–268.

Redfield, R. 1947. The Folk Society. *The American Journal of Sociology* 52: 293–308.

Relph, E. 1976. *Place and Placelessness*. London: Pion.

Revenge of Geography, The. 2003. *The Economist*. March 15.

Salih, A. 2006. Qanats a Unique Groundwater Management Tool in Arid Regions: The Case of Bam Region in Iran. Paper presented at the International Symposium on Groundwater Sustainability (ISGWAS), January. Available online at: http://aguas.igme.es/igme/ISGWAS/Ponencias%20ISGWAS/6-Salih.pdf.

Sauer, C. O. 1962 [1931]. Cultural Geography. In *Readings in Cultural Geography*, eds. P. L. Wagner and M. W. Mikesell, 30–34. Chicago: University of Chicago Press.

Shortridge, J. 1996. Keeping Tabs on Kansas: Reflections on Regionally Based Field Study. *Journal of Cultural Geography* 16(1): 5–16.

Teather, E. K., and Chow, C. S. 2000. The Geographer and the Fengshui Practitioner: So Close and Yet So Far Apart? *Australian Geographer* 31(3): 309–332.

Tunbridge, J. E., and Ashworth, G. J. 1996. *Dissonant Heritage: The Management of the Past as a Resource in Conflict*. New York: John Wiley.

United Nations Conference on Trade and Development (UNCTAD). 2008. *World Investment Report: Transnational Corporations and the Infrastructure Challenge*. New York: United Nations.

United Nations Conference on Trade and Development (UNCTAD). 2009. *World Investment Report: Transnational Corporations, Agricultural Production and Development*. New York: United Nations.

United Nations Educational, Scientific and Cultural Organization (UNESCO) 2009. World Heritage List. Available online at: http://whc.unesco.org/en/list.

UNCTADstat. 2012. Foreign Direct Investment. Last modified July 18, 2012. Accessed March 15, 2013. http://unctadstat.unctad.org/.

Van Elteren, M. 2003. U.S. Cultural Imperialism Today: Only a Chimera? *SAIS Review* 23(2): 169–188.

Wagner, P. L. 1994. Foreword: Culture and Geography: Thirty Years of Advance. In *Re-reading Cultural Geography*, eds. K. E. Foote, P. J. Hugill, K. Mathewson, and J. M. Smith, 3–8. Austin: University of Texas Press.

Wayland, C. 2001. Gendering Local Knowledge: Medicinal Plant Use and Primary Health Care in the Amazon. *Medical Anthropology Quarterly*, NS 15(2): 171–188.

World Health Organization (WHO). 2002. *WHO Traditional Medicine Strategy 2002–2005*. Geneva: WHO.

Chapter 3

Boserup, E. 1965. *The Conditions of Agricultural Growth*. London: G. Allen & Unwin.

Carling, J. 2005. Gender Dimensions of International Migration. *Global Migration Perspectives No. 35*. Geneva: Global Commission on International Migration.

Castles, S. 2002. Migration and Community Formation Under Conditions of Globalization. *International Migration Review* 36(4): 1143–1168.

Central Intelligence Agency (CIA). 2009. *The World Factbook 2009*. Washington, DC: Central Intelligence Agency.

Chan, K. W. Forthcoming. China, Internal Migration. In *The Encyclopedia of Global Human Migration*, eds., I. Ness and P. Bellwood. Hoboken, NJ: Wiley-Blackwell.

Democratic People's Republic of Korea (DPRK). 2005. *DPRK 2004 Nutrition Assessment Report of Survey Results*. N.p.: DPRK Central Bureau of Statistics. Available online at: http://www.unicef.org/dprk/dprk_national_nutrition_assessment_2004_final_report_07_03_05.pdf.

Ehrlich, P. R. 1978. *The Population Bomb*. Rev. ed. New York: Ballantine Books.

Ehrlich, P. R., and Ehrlich, A. 2009. The Population Bomb Revisited. *The Electronic Journal of Sustainable Development* 1(3): 63–71.

FAOSTAT. 2012. Production. Available online at: http://faostat.fao.org.

Harper, K., and Armelagos, G. 2010. The Changing Disease-Scape in the Third Epidemiological Transition. *International Journal of Environmental Research and Public Health* 7, 675–697.

Hinrichsen, D. 1999. The Coastal Population Explosion. In *Trends and Future Challenges for U.S. National Ocean and Coastal Policy, Proceedings of a Workshop,* eds. B. Cicin-Sain, R. W. Knecht, and N. Foster, 27–29. Silver Spring, MD: NOAA, National Ocean Service.

Hoefer, M., Rytina, N., and Baker, B. C. 2009. Estimates of the Unauthorized Immigrant Population Residing in the United States: January 2008. Washington, DC: U.S. Department of Homeland Security. Available online at: http://www.dhs.gov/xlibrary/assets/statistics/publications/ois_ill_pe_2008.pdf.

International Organization for Migration (IOM). 2005. *World Migration 2005: Costs and Benefits of International Migration*. Geneva: International Organization for Migration.

International Organization for Migration (IOM). 2008. *World Migration Report 2008: Managing Migration Mobility in the Evolving Global Economy*. Geneva: International Organization for Migration.

Kenya National AIDS Control Council. 2009. *Kenya: HIV Prevention Response and Modes of Transmission Analysis*. Nairobi: Kenya National AIDS Control Council.

Lee, E. S. 1966. A Theory of Migration. *Demography* 3(1): 47–57.

Lee, R. 2003. The Demographic Transition: Three Centuries of Fundamental Change. *Journal of Economic Perspectives* 17(4): 167–190.

Lopez, A., Mathers, C. D., Ezzati, M., Jamison, D., and Murray, C. J. L. 2006. Global and Regional Burden of Disease and Risk Factors, 2001. *The Lancet* 367: 1747–1757.

Malthus, T. 1997 [1798]. *An Essay on the Principle of Population*. London: Electric Book Company.

Marcus, A. P. 2009. (Re)creating Places and Spaces in Two Countries: Brazilian Transnational Migration Processes. *Journal of Cultural Geography* 26(2): 173–198.

Méda, D., and Pailhé, A. 2008. Fertility: Is there a French Model? *The Japanese Journal of Social Security Policy* 7(2): 31–40.

Population Reference Bureau (PRB). 2009. *World Population Data Sheet: 2009*. Washington, DC: PRB.

Population Reference Bureau (PRB). 2012. *World Population Data Sheet: 2012*. Washington, DC: PRB.

Ratha, D., Mohapatra, S., and Silwal, A., comps. 2011. *Migration and Remittances Factbook 2011*. 2nd ed. Washington, DC: World Bank. Available online at: http://go.worldbank.org/QGUCPJTOR0.

Ravenstein, E. G. 1885. The Laws of Migration. *Journal of the Statistical Society of London* 48(2): 167–235.

Ravenstein, E. G. 1889. The Laws of Migration. *Journal of the Royal Statistical Society* 52(2): 241–305.

Riley, N. E. 2004. China's Population: New Trends and Challenges. *Population Bulletin* 59, no. 2. Washington, DC: Population Reference Bureau.

Roseman, C. C. 1971. Migration as a Spatial and Temporal Process. *Annals of the Association of American Geographers* 61(3): 589–598.

Simon, J. L. 1981. *The Ultimate Resource*. Princeton, NJ: Princeton University Press.

Simon, J. 1996. *The Ultimate Resource 2*. Rev. ed. Princeton, NJ: Princeton University Press.

Skinner, G. W., Henderson, M., and Jianhua, Y. 2000. China's Fertility Transition Through Regional Space: Using GIS and Census Data for a Spatial Analysis of Historical Demography. *Social Science History* 24(3): 613–652.

Suzuki, M., Willcox, C., and Willcox, B. 2007. The Historical Context of Okinawan Longevity: Influence of the United States and Mainland Japan. *The Okinawan Journal of American Studies* 4: 46–61.

Torres, A. B. 2006. Colombian Migration to Europe: Political Transnationalism in the Middle of Conflict. *COMPAS Working Paper No. 39*. Oxford: Center on Migration, Policy and Society.

UC Atlas of Global Inequality. 2009. Available online at: http://ucatlas.ucsc.edu/cause.php.

United Nations, Department of Economic and Social Affairs (UNDESA). 2009. World Population Prospects: The 2008 revision. Available online at: http://www.un.org/en/development/desa/population/publications/index.shtml.

United Nations, Department of Economic and Social Affairs (UNDESA). 2011. World Population Prospects: The 2010 Revision. Available online at: http://www.un.org/en/development/desa/population/publications/index.shtml.

United Nations, Department of Economic and Social Affairs (UNDESA). 2012. Trends in International Migrant Stock: Migrants by Destination and Origin. Available online at: http://esa.un.org/MigOrigin/.

United Nations Population Fund (UNFPA). 2008. *State of World Population 2008*. New York: UNFPA.

United Nations Program on HIV/AIDS (UNAIDS). 2008. *2008 Report on the Global AIDS Epidemic*. Geneva: UNAIDS.

United States Census Bureau. 2012. Inmigration, Outmigration, and Net Migration for Metropolitan Areas: 1985–2012. Available online at: http://www.census.gov/hhes/migration/data/cps/historical.html.

United States Census Bureau, International Data Base. 2009. Available online at: http://www.census.gov.

United States Census Bureau, International Data Base. 2012. Available online at: http://www.census.gov.

United States Department of Homeland Security 2012. *Yearbook of Immigration Statistics: 2011*. Washington, DC: U.S. Department of Homeland Security, Office of Immigration Statistics.

Watts, M., and Bohle, H. 1993. Hunger, Famine, and the Space of Vulnerability. *Geojournal* 30(2): 117–126.

World Bank. 1986. *Poverty and Hunger: Issues and Options for Food Security in Developing Countries*. A World Bank Policy Study. Washington, DC: World Bank.

World Bank. 2011. Migration and Remittances Data. Available online at: http://econ.worldbank.org.

World Health Organization (WHO). 2011. Fact Sheet 310: The Top 10 Causes of Death. Available online at: http://who.int/mediacentre/factsheets.

Zhu, W. X., and Lu, L. 2009. China's Excess Males, Sex Selective Abortion, and One Child Policy: Analysis of Data from 2005 Intercensus Survey. *British Medical Journal* 338(18 April): 920–923.

Chapter 4

Ardila, A. 2005. Spanglish: An Anglicized Spanish Dialect. *Hispanic Journal of Behavioral Sciences* 27(1): 60–81.

College Atlas of the World. 2007. Washington, DC: National Geographic.

Crystal, D. 1997. *English as a Global Language*. Cambridge: Cambridge University Press.

Crystal, D. 2003. *The Cambridge Encyclopedia of the English Language*. 2nd ed. Cambridge: Cambridge University Press.

Delahunty, J. L. 2009. Yew Tree Toponyms and Their Connection to the Irish Landscape. *Focus on Geography* 51(4): 1–6.

de Swaan, A. 2001. *Words of the World: The Global Language System*. Cambridge: Polity Press.

Diamond, J., and Bellwood, P. 2003. Farmers and Their Languages: The First Expansions. *Science*, New Series 300(5619): 597–603.

Dictionary of American Regional English (DARE). 2013. Available online at: http://dare.wisc.edu/.

Frawley, W. J., ed. 2003. *International Encyclopedia of Linguistics*. 2nd ed. Oxford: Oxford University Press.

Gamkrelidze, T. V., and Ivanov, V. V. 1990. The Early History of Indo-European Languages. *Scientific American* (March): 110–116.

Gordon, R. G., ed. 2005. *Ethnologue*. 15th ed. Dallas, TX: SIL International.

Graddol, D. 2004. The Future of Language. *Science* 303(5662): 1329–1331.

Greenberg, J. H. 1987. *Language in the Americas*. Stanford, CA: Stanford University Press.

Grounds, R. A. 2007. English Only, Native-Language Revitalization and Foreign Languages. *Anthropology News* (November): 6–7.

Hale, K., Krauss, M., Watahomigie, L. J., Yamamoto, A. Y., Craig, C., Jeanne, L. M., and England, N. C. 1992. Endangered Languages. *Languages* 68(1): 1–42.

Hinton, L., and Hale, K., eds. The Green Book of Language Revitalization in Practice. New York: Academic Press.

Kurath, H. 1970 [1949]. *A Word Geography of the Eastern United States*. Ann Arbor: University of Michigan Press.

Language Hotspots Project. Living Tongues Institute for Endangered Languages. http://www.livingtongues.org/hotspots.html.

Leutwyler, K. 2000. Preserving the Yuchi Language. *Scientific American*. December 12. http://www.scientificamerican.com/article.cfm?id=preserving-the-yuchi-lang.

Lewis, M. P., ed. 2009. *Ethnologue: Languages of the World*. 16th ed. Dallas, TX: SIL International.

Lieberson, S. 1981. *Language Diversity and Language Contact*. Compiled by A. S. Dil. Stanford, CA: Stanford University Press.

Linn, M. S. 2000. A Grammar of Euchee (Yuchi). Ph.D. diss., University of Kansas.

Mackey, W. F. 1991. Language Diversity, Language Policy and the Sovereign State. *History of European Ideas* 13(1–2): 51–61.

Maurais, J., and Morris, M. A., eds. 2003. *Languages in a Globalizing World*. Cambridge: Cambridge University Press.

Mazrui, A. A., and Mazrui, A. M. 1998. *The Power of Babel: Language and Governance in the African Experience*. Oxford: James Curry.

McArthur, T. 1998. *The English Languages*. Cambridge: Cambridge University Press.

Mufwene, S. S., Rickford, J. R., Bailey, G., and Baugh, J., eds. 1998. *African-American English: Structure, History and Use*. London: Routledge.

National Geographic Magazine. 2005. Geography of Everyday Life. *National Geographic*, December, n.p.

National Geographic Magazine. 2008. Birth of a Sign: The Peace Symbol is Fifty Years Old. *National Geographic*, August, p. 24.

Nettle, D. 1998. Explaining Global Patterns of Language Diversity. *Journal of Anthropological Archeology* 17: 354–374.

Renfrew, C. 1989. The Origins of Indo-European Languages. *Scientific American* 261(4): 106–114.

Ruhlen, M. 1987. *A Guide to the World's Languages*. Vol. 1, *Classification*. Stanford, CA: Stanford University Press.

Sappenfield, M., and Joshi, S. 2006. Tear Up the Maps: India's Cities Shed Colonial Names. *Christian Science Monitor*, September 7.

Schmemann, S. 1991. Leningrad, Petersburg and the Great Name Debate. *New York Times*, June 13.

Tonkin, H., and Reagan, T., eds. 2003. *Language in the Twenty-First Century: Selected Papers of the Millennial Conferences of the Center for Research and Documentation on World Language Problems*. Amsterdam: John Benjamins Publishing Company.

U. S. English. 2013. States with Official English Laws. Available online at: http://usenglish.org/.

Web Atlas of Oklahoma. 2005. Available online at: http://www.okatlas.org/.

Williams, C. H., ed. 1988. *Language in Geographic Context*. Philadelphia: Multilingual Matters.

Wolfram, W. 1991. *Dialects and American English*. Englewood Cliffs, NJ: Prentice Hall.

Chapter 5

Barrett, D. B., and Johnson, T. M. 2001. *World Christian Trends, AD 30–AD 2200: Interpreting the Annual Christian Megacensus*. Pasadena, CA: William Carey Library.

Barrett, D. B., Johnson, T. M., and Crossing, P. F. 2005. Missiometrics 2005: A Global Survey of World Mission. *International Bulletin of Missionary Research* 29(1): 27–30.

Bellah, R. N. 2005 [1967]. Civil Religion in America. *Daedalus* (Fall): 40–55.

Bhardwaj, S. M. 1998. Non-Hajj Pilgrimage in Islam: A Neglected Dimension of Religious Circulation. *Journal of Cultural Geography* 17(2): 69–87.

Bird, W., and Thumma, S. 2011. *A New Decade of Megachurches: 2011 Profile of Large Attendance Churches in the United States*. N.p.: Leadership Network. Available online at: http://www.leadnet.org.

Bogan, J. 2009. America's Biggest Megachurches. *Forbes*, June 26.

Breuilly, E., O'Brien, J., and Palmer, M. 1997. *Religions of the World: The Illustrated Guide to Origins, Beliefs, Traditions & Festivals*. New York: Facts on File, Inc.

Chatwin, B. 1987. *The Songlines*. New York: Penguin Books.

Encyclopaedia Britannica, Inc., and NetLibrary, Inc. 2008. *Britannica Book of the Year 2008*. Chicago: Encyclopædia Britannica.

Foote, K. E. 1992. Stigmata of National Identity: Exploring the Cosmography of America's Civil Religion. In *Person, Place, and Thing: Interpretive and Empirical Essays in Cultural Geography*. Geoscience and Man, vol. 31, ed. S. T. Wong, 379–402. Baton Rouge: Department of Geography and Anthropology, Louisiana State University.

Foote, K. E. 1997. *Shadowed Ground: America's Landscapes of Violence and Tragedy*. Austin: University of Texas Press.

Francaviglia, R. V. 1971. The Cemetery as an Evolving Cultural Landscape. *Annals of the Association of American Geographers* 61(3): 501–509.

Griswold, E. 2008. God's Country. *The Atlantic Monthly* (March): 40–55.

Jenkins, P. 2002. The Next Christianity. *The Atlantic Monthly* (October): 53–68.

Johnson, T. M., and Chung, S. Y. 2004. Tracking Global Christianity's Statistical Centre of Gravity, AD 33–AD 2100. *International Review of Mission* 93(369): 166–181.

Kong, L. 2001. Mapping "New" Geographies of Religion: Politics and Poetics in Modernity. *Progress in Human Geography* 25(2): 211–233.

Lehren, A., and Ericson, M. 2007. Where Megachurches Are Concentrated. *New York Times*, October 23.

Pew Research Center. 2006. *Spirit and Power: A 10-Country Survey of Pentecostals*. Washington, DC: Pew Forum on Religion & Public Life. Available online at: http://religions.pewforum.org.

Pew Research Center. 2008. *U.S. Religious Landscape Survey*. Washington, DC: Pew Forum on Religion & Public Life. Available online at: http://religions.pewforum.org.

Pew Research Center. 2009. Religious Groups' Views on Global Warming. April 16. Washington, DC: Pew Forum on Religion & Public Life. Available online at: http://religions.pewforum.org.

Rinehart, R., ed. 2004. *Contemporary Hinduism: Ritual, Culture, and Practice*. Santa Barbara, CA: ABC-CLIO.

Rose, D. 1996. *Nourishing Terrains: Australian Aboriginal Views of Landscape and Wilderness*. Canberra: Australian Heritage Commission.

Smart, N., ed. 1999. *Atlas of the World's Religions*. Oxford: Oxford University Press.

Sopher, D. E. 1967. *Geography of Religions*. Englewood Cliffs, NJ: Prentice-Hall.

Stahnke, T., and Blitt, R. C. 2005. *The Religion-State Relationship and the Right to Freedom of Religion or Belief: A Comparative Textual Analysis of the Constitutions of Predominantly Muslim Countries*. Washington, DC: United States Commission on International Religious Freedom. Available online at: http://uscirf.gov.

Stoddard, R. H., and Morinis, A., eds. 1997. *Sacred Places, Sacred Spaces: The Geography of Pilgrimages*. Geoscience and Man, vol. 34. Baton Rouge: Department of Geography and Anthropology, Louisiana State University.

Stump, R. W. 2008. *The Geography of Religion: Faith, Place, and Space*. Lanham, MD: Rowman & Littlefield.

Teather, E. K. 1998. Themes from Complex Landscapes: Chinese Cemeteries and Columbaria in Urban Hong Kong. *Australian Geographical Studies* 36(1): 21–36.

Teather, E. K. 1999. High-Rise Homes for the Ancestors: Cremation in Hong Kong. *Geographical Review* 89(3): 409–430.

White, L. 1971 [1967]. The Historical Roots of Our Ecological Crisis. In *Man's Impact on Environment*, ed. T. R. Detwyler, 27–35. New York: McGraw-Hill Book Co.

Zelinsky, W. 1994. Gathering Places for America's Dead: How Many, Where, and Why? *Professional Geographer* 46(1): 29–38.

Zelinsky, W. 2001. The Uniqueness of the American Religious Landscape. *Geographical Review* 91(3): 565–585.

Chapter 6

Airriess, C. A. 2007. Conflict Migrants from Mainland Southeast Asia. In *Contemporary Ethnic Geographies in America*, eds. I. M. Miyares and C. A. Airriess, 291–312. Lanham, MD: Rowman & Littlefield.

Anderson, K. J. 1987. The Idea of Chinatown: The Power of Place and Institutional Practice in the Making of a Racial Category.

Annals of the Association of American Geographers 77(4): 580–597.

Australian Bureau of Statistics. 2009. Experimental Estimates of Aboriginal and Torres Strait Islander Australians, June 2006. Available online at: http://www.abs.gov.au.

Bonnet, C. 1779–1783. *Oeuvres d'histoire naturelle et de philosophie de Charles Bonnet*. 18 vols. Neuchatel: S. Fauche.

Bullard, R. D. 2000. *Dumping in Dixie: Race, Class, and Environmental Quality*. 3rd ed. Boulder, CO: Westview Press.

Christopher, A. J. 1994. *The Atlas of Apartheid*. London: Routledge.

Central Intelligence Agency (CIA). 1979. *Racial Concentrations and Homelands* [map]. Scale not given. N.p.: CIA. Available online at http://www.lib.utexas.edu/maps/africa/south_africa_racial_1979.jpg.

Eltis, D., and Richardson, D. 2009. *An Atlas of the Transatlantic Slave Trade*. New Haven, CT: Yale University Press.

Gans, H. 1979. Symbolic Ethnicity: The Future of Ethnic Groups and Cultures in America. *Ethnic and Racial Studies* 2(1): 1–20.

Hattam, V. 2005. Ethnicity & the Boundaries of Race: Rereading Directive 15. *Daedalus* (Winter): 61–69.

Human Rights Campaign (HRC). 2010a. Marriage Equality & Other Relationship Recognition Laws. Available online at: http://www.hrc.org/state_laws.

Human Rights Campaign (HRC). 2010b. Statewide Marriage Prohibition Laws. Available online at: http://www.hrc.org/state_laws.

International Labor Organization (ILO). 2005. *A Global Alliance against Forced Labour*. Geneva: ILO.

Levi, J., and Maybury-Lewis, B. 2010. Becoming Indigenous: Identity and Heterogeneity in a Global Movement. In *Indigenous Peoples, Poverty and Development*, eds. G. Hall and H. Patrinos, 1–44. Available online at: http://siteresources.worldbank.org/EXTINDPEOPLE/Resources/407801-1271860301656/Chapter_2_Becoming_Indigenous.pdf.

Li, W. 1998. Anatomy of a New Ethnic Settlement: The Chinese Ethnoburb in Los Angeles. *Urban Studies* 35(3): 479–501.

Longhurst, R. 2000. Geography and Gender: Masculinities, Male Identity and Men. *Progress in Human Geography* 24(3): 439–444.

Mahgoub, E-T. M. 2004. Inside Darfur: Ethnic Genocide by a Governance Crisis. *Comparative Studies of South Asia, Africa and the Middle East* 24(2): 3–17.

Massey, D. 1994. *Space, Place, and Gender*. Minneapolis: University of Minnesota Press.

McDowell, L., and Sharp, J. P., eds. 1997. *Space, Gender, Knowledge: Feminist Readings*. London: Hodder Arnold.

Merchant, C. 2003. Shades of Darkness: Race and Environmental History. *Environmental History* 8(July): 380–394.

Miyares, I. M., and Airriess, C. A., eds. 2007. *Contemporary Ethnic Geographies in America*. Lanham, MD: Rowman & Littlefield.

Morning, A. 2008. Ethnic Classification in Global Perspective: A Cross-National Survey of the 2000 Census Round. *Population Research and Policy Review* 27(2): 239–272.

Pastor, M., Sadd, J., and Morello-Frosch, R. 2007. *Still Toxic after All These Years: Air Quality and Environmental Justice in the San Francisco Bay Area*. Santa Cruz: Center for Justice, Tolerance & Community, University of California, Santa Cruz.

Prewitt, K. 2005. Racial Classification in America: Where Do We Go from Here? *Daedalus* (Winter): 5–17.

Pulido, L. 2000. Rethinking Environmental Racism: White Privilege and Urban Development in Southern California. *Annals of the Association of American Geographers* 90(1): 12–40.

Reddy, G. 2005. *With Respect to Sex: Negotiating Hijra Identity in South India*. Chicago: University of Chicago Press.

Sciorra, J. 1989. Yard Shrines and Sidewalk Altars of New York's Italian-Americans. *Perspectives in Vernacular Architecture* 3: 185–198.

Silvey, R. 2004. Transnational Domestication: State Power and Indonesian Migrant Women in Saudi Arabia. *Political Geography* 23: 245–264.

Statistics South Africa. 2012. *Quarterly Labor Force Survey*. Pretoria: Statistics South Africa. Available online at: http://www.statssa.gov.za.

Strauss, S. 2005. Darfur and the Genocide Debate. *Foreign Affairs* 84(1): 123–133.

Suchan, T. A., Perry, M. J., Fitzsimmons, J. D., Juhn, A. E., Tait, A. M., and Brewer, C. A. 2007. *Census Atlas of the United States*. Series CENSR-29. Washington, DC: U.S. Census Bureau.

Townsend, J. 1991. Towards a Regional Geography of Gender. *The Geographical Journal* 157(1): 25–35.

U.S. Census Bureau. 2000a. American FactFinder, Census Tract 2132.01, Los Angeles County, California. Available online at: http://factfinder.census.gov.

U.S. Census Bureau. 2000b. *Ancestry 2000 Census Brief*. Available online at: http://www.census.gov.

U.S. Census Bureau. 2000c. Census Tract Outline Map: Los Angeles County, California. Available online at: http://www.census.gov.

U.S. Census Bureau. 2010a. American FactFinder, Census 2010 Summary File 1. Available online at: http://factfinder2.census.gov.

U.S. Census Bureau 2010b. *The 2010 Statistical Abstract: The National Data Book*. Table 685, Median Income of People with Income in Constant (2007) Dollars by Sex, Race, and Hispanic Origin: 1990 to 2007. Available online at: http://www.census.gov/compendia/statab.

Vestal, C. 2009. Gay Marriage Legal in Six States. Updated June 4. Available online at: http://www.stateline.org.

Wood, J. 1997. Vietnamese American Place Making in Northern Virginia. *Geographical Review* 87(1): 58–72.

World Economic Forum. 2007. *The Global Gender Gap Report 2007*. Geneva: World Economic Forum.

Zelinsky, W., and Lee, B. 1998. Heterolocalism: An Alternative Model of the Sociospatial Behavior of Immigrant Ethnic Communities. *International Journal of Population Geography* 4: 281–298.

Chapter 7

Agnew, J. 1998. *Geopolitics: Re-visioning World Politics*. 2nd ed. New York: Routledge.

Central Intelligence Agency (CIA). 2009. *The World Factbook 2009*. Washington, DC: Central Intelligence Agency.

Chan, P. C. W. 2009. The Legal Status of Taiwan and the Legality of the Use of Force in a Cross-Taiwan Strait Conflict. *Chinese Journal of International Law* 8(2): 455–492.

Child, J. 2005. The Politics and Semiotics of the Smallest Icons of Popular Culture: Latin American Postage Stamps. *Latin American Research Review* 40(1): 108–137.

Council of the European Union. 2009. *Independent International Fact-Finding Mission on the Conflict in Georgia Report*. 3 vols. Brussels: Council of the European Union. Available online at: http://www.ceiig.ch.

Farrell, D. M. 2001. *Electoral Systems: A Comparative Introduction*. New York: Palgrave.

Flint, C., and Radil, S. M. 2009. Terrorism and Counter-Terrorism: Situating al-Qaeda and the Global War on Terror within Geopolitical Trends and Structures. *Eurasian Geography and Economics* 50(2): 150–171.

Guibernau, M. 2000. Spain: Catalonia and the Basque Country. *Parliamentary Affairs* 53(1): 55–68.

Hartshorne, R. 1950. The Functional Approach in Political Geography. *Annals of the Association of American Geographers* 40(2): 95–130.

Huntington, S. P. 1996. *The Clash of Civilizations and the Remaking of the World Order*. New York: Simon & Schuster.

Jackson, R. 1999. Sovereignty in World Politics: A Glance at the Conceptual and Historical Landscape. *Political Studies* 47: 431–456.

Mackinder, H. J. 1904. The Geographical Pivot of History. *Geographical Journal* 23(4): 421–437.

Mackinder, H. J. 1942 [1919]. *Democratic Ideals and Reality: A Study in the Politics of Reconstruction*. Reprint, with a new introduction by S. Mladineo, Washington, DC: National Defense University Press Publications, 1996.

Murdock, G. P. 1959. *Africa: Its Peoples and Their Culture History*. NY: McGraw-Hill.

National Consortium for the Study of Terrorism and Responses to Terrorism (START). 2012. Global Terrorism Database. Retrieved from: http://www.start.umd.edu/gtd.

Philpott, D. 1995. Sovereignty: An Introduction and Brief History. *Journal of International Affairs* 48(2): 353–368.

Philpott, D. 1999. Westphalia, Authority, and International Society. *Political Studies* 47: 566–589.

Rosendorff, B. P., and Sandler, T. 2005. The Political Economy of Transnational Terrorism. *Journal of Conflict Resolution* 49(2): 171–182.

Shelley, F. M., Archer, J. C., Davidson, F. M., and Brunn, S. D. 1996. *Political Geography of the United States*. New York: Guilford.

Shughart, W. F. 2006. An Analytical History of Terrorism, 1945–2000. *Public Choice* 128(1–2): 7–39.

Smith, A. D. 1987. *The Ethnic Origins of Nations*. New York: Blackwell.

Symonds, P., Alcock, M., and French, C. 2009. Setting Australia's Limits. *AUSGEO News* 93(March): 1–8.

Chapter 8

Abu-Lughod, J. 1987. The Islamic City—Historic Myth, Islamic Essence, and Contemporary Relevance. *International Journal of Middle East Studies* 19(2): 155–176.

Acioly, C. 2007. The Challenge of Slum Formation in the Developing World. *Land Lines* 19(2): 1–6. Available online at: http://www.lincolninst.edu.

Adams, J. S. 1970. Residential Structure of Midwestern Cities. *Annals of the Association of American Geographers* 60(1): 37–62.

Beaverstock, J. V., Smith, R. G., and Taylor, P. J. 1999. A Roster of World Cities. *Cities* 16(6): 445–458.

Bonine, M. E. 1990. The Sacred Direction and City Structure: A Preliminary Analysis of the Islamic Cities of Morocco. *Muqarnas, An Annual on Islamic Art and Architecture* 7: 50–72.

Burgess, E. W. 1925. The Growth of the City. In *The City*. University of Chicago Studies in Urban Sociology, eds. R. E. Park, E. W. Burgess, R. D. McKenzie, and L. Wirth, 47–62. Chicago: University of Chicago Press.

Congress for the New Urbanism. 1996. Charter for the New Urbanism. Available online at: http://www.cnu.org/charter.

Federal Housing Administration. 1936. *Underwriting Manual; Underwriting and Valuation Procedure under Title II of the National Housing Act; with Revisions to April 1, 1936*. Washington, DC: Government Printing Office.

Ford, L. 1996. A New and Improved Model of Latin American City Structure. *Geographical Review* 86(3): 437–440.

Getis, A., and Getis, J. 1966. Christaller's Central Place Theory. *Journal of Geography* May: 220–226.

Grant, R., and Nijman, J. 2002. Globalization and the Corporate Geography of Cities in the Less-Developed World. *Annals of the Association of American Geographers* 92(2): 320–340.

Griffin, E., and Ford, L. 1980. A Model of Latin American City Structure. *Geographical Review* 70(4): 397–422.

Harris, C. D., and Ullman, E. L. 1945. The Nature of Cities. *Annals of the American Academy of Political and Social Science* 242(November): 7–17.

Hartshorn, T. 1992. *Interpreting the City: An Urban Geography*. 2nd ed. New York: John Wiley and Sons.

Hoyt, H. 1939. *The Structure and Growth of Residential Neighborhoods in American Cities*. Washington, DC: Federal Housing Administration.

Jackson, K. T. 1985. *Crabgrass Frontier: The Suburbanization of the United States*. New York: Oxford University Press.

Kaplan, D., Wheeler, J. O., and Holloway, S. 2008. *Urban Geography* 2nd ed. New York: John Wiley and Sons.

Kreja, K. 2006. Spatial Imprints of Urban Consumption: Large-Scale Retail Development in Warsaw. In *The Urban Mosaic of Post-Socialist Europe: Space, Institutions and Policy*, eds. S. Tsenkova and Z. Nedovic-Budic, 253–272. New York: Physica-Verlag.

Larsen, K., and Gilliland, J. 2008. Mapping the Evolution of "Food Deserts" in a Canadian City: Supermarket Accessibility in London, Ontario, 1961–2005. *International Journal of Health Geographics* 7: 16. Available online at: http://www.ij-healthgeographics.com/content/7/1/16.

Morrill, R. 2006. Classic Map Revisited: The Growth of Megalopolis. *Professional Geographer* 58(2): 155–161.

Mutlu, S. 1989. Urban Concentration and Primacy Revisited: An Analysis and Some Policy Conclusions. *Economic Development and Cultural Change* 37(3): 611–639.

Palca, J. 2008. Abu Dhabi Aims to Build First Carbon-Neutral City. National Public Radio, May 6. Available online at: http://www.npr.org/templates/story/story.php?storyId=90042092.

Park, R. E., Burgess, E. W., McKenzie, R. D., and Wirth, L., eds. 1925. *The City*. University of Chicago Studies in Urban Sociology. Chicago: University of Chicago Press.

Population Reference Bureau (PRB). 2011. *World Population Data Sheet: 2011*. Washington, DC: PRB.

Short, J. R. 2004. *Global Metropolitan: Globalizing Cities in a Capitalist World*. London: Routledge.

Taylor, P. J. 2001. Urban Hinterworlds: Geographies of Corporate Service Provision Under Conditions of Contemporary Globalization. *Geography* 86(1): 51–60.

United Nations Human Settlements Program 2003. *The Challenge of Slums: Global Report on Human Settlements 2003*. London: Earthscan.

United Nations, Department of Economic and Social Affairs (UNDESA). 2008. World Urbanization Prospects: The 2007 Revision. NY: United Nations.

United Nations, Department of Economic and Social Affairs (UNDESA). 2012. World Urbanization Prospects: The 2011 Revision. NY: United Nations.

United Nations Human Settlements Program 2008. *State of the World's Cities 2008/2009: Harmonious Cities*. London: Earthscan.

United Nations Population Division. 2008. *World Urbanization Prospects: The 2007 Revision, Highlights*. New York: United Nations.

Vance, J. E. 1964. *Geography and Urban Evolution in the San Francisco Bay Area*. Berkeley: Institute of Government Studies, University of California.

Chapter 9

Blaikie, P. 2000. Development, Post-, Anti-, and Populist: A Critical Review. *Environment and Planning A* 32: 1033–1050.

Brandt, W. 1980. *North-South: A Programme for Survival: Report of the Independent Commission on International Development Issues*. Cambridge, MA: MIT Press.

Congressional Budget Office (CBO). 2011. Trends in the Distribution of Household Income Between 1979 and 2007. Washington, DC: CBO. Available online at: http://www.cbo.gov/publication/42729.

Dicken, P. 1998. *Global Shift: Transforming the World Economy*. 3rd ed. New York: Guilford Press.

Dickenson, J., Gould, B., Clarke, C., Mather, S., Prothero, M., Siddle, D., Smith, C., and Thomas-Hope, E. 1996. *A Geography of the Third World*. 2nd ed. London: Routledge.

Dikhanov, Y. 2005. *Trends in Global Income Distribution, 1970–2000, and Scenarios for 2015*. Occasional Paper, Human Development Report, 2005. New York: United Nations Development Program.

International Monetary Fund (IMF). 2006. *Albania: Poverty Reduction Strategy Paper Annual Progress Report*. IMF Country Report 06/23. Washington, DC: IMF.

Mistiaen, J. A., Özler, B., Razafimanantena, T., and Razafindravonoma, J. 2002. Putting Welfare on the Map in Madagascar. Africa Region Working Paper Series, No. 34. Washington, DC: World Bank.

Organization for Economic Cooperation and Development (OECD). 2008. *OECD Annual Report*. Paris: OECD.

Paternostro, S., Razafindravonona, J., and Stifel, D. 2001. Changes in Poverty in Madagascar 1993–1999. Africa Region Working Paper Series, No. 19. Washington, DC: World Bank.

Population Reference Bureau (PRB). 2011. *World Population Data Sheet: 2011*. Washington, DC: PRB.

Revkin, A. C. 2005. A New Measure of Well-Being from a Happy Little Kingdom. *New York Times*, October 4.

Rostow, W. W. 1971. *The Stages of Economic Growth: A Non-Communist Manifesto*. 2nd ed. Cambridge, MA: Cambridge University Press.

Sachs, J. D., Mellinger, A. D., and Gallup, J. L. 2001. The Geography of Poverty and Wealth. *Scientific American* 284(3): 70–76.

Slater, D. 1997. Geopolitical Imaginations across the North-South Divide: Issues of Difference, Development, and Power. *Political Geography* 16(8): 631–653.

Smith, N. 1984. *Uneven Development: Nature, Capital, and the Production of Space*. New York: Blackwell.

Taylor, P. J. 1992. Understanding Global Inequalities: A World-Systems Approach. *Geography* 77: 10–21.

Therien, J. 1999. Beyond the North-South Divide: The Two Tales of World Poverty. *Third World Quarterly* 20(4): 723–742.

United Nations. 2013. Millennium Development Goals. Available online at: http://www.un.org/millenniumgoals/.

United Nations Development Program (UNDP). 2005. *Human Development Report: International Cooperation at a Crossroads: Aid, Trade and Security in an Unequal World*. New York: UNDP.

United Nations Development Program (UNDP). 2007. *Human Development Report 2007/2008: Fighting Climate Change: Human Solidarity in a Divided World*. New York: Palgrave Macmillan.

United Nations Development Program (UNDP). 2011. *Human Development Report 2011: Sustainability and Equity: A Better Future for All*. NY: Palgrave Macmillan.

Wallerstein, I. 1974. *The Modern World-System*. 3 vols. New York: Academic Press.

World Bank. 2008. *Poverty Data: A Supplement to World Development Indicators 2008*. Washington, DC: World Bank.

World Bank. 2013. World DataBank. Available online at: http://databank.worldbank.org/data/home.aspx.

Zurick, D. 2006. Gross National Happiness and Environmental Status in Bhutan. *Geographical Review* 96(4): 657–681.

Chapter 10

Bairoch, P. 1982. International Industrialization Levels from 1750 to 1980. *Journal of European Economic History* 11: 269–310.

Benko, G. 2000. Technopoles, High-Tech Industries and Regional Development: A Critical Review. *GeoJournal* 51(3): 157–167.

Berry, B. J. L., Conkling, E. C., and Ray, D. M. 1997. *The Global Economy in Transition*. 2nd ed. Upper Saddle River, NJ: Prentice Hall.

Dedrick, J., and Kraemer, K. 1998. *Asia's Computer Challenge: Threat or Opportunity for the US and the World*. NY: Oxford University Press.

Dicken, P. 2011. *Global Shift: Mapping the Changing Contours of the World Economy*. 6th ed. NY: Guilford Press.

Engman, M., Onodera, O., and Pinali, E. 2007. Export Processing Zones: Past and Future Role in Trade and Development, *OECD Trade Policy Working Papers*, No. 53. Paris: OECD Publishing.

Gereffi, G., and Memedovic, O. 2003. *The Global Apparel Value Chain: What Prospects for Upgrading by Developing Countries?* Vienna: UNIDO Strategic Research and Economics Branch.

Hayter, R. 1997. *The Dynamics of Industrial Location: The Factory, the Firm and the Production System*. New York: John Wiley & Sons.

Ho, A. L. 2007. Breaking into the Tennis World a Ball at a Time. *Philippines Daily Inquirer*, May 20. Available online at: http://business.inquirer.net/money/features/view/20070520-67042/Breaking_into_the_tennis_world_a_ball_at_a_time.

Innis, H. A. 1933. *Problems of Staple Production in Canada*. Toronto: University of Toronto Press.

International Fur Trade Federation (IFTF). n.d. *The Socio-Economic Impact of International Fur Farming*. Available online at: http://www.iftf.com.

International Labor Organization (ILO). 2007. Equality at Work: Tackling the Challenges. Report of the Director General,

International Labor Conference. 96th Session 2007. Geneva: ILO. Available online at: http://www.ilo.org.

International Labor Organization (ILO). 2012. *Global Employment Trends: Preventing a Deeper Jobs Crisis*. Geneva: ILO.

Kraemer, K. L., Linden, G., Dedrick, J. 2011. *Capturing Value in Global Networks: Apple's iPad and iPhone*. Irvine, CA: Personal Computing Industry Center.

Mackintosh, W. A. 1923. Economic Factors in Canadian History. *Canadian Historical Review* 4: 12–25.

Maddison, A. 2001. *The World Economy: A Millennial Perspective*. Paris: OECD Development Center Studies.

Maddison, A. 2003. *The World Economy: Historical Statistics*. Paris: OECD Development Center Studies.

Phillips, D. R., and Yeh, A. G. O. 1990. Foreign Investment and Trade: Impact on Spatial Structure of the Economy. In *The Geography of Contemporary China: The Impact of Deng Xiaoping's Decade*, eds. T. Cannon and A. Jenkins, 224–248. London: Routledge.

Rowthorn, R., and Ramaswamy, R. 1999. Growth, Trade, and Deindustrialization. *IMF Staff Papers* 46(1): 18–41.

Skov, L. 2005. The Return of the Fur Coat: A Commodity Chain Perspective. *Current Sociology* 53(1): 9–32.

Stearns, P. N. 2007. *The Industrial Revolution in World History*. 3rd ed. Boulder, CO: Westview Press.

Taylor, F. W. 1998 [1911]. *The Principles of Scientific Management*. Mineola, NY: Dover Publications.

United Nations Conference on Trade and Development (UNCTAD). 2008. *Development and Globalization: Facts and Figures*. New York: UNCTAD.

United Nations Industrial Development Organization (UNIDO). 2009. *Breaking In and Moving Up: New Industrial Challenges for the Bottom Billion and the Middle-Income Countries*. Vienna: UNIDO.

United Nations Industrial Development Organization (UNIDO). 2011. *Industrial Energy Efficiency for Sustainable Wealth Creation: Capturing Environmental, Economic and Social Dividends*. Vienna: UNIDO.

United States Agency for International Development (USAID). 2000. *Latin America and the Caribbean: Selected Economic and Social Data, 1999*. Retrieved from LexisNexis Statistical.

World Bank. 2013. World DataBank. Available online at: http://databank.worldbank.org/data/home.aspx.

World Trade Organization (WTO). 2002. *Annual Report 2002*. Geneva: WTO.

Yeung, Y., Lee, J., and Kee, G. 2009. China's Special Economic Zones at 30. *Eurasian Geography and Economics* 50(2): 222–240.

Chapter 11

Angelsen, A. 2007. Forest Cover Change in Space and Time: Combining the von Thunen and Forest Transition Theories. World Bank Policy Research Working Paper 4117. Washington, DC: World Bank. Available online at: http://econ.worldbank.org.

Bauman, P. R. 2008. Grand Prairie of Illinois: Cash Grain Farming. *Geocarto International* 23(3): 235-244.

Borlaug, N. E., and Dowswell, C. 2004. The Green Revolution: An Unfinished Agenda. CFS Distinguished Lecture Series. Committee on World Food Security, Rome, 20-23 September. Available online at: http://www.fao.org/docrep/meeting/008/J3205e/j3205e00.htm.

Chisholm, M. 1968. *Rural Settlement and Land Use: An Essay in Location*. 2nd rev. ed. London: Hutchinson University Library.

Clement, C. R. 1989. A Center of Crop Genetic Diversity in Western Amazonia. *BioScience* 39(9): 624–631.

Cowan, C. W., and Watson, P. J., eds. 1992. *The Origins of Agriculture: An International Perspective*. Washington, DC: Smithsonian Institution Press.

Evenson, R. E., and Gollin, D. 2003. Assessing the Impact of the Green Revolution, 1960 to 2000. *Science* 300(5620): 758–762.

FAOSTAT 2010. Milk Production, 2008. Available online at: http://faostat.fao.org/site/339/default.aspx. Last accessed May 5, 2010.

FAOSTAT. 2013. Cereal Production. Available online at: http://faostat.fao.org/site/567/default.aspx#ancor.

Goodman, M. K. 2004. Reading Fair Trade: Political Ecological Imaginary and the Moral Economy of Fair Trade Foods. *Political Geography* 23: 891–915.

Grimes, K. M. 2005. Changing the Rules of Trade with Global Partnerships: The Fair Trade Movement. In *Social Movements: An Anthropological Reader*, ed. J. Nash. Malden, MA: Blackwell Publishing, 237–248.

Hammond. 2004. *Hammond Comparative World Atlas*. Union, NJ: Hammond World Atlas Corporation.

Hart, J. F. 2003. *The Changing Scale of American Agriculture*. Charlottesville, VA: University of Virginia Press.

Hawkes, C. 2006. Uneven Dietary Development: Linking the Policies and Processes of Globalization with the Nutrition Transition, Obesity and Diet-Related Chronic Diseases. *Globalization and Health*. Available online at: http://www.globalizationandhealth.com/content/2/1/4.

International Food Policy Research Institute (IFPRI). 2002. Green Revolution: Curse or Blessing? Washington, DC: IFPRI. Available online at: http://www.ifpri.org.

International Labor Organization (ILO). 2012. *Global Employment Trends: Preventing a Deeper Jobs Crisis*. Geneva: ILO.

International Service for the Acquisition of Agri-Biotech Applications (ISAAA). 2008. *Global Status of Commercialized Biotech/GM Crops: 2008*. ISAAA Brief 39-2008. Available online at: http://www.isaaa.org/default.asp.

Malcolm, S. A., Aillery, M., and Weinberg, M. 2009. *Ethanol and a Changing Agricultural Landscape*. Economic Research Report 86. U.S. Department of Agriculture, Economic Research Service. Available online at: http://www.ers.usda.gov.

Mannion, A. M. 1999. Domestication and the Origins of Agriculture: An Appraisal. *Progress in Physical Geography* 23(1): 37–56.

Mitchell, D. 2008. A Note on Rising Food Prices. Policy Research Working Paper 4682. Washington, DC: World Bank, Development Prospects Group. Available online at: http://econ.worldbank.org.

Nair, P. K. R. 1993. *An Introduction to Agroforestry*. Dordrecht: Kluwer Academic Publishers in cooperation with International Center for Research in Agroforestry.

O'Brien, D. 2010. U.S. Grain Supply-Demand Projections for 2010 from the USDA Agricultural Outlook Forum. Manhattan, KS: Kansas State University Research and Extension. Available online at: http://www.agmanager.info/marketing/outlook/newletters/archives/.

Parayil, G. 2003. Mapping Technological Trajectories of the Green Revolution and the Gene Revolution from Modernization to Globalization. *Research Policy* 32: 971–990.

Pingali, P. 2006. Westernization of Asian Diets and the Transformation of Food Systems: Implications for Research and Policy. *Food Policy* 32(2006): 281–298.

Piperno, D. R., and Pearsall, D. M. 1998. *The Origins of Agriculture in the Lowland Neotropics*. San Diego, CA: Academic Press.

Ramankutty, N., Evan, A. T., Monfreda, C., and Foley, J. A. 2008. Farming the Planet 1: The Geographic Distribution of Global Agricultural Lands in the Year 2000. *Global Biogeochemical Cycles* 22, GB1003.

Robbins, P. 2004. *Political Ecology: A Critical Introduction*. Malden, MA: Blackwell Publishing.

Smith, B. D. 1994. Origins of Agriculture in the Americas. *Evolutionary Anthropology* 3(5): 174–184.

Spencer, J. E., and Stewart, N. R. 1973. The Nature of Agricultural Systems. *Annals of the Association of American Geographers* 63(4): 529–544.

Sunderlin, W. D., and Resosudarmo, I. A. P. 1996. *Rates and Causes of Deforestation in Indonesia: Towards a Resolution of the Ambiguities*. CIFOR Occasional Paper No. 9. Jakarta: CIFOR.

Timmer, P. 1969. The Turnip, the New Husbandry, and the English Agricultural Revolution. *The Quarterly Journal of Economics* 83(3): 375–395.

Turner II, B. L., and Brush, S. B., eds. 1987. *Comparative Farming Systems*. New York: Guilford Press.

United States Agency for International Development (USAID). 2009. Global Food Insecurity and Price Increase Situation Report #1. Available online at: http://www.usaid.gov/our_work/humanitarian_assistance/foodcrisis/.

USDA, National Agricultural Statistics Service. 2001. *Agricultural Statistics, 2001*. Washington, D.C.: U.S. GPO. Available online at: http://www.nass.usda.gov/Publications/Ag_Statistics/index.asp.

Willer, H., and Yussefi, M., eds. 2007. *The World of Organic Agriculture: Statistics and Emerging Trends 2007*. Bonn, Germany and Frick, Switzerland: International Federation of Organic Agriculture Movements and Research Institute of Organic Agriculture.

Willer, H., and Klicher, L., eds. 2009. *The World of Organic Agriculture: Statistics and Emerging Trends 2009*. Bonn, Germany and Frick, Switzerland: International Federation of Organic Agriculture Movements and Research Institute of Organic Agriculture. Available online at: http://www.organic-world.net.

Chapter 12

Berg, L. and Hager, M. C. 2009. *Visualizing Environmental Science*. Hoboken, NJ: John Wiley & Sons.

Blaikie, P., and Brookfield, H. 1987. *Land Degradation and Society*. London: Methuen & Co.

Boden, T.A., Marland, G., and Andres, R. J. 2012. Global, Regional, and National Fossil-Fuel CO2 Emissions. Carbon Dioxide Information Analysis Center, Oak Ridge National Laboratory, U.S. Department of Energy, Oak Ridge, TN. doi 10.3334/CDIAC/00001_V2012.

BP 2008. *BP Statistical Review of World Energy June 2008*. Available online at: http://www.bp.com/statisticalreview.

BP 2012. *BP Statistical Review of World Energy June 2012*. Available online at: http://www.bp.com/statisticalreview.

Cavallo, A. J. 2002. Predicting the Peak in World Oil Production. *Natural Resources Research* 11(3): 187–195.

Cavallo, A. J. 2004. Hubbert's Petroleum Production Model: An Evaluation and Implications for World Oil Production Forecasts. *Natural Resources Research* 13(4): 211–221.

Earth Pulse: The Essential Visual Report on Global Trends. 2008. Washington, DC: National Geographic.

Ecological Society of America. n.d. *Ecological Principles for Managing Land Use*. Available online at: http://www.esa.org/science_resources/publications/landUse.php.

Ecological Society of America. 1997. Ecosystem Services: Benefits Supplied to Human Societies by Natural Ecosystems. *Issues in Ecology* 2: 1–16.

Ellis, E. 2007. Land-Use and Land-Cover Change. In *Encyclopedia of the Earth*, ed. C. J. Cleveland. Washington, DC: Environmental Information Coalition, National Council for Science and the Environment. Available online at: http://www.eoearth.org/article/Land-use_and_land-cover_change.

Energy Information Administration (EIA). 2008. International Energy Statistics. Available online at: http://www.eia.gov.

Energy Information Administration (EIA). 2009. *Monthly Energy Review* (January). Available online at: http://www.eia.gov/mer.

Energy Information Administration (EIA). 2010. International Energy Statistics. Available online at: http://www.eia.gov.

Energy Information Administration (EIA). 2013a. *Short-Term Energy Outlook* (April). Available online at: www.eia.gov/steo.

Energy Information Administration (EIA). 2013b. *Monthly Energy Review* (January). Available online at: http://www.eia.gov/mer.

Energy Information Administration (EIA). 2013c. International Energy Statistics. Available online at: http://www.eia.gov.

Foley, J. A., DeFries, R., Asner, G. P., Barford, C., Bonan, G., Carpenter, S. R., Chapin, F. S., Coe, M. T., Daily, G. C., Gibbs, H. K., Helkowski, J. H., Holloway, T., Howard, E. A., Kucharik, C. J., Monfreda, C., Patz, J. A., Prentice, I. C., Ramankutty, N., and Snyder, P. K. 2005. Global Consequences of Land Use. *Science* 309: 570–574.

Gearheard, S. 2008. What Changes are Indigenous Peoples Observing in the State of Sea Ice? National Oceanic and Atmospheric Administration (NOAA) Arctic Theme Page. Available online at: http://www.arctic.noaa.gov/essay_gearheard.html.

Global Wind Energy Council (GWEC). 2008. *Global Wind 2007 Report*. Brussels: GWEC.

Hardin, G. 1968. The Tragedy of the Commons. *Science* New Series 162(3859): 1243–1248.

Hardin, G. 1985. Human Ecology: The Subversive, Conservative Science. *American Zoologist* 25(2): 469–476.

Hardin, G. 1998. Extensions of "The Tragedy of the Commons." *Science*. New Series 280 (5364): 682–683.

Intergovernmental Panel on Climate Change (IPCC) 2007. *Climate Change 2007: Synthesis Report*. Contribution of Working Groups I, II and III to the Fourth Assessment Report of the Intergovernmental Panel on Climate Change, eds. R.K Pachauri and A. Reisinger. Geneva: IPCC.

International Atomic Energy Agency (IAEA). 2008. *Energy, Electricity and Nuclear Power Estimates for the Period up to 2030*. Vienna: IAEA.

International Energy Agency (IEA). 2006. *World Energy Outlook 2006*. Paris: IEA.

International Energy Agency (IEA). 2007. *Key World Energy Statistics*. Paris: IEA.

Laidler, G. 2006. Inuit and Scientific Perspectives on the Relationship between Sea Ice and Climate Change: The Ideal Complement? *Climatic Change* 78: 407–444.

Le Treut, H., Somerville, R., Cubasch, U., Ding, Y., Mauritzen, C., Mokssit, A., Peterson, T., and Prather, M. 2007. Historical Overview of Climate Change. In: *Climate Change 2007: The Physical Science Basis. Contribution of Working Group I to the Fourth Assessment Report of the Intergovernmental Panel on Climate Change,* eds. S. Solomon, D. Qin, M. Manning, Z. Chen, M. Marquis, K. B. Avery, M. Tignor and H. L. Miller, 95–127. Cambridge: Cambridge University Press.

Lyles, L. D., and F. Namwamba. 2005. Louisiana Coastal Zone Erosion: 100+ Years of Landuse and Land Loss Using GIS and Remote Sensing. *Proceedings of 5th Annual ESRI Education User Conference*. Available online at: http://proceedings.esri.com/library/userconf/educ05/papers/pap1222.pdf.

Mann, M. E., and Kump, L. R. 2009. *Dire Predictions: Understanding Global Warming*. New York: DK Publishing.

Meyer, W. B., and Turner II, B. L. 1994. *Changes in Land Use and Land Cover: A Global Perspective.* Cambridge: Cambridge University Press.

Moran, S. 2007. The Energy Challenge: Strangers as Allies. *New York Times*, October 20.

Mwangi, E., and Ostrom, E. 2009. Top-Down Solutions: Looking Up from East Africa's Rangelands. *Environment* 51(1): 34–44.

NEA and IAEA 2008. *Uranium 2007: Resources, Production and Demand*. Joint Publication of the OECD Nuclear Energy Agency (NEA) and the International Atomic Energy Agency (IAEA). Paris: OECD Publications.

Ostrom, E. 2008. The Challenge of Common-Pool Resources. *Environment Science and Policy for Sustainable Development* (July/August). Available online at: http://www.environmentmagazine.org/Archives/Back%20Issues/July-August%202008/ostrom-full.html.

Robbins, P. 2004. *Political Ecology: A Critical Introduction*. Malden, MA: Blackwell.

Soublière, M. 2006. Meltdown: Climate Change Hits Home. *Inuktitut* (Winter): 23–31.

Sutton, M. Q., and Anderson, E. N. 2004. *An Introduction to Cultural Ecology*. Walnut Creek, CA: AltaMira Press.

Turner II, B. L., Clark, W. C., Kates, R. W., Richards, J. F., Matthews, J. T., and Meyer, W. B. 1990. *The Earth as Transformed by Human Action: Global and Regional Changes in the Biosphere over the Past 300 Years*. Cambridge: Cambridge University Press.

Turner II, B. L., and Robbins, P. 2008. Land-Change Science and Political Ecology: Similarities, Differences, and Implications for Sustainability Science. *Annual Review of Environment and Resources* 33(8): 295–316.

United Nations 2003. *Integrated Economic and Environmental Accounting*. Handbook of National Accounting, Studies in Methods, Series F, no. 61. New York: United Nations.

United Nations Development Program (UNDP). 2007. *Human Development Report 2007/2008: Fighting Climate Change: Human Solidarity in a Divided World*. New York: Palgrave Macmillan.

United Nations Environment Program (UNEP). 2005. *One Planet Many People: Atlas of Our Changing Environment*. Nairobi: UNEP. Available online at: http://na.unep.net/atlas/onePlanetManyPeople/book.php.

United Nations Environmental Program (UNEP). 2007. *Dams and Development: Relevant Practices for Improved Decision-Making*. Nairobi: UNEP.

United Nations Framework Convention on Climate Change (UNFCC). Local Coping Strategies Database. Available online at: http://maindb.unfccc.int/public/adaptation/.

United Nations Framework Convention on Climate Change (UNFCC). Kyoto Protocol. Available online at: http://unfccc.int/kyoto_protocol/items/2830.php.

World Commission on Dams (WCD). 2000. *Dams and Development: A New Framework for Decision-Making*. London: Earthscan Publications.

Index

natural or environmental amenities
and, 84
net migration and, 81
principles of, 82
push and pull factors and, 82
Ravenstein's principles and, 82
rural-out migration, 84–85, 85f
urban-out migration, 85–86, 87f
urbanization and, 235
Milkshed, dairy farming and, 342
Millennium Development Goals (MDGs),
287–290
Milpa, 336
Mixed crop and livestock farming,
342–343, 343f
Mixed-use development, 256–257
Modernism, religion and, 150
Moksha, 137, 155
Monoculture, 331
Monotheistic religions, 132
Monsanto, 333
Mormon settlements, 147
Mortality rates, 71–72
Mosques, 155
Mountain geography, 6
Mountaintop removal, coal and, 368–369,
368f
Muhammad, 135–137
Multinational corporations, 37–40, 38f–39f,
42, 305–307
Multinational states, 200–201, 200f–201f
Multinationalism, 210, 210f
Multiple nuclei model, 244–245
Mutual intelligibility, languages and, 97
Mystical ecology, 55

N

Nation-state, 200
Nationalism, 200
Nations and states, 199–201
Natural capital, 358–359
Natural languages, 102
Nature-culture dualism, 5
Neo-Malthusians, 79
Neoliberalism, 286
Neolocalism, 43, 43f
Nepal, migration and, 85f
Net migration, 81, 87–88, 88f
New renewables, 371
New urbanism, 256, 257f
Newly industrialized economies (NIEs),
310–311, 310f–311f
Nigeria, smallholder crop and livestock
farming and, 338–339, 339f
Nike, 42, 308, 314
Nitrous oxide, 376–377
No-till farming, 347
Noncommunicable diseases, 80
Nonmaterial culture, 44

Nonrenewable energy resources, 359,
362–370
coal, 367–369
global energy consumption by fuel, 362,
3622
nuclear energy, 369–370
oil and natural gas, 362–366
oil production and consumption,
363–365
oil reserves, 363f
peak oil and, 363
reserves-to-production ratio (R/P ratio),
362–363
shale oil production, 365–366
Normative developmental studies, 264
North American Free Trade Agreement
(NAFTA), 312
North American urban structure, 243–246
concentric zone and sector models,
243–244, 244f
edge cities and, 245–246
filtering and, 244
multiple nuclei model and, 244–245
transportation and urban form,
245–246, 245f
urban realms model and, 245
North Korea
food insecurity and, 80f
traditional medicine and, 52
Nuclear energy, 369–370, 369f
Nutrition, as sociodemographic indicator,
267
Nutrition transition, 349

O

Observational scale, 22
Occupy Wall Street movement, 278–289
Office of Management and Budget (OMB),
176
Official English laws, 110, 110f
Official languages, 110, 110f
Offshoring, 308, 313–314
Oil and natural gas, 362–366
global energy consumption by fuel, 362f
oil production and consumption,
363–365, 364f, 365f
oil reserves, 363f
shale oil production, 365–366, 366f
Okinawa, Japan, 72f
Oklahoma City, Oklahoma, 252f
One-child policy, 70, 71f
Open-access resources, 360
Optimal market areas, 239, 239f
Organic agriculture, 348, 348f
Organisation for Economic Co-operation
and Development (OECD),
277–278, 278f
Organization of Petroleum Exporting
Countries (OPEC), 363–364, 364f
Othering, 172

Outsourcing, 308, 309f
Overfishing, 359, 359f

P

Palestine, 140–141
Pan-Islamic Caliphate, 218
Pandemics, 16
Passive solar collection, 373
Pastoralism, 337–338, 338f
Patriotism, 200
Peace of Westphalia, 197
Peak oil, 363
Pennsylvania, deindustrialization and, 317f
Perceptual regions, 11, 11f
Peripheral regions, development and, 284
Permeable barriers, 17
Personal approach, traditional medicine
and, 51–52
Peru, smallholder crop and livestock
farming and, 338–339, 339f7
Petroleum, 362
Petty apartheid, 170
Philippines, high-tech manufacturing
and, 311f
Phoenix, Arizona, 253f
Photovoltaic cells, 373
Physical geography, 5
Physiographic boundary, 204
Physiological density, 67
Pidgin language, 111–113
Pidginization, 112
Pieterse, Jan Nederveen, 43
Piety, 133
Pilgrimages, 146, 146f–147f
Place, 12–14
Placelessness, 42, 42f
Plantation agriculture, 340–341, 340f
Pluralism, 178
Pocock, Douglas, 48–49
Polarization, globalization and, 42–43
Political ecology, 8
Political geography
boundaries and, 204–207
centripetal and centrifugal forces,
208–209, 209f
colonialism and, 201–203, 202f
development of the state, 197–199
divided states, 198f–199f, 199
electoral geography, 220–223
global geopolitics, 214–219
globalization and terrorism,
218–219, 219f
imperialism and, 201–203
internationalism and, 211–214
multinational states, 200–201, 200f–201f
nation-states, 200
nations and states, 199–201
political landscapes, 223–224
political map of world, 196f–197f
self-determinism and, 203

Remote sensing, 23–25, 24f–25f
Renewable energy resources, 359, 370–375
  biomass energy, 371–372
  geothermal energy, 374–375
  hydropower, 372–373
  new renewables, 371
  solar energy, 373
  wind energy, 374
Renewalism, 152–153
Replacement level, population and, 67
Research and development spending, service sector and, 320
Research Triangle, North Carolina, 320
Reserves-to-production ratio (R/P ratio), 362–363
Residential change, public policy and, 250
Reverse hierarchical diffusion, 41, 41f
Revolutionary terrorism, 218–219, 219f
Ritual commemoration, sanctification and, 149f
Rituals, religions and, 133
Riverine wetland restoration, 360, 360f
Roca, 336
Roman Catholicism, 135
Romance languages, 107
Rostow, Walter, 282
Rostow's states of development, 282–283, 283f
Rousseau, Jean-Jacques, 286
Rural-out migration, 84–85, 85f
Rural-rural migration, 84
Rural-urban migration, 84
Russia, life expectancy and, 72
Rust Belt, 317f
Rwanda, refugees and, 202f, 203

S

Sacred places, civil religions and, 148–149
Sacred space, 144–149, 144f–145f
St. Louis, Missouri, 250, 250f
Salinization, 347
Same-sex marriage, 185f
Sanctification, 148–149, 149f
Santa Fe, New Mexico, 43f
Santeria, 132
Saskatchewan, Canada, 344f
Sauer, Carl, 9
Scientific farming, 331
Seagate, 310–311
Second agricultural revolution, 330
Secondary hearths, religions and, 140
Secondary industry, 299f, 300–302
Sector models, urban structure and, 243–244, 244f
Secularization, religion and, 150
Security landscapes, 224, 224f
Self-determinism, 203
Self-stabbing rituals, 152
Semiperipheral regions, development and, 284

Semitic hearth, religions of, 140–142
Sense of place, 14
Separatism, 209–210, 210f
September 11 terrorist attacks, 218
Serbia, centrifugal and centripetal forces in, 209, 209f
Services
  deindustrialization and, 316–317, 317f
  employment trends and, 319, 319f
  knowledge-based economy and, 319
  postindustrial societies and, 319
  quaternary services, 318
  quinary services, 318
  research and development spending and, 320
  technopoles and, 320–321, 320f
  tertiary services, 318
  types of, 317–318, 318f
Sex ratios, 75–76, 75f
Sexuality
  harassment and discrimination and, 185
  heterosexual norm, 184–185
  identity and space, 184–185
  public space and, 185
  same-sex marriage, 185f
Shahadah (profession of faith), 136f
Shale oil production, 365–366, 366f
Sharia, 151, 152f
Sheep grazing, 344f
Shenzhen, China, 254f
Shias (Shiites) Muslims, 137
Shifting cultivation, 336, 336f–337f
Shiva statue, 137, 137f
Short, John Rennie, 242
Shortridge, James R., 43
Siddhartha Gautama, 138
Sign languages, 101
Sikhism, 139, 142–143
Silicon Fen, Cambridge, England, 320
Silicon Valley, California, 320
Singapore, high-tech manufacturing and, 311f
Sip-wells, 55
Site and situation, 12, 13f
Slash-and-burn agriculture, 336, 336f
Slavery, 166–167, 166f–167f
Slums
  alleviation of, 256
  formation of, 253–255, 254f–255f
Small hydropower, 373
Small-scale maps, 21–22
Smallholder agriculture, 338
Smallholder crop and livestock farming, 338–339, 339f
Smallpox, 80
Smith, Adam, 275, 286
Snowbirds, 82
Social capital, 51
Social construction, 9, 164, 165f
Social dynamics, 5

Social factors, languages and, 98
Social networking, 14
Social space, religous law and, 151
Socialist cities, 246
Sociocultural transnationalism, 90–91
Sociodemographic indicators, 267–270
Socioeconomic distress, 240, 240f
Soil conservation techniques, 348, 348f
Solar cooking, 290
Solar energy, 373
Solar hot water heaters, 373
Sophia Antipolis technopole, France, 321
South Africa, apartheid and, 170–171, 170f–171f
South Korea, traditional medicine and, 52
Sovereignty, 197–199
Soviet-era housing estates, 246–247, 246f
Soviet Union fall, 200–201, 200f–201f
Space, 14–15
Spain, multinationalism and, 210, 210f
Spanglish, 112
Spatial arrangement of central places, 239, 239f
Spatial association, 15, 15f
Spatial data, 27, 27f
Spatial diffusion, 16–17
Spatial interaction, 17–20, 19f
Spatial perspective, 15
Spatial variations, agriculture and, 344–345, 345f
Special economic zones (SEZs), 313, 313f
Specialized languages, 102, 102f
Sports, cultural commodification and, 47–48
Sprawl, 252–253, 253f
Squatter settlements, 255
Sri Lanka, migrants and, 254f
Standard dialects, 124–125
Staple theory, 298–299
Starbucks, 42
Stateless languages, 110
States
  boundaries and, 204–207
  centripetal and centrifugal forces and, 208–209, 209f
  definition of, 198
  divided states, 198f–199f, 199
  enclaves and exclaves and, 207–208
  federal systems and, 208
  multinational states, 200–201, 200f–201f
  nation-state, 200
  nations and, 199–201
  separatism and devolution and, 209–210, 210f
  shapes of, 207, 207f
  unitary systems and, 208
  world's ten largest states, 207t
Stiglitz, Joseph, 287
Stillwater, Oklahoma, 232, 232f
Stimulus diffusion, 16